W9-CFO-455

PENGUIN BOOKS

Heartbreaks Along the Road

Over the last twenty-five years Roch Carrier has taught, lectured and, most importantly, written some of the most beloved books to come out of Quebec. The author of such well-known works as *La Guerre, Yes Sir!* and the children's classic *The Hockey Sweater*, Carrier's work continues to be widely read in both its original French and in English. He has lectured extensively in Canada, the United States, England, Europe and Australia. As well as serving on a number of cultural boards, Carrier was Chairman of Montreal's Salon du Livre for several years. A varied and expansive career has also steered Carrier into the worlds of film, jouralism and fine art — Carrier wrote the text for *Canada Je T'aime/ I Love You,* a collaboration with painter Miyuki Tanoube.

Sheila Fischman is a Governor General's Award-winning translator who has become well-known for her translations of many Quebec classics. In addition to Carrier, she has translated novels by Anne Hebert, Marie Claire-Blais and Michel Tremblay.

ROCH CARRIER

Heartbreaks Along the Road

Translated by Sheila Fischman

Penguin Books

PENGUIN BOOKS
Published by the Penguin Group
Penguin Books Canada Ltd, 10 Alcorn Avenue, Toronto,
Ontario, Canada M4V 3B2
Penguin Books Ltd, 27 Wrights Lane, London W8 5TZ, England
Penguin Books USA Inc., 375 Hudson Street, New York,
New York 10014, U.S.A.
Penguin Books Australia Ltd, Ringwood, Victoria, Australia
Penguin Books (NZ) Ltd, 182-190 Wairau Road, Auckland 10,
New Zealand

Penguin Books Ltd, Registered Offices: Harmondsworth,
Middlesex, England

First published by House of Anansi Press, 1987

Published in Penguin Books, 1991

10 9 8 7 6 5 4 3 2 1

Originally published in French as *De l'amour dans la ferraille*
Copyright © Editions internationales Alain Stanké, 1984

*Publisher's note: This book is a work of fiction. Names, characters, places
and incidents either are the product of the author's imagination or are
used fictitiously, and any resemblance to actual persons living or dead,
events, or locales is entirely coincidental.*

Manufactured in Canada

Canadian Cataloguing in Publication Data

Carrier, Roch, 1937-
  [De l'amour dans la ferraille.   English]
  Heartbreaks along the road

Translation of: De l'amour dans la ferraille.
ISBN 0-14-012757-7

I. Title.   II. Title: De l'amour dans la ferraille.
English.

PS8505.A77D3813   1991   C843'.54   C91-093152-6
PQ3919.2.C25D3813   1991

American Library of Congress Cataloguing in Publication Data
Available

I dedicate this novel to my daughters Capucine and Frédérique who, like all children, make life more beautiful.

Translator's note

The "Chef" who appears in these pages directs, not the operations of a kitchen, but the activities of an entire province, down to the insertion of the last lightbulb. He is a political leader, not a cook. And he is identified here by the nickname given to a man who was, perhaps, one of his followers or predecessors, the late Quebec Premier Maurice Duplessis.

He is assisted in keeping a vigilant eye on his Province by "good Curé Fourré." The priest's name provides more than a rhyme: *fourrer,* to stuff (a chicken, celery, a feather-pillow) also means to stick, to shove — and by extension, a familiar vulgar expression often rendered in English as "to screw."

— S.F

I

The village isn't dead, it's just asleep

In this place, nothing would happen. Trees would get taller, children would grow up, old people would fall asleep. One season would give way to the next. Each season would approach, settle in, have its day, then disappear. In foreign lands a war had been going on for a long time. No one wanted to travel so far. Why should they?

The City of Quebec was nearer. It was the Capital. Rich men's wives, who would rather go without underwear than shop in Saint-Toussaint-des-Saints, went there every week. They came home with more trinkets than were to be found in the whole general store. Ordinary people didn't visit the Capital even once a year. Some, who weren't even in poor health, had never seen the bridge to Quebec.

In the dense forest, trees choked each other, then slowly rotted. The young shoots, too, would strangle each other one day. There were so many swamps it seemed that the God of the Bible had forgotten to divide the waters from the firmament. There were so many stones, they were like flocks of sleeping sheep. The whine of mosquitoes overjoyed at their moist surroundings often could be heard as far away as the village. Houses lined the single street. The church stood on the tip of the hill that formed a bump like a knee under a sheet. Some houses were brightly painted. Others wore the color of the barns, the color of wood that has been soaked in the rain, scoured by winds, lashed by storms. The street stopped at the village limits.

The air smelled of grass and the grass had the fresh taste of rain-scented air. Butterflies moved their wings: their task was to scatter bright pigments that would gleam in the grass and glow in the dust of the road. The light was as beautiful as the water in a stream, scarcely licking the stones. Cows lowed and in the distance other cows answered. Somewhere a horse whinnied. The echo repeated the clanks as the blacksmith pounded a fire-softened horseshoe on his anvil. Men gazed at these acts as if they were their own past and future: idle men, waiting now for nothing but death. Some of the youngsters were sad because childhood lasts so long. A car drove slowly through the village, gently, not making a sound, not raising dust. The villagers marveled once again at how silent and clean the street had been ever since the Right Party, during the previous election campaign, had covered it with a layer of blue asphalt.

Children's voices chirped. A sob burst from an open window. Here and there curtains swayed in the wind. A cock proclaimed imperiously that it was morning: it was past noon. A hammer struck a nail: the carpenter was fixing the Curé's stair. Wood thrushes proudly thrust out speckled breasts. Sparrows pecked at manure. Far away, a nuthatch sang its nasal song. In a hollow trunk, a woodpecker was furiously at work. Above the forest, a marsh-hawk shrieked and glided over his domain. Every house breathed like a fat sleeping woman. On verandas old people rocked in their chairs; their thoughts were in another time. Swallows perched on a wire the Right Party had put up during the last election campaign and picked lice from their feathers. A song on the radio, that made the hips of women busy at their tasks move in three-quarter time, was abruptly interrupted:

"Ladies and Gentlemen, *Mesdames et messieurs*, our news department has learned just this minute that, apparently, if various rumors turn out to be accurate and well-founded, the people will very shortly be called upon to go to the polls to elect the next government. The honorable ministers are presently holding a meeting — a secret meeting. The room where they are presently sitting around an oak table has no windows or doors. Sorry, there's one door; the honorable ministers aren't packed into this room like sardines in a tin. The door is soundproof, draughtproof, padded and guarded by a big policeman. None of the honorable ministers' words can get out. The room has no windows so nobody can peek inside. However, your favorite radio station is in a position to tell you, between two waltzes, that shortly we'll be having an election!"

II

With the province's bigwigs

First, Le Chef slapped the table. His ministers jumped; they were drowsy after a copious meal washed down with heavy beer. The July heat was oily.

"The province needs an election: I therefore declare the election campaign open. We have a raspberry season, we have a blueberry season: if you Gentlemen of the Cabinet had as much political sense as the Honorable Minister of Agriculture's cow, you'd know that the Right Party needs an election, that the populace needs to return us to power one more time, bless their hearts. Before the apple season, we'll have an election season. The populace is in bloom. You, Gentlemen of the Cabinet, will give the populace the appropriate watering, you will poison the Opposition caterpillars and fertilize the flowers that contain all the promises in the world. If you're good gardeners, Gentlemen of the Cabinet, the Right Party will have the finest harvest in its history, and you'll be able to take your seats around this table again and snore like stuffed pigs; if you're bad gardeners you'll lose the election, and you'll be . . . you'll be . . . Has the Honorable Minister of Agriculture learned enough about his Ministry to tell me the principal by-product of the bovine digestive process?"

The smoke from their cigars was dense. Big eyes dulled by an undeniable urge for sleep sought the Minister of Agriculture and watched him reflect, with the air of a man making an important decision. As if it were a sacred word, he named the by-product in question.

"That's what you'll be worth if you lose your election! Meaning you won't be honorable any more. Today, the populace thinks everybody around this Cabinet table is an honorable gentleman. But remember: a politician that loses an election stops being a politician. He's a member of the Opposition — and the Opposition isn't worth . . . it isn't worth . . . Will the Honorable Minister of Agriculture tell me again: what's the principal by-product of the bovine digestive process?"

The gallant Minister wasn't accustomed to receiving so much of his Premier's attention; a pinch of contempt from Le Chef was worth more than a great deal of indifference. Le Chef had singled him out from the others by honoring him with his sarcasm. He repeated the word as his Chef had requested. Resuming his chair, Le Chef stared at them with all the certainty of his superiority.

"Honorable Ministers, he who would harvest first must sow; to harvest votes, you must sow roads. You're going to scatter strips of road all across this province. Every person who votes for the Right Party will have his strip of road by voting day. Every benighted soul who might be considering giving his vote to the Opposition has to have his strip of road. Every Curé in the Province has to have his strip of road so his parishioners don't have to skip Mass if the rain comes down like the Flood; the populace mustn't be kept from confessing their sins just because their horses might break a leg in the morass. And if you don't know what a morass is, ask the Honorable Minister of Culture; he'll ask his deputy minister, who'll ask his wife, the schoolteacher, and she'll look it up in her dictionary. Every rural part of this Province has to have its strip of road, because roads are the arteries of a country — and politics are its life."

III

Life seems complicated if you haven't lived

In a college on the other side of the Appalachians, Innocent Loiseau was the last student to hear the bell that summoned them inside. He was the last to put an end to his games, the last to obey the call, the last to enter the building that reeked of incense, tobacco, and heavy woolen clothing soaked with sweat. From the meal that was cooking at the end of the corridor came a disgusting smell. Spring was glistening, the grass of May was turning green and trees were bursting into leaf. The door was locked. On the balcony, a trunk stood in the sun. He recognized it as his own. He knew the meaning of this sign. More than once he had seen the ritual performed. He was being expelled. Turned away. Anathema had been cast upon him. Behind the bolted door stood a black-robed man, arms crossed on his chest. It was the tallest of the priests. The fattest. He filled the doorway. He stood there like a wall, reinforcing the door. The boy would not go back inside. The priest's eyes didn't see him. They didn't see the student's anxiety or his distress. The eyes were two little holes in a wall. What was he to do? He'd been kicked out of school and now all the roads in the world were opening at his feet. His trunk stood beside him. The priests had assembled his belongings, his books, his clothes. He tested the weight of the trunk. It was heavy. Gardeners had wheel-barrows. He'd make off with one. It would be sweet revenge on the school. Nothing to it. He loaded his trunk and descended the long hill on top of which stood the college. He was even happy: his life was about to begin. Back home, his mother would weep in despair, his father would punish him, Curé Fourré would sprinkle him with holy water to extirpate the devil from his schoolboy's possessed body. All that would come later. His sweet delight at finally being born into real life would be well worth the tears, the recriminations and the blows that would greet his return. But now, as he awaited the inevitable storm, he must allow nothing to tarnish his splendid joy at simply being freed from school.

It was the month of May. The last patches of snow were turning to water. Innocent Loiseau was pushing his wheel-barrow, happy as a calf let out of the stable. He was so happy. All roads were open to him — but where does an adolescent go who knows nothing but the inside of the egg where he's been living? An animal instinct had led him quite naturally onto the road to his parents' house, the house he'd left to come to college and learn about life. He was obeying a law like the one that makes birds return to their nest after long journeys across continents. On the map, his father's house wasn't far from the school. A brief zigzag represented the road. At school he had journeyed through centuries and continents. From Saint-Toussaint-des-Saints, from the forest, he had come to a town where the houses were set out like the squares in a crossword puzzle. He had passed from childhood into adolescence. Not yet a man, he knew that some day he'd become one, but he didn't know what being a man consisted of; however, he was no longer a child, and he didn't want to be one now. He had left his calm and peaceful village marked by the church bell sounding the hours, by farmers squabbling across their split-rail fences, by the shouts of mothers trying to instill some discipline in their wild brats who behaved like the animals in the forest, and crossed through periods of history torn by war and bloody conquests, shaken by philosophical or theological crises. He had travelled into the past; he had ventured far beyond the distance that separated his house and his school.

Innocent Loiseau came home filled with knowledge and memories. Even though he was no longer a child, even though he had learned a great deal that was unknown in Saint-Toussaint-des-Saints, he was once again as alone as a child. He would go home to his mother and father. How could he use his knowledge? The birds sang the same way for those who didn't know how to read as for those who had spent long years hunched over books. Ancient times were absolutely useless: they no longer existed for the road that climbed up the hills or for the houses and barns scattered along either side, with dogs that barked as he passed and cows that mooed. He had studied physics, but his trunk was no lighter, his wheel-barrow no easier to push. Who was he? He was not a man. He was not a child. His memory contained other memories as if he were a thousand years old, but he had not yet lived. Who was he? Just an adolescent, whose legs felt heavy, pushing his belongings in a wheel-barrow. Blisters seared his hands as they gripped the handles. It was no longer day. It was growing dark. He wouldn't reach his father's house before night. There was a lot of road yet to cover. Turning to measure the distance he had come, he still saw the dome of his school against the grey of the sky. He hadn't even erased it from his horizon.

Innocent Loiseau was a vagabond, a bohemian, he was Rimbaud, he would sleep in the fields, at the Inn of the Shooting Star. He had no need to be greeted, to eat strawberry jam on fresh bread, to sleep in a kitchen with dogs huddled about him.

A few cars had passed, slowing down to give the passengers a better look at this beggar, who was not in rags, who was so young, who was pushing a wheel-barrow that contained all his worldly goods, then accelerating amid a cloud of dust and a shower of pebbles. His hands were bleeding. His arms wanted to tear themselves from his shoulders. His legs refused to take another step: they wouldn't bend and his shoes were now too narrow for his feet. He recalled his grandparents' stories that he'd heard at so many family gatherings. "Back then they didn't have good roads like nowadays. The road, she was just two ruts hollowed out by the cart-wheels. Why'd the good Lord give us so much misery? You look at those fine roads they got nowadays, that run on as straight and sharp as the school-teacher's handwriting, and you ask yourself why the good Lord's spoiling the younger generation, when He gave us so much misery. We ate his misery three times a day, all our lives, and we didn't like it any more than the younger generation would. There's mysteries in life we'll never understand till we've passed on . . . True, back then if you wanted to make your way you had to carve out your own road, you had to fell a tree before you took your next step. You had to know just where you wanted to go. Youngsters now though, they just have to take those fine roads stretching out ahead of them like carpets . . . Young people now, they don't even have to know where they want to go, they just have to follow . . . Oh, it's easier now . . . Following's easier than building . . . A young fellow today, he can go anywhere on this earth, along fine roads, without even knowing where he wants to go . . . There's more roads nowadays than tilled soil."

At his wheelbarrow, Innocent Loiseau could hear their voices, made husky and rasping by the years. He was going home to his parents, but that wasn't really going anywhere. He was as lost as if there were no road, as in the olden days. He was sleepy, dirty, exhausted, famished.

He decided to stop. At the little house covered with cedar shingles, walls and roof, he was greeted not by dogs, but by a slender woman who scampered to the door, her hair disheveled. She peered at him through the screen-door. What did he want? Didn't he know anybody else along the road? Why didn't he have a car or a horse? Did he have any baggage? He had to answer all her questions. She wanted to know everything. She dared not let him in because her husband was jealous. So jealous. She didn't need dogs to protect her, for her husband could smell visitors — especially if they were men — better than any dog. He told her he hadn't eaten all day. Finally she agreed to let him in. Was he sure he wasn't afraid of her husband who would come home and bark louder than an angry dog at the sight of a young boy inside the house with his wife? He replied that he had no reason to be afraid of a man: weren't all men brothers? Her husband would see that he was only a poor schoolboy who'd been turned out into the

17

woods. She assured him that the schoolboy was deluding himself, that her husband would be fiercely jealous and that he was probably already aware of the odor of young man. She went into the bedroom and came out again with her hair combed. She was holding a towel. ("My husband's not only jealous, he hates boys with dirty faces.") Without asking his permission, she began in a motherly way to wipe his face clean of the dust of the road, which his sweat had turned to a muddy crust. Then she took a cloth from the chest and spread it on the table, she set out a plate, a knife, a fork and a glass, and took from the refrigerator a roasted leg of veal and some milk; she offered him bread with butter that smelled of milk, fruit relish, jam: enough to feed Gargantua. His appetite was huge. She watched him.

"If you're telling the truth, the good fathers abandoned you."

"I'm glad to be gone."

"Strange," she said. "My man said the same thing, word for word."

"Where *is* your husband?"

"What about you — where are you going?"

"Home to my parents. My father will beat me, my mother will cry, but I'm going home. To become a man you must hurt somebody. I was out of place in school, as if I was in somebody else's skin. My parents won't understand that. They thought they were giving me a gift, putting me in that skin — the skin of bearded women like the priests. I've had enough of school, now I want life. I don't want to sit at my desk, watching life pass by in other countries and centuries, and never touching it. I want to touch life. I don't just want to learn, to remember: I want to do. I don't want to be a barren apple-tree, Madame, I want to yield fruit. My hands aren't dead branches. The sap hasn't dried up inside me. I don't want to spend my life remembering what other people have lived. I don't want to settle for knowing there are roads that lead to fabulous lands, I want to travel them, Madame." (He shoved a lump of potatoes and gravy into his mouth.) "That's what I'll tell my father and mother. He'll hit me. She'll cry. They gave me life, but they can't stop me from living."

The young woman listened, smiling attentively. Her nose was too short. That was what made her look as if she was smiling. He spread some rather hard butter that smelled of milk onto a piece of brown bread, and draped a slice of veal over the buttered bread. Before biting into it he declared:

"As soon as you're out of school you meet real life along the road."

"And I think you do too much thinking. A man's head, or a woman's, is very small. If you cram it full of ideas that are too big for you, you're like somebody with feelings too big for his heart; the heart breaks, the head cracks open and he goes a little crazy . . . "

"Thanks for your hospitality, Madame. It's good to eat food that tastes of life."

And licking his lips he spread some relish on the roast veal.

"Eating is a kind of happiness. Men have suffered so much in their search for happiness and many of them have lost their lives; they've crossed oceans and deserts, forests and jungles and mountains, they've conquered countries. And all that time, happiness might have been as near as their dinner table."

"You've got too many ideas in that little head of yours. It could crack. And don't forget, my husband's very jealous. He knows you're in the house with his wife. He's smelled you, I know he has. He's very jealous and he says he's the only one entitled to eat his wife's food. He always comes home when there's a man in the house. And he's furious. He beats me."

"Madame, doesn't that prove your husband loves you?"

His hunger had vanished. Now anxiety was slowly clutching his belly.

"Oh yes, my husband's jealous, but he loves me so much! Too much! He's very jealous, my husband. He can smell your presence. He'll come back, and you'll be scared, like the others. He's got too many ideas in his head and too many feelings in his heart. His heart and his head are a little bit cracked."

He didn't want to eat any more. He stood up. It was time to be on his way. He no longer felt his fatigue. The

19

fear that stabbed his body like electric shocks had dissipated his fatigue.

"I'll be going now."

She gazed at him, incredulous.

"Thank you for giving me some of your food: God will return it a hundredfold. And now I'll be on my way."

"No," she pleaded, her soul so distraught, such fear in her eyes that he shuddered, "don't go! My husband will be waiting by the roadside, to catch you unawares. He knows you're with me. Stay here where you'll be safe. My husband's so jealous."

She gripped his hands. He was paralyzed by all the strength in the woman's fingers. He tried to resist, but she pulled him toward her, then into the bedroom; she pushed him onto a bed and threw herself upon him; she clasped him in her arms, she wrapped her legs around his and whispered in his ear:

"Rest. You're so tired. Don't show yourself on the road at this hour of the night. It's so dark. My husband's so jealous. He knows you're here. He'll follow you. He'll find you. Rest. Don't think. You have too many ideas. Your head will split open. My husband's so jealous."

She must have sensed that he was surrendering; she loosened her grip. As he had stopped moving, she pulled the covers over him. Then she started to take off her dress.

"He'll come back," she repeated. "He'll fly into a terrible rage. We'll hear him, because he makes a terrible racket. So slip out of bed now, don't make a sound, and hide underneath. I'll tell him I'm alone and that'll set his mind at ease. He'll go away and you can get back in my bed and rest, because you're such a tired little boy. You must be so handsome when you're asleep."

Innocent Loiseau was terrified. To what madhouse had the road brought him?

"Sleep, child, I'll love you very gently. Don't think; let your ideas go to sleep. A man's ideas are useless at night."

His blood was frozen. His heart had stopped. His skin must be as icy as a dead man's. He felt only fear: the fear that makes a man like all the other beasts.

"You think too much. Relax."

Talk. He needed to talk.

"Madame, your husband, your jealous husband, where is he?"

"Where? He doesn't tell me. So I don't know. He's been dead for seven years and six months. Where is he? Probably dragging himself along the roads in the land of the dead . . . "

"Your husband's dead!"

Innocent realized that he was pushing his wheel-barrow. His trunk was as light as a cloud. The handles no longer felt like red-hot iron. His back was no longer dislocated by his exertions. The night veiled neither the road nor the fields; the moon shed as much light as a sun. In this night no ghost, no soul of a dead jealous husband could find enough shade to hide in. Innocent was running. His heart beat fast enough to burst his arteries. He had wrenched himself from the mad widow's arms. He seemed to have acquired the ability to move through walls. He didn't remember his escape from the demented house inhabited by nightmares. Did the house exist? Had the madwoman really held him in her arms? Did the jealous husband exist? Was he really dead? Was he one of those lost souls that roam the earth because they're still trying to understand the reasons for their unhappiness? But what exists? What does not exist? Yes, the madwoman's house existed. The proof was his wildly pounding heart. What confusion in his thoughts!

He set down the wheel-barrow. The night shed a milder light than the day. He wiped his brow. His head was ablaze. Sweat dripped down his temples. It was quite true that he thought too much. He was only a child and he was trying to cram all the thoughts in the world into his head. He was following this road like an exile, cast out of his country. He advanced uneasily, fearful of blows, without regret but with a sense of guilt; he had walked knowing he was heading in the wrong direction; he should have gone elsewhere, not to the house of his childhood, but toward the main roads that would show him the world. Why were ideas pursuing him like a swarm of wasps? Why couldn't he be a young man walking along in the daytime, whistling and carefree? He thought too much. He was falling asleep.

Several hours later his eyes opened. He gave them time to grow accustomed to the light and see where he had slept. Innocent Loiseau remembered a nightmare. He was at the side of the road. His wheel-barrow had capsized and his trunk had rolled into the ditch. He had slept as soundly

as if he no longer existed, but he did remember a little
house where a crazy widow lived. He could no longer sort
out real life from the life of dreams. Perhaps he shouldn't
try. He thought too much. It was still a long way to his
father's house, and thinking wouldn't get him there any
faster. He pushed his trunk, hoisted it into the wheel-
barrow and set off again. There was no fruit on the trees
yet. He had nothing to eat. At the next house he would
ask for a piece of bread. He had slept like a tired beast.
No vehicle had wakened him. The road was untraveled.
Why had he set out on this road that would take him back
to his childhood? Why follow a road that leads nowhere,
when other roads lead to life, the greatest adventure in
the world? Why was he exhausting himself, pushing this
trunk that held his few poor possessions? He should have
entered life as naked as a newborn. Why fill his head with
old ideas that weighed down his soul like a rock and an
old man's fatigue when he need only look at the sky to
realize that nothing can be explained, that the smallest
particle of the universe is vaster than mankind's greatest
idea? He thought too much. What virus had given him the
disease of thinking? What force of attraction was leading
him where he was going? He obeyed, knowing it would be
better to head in another direction. Alongside the roads
built by men are other roads, beneath and above them,
that travel in every direction; humans follow invisible roads
while seeming to follow sensibly the ones they have laid
out.

Hunger was scorching him, his thoughts were on fire.
He would never reach his father's house with his stomach
in such torment. Yet he'd been amply fed at the crazy
widow's house. That was a nightmare, and the tasty veal
on buttered bread was unreal food. He would stop at the
next house.

Strange! It was covered with cedar shingles painted grey
by age. Innocent recognized the house, he had seen it
before! He had more than a vague recollection of it. He
knocked at the door. A gruff voice shouted:

"Make yourself at home."

Entering, he recoiled at once. He was back in the crazy
widow's kitchen, with the same table, the same chairs, the
same flowered linoleum, the same stove and the wall painted

the same green. The rough authority of the gruff voice brought him back like a heavy hand pulling his arm.

"Whaddya want? You musta come here for something."

"I'm hungry, Monsieur: would you have a crust of bread?"

"You got too many manners, my boy, where you from? You got more sugar in you than a sugar pie. Were you boiled in maple syrup like candy? Did they shove you up on the shelf next to the jam jars?"

He was a big, dark, bearded man with a square head, a square brow and square shoulders; even his belly was a swollen cube; his big hands were square as well.

"I come from the college, Monsieur."

"Monsieur? Just who do you think you're calling Monsieur. That's an insult! The name's Procule Ponton, not *Monsieur*!"

"I was expelled from the college, Monsieur Ponton."

"So that's where the sugar comes from. You spent some time in Father Superior's honey keg . . . Monsieur Ponton . . . Nobody ever calls me that. The name's Procule Ponton. When you're a man, that's what you'll call me. Procule."

"I understand, Mons . . . "

A single glance from the big dark man cut off his words, and he couldn't leave, couldn't escape.

"So they kicked you out of the college," the voice rumbled, with a sound like an iron-rimmed wheel on gravel. "Thank the Lord. He loves you better than the boys he leaves steeping in honey. You'll end up with your feet on real earth. Our father Adam was made out of earth, not honey like a doughnut. Man's made out of earth so he can live on the earth."

"Adam might be just a legend."

"Everything they tell us is a legend. Nobody knows enough to tell something that's true. Everybody tells legends. Who told you our father Adam was a legend? Not the priests!"

"No, it's a personal reflection."

"You think too much, my boy, your head's going to be so full of ideas it'll crack like a plate."

Someone had already predicted such a disaster. He searched in his rather muddled memory. Where had he heard that comparison with a cracked plate? When had he heard the words Procule was saying now? Had he lived this before? Had he seen this house before? Was he re-living an earlier experience? Was he discovering a gift for knowing things that didn't yet exist? He had been in this house before. He thought too much. Wasn't this strange sensation of re-living what had been experienced before, or of knowing in advance what he was going to experience, wasn't it the start of the unsettling of his ideas and his soul?

"Procule, would you let me have a piece of bread and butter?"

"When you respect a man you don't beg like that, you *tell* him what you want. There's nothing more hypocritical than begging from a man."

"Procule, I'm hungry."

"I took a good look at you. You're as skinny as a fishbone, you're as white as paper, you're as pale as a little girl saying her prayers, you're as flimsy as a blade of grass, you're as nervous as a vicar taking up his first collection for charity; you look as sick as if you just got out of the hospital. You could pass for a dying man hunting for the graveyard. And you don't look like that because you're hungry. I know, I've been hungry. You think too much. Stop think-ing so much and live! Life is health. No reason for you to die just because you think about life too much."

Procule Ponton brought some butter, bread and a piece of meat on a plate. He offered it to Innocent.

"It's roast veal."

Innocent looked away. Was last night a dream, or had he really eaten roast veal?

"So you don't like roast veal. Everybody likes what he likes and hates what he hates."

To give himself strength, Innocent Loiseau chewed some bread with farm butter that tasted of milk, then he looked up at the man drawn in broad black lines. He hoped to read in his eyes the answer to a curious mystery, but Pro-cule Ponton was staring back. He felt his eyes melting like butter, so he merely whispered:

"I think I already ate roast veal tonight."

A sort of giddiness was making his eyes swim.

"When I walked in your house I had the feeling I'd been here before. But I wasn't dreaming. I remember how the roast veal tasted. It was in your house. I don't understand: I walked part of the night, I pushed my wheel-barrow with

24

my trunk in it, then I slept by the side of the road, and now I'm back in the same house, but it's you Mons . . . "

"Procule."

"It's you, Procule, that lives in this house, not a crazy widow."

"Ah!" said Procule, "I understand. You went to my wife and she told you I was dead. But I'm not. I left the house I built with my own hands, from lumber I cut on my own land, put together with nails I forged myself, on my own anvil. So she told you she's a widow. But I'm still alive. She told you I'd passed away, but I only moved. I liked that house of mine, so I re-built it by the side of the same road, with the same poplars and spruce trees out front, behind the same hill, and I built it the same way, with my own hands. I fixed up the inside just the same, to help me forget I had to leave a house I loved, that I'd built around me like the peel around an apple. I was *forced* to leave it. There was too much suffering in that house. My wife, she suffered as much as one woman can suffer because of a man. She thought I didn't love her, but of all God's creatures she was the one I loved the most. And of all God's creatures, my wife's the one that caused me the most pain. I loved her though, and the more I loved her, the more she suffered because of me and the more I suffered because of her. The more I loved her, the more she thought I didn't love her. I loved her. Without her, I'd be like bread without yeast. If she hadn't been there it'd be like there was no sun in the sky, like I had no air in my lungs. She was my beating heart. You can't understand that, my boy, because it's love. Me, I was happy, and when she made me suffer I was happy because suffering seemed to prove that it was love. I thought it was normal for a man, a real man, to live for a woman. She loved me too. And because she loved me, she was jealous. My boy, if your woman's not jealous, it proves she doesn't love you. My wife was jealous. If she could see or thought she saw a glimmer of a thought in my eyes, she was positive I was thinking of another woman, that I'd rather dream about some other woman than love her in the flesh. So then the crying started, and the accusations and the tears and the denials and the fighting. And after that came the loving, as fierce as our fights. When I was loving her, she'd say, 'I know you're thinking

25

about another woman,' and me, I'd hardly hear her, I was so lost in my love for her. She'd scream: 'You don't love me, who do you love?' If I came home tired, it was because I'd loved some other woman too passionately. She'd sidle up to me, she'd smell me, then she'd say, all cheeky, after she got a whiff of my sweat: 'You stink of a man that's spent himself on a female.'

"She suffered and I suffered and we were both unhappy. She loved me too much and I loved her too. We loved each other enough to destroy us. We wanted to die so we'd be resurrected together. Ten times a day we'd kill each other with hatred then be resurrected with love. You have to live that, my boy, to understand it. Love drives you crazy. I'd look up at the sky to see what the weather was going to be and she'd be sure I was dreaming about a woman. If a car slowed down outside our house, my wife was positive some woman was coming to see me. We'd get a letter and she'd tear open the envelope before I had time to read the letter she thought was written by a woman, even if it was in a government envelope. She followed me everywhere. I could hear her footsteps creaking in the straw because she'd spy on me in the stable, from behind the wall full of knot-holes. Many times when I went out to fell trees in the forest I'd hear an animal tiptoeing across dead branches that broke under its weight: my wife. I was always alone; she never caught the woman that was supposed to be with me, so she figured I did a good job of hiding her and she'd spy even harder. She loved me. When I saw how much she loved me I tried with all my might to love her just as much. I never loved anybody else. I never loved another thing. My boy, after you've held a woman in your hands instead of books, when you walk on the dirt roads thinking about a woman's body instead of lines of black words on paper, then you'll understand."

Innocent Loiseau had stopped eating. He'd heard too much talk of love that night. He wanted to run away. He wanted to hear nothing but the voice of the cicadas, chickadees and squirrels, who talk for the sake of talking, who instead of expressing universal madness sing of their great, gratuitous, meaningless joy, beautiful and ephemeral. He got up to say thanks and goodbye and get back on the road. The powerful square hand matted with black hair squeezed his shoulder.

"My wife had nothing left but revenge. She decided to make me suffer as much as I'd made her suffer. That's what love is: giving happiness and causing suffering. Sharing everything. It was a lonely road we lived on. My wife decided she'd fill her life with men. She'd stand by the side of the road and when a car drove up she'd wave, make signs of distress so it would stop. I've seen her do it. Sometimes the car would stop. I'd come back to the house and the bedroom reeked of tobacco. The sheets would be off the bed. Sometimes I'd find glasses or a watch or a rosary I'd never seen before. If the car didn't stop at the roadside, she'd hike up her dress. I've seen it. She'd open her dress to the winds and show herself, bare naked, to the driver of a car who stopped in a cloud of dust the size of a storm cloud . . . I've found empty beer bottles on the kitchen table, though I don't drink that poison. On my way back to the house I've seen a car scoot away like a scared rabbit. There's been times I found our bedroom door shut; I pushed, it was blocked, then suddenly my wife would open it, wild-eyed and puffy-faced, and I saw the window open, I saw the curtains waving in the breeze, I practically saw the shadow of a man running away. She wanted to make me suffer and I suffered. The more I suffered, the more I loved her, and the more I loved her, the more my wife thought I was hiding my other loves from her, and the more she thought I was hiding my other women, the more she wanted to make me suffer, and the more cars she'd stop by the roadside. If I'd been able to catch one of her visitors, crush him like a strawberry, it would've poured a little cold water on the fire of my suffering, but there's nothing craftier than a woman: as soon as I showed up, making no more sound than a mosquito, the man was already on his way. We loved each other, but instead of simply loving we hurt each other more than if we'd hated. When there was too much pain in my soul I'd go in the forest as deep as I could, I'd look for the biggest maple standing and I'd cut it down. I'd come home drained of my sadness, tired and calm; my wife would explain my fatigue by the love I'd given some woman in the forest.

I'd see the tangled sheets on the bed; I'd see a cigarette butt in an ashtray on the table, though I only smoke a pipe . . . Strangers had taken my wife and I wanted to get her back.

"Once, the battle was too hard. I'd wrenched my wife away from a stranger, I wanted to keep her, I held her tight against me. They told me she was dead. They went away with her, they took my wife away and buried her, they hid my wife in the ground so I couldn't see her.

"Then they came back to our empty house and asked me questions, they wanted to know everything, they wrote the answers in their notebooks, they kept asking the same questions and they didn't like my answers, they got impatient, they threatened, they hit me. Me, a man of honor, that can face up to another man, I let myself be beaten: like a child, I wept because their questions scared me. They tried to make me admit my wife was dead. I knew she wasn't dead because I loved her.

"One day I decided there'd been too much unhappiness in my house and I took to the road. I kept on till I felt like stopping — here. The place was like the one I'd left. I built a house. I built my house just like the one I'd left. I covered it with cedar shingles and when I'm not too sad, I cook the same kinds of meat my wife used to make for me. The way she roasted veal, it tasted like almonds. But she's not dead, my wife. She comes back. She spies on me. She doesn't let me look at another woman. I don't look at them. I won't touch another woman. She comes back to spy on me. She isn't dead, I know it. I spy on her. She still entertains men in my house, she entertains them in my bed. I know it, I can smell it when there's a man with my wife."

The big man with the square black head had tears in his eyes; Innocent felt his heart shudder and his knees tremble as if he were standing at the edge of a dangerous cliff. Here, in the bright light of day, the student knew he wasn't dreaming. If he didn't recoil, if he didn't leave, he'd be dragged into a nightmarish abyss. The man was suffering. The man was mad. He ought to leave, tear himself away from the giddy fascination the dark man's story created. Slowly, cautiously, slyly, Innocent Loiseau minced backwards, toward the door. When his heel skimmed the door-step, he said:

"It's true, your roast veal tastes of almonds."

He pushed the door:

"Thank you for feeding a hungry man; the good Lord will return it."

When the door was shut he added:

"I know you love your wife. I'll tell everybody you love your wife."

"You do that! Tell them I love her and they'll all say I killed her."

"I know your wife's alive; I'll tell them!" he promised, racing to his wheelbarrow.

What a joy it was to hear the rustling of leaves, the voices of the cows, the hymns of the dogs and the songs of the birds! He wouldn't reach his father's house before night. He knew that he thought too much. He mustn't let ideas peck at him like a flock of carnivorous birds. His father would beat him because he'd been expelled from the college; his mother would weep bitter tears as if her son had been struck by a shell. He knew he would never understand love, never understand life, but he wanted to live.

He would go back to the house of his childhood. This road had crossed through the dreams of night, and now it was leading Innocent Loiseau toward daylight dreams. At the end of the road there awaited not his childhood, but his life as a man.

IV

The redemptive value of work

"Election!" Germaine shouted from the stool where she stood, nylons rolled around her ankles, as she painted the kitchen ceiling. She jumped down and ran to the rocking chair where her husband Mozusse was snoring, head thrown back and mouth agape.

"Mozusse Chabotte! There's an election coming! Get in the car! Get your hide over to the Minister's office! When there's an election jobs grow like weeds! Mozusse!"

The man went on snoring. The echoes of political life weren't loud enough to break down the wall of his sleep.

"Mozusse!"

He was not of this world. With one of those brisk movements an emergency can provoke, she slapped his face with her paint-brush. At the shock, an eyelid flickered.

"Mozusse Chabotte!" Germaine roared, "if everybody was like you they'd all be just as poor. I tell you there's going to be an election and you just sleep as if everything was normal. You ought to be at the Minister's office by now. If he wants your vote he has to give you a job. You just sit here asleep in your rocking chair while your wife spends her life with a rag in her hand, rubbing and scrubbing, dusting and washing, painting and painting."

Once again the paint brush landed splat on the face of Mozusse Chabotte, limp and greasy. Rather than grimace, he merely remained in the utter bliss of a cozy nap. Before sinking into happiness altogether, he muttered words his wife could decipher only too well:

"If the Minister has to give me a job to get my vote, I'd just as soon wait and ask him for it next week. I've never needed sleep so bad. Germaine, your husband's entitled to his rest."

With the brush in one hand and the bucket of paint in the other, she dived into the screen door, which slammed against the wall. Planted on the veranda, she shouted in the direction of the house across the street:

"Armanda! Yoo hoo! Armanda Binette! Armanda! Are you fast asleep like my husband?"

All seemed peaceful in the little house Armanda had just painted yellow. ("A color for people with no taste," in Germaine's opinion. "I can't sleep at night since that house was painted like a canary.")

"Armanda Binette!" she cried insistently.

Germaine knew Armanda was inside; she hadn't seen her go out.

"Armanda!"

The screen-door opened. Armanda Binette appeared, buttoning her dress and breathing hard.

"Didn't you hear me, Armanda Binette?"

"I heard you shout, but there's times, when my man's at home, I can't just come running."

"Armanda Binette, the radio just said there's an election on the way."

"Germaine Chabotte, you can always smell an election coming."

"Armanda Binette, Le Chef wouldn't let the radio announce an election if there wasn't going to be one. Le Chef doesn't let lies get around. The radio said so. I heard it with my own two ears: there's going to be an election!"

"So they'll be bringing out their little pieces of new road."

"Whenever men want us, Armanda Binette, they always bring out a little piece of something."

"What a joker you are, Germaine Chabotte!" Armanda cooed, buttoning her dress. "You're so silly you make me blush. You don't have to tell the whole village about my Ephrem's . . . "

The neighbor's screen door opened and Idola Couture, long and thin as a mop handle, came running out, all ears.

"You know I don't usually listen in on other people's conversations, but did I hear you say there's an election coming?"

"That's what the radio said."

"The radio isn't the Pope."

"When the Pope wants to tell the truth he tells it on the radio."

Armanda Binette looked skeptical.

"The Right Party can't have an election without giving us a piece of new road."

She went inside. The screen door slammed. Idola Couture excused herself:

"I'm going in; I just came out to sniff the air."

"I'm going back to my painting, and I've got a strawberry pie in the oven," said Germaine Chabotte.

Silence returned to the street, broken only by the occasional crying child. Germaine climbed back up on her stool. She dipped her brush in the thickened paint. The fire crackled in the stove. It was too hot. This was no weather for baking pies. But a body has to eat. ("The good Lord brought us into this world starving.") It was no weather for painting either. Mozusse went on snoring. He'd become so good at it he could rock his chair as he slept. They were playing a waltz on the radio. The brush glided over the ceiling in time to the music.

A car started up. Germaine recognized its cough. It belonged to Ephrem Binette, Armanda's husband. He must be on his way to the Minister's office.

"Some men pull their pants on even faster than they pull them off," Germaine sighed. "And there's mine, fast asleep."

Another car started up. Armanda got down from her stool and looked out the window. She knew it, it was Attila Couture, Idola's pot-bellied husband, hurrying to get to the Minister before Armanda Binette's husband.

Germaine Chabotte was shaken by a powerful volley of rage, a sudden surge, like one of those waves of fire that tear apart the earth's crust. She rushed at the sleeping man. She held the bucket of paint above his head, hesitating because she knew she'd be the one who had to wipe it up. A force was urging her on and she could only obey. Just as you throw cold water on a person to wake him up, she poured the paint on the head of her husband, who snored away, unconcerned about the elections and the list to which he must add his name to get a job. Mozusse Chabotte was unaware of the sticky mess. It wasn't till later, when his wife had almost finished cleaning up, that his eye opened.

"You know Germaine, I been thinking it over, and if there's one thing in this life I don't give a hoot about, it's politics."

Very industriously and very gently, as if she were washing a baby's delicate skin, Germaine wiped his face.

"You'll have to take off your shirt and pants."

"Did you think I was the ceiling, Germaine Chabotte?"

His wife was sitting on his knees. The fiery weight of her crushed him and the rocking chair bent and swayed, pitching dangerously like a boat about to capsize.

"You don't want anything to do with politics, Mozusse Chabotte, but maybe you'd like to do something for your wife. Maybe you could be good to me like Armanda Binette's husband."

"As the years go by, Germaine Chabotte, sex don't interest me much more than politics."

She tore herself from him, grabbed her paint brush and roared like a furious lioness:

"Do you think you need another woman to bring you back to life, Mozusse Chabotte? Well you're keeping the same wife — and the same Chef!"

"When a woman makes good soup and Le Chef gives us a strippa new road, a man don't have to change either one."

"That strippa new road's going to bring this parish a flood of dollars."

"And who'll get the blisters and sprain their ankles and wrench their backs and bust their guts and get the rheumatics, doing the road work? The poor people, the little guys. Not the politicians: they don't work. Never lift a finger. All they do is promise. The poor people work

33

their hearts out, but did you ever see a politician die of an overdose of promises?"

"I'm going to shut the door so those communist words can't get out and corrupt our youngsters. Until you officially agree to go to work, Mozusse Chabotte, I declare myself forbidden territory. Hands off! I tell you, if a man hasn't got it in him to heave a shovelful of dirt when it's his turn, on the strippa new road the Right Party's going to give us as a present, that man's heart isn't strong enough to take on his wife."

"Germaine Chabotte," he sighed, "you're always right. I'll run to the Minister's office as fast as I can and ask his permission to add my drop of sweat to the others on the new road."

He stayed glued to his chair. He shut his eyes again.

"Well," Germaine insisted, "are you going? Yes or no?"

"I'll just have a little snooze first."

"You'll be the last one there."

"Ain't my fault if I have to think before I act. It's human nature."

V

Even normal folks can't understand everything

"Election! Election!"

Young Opportun had forgotten all the words he'd learned; all he could say was:

"Election! Election!"

"This time," said one of the bearded men who had got together to comment on the news, "you're right."

His big callused hand roughly stroked the child's head buried in its hunchback's shoulders.

"Been years now you've been announcing an election, Opportun, but this time you got it right."

"If you keep announcing something, it'll happen," said another of the men. The seat of his pants was worn thin by his tractor.

The first man ran his fingers through the jubilant child's tousled hair the way you pet a faithful dog. They loved this child, who followed them around like a pet.

"Election! Election!"

After the accident the child had forgotten everything. He no longer knew who his father was, or his mother. He no longer recognized his house. Like a trusting dog, he followed people. He would go to the fields with one or the other. He was gentle. He asked for nothing. He would linger until someone patted him or fed him. No one was mean to him as they were to other cripples. ("It's such a sad story.") The doctors at the big hospital in the Capital had said that Opportun would never get back the words he'd lost, that he'd never recognize his father or mother again. The accident, explained the doctors, had broken his brain. Only one word had been spared. Why that one? God has His secrets. That was Curé Fourré's reply. The words in Opportun's vocabulary had been shattered like eggshells. The doctors in the big hospital didn't even know if the child would grow. The accident, they explained, had broken an essential little bone. Because that little bone was in crumbs, the child's skeleton had become a cage. The child remembered nothing and could learn nothing. In rain or wind, amid squalls of snow or colored butterflies, at weddings and funerals, auction sales and processions, the child would walk behind the last person who had shown him any affection and proclaim:

"Election! Election!"

"This time, the good Lord struck like lightning! He struck the one that didn't deserve to be punished."

These words had been repeated to Curé Fourré by Mademoiselle Exupérance, the Grade Two teacher, who had heard them from the mouth of Uguzon Dubois, a logger famous for winning every cursing contest in the forest area of the Appalachians. The Curé had organized a public prayer to ask forgiveness of God's infinite justice.

Perched in the pulpit, Curé Fourré had leaned toward his assembled flock and pointed an accusing finger at a back corner of the church. All heads turned, all eyes sought Uguzon Dubois. People realized he was the author of those insults to God. The logger got to his feet.

"If you don't mind me saying so, Monsieur le Curé, I'd like to believe every goddamn one of your holy words. But *hostie*, Monsieur le Curé, it don't make no sense to me that He'd hit a poor little bugger that never hurt a fly with a goddamn lightning bolt. Why didn't He punish me, for Christ's sake? Why didn't He squish me like a pile of shit, if you don't mind me saying so, Monsieur le Curé? How come the Lord if He's so goddamn holy, how come He punished a child as innocent as the goddamn halo around the Baby Jesus' head? Even me, with my goddamn pig's head, I'd never think of a thing like that, *calvaire*."

The Curé asked his flock to pray to erase these impious words that had besmirched the incense-filled air of his church. Then he explained God's justice:

"The acts of God that seem unjust to man are probably the ones that are most just. Man can't understand justice because he himself has so little capacity for justice."

Despite the Curé's inspired efforts, the parishioners still didn't understand why God had punished young Opportun.

The disaster had occurred four years earlier. The child was in the house. The family was eating in silence. The children — they were nine around the table — had learned to be quiet and to chew without making too much noise, for their father, who came in from the fields to eat, liked to find out what was going on in the world before he went back to the fields "to tell the grasshoppers and the snakes" as he put it. That noon, the radio announced the Right Party was about to call an election. "Now that's the best news we could hear!" exclaimed Poutine Lachance, in his excitement spilling his tea. He stood up so energetically he pulled the cloth off the table: plates skittered, glasses overturned and shattered. Pounding the table with his fist, he promised:

"We'll smash the Opposition like an egg!"

Opportun, who was six years old, charged at the screen-door proclaiming:

"Election! Election!"

The main street was peaceful and silent as if no one had heard the great news. The child must spread it. He ran along shouting:

"Election! Election!"

Opportun could tell from his father's expression that an election was a very important matter; he didn't know what it was, but in his child's soul there was a need to shout it to every corner of the village.

"Election! Election!"

He shouted it as he would have shouted: "Light! Light!" if, by some miracle, day had broken in the middle of the darkest night. With the same vigor he would have shouted: "Flowers! Flowers!" if spring had come in January. The word rose to his mouth; he existed only through the word!

"Election! Election!"

He ran down the middle of the street:

"Election! Election!"

He felt as if his voice, repeated by the echo, was striking the horizon and returning to the village, that his voice was rising as high as the steeple and flying as high as the birds.

He didn't see Domitius Vacher's Chevrolet, which hit him. His little body was hurled into the air.

At noon on the day in question, Domitius Vacher too was listening to the news. When he heard the election announcement he dropped his spoon in his bowl of soup and sat there, stunned with surprise. In his opinion Le Chef was making a mistake to call an election at this time of year, when the farmers were more concerned about the haying than politics.

"Domitius Vacher!" cried his wife. "Get off your cloud and come back to earth. When they make an election it means they're going to make a strippa new road. Now you jump in your Chevrolet and run to the Minister's office and ask for the favor of working on the new road."

"The Opposition," he reasoned, "seems tougher than in other elections."

"Domitius Vacher! There's an election on: this is no time for politics. You should be driving off in a cloud of dust to see the Minister. Do you want to work on the new road or not?"

"Sure I want to work on the new road, Romualdine, but a man's entitled to eat his lunch."

"Don't ask me, Domitius Vacher, why we're such a backward people. It's because we always take time out to eat our pea soup before we do anything. If you don't hightail it over to the Minister to ask the favor of working on the new road, Domitius Vacher, your mother-in-law's going to hear about it! And if you've never seen the Devil in person, you'll get an eyeful. Domitius, your loving wife wants you to be the first man the Minister hires for the new road."

Domitius Vacher dragged himself off to his car, but once he was at the wheel the motor gave a frenzied roar. Spitting pebbles and gushing black smoke, Domitius Vacher's car sped down the road. He would be the first one at the Minister's office.

Meanwhile, Opportun was running across the street announcing:

"Election! Election!"

He didn't see Domitius Vacher's fire-breathing car, whose driver didn't see the child. Young Opportun "just rose up in the air like a little saint," some village gossips would say later. Two old men were silently smoking their pipes, their rocking chairs creaking on the wooden gallery as they watched time pass on the village street. They also witnessed the accident.

"If you ask me, shooting up in the air like that don't do the health no good."

The little body came briefly to a standstill, then started crashing down.

"Wanta know my opinion, if the kid didn't get killed on the way up, he'll smash like an egg when he lands."

Opportun was saved by Malice Blanchette.

Malice Blanchette lived in the part of the parish the Old Folks had christened Mud Lake Overflow. Nowhere in the Appalachians was there land so wet. When the fields in other places were dying of drought after weeks when the good Lord refused to send His rain, at Mud Lake Overflow the mud clung to men's shoes and horses' hooves. Mud Lake Overflow had given rise to a number of strange stories. It was said that the earth had swallowed up a farmer and his horse as if it were the sea. They'd never been found. The explanation for this troubling event, it was said, was that there were lakes, ponds and streams hidden everywhere under the earth in that part of the country; at times the covering layer of earth was no thicker than a woman's fancy knickers.

Malice Blanchette knew those stories; as he put it, he knew his ground as well as his mattress. He wasn't worried. If the moisture in the soil had certain drawbacks, it gave his hay a color and a taste that were famous all over the Appalachians. Farmers who wanted to treat their cows before calving so they'd produce happy offspring would feed them nothing but Malice Blanchette's hay.

On the day Domitius Vacher's car catapulted young Opportun, Malice Blanchette was carting the new hay he'd sold to Fidèle Beaupré, a rich farmer who fed his cows the special hay not just at calving time, but even during what he called the courting season. As Malice Blanchette was bringing his load of hay from Mud Lake Overflow, the faithful Fidèle was saying:

"If it ain't Malice Blanchette with a fine load of hay! Nothing better for a bull in love than a happy cow. When my cows see you comin', Malice, they grin!"

The animals thanked him for the fine fodder he'd brought. Whatever he sowed grew higher or bigger than anywhere else: the biggest potatoes, the leafiest lettuce, the heaviest cabbages, the reddest beets. In other areas the land was barren, but at Malice Blanchette's, everything grew in profusion. He was overwhelmed.

He would have been utterly content if only he could drive a truck like other well-off farmers. Unfortunately, though, the road at Mud Lake Overflow was as swampy as the fields. It was awash in brown water. The ruts looked like ponds. No truck was powerful enough to drive this muddy, rough and winding road. Only a horse-drawn cart could pass; only a very strong horse could pull the haywagon through the mud that sometimes came up to the hubs of wheels and the animals' knees.

If Malice Blanchette had driven a truck, the gossips explained to the two old men out rocking on the gallery, who had seen young Opportun shoot up in the air, the truck would have been far away when young Opportun came back to earth; his little body would have been shattered to bits on the hard asphalt road. However, Malice Blanchette's horse, trotting placidly, had driven up with its load of hay just in time to receive young Opportun. The good Lord, the gossips confirmed, had given Malice Blanchette a slow horse instead of a fast truck so as to save young Opportun.

"If the good Lord wanted to save Opportun, why'd He let him get hit by a car in the first place?"

"So He could save him and give the world proof of His goodness."

"I'd like to know how knocking out a kid's a sign of goodness."

"Shut up, communist, or I'll tell Curé Fourré."

"Instead of insulting the Lord you should be praying He won't send you to Hell."

They saw young Opportun's head loom up above Malice Blanchette's green hay, they saw him walking in the hay; with his little hands clutching at the sides of the cart they saw him get off, jump to the ground and dart through the village proclaiming:

"Election! Election!"

To those who didn't understand the child's illness, his father, Poutine Lachance, explained:

"A child's like jam. But instead of little jars of raspberries and currants and blueberries and wild strawberries, they got instincts and feelings and manners and all them things they learn in school. When the car hit my Opportun, all the jars of jam fell off the shelves where the good Lord had put them for my Opportun's lifetime. Everything busted. All the jars of jam got mixed up. My Opportun's shelves are empty now. When the good Lord made him, He made him different from other youngsters. I'm only a man, I can't tell the Lord He made a mistake, but what I do tell Him is: 'I got a gullet full of lumps, I'm so unhappy; why, in Your holy will, are you making my poor Opportun suffer so bad?' If He gave me a straight answer maybe I'd understand, but the good Lord ain't in the habit of answering His creatures. Which means my Opportun can't even talk. Talking, you see, it's something like a violin. The car that attacked my Opportun, it broke the violin that makes him talk. Understand? All he's got is a tiny piece of violin string at the back of his throat, and it can only play two notes: 'Election! Election!'"

Opportun stopped growing. Even the hump on his back had stopped growing. He seemed to be carrying around a pumpkin. With his hump and his small head that kept dipping a little lower toward the ground, with his short legs, one longer than the other, Opportun resembled a big awkward bird that followed behind the humans cheeping:

"Election! Election!"

Young Opportun followed the noisy, be-ribboned marriage processions: "Election! Election!" He would join black funeral corteges, crying amid the tears: "Election! Election!" He would skip among children playing ball: "Election! Election!" He would walk through groups of endlessly arguing men: "Election! Election!" Often, while the Curé

41

was preaching a sermon to say that hell was going to open and swallow up the sinners, young Opportun would call for "Elections! Elections!"

He hardly slept any more, but roamed from bedroom to bedroom whining: "Election! Election!" At night when there were parties in the village, especially at the Good Drink Inn, he'd spy on cars in the night. Embracing lovers often saw his dazed face pop up in the midst of their revels, his eyes bereft of intelligence would come up to the window and watch as if he couldn't see, he would linger and then leave, saying: "Election! Election!" When his father, Poutine Lachance, pasted his ear to the radio to listen to the news, young Opportun would do the same: he too would stick his ear against the cabinet; like his father, he would listen, and then Poutine Lachance would smile briefly, for he knew that since the accident his child understood nothing.

Thanks to Malice Blanchette, the accident had not been fatal. Poutine Lachance wasn't sure if he should be happy or sad about that. Young Opportun was hunchbacked, he'd never grow, he'd never speak, he could never work. He was still alive, and his child's fate was less painful than the fate of children in the countries that were at war. Poutine Lachance was convinced that to the end of his days, his son would be like a big featherless chicken who ate at the table with his other children, but would never do a lick of work.

Poutine Lachance was determined to accept this son who wasn't really a son. He'd got used to seeing him limp. It no longer grated on his nerves when the boy croaked like a frog, he no longer noticed the neck sunk into the child's little body.

Since the accident, time had passed: four years. Poutine Lachance and Opportun, ears pressed to the radio, had heard that Le Chef was giving the populace an election. In Poutine Lachance's opinion, the few members of the Opposition who had weathered the storm of the previous election would fall like rotten apples.

Already young Opportun was limping and skipping from house to house, his little hump shaking, announcing breathlessly:

"Election! Election!"

"If you wanta know what I think," said one of the men with a pitying smile, "I think that little hunchback understands a hell of a lot more than we give him credit for."

"Lots of normal people that aren't hunchbacked don't understand nothing," said another.

Young Opportun stood in the middle of the road, proclaiming:

"Election! Election!"

A car shot forward, a horn blared, tires squealed. The wheels traced two black lines on the pavement. The car zigzagged as if the road were slick with ice; there was a little muffled sound as Opportun's body was struck by the car. The shock hurled him up in the air. While the frail victim rose into the sky, the car stopped and through the open door, a man fell to his knees crying:

"The second time! God, what harm has that child done, to make me hit him with my car every time I see him?"

It was Domitius Vacher. The one who'd struck young Opportun the first time.

Deep in his heart, from the wellspring of the tears that scalded his face, he hated his wife, Romualdine; it was her fault that he'd hit young Opportun again; if she hadn't forced her husband, under pain of separate beds, to go and ask the Minister for work on the new road, he'd never have hit young Opportun. Not even once.

Two black-clad gossips on their way to church caught sight of a child flying, very high.

"It's an angel going to Heaven," said one.

"No," said the other, "that's no little saint. Take a good look, he's coming down to earth."

Young Opportun was flapping his hands and feet like a child splashing in the water, trying to swim. He hadn't been killed by the impact of the car then, but he would shatter like china when he hit the ground. Domitius was weeping. The villagers following the events were silent and still as if they had suddenly heard the end of the world being sounded. Eyes riveted on Opportun's body as it sped back to earth, muscles tense in preparation for the hideous sight of a child's body smashed like a quart of milk dropped on a stone, the gawkers hadn't noticed the slow approach of Malice Blanchette's horse, hitched to a cartful of the

sumptuous hay from Mud Lake Overflow. Malice Blanchette's hay would rescue Opportun. A miracle! Opportun
jumped nimbly out of the cart and someone heard him
ask:

"Do you think I could get a man's job on the new road?"

The gawkers came running, drawn by the screeching
tires, by the exclamations and prayers. The hunchback's
back had straightened under the impact, Opportun had
at one stroke been hammered smooth as a car bumper
after body-work. His spinal column had straightened out.
It was a miracle. Opportun was straight again, like other
children his age who grew with the slender pride of the
young maples that blanketed the Appalachians.

Did they owe the miracle to the Blessed Virgin or the
patron saint of the village, who had roasted over the coals
like a barbecued chicken? Did they owe it to the Baby Jesus
or to the good Lord? Had these favors been cast upon
young Opportun by Saint Expédite herself, the unher-
alded saint to whom the two black-clad old ladies on their
way to the church insisted on praying? During the discussions Poutine Lachance, young Opportun's father, had fallen
to the ground, his face in a patch of grass.

"Poor man," said Malice Blanchette, seeing him in this
position, "he's so happy his legs won't hold him up!"

Only later, well before the end of the controversy re-
garding the author of young Opportun's miracle, did they
realize that Poutine Lachance wasn't breathing. He was as
stiff as a log.

"There's one," said Domitius Vacher, "that won't be
working on the new road."

VI

Is it necessary to please the boss?

The young reporter from *The Provincial Sun* would no longer be restricted to describing minor fires in working-class sections of the Capital. (When the blaze was fierce and devastating, a more experienced journalist was called in.) Often in his room at night he would describe imaginary fires. He had drawn up a vocabulary which he used like a painter's palette. His descriptions of fires were more vigorous, more inspired, smelled more of smoke, sounded more like wood chewed by flames than the elder journalist's accounts, but in the newsroom, where all the journalists looked like a class of seminarians weathered by the years, only grey hair and bald heads counted. Real talent like Achille Bédard's was wasted on dull descriptions of the distribution of school prizes, on descriptions of Monsignor the Bishop's visit to a convent, on transcribing press releases advising the public there would be no garbage collection on the Feast of the Immaculate Conception. The good Lord had given the young reporter the gift of describing things as they really were. Until now, he had thrown away his talent like those pianists who lower themselves by playing cheap music in vulgar places.

This sad period was drawing to an end. Today, Achille Bédard was starting out in Politics. He must not regret his painful apprenticeship. It must have taught him something. What? He'd find out later. That period of suffering was a trial life imposed on all those who would conquer it. It would resist at first, then yield — to those who pushed it. Some would not pass the test: their weakness wouldn't allow it. They would give up, discovering that they didn't want to conquer life. Their dream was only a dream.

He would become a great journalist. His name would be inscribed in the literature: not only his name, but his photograph as well. Selected portions of his articles would be reproduced and future generations of students would read them as he himself had read the elders who had come before. He was the only one in this newsroom who had the inspiration that enables great people to accomplish great things. A hundred years from now, students would memorize the dates of his birth and death. He would not have lived in vain; he would have left his mark.

Today he was turning his back on prize-givings, on summaries of Monsignor's sermons, on minor fires, on third-rate burglaries. Today, he was entering Politics. Without reading the article that Achille Bédard had just set on his desk, the editor-in-chief took a pencil from the sheaf in front of him and circled a letter in red:

"Politics," he snapped, "takes a small p. Nothing in politics deserves a capital. Not even the politicians' names."

Sautereau, the editor-in-chief, was a man with yellow rings around his eyes, like a bruised and battered boxer. He read too much. Others said that his liver was diseased and the bile was rising to his head. He was a pale man, the color of aging paper, and tall, with a body as slender as a pencil. He looked like a snake standing on its tail. He walked with his head bowed as if he was afraid of bumping into the ceiling. He lifted his feet off the floor as if it were strewn with traps. He was a man who never looked happy; he never slept, he had stomach trouble, he didn't laugh, he talked about nothing but work. His mustache resembled a minuscule porcupine that had strayed under his nose. He had been at the newspaper forever. Though he was unhappy there, it was said that the only thing on earth he enjoyed was his unhappiness. Le Chef had made a historic jibe about him:

"Sautereau don't look sautéed, he looks boiled!"

Young Achille Bédard had very little respect for the older man, who had been beaten like an egg in an omelet. Sautereau had pains in his back, pains in his liver, pains in his eyes; he didn't sleep, he had indigestion and aching joints. He cared less about politics than his illnesses. The young journalist was interested in politics above all. He was prepared to shun marriage and family to devote himself to politics. A man committed to politics can get along without women and children. For isn't politics where all human feelings exist most intensely? Cannot politics satisfy all human ambitions? Can it not fulfill all of man's desires, those that spring from his primitive hunter's instincts as well as those that belong to the more highly developed mind of urban man? Cannot politics supply all the emotions needed by a man who wants his life to shudder like a wind-swollen sail? Is politics not life? For Achille Bédard, politics took a capital P.

"Remember," Sautereau repeated, "politics is written with a small p."

The young journalist kept his protests clamped tightly inside in his throat. His editor-in-chief circled all the capital P's he'd spotted with one professional glance, then began to read the article. As he read, he would draw a thick red line through the words. The young man was silent. The first page was scarred with horizontal red lines. Before turning to the second page, Sautereau was careful to criss-cross it with assiduous, emphatic, carefully parallel strokes. When this was done, before he continued his reading, without a word he crumpled the page to throw it in the waste-basket, then he stopped; instead of dropping in the wad of paper, he handed it to the young man and, again without a word, waited for him to take it.

Achille Bédard dug his thumbnail into his palm. He held back his anger. In politics, you must know how to shut up. Sautereau wouldn't always be in his way. In politics there are obstacles to be torn down, and others that break up by themselves. Le Chef had installed Sautereau at *The Provincial Sun*. Whatever power Sautereau possessed came from

Le Chef. Alone, without Le Chef's protection, Sautereau was nothing but a diseased liver, aching joints, a scrawny frame, afflictions and shadowed eyes.

The editor-in-chief went on with his reading. He crossed out every line before starting on the next. He stopped for a moment, got up, went to the pencil-sharpener that was screwed into the window-frame and turned the handle, not looking outside. He crossed out the rest of the article. This time he didn't bother to make his lines straight and parallel; he condemned the article not word by word, line by line, with the pleasure to be derived from torturing a fly, slowly pulling off its wings, removing its legs one at a time, but with a fury he couldn't contain. The page was a smear of red circles, but Sautereau kept crossing out, making jerky zigzags and spirals; relentlessly, he scored the page, the red pencil struck the paper like lightning and he didn't even crumple it before throwing it in the basket, stamping on it with his foot as viciously as if he were stomping on a man.

The young reporter was silent. Sautereau was the man whom Le Chef had placed at the newspaper to see to the Right Party's interests. The young reporter had been rash to write such an article. Would Sautereau send him back to Monsignor's ceremonies, to prize-givings, minor fires, car accidents where no one was hurt? He hadn't intended to attack Le Chef. The time wasn't right. He had only tried to take advantage of the opportunity to point out, with some humor, a few necessary truths. Sautereau was no longer pale but red, as red as the pencil he'd used to attack the article.

The editor-in-chief had opened the door to the penal colony where Achille Bédard was condemned to forced labor on short, useless articles. He'd been required, for example, to write about the death of a city councilor's wife's cat that had been turned to mush by a motorcycle. Sautereau had invited him to approach Politics, then returned him to penal servitude.

It was said that they had Sautereau by the throat. It was whispered that he wasn't free to act as he wished. At the tavern after work, some of the older journalists insinuated that Sautereau must have scores to settle. With whom? The older journalists would answer evasively, their laughter

48

laden with innuendo. "Sautereau's being watched," the oldest conceded. When the young journalist asked for details, the older man got up, on the pretext he had to go back to the office.

"Le Chef could make Sautereau sing," insinuated another man, the one who always had a dead butt, like a tobacco wart, at the corner of his mouth.

"Sing what?" the young journalist asked naively, the first time his colleagues broached this shadowy subject that was mentioned only among the initiated. Another of the elders, the one who wore huge shoes, answered with a smile:

"Sautereau could sing opera with a quaver in his voice like a guy with his you-know-what caught in a vise."

And that was the man who was showing the young reporter the way into Politics. Sautereau was despicable, that was certain. A man who is subject to blackmail is not altogether a man. A man who can be made to dance like a puppet has no dignity. A man who doesn't react like a tiger when life has wounded him deserves no respect. Achille Bédard would simply tell him:

"I'll do the article again, Monsieur Sautereau."

All the tavern conversations came back to him, the innuendo, the laughing silences at the end of unfinished sentences, he saw again the winks of complicity between the elders, the gestures that completed what words would not confide. Standing, his hands behind his back, the young journalist heard himself tell his editor-in-chief:

"Monsieur Sautereau, I realize you aren't comfortable in your situation; I realize you can't allow the truth."

Instantly, as if he'd suddenly been drained of all his blood, the editor-in-chief turned paler than the young man had ever seen him. The pinch of hair under his nose quivered; he started to pound his desk, but his hand came down gently on the green blotter. He seemed to be preparing to roar, but from his shrunken lungs there issued only a wisp of voice:

"I knew you were a bird-brain, but I didn't think you were a bird of prey. It's not so long since your mother was changing your diapers, and now you want to attack our Chef. If it hadn't been for him you wouldn't be at this paper and I wouldn't have read your job application right through. Know-it-alls like you see themselves first, then

49

the world around them. Newspapers aren't made by people like you. You came to *The Provincial Sun* because you got a push from Le Chef. You haven't even got the decency to be grateful for the food in your belly. You bite the hand that gave you alms. You're a down-and-out, a miserable down-and-out because you have a stingy heart. Your article is an underhanded attack on Le Chef. At this newspaper, young man, I see to the interests of Le Chef just as Le Chef sees to the interests of our populace."

The editor-in-chief replaced the cushion on his chair and his bony rear end dropped onto it. He held his little head in his long hands. He was sorry he hadn't controlled his anger. He held his position because of his strength of character. Le Chef had pushed him into this position at the newspaper. But would Le Chef have noticed him if he hadn't had the strength of character that is the source of authority? His headache was back. Why had he lost his temper? Every time he gave in to anger he felt as if his brain was growing inordinately big, becoming as hard as a biceps, that his skull had shrunk and was choking the sensitive organ. The young journalist was nothing but an ambitious little cynic. Sautereau should have simply thrown his article away, without getting so worked up. Ah! but the swaggering little rooster had gumption! Le Chef had a nose for men like him. Sautereau used to be like that himself: loathsome and despicable. Sautereau too had got his hackles up and crowed. The young reporter would get his turn. One day a big invisible hand would squeeze his throat swollen with cries; when that hand was on his neck he'd think twice before he even let out a sigh. His head was splitting! He wished he could take it off, as he often took off his shoe to relieve the corn that tormented him as well.

Achille Bédard re-read his article. He hadn't been very adroit. Sautereau was right to reject it. The young reporter had wanted to introduce some humor into the pages of this paper where sports news, international news and the editorial all had the same tone as the death notices. He learned that a sense of humor wouldn't take him far in politics. Humor is the shadow of a doubt cast over things. Politics must not doubt. He had been wrong to write: "At the end of winter, when country-dwellers see the crows arriving, they exclaim: 'Spring's coming!' And when they see government tractors drive into their villages, they exclaim: 'Election's coming!' "

This article had been neither well-written nor clever nor amusing. The editor had been right to reject his attempt at humor: politics should not be fun. Sautereau had lost his temper; he was quite justified. The young reporter would write the news differently: "Determined to pursue its commitment to build a highway network unique in the world, to be followed by a hydro-electric network that will be the envy of the most affluent nations, determined to pursue a struggle for freedom against the outside forces that threaten us, resolved to reduce taxes, and anxious to be supported at every stage of its government by the deepest will of the people, the Right Party has called an election."

Sautereau would be satisfied. Perhaps Le Chef would be pleased with him as well. Then the young reporter would be corrupt. Achille Bédard refused that path.

VII

Men and women together will build the roads of the future

At first it seemed like a fly that buzzes around a cake before it lands. The Local Riding Minister's hydroplane was hovering very high in the sky, making concentric circles that, instead of shrinking around the lake, were expanding around the village. What could be attracting the Minister's attention? They waited.

Like God in His Heaven, the Minister was looking down upon the land and those who dwelled on it. He was admiring his lake. He could say "my" lake the way others would say "my" trousers or "my" hat. The Right Party's government had lent him the lake for ninety-nine years. Around the lake, the Minister could count the colored roofs of houses. The Right Party's government had made him responsible for populating this beautiful section of the Appalachians where there were too many trees and not enough loggers. The joyous colors of the roofs glowed through the spruce trees.

The Minister had brought Le Chef a map of his riding and pointed out his lake; he had drawn a line around it with a pencil. "This is a road. I've suggested calling it 'Le Chef's Road.' "

Le Chef had smiled:"That way your goddamn farmers'll always be on the right road!"

The Minister laughed hard. Le Chef added: "You couldn't say that if they named it after you."

Then Le Chef laughed. The Minister had to laugh as hard as his Chef. Next he drew lines that started at his lake and went into the countryside in all directions. "I'll be needing some roads," the Minister said confidently. And instead of peering at the map, Le Chef had looked him in the eye:

"Would you mind telling me, you clever son-of-a-bitch, why all your roads go through land you own?"

"Chef, you told me yourself, the province'll never be a country as long as there's areas the size of the ocean that aren't cultivated or inhabited."

"Some times I look at the world: there's the Devil and there's the good Lord. And I ask myself which one's in Power and which is the Opposition. Who's a better politician? The good Lord? The Devil? We can't know. All we can do is go on with our politics, not knowing which we are — the good Lord or the Devil."

Devil or God, the Local Riding Minister was up there in his hydroplane, closer to God than the Devil. He didn't want to land right away, but fly over his territory again. The hydroplane wasn't climbing or descending, it was gliding. The Minister knew where he'd have to hand out strips of road. He knew that such-and-such a hill was so steep, the horses couldn't pull log-laden sleighs up it come winter; elsewhere, the road got so wet in summer, people often couldn't walk to Mass; and somewhere else a dusty road ran through an oatfield and made the crop taste so strongly of sand that in winter the animals wouldn't eat it.

Of his childhood friends the Minister had gone to school with, some had got better marks, others the teacher had liked better, but now they were leaning against a cow, squeezing meager spurts of milk from grimy teats. He, though, was up above. The people in his riding would look at him with the same respect as when they gazed at the horizon, wondering if their fields would be given rain or sun. He was that riding's representative, and its Minister.

He'd been re-elected several times and he'd be re-elected again. There was a force that kept supporting the Minister, like the one that supported his plane. He would sow strips of road through his riding. Anyway, wasn't he a friend of Le Chef? Well, not really a friend, for Le Chef was a free man and a free man stands alone. The Minister too was alone. There were times, though, when Le Chef spoke to him as to a friend . . . Le Chef had confided that the only quality he respected in a man was his having had a humble start in life: "A good man's like a good fruit — self-made." The voters knew that Le Chef respected their Minister. They also knew that the Minister often talked about them to Le Chef. Their riding had obtained more strips of road than any other riding. He would remind them of that and he'd be re-elected again.

The Minister had had a very humble beginning. He'd told the story so often, yet thinking about it again, high in the sky, he smiled. Even as a child, he knew he couldn't bear to be a farmer like his father. He detested the smell of animals, the smell of milk, the smell of the earth. He wouldn't get his hands dirty. He had noticed that the farmers bowed to the ground so much they couldn't straighten up. Even on Sunday, when they headed for church in their clean, pressed suits, their arms seemed to be swinging a pick, their eyes seemed to looking for the tops of weeds; never did they look up to the vast sky, dwelling-place of the good Lord to whom they prayed, where today the Local Riding Minister was light-headedly flying in his hydro-plane, as if he had sprouted vast wings. Never did they look up to the sky without fearing that too much rain or too much sun might fall on their land. As a child, he used to stop playing to study the clouds that resembled curled-up cats or human heads, he would watch the clouds drift by, he would look into the expanse of blue, he would peer into the sky as if it were the water of a well, and gradually, everything swayed. The sky would whirl under his feet, he felt giddy, his head spun; if he shut his eyes he felt as if he were flying. Much later, during his first trips in an airplane, the Minister experienced that same troubling sensation again.

As a child he hated the earth. It felt slimy, like the worms he used to bait his hook when he went fishing in the Famine

River. Farm animals, pigs and cows, dumb beasts that can learn nothing, disgusted him. They forced men to a lifetime of work to feed them and to gather up their stinking dung. Little by little they made men as stupid as they were themselves, with their eyes always looking at the earth. As a child, the Minister had vowed he would never be a servitor to animals. When his father struck him as punishment for not being a good servant to the dirty, stinking beasts, he became hardened to it; with tears prickling behind his eyelids, he tolerated it, swearing that he wouldn't follow his father's road through life. Instead of anger, instead of having his veins bristle with rebellion, he was filled with indulgence for this man who smelled of animals, of their dung and their forage, who, from living with animals, now understood only cries and blows. One day, that man would stop striking him. The child would run away. He often thought about that at school. At night, in the house, before the books spread open on the kitchen table, in the yellow light of the lamp whose nervous flame made the shadows dance, his fingers clutching his pen would stop drawing letters or numbers and he would dream about leaving the farm. He always came back to his scribbler, he always came back to his books, for that was where he would learn what he needed to get by, after he left the land and the animals.

He was still only a child, but already he had left school and his father's house. He didn't go far, just to the village where he got a job with the butcher. He was still living with animals. His hands couldn't get used to touching them, even though they were dead and cut into pieces. He was covered with blood. It made him sick. At night, in his room, he had books, magazines, the newspaper. Almost every week the butcher would see reading material arrive, addressed to his apprentice. The butcher kept an eye on him: one day all that reading would give the apprentice communist ideas. The butcher knew that reading causes immoral ideas, or else it disturbs the brain. Already the apprentice was absent-minded. Once, at the slaughterhouse, as he filled the truck with decaying carcasses for the fox-farmer, the apprentice had slipped and fallen among the stomachs of cows and pigs, the intestines that formed an ooze of slimy, bleeding phlegm. He had tried to swim; like a cat in water, he squalled. He would probably have drowned in the waste if someone hadn't managed to hold out a broomstick. He clutched at it. When they brought him out he was as slippery as the guts. The butcher told him: "If you didn't read so much you wouldn't be so stunned, you could stand on your feet like a man." The butcher, in his thickheaded judgment of a lout who had decided not to be dominated by animals, but to kill them and subject them to his knife, wasn't altogether wrong. The apprentice, who clambered up on the slatted side of the truck, had been distracted by what he'd been reading: how the voice is transmitted by the telephone.

Often, after that, he would explain it behind the counter while he cranked the meat-grinder as it filled pig's intestines with ground meat to make sausages. At the end, he would predict:

"Before I have my first white hair, you'll see a telephone in here, hanging from the wall."

One day when he was repeating this story for perhaps the hundredth time, Armorique Légaré, who had been a pensioner so long nobody could remember what he'd done before, told him with the incredulity of someone who has been watching life for a very long time:

"Listen to him, still wet behind the ears; he talks about the telephone, says it'll come here in a flood like the frogs that invaded La Crapaudière in ought ten . . . Keep listening to him and he'll tell you there'll be folks landing on the moon, to take a leak . . . "

The pensioner guffawed. His worn old voice and his bare gums grimaced at a young man's dreams and at the youth he'd lost forever. The apprentice pointed at old Armorique Légaré, the pensioner:

"I predict there'll even be a telephone on your coffin . . . Only you'll be too hamfisted to make it work!"

The customers' faces were contorted by guffaws that filled the shop. These young ignoramuses were laughing at old age. Flushed with indignation, Armorique Légaré slammed his package of pork chops on the counter.

"If this here's the headquarters for public insults to the pioneers of our village, I'll never set foot in here again. For as long as the good Lord gives me, I'm eating sardines. No more meat wrapped up in insults. Sardines for me!"

The apprentice shouted, still cranking the sausage-machine:

"There's lots of good to be said for the telephone, but it can't keep a man from his grave."

Was his impertinence the last straw? Old Armorique Légaré crashed into the door, his feet powerless to lift him over the threshold. The apprentice was on the verge of regretting the ardor of his words when he felt a hand clutch his wrist and another grasp the seat of his pants; he was lifted up, he went soaring over the old pensioner's prostrate body. When he touched the ground, which took big bites from his hands and knees, he gathered that his days as a butcher's apprentice were over. He got to his feet. His palms were bleeding. His knees too. Limping, he looked at the road which, in one direction led back to his father's house, to the stable, the cows, the fields. In the other direction, the road went behind the Appalachians, to the cities . . .

In his hydroplane, the Local Riding Minister felt his heart swell. He couldn't stop the tears that blurred his vision and slipped down his cheeks as he thought of the child who didn't want to follow in his father's footsteps. That child was alone, as children who dream are alone. The Minister couldn't help him. He didn't wipe his tears because no one could see him cry.

Suddenly, the child was almost a man. There came the monthly meeting of the town council. The mayor and councilors were seated around a green felt-covered table, strapped into their Sunday suits, holding frail papers in their rough farmers' hands. Opposite them, as rowdy as schoolboys, were taxpayers dressed in their everyday clothes, loggers, farmers, truck-drivers and some who didn't have to get their hands dirty — the postmaster, the restaurant-owner, the general storekeeper, the horse dealer. At the front was a youth in his Sunday suit. He had grown. His arms hung out of his sleeves and his shins showed below his trouser cuffs. He asked for permission to speak. His shirt was wet. He was going to get up in front of these men and force them to listen. If they didn't, he'd have to go back to his father's house, to the stable, the fields. He was shaking so hard, one of his shirt-buttons went flying.

He was granted permission to speak even though he was still a minor, even though he wasn't a tax-payer or a property-owner. As he faced these men who had lived so much, how could he fail to dissolve? What would he say to them? The Local Riding Minister does not remember. That moment of his life is not engraved on his memory. The Minister has forgotten all the words that were in his mouth at that moment, but he'll never forget the persistent notion that came to him as he was talking to these men who knew about life and animals and the land: he did not want to go back to his father's house. Abruptly, he told them everything. Then he stopped. There was applause. Those faces, baked by the sun and furrowed by the winter winds and the years that had passed, faces rough and hard as stone, suddenly mellowed in a smile and he saw the big hands come up and strike against one another. They were applauding him!

"Little bugger's got a tongue like an angel: if he don't wanta be a priest he oughtta at least run for Parliament."

In his hydroplane, the Minister thought once more of that meeting and once again he couldn't hold back his tears. Did these men, who knew the past so well, know the future too? They listened to the winds, they observed the movements of the stars, they listened to the night. That was probably the source of their knowledge. The Minister was not at all like them. The sky was something he saw when his travels required him to take a plane. Of the night, he knew that it was as black as the time lost in sleep. The wind no longer spoke to him except, at times, when he remembered his childhood, and then the wind would sing. How had he — a shy and puny youth — been able to convince those men?

He had told them about the telephone. He explained why the telephone would become as common as a knife and fork. Every man would have his telephone just as he had a pencil. Already there were men in city skyscrapers who had drawn on a map that showed every hill, every pond, every house in the parish, the lines that would start at the main line and bring the voice of the telephone into every house; those men in their offices knew how much wire would be needed between every house; they already knew the thickness of the walls they'd have to pierce to insert the wire. The time of the telephone would come, that was certain, just like haying time. The Telephone Company would appear with its huge rolls of wire, workmen eager to put in telephones everywhere, and eager to unroll the wire that would form a kind of immense spiderweb between all the houses. To support the web they would need posts; the Company would come with the longest trucks the village had ever seen, laden with posts, and eager workers would plant the posts all over, in fields and gardens, next to houses and barns. The posts would stay there forever, and the horses would bump their heads against them, mowers or carts would collide with them, they'd attract lightning: animals would be killed for sure. The Telephone Company was powerful; it had a contract with the government. Which meant it could do whatever it wanted. That would come. It wasn't the future, it was already part of the past, because the Company had already gone into regions not far from the Appalachians. They mustn't let a company decide the laws for Saint-Toussaint-des-Saints. The local population must unite and stop the Company from trespassing on their land and planting posts all over, like weeds. To the Company, a single farmer was no more important than a cow plop, but if all the farmers were united, they would become a Company too, and then the Telephone Company would have to be polite and put on white gloves and lift its hat before it spoke to them.

After this speech to the town council, the young man went back to his father's house. At dawn, when the household was awake, he got up and put on his work clothes. He recognized the sounds of pots and pans in the kitchen, the cries of roosters, the cheeping of the hens, the lowing of heavy-uddered cows calling to be milked. When he got to the table where his brothers were slurping their porridge, muzzles in their bowls like dogs, his father looked him straight in the eye. After a long pause, he said:

"I hear tell you made quite a speech to the town council. Sounds like you might have the makings of a politician. In our family we've brought down trees, we've dug roads, we've built houses, we've cut the stones to build the church — but we've never had the honor of talking in Parliament. Now listen, the rest of you — listen to what I've got to say!"

He had shouted. Bowls thudded onto the bare table.

"As of today," declared the father, pounding the table to emphasize the importance of his words, "I forbid this youngster to dirty his hands. Him and him alone, he'll have the right to eat without getting his hands dirty first. Since he won't be touching the dirt with his hands, he won't have the right to touch any inheritance either. And if I hear a squeak out of the rest of you because he's kept his hands clean, whoever squeaks'll lose his right to the inheritance too. That's all I got to say. Now there's been too much eating and not enough working. If the sun got up as late as us, he wouldn't have time to light up all the corners of the earth."

Pulling on his battered, sweat-stained straw hat, the father murmured:

"That one with his little white hands, he's gonna have more property than our family's ever touched."

His father didn't live long enough to see his son realize his prophecy. One winter, just as he'd swung his axe to fell a maple, he slumped into the snow, which was very deep that year, his foot got wedged in the bushes and the tree fell on top of him. They found him the next day. The place was marked by a large blood-stain. All around there were signs of wolves.

The Local Riding Minister often thought of his father when he was travelling by plane. There was surely a Heaven for men who believed in it as his father had. God would be very unjust to such men if He didn't give them the Heaven they'd believed in all their lives. Perhaps his father's soul was in that white cloud, or in the dazzling glint on the windshield, or flying about in the sky. When his father's soul saw the hydroplane passing, he would push the old straw hat to the back of his head with that proud gesture he used when he still lived on the earth, he'd hook his thumbs in the suspenders of his work clothes and, proudly sticking out his belly, proclaim to the other tender souls:

"That's my boy, the one with clean hands. He's a Minister in the Right Party."

The Minister imagined the smile on his father's soul. He wasn't aware that his own face bore that very smile.

After his speech to the town council, the young man made the rounds of the parish. He explained what the telephone was, how it was useful, how you could talk from house to house, from parish to parish, without seeing one another, he dispelled fears that the machine would enable people to hear what was being said in the house. The young man who had hands like an altar boy's, who was skinny, whose thin arms had no biceps, this youth who was still growing, put them on guard against the Company — as powerful as the United States — that was going to come and plant posts all over their fields, their gardens, along their road, putting up wires everywhere. He exhorted the population of his parish to unite and protect their ancestral land. In the end, no one refused to sign the contract he proposed: only he would have the right to plant telephone posts on their land, and he would have the exclusive right, after concluding an agreement with the client, to put up a telephone box on the wall.

How could he, so young, so ignorant about life, make these people listen to him? They sat him down at the kitchen table, with everyone around him — the man of the house, the mother with a child in her arms, and all the other children clustering around him. They listened to him as if he were right.

Once he had collected a dozen duly signed contracts, he decided it was time to advise the government of the new situation. He wrote on the writing paper his mother kept in her dresser drawer for special occasions.

"Monsieur the Right Honourable Premier of the Province:

"The present is to inform you [to make himself sound like an administrator, he'd copied the formula used by the town secretary] of the founding, on the fifteenth (15th) of the present month, of the Company for the Union and Protection of the County Telephone, hereinafter referred to as the Company, which possesses exclusive rights to plant telephone poles on private and public lands in Appalachian County and to install telephone boxes in public and private locations. Any individual or corporation contravening these inalienable rights will come up against the opposition of the original proprietors of the aforementioned exclusive rights which have been ceded to the Company and will risk legal proceedings on the part of the Company and its sole shareholder, Joseph-Amédée

Lasouche. (Signed) Joseph-Amédée Lasouche, age 16, Presi-. dent. (Co-signed) Joseph-Athanase Lasouche, his Father.

"P.S. Kindly send at your earliest convenience all documents required for the legal registering of my Company.

"P.S. #2. Kindly inform the Telephone Company, as quickly as possible, of the existence of my Company for the Union and Protection of the County Telephone, and advise them that our motto is 'Stand like a man.'"

"P.S. #3. Thanks a lot."

And that was how the Minister got his start.

It was time to come down, but the Local Riding Minister wanted to linger in the sky. He made another pass around his hills, his village and his lake. In the plane, he felt as if the sky was entering his body, and he allowed himself to be transformed. Once he was back on the ground, he'd be a hostage to politics again. That didn't displease him. He needed it.

People were waiting for him down on the ground. News of the election was drawing the electorate to his office. From the hydroplane he could see, on roads that he had built, clouds of gravelly dust raised by cars that were hurrying — he was sure of it — in the direction of his office. That was business. The Minister would offer the local people jobs on the construction of the new road, and they would repay him with their votes. His profit: re-election.

The hydroplane approached the lake. The shore was packed with cars. People waved to greet the returning Minister, they hopped up and down on the roofs of their cars; others tore off their shirts and waved them like banners; still others trumpeted their enthusiasm on the horns of their automobiles. Each one hoped to land one of those jobs that don't tire the arms: holding the red flag to slow down motorists, warning the population about dynamite blasts, or being in charge of the cold water to cool off the workers. These tasks were assigned to the Minister's best friends.

The hydroplane rumbled overhead. Its wings whistled above the crowd. It sounded like a sabre thrust in the air. The plane descended and touched down on the lake, which shuddered. There was applause. The plane glided over the water and came to a stop. They waited. Would the Minister appear? They were silent as at Mass, when the bread is about to be changed into the flesh of God. A motor on board backfired, shattering the silence. A skiff was released from shore and headed for the hydroplane. The door opened. They saw the Local Riding Minister, his arms so weighted down with files he couldn't wave to the voters who had turned out to meet him.

At that moment, fifty or sixty canoes, rowboats and rafts all left the shore together. They paddled and rowed toward the Minister. Amid these craft, people swam, naked as fish or in neckties and shoes; others floated in inner-tubes, while still others straddled the trunks of trees. They shouted, wriggled, waved, gesticulated. Arms, oars, paddles, feet pushed at the water, all heading for the skiff in which the Minister stood like the Frenchmen you see in old pictures, coming ashore among the Indians. Suddenly, the man who was straddling his tree-trunk was unseated. The one who was rowing collided with him; hands gripped gunwales and bodies tried to hoist themselves up. The one on the raft sank: his head was in the water. The swimmers were grasped by hands terrified of drowning. The entire mass flapped and fluttered, howled and waved their arms and legs, they swallowed water, spat out water, scanned the smooth water for something to cling to, they tried to swim, tried not to be swept to the bottom of the lake; but they had to float, not give way, not be swallowed up in the water; they mustn't swallow water, they must make themselves as light as water, they must struggle to keep from being smothered in its liquid arms, they must wrest themselves from the water as from the tentacles of an invisible octopus lurking at the bottom of the lake that was flinging up bodies. In this struggle to the death, they had lost shoes and socks; trousers had slipped down haunches and, weighted down by the water, sunk. Paper money, fallen from pockets, was floating. Some hands grabbed it, others hesitated, not knowing if they ought to close around the bills or open out in the water and swim. You had to live if you wanted to approach the Minister and request the privilege of working on the new road he would build before the election. Those who drowned wouldn't get jobs. Hands and feet churned to stay alive. They swam toward the Minister who, when he saw all these bodies stripped bare by the water and glistening in their nakedness, suddenly thought of the

Opposition. They would accuse him of public indecency. The Opposition would publish stories claiming that the Right Party sponsored lewd aquatic orgies during the election campaign, that the Right Party exploited sex to garner votes, that the Right Party was shameless, that it would lead the population into sin and that such sexual transgressions would bring down on the populace the thunder of a raging God. Standing in his boat, the Local Riding Minister felt his head reel. He was dazed. The Opposition would accuse him of being the high priest at a black mass celebrated in the lake to call on the Devil to protect the Right Party. That would be enough to make him lose his election. The Minister brought his hands to his head. His documents took flight. All around him people were jostling, shoving, pushing, spattering, dipping heads under the water, trying to strangle, exchanging kicks, blows, insults, egging on, sinking down, then coming back to the surface of the water. The Minister remembered that Jesus Christ, in the Gospels, had officiated at a baptism during which people had come down and immersed themselves in the water. He would retort to the Opposition that the Right Party was simply following the example of Jesus Christ. The Opposition would be imprisoned by its own strategy. The Local Riding Minister smiled.

Near his boat a big pink body gazed at him with suspicious little eyes; it was not a voter but a pig. On the other side, another pig was floating. Everywhere, among the voters, there were pigs. It was easy to tell the voters from the pigs; the voters flapped around as they swam, while the pigs merely floated like great pink logs. The Minister mused that it's harder to be a man than a pig. He understood at once: the pigs' presence at the launching of his election campaign could be explained as Opposition tactics. The Minister knew his adversaries well. When he spoke into the microphone he would simply point to the pigs and state: "I notice there's some Opposition members in the crowd that's turned out to welcome your Minister." He would use laughter to defuse the Opposition's strategic bomb. He was approaching the shore. Everything that was splashing, swimming, floating, fluttering, was following the Minister's boat. The Minister would announce the construction of several strips of road in the Appalachians. He replaced his fedora with the blue feather in the band, pushing it to the back of his head to uncover his brow; he adjusted the knot in his polka-dot tie.

Le Chef said: "The road of our populace was laid out long ago in the big book on the good Lord's table. Now it's up to the Right Party to build it. Today, we can be proud of what we do. A Right Party man is a man who's as proud as a man who's built his own road by himself." The Local Riding Minister was proud Le Chef talked like that, he was proud to be a member of the Right Party, and his polka-dot tie flapped against his chest like a flag. His skiff was about to touch the shore. ("A country's roads are like the veins and arteries in a man's body," Le Chef said as well.)

Suddenly, the boat was jolted. The Minister saw a person burst out of the water, all draped in hair or seaweed; the person shouted and with widespread arms embraced and clung to him, roaring:

"Me too, I wanta work on the Right Party too! Just because I'm a woman doesn't give you the right to not give me a job. My arms are stronger than my husband's, Origène Rossignol. My backbone's tougher than his, Monsieur. (She pounded her belly.) My backbone carried seventeen children in this here sack. And my Origène made big ones! Just because I'm a woman doesn't mean I can't swing a pick or roll stones or push a barrow or tell dirty jokes. I know some that are better than what you'd hear from my Origène. If I don't get a job on the new road, I'm voting against the Right Party. And my Origène too. Mister Minister, it's high time you came out and said whether you're with us women or against us. If you want new roads, those roads haveta be built by men and by women; we sleep in the same bed, Mister Minister, we live in the same house; so why shouldn't I, Pommette Rossignol, have the same rights as my Origène? Just because I wear a dress with a neck you can see down when I go visiting, is that any reason I shouldn't get a job on the new road? Listen, I can even drive a truck. Mister Minister, when you've been running a man for twenty years, you can make a truck do what you want."

The Local Riding Minister had set foot on the terra firma of his riding. He declared:

"The good Lord gave men the duty to govern this province; the good Lord gave women the power to populate this province; but this province also needs strong arms; and I wouldn't dream — I, who was brought up on the Right Party's philosophy — I wouldn't dream of refusing a woman's arms. I'm not one of those men that's been perverted by the Opposition's ideas, who'd refuse a woman the right to work, under the false pretext that she already enjoyed the right to vote. Women have the right to vote so they can pick the men the good Lord gives His authority to. Those men have to allow the women that vote for them to work. One of the Right Party's fundamental ideas is that men and women — together — must build the roads to the future."

The Local Riding Minister had spotted the journalist from *The Provincial Sun.*

"If you don't report what I've just told this electress — *word for word* — to open my election campaign, you'll be kicked out to starve to death along with the Opposition newspapers the Right Party's going to ruin, one after another. Understand?"

"Monsieur le Ministre, the statement you made to Pommette Rossignol was too magnificent to be consigned to oblivion."

"You're as cunning as a snake, you; I sometimes worry about a fatal bite."

"What are you talking about, Monsieur le Ministre? I've got too much respect for you and for the Right Party."

"Too much respect worries me a lot more than not enough," the Minister rejoined.

He was caught in a wave of electors who'd washed up on the beach like surf and now encircled him. Clothes dripped, the cloth clinging like mud, hugging bellies and bosoms. Hair was pasted to faces. The people were barefoot or had lost one shoe and were dancing on one shod foot. They clamored for the Minister's attention, they bickered, shoved and elbowed one another. The pigs were back on land now too, grunting as loud as the electorate. The Minister was greeted triumphantly; the voters' welcome was a sign of imminent victory. Yes, he'd give work to all those who asked for it. Yes, he was proud, as a member of the Right Party, to open roads so the fine freedom of a free country could circulate. Yes, he was proud to build roads along which people would build houses to fill with children, schools to teach those children how great countries are made, and factories where the populace would produce goods that would be shipped along our roads to countries all around the world.

The Minister finally reached his waiting limousine. Before driving off, he rolled down his window to say goodbye to the electorate and remind people to vote for him. They hoisted themselves up on the limousine, slipped, clung, clutched bumpers, tried to open doors, got hit, ripped clothes, kicked, shouted, threatened. The pigs were calmer. There were pleas and tears. Suddenly Mathusalem Laforce's widow stuck her head in the window to plead her cause, her creased old face smack against the Minister's.

"My Mathusalem, he wanted to work on the road, but he passed on. If he wasn't dead I know he coulda worked. He was a good age, my Mathusalem, but he was as fresh as plenty of youngsters. Take yourself, Minister, Sir, with all due respect, can you mount your woman three times a day, regular as you sit down at the table? My Mathusalem did. He can't any more, because he's passed on. Minister, Sir, my Mathusalem he always voted for you and your Right Party. But now he's passed on. He wanted to work on your new road one last time. In every one of your elections, my Mathusalem worked on your new road. He wanted to this time too. But he passed on. Which means he can't work with his body, but I know my Mathusalem's going to work on your new road with his soul. And I know my Mathusalem's soul's gonna vote for you and your Right Party. But what I want to know is, seeing how his soul's going to work on your new road, how about sending his pay to me?"

The Minister reassured her in a fatherly way. Very slowly, very patiently, the limousine advanced. The Minister glanced out the rear window. The pigs weren't following him.

VIII

And there was no light!

The postman waved a letter:

"Prudentiel Ladouceur, you got a letter from the Minister."

The small grey frame house was stuck in the middle of a meadow where there wasn't even a dirt road. Some shingles were torn off the roof; whenever the postman came he thought the rain must fall inside as well as outside. Strips of tarpaper hung from the walls and swayed in the wind. A shingle flew off the roof, a brick was wrenched from the chimney, a piece of paper was carried off by the wind, a rotten plank came loose from the wall, a window-pane crumbled to the ground. Prudentiel never fixed anything, he never hammered a nail, never climbed a ladder. Prudentiel smoked. He spent the summer sitting on the gallery that hugged the front of his house, all askew because the pillars were more or less in ruins. His wife Hermeline grumbled:

"Instead of wasting your energy smoking, you ought to get a job and work up a sweat."

After long reflection, accompanied by lengthy rocking of his chair (he rocked deeply the way other people breathe deeply), Prudentiel Ladouceur retorted:

"A man needs a little smoke to chase away the epidemic of mosquitoes the good Lord sends us like an Egyptian plague."

He rocked again, reflecting, then stopped and glared furiously at his wife.

"Hermeline Ladouceur, I think you raise your voice a little too much to a husband that's got a weak heart and bad lungs and won't make it through the next winter."

"Prudentiel Ladouceur, you got a letter from your Minister," the postman repeated, shoving it into the cage-shaped mailbox perched on a post.

"I don't want no letter from the Minister. If the good Lord spares me till election time, I'm voting against him."

For a long time, Prudentiel rocked and smoked. As he reflected, his eyes were creased like the eyes of a man with a lot on his mind.

In the last election, Prudentiel and Hermeline had stated publicly that they wouldn't vote for the Right Party because it hadn't given them anything. Prudentiel had made the declaration on his gallery to the mailman who distributed rumors, facts and tales along with letters. On the morning of voting day, the Right Party's Local Organizer suddenly appeared outside Prudentiel and Hermeline's house, along with a man carrying a box of implements and wearing a leather belt with a whole array of tools hanging from it.

"Good day!" exclaimed the organizer. "Today's the day of light! Ah yes, the Minister asked me personally to bring the electricity to you. The Minister promised rural electrification. Ah yes! As of today you can throw out your old coal oil lamp; you're going to get your light the same way they get it in town: from electricity. All the Minister asks is for your vote today."

The man with the toolbox was already inside the house. He glanced up at the ceiling, set down his chest, opened it, pulled out wire, pliers, a hook, a screwdriver. He climbed up on a chair and screwed a hook into the ceiling. Then he knotted some wire around the hook. On the end of the hook, with quick, sure motions of his hands and screwdriver, he attached a socket and screwed in a bulb, which he carefully blew on to get rid of the dust. Then he jumped off his chair, put it back where he'd got it and replaced his tools in the blue chest.

"That's rural electricity!" exclaimed the Right Party's Local Organizer with an impatient look at his watch. "Time's flying, it's time to go and vote. Ah yes! For the Minister!"

Prudentiel, from his rocker, had been keeping an eye on the work. He said:

"Now that me and Hermeline's been rurally electrocuted by the Right Party we'd be ready to go and put our X by the Minister's name . . . But I think me and Hermeline'd be more likely to vote the way you want if we were like everybody else, if we had our electrical wire hanging between a pair of posts out front of the house."

The Right Party's Local Organizer grimaced and went pale.

"The day's nearly over, ha ha! Polling stations'll soon be closed."

He put his hand on the nape of Prudentiel Ladouceur's neck to pull him out of his chair and into the car that would take him to the polling station. Prudentiel smoked as he mulled things over.

"Only thing me and Hermeline want is a length of electrical wire out front of our house. You haveta understand, if the Right Party just does a halfway job of rural electrocution, well then me and Hermeline, we'll just give the Minister half a vote."

Impatient, the Local Organizer didn't know what to think. Persuading this old couple to come out and vote was as arduous as explaining politics to a stump before you pulled it out of the ground. Should he give up on these two votes? The book entitled *How to Win an Election* had taught him to "Promise; if the voter doesn't believe you, promise again. If he thinks you're lying, promise more. The more you promise, the more they'll believe you and vote for your candidate." The Local Organizer assured them that the day after the vote — the day after the Minister's victory — men would come and plant two fine posts, the straightest and tallest in the region, outside the house of Prudentiel and Hermeline Ladouceur.

When he heard the promise, Prudentiel rolled his eyes. Did the gleam in his eyes, behind lids wrinkled and almost shut, indicate incredulity or naiveté? Prudentiel Ladouceur dumped the contents of his pipe in his hand and dropped the black tobacco residue in his shirt pocket. With a typical gesture, he rubbed his balding head, smoothing unruly hair that hadn't been there for a long time. Then, from the other pocket of his shirt, he took a tobacco pouch made from a pig's bladder, the way his late father knew how to make them, he stuffed his pipe, struck a match which he kept from his pipe until the flame had licked his fingers and then, from his cloud of smoke, said:

"If folks going past our house don't see no posts or electrical wire, they're gonna say: 'Hermeline and Prudentiel, they're still living like their ancestors: no electricity. They aren't up-to-date, those two.' No wire, no posts — how d'you expect me and Hermeline to be satisfied with the Right Party? A voter that isn't happy with the Right Party can't vote for it."

The Right Party's Local Organizer did his best to uproot these two from their house, but he mustn't let his bad mood show. His impatience had a strong salty taste in his throat, but he had to smile at these two idiots as if he had honey on his tongue. Time passed. Prudentiel sucked on his pipe. The smoke was time burned up doing nothing. After the election, they'd add up the number of votes brought in by each of the Right Party's servitors. The Local Organizer would have accounted for fewer Xs than the others and they'd conclude that he was "slipping," that he "wasn't as good as he used to be," that his grip wasn't as firm as "back in the good old days when he drove the voters with a whip" and he'd be fired because of these two stubborn old fools. His blood was boiling with rage. He'd lose the title of Local Organizer. Once a man lost his standing with the Right Party, he'd best do like Job and go and sit on a dung-heap.

The Local Organizer turned on his heels and left, head drooping, defeated. He dusted his black car with his handkerchief, rubbed the chrome ornaments, and slowly drove away without raising any dust. Prudentiel took his pipe from his mouth and a broad smile stirred the long bushy hairs of his grey beard.

"For once, Hermeline, the Right Party didn't screw us!"

Just then there was a growl of motors amid a cloud of dust. A truck brought two long posts with the Right Party's blue flag dangling from one end. In front of Prudentiel and Hermeline's house, workmen jumped over the slatted sides or sprang out of the cab of the truck. The Local

71

Organizer got out of his car and set to work polishing it with his white handkerchief until it gleamed. Then picks, pickaxes and shovels attacked the earth. In less time than it takes a cat to hide his turd, two holes had been dug for the two long wooden posts. The workmen grabbed hold of one that must have stood as high as eight or ten men. The post was planted like a candle in a birthday-cake. Then they repeated the operation, lining up the second post with the same sighs and movements. When both posts were standing in the ground, the man with climbing irons on his boots clambered up like a squirrel, unwound some wire, attached it to the head of the post, clambered down as fast as he'd gone up, ran to the other post, scurried up even faster, unwound his wire, pulled it tight between the posts, knotted it and slid down to the ground with his legs wrapped around the post.

Prudentiel and Hermeline were rocking. They hadn't shown the faintest sign of interest in the rural electrification work. It was as if the smoke from Prudentiel's pipe had hidden it. The Local Organizer came up to them wreathed in the sweet smile of a generous man.

"Now then, ahem, you're going to come and give the Minister your vote. Right now!"

Prudentiel cautiously got to his feet. Hermeline did the same.

"It's the truth, Hermeline! The Right Party gave us light: let's go give it our vote!"

Nowhere on earth was there a feather lighter than the Local Organizer. He'd succeeded in moving those two mountains and no voter could resist him now.

They put their X in the little square reserved for the Right Party's Minister. Prudentiel Ladouceur's hand hadn't shaken so hard since he'd signed his will in the Notary's office; Hermeline's hand was calmer when the wedding ring was slipped onto her finger. They went home hoping for night to come quickly so they could enjoy their electric light.

Prudentiel was smoking. Hermeline was silent. They rocked in their chairs and gazed at the sun, still high in the sky. Prudentiel said:

"He's stayin' put."

Hermeline agreed. The smoke from his pipe was suspended before him, a big balloon unmoved by any wind. He repeated:

"He's stayin' put."

Man and wife both stared at the big red ball screwed into an unchanging sky. He smoked. She was silent. They rocked. Night would come late. No clouds. Flowers made multicolored stains on the grass. No frogs sang. Hermeline didn't see a single butterfly.

"He's stayin' put."

Nothing was more beautiful than the wire stretched out between two upright posts in front of their house. Suddenly the sun sank like a pebble in the blue water of the sky, now tinged with the blood-color of the evening star, but soon to resemble a dark pond filled with strange grasses. The sun was already extinguished. Prudentiel turned his head toward his wife, who was rocking beside him. He couldn't even see her. Night had returned.

"Hermeline, we don't have to sit out here looking at the stars now we're on the rural electricity. Come on inside."

Inside the house, chairs and table blended into the night. The windows were as opaque as the walls. Like a magician, a sorcerer, like the good Lord at the beginning of the world, Prudentiel would create light. The night would bolt like a black horse that's been whipped. He would cover the night with light as you cover a wall with fresh paint: not the wan, yellow, pissy, hesitant, trembling light of the coal-oil lamp that shed its grimy illumination in the room. It would be beautiful electric light, as bright as the noonday sun, beautiful rural electrification light, a gift of the Right Party to the good people of the province. The electric wire was stretched between two posts in front of the house. The bulb was attached to the wire. The wire hung from the ceiling. He had only to press the switch. Light would pour out onto everything in the room and spill out the windows. With numb fingers Prudentiel groped for the switch. He felt the button. Prudentiel shut his eyes.

"Hermeline, you shut your eyes too. Don't open them till I tell you."

He pressed the button. He waited a moment, feet rooted to the floor as if he were preparing to receive a shock.

"All right, Hermeline, we can open our eyes. Not too fast though, the electric light might blind you."

Gently their eyelids moved, slowly Hermeline and Prudentiel's eyes opened and they saw nothing but night, plain ordinary night as if the light at the end of the wire, which they couldn't see, contained not light but night.

"Wait a bit, Hermeline, maybe it takes a while for the light to get to the bulb."

They waited, eyes open in the night, unmoving, ready to be blinded by a sudden burst of light. The night was still black. Hermeline stirred, he could hear her walking, he heard a cupboard door creak as she opened it. She was rummaging among the glasses and dishes. A match was struck and in the spot of light, Prudentiel saw that Hermeline was lifting the globe off the coal-oil lamp so she could light it.

"If you ask me," Prudentiel muttered, "we ain't been rurally electrocuted."

Quite calmly, with deceptive, almost meek tranquillity (there'd be time for revenge, there'd be another election and he'd give his vote to the Opposition), he waited for Hermeline to set the lamp on the kitchen table. Dragging his feet, he went to his chair beside the table, beside the coal-oil lamp, because he liked to watch himself smoke.

"I think, Hermeline, the Right Party's screwed us."

In the election, the Right Party triumphed. Time passed. In the first weeks, Prudentiel often fiddled with the switch, hoping without admitting it that he'd see electric light burst out like durable lightning. He had to resign himself; he would continue to live in the age of the lamp. His ancestors had lived out their lives without rural electrification, by the light of a coal-oil lamp. Hermeline often pressed the switch, surprised each time when nothing happened, hoping each time that the wire hanging from the ceiling would suddenly be filled with electric power. More weeks passed, more months sped by. The dream was slowly forgotten, the way that real things wear out. Years passed. They stopped seeing the electric wire and the two posts outside the house when they looked at the forest which disappeared behind the horizon. They stopped seeing the dead bulb hanging from a wire that had no electricity. The coal-oil lamp still illuminated their evenings as it had done since they were children.

And now the radio had announced another election. They began to see again, outside their house, the wire with no electricity in it and the bulb hanging from their kitchen ceiling that had never been visited by the smallest electric spark. This time they would vote for the Opposition. The postman came with a letter from the Minister, who had written every voter to announce his promises.

"Read your letter, Prudentiel," exclaimed the postman, "I know what the Minister said in it, but read it with your own eyes cause it ain't every day a Christian gets a letter from the Right Party."

Prudentiel took a few puffs as he rocked; the postman left for the neighbor's, far away. At the sound of Prudentiel's voice he turned and came back.

"What're they promising for their election this time?"

"They want to put down a strippa new road outside your door."

"You can keep your Minister's letter to wipe your you-know-what. Me and Hermeline, we'll vote for the Right Party when we see the new road outside our door — and not before."

IX

Heaven and earth shake hands

"Monsieur le Ministre, our blessed Curé wishes to speak with our Minister."

His secretary spoke in the same low, circumspect voice she must use in the confessional to acknowledge her imperfections to the priest. She had no children, she had no husband, she had no friends, she refused to travel, she wouldn't even take a vacation. Her whole life was lived in the Local Riding Minister's office. She would not allow a single piece of paper to go unfiled. She would not allow a single grain of dust to settle. All transactions were inscribed in her memory. She remembered everything the voters had ever asked for. She knew every promise the Minister had ever made. She recorded, so it would never be forgotten, everything the Minister had given his voters, everything he'd refused to give his enemies in the Opposition. At the Minister's request, she could rhyme off a list of grants awarded, the numbers of the lots ceded for private development, the names of the beneficiaries; she knew precisely where the Right Party had built strips of new road, whose lots had been expropriated, the sums paid in compensation, she could draw up the list of contractors and an inventory of their machines, she could name those who had been late in starting their contracts and those who were late in finishing; she had identified the ones who exceeded their allotted budgets. As for the party's campaign fund, she knew the list of contributors, she knew whether they had contributed more or less than in earlier campaigns. The documents filed impeccably in their folders, as carefully as nuns stored the sacred vestments, seemed to exist only to prove that the secretary had never made a mistake.

"I'm expecting the blessed Curé," said the Minister loud enough to be heard by all his visitors.

Mélanie Binette had been a mere adolescent, just out of the Reverend Sisters' School for Matchless Women, where she learned typing, bookkeeping, accounting, knitting and English, when she went to work for the Local Riding Minister. He was a very young businessman at the time and Mélanie Binette had been with him ever since. He had become an important man in the riding, had got himself elected first municipal councilor, then mayor, then a member of the provincial legislature; he'd been named a Minister by Le Chef and become one of Le Chef's pampered Ministers. He had built roads in the riding, he had travelled all across the country, he often went to the United States, he went to Europe every year, he'd even been to Africa. Mélanie Binette had stayed with the Minister. He had never once criticized her, though he was a man feared by all.

When she first saw the new minister come into her office, Mélanie Binette felt herself blush. Her legs went rubbery and she had to sit down. She held her arms folded across her bosom and couldn't keep from trembling. She could, however, conceal the pounding of her heart. Her boss a Minister! What an honor! Le Chef hadn't picked some other secretary's boss, he'd chosen hers. She was working for a Minister who had been chosen by Le Chef. She went out in the field behind the church and picked some flowers. She set a bouquet on the Minister's desk, put a tiny bunch of everlastings on her own desk, then braided a garland of flowers and draped it around a large photograph of the Minister she had hung on the wall. She also slipped some daisies in her hair. In spite of all the emotion, she managed to utter: "Good morning, Honorable Minister."

The great man started.

"Mélanie Binette (there was real anger in his voice), if you call me 'Honorable' again you can get the hell out. I'm no more honorable than I was before I got to be Minister. Now that Le Chef's given me the combination to the safe, I suspect I'll be even less. I'm counting on you, Mélanie Binette, to be my guardian angel, my conscience."

His man's eyes sought Mélanie Binette's. She tried to look away but couldn't, she tried to lower her gaze but was unable to do so; she could feel a blazing heat in her eyes. It was no longer she who directed her gaze, but the Minister. He was looking at her now as he'd never looked at her before.

"Mélanie Binette, we've spent quite a few years together. You're a woman, I'm a man; I've never seen what's under your dress; Mélanie, show me how the good Lord made you."

When he had that man's look in his eyes she couldn't disobey him; she unbuttoned her dress, loosened it and let it fall to the floor; unhesitatingly she took off her slip, unhooked her brassiere; the Local Riding Minister looked her smack in the eyes as if he hadn't seen her swelling breasts.

"What a waste!" she heard. "The good Lord makes a woman who's a masterpiece, and she's hidden away in the office of a Right Party M.P., and even he can't get a look at her till he's a Minister."

The Minister was no longer looking into her eyes. She saw him come toward her, hands out as if to gather fruit.

"Honorable Minister," she said, "hands off. I'm going to give you the weekly report, starting with the phone calls, then the visits, then the mail . . . "

"Another time," said the Minister, making a half-hearted effort to leave the office.

She heard him breathing hard as if he'd been running.

"Honorable Minister!" she said again.

He stopped, but didn't turn around.

"Honorable Minister," she repeated, "I've often thought of what I'm about to tell you. I've thought about it every day, I've thought about it every night. Many nights I haven't slept a wink from thinking about it so much. So what

I'm about to tell you isn't some little girl's dream, it's a woman's thoughts. Here it is: we don't know what road the good Lord's laid out for us in the future, but if it should happen that it's your destiny for the good Lord to take your wife and call her back to Him in Heaven, I'd like it to be on my route for me to give myself to you, and I'd like it to be on your route to want me to give myself to you. Honorable Minister (she stammered and realized that her lips couldn't say everything that had to be said), I've thought about that often (her heart was pounding even harder): I'd like to be in your wife's place. I've often thought about it even here in the office, while I was at work. I'll never try to take your wife's place by myself but I'll gladly take it if the good Lord gives it to me. Honorable Minister, if the good Lord takes your wife away, I'd like Him to give me to you. If He gives me to you, I'd want to be as fresh and new as a perfect apple that hasn't been picked, a fine apple that's still attached to the branch and has never been eaten by a worm."

The Local Riding Minister turned to her and gazed deep into her eyes again. This time she didn't feel her own eyes burning. His face was flushed.

"Mélanie Binette, I want to see your bum."

She turned her back and slipped her briefs off her buttocks and down her thighs. The Minister gazed and murmured:

"What a waste!"

"I've never wished your wife any harm, Honorable Minister. If I let your hand touch my body, I think it would hurt your wife terribly, but if the good Lord were to take her away and if the good Lord were to give me to you in her place, then I'd be yours entirely, Honorable Minister, and you could work me like your land."

Again the Minister murmured,

"What a waste! I'm going to take a rest."

She heard him breathing very hard again, then his office door was opened and shut. She put her clothes on, weeping, but she didn't leave her desk. She had been given the helm of this office and she wasn't one of those women who abandon their responsibilities just because of some tears in their eyes.

The next day, the new Minister entered the office in his usual way, as if he would rather knock down walls than walk through doorways. He stopped abruptly in front of his secretary.

"Mélanie Binette," he said, "I thought about you during the night."

"Honorable Minister . . . "

"I forbid you to call me that!"

"And I, Honorable Minister, forbid you to think about me in your bed at night, when Madame's asleep beside you. If I know you're thinking about me in the big bed you share with Madame, I'll feel guilty of a great sin; I don't want to commit that sin, I'm not that wicked. Only one of us is entitled to think of the other at night, and that's me. Because I'm alone in my bed and I get all sorts of ideas that keep me awake. I'm always thinking about my work, about what I've done and what I have to do, about the letters to be written, the bookkeeping, the forms to fill out. Which means that I think about you. I'm entitled to do that, because I'm not lying next to the person I married for life."

The Minister came near her desk, rested his hairy man's hands between two piles of documents and, leaning toward her, closer than he'd ever been, told her in a voice that was almost tender:

"Mélanie Binette, I wish that all the roads I build across my riding were as solid as you."

She had learned at the Reverend Sisters' School for Matchless Women that, between the man who was boss and his devoted secretary, there must always be a grille "similar," they said, "to the one that separates the cloister from civilian life." If that grille were taken down, secretaries would no longer be respectable and respected. "When bosses touch their secretaries," she'd been taught, "they leave indelible stains like sins that may be forgiven but not erased." Mélanie Binette stopped herself from touching the Minister's hand with her own. But her heart was pounding and the Minister, who was staring at her bosom, must be able to see it beating through the dress stretched tight across her breasts. She didn't have the right to touch this man who belonged to another woman, but she felt a strange urge to tear off her dress and throw herself against the body of her Minister, who smiled suddenly and said, laughingly:

"The difference between you and my roads, Mélanie Binette, you aren't open to traffic."

And he withdrew into his office.

"What a waste!"

The Minister had forgotten these moments, just as he often forgot his glasses: never finding them, never bothering to look for them, forgetting he'd forgotten them. Mélanie Binette had forgotten nothing. Some years later, she thought about them again during endless and exhausting bouts of insomnia in her big spinster's bed that saw time speed by and bring her only solitude. Her sisters were married, her parents were old, she had cared for them until they died, almost at the same time, just as if they had wanted to set off together on the long journey into the eternally-silent night. She found herself alone in a house that was far too big for her, without a man or a child; she sold it and rented an apartment in a house where the children were big enough to laugh at her because she didn't have a husband. The good Lord hadn't chosen her to be this man's wife, but He had selected her to be this Minister's secretary and to accompany him through the storms, the ups and downs, the weary stretches and all the traps and pitfalls along the road of his political life. Perhaps that was as important as being the wife of a Minister who never saw her husband in his office, where he lived his real life, but saw him only in her bed, with unruly hair rumpled by sleep, without a shirt or tie, Ah! barefoot, with his ugly toenails, Ah! a man in his underwear, Ah! She hadn't taken a wrong turn. She considered herself lucky to have been chosen as her Minister's secretary.

"What're you thinking about, Mélanie Binette?" the Minister asked. "There's no need to announce Monsieur le Curé. Just show him in. He's at home here. In the pulpit Monsieur le Curé shows his flock that the Right Party's a little like Heaven, while the Opposition's a lot like Hell. What can I do for you, Monsieur le Curé?"

Political power extended its hand to divine power. The two hands were clasped confidently, joined like beams supporting a house. The Minister kept his eyes to the ground where he exercised his power, while the priest looked up to Heaven where he had a certain influence.

Curé Fourré seemed not to have a body, as if the loose soutane were draped over his soul. The man of God had a greenish complexion. As a young seminarian, his piety foretold a future saint. His name was even mentioned to the bishop of the diocese. Once, following the long prayers in the service on the Friday of Christ's death, turned away from life here below and with all his thoughts directed to Heaven, transported by his prayers, the seminarian had kissed the crucifix on his rosary with so much avid piety, he swallowed the rosary. Facetious fellow-priests who hadn't attained his degree of spirituality and didn't share his respect for religious objects, invented — no doubt inspired by the demon himself — a whole epic of adventures for the rosary in seminarian Fourré's body. The rosary remained inside the young man's body and he saw himself as the receptacle of a consecrated object. He had learned to consider himself as worthy as the monstrance that contains the sacred Host. It was said that he owed his greenish coloring to the crucifix, which had tarnished in his body and tarnished his skin as well.

"Monsieur le Ministre, there has been a miracle in Saint-Toussaint-des-Saints, where not all our parishioners are saints and many sins of the flesh are committed. A number of our parishioners saw this miracle with their own eyes. Monsieur le Ministre, God Himself has travelled the road of our village, and wrought a miracle. Monsieur le Ministre, don't you think we ought to give thanks to God?"

"Monsieur le Curé," said the Minister, "must we not always give thanks to God, without even waiting for a miracle? Myself, for instance, when I think that I'm alive, that's already quite a miracle. And I thank the good Lord . . . But you tell me, Monsieur le Curé, you tell me the Lord has worked a greater miracle in our village than the one that bestowed life on your Minister?"

"Monsieur le Ministre, do you remember young Opportun, the son of Poutine Lachance, one of the believers in the Right Party, a man who's never voted for the Opposition? Do you remember how the good Lord, for reasons incomprehensible to us with our fallen angels' intelligence, took away his power of speech? Do you

82

remember the touching little frog who used to hop around croaking: 'Election! Election!'? Very well: the good Lord, blessed be His name, has restored young Opportun's power of speech. It is a very great miracle. We must give thanks to God. Man, a mere insect upon this earth, does not have the right not to sing the praises of his Creator when He has given evidence of so much love for one of His children. Do you agree, Monsieur le Ministre?"

"Monsieur le Curé, you're expressing my very thoughts. Of course I agree, and when I tell my Chef, he won't think otherwise. He'll certainly respect a Curé who attracts miracles. Monsieur le Curé, we need miracles in this province which is threatened by a constantly criticizing Opposition. Monsieur le Curé, we're both men of authority, we share the same ideas, so tell me what you want. 'Ask and ye shall be given.' We in the Right Party, we respect religion, and the Right Party doesn't tolerate communists the way the Opposition does."

Curé Fourré remained standing, looking up at the ceiling as if there were no obstacle between him and Heaven. His skinny hands, their long fingers accustomed to delicately turning the pages of his breviary, were crossed on his chest.

"The good Lord has inspired me to organize a grand procession. The good Lord has inspired me to have all the statues in the church take part in the procession too. Unfortunately, the saints won't be proud of the statues that represent them: they're old and peeling; the hands and noses have been broken and glued back together. On some, the head has been removed and replaced by the head from another statue. No, the saints who take part in our great thanksgiving procession won't be proud at the sight of themselves."

The Local Riding Minister often had dealings with the clergy and was quick to understand their language.

"Granted!" he replied, rather un-clerically.

Curé Fourré bowed his head slightly, his eyes still gazing at Heaven. The Minister called his secretary.

"Mélanie Binette, you're a woman, you've got good taste, go and help Monsieur le Curé buy some new statues for the church. The Right Party wants to thank the good Lord for His miracle."

"Modern art makes fine-looking statues," said the Curé.

"The Right Party promises, Monsieur le Curé, it'll be with you in your procession. Monsieur le Curé, will you be with us in the election?"

"God creates men and lays out their path," said the prophet.

Curé Fourré left, singing a *Te Deum* in his head. Children, spying the Curé, came and joined him, the priest let the words to the hymn of gratitude escape his lips, the children began to sing along with him, other children came and swelled the group and the procession giving thanks to God accompanied the holy man to the presbytery.

"Mélanie Binette, get me Pomerleau's number: Pomerleau the Minister. That bugger sells typewriters to the Government and statues to the Church. He drinks from both tits."

"You, Monsieur le Ministre, you have roads . . ."

"It's true, the future's at the end of the road . . . Pomerleau's going to give me a good price on those statues. The bugger owes me a few strips of road . . . You remember that, eh, Mélanie Binette."

X

When Caesar or Napoleon
lost everything

The voice on the telephone was as sharp as the saber thrust that slices a man in half.

"You'll never get another contract from the Right Party, Verrochio. You're going to lose everything you've ever got from the Right Party. You'll be naked in the street, as naked as the day you were born. You'll have to mortgage your asshole. You're going bankrupt Verrochio, and you know why."

Nino Verrochio was sure his hair had turned white all at once. He was ruined, he'd stopped breathing, he was a dead man.

"The Right Party made you like God made the first man: out of nothing. The Right Party made a businessman of you. In all your machines there's not one screw the Right Party didn't pay for. In your fine house on the heights of Quebec there's not one nail the Right Party didn't pay for. Your wife dresses better than the Queen of England, and there isn't one thread in her wardrobe the Right Party didn't pay for. Even you, Verrochio you son-of-a-bitch, you haven't got a fly-button you don't owe to the Right

Party. Is it true, what I just said, or am I a goddamn liar, a two-faced hypocrite like you?"

"I'm think I'm owe a big debt to the Party."

"To the Right Party. You owe more than a big debt. If it wasn't for the Right Party you wouldn't be here."

"Maybe I could talk to your boss, explain him a few things."

"Explain what? My boss wants to kill you, you son-of-a-bitch. And you know why . . . Right in the middle of an election campaign, when we have to do everything we can to be sure the Right Party triumphs, you go and make a thousand-dollar charitable donation to the Opposition."

"And I'm tell you, that's not true. All the money I've got to give at election time, I'm give to the Right Party. I've got *onore*."

"We know everything that goes on in the Opposition, it's the Right Party that controls their purse-strings."

"Cars, they got a bumper in front and a bumper in back, to protect from shocks. The Right Party, she's going to win the election, that's for sure. But if the Right Party loses, me, I'm a businessman, I need my bumper. A thousand smackers to the Opposition, that's the price for my bumper. A thousand little smackers, that's not mean I'm stop being a friend of the Right Party. If she lose the election, my company gets contracts from the Opposition. Then I'll be a friend that can invest in the Right Party's campaign fund and help you get back in power. You're gonna need friends you can count on like me and I'm need friends I can count on like you — my good friends in the Right Party."

"Don't try and bamboozle me with your sweet talk all twisted and tangled like spaghetti, Verrochio. You listen to me like you'd listen to a judge that's reading your death sentence. First of all, you owe your life to the Right Party. Second of all, the Opposition's going to be wiped out like a fly, so you can kiss your thousand smackers goodbye. Third of all, the Right Party's going to be elected because that's who the people want. Verrochio, you're a dead man, defunct, a goner. The Right Party washes its hands of you, you son-of-a-bitch. Your machines won't be hauling one goddamn pebble. A man without a heart can't live long. You're going to end up like you started, penniless. If you were smart you'd go back where you came from, back to the wilds of Italy. You'd be even better off six feet under. Warn your wife, you won't be leaving any estate. Such a good-looking dame . . . She'll make a handsome widow, nice and round where a broad's supposed to be round . . . When you gave the Opposition a hand, Verrochio, you slipped the rope around your own neck. The undertaker'll have to bury your hide on credit."

He hung up. Nino Verrochio's legs had turned to jelly, his arms were limp and all the muscles in his body had gone flabby. His heart was as heavy as a stone and couldn't beat. He needed air. Nino Verrochio dragged himself outside. He thought he was crawling but he was walking, walking like a drunken man past his secretaries, who thought the boss had drunk too much wine. He was pale as he ran outside to vomit. Air, air! The Capital was baking in the sun, which smelled of oil. He was suffocating as if his chest was filled with cement. His ears were buzzing. The veins in his temples were too small for the blood that was swelling them. Air! He collided with a truck. He realized he couldn't see. He brought his fingers to his eyes. They were awash in tears. Nino Verrochio was ruined.

Yesterday he had been a rich man. Today he was poor. Without his contracts from the Right Party he couldn't keep up his mortgage payments. His creditors belonged to the Right Party and now that he'd fallen they'd show a renegade no pity. Though he kept saying, "I'm ruined," he still couldn't believe it.

Whenever he approached one of his roads under construction, he liked to stop his Cadillac on a hill and, proud as Napoleon before the pyramids, gaze at the machines that bore his name: Verrochio Construction International. He would admire his machines that crunched up forests and swamps, he would listen to the music of his bulldozers, tractors, trucks, steam shovels, his graders whose harsh voices rumbled above the hills. He stopped and meditated. The mechanical chorus sang in his ears: "You're a rich man, Nino Verrochio." Then he'd get back in his Cadillac and make straight for his worksite. He'd pull up in a cloud of dust, spring from the Cadillac like a lion bounding from his cage and talk to his men the way people used to talk to him when he was poor. Then he'd take off again. He didn't believe he was rich, yet he was no longer a barefoot child in the swamps of Sardinia; he was no longer the youth who one morning kissed his mother and father, brothers and sisters, and left *casa* and *paese*; he was no longer the tearful traveller standing in the wind at the back of a boat jolting across an endless sea; he was no longer an immigrant with hands flayed by hard labor; he was no longer a gardener dazed by the sun, tending flowers as he knelt on the ground; he was no longer the young man so exhausted he'd forgotten his *paese*, his *casa* and his *mamma*, who was working now because in America, gold comes to the man who sweats day and night. Now he was a man with grey hair. The top of his skull was slightly bald. He'd never gone back to Sardinia. He'd shed the poverty that clung to him like his accent: he had worked and he had grown rich. As he drove his Cadillac to another worksite he'd started because he was on good terms with the Right Party, he couldn't believe he was rich.

The telephone call had struck like lightning. His empire was crumbling like a burning building. He walked like a sick, sad old man. The flock of machines in the parking-lot bore the name of the child from Sardinia who had got rich in America. The machines gleamed. They weren't covered with the grey grime of the worksites. They hadn't been spattered with the black grease that is the sweat of machines. Their steel wasn't aching with effort. The tractors, bulldozers, graders, crushers, compacting cylinders and cranes were motionless, silent and cold. Already his machines had abandoned him.

Nino Verrochio was once again as poor as he'd been in Sardinia. He was as poor as if he'd never left the earth of his *paese*, poorer than the young man on the ship who was never separated from his leatherette suitcase, so afraid he was that his clothes would be stolen. He was a ruined man. His heart was so terrified it dared not beat.

He was leaning against a crusher. His suit was wet, as his clothes used to be when he'd been working under the blazing sun. His machines would be seized. His warehouses would be taken away, he'd lose his land, his houses, the bank would withdraw his credit, he'd lose his house, and he'd discover again the *poverta* of the young man from Sardinia.

He hadn't lacked *onore* as far as the Right Party was concerned. By contributing to the Opposition's campaign fund he'd only been acting like a cautious contractor. There was a big sweat stain on the back of his pale blue jacket when he leaped inside his Cadillac. The wheels tore up the dirt. The accountant looked up from his adding machine. The black Cadillac sped by as if there were no other cars on the street, no children playing their carefree games. Nino Verrochio knew where he was going. A victim, Nino Verrochio would rather smash his head against a brick wall than be smashed by the Right Party. Nino Verrochio had never returned to his native land. He had never felt rich enough to show his face in Sardinia. He'd go back there one day, and people would agree that he'd been right to leave his homeland and his family. Nino wasn't one of those people who open a cobbler's shop or a pizza stand and then declare, in letters that dazzle the cousins who haven't had the courage to flee their misery, that they've made their fortune in America. Nino Verrochio was a builder: he had built houses, he had built roads, he would build cities. America had given Nino Verrochio the frenzy for life that sets fire to a man. No miserable political clerk was going to stop him from building. Building was his *life*! The Right Party would give him other contracts. He wouldn't go bankrupt. He would fight like a man who refuses to die. The bank wouldn't come and seize his machines or his warehouse or his property or his houses.

If Nino Verrochio had stayed in Sardinia like the rest of his family, he would never have known the thrill that comes from fighting an adversary far more powerful than he. How he loved this new country where a man can fight Goliath and win! He would not be ruined. He would fight as he'd never fought before. Sure, he'd contributed to the Opposition's campaign fund, but so had some of the Right Party's honorable ministers. His name would stay in big letters across his warehouses and garages. Soon his machines would thunder across the worksite for the new road. Nino Verrochio would bind himself, on his *onore*, to pay what he owed. He would fight the way a desperate man swims. The tires of his Cadillac shrilled along the pavement. He didn't obey the stop lights. Impulsively, he blew his horn.

He knew where he was going. Nino Verrochio was going to the Kerhulu Restaurant where the Ministers often ate their meals. A number of times, Nino Verrochio, child of a poverty-stricken Sardinian village, had been the guest of one of these ministers, who called him Nino, like a friend.

He left his car beside the sidewalk. Business is sometimes cruel. He had once known a gardener who, like him, came from Sardinia — Ermenegildo, an old man who'd lost the power of speech. This compatriot was far younger than you'd think from his wrinkles and white hair; he had once been a millionaire, but during the Depression, he lost everything in a financial operation, through fear and despair. It was said that Ermenegildo's hair had turned white overnight. In a single night the back of that man of steel had bent like the backs of men who perform the humblest tasks. After going bankrupt, Ermenegildo had resumed the humble work he'd done when he arrived in the new country. This silent man seemed deaf as well; he wrapped himself in the silence of a wordless dream. Nino Verrochio would fight. Pirates wouldn't come and take away his spoils. He would plead his cause. In great haste he dashed up the stairs to the restaurant. The maître d'hôtel greeted him unctuously. In his usual place by the window, the Minister of Roads and Bridges was in conversation with some strangers, amid clouds of cigar smoke. Nino Verrochio wouldn't let himself be skinned alive.

"The Honorable Minister of Roads and Bridges is expecting me."

The maître d'hôtel showed him to the Minister's table.

"Monsieur le Ministre," the contractor led off, "I wanna talk about an important problem."

The Minister looked up and seemed astonished at the sight of Nino Verrochio.

"I wanna talk to you . . . "

"Verrochio," the Minister of Roads and Bridges exploded, "if I see your face for one more second I won't be able to digest my lunch."

"Monsieur le Ministre," Nino Verrochio pleaded, both hands extended like a castaway, "I just wanna tell you . . . "

"Ask the Opposition for help, Verrochio, since you're such great friends."

Nino Verrochio refused to let the Minister's reply upset him. The Minister probably saw only a businessman wanting to negotiate a contract. Nino Verrochio hadn't lost often. His luck had turned, like the wind, abruptly. Today there was an adverse wind, luck was running against him, but he must make his bid and he must win. His venture had been shaken like a fisherman's small craft on the Sardinian sea. Nino Verrochio would not run aground.

Usually, the last clause in a contract for building a road or a bridge specified a "usual deduction of ten percent" — a portion of the total cost of the contract that went directly to the Right Party's war chest. In addition, to pour a little oil in the gears, as they said, the contractor would pay the Minister one or two per cent.

"Monsieur le Ministre, I wanna tell you, instead of the usual ten percent, I'm prepared to sign over up to twenty per cent to the Right Party. Monsieur le Ministre, do you know any better contractor than me?"

The great man took a long drag on his cigar, pretending to reflect.

"Verrochio, you'd mortgage your blessed mother's bed in Italy to make a buck."

The Minister resumed his conversation with his guests. The contractor, though shaken, must appear as unyielding as the bedrock that sometimes resisted his dynamite. Verrochio had come to land a contract that would enable his machines to growl, to roll, to dig again. He looked stunned, like a boxer who's received a strong hook to the jaw, but he wouldn't leave until he'd rescued his business.

A hand was laid on his shoulder, almost warmly. Nino Verrochio turned around to face a friend.

"Goddamnit Verrochio, don't you get the picture? The Right Party doesn't wanta see your face."

It was one of the Minister's bodyguards: eyebrows as thick as a cat's tail, forehead bulging above his eyes, a belly you could cart in a wheelbarrow and a voice like an ox with laryngitis. He asked the Minister,

"You want us to chuck this asshole down the stairs?"

"I don't want you hurting Verrochio; it'd be too hard on his lovely wife."

The Minister's teeth still clenched his cigar. The big hand loosed its grip. The contractor's shoulderblades felt crushed. The Minister's voice went on:

"Madame Verrochio's a pearl. When I think of a pearl like that belonging to this pig Verrochio, that gives the Opposition a thousand dollars . . . What is it about women like that, pearls that stick with spineless wonders, while men like me — prestige, power, good looks, savoir-faire — we attract fish? Beats me, life."

The Minister disappeared behind a cloud of smoke, eyes riveted on a vision that appeared divine.

Nino Verrochio, pushed by the muscle man, had landed on a chair at another table. Since the phone call from the clerk with the cutting voice, he hadn't thought of Lucia, his *amore*. Would Lucia still love a man dishonored by bankruptcy? If Lucia tried to leave him he'd slit her throat. Though she was as beautiful as a Roman society lady and dressed like an Italian fashion plate, he'd slash her with a knife, he'd fire a bullet, two bullets at her: one into the face, to make her ugly, the other into her heart, to kill her; yes, he'd murder her while her lips, as beautiful as Sardinian grapes, and her teeth, made for a happy smile, formed the word *addio*. Lucia belonged to him. How could she live with a man who was poor? Lucia had been created for a rich man. Lucia could not walk in shoes that didn't have new soles: she'd twist her ankle. Could she cover her legs with those coarse grey stockings that poor women wear? She wouldn't want to live with a ruined man. How he loved her! Only rarely had he taken another woman to a hotel room. He loved his Lucia. It wasn't really cheating, because whenever he was with another woman he knew he loved Lucia even more than he had realized. But would Lucia still love him when he was a fallen man? In the kingdom of construction, he had been an emperor, a Caesar. If ever the good Lord, Creator of all things, had created a woman for a man, He had created Lucia for Nino. Lucia hadn't known him when he was poor. When they met, contracts from the Right Party were dropping onto his desk like autumn leaves on the lawn. Would Lucia have loved Nino Verrochio down on his knees in a garden, his clothes torn by branches and stones, hands covered with earth, body soaked in sweat that had combined with the dirt to form that moldy mud he could smell even now?

Nino Verrochio wouldn't let Lucia be taken from him. Other businessmen envied him Lucia. When he showed up with his wife on his arm, he could see their eyes spin. They didn't know where to look; it was as if Lucia had blinded them. She was always beautiful, desirable. He wouldn't let himself topple into the abyss of failure, with his machines, his warehouses, his houses. Despite the habit of years, each time he caressed Lucia her body was the most feverish of all the ones he'd touched. He loved her body which, under the pretty dresses he delighted in buying her, was a flame he could touch with his hand. When he came home from a trip and got out of his Cadillac covered with the dust of the roads, he sometimes desired her as if she had never been his wife. Lucia had given herself to him, but he never felt that she belonged to him altogether, not like his Cadillac or his machines or his houses. Can anyone possess fire? Whenever he thought about Lucia — and on the road he thought about her often — he told himself she was a far-off light, the light in his house. That light was where he really lived. He worked hard to keep it from going out. When he felt exhausted or lost or when he had no reason to go on working, he would turn to Lucia: she shed light like the light of the sun. In all his life, Lucia was the only thing that would endure. In all his life, only Lucia did not seem like a dream. And yet, Lucia always seemed a little aloof. He never stopped desiring her. When he held her in his arms he needed to desire her even more.

The first time Lucia's father had deigned to talk to Nino Verrochio, it was to tell him:

"My Lucia was born with a golden spoon in her mouth. If her future husband ever forgets that, he'll be asking for plenty of trouble. I want that golden spoon to inoculate my Lucia against poverty. I've been poor myself and I know what pain and suffering it can cause. It's a disease and I don't ever want my Lucia to come within touching distance of it."

Nino Verrochio had promised that Lucia would never hear the word poverty uttered in his house. Then he said something that overwhelmed the old grocery importer.

"Signor," he'd said, "I know that your daughter wants only the best for the two of us and for the children we'll have."

Tears pricked at the older man's eyes. He took Nino's hands and clasped them for a long time in his big hands that still remembered the rough work the immigrant had been forced to do before he became an importer.

"Young man, my wife and I have no reason for living except Lucia. The man who marries Lucia must have no other reason for living either. If not, Lucia will be very unhappy."

As he spoke that way, in the language of the old country, the old man peered into Nino's eyes. There too, he saw tears. The old man watched them fall from his lashes and run down his cheeks. Nino couldn't rub his sleeve against his cheek to wipe them away because the old man was still clasping his hands. He released them and offered Nino a cigar. They smoked together, without talking. The old man was probably seeing his entire past again, while the prospective son-in-law, dazed by the present, was trying to imagine the future.

Now, years later, Nino Verrochio still loved his wife. He travelled a lot between worksites. After all his worries, after overwhelming pressure from creditors, fears of going over budget, labor conflicts, mechanical breakdowns and the exorbitant costs of repairs, every homecoming was a sweet and tender celebration. Lucia wouldn't leave him. Even though she'd been born for the life of the rich, Lucia wouldn't abandon him if he went bankrupt. Lucia wouldn't turn her back on her husband as he toppled into the abyss. Even if he became a gardener again like old Ermenegildo, Lucia would stay with him. He loved her and she loved him. Lucia wasn't one of those women who would abandon her husband when trouble struck. For Nino Verrochio the fight wasn't over. The more menacing the disaster, the stronger he became. He asked the waiter for some writing paper. The tip of his nervous pen scraped the paper as he wrote:

"Monsieur le Ministre, the undersigned confirms his proposal to cede to the Right Party 25% of the value of all contracts awarded by the Right Party; this offer is valid until the elections. The undersigned intends thereby to express his faith in the future of the province and of the Right Party." His hand trembled as he signed it.

Then he asked the waiter to take the message to the Minister. The waiter brought the Minister's reply. Feigning calm, he unfolded the paper. On it was a clumsily drawn rope, with a hanging knot that suggested a noose to be slipped around a doomed man's neck. Crude laughter erupted behind his desk and moved over to crush him. Verrochio took another sheet of paper and wrote on it with a hand that he kept from trembling: "Monsieur le Ministre, this is my guarantee that for any contract the Right Party awards to Constructions Internationales Nino Canada Ltd., 30% of the total amount will be reinvested by the undersigned in the Right Party's war chest." He asked the waiter to take this message to the Minister.

He waited for the laughter. There was only silence, more oppressive than mockery. The waiter returned, bearing a crumpled paper on his tray. Hands shaking, fingers numb and, strangely, cold, he smoothed out the wad. The Minister had written the letters RIP, which the former gardener had seen on all too many tombstones.

Verrochio decided to telephone from his office.

"Lucia carissima, I think I'm finished! I been cut off by the Right Party. Si, I saw the Minister. No contracts for me, Lucia carissima. But I'll fight. The more they ruin me, the harder I fight. But with no contracts, Lucia carissima, we lose everything. I want you to go out right away and buy all the jewels you want. Si, carissima, all the jewels. The ones I never gave you . . . Si, on the company account. Those jewels, carissima, they can't take them away from you. Ciao. I'll be home late. Ciao."

Verrochio sat at his desk for a long time. He didn't answer the telephone. He doodled lines and circles on sheets of paper, then diligently threw them in the wastebasket. The pencil seemed to be moving of its own will in his fingertips, which felt paralyzed. Night had fallen and he hadn't even noticed. All his employees had long since gone. He was alone in the midst of everything he was about to lose. Already, all around him, his offices, his machines, his buildings, seemed like memories. Only he, Nino Verrochio, was real. He was ruined. Perhaps that too was a dream. Nothing really existed. His useless machines were drowned in the pitch-black night which erased the things that no longer belonged to him. He would fight.

That night Lucia came home later than Nino. He had tried to sleep, but he was in too much pain because he was on the brink of ruin and because he didn't know where his wife was. His heart wanted to leap out of his chest. He picked up a newspaper. Lucia found him slumped in his easy chair, draped in the newspaper like a blanket. Lucia smiled at him. She seemed to smell of alcohol and tobacco. (At tender moments he would proclaim that her body smelled like a bouquet of rare flowers.)

"My love," she told him, "you'll get your contract."

She had drunk liquor. Her hair and her dress were steeped in the powerful smell of strong tobacco.

"I saw the Minister," she said.

She went to the bedroom, shut the door and locked it. Tears filled Nino Verrochio's eyes. His face crumpled like the face of a child on the verge of tears.

"Lucia! Lucia!"

The bedroom door stayed shut.

"Lucia! Please tell . . . please just tell me where it is, the strippa new road I'm to build."

XI

The woman taken in sin repents and swings out with a hen

In the newsroom of *The Provincial Sun*, typewriters were clattering. With wild enthusiasm bells dinged and carriages gobbled up paper. No one was leaning back in his chair, balanced on the two back feet; no one was daydreaming with his shoes on his desk. On tables, on the floor, everywhere, there were newspapers — open, stacked, crumpled. The room was thick with tobacco smoke. The windows couldn't be opened because the wind would blow the papers away. Grime from necks and hair made rings on damp shirt collars. In a few minutes it would be time to put the paper to bed. Articles had to be completed, marked 30. Elections were such marvelous times! Events popped up during election season like raspberries on bushes: you just had to hold out your hand and pluck them. Sautereau, the editor-in-chief, had laid down the following guidelines:

"At ordinary times, stretch out your news; at election time, shorten it. It's simple. Elections: shorten; no elections: stretch."

Sautereau went from office to office, keeping an eye on what was being written, now and then pinching with his white fingers the corner of the page going through the typewriter, advising, correcting, jibing. His eyes watered from the smoke. All his bending over to keep an eye on the reporters had inevitably led to back problems. The tobacco smoke made him cough. Though he'd never tasted a cigarette, his lungs must be clogged like a chimney. But didn't the smell of paper irritate his lungs as well? In his youth he had dreamed of becoming a journalist and now he was editor-in-chief of the biggest paper in the Capital. At times, when he thought of his youthful ideal, Sautereau hated the naive young man he'd once been. He maintained that if a magician, or the Devil, were to offer him a magic potion with the power to blot out the mature man he had become and bring back the naive adolescent, he would refuse it.

"Naiveté," he frequently declared, after reading a piece by a young journalist, "is the cancer that gnaws at youth."

Life is what it is, men are what they are, better to want something than possess it, he thought. He had wanted to become a journalist. He'd become one. If he had his life to live over he wouldn't become a journalist. What would he choose? The same profession? To fight for truth . . . Young journalists never pondered the nature of truth. It was what they thought it was. A man who has lived knows that truth perhaps doesn't exist . . . His headache stepped up its attack. It was crawling under his temples, creeping between his brain and his skull. He thought too much. Why couldn't he stop? Now his blood was pounding at his brain like a hammer and his temples were vibrating like a drum. He went to his office to swallow a couple of pills. His top right-hand drawer contained everything he needed to deaden the pain.

"Monsieur Sautereau! Monsieur Sautereau!"

It was young Achille Bédard who, once again, had brought his bicycle into the newsroom.

"I've turned up a scandal, Monsieur Sautereau! Don't go to press till I write it up."

"Put your bike outside! This is a newsroom, not a dump!"

Because Achille Bédard wanted to stay in the good graces of Sautereau, who would further his journalistic progress, he restrained himself from observing that the newsroom was the dump for human actions. He made a note of it though. It would be useful later. He would make it ring out in an impassioned article once he'd become a great journalist.

"I've uncovered a scandal. A nice smelly political scandal."

"I hope your scandal's in the Opposition."

This time, the young reporter couldn't hold back another remark that he'd add to his notebook.

"If a party's not in power it can't be corrupt."

Sautereau turned even paler: all at once the blood in his grey face had gone white. The pinch of hair under his nose was quivering. He pointed to the door.

"Get that bicycle out of here *now!*"

Achille Bédard had no choice. He left, muttering:

"Covering up scandals doesn't serve the truth."

Sautereau had heard; he began to preach, his voice like an altar boy's with a cold.

"The truth? The truth? What is the truth? Is it writing down all the gossip making its way around the province like the worms that appear on the sidewalk after a rain? Truth? Is it tarnishing reputations? Is it throwing turds at the men who are trying to bring the province out of the poverty, the Middle Ages where it's been kept by those who are on the Opposition side today? Truth? Is it printing in my newspaper everything that goes through the head of a young man whose brains are as soggy as cat food? Truth? Is it letting him report the scandals he thinks he sees before he's seen anything of life?"

Achille Bédard didn't listen to the entire speech. He'd gone down to put his bicycle away and now he was coming back upstairs. Sautereau's harangue was still going on. He interrupted:

"If we put all the Right Party's scandals together, they'd stretch as far as all the roads they've built in the province."

"Youth! Ah, youth! Always ready to insult, to abuse, to despise those who've gone before. Freud called that wanting to kill the father."

Sautereau had employed diversionary tactics. He wanted to lead the high-spirited young reporter away from political scandal. But Achille Bédard wouldn't budge. He stared at his boss. When anyone looked Sautereau in the eye, he turned his head away.

"Monsieur Sautereau, is *The Provincial Sun* an independent paper or a paper where journalists have to believe in the Right Party, the way the editors of the *Annales de Sainte-Anne* believe in their saint?"

"Quiet, you young harebrain! You'll find yourself out on the street with your bicycle."

"Monsieur Sautereau, you're barking again; but you know, watch-dogs are tied up by the neck. Is it true, Monsieur Sautereau, that the Right Party's got you by the neck?"

"What about you?" snapped Sautereau, "Who opened the doors of *The Provincial Sun* to you? Who gave you your first job, you little scribbler that knows nothing about spelling or life or politics?"

"Nobody's going to squeeze me by the throat if I say the wrong thing about the Right Party."

"Damn you, Bédard, I'll wring your neck!"

Sautereau, more livid than ever, reached out to Achille Bédard, to seize his throat, thumbs ready to press his Adam's apple. Ashamed at his burst of rage, he fled to his office and shut the door. He probably regretted doing so, for he opened it again at once.

"Go ahead, write up your scandal. It won't be said that I, Sautereau, practised censorship. Tell your truth, but remember, the truth often hurts the one who tells it, and scandals cause more harm to the one who denounces them than the one who commits them, and it's often the one who denounces who gets punished."

"Monsieur Sautereau, are you the victim of a scandal you denounced?"

Achille Bédard recognized the grief in Sautereau's voice when he heard:

"If denouncing scandals could change anything, the whole human race would be angels. Young people see just one thing: denouncing scandals ... But what exactly is a scandal?"

"And what is the truth?" mocked Achille Bédard, who had already inserted in his typewriter the paper on which he would denounce the scandal. The truth, he repeated, is what a man says when he's free. The truth is what appears in a newspaper when it's free.

Sautereau had come up to his desk. Now he leaned over and whispered in his ear:

"You tell me about freedom: you got your job at this paper because you were protected by the Right Party."

"The Right Party thought they were getting a pawn they could move around according to their whims, but instead they're going to find a free spirit — a Voltaire, a Léon Bloy."

"Young people are snakes that bite the hands that feed them. You want to become a journalist. Very well. When sailors decide what port they're bound for, they study the wind and use it rather than run counter to it. You want to become a great journalist. Very well, study the way the wind is blowing. It's blowing in the direction of the Right Party being re-elected. As for me, I'm on your side."

"My article will stir up a little adverse wind."

Sautereau grimaced and shrugged dejectedly. He went back to his office. His attempt at persuasion had failed. He would let the impetuous youngster write his piece and once it was on his desk, he'd run a red pencil through it.

Achille Bédard's fingers rested on the keys of his big black typewriter, which gleamed brighter than the others because he polished it every day with a substance his mother used on her furniture. One day he would be a great journalist. A great journalist is one who allows the whole truth to circulate. The whole truth and more. That would be a good headline. He had entitled his article: "A road that will smell like a woman." He crossed it out and replaced it with: "The whole truth about a deal for a contract for building new roads." Sautereau would reproach him for using so many prepositions. Achille was already behind the times: he knew nothing about modern techniques for writing snappy headlines. Wouldn't "The Whole Truth" be a good slogan for a journalist? Great men's strength came from regularly and constantly applying the principle behind a slogan. "The Whole Truth." Achille Bédard had just found one for himself.

Today he would swing into action. He had given up poetry. Dreamers, he had learned, are not alive, because life springs only from reality: dreaming about a bouquet of marvelously colored flowers doesn't bring the bouquet to life; you must gather them, or sow or plant, you must turn over the earth, water, prune. "The Whole Truth." With the words: "and more" added. Henceforth that would

101

be his slogan. Later, it would be the title of his autobiography. It was also the heading for the article he was writing. The words came quickly. His fingers couldn't move fast enough on the keys. Riding his bicycle to work, he had already composed the whole article in his head. Now he just had to put it down on paper.

The Whole Truth and More about a Road Construction Contract
by Achille Bédard

Quebec (A.B.)
When fruit has been on the branch long enough, it either falls or rots. The same principle applies to governments.

Everyone knows how the Right Party rallies voters: to every citizen the Right Party offers a strip of road. Country roads, roads to the churches for the dear priests who shower the regime with an incense-burner that should offer its sacred smoke only to Almighty God; roads to stables, roads for cows. When everyone has his strip of road, his handful of gravel or his shovelful of asphalt, the populace, thinking it has the best road network in the world, says thank you to the Right Party.

Will anyone dare to come out and say that every patch of road scattered across the province is made not only of sand, stone and gravel, but above all of embezzlement, blackmail, plundering, misappropriation of public funds, petty speculation, fraud and piracy?

This writer has learned from a safe, reliable and credible source the following irrefutable points:

a) The Minister of Roads and Bridges received in his hotel room a lady who left the room two hours later, "her hair not quite as carefully arranged as when she went in," according to our witness;

b) This same lady enjoys a favorable reputation in the city of Quebec because of her role in various charitable works and in the Organization to Popularize Great Music (OPGM).

c) The disheveled beauty is the wife of a bald highway contractor. (The young reporter crossed out the word bald. If he gave no identifying characteristics, a number of building contractors would feel queasy enough to make a confession. They'd make good subjects for future articles.)

This writer has also learned, from another reliable source, that the highway contractor had been struck from the list of official Right Party builders because he had made a contribution to the Opposition campaign fund.

As good stories always have a happy ending, this writer has learned that, following a secret meeting in a luxurious room at the Château Frontenac (the number is known), at which the Minister of Roads and Bridges met privately with the wife of a highway contractor, the aforementioned contractor was offered a contract. In a few days' time, the contractor will start building a road on a green, wooded hillside in the remote countryside.

One question: why is the Minister of Roads and Bridges sending the lady's husband so far from the Château Frontenac?

These are the facts. If anyone can contradict them it won't be the Minister of Roads and Bridges or the Contractor's Lady or her poor husband who was first ruined, then saved by the Right Party.

This is not an isolated incident.

-30-

Achille Bédard started to reread his article. He had a knack for opening paragraphs that hook the reader. He was also skilled at uncovering information. He had eyes, as he put it, at the Château Frontenac hotel. His friend Jeannot Tremblay was a bellhop there. Jeannot wanted to become a politician after law school; Achille Bédard had decided not to complete his education because, he said, journalism can be studied only in the university of life. And so the two friends had made a pact. Achille Bédard would become a journalist, a great journalist, then he'd help Jeannot Tremblay become a great politician. They shared the same ideas. They had long conversations in streets where the old stones of the houses or streets still held the aromas of time past. They commented on articles in the *Revue Nationale*, they quoted from the dossiers of the *Club Patriotique*. When they passed the Plains of Abraham they were silent, only listening, as if they could hear the rumbling cannons of the unforgettable defeat that must

103

be avenged. In their students' uniforms, tight now because they had grown, under a sky that reflected the light off the river, they suddenly felt singled out by God to be the saviors of their people. Jeannot Tremblay always found a bench, a wall, a fence to perch on and spout a patriotic speech worthy of a great orator. Jeannot would be a politician. Their entrance into History was well-timed. Was it not providential? Achille Bédard would found his own newspaper; Jeannot Tremblay would take power. Achille Bédard would bring down his enemies with a pen he would sharpen like the tip of a bayonet. Driven by their fervent faith in the future, they promised the people more liberty, more honesty and more knowledge. They dreamed they would banish war from the earth. Achille Bédard prophesied that "One day, soldiers will become extinct, like dinosaurs." And Jeannot Tremblay, with a politician's practical sense, replied: "We'll have to find something to replace them with." The two friends supported each other. They had read books about secret societies. They understood how mutual support had helped the Freemasons gain control over certain countries that believed themselves obedient to other leaders. One day the two friends made a pact. With one hand on his heart, each wrote on a piece of paper: "I swear by my life that I will always help my friend until the ultimate conquest of Power." They rolled up the papers, stuffed them in a bottle, sealed it with a cork and wax and then, clasping one another tightly, cast the bottle into the river which, like their lives, was flowing toward the unknown sea.

Some weeks later, they were talking about politics and the future as usual when, in the middle of a vehement outburst about how power corrupts, Jeannot Tremblay choked and burst into tears. His tears were more like cries. He would not disclose the reason for his grief. Achille Bédard told him that suspicion was a breach of the pact of friendship and mutual support they had launched into the vastness of the sea. Gradually then, through his sobs, Jeannot Tremblay gave in and consented to speak.

Jeannot Tremblay's father was a land surveyor. A member of the staff of the Minister of Roads and Bridges, he had laid out a number of the roads built by the Right Party. Jeannot had never seen his father laugh. At home, he spoke little; he smoked a lot. Jeannot remembered him always hidden in a cloud of smoke. He seemed to be afraid, like a hare hiding in the lower leaves of shrubs. His features were always contorted. He never seemed to think about anything enjoyable. He never laughed. His thoughts seemed only sad. He never brought back funny stories from his trips, like the fathers of Jeannot's friends. He remembered only the bad weather, the rain that was so cold, the sun that was so hot, the bumpy road that jolted the car, the farmers who had insulted the government, the overcooked meat served in hotels, the mosquitoes that had eaten him alive. At times he would sigh, complaining about the MP in the riding where he'd gone to lay out a road. "He seems to think you can lay out a road across private land with a stroke of a pen, like signing a cheque." Jeannot Tremblay's mother heard these words like any others, but Jeannot noticed that when his father said them, he always bowed his head and added: "But I shouldn't talk about that." At once, his mother would change the subject. A few times, he had tried to penetrate the secret that was eating away at him, but he was used to his father being closemouthed. He never went fishing in far-off lakes like the fathers of Jeannot's friends, he never danced at parties. Jeannot was used to his moodiness. Then he entered adolescence and became preoccupied with school, his future and politics. He realized that his father was old. Wasn't it normal for old people to be sad because their youth was gone?

His father died far away, in a remote part of the country. He was on his way back to the city. A truck laden with new tractors was heading into the countryside. On a curve, the truck rolled onto the surveyor's car. It was he who had laid out the road and calculated the degree of the curve. The coffin was closed. Jeannot Tremblay bought a black tie, his mother, some black dresses. She cried a lot. He hadn't yet shed a tear but at the graveyard, in the muddy earth, before the hole that was filling up with water as if there was a spring beneath it, he suddenly felt wrenched apart and then the sobs came. His face was covered in tears that finally unleashed his sorrow. He thought that he became a man at the moment the coffin slipped from the cables and dropped into the muddy grave. His mother hugged him to her. She hadn't done that for a long time. With both arms, she clung to him. He felt her body's roundness flattening against his own skinny body and he didn't like the sensation. He moved away. After that, she often wept. He noticed that he resembled his father. He was taciturn. He didn't talk in the house. At school, he never laughed, never told dirty stories, never pulled pranks. He stayed off to one side, silent, as if he wanted to devote all his thoughts to some grave secret. He resembled his father and he hated the similarity. His mother still wept. She put the house up for sale. It had become too big and it held too many memories.

"You know now your father isn't here, we're alone . . . there's no pay-cheque coming in every month. With your father's salary we lived well. But now we're alone. (She wept and the tears fell onto her black dress.) Now we have to struggle along as if he'd never been there. (His mother had an amazing bosom inside her tight-fitting black dress, like the actresses whose pictures the boys traded in school. Her breasts were like Shelley Winters' in her angora sweater.) Your father was a land surveyor. It's a noble trade. But he wasn't a millionaire . . . You don't make a fortune laying out roads . . . Your father couldn't afford a big insurance policy . . . It was his fault (her words were drowned by tears) his mistake that caused the accident . . . so the insurance . . . isn't generous . . . We need a new car. Jeannot dear, I'd like to have a brand new car to take you to school in, like other parents."

Achille Bédard and Jeannot Tremblay took a long walk through the city. Achille told him that his father had died a long slow death at home. Afterwards Achille had been completely transformed, his soul in disarray, his mind a shambles; he was a different person. He felt as if his father's soul had entered him and mingled with his own. Achille had described Death with a great scythe in his hands.

"We men stand before her like a wheatfield. This time Death struck down our fathers. The next stroke of her scythe will be for us. But before that we have our whole lives to live."

They walked on, talking about the great men they admired. Meanwhile, though, Jeannot Tremblay was looking for an easy job so he could help his mother.

"Why not be a bellhop at the Château Frontenac? I work there a few hours every night and the tips are good. There's plenty of politicians. I serve cabinet ministers every day. There's plenty of MPs and civil servants buzzing around them like flies around . . . So I keep my eyes open. I learn. I make myself known. The Château Frontenac is the citadel of politics. Let's both of us enter it, not hidden in a Trojan horse, but more subtly, disguised as bellhops, as well-trained servitors of the Right Party, making the necessary bows to corruption . . . What's the title of that play by de Musset where . . . ?"

"Lorenzaccio."

Jeannot Tremblay had read it too.

One night some time later, Jeannot Tremblay was donning the white jacket worn by the Château Frontenac bellhops. He stood stiffly at the mirror and adjusted his black bow-tie.

The tray he held was trembling and the glasses rattled with a hideous crystalline tinkling as he pushed open the door to a room. He often recognized faces from the newspapers. How thirsty these men were! Their talk sounded like insults, they shouted, they pounded their fists on the table, then they all burst out laughing. Other rooms were more peaceful. Jeannot preferred to bring a tray laden with bottles and glasses to a dozen men squabbling in a cloud of tobacco smoke as thick as if the mattresses had been set on fire, than to arrive at a bed where some fat man was smiling beatifically at the young woman beside him. He always had to watch where he stepped because there were clothes and shoes scattered all over the rug. Politics and business were awash in strong liquor and thick beer, while champagne sparkled for love.

"Here," said the headwaiter, "deliver this. Keep your white gloves on, you'll be meeting Madame Right Party in the flesh."

"In the raw, you mean!" said another waiter.

They seemed to have made a joke. Jeannot didn't understand. He didn't see anything funny.

"Why," Jeannot asked, "is she Madame Right Party?"

"Because she sleeps with all the Right Party MPs, one after another."

Jeannot walked into room 519, dropped his tray and vomited on his black trousers and on the carpet. Beside a man who hid his face with *The Provincial Sun* he saw his mother.

For several days, Jeannot didn't go home. Suddenly the taciturn young man was talking to everybody, arranging to be invited home by fellow-students he'd never said a word to in the past. His zeal in class surprised his teachers. He turned out to be a very skillful pilot of paper airplanes. Adolescent crisis, the learned men diagnosed. He was summoned by the Father responsible for the students' spiritual guidance. Battling with sin in the school had given the priest a face like an old soldier's. He seated Jeannot opposite him and took the boy's hands in his own, which were strong and warm.

"My child," he began, in a whisper, "I am bound by the secret of the confessional and I would be eternally damned if I revealed what your mother confided. I gave her absolution and God has forgiven her. If God can pardon her sin, so should you, her only child."

Jeannot bridled. Straightening up on his chair, he yanked his hands from the priest's. The confessor took them back and gripped them even harder.

"My dear child, your mother is a saint. Your irrational behavior shows that you think you have the right to judge her. My child, you are the one who's a sinner."

At these words the priest's expression became an unbearable torment and the big pious hands held Jeannot's in a trap that didn't hurt, but would not open.

"My child, you are sinning against God's fourth commandment, the one in which He told men to honor their father and mother. By not going home, you are torturing your mother as if she'd committed some wrong. My child, your mother spreads love about her the way birds offer up their joyous song, the way flowers offer up their perfume: for the greater glory of God. Kneel, my child, and confess the grief your behavior is causing that saintly woman."

The spiritual advisor's hands tugged Jeannot Tremblay until he slid from his chair and fell to his knees. Instead of kneeling, though, he cried out as the pain he could no longer hold back tore at his throat. The pious hands released their grip. Fleeing, Jeannot knew where to go. He would go home and stab his mother.

He flung himself at the door and ran to the kitchen for a knife, then stopped as if he'd been flattened by a pane of glass. His mother was standing at the stove, the knife in her hand. She was using it to cut up a chicken.

"I'm making you chicken with honey for dinner," she said in her usual voice, as if no disaster had struck.

Jeannot was experiencing too much grief, too much pain; there was too much hatred in his soul; the urge to vomit was too insistent in his throat. He raised his arm toward his mother as if he were wielding the knife, but instead of striking he screamed, spitting out the words:

"You had to tell the priest you're the biggest whore in the Château Frontenac. You thought Father Confessor had to know that Jeannot Tremblay's the son of the Right Party's whore. I've just got one thing to tell you: we can't choose our mothers, but I wouldn't even choose you as a whore!"

Stunned, he crumpled to the floor. His blood was flowing. He thought his mother had stabbed him with the knife. Holding his neck in both hands to keep his head from falling, he screamed:

"Help! The whore murdered me!"

The next blows fell even harder. His mother had swung the chicken. The first time it bloodied his nose and smeared his hair with honey. Now it was dripping off him, along with mingled blood and tears and snot. Her son was as dirty now as when he came into the world. She bent down to help him get up.

"Don't touch me! Your hands stink of the Right Party men."

With the back of her hand, she slapped him even harder.

"Go ahead, hit me, kill me; you don't love me. Whores can't love."

He waited for the blow; he shut his eyes, tensed himself. The blow didn't fall. He opened his eyes. His mother was washing the chicken at the sink and there were tears in her eyes.

Very ostentatiously he reached in his pocket, took out a bill, unfolded it and held it out.

"Mamma, if I pay you, will you love me?"

"I'm not talking to you again till you're a man."

"A whore knows about men, doesn't she Mamma?"

His mother's face was creased like the face of a child with a sorrow too great to bear. She heaved a tremendous sigh, holding back her sorrow.

"My little boy (her voice quavered; the words were wet with tears), you think you're humiliating your mother. You're fairly refined compared with some of the ones I put up with. Humiliation is the price I have to pay to keep my son clean and well-groomed, in a white shirt that mustn't have a threadbare collar or worn cuffs, in well-pressed grey trousers, in a spotless navy blazer with shiny buttons; humiliation is the price I have to pay to keep my clean little boy in a school where all his friends are well brought-up and rich, where the teachers are learned, pious priests. Son, whores work for a pimp. Didn't the priests teach you that? You've decided your mother's a whore. Well, I've decided that since I give you everything I earn, you're my pimp. Never forget that: whenever you think of your mother as a whore, don't forget you were my pimp because you were the one who gathered the fruit of my labor."

The telephone rang. With sobs still in her voice, Jeannot's mother explained that she couldn't go out, she had a headache, she hadn't slept that night, she was worried about her son, he'd had a troubled adolescence, luckily he hadn't yet started to smoke, she was tired, her skull throbbed with every beat of her heart and she wasn't free. Then she listened; it seemed that she was being forced to listen. Finally, dutifully, she gave in.

"Very well. If that's how it is I'll be there."

She went to her room and emerged half an hour later with her hair done, wearing a necklace and a low-cut dress. The tips of her breasts seemed about to pierce her dress. Her thighs seemed about to burst her seams.

"Whore!"

She went out, leaving behind the clinging odor of her perfume. Jeannot staggered to the door, blinded by tears.

"Whore!" he cried, so the whole neighborhood could hear and his mother would be so ashamed she wouldn't dare to show her face.

She got into a shiny black car driven by a chauffeur.

Jeannot Tremblay picked up the carving knife, rubbed it against the whetstone and, before he slit his throat like Guy de Maupassant — as his literature teacher had described it — he touched the cutting edge of the blade. He'd never be brave enough to slit his throat. Instead he ran to the bathroom, opened the medicine cabinet and spilled a handful of aspirins — he knew they were fatal — into his shaking hand, for he had decided to die. He couldn't live with the knowledge that his mother was a prostitute so he gulped down the handful of aspirins; they were as dry as sand so he tossed back a glass of water, then lay in his bed and waited for death. He wanted to die without forgiving his mother. Dying was no harder than falling asleep. Why were people so afraid of death? It was so gentle, so easy. He felt himself dying slowly, very slowly. It really was like drifting off to sleep.

Long afterwards, when he opened his eyes again, he recognized his mother through the fog. He wanted to cry out "whore" but he couldn't, because there was something sharp and pointed in his throat. It was a plastic tube. He was in the hospital.

"Jeannot, can you hear me?"

He tried to pretend he could hear nothing, but his mother knew from the furious light in his eyes that she could talk to him.

"You behaved very badly."

She came back to see him several times. Every day she talked to him for a long time. He was silent and hated her. He was eager to recover so he could go home and kill himself. This time he'd have the courage to take the carving knife and slice his jugular vein. He would close his eyes and kill himself because he lacked the strength to kill his mother. She talked on and on. Couldn't she shut up?

Jeannot Tremblay's father, she told him, had never been a land surveyor. He didn't have the necessary education. He had no diploma. All he'd done was work with a surveying team. He was just an assistant in the team when a man from the Right Party came for him. The man explained that the Right Party could have him appointed a land surveyor. The salary was attractive. At first he had the help of some real land surveyors who showed him how to lay out a road on graph paper, how to draw levels. His father learned fast, he enjoyed it. He was especially glad the Right Party was giving him a chance to escape the fate of a common laborer. Some weeks later, when his father was all decked out like a real land surveyor, with his book of measurements, he realized what his job entailed: he was supposed to put his signature at the bottom of the plans and estimates that were brought to him. He was supposed to demand from the contractors and suppliers what was described as the "usual" contribution of ten per cent or more to the Right Party war chest. Where would the roads go? Across whose property would the government expropriate a piece of farmland? How high would the embankments be? What sort of gravel would be used? These decisions were made by others, but Jeannot's father was supposed to act as if he was the boss. How many documents his father had signed! Sometimes he was afraid he'd end up in jail. He was afraid, too, that the Right Party might abandon him. What could he do? Go back to doing odd jobs? No one would give work to a land surveyor who didn't want to do that any more. All his life, the poor man had been afraid. It was a serious matter to usurp the title of land surveyor. The Right Party had dug up some certificate from a mail-order course in the United States, but if anyone looked at the diploma on his office wall, he trembled. He signed documents. That was worth more than doing odd jobs. He asked no questions, he just signed. He didn't say anything about anyone because his position was so delicate. Finally, he didn't say anything at all. He was silent, he smoked. Before the Right Party had got its claws in him, though, Jeannot's mother had seen him happy. Doing odd jobs, he never worried. In those days he was always laughing. In the fields, as he was holding the marker, striped red-and-white like a barber pole, the farmers would come and talk to him. He always had stories that made them laugh. After the Right Party made him a land surveyor, he couldn't talk to them without authorization. ("Your father was like a mask.") He never knew what wheeling and dealing had led to the decision. ("It didn't always smell like roses. And sometimes it smelled so bad your father was sure people would notice there was something rotten under the Right Party's roads. And he realized he'd be the first one to be accused, because his name appeared on that rot.") The poor man could no longer open a newspaper without trembling at the prospect of being found out. A man cannot hide his fear. He was silent. He smoked. What would the Right Party do with a man who was afraid? They replaced him with a very determined young man who could walk in gutters up to his chin without losing his smile. To Jeannot Tremblay's father, who knew too many secrets, they gave a warning: "If you ever open your mouth about what you know, we'll denounce you to the Professional Association of Land Surveyors for falsifying a diploma."

The Right Party sent Jeannot's father to the most remote parts of the province. His job was to pretend he was determining the best possible alignment for a road, but to follow the one the Right Party's local organization had decided on. Jeannot's father would sign his name and he always added, as was expected, "Land Surveyor." Because he was afraid, because he lacked assurance, because he was racked with doubt, because he was responsible only for small-scale projects in remote parts of the province, he hadn't had a raise for a long time. But he wasn't a real land surveyor so how could he expect to be paid like one? Besides, he'd made a few miscalculations and he'd drawn some rather alarming curves through flat fields. The Professional Association of Land Surveyors had asked questions about these alarming alignments. The Minister of Roads and Bridges, ill at ease, had to answer them. An employee of the Ministry of Roads and Bridges discovered that Jeannot's father only had a diploma from some unknown school in the United States that had since gone bankrupt. His report read: "In such universities, the courses often consist of simply sending in your hundred dollars; no other correspondence follows." Then his salary was cut. He had to keep living in the style of a land surveyor. Jeannot Tremblay's mother had to dress like a land surveyor's wife. Jeannot had to go to the school attended by the sons of professionals, he had to be dressed like the sons of professionals; the family had to live in a neighborhood where other professionals lived; his father had to drive a car a land surveyor could be proud to drive along the roads he'd built. Their house had to suggest a certain wealth. The father went into debt. He was afraid his duplicity

113

would be uncovered. He was silent. He locked himself in silence so as not to betray himself. He smoked. He was afraid. ("My poor husband — your father — was eaten up by fear the way others are eaten up by cancer.")

Jeannot Tremblay knew nothing about his father's life. He had lived in the same house, he had been raised by him, he had been brought into the world by him, he was part of him, yet it was as though this man, his father, was a stranger. Jeannot had never suspected his father's suffering. A man who lived such a painful life deserved a great deal of respect. He turned to his mother and for the first time since he'd surprised her in room 519 of the Château Frontenac, naked in the bed of a big hairy man, he looked her in the eyes.

"Whore!" he spat.

She drew the covers up to his chin and around his shoulders as she'd done when he was a child. Then he added:

"You'll have to sell the house and move to an apartment. I don't want to go to school. I'm going to work. I'll support you."

"You know, Jeannot, I'm just an ignorant woman. In my day, people thought that being a woman was enough. Nobody taught me anything about life, Jeannot."

"You should have told me . . . I wouldn't have let you do that."

"Sometimes the truth is frightening . . . We hide it from others and even from ourselves."

"Mamma, I'll be responsible for you from now on."

Then, bitter again, he pulled the sheet over his face.

"Jeannot, it's true that I confided in your spiritual advisor. I was worried. What can happen to a son if his mother deceives him? I didn't know where you were. I hadn't heard from you. I could have found out they'd dredged your body out of the St. Lawrence. Lots of young boys take . . . " (she didn't add the words "their lives". He, of course, had tried to take his life. Could she have forgotten already?) "I just told your spiritual advisor I was taking care of some handicapped people."

"That's what your Right Party MPs are, all right — cripples and morons!"

"The Jesuits don't know anything. Only you and I know . . . "

"I'll never forget it!"

"What about me, do you think I'll forget?"

After Jeannot Tremblay recovered, he didn't go back to school. He took a full-time job at the Château Frontenac. He didn't miss the Jesuits. He was learning from life now, not from ancient books; he wasn't studying the life of olden times but the life of here and now, in the hotel rooms where it was lived.

XII

Can a boss be free?

"Your article must be good, Achille Bédard. You've been staring at it for half an hour."

It was the shrill hoarse voice of Sautereau. He held out the article: "The Whole Truth and More About a Road Contract." Sautereau took the article into his office to read. He shut the door, then came out at once, waving the pages of the article and hopping about in his baggy trousers and oversize shoes with turned-up toes.

"Can you give me one good reason why we should publish this sewage? Just one?"

The young reporter drew himself back on his chair, hooked his thumbs complacently around his suspenders and snapped them, and looked Sautereau in the eye as he answered:

"The truth."

"*Your* truth, you mean. Our paper doesn't exist to publish *your* truth. The mandate of *The Provincial Sun* is to inform the people so they'll love their province. With love, everything becomes possible. It's possible to consider a great future."

"If I hear you right, Monsieur Sautereau, you're saying that *The Provincial Sun* looks at politics and says 'What wonderful shit the Right Party's giving us. Don't we love

116

it! The future will grow like a big fat pumpkin!' Is that your philosophy?"

"Would you prefer idle gossip that saps a people's confidence in its government?"

"Monsieur Sautereau, it must be true they've got you by the throat . . . "

Sautereau folded the pages and meticulously shredded them into tiny pieces, concentrating on making them unreadable. Instead of throwing them out he put them in his pocket.

"*The Provincial Sun* won't publish cheap gossip even our enemies wouldn't dare to invent."

This time Sautereau looked straight into Achille Bédard's eyes, so forcefully that the young reporter was shaken. He looked away.

"When you're a real journalist, Achille Bédard, you'll know how to tell the difference between news and bellhop's gossip. He sells his imagination the way his mother sells her ass. Like mother, like son . . . His father cheated the government by passing himself off as a land surveyor. He couldn't add two and two, but he bought fake diplomas and with them — and the people's money — he built badly laid-out roads . . . The son can add though: money and whores. He's treating himself to all the whores in the Capital, one after the other . . . That is also the truth."

The clattering of typewriters in the newsroom had broken off. The other journalists were forming a circle around Sautereau and the young reporter, their expressions amused and attentive like spectators at a fight.

Achille Bédard couldn't answer Sautereau. Dazed, with quivering knees and downcast eyes, he left the room. The sky above Quebec was high and clear. The stars were as distant and beautiful as flowers in the meadows. The air that rose from the river smelled good, like fresh water. He got on his bicycle and pedalled along several streets at random without going anywhere. He breathed deep to rid his body of the newspaper's tainted air. He felt as if the night that was slipping into his hair and onto his face was washing him as well. He rode around for a long time.

Jeannot Tremblay had changed. During their most recent walks together, Jeannot had talked more about women than politics. The oath they'd sworn to assist each other in

117

their political projects was drifting out to sea. Jeannot's life hadn't been easy. The trials he'd endured would toughen him. They saw less of each other now. When Jeannot talked about women it was always with a certain contempt. If he thought that way, it was because of his mother, of course. It must be a shock to discover that your mother is selling herself, like meat in a butcher's stall. Jeannot would soon be cured. He would regain his youthful idealism. An interest in politics lay dormant in him. Achille Bédard had proof in the information he called in to the paper from time to time. Jeannot Tremblay would have experienced human suffering. He'd know how to get back on his feet after a disaster. Jeannot had been shaken by life. Such experience couldn't be derived from books. The difficulties one surmounts form the character of a man who will be a leader.

Achille Bédard rode his bicycle for a long time. It was so light he felt as if he was flying. The walls, the lighted windows and the dark doors that filed past on either side of him seemed as intangible as the sky above the city. Though he was pedalling, he was travelling as much in his thoughts as along the ancient streets. At last he was outside his house. Everything was asleep. He jumped off his bicycle. His feet struck the hard reality of the pavement. A shadow moved in the shadows. He started and gripped the handlebars. In a breathless, nasal voice the shadow said:

"One day you'll be glad I stopped you from publishing that article."

"It was the truth."

"I couldn't publish it in *The Provincial Sun*."

"Right, they've got you by the throat, but I . . . "

Sautereau drew closer. Achille couldn't see his face, which was cast down, the chin drawn into the collar of his trench-coat. Sautereau took his hands out of his pockets and placed them on the handlebars.

"I'm married to a woman who's a good wife and mother, I have four children . . . "

"They've got you by the throat, they make you dance . . . Sautereau, they make you sing whatever they want . . . "

The editor-in-chief made no reply, but Achille Bédard saw him nod in a vague sign of assent.

"There aren't many free men on the roads of this province."

"The truth is free. What do you put in *The Provincial Sun*, Monsieur Sautereau, when that shady character Verrochio got a big contract because the Minister of Roads and Bridges managed to plant his little post in Verrochio's wife?"

"I have a wife and four children . . . "

"They tell you to sit up and beg and you lift your paws like a well-trained dog. A man who's decided to be free is already a free man."

"Your friend Jeannot Tremblay needs help. Your friend's been cast adrift."

"And you, Monsieur Sautereau?"

"Your friend's going to run aground. The poor child has been offering his mother's services to customers."

"Monsieur Sautereau, if you say one more word against my friend I'll denounce you."

"So you're not so fond of the truth now!"

Achille Bédard protested.

"You're lying! You want to tarnish his reputation because he's told me about your moral decay."

Sautereau took his hands off the handlebars.

"Achille, for the love of God help your friend."

He took a few steps, then came back to the young reporter.

"Children, don't let yourselves fall into their hands . . . "

This time he walked away. Achille caught up with him.

"So it's true the Right Party's got you cornered?"

Sautereau quickened his pace and soon vanished into the night. Achille ran up behind him.

"Monsieur Sautereau, would you like to ride my bicycle home?"

There was no answer.

Achille Bédard would rescue Jeannot Tremblay. One day he would know what the rope the Right Party had dropped around Sautereau's neck was made of.

XIII

Can a politician lay an egg?

Word spread throughout the Appalachians that a great procession would be held in honor of the miracle at Saint-Toussaint-des-Saints. It seemed important to celebrate this new favor in a Christian way. All those who had any relatives in the village, those who had passed through the village, those who knew the name of the village, those who knew someone who knew the village and, finally, all those who lived in the Appalachian Region where the miraculous village was perched, felt touched by the blessing God had showered upon young Opportun, son of Poutine Lachance. They felt an obligation to come and thank the Lord for His goodness. Every one of them was grateful. Every one bore on his body a few grains of the pollen of divine benediction.

There were some who didn't believe they'd been touched by the miracle; however, they had been touched by the Right Party's blessings. Like those who had benefited from divine grace, everyone in the Appalachian Region who had received the blessings of the Right Party was travelling to the village to give thanks unto the Local Riding Minister and to the Minister of Roads and Bridges. Those who knew someone who had been a recipient of the Right Party's blessings felt favored as well, and they hoped the blessings soon would touch them.

All these people had come to the good Lord's miracles, to the Right Party's blessings, as naturally as children's lips reach out to the maternal breast. To acclaim the good Lord and the Right Party, people from all over had come down from their hillsides, they had risen from their valleys. They had donned the garments they saved for Sunday, for weddings, for baptisms and burials. It was the first time in the history of Saint-Toussaint-des-Saints that so many people had come together. The hotel was full. Every house was taking in visitors. Cars were packed together, one behind the other. Not even in the Capital were there so many cars. Some had made the journey from distant parishes by horse and buggy: the horses were parked among the automobiles. The more distant the parishes, the darker and heavier were the visiting parishioners' clothes, and the shinier their shoes. The two restaurants were full: to get a sandwich you had to wait your turn, standing in line as if in school. Some visitors took their meals with villagers who had offered hospitality. Others, afraid of going hungry, had brought baskets heaped with egg and ham and tomato sandwiches and bottles of yellow Kik that splashed their faces when they popped the cap. Everywhere there were children crying, children begging to go peepee, children joining their little hands in prayer.

Along with the crowd, strange cars had appeared. They were parked along the road that the procession would follow. They were old cut-down buses, old delivery trucks with holes carved out of their sides; they were stalls mounted on farm-carts, drawn by meticulously groomed horses with gilded collars, their harnesses decorated with shiny buttons. Some were nothing more than a house the size of a bird-cage that had been erected in a wheelbarrow pushed by a hunchback or a man with a clubfoot. All these stalls had a smoking chimney cut into the roof. The stalls were red, they were yellow and green. As they drove through the village they left a clinging odor that dug hunger deep into stomachs. On the sides of the travelling stalls were painted in garish colors: LE GEANT DE LA SANDWICH or THE KING OF FRENCH FRIES FRIED IN SPECIAL

FAT or THE EMPRESS OF COUNTRY-FRESH SUGAR PIE or THE MAGICIAN OF HOT ROASTED PEANUTS or NATIONAL PICKLED EGG CHAMPIONSHIP. One might also observe THE PALACE OF HOTDOGS THAT STICK TO YOUR PALATE; or lick one's lips when MOTHER'S HOME-MADE COUNTRY BREAD WITH CITY JAM appeared. Children grew feverish at the sight of an igloo-shaped stall painted white, with blue-and-grey lettering that suggested glittering icicles and read: ICE-COLD ICE CREAM DIRECT FROM THE NORTH POLE.

All day long the village air was pierced by the cries of children being refused some treat. The effluvia from the stalls were staggering, and from the cracked mouths of loudspeakers came wild carnival music that filled children with desire, that made their mothers twitchy and lured the men. Never had so many people been seen in Saint-Toussaint-des-Saints. As they strolled, everyone was eating something that dripped between their fingers, stained their faces and soiled their clothes. At mealtime, the tables were deserted. Mothers moaned because they had needlessly prepared food that was going to go to waste "while children in other countries are starving to death." Gradually, one at a time, the women capitulated. Like their husbands and children, they too would indulge in the rare treats. Around the stalls scattered the length of the street flocks of people were eating where they stood, noses in their feasts, and at every window in every former delivery truck that exuded the aroma of hot fat or a sugary perfume, customers stamped their feet as they waited their turn at one of the dripping delights.

Suddenly, at a certain point in the afternoon, there was no one outside any of the stalls except the one where the National Pickled Egg Championship was being held. All the villagers and all the visitors had gathered there. The man who would be chosen National Champion would be the one who tucked away the largest number of pickled eggs. These were ordinary hen's eggs that had been hard-boiled, then shelled and put up in vinegar. As the competition got under way, some children were taking part. They quickly realized, however, that this was a matter for men, and that they must wait another few years before they could take a stab at the national pickled egg championship. Much later, one of the men gave up. He left, ashamed and humiliated, face bloated and red; one hand covered his mouth, the other clutched his belly. Suddenly the children thought the fellow's big belly had burst. It looked to them as if it had opened up the way a pig's belly does when it's sliced with a knife in the slaughterhouse and the guts come pouring out. The contest went on. One after the other, the men gave up. They disappeared, vanquished, mortified. You could hear them gasping and moaning, behind fences or bushes. Soon, in the center of the crowd that was applauding and jostling and egging them on, only a few contestants remained. After a few dozen pickled eggs, they could have swallowed nails. They crammed the eggs into their mouths, one after another; their stomachs were like sacks into which eggs dropped as if it were the most normal thing in the world. Suddenly their legs would give way, unable to support such weighty bodies, and they crashed to the ground, blue in the face, paralyzed, unable to move, like rocks. The crowd guffawed. They teased, insulted, humiliated the poor victims. Grabbing them by the arms and legs, people jeered as they dragged them from the battlefield.

In the end only two men were left. One of them, Malice Blanchette, lived at Mud Lake Overflow; the other, Albéric Racine, beside the future new road. One would vote for the Opposition, the other for the Right Party. One would be condemned to drive his horse along a muddy road where the wheels would sink up to the axles; the other would receive the favor of a new road laid out nice and straight, hard, free of dust and mud, hemmed by fine ditches to catch the runoff. The road would eat up a piece of his property, but the Right Party had promised to pay generously for the land. The men were face to face, like boxers, sweating and puffing, eyes were swollen and full of pain; but rather than exchanging blows, each one brought to his mouth an egg, which he bit, which he chewed, which he swallowed while his body quivered, like a boxer's as he lands a blow. They were so full, their mouths were so pasty that they couldn't talk. The two angry men didn't punch each other, didn't touch each other, they grunted. Someone translated their grunts, all smeared with chewed-up eggs.

"Maybe I won't have a strippa new road, but I'll have the national championship!"

"I'm the champion. I'll have a strippa new road and the championship. And I'm gonna win my elections. I'm gonna smash you like an egg."

Those who were going to vote for the Right Party applauded. The two men kept cramming in eggs with both hands. Their red cheeks were swollen sacks. Now they were sitting on the ground. Before each one sat a plate heaped high with pickled eggs. An upright old villager named Timoléon Tassé, a man renowned for never having brought to his lips even a blade of grass that didn't belong to him, had been charged with counting the number of eggs wolfed down. He gave the score very loud as soon as he was certain the egg would not be rejected.

"Hundred and eighteen . . . Hundred and nineteen."

Applause rang out. The champions unfastened their belts. Their pants had become too tight. Their bellies were as bloated as their cheeks.

"Hundred and twenty-one."

Applause!

"Keep going! The national champion of Japan downed nine hundred and eighty-seven!"

"Eggs in those countries are smaller than ours."

"I'll tell your wife, Foufoune Labrecque: you've been studying foreign chicks!"

"Hundred and twenty-seven to hundred and twenty-seven!"

The contestants were tied. The bystanders were jumping up and down. These fat men, these fat women, weighted down by their work, danced and giggled nervously like overwrought little girls.

"A hundred and thirty-three to a hundred and thirty-three!" proclaimed the incorruptible Timoléon Tassé.

Suddenly, one of the champions — both of them now lying on the ground — was no longer bringing eggs to his mouth but holding them in his hands, at the end of outstretched, motionless arms.

"He's dead."

Applause! What a champion! The applause quickly ceased. The dead man wasn't as great a champion as the man who was still cramming eggs into his mouth. A man who was not from the village came up to the one who was dead. He said something in his ear. The dead man didn't move. The other men kept talking to him, urging him to eat more pickled eggs; the man forebade him to abandon the struggle so cravenly; the man shook him, tried to stir up his pride, to wrench him from his inertia. Soon he was shouting:

"Which side are you on: the Right Party or the Opposition? The Right Party's going to give you a new road without no dust, but you can't even swallow a dozen little eggs for the Right Party! You claim you're loyal to the Right Party but you're gonna let the Opposition walk away with the championship."

"Hundred and fifty-eight!" proclaimed the incorruptible Timoléon Tassé.

Applause. The champion went on without hearing, without seeing how much his prowess was appreciated. He ate his eggs blindly because his puffy lids were shut tight over his eyes; he ate not knowing he was the national champion.

"A hundred and eighty-one pickled eggs," proclaimed Timoléon Tassé.

Applause.

"One hundred and eighty-eight pickled eggs."

Applause. It continued for a long time. At the end, nobody was applauding.

"Two hundred and nine pickled eggs!"

Nobody was left to admire the champion, who didn't realize he'd lost his audience. His was a struggle for ideas: the Opposition must outstrip the Right Party in pickled eggs.

"Two hundred and nineteen pickled eggs," announced Timoléon Tassé, his chin thrust out, his wart-hairs trembling. He grumbled,

"Politics, politics . . . not a politician alive could lay an egg."

Outside some of the other wheeled stalls, the children's faces were smeared with green mustard and pink ice cream. On all sides, customers were jostling one another: women squeezed by men, children trampled by each other. On all sides the shouts of impatient customers alternated with the replies of short-tempered salesmen. Famished customers were assailed by the warm scent of melted butter, of oil, of toasting bread, of roasting sausages, mingled with the fresh aromas of ice cream made from various rare fruits. Off-color jokes were greeted by throaty laughter. Coins jingled.

"Eat up, eat up while the Right Party's still in power. If the Right Party loses, who knows what'll happen."

Along with the wheeled stalls had come all sorts of dented, rusted panel trucks, squashed under the weight of boxes, bags and suitcases. On the door or side an awkward hand had painted names like UNIVERSAL CIRCUS, AMUSE-MENTS EAST AND WEST or HEAVEN AND HELL LTD or THE SURPRISE NEST EGG or MAJOR LEAGUE FISHING ETC. These trucks were parked along the street, behind the food-stalls. Strangers, men and women who rolled their "r"s and wore garishly colored clothes, untied ropes, opened crates and suitcases, unrolled canvasses. Soon, beside each truck a tent had been pitched; it was nothing more than a canvas roof supported by posts and held by cables tied around pegs that had been driven into the ground. For a few cents you could spin a wheel of fortune, you could place bets on heaven or hell: in fact, a white mouse had been tossed onto a turntable with two holes in it. One represented heaven, the other hell; you just had to guess which hole the mouse would choose. Its paws would slip across the painted table, it would fall, and coarse laughter would send the bets up. You could cast a line, as if you were fishing, behind a canvas on which were painted waves, sailboats, fish, whales with their spouts draped over their heads like cloaks; when you reeled in your line the basket at the end of it had snagged a gift-wrapped present — a ring, a tie-clip, a pencil, gum, a candy, an orange, a pair of socks, a necklace, an old boot, a chocolate fish, a pussy-willow. In another tent you could throw a hoop and keep whatever it landed on: cigarettes, a doll, a bottle of wine, a bracelet, a shell in which you could hear the sea, a lamp, kid gloves, a genuine natural pearl necklace, an official photograph of Maurice Richard, a necktie that once belonged to Charlie Chaplin. You could enter a closed tent and lay your palm flat on the table and a great master, trained by a Hindu hermit, would read the future and the past in your hand. The tents were surrounded by a seething, impatient, rollicking crowd, whose laughter kept bursting out, whose shouts exploded. Then everything was quiet, as the religious ceremony in honor of young Opportun's miracle and the inauguration of work on the new road being built by the Right Party got underway.

Opportun, the child who had been miraculously cured, had missed out on all the treats. All afternoon he had squirmed uncomfortably in his new suit, whose sleeves and legs his mother had rolled up because they were too long; she would unroll them as her now-normal child grew taller. He had had to sit quite still, between the Curé and the Local Riding Minister, while people paraded past, shaking the Minister's hand as they asked some favor for themselves or a relative, genuflecting before the Curé who would draw a little cross with his thumb upon their piously bowed heads. Then they gazed at Opportun, their eyes looking for some sign of the miracle. The ladies kissed Opportun and he could feel a sticky lipstick mark on his cheek. All the ladies wore perfume that stank, he thought, like a skunk's rear end. The gentlemen, who reeked of tobacco, patted his head, or his shoulder or cheek. In the end he was dazed, he felt dirty. It went on and on: people kept parading by as if they were looking at a coffin. The children who walked past Opportun looked away as if he were a dog turd, he thought. The Minister promised favors and the Curé handed out benedictions. When it was finally over, young Opportun, who had seen nothing of the stalls on wheels that promised so many delicious treats, or the tents that offered such amusing games, was dragged off to church for the ceremony. They were going to thank God for working a miracle that had awakened his "intelligence" as his mother explained.

XIV

A sermon on the fog of this world

The point of the church steeple disappeared into the sky; many times in the course of the year the villagers, who had never seen anything so high, could see neither the cross at the very tip nor the rooster perched on the top of the cross. The rooster was so close to God, He must stroke its head. When the villagers were building the church, they had decided to erect the tallest steeple in the Appalachian Region to prove that they didn't suffer from vertigo and that they could climb higher than any men in the region and plant the sacred rooster at the top of the tallest church.

Inside, there was so much light and so much fervor it seemed as if heaven itself had overflowed into the church. The singing was so beautiful that if the villagers hadn't turned toward the choir loft and seen Célanire Pigeon waving his slender arm like a whip in front of the joint choir of the Daughters of the Virgin and the Sons of the Sacred Heart, they'd have thought the song was produced by angels. The organ's powerful voice was like the voice of a happy God singing to Himself in the flowering gardens of His Heaven.

On the wall over the crucifix and above the altar was a sky painted a perfect blue, except at the top where a few tufts of clouds reminded you that it was the sky and not the wall of the church. A throne was set in the sky. Seated on the throne was the good Lord, His face impassive and severe, but His eyes mild and kind. His hair and beard tumbled down over His face like a river's waves. A crown on His head was set with precious enamels and gems. His scarlet tunic formed broad swirls on His knees. His left hand held a sealed volume, while His right was raised in benediction. Above the throne there shone a rainbow, while before it, at the good Lord's feet, came together — terminating and arriving at their destination there — a number of roads that blended into one, and upon these roads, in the distance, could be seen groups of people with differently colored faces and odd sorts of clothing, who were approaching the throne. Before they reached it, though, they must pass a frightful animal that was curled up and hiding behind a shrub, a fearsome animal, a serpent with claws, spitting fire, winged but with a lion's head.

Curé Fourré made his way to the pulpit of truth. Célanire Pigeon silenced his choir with a snap of his fingers. The organ was silent too. Fat Iphigénie Lamontagne was out of breath from playing with such sincerity. Missals closed with a little thump. Rosaries clicked in their leather cases. On the great crucifix in the choir, above the altar, the dying Christ, the body violet and covered with bruises from the blows it had received, smiled at the faithful because there was such fervor in the church. They sat down; God's messenger, their holy Curé Fourré, had news for them. They coughed diligently, as if trying to expectorate everything they could. The man of God stretched out his arm and his body wrapped in the white alb, arrayed in stole and maniple, was as rigid as the crucifix above the altar.

"My dear, my very, my most very dear brethren: the good Lord wanted us to be together. And here we are, like a big family of brothers and sisters and cousins. I, whom God has given you as a spiritual father, I see you here and I am happy, for I can feel that you love one another with a Christian love and I love you with that same spiritual love, which doesn't create children but doesn't deteriorate either, as carnal love frequently does, and in all too many cases, rots like old potatoes left out in the field. We are gathered together here with a number of our friends; I note in particular our very honorable Local Riding Minister who is the intermediary between our parish and Le Chef, just as I am the intermediary between my parishioners and the Almighty. We thank you from the bottom of our heart. We aren't allowed to applaud you in this sacred temple, but I can assure you that the hearts of all our parishioners are beating in gratitude." (He stopped for a moment and cast a blistering glance at certain parishioners.) "Unfortunately, the Right Party's blessings are not always received with gratitude. The Devil sows ingratitude. Most very dear brethren, you have seen in the niches around the church our dear saints who watch us as they pray for us. These new statues, which are fireproof and inspired by modern art, are also a gift: the honorable Local Riding Minister, his Chef and the entire Right Party have made us a gift of these saints who will inspire our meditations and our thoughts. In the name of all my parishioners, Honorable Minister, I will pray for the Lord to enlighten the spirits of my parishioners on voting day. You, Honorable Minister, are concerned with laying out roads on this earth; these saints you have given us show us the roads we must follow to arrive at the house of the Father.

"Our great family here in Saint-Toussaint-des-Saints also welcomes a visitor, a great contractor, a man who builds to last, a craftsman who builds roads with future generations in mind, one of Le Chef's chosen and favorite contractors — Monsieur Verrochio. His name isn't French-Canadian like yours and mine, but you'll learn it fast because it's written on every one of the trucks and every one of the machines he's bringing here. Monsieur Verrochio is a foreigner, but we're honored that he's come from Italy, the country of our Venerated Holy Father the Pope and of the Holy See of the Holy Church. Monsieur Verrochio has lived under the same sun as our true father, the Pope. He has travelled a long road to come here and work with us. The road he will build is meaningless if it does not lead us all to Italy, to Rome, to the feet of His Holiness the Pope.

"Most very dear brethren, the roads of God are often impenetrable. Where do we come from? Where are we going? Above the road of our lives hovers a dense and clinging fog. Suffice it to say, to think, that we are on the road where the good Lord has set us, with all the love a father has for his children. On this earth, most very dear brethren, we can understand nothing. We are in a dense fog, but let us remember that we are on the road to God.

"How, for example, can we understand the miracle of which we all are witnesses? Young Opportun Lachance was a child like every other child; suddenly the good Lord took away his intelligence; for years, young Opportun had a child's body but no intelligence. Young Opportun had no more intelligence than a butterfly, but without the instinct of settling on flowers. Suddenly, God struck young Opportun again, but rather than strike him with death, God restored his intelligence. Everything God touches is sanctified; the intelligence of our young Opportun Lachance has undoubtedly been ameliorated. You will recall, most very dear brethren, that God once touched some loaves of bread and some fish, and that those loaves of bread and those fish were multiplied. Our young Opportun's intelligence has undoubtedly been multiplied, just like that bread and those fish.

"Most very dear brethren, that miracle is what we shall celebrate today, by forming a fervent procession. We shall thank the good Lord for giving young Opportun back his intelligence and we shall give thanks to the Right Party for giving us a new road. At one and the same time we shall follow the path of God and the road of the Right Party."

XV

Eating french fries can be fatal

When the church door opened, those who had been unable to attend the ceremony and had assembled along the street might have thought the sky had melted into the mild June night. Light poured from the church and onto the summer-baked fields: the roots of everything that grew were dry that summer. They needed rain. The earth was returning to dust. If it didn't rain the seeds would burn. Those who had stayed outside heard hymns sung loud enough to be heard by the good Lord, who is so far from the earth. The prayers of the faithful had made the stone walls vibrate! Surely angels had come and joined in this piety. Now that the doors were open, the angels had probably gone out; perhaps they were flying around like invisible butterflies. There was night everywhere, but the church was surrounded by a halo of light, as if the walls had become transparent. In the light, the church stood like an island. The sky was black. It wasn't one of those pale June nights from which the sun refuses to withdraw completely. There seemed to be anger in this sky. The night was tumultuous waves, like a discontented sea. And yet the air was mild. No dew would fall upon the earth. The soil still held its daytime warmth. The women didn't have to drape sweaters over their shoulders. They wore dresses of light flowered cotton and the men ogled their discreet necklines to see what treasures they concealed. In the main doorway an altar boy could be seen carrying the cross at the end of a long pole.

Opportun, sitting next to the Local Riding Minister, in a big armchair upholstered in red velvet, had been present at the whole ceremony; he had knelt when necessary, he had joined his hands when necessary, he had bowed his head at the proper time, he had made the sign of the cross and genuflected when it was appropriate, he had listened religiously to the prayers, the hymns and the sermon, he had said amen when the others said amen, even when the Local Riding Minister absent-mindedly forgot to do so. People wanted Opportun to thank the good Lord for the miracle that had been wrought for him, so he thanked Him. They wanted him to thank the Right Party for the new road that would be built, so Opportun thanked the Right Party. They sensed in him the grace that divine miracle had lodged there.

When the ceremony had ended and the procession was being formed, each person waiting his turn to step behind the altar boy in a too short soutane who was carrying the cross, Opportun slipped away. He disappeared without anybody noticing. During the ceremony, he had submitted to all the rituals, but it wasn't the idea of God that dwelled in him, it was the profane notion that all along the street those stalls on wheels, shimmering and brightly colored, were filled with extraordinary treats. The aromas of all the good things that were cooking or boiling mingled with the incense smoke. Opportun longed for french fries! There were coins in his pockets. He could feel them against his thigh. With these coins he would buy french fries and sprinkle them with vinegar; he would buy strawberry ice cream with butterscotch sauce; he would buy a mountain of pink candy floss; he would buy popcorn that he'd drown in melted butter. When he'd eaten everything he'd start again, he'd go back and buy more french fries that smelled of oil and vinegar, more ice cream with more strawberries and more butterscotch; he would eat more pink candy floss, and more popcorn. When he was no longer hungry he'd go down to the tents to investigate the games that were so much fun. He'd win money, because some of the games were the kind at which you could win money. Then he'd go back to the stalls where they sold all the marvelous treats. He would eat more french fries, dipping them in ketchup, he'd eat more ice cream, more candy floss, another cone of popcorn.

Opportun ran to the french-fry stall. The perfume of the oil was sweeter than the incense in church. The stall was beset by a mob of customers jostling to get at the wicket through which the salesman held out cones of french fries. The customers fought over them with cries of wonder, with insults and exasperated sighs.

"I want french fries!" said Opportun with all the authority that was due him as a miracle cure.

People recognized at once the boy whom God had virtually raised from the dead.

"I want french fries!"

His words sounded like a divine command. In a way it was God they heard speaking through Opportun's voice. The child who had been touched by God must take precedence over all the others: he was more than a priest, more than a cardinal, he was a saint, like Saint Tharcisius or Gérard Raymond, who wore a hair-shirt under his tennis clothes. Opportun was lifted bodily, hoisted above the heads of the customers in front of him. "Let our saint through!" Other arms grasped him, pushed him. He was carried at arms' length. "Make way for our little saint!" Other arms hoisted him over other customers. "Let our little saint get through!" Opportun, light as a bird, soared above the mob. Now he was close to the french-fry stand. The hot fat smelled so good. Hands grasped his little body, projecting it further, and other hands caught it and tossed it again. Suddenly Opportun was at the wicket, but before he could demand, "I want french fries," his body was hurled through the wicket and he collided with the firm bosom of a fat lady holding a basket of potatoes in a vat of boiling oil. Opportun took a dive into the oil and it spilled over onto the fire. Before a single throat could release a cry, the stall was in flames.

XVI

What is life but a procession?

The altar boy whose soutane was too short, who was carrying the processional cross, emerged from the church.

At the foot of the hill, a fiery tree was swaying in the night. Was it a house? Whose house was on fire? Who was the good Lord striking with such a scourge? All those who had been unable to get into the church left the places on either side of the street that they'd selected and held, for which they'd waged war. They ran toward the flames. They jostled, they pushed, they restrained one another. Old men and old ladies were hurrying as fast as the children; the sick, the infirm, those with weak hearts or sick lungs were running as fast as everyone else.

Seeing the deserted street and a column of fire and a plume of sparks at the bottom of the hill, the altar boy hesitated, uncertain what to do. Emérentienne Gousse, the eldest Daughter of the Virgin, ran down the aisle toward the choir, and her cane and the metal taps on her shoes made it sound as if she had three feet. She summarized the tragedy to the sexton, Théophile Labbé, who rushed off to whisper something in the ear of Curé Fourré, who was already sitting under the canopy, at the side of the Local Riding Minister who was worried because the Minister of Roads and Bridges was late. Curé Fourré turned pale, staggered and, to keep from falling, leaned against one of the poles that held up the canopy. He inhaled and exhaled several times, finally regained his balance, then held out his arms in a papal gesture.

"My dear, my very, my most very dear brethren, God has just wrought another miracle in our parish. When He took young Opportun away from us, letting him be struck by a car, we all grieved and found it hard to understand the good Lord's will. Then he gave young Opportun back to us by having him hit by a car again; we rejoiced, not really understanding the good Lord's will, though we thanked Him here in this church. Now I have just learned that the good Lord has taken young Opportun from us yet again. I don't think the good Lord can give him back this time, despite His infinite powers; this time again, we do not understand the good Lord's will. We do not understand the good Lord, but we are going to thank Him with the grandiose procession He has allowed us to organize."

The Local Riding Minister emerged from under the canopy and, like Curé Fourré, held out his arms in a papal gesture.

"The new road I'm going to give you, thanks to the Right Party's cooperation, will bear the name of the little saint from this village who rose up to Heaven in a spectacular bonfire. The road will be called Chemin Opportun. That's the name we'll put on all the maps. If the Opposition came to power I don't know what they'd call our new road . . . That's why I'm officially baptizing the road with Opportun's name here and now."

Curé Fourré swooped in front of the Local Riding Minister, raised himself to his full biretta-ed height and extended his arms in a magnificent gesture that displayed the broad sleeves of his alb in all their splendor. This move caused the Local Riding Minister to disappear behind him.

"My dear, my very, my most very dear brethren, only the Church, whose humblest apostle I am, has the power to baptize. And so I baptize the new road, to be built thanks to the Right Party's generosity, to which we will all be grateful, I baptize that road to the future the Chemin Opportun."

At these words, the church trembled. No violence; it was shaken gently. The Curé, the Minister, the faithful and the altar boys thought they were about to see an appearance by God Himself. They saw nothing. Everything was once again as quiet as if the church had never trembled on its foundations. People shot questioning, astonished looks at one another. Some of the women were upset.

"Most very dear brethren and sisters," Curé Fourré assured them, "the soul of our sainted Opportun has just passed through our church, which is located on the road that leads to the good Lord."

"Is the Minister gonna try and tell us the Right Party built that road?" shouted the disrespectful logger Uguzon Dubois, a non-believer from the Opposition.

Curé Fourré's face turned red with rage at the infidel who had once again broken the silence in this holy place. As a priest of God his role was only to forgive and he took pains to do so. He dropped his dry, pointed chin onto his flat chest to collect his thoughts. The Local Riding Minister spoke:

"The Right Party builds roads where the good Lord wants 'em, when He wants 'em. The good Lord wants the Chef of the Right Party to build a road right here in Saint-Toussaint-des-Saints, for the populace, old and young. When the Opposition was in power — for too long — the good Lord asked them to build roads for the people too, but the Opposition didn't listen to the good Lord's voice. It didn't build any roads and it didn't build any bridges. The Opposition doesn't follow the voice of God, because there's too many communists in the Opposition: communists that don't even respect the House of God, that shout insults at established power and show no respect for the holy tabernacle that contains the body of Christ."

There were sputterings of applause. Curé Fourré didn't take offence at this unaccustomed tumult in the House of God. He thanked God that the Minister had gone into politics and not the priesthood. Compared with such a priest, who knew how to stir up a crowd, Curé Fourré would have cut a pale figure with the bishop. The Minister listened to the applause and thought again of the Minister of Roads and Bridges, who was very late.

The Minister of Roads and Bridges, who was to honor the important procession with his presence, had kept to the schedule that was drawn up. At the appointed hour, his airplane had taken off from the Capital. He had brought along a secretary, an adviser and some boxes of personal letters on which he was supposed to inscribe his signature. The Minister of Roads and Bridges reminded the voters of all the blessings the Right Party had sown in the Appalachian Region. When he was handed the letters to sign, the Minister pushed them away, saying: "Put my personal signature there yourselves; yours are realer than mine." He settled back in his seat, stretched out his legs and fell asleep. He was very likely dreaming about politics, which gave him so many splendid opportunities to live high off the hog. He was smiling as he dreamed, as he did in the publicity photos that showed him shaking the hands of women voters clustered about him. He sighed. He snored. The clouds were draped in soft pink evening light. The airplane followed the river that was like a slack blue road, then it turned south and flew over flat fields that rose suddenly into rugged hills. The land raged like a sea. The hills, which rose higher and higher, were covered by an ever harsher forest. Here and there, a rent in the forest showed houses scattered along roads that zigzagged through fields, circled hills and crept between the houses clustered around a church like chicks around a hen. Steeples rose in the sky like tall pointed trees without branches. The functionaries signed his electoral messages. They said nothing, but they were thinking that the Minister of Roads and Bridges was less adroit than the Local Riding Minister. Throughout their careers as servants of the State, they could not recall a Minister ever organizing a procession in honor of a local saint to inaugurate construction of a segment of road. True, such a tactic could be effective only in a backward region. Whenever they talked about political strategy, one of the functionaries was in the habit of declaring that what was effective in backward regions should work in the Capital too.

"Go back a couple of generations and you'll see your shiny city-dweller sitting down to milk a cow."

Then the sociological discussions would flare up. This time, in the airplane, the Minister of Roads and Bridges was snoring. It was the functionaries' duty not to disturb him and to watch over the safety of the State — menaced by the Opposition's coming to power — by inscribing the personal signature of the Minister of Roads and Bridges at the bottom of his missive.

In the central doorway of the church, the altar boy who was carrying the cross gazed questioningly at Heaven. At the bottom of the hill, flames thrust violent red tongues into the night. Above his head, the church steeple shook. Then, nothing moved. The altar boy had waited for a stone, wrenched from its mortar, to drop, or for the copper rooster at the tip of the steeple to crash to his feet. The altar boy saw nothing fall.

The sexton uttered a word that was not part of the language of worship.

"Giddyup!" he shouted, as if he were commanding a horse.

The altar boy raised the processional cross high and parallel to his body. This marked the start of the procession. He was followed by the other altar boys, their lace surplices carefully starched by the nuns' patient fingers, but spotted with jam or ink; there had been some wrestling before the ceremony. Their robes had not followed the example of the tunic of Jesus Christ, which had grown along with His divine body.

Mothers examined their children from head to toe. Under the soutanes coarse wool trousers could be seen: it was summer now, but winter would inevitably come, and it was better to be too hot in summer than too cold in winter. The trousers under the soutanes were pressed or as round as stove-pipes: this said something about the way the mothers took care of their families. Some trousers dropped onto shoes and dragged in the dust; the mothers of those children were provident: they had thought of the future when they bought their trousers; the child would grow. Other trousers were short, revealing socks: the mothers of these children were thrifty rather than provident: they waited until the child could no longer get into his trousers before buying him another pair. All the altar boys wore black shoes, too big for them, that scuffed along the pavement.

These children were wearing men's shoes and struggling to take men's strides. In a few years, they would work with their arms like real independent men. Under the soutanes, the long shoes glided, all at the same rhythm, together, in a rubbing of leather on pavement. It seemed to be a whispered prayer. The torches they carried traced a fine and frenzied lace.

Next came a white satin banner fringed in gold, on which was painted the Virgin clad in a blue tunic. She joined her very delicate hands, which had never touched the strong lye that burned ordinary women's hands. Her red heart, painted on top of her white robe, was pierced by seven daggers, representing the seven sorrows the Virgin suffered during her life on earth. Her feet stood on a globe on which the seas and continents were outlined. But if you looked closely, despite the gathering dark, you could see her bare feet flattening a serpent that strangled the globe. Under the Virgin's ivory feet, Satan must have been releasing his grip on the earth.

Behind their banner, the Daughters of the Virgin advanced with a smile so sweet they seemed to be marching toward Paradise, breathing its perfume. These young girls wore scarves as blue as the Virgin's tunic. Some had already been promised; they looked at nothing, for fear of letting their gaze settle on a man who wasn't theirs. The others, those who hadn't found a husband yet, raised their eyes as they recited prayers. They looked out cautiously, their expressions like deer that know they're being hunted. A glance that settled too long, too directly, would have been interpreted as a call unworthy of a Daughter of the Virgin. They would have been placed in the category of young girls with frivolous ideas. ("If they've got crazy ideas before the wedding, imagine what they'll be like afterwards.") Those who showed themselves to be frivolous had many suitors, but few marriage proposals. In many cases they were the ones who married last. And so, white-skinned, plump-cheeked, with lush bosoms that could nurse many children, with muscular calves and strong legs from frequently climbing up and down the road that sat on the hill like a saddle on a horse's back, the Daughters of the Virgin advanced, with pious looks, bowed heads, folded hands, in colored dresses with collars tight about their necks, and sleeves that fell to the wrists. So often had they come this way, so often would they come again: down the village street they would parade amid ribbons and automobile horns on their wedding days; down this street, the children they would have, would head like them to school; down this street, they would grow old and their legs would no longer be able to climb up to the church. The Daughters of the Virgin minced along in shoes that compressed their feet. Perhaps some night they would go out on the new road, in the well-waxed automobile of a man who would say words as strong as the drink that muddles your thoughts. Along this road, they might leave the village for distant towns with shop-windows as beautiful as dreams. Perhaps it would be down this new road that a stranger would come with whom, later, they would go away. Hands folded like the Virgin's, they prayed fervently but without thinking of the words they were mouthing. With all the multi-colored flowers planted in their hats, they carried gardens on their heads.

A banner of the Sacred Heart separated the Daughters of the Virgin from the Sons of the Sacred Heart. These young men were no longer adolescent, but weren't yet real men because they were still bachelors. A number had already found their future wife, who was marching with the Daughters of the Virgin. The others were looking, or waiting. All were somewhat dazzled by the women's per-fumes that reached their noses from the other side of the banner. All felt their hearts shiver at the hush of muslin in which the young girls dressed their bodies. On their lips there were prayers, but from His banner the Sacred Heart could read the thoughts that were tumbling about in their souls, and He knew why his sons had goose-flesh: too many blazing thoughts, too many impossible desires . . . From His banner, the Sacred Heart was judging them with eyes so pure, it made the impure feel ashamed. At the sight of Him like that, showing His bleeding heart, wounded by the crown of thorns that had been planted there by sinners, the Sons of the Sacred Heart blushed at the sins they had not yet committed, and lowered their heads. They were guilty, certainly, of letting their thoughts roll about in the perfumes of young girls and the disturbing whisper of their robes, but hadn't the good Lord created women?

Hadn't the good Lord decided that, in the presence of women, men would be as wild as moose in rutting season? Anyway, weren't they young? Wasn't youth a fire whose flames were quickly doused? Wasn't it inscribed in nature that young men and young girls consume their youth together, in a great fire? The time for cold ashes would come soon enough. Then the Sons of the Sacred Heart would resemble their fathers. The Daughters of the Virgin would resemble their mothers. That would be old age. And they would regret the time of their youth. The road between the two was very short. So much was forbidden. Only prayer could help take their minds off those forbidden desires that made their bodies, swollen with guilty dreams, too small for their souls. They prayed more intensely and pressed their fingers of their joined hands harder together, but if they had dressed in their new suits, if they'd buttoned their starched collars, if they'd tied around their thick necks colored neckties with bright flowers, if they'd dashed a little French cologne on their faces, it wasn't for the good Lord and it wasn't for young Opportun.

The Sons of the Sacred Heart tried not to think about the Daughters of the Virgin. Some of them, it was said, weren't afraid of their mothers: they dared to come in after midnight, to get in a car with a boy and go for a drive along dirt roads where only hares could spy on them. These girls wouldn't protest when the car stopped in a field so they could look at the sky, the stars, as if there were a sea up above them on which they might sail away . . .

They must pay attention to their prayers. If profane thoughts in the hearts of His sons brought suffering to the Sacred Heart, why didn't He drive them away? Why did the good Lord's breeze smooth the dresses of the Daughters of the Virgin against their bodies? Why did the good Lord breathe that dizzying perfume of grass and flowers mingled with an odor of flesh like a baby's? ("Forgive us poor sinners, now and at the hour of our death. Amen!") Their hearts weren't in their prayer, but wasn't that a fact of youth? They would pray later, when they were as old as their parents, when they were old . . . The new road would change many things. Life would be different when it was easier to get around . . . What new things would come to the village along the new road? What would leave? A road was as unknown and unpredictable as life.

Next came the Knights of Columbus, who seemed to be disembarking from another time. From their shoulders fell the sumptuous folds of red-lined capes. In their shiny top hats, they didn't look like village men. They were encased in swallow-tail coats. Some, the most important, wore heavy silver charms around their necks. They followed the procession, chins high, heads thrown back, without glancing around them, as if they had only contempt for the admiring crowd. A long sword shone on their right side. Their hands gripped the shank and they stood ready to obey the order to unsheathe them. Their left arms swung rigidly, like soldiers'. The goal of the Knights of Columbus was to defend truth on the earth. The Knights seemed determined to fight to the last drop of their blood. To see them you'd think the enemy was approaching from the other end of the road. The Knights of Columbus were a secret society: they shared the knowledge of a magic and powerful secret. Was that what made them seem so strong? You couldn't help but respect them. In the procession, you wanted to follow them, follow in their footsteps.

For their secret initiation, the windows of the parish hall were blocked with wooden panels. A fence guarded by the sturdiest Knights was unfurled around the room. The Knights reappeared at the end of the day, exhausted, sweating, their clothes wrinkled and wet; they were drunk but didn't reek of alcohol, though they laughed and laughed and couldn't talk. Some wives thought the well-kept secret had to do with those women without religion or virtue who come from the cities, but they dared not say so openly. They sighed; they feared their husbands, who now belonged to a powerful order. And so the wives were silent, they pouted and heaved great suffering sighs. As for the Knights, they walked in the way of God.

If you were to see them marching in the procession in their ceremonial clothes, sword at their sides, top hats and red capes like a hero of olden times, you would discover that these tremendously powerful men disguised themselves on ordinary days as very ordinary folks, the better to carry out the secret tasks assigned them by the Order.

If the Knights of Columbus were taking part in the procession to honor young Opportun and the new road, you could be sure they'd told the Pope about the miracle wrought on Opportun's behalf. And then the Pope would bless the Chemin Opportun.

"Gaze out with love upon the River's shore:
A still young nation trembles with a surge
How often hast thou saved it from the scourge
Now grant Thy boon, watch over us the more."

Marching in step, a line of girls and a line of boys were separated so they couldn't touch. Their eyes were shut so they'd think of nothing but their song. Their hands were joined but held away from their bodies so their arms wouldn't squeeze their lungs. To the boys assembled by the side of the street the girls' bosoms had never looked so prominent. Suddenly a cry erupted through the melody: the pressure had burst open the buttons on a dress. A lavish bosom popped out ("tits like pumpkins"), but after the exclamations, the young spectators withdrew into a sullen, disappointed silence. Angèle Leboeuf's bosom was held in by countless undergarments. Other spectators looked at the open mouths and they thought they saw, in the chillier air of evening, the song rising up in a sort of smoke almost invisible to human eyes. The choir passed and their singing entered every one of the spectators. Suddenly, each one felt his chest swell, mouths opened, heads were raised toward heaven, and the hymn surged powerfully up to God, who could not be indifferent. He would come to help these men and women build their new road across the land He had created for them. As they looked at the vast night sky, everyone knew that God made no distinction between voices; He listened to the voices of their hearts:

"Now grant Thy boon, watch over us the more."

Through the toil of their bodies, of their arms, they would build a new road, but now their song was tracing a path through the sky.

Next came the pioneer men and women of Saint-Toussaint-des-Saints, with rosaries wound about their wrists, dressed in black dresses or suits, as they would be in their coffins. They disapproved of what was taking place under

144

the rule of the young. They could not forgive the young for leaving the land where they were "kings" and fleeing to the city where they were "slaves." They would be slaves all their lives, pale from never seeing the sun, pale as the dead, and deaf "before their time" from the noise of machines. The pioneer women and men also warned the young that in the cities they would forget the good Lord and the true religion. ("The black smoke from the factories hides the blue sky and if you can't see the sky you forget the Lord.") The pioneer women and men were unhappy too because the young girls scorned boys who worked on the land. The girls were running off to the cities too. Instead of being queens on their own land, they would go and clean the filth in the castles of the rich who practised another religion and spoke another language. The young people reproached the pioneers for grumbling, for muttering, for being gloomy, for always being unhappy, for thinking only of the past, for not accepting progress. The old people didn't understand why the young got rid of horses that needed only oats, replaced them with delicate machines that ate up all their savings, that were always thirsty and didn't obey a good flick of the whip. The pioneer women didn't like to see the younger women with a cigarette in their lips from which ashes fell onto their food. It was something they had learned from the women who came back from the cities with faces painted like the women in the Coca-Cola ads, with husbands who didn't even speak their good country language, and strange children who didn't have the family look about them. The pioneer women had no reason to be proud of the modern women: instead of feeding their babies at their breasts, as the good Lord surely wanted since He had given women milk, modern women fed their children water and powders that came from the city in cans; did they think they could build a strong race from water and powder? As for the breasts the good Lord had given them to feed their children, modern women decked themselves out in complicated harnesses, suspenders, and pads, then exposed themselves like the oranges and apples in the general store. Oh! they had lots to be sad about, the old people. They had plenty of reasons to be grouchy and to let their minds wander, with tears in their eyes. When you asked them, "Hey, Gramps, are you weeping over your old sins?" or "Say, Granny, are you lonesome for your first lover?" they felt there was nothing more for them to do on this earth, in this time; and without anger or impatience, without complaining, asking nothing of these young people who could give them nothing, the old people would get out of their rocking chairs and announce: "I guess I'll go to the church, and offer the good Lord some prayers for the rest of you." Praying to the good Lord meant that in their usual places in the church they would kneel, drape a rosary around their wrists, cross their hands and, lifting their eyes to the big crucifix behind the altar, say: "I'll be ready to go Lord, when You're ready to come for me."

That night, they dragged their heavy feet in their old-fashioned shoes. (It would be a waste to buy new ones because they'd soon be "departing.") With ankles swollen because their old bones were worn and their old arteries dried up, with legs made heavy by age, numbed by rheumatism, swollen by phlebitis and tortured by arthritis, the pioneers moved slowly, painfully, sadly. They wouldn't spend much time on that new road the Right Party had just given them. That new road was the road of youth, of children. Their eyes wouldn't see what was going to come down that road, what was going to disappear along it. Their eyes would be closed forever, their hands frozen in the endless cold of death, but along that road their descendants would continue to walk, children would run, cars would drive, trucks rumble, bicycles clatter as if they, the old people, were not dead, as if they had never been alive, as if life had not dried up in them.

Far away, in the cities, life was no longer as the good Lord had made it, no longer good as it had been in the olden days. People no longer believed in religion's holy truths; they wanted to change their wife or husband like a shirt; children were no longer a blessing but a trial; many pregnant women were ashamed of their bellies, as if they were an infirmity; women refused to obey their men; now they were refusing to let themselves be seeded, and what is a field without seed? Children no longer obeyed their parents and parents no longer even wanted to be obeyed. Workers in factories didn't want to work: work had become a curse. They carried placards that insulted their bosses.

Workers wanted to keep their hands clean. When the new road was built, this new life would flow along it like a river: the village would change greatly too. Perhaps it was better to be condemned not to endure, not to live too long? The old people did not sing the new words to the hymns; in their silence they recited ancient prayers. Hands folded, wrists joined by rosaries, heads bowed piously before the power of omnipresent God, they were submissive to life, submissive to death.

They were the pioneers: before them there had been the forest covered with brushwood. When they arrived, there had been no road but the one their axes slashed through the forest, which had been the way it had grown since the creation of the world. Because they were looking for a place to live, they had built a road. Today, their children might use the new road to run away from this place to which the good Lord had brought them. The weakness of youth resulted from having open roads before them. Men and women are born to open roads. The young people were idle, sad and hopeless. All the roads had been laid out before them. The village stood there, with its painted houses on smooth lawns, with ribbons of flowers. The road ran before them; on it they were like fish in water. The young people had no desires, they had no need of anything, they asked nothing of the good Lord, they had stopped believing in Him. Oh! the pioneers' footsteps were weighty in this procession: their shoes dragged on the pavement and the sound they made was louder than the murmured prayers.

Following after them, the saints which the Right Party had given to the church and to good Curé Fourré were carried by altar boys on palanquins trimmed with gilded fringe.

St. Francis had birds perched on his outstretched arms. After the admiring "Oh"s came the whispers: they'd have liked to penetrate his secret and learn how to talk to the birds and hold them in their hands, for around here the birds flew away even if you threw them seeds. St. Joseph the carpenter, father of Jesus, came next, carrying his tools in his firm, muscular arms. What was he making? A cradle for baby Jesus. They recognized the set square, the auger, the chisel and especially the "saint-joseph" (the name they'd given to the village carpenter's long wood-plane).

"Who's that saint tied to the wheel?"

"St. Catherine of Egypt," said an altar boy to whom Curé Fourré had told the story of Catherine, a Christian woman punished by an evil pagan emperor for refusing to marry him; he had tied her to a great wheel with steel teeth that bit into her pure white virgin's body.

"Did she get saved by a miracle?"

"If she'd been saved by a miracle she wouldn't be a plaster saint today," was the altar boy's reply, tinged with contempt for the other's ignorance. And he continued Curé Fourré's feverish account:

"St. Catherine died after days and days of torture on the jagged wheel. The good Lord sent a bird that dropped food between her lips."

"What kind of food? Worms?" asked a stranger with a pagan laugh.

"Communist!" shouted a visitor behind him. "The good Lord gives us a fine new road and you mock His saints. A road sown with blasphemy is a road that leads to the devil."

"Where else do you expect it to go, if the Right Party's building it?"

The communist was jostled and pushed and kicked in the shin and he had to go elsewhere to watch the procession.

Next came St. Julian, with his bow and arrow and, beside him, kneeling, the deer with the cross of light that had appeared between its antlers just as the saint was about to kill the good Lord's creature.

"If deers here ran around with a flaming cross on their heads they'd be out of luck: we hunt with rifles, and we shoot anything that moves!"

"When the Daughters of the Virgin went past I saw some pretty little round things move inside their summer dresses, but nobody fired a shot. Ha ha!"

Laughter erupted on all sides, steeped in the sour smells of onions and frying fat. A few visitors plugged their ears to keep out such obscenities: would the new road be used only for insulting the saints?

Next, on a palanquin covered with white cotton fringed in red, came Maria Goretti, a young girl who had died shouting NO! to the wicked men who tried to take advantage of her virginal body. The nuns at school had told the story of this brave young saint a hundred times. The young girls knew that wicked men could burst out from behind bushes, tall grass and trees, wanting to sully their bodies. As if they themselves had fled, they repeated very loud, in their souls: NO! And when they described their fright, their mothers would sigh:

"You're right. When a man walks down the road that road belongs to him, while a woman . . . "

On a larger palanquin, four altar boys carried the eight Holy Canadian Martyrs tortured to death by savage Indians. The youngest, René Goupil, had written a poignant letter to his mother as he lay dying. When the boys went out to play in the forest, they would sing René Goupil's lament to his mother at the top of their lungs, to drive away their fear and reassure themselves, for along all the paths they could see savage shadows moving among the bushes. Like the Canadian missionaries of old, the boys would suffer martyrdom as they looked up at the sky, their one true fatherland, to which the earthly roads would lead them.

How beautiful the saints were! How good it would be to kneel before them once they were settled in their niches! How kind the Right Party was, to give a new road to the village and new saints to the church. People would come and join the community, others would leave it, but the saints would remain in the church; like the true religion, they would not change.

Pretty angels followed after the saints. They were little girls in long white robes and white shoes; they walked along, contemplative, sweet, light, ready to fly into the blue sky. Their tinfoil wings could have lifted them from the earth where there was so much evil to stain their white robes. Their little hearts shuddered. They held lighted candles. If the breeze blew them out, they would piously seek a light from the next girl: so must God's children help one another. They must share the light that He had created on the first day of the world. From up above the good Lord could see their flames flickering in the night. For them He would create more light. God would not allow His angels to be spattered with the mud where adults crawl.

No, God would spare some of his white angels. He would come and gather some of these young girls before life turned them into women. Under the vast starry sky, the hearts of the white-robed angels throbbed. The tinfoil wings at their backs could have made them rise up to the sky. They were dazed by the vertigo of being drawn to the sky, as if they had invisible wires, like puppets, which the good Lord could tug to draw them back to heaven. The flickering candle flames were warm like the breath of God.

Behind the white angels came black-dressed men hunched under the sacks they carried on their backs. These were the sinners. The burden, Curé Fourré had explained, was the visible sign of sin, which weighs down the sinner's shoulders. The burlap bags were full of ashes, the Curé had explained further, to remind the faithful that one who has sinned "will burn in the flames of purgatory, for venial sins, or in the eternal flames of hell (much hotter than the flames in the boiler that heats our church in winter) if the sins were mortal. Of the sinner," he had added, "nothing will remain but ashes and dust." Curé Fourré, who alone "with God" knew the sins of Saint-Toussaint-des-Saints, had asked some of the strongest men to bear all the sins committed in the parish since its founding, and all the sins that would be committed against God until the parish was no more. These men, already weary, panting, sweating, staggering, faces black from ashes mixed with sweat, carried the sins of their fellow citizens on their shoulders. Those who had admired the angels shut their eyes. Everyone, through his sins, had added some ashes to the sacks: the children through lying, through gluttony, had placed a pinch of ashes in the sacks; but the young men and young girls who, in the fire of their unbridled senses, had done what the beasts do in the fields, the wives who refused their conjugal duty, the men who, angry at their animals or machines, at an overly tough tree, an overly heavy stone, an overly tenacious root, raised their fists and railed against God for having created things as He had created them: all the inhabitants of Saint-Toussaint-des-Saints had contributed something to the black sacks borne by the penitents. Bystanders along the road lowered their gaze. One day God would come to reclaim the soul He had lent them. It must be as white as the angels' robes. At the sight of these men bent under the ashes of their sins, the villagers knew that they had greatly offended God. They too bore on their shoulders an invisible sack crammed with the ashes of guilt. Their backs were bowed by the burden and one by one, crushed by the weight of their sins, they fell to their knees as the men in black passed by. Trembling, they prayed. They had sinned like those people in the village destroyed by fire, or in countries drowned by a flood. Would God not tire of forgiving the sins that people kept committing, unrepentant? If the fires of Heaven were to rain down on the village, if a sea of water were to descend on the village, would they be able to escape? True salvation consists not of fleeing, but of regretting one's sins. They watched the passage of these men who bore the ashes of the parish sins, and their terror was as great as the terrors of childhood.

Then the villagers got up, shaking the dust from their trousers or skirts. Next came the nuns. They had no bodies: only a white coif, feet that moved below their robes, and small white hands. They weren't altogether women, they were almost angels. Their long black robes drifted in the night; they seemed to be flying, like angels. Their slight imperfections weighed lightly in the penitents' sacks. When they returned to the ashes and dust whence they had come: "Remember, O man, O woman, thou art but ashes and dust," the dust and ashes of their bodies would be a benediction for the earth that would receive them. They sang, there were seven of them, they walked in twos, preceded by their Superior. You could not see their faces. Night drew a circle of shadow under their coifs. Their voices were sweet. They sang politely: "Lord, have pity on us!" Not for themselves did they beseech God's grace, but for all those who had loaded sins into the penitents' sacks. They had not had children but the village children had learned more from them than from their own mothers. They taught reading from the great book of God. Where did they come from? They would spend a few years in Saint-Toussaint-des-Saints, then take the road to which God called them. There were always seven of them in the village, following their Superior two by two. They went outside only to walk from their school to the church. It wasn't the nuns who needed the new road. Some of the

151

penitents had agreed to carry sacks of ashes in the hope that Curé Fourré would recommend them warmly to the Local Riding Minister and they'd get jobs on the new road, but the holy nuns had no other reason to take part in the procession than to ask God to bless the work of all the men on the new road. Above all, they had come to thank the good Lord for His miracle on behalf of young Opportun. The Superior had assured Curé Fourré that she and her nuns would vote for the Right Party, out of natural gratitude. The Local Riding Minister had already given the church a gift of fine modern plaster saints, "that won't burn like those crummy wooden statues that used to decorate the temples in the olden days." He had asked Curé Fourré to tell the nuns that while the new road was being built, trucks would come and pour fine soil, free of weeds and insect-proof, onto the schoolyard; construction men would rake it smooth so the nuns could plant their vegetables and flowers. The Superior had said: "We nuns would be ungrateful if we didn't tell our children that the Right Party gave the saints to the church and a garden to its nuns. We'd be ungrateful if we didn't ask our children to tell their parents." The Curé had said: "Any men who go near the nuns or their garden must be worthy of being in the presence of virtue. I'll see to it that the men who work for you have the necessary innocence. I'm considering sending you the penitents who will carry the sacks of sinful ashes in the procession."

The Superior gestured to her nuns to sing God's praises even louder. Some of the faithful struck up the refrain along with them.

The holy nuns didn't need a new road: they followed different paths along this earth. The roads to holiness have no need of surveyors or bulldozers or trucks. The nuns went through life like angels. In the night they were angels dressed in black robes. The village women, rounded by child-bearing, were somewhat envious of the nuns. They felt a shudder of remorse for having given to a man who smelled of sweat and tobacco the virginity that would have turned them into angels. As punishment, they were condemned to follow roads laid out by men.

They looked like angels too, these young girls who were going to offer their virginity to a man, these future brides who kept their hands folded together like the nuns. Their bosoms sighed, too narrow to contain a heart that leapt at the imminent arrival of the day they had anticipated since distant childhood, the day when they would become women. The breeze blew the organdy and tulle against their bodies: they had donned their bridal gowns for the procession. In a while, the children born of their bodies would walk along the road that wasn't built yet. Later, the children would drive fast cars, as if they wanted to catch up with death, their throats filled with frenzied laughter. These children, who were still only a dream, would stop along the road one mild evening, they would seek an oasis of greenery hidden under the whispering leaves, and young men and young women would give themselves to one another, dazzled; as their blood became magical, they would feel an urge to cry out to God, behind the stars, that they had never been so happy as in sinning against Him, that by trespassing against Him they had been re-born as men and women! Tears clung to the lashes of the future brides: these children would also have children, who would run along the new road, but by then they would be old. Their children, alas! would grow old too; then they would be dead and in the ground, they would be only a vague memory for the old children who, at the end of their years, would feel nostalgic for their mothers. How strange was the road that God had laid out for women upon this earth. They were still only young girls, they weren't yet married, they would not marry until June when bouquets of fresh-blown flowers would be draped over their missals, yet already their hearts were sad as if their lives were over. Young Opportun was not their child and mattered less than the children who would be born to them later. The new road was not important because even without it they would have been able to love, to be loved and to marry. Curé Fourré had asked them to join the procession because they had been chosen above all others, he explained, to make children so the new road would not be deserted and covered with grass. ("This land needs roads and men to travel those roads. If the Right Party's given us roads, you, the future women of this land, must give children to the roads.") That was what Curé Fourré had told the future brides. They followed right behind the holy nuns. They walked cautiously because they didn't want to scuff the white shoes they would wear at their weddings. There were seven of them, like the nuns. The breeze stirred their gowns, but unlike the nuns they didn't seem to fly. At the side of the street, the men's gazes were fixed on the white gowns, trying to penetrate the mysteries of the organdy. Fat, older women elbowed their husbands: "I was once a beauty like that, y'know," but they didn't believe it and their husbands didn't remember. So many years had passed on this street since they had walked out of the church, married: so many other newlyweds, so many newborns, so many processions, so many funerals; so many more things would arrive along the new road. The future brides walked on, and the people were looking at no one but them. No one would have looked up toward the stars. They were the most beautiful things in the universe, and people knew that beneath the tulle and lace, in their bodies as beautiful as youth, was concealed the future of the village. A few smutty remarks were spat out, but they were covered at once by reproval and reproaches. The future brides were admired with the respect usually reserved for tabernacles.

A few steps behind their fiancées came the future bridegrooms. Curé Fourré had ordered the man at the head of the group to respect the distance of fifteen paces ("or more"). It was not proper for young men, their senses fired by their approaching marriage, to stand too close to young girls whose dreams were inflamed by the proximity of that event. There were eight future bridegrooms in the black suits they would wear on their wedding day. They marched in twos. They were eight. Seven fiancées had been counted. No one was surprised at the extra man. Polycarpe Poisson was a familiar sight. He wore his nuptial costume but he had no fiancée. He had never had a fiancée, but was always announcing his imminent marriage. He had been announcing his marriage for years. He was looking for a wife, but he had never found one. And yet he was a man of property as they said. His father had turned it over to him, as they also said, in exchange for a meager wage paid to the Widow Chérubine Haché to take care of the old man, to serve him tea and dry biscuits, wash him, wash his clothes when he consented to take them off, and endure the stench of his tobacco. Fall and winter, Polycarpe Poisson went up

154

to the logging camps in the Abitibi forests. He shut up the house and stable; he sold off his calves, cows, hens and pigs. When he returned in the spring, Polycarpe Poisson would re-open the house which despite the sun's rays long retained a memory of glacial cold, he would collect his father from the Widow Chérubine Haché, and buy the calves, bulls and piglets that his father would fatten up over the summer. These useful tasks kept the old man from dying of boredom. Polycarpe looked after the fields and the woods. In the autumn, he had animals, wheat, hay, alfalfa and fire-wood for sale. So Polycarpe Poisson had property; he'd never withdrawn a cent from the *Caisse Populaire*: what he deposited there must stay and bear fruit. ("When you plant a potato you don't dig 'er up and eat 'er till she's ripe . . . ") That was his philosophy. With such ideas, he felt he'd be shown some respect when he showed up at the *Caisse Populaire*.

"Work and save," he proclaimed to the town council one day. "That's the strut and the upright of the cross that brings man's salvation."

"It can crucify a fellow too," replied a joker. Polycarpe Poisson hadn't paid much attention to him, because his own property was slight.

Before Mass on Sunday, Polycarpe Poisson would dust off his black Ford, he would apply a thin coat of wax and rub and polish until the chrome and hub caps gleamed. Then he would deck himself out for Sunday, as he put it. Polycarpe Poisson was dressed like a *monsieur* from town. No one in the village had suits as fashionable as his, not even the notary or Curé Fourré under his soutane. When Polycarpe came down from the Abitibi camps, he always stopped off in the Capital to buy himself a suit. Every time, he was sure he'd be marrying that summer. Others who got married had worn-out suits; Polycarpe would never marry, but he was resplendent in the most up-do-date fashion for newlyweds. Polycarpe Poisson told himself that the good Lord, in His wisdom, hadn't wanted to give him a wife because his time had not yet come.

After Mass, he took off in his gleaming car with the sunlight glinting off it through the dust stirred up by the road. Polycarpe was going fishing for a wife, as he put it. He'd been trying to lure one for years now, but he still hadn't given up hope. Somewhere there was a woman the good Lord had created for him. All dressed up in his fine suit, Polycarpe Poisson went out to look for the woman who was waiting for him. First, he made the rounds of the village houses; he knew where the spinsters nested, he knew where children had suddenly become young girls ripe for marriage. Polycarpe acted openly, he got straight to the point in a manly way, without hypocrisy, without hiding anything.

"Hello there," he would say, "fine day we're having (even if it was raining). Good weather for haying . . ." (These last words would be addressed to all the people he noticed.) Then he would address the father:

"Y'see, I'm looking for a wife. I don't drink, don't smoke, don't curse, don't chase women (except now that I'm lookin' for a wife), I got my nest egg in the *Caisse Populaire* and land under my feet. It won't be long before my pa packs up for the graveyard, so pretty soon the house'll be empty except for me. My wife wouldn't have to put up with the old man for long. At his age he won't make it through the winter, and even if he does make it to spring, he'll be gone when the dandelions go to seed. It's a fine house for a young woman. So I'd be prepared to marry that daughter of yours — what was her name?"

After he'd fished, as he put it, in all the houses in the village, he'd get back in his black Ford and try to reel in a wife from all the houses scattered through the parish. He always knocked politely at the door, like a *monsieur* from town.

Very late at night, long after the sun had gone down, the black Ford would come back, all dusty and driven by a man who'd come home empty-handed. As he hadn't found a wife at home, he would explore the neighboring parish. Every Sunday he would take a different road, stopping at every house, asking if there was a marriageable woman, if there was one at the neighbor's or on the next road. Every spring when he came down from the logging camps, he set off on his rounds again, but never did he find what he was looking for.

Why didn't the young girls want to marry him? He knew that modern girls don't like agriculture. They preferred cars to cattle. Was his black Ford too old? It was still spotless, luxurious. It would be wasteful to part with it and buy a new one. He decided to rejuvenate it instead. He bought paint, a modern color: canary yellow. Meticulously, he painted the Ford. His powerful logger's hands, accustomed to felling tall, hard trees, carefully avoided smudging the chrome or the windows. The Ford was as yellow as the dandelions in the field. Polycarpe Poisson still didn't find a wife.

Was it because they didn't like his smell? A man who, every day of his life, soaks his shirt in the sweat of his muscles, who works amid the acrid odor of animals and trees, has a particular smell that clings to him. He wrote to the store in the Capital where he went every spring to buy himself a wedding suit, and asked them to send him a flask of perfume. "I want to smell good like they smell in Paris, so don't send me nothing but expensive French perfume."

His car was the shiniest, his perfume concealed any human exudation, but still Polycarpe Poisson found no one to marry.

None of the men who had found a wife had as much property as he. And all those men swore, they drank like pigs, they chased women and spent three or four days in the Capital visiting the wicked houses on the rue Saint-Paul when they came down from the Abitibi forests. No one was as good as Polycarpe Poisson. Yet no woman wanted him. Was it because he was too short? In the olden days such details didn't matter. In these modern times, since the movies, women dreamed of actors who had bodies like young ladies and stood at least a head taller than their partners. Polycarpe Poisson was too short. That was probably why he hadn't found someone to marry. Why hadn't he realized it sooner? Fortunately, he saw an advertisement in the *Bulletin des Fermiers* offering a foolproof and miraculous way to grow instantly taller. On one side they showed a man who was short, lonely, pitiful, defeated. That was before the application of the miracle method. On the other side the same man was surrounded by young girls who were clustered against his chest. He stood head and shoulders above all these beauties. That was after the application of the miracle method. Women, the advertisement explained, don't want to tower over a man; it's in their nature to need to take shelter against a sturdy man as tall as a tree. Polycarpe Poisson sent a cheque to the address given. While he waited for a reply and the miracle that would transform him into a man who would be loved by women, he painted his Ford black again and returned the perfume to the store in the Capital, asking for a refund because it hadn't worked.

After several weeks he received a reply to his order: two thick wooden soles to place under his shoes. With them he couldn't not grow taller. Guaranteed. Polycarpe Poisson followed the instructions to the letter. The magic soles attached to his shoes really did make him taller. He couldn't believe what he saw in the mirror: he was as tall as those actors the women liked so much.

The actors, though, weren't bald. Working hard and sweating under his cap had burned the roots of his hair. His forehead now extended to the back of his head. After mulling it over several evenings, Polycarpe Poisson went to the ladies' hairdresser in the village, who would understand his problem better than the barber. Napoléon Labrosse just knew about cutting and shaving. For years, he'd been the enemy of anything that resembled a hair. Besides that he had a big mouth, bigger than the worst gossips. He'd tell everybody and his uncle that Polycarpe wanted to grow artificial hair. The village hairdresser understood. She ordered him a toupee as blond as the American movie stars who made her cry so much. The hair he still had on his head was black, but now he could think of nothing but the blond toupee that would make the young girls dream.

A few weeks later, the toupee finally arrived. He arranged it on his head like a beret, combed it and combed the hair around it too, the black hair. He wasn't aware that the toupee looked like a floppy pancake on top of his black skull. He gazed at length in the mirror, for he didn't recognize himself; he had become another man. Perched on his miraculous soles, with the blond wig on his head, Polycarpe Poisson was taller and handsomer than all the men who had found a wife or strolled arm-in-arm with their fiancées on Sunday. He had a foreboding that on this day he would meet the woman the good Lord was reserving for him.

With that idea in mind, as sweet as a dream, and with his heart in his chest like a bird who shudders as he sees his cage door open, Polycarpe Poisson descended the stairs from the balcony. His black Ford, which he had waxed and polished, was gleaming in the sun. For the fiancée he would have at last, his car must shine like a royal carriage. At the foot of the stairs his dog barked, angry and threatening. He didn't recognize his master dolled up like an American movie star. Not yet accustomed to his elevated shoes, his head giddy with joyful thoughts, Polycarpe Poisson lost his footing and tumbled down the stairs. His wig fell off and the dog, who had kept up his vicious barking, snatched the blond object and ran away with it, growling. Polycarpe couldn't get to his feet unassisted: he had broken his ankle. That was why he limped. Barring a miracle, he would always limp. He asked God to find him a wife. With her, in his Ford that would be repainted white, he would go away, his heart so swollen with happiness that the Ford would be too small to contain it. He would raise a cloud of dust on the new road!

Newborns drowning in the lacy folds of blue or pink gowns squalled because they didn't know where they were. Where were their parents taking them, in baby-carriages that dripped with ribbons and wildflowers, strutting as stiffly as if the procession was in their honor?

Some months earlier, Curé Fourré had received a commandment from God to communicate the message that He, in His infinite wisdom, wanted married men and women to have more children.

"A village that doesn't produce more children is a village doomed to death," the Curé had said. "A village whose inhabitants don't produce children is like an apple orchard filled with barren trees. If men and women don't produce children it means they've chosen death, that they no longer want to live. O men, the Almighty has asked me to tell you: see to your women, as your ancestors in days gone by devoted themselves to ploughing the fields. That's what makes fine harvests. Woe unto barren fields! said the Almighty in the Holy Bible. O French-blooded men, are you less potent than *les Anglais*? O women of the holy Catholic faith, are your bellies less fertile than the Protestants? O men, O women of French and Catholic stock, the Protes-

159

tants are spreading all around you like an ever-rising tide; are you prepared to stem that tide with a dike of children to protect your language and your faith? My dear, my very, my most very dear brethren, if I look in my register, I note that the population of our village is precisely 1,987 souls (including old Fatima Labbé who is dying of old age even as I speak to you: she won't last the night)."

There was an insistent squeak, like a mouse trying to make itself heard. "I may be dying, Monsieur le Curé, but I ain't dead yet!"

The dying woman to whom he had administered the last rites just that morning was here in the church! He had seen her languid with death only a few hours before.

"Dead or not, Fatima Labbé, you aren't eternal. We have to think about young people to replace you. Doesn't the future mean replacing old age with childhood?" The priest was getting fired up. "One thousand, nine hundred and eighty-seven Catholic souls, one thousand nine hundred and eighty-seven Catholic mouths: that's not enough to keep this continent from becoming English and Protestant, my most very dear brethren. The Almighty doesn't like to see just 1,987 Catholics that speak French in our village. Did you know that in the next parish Curé Bouché can count 1,976 souls in his parish register? If he adds all his pregnant women, he predicts that the population of his village will outstrip Saint-Toussaint-des-Saints. The Almighty, who allowed our village to be founded before Curé Bouché's, would never forgive me for a poor harvest of children. Do you want to give the Almighty a smaller tithe than Curé Bouché's?"

After Curé Fourré's urgent appeal, the children were put to bed early that night. Those who put up a fuss got a slap. Soon they were all fast asleep, huddled under the blankets. The tears had dried on their cheeks. When the houses were silent, the parents made their way to the conjugal bed-chamber. The women called on the Almighty to make them fertile to the seed of their husbands, who flung themselves upon them like bulls set loose on the vast plains.

Later, as Curé Fourré watched his female parishioners enter the church, he began to smile. When he saw the swollen bellies under flowered dresses, he knew that his message had been heard. Soon the two thousandth inhabitant would be inscribed in his register. His tithe would be higher than that of Bouché, a fellow seminarian who always stood far behind him not only in Latin, but in Mathematics, Sacred History and Comprehension of the Breviary. Curé Fourré gazed at the young women pregnant with the children he would have the privilege of presenting to the Almighty during the baptismal ceremony. ("Our young mothers as dazzling as the monstrances that bear the body of Christ.") The males of Saint-Toussaint-des-Saints had taken better care of their women than those in Curé Bouché's parish next door.

Because of their hard labors in the fields, or because of some physical weakness, some mothers lost their babies before term. Curé Fourré sprinkled holy water over these little objects that hadn't had time to be born (just in case they possessed a living soul) and they were buried. To console the mothers, Curé Fourré said:

"That's one more little angel to fly over our village among the birds and butterflies and grasshoppers."

Charlemagne Papillon had retorted,

"Now I'll be scared to slap mosquitoes on my face, for fear I'd do in one of our baby saints."

Since that quip, Curé Fourré had stopped talking about angels when a child was buried; philosophically he would say:

"The road of life passes by way of death and the road of death passes by way of the road of life. Where there is death, the good Catholic introduces life."

Grieving parents took consolation from the thought that not all seeds produce vegetables and that, in life, as long as a job isn't finished, you can only start it over again.

Proud mothers pushed their newborns, heads high, breasts swollen by milk. They wouldn't allow the coarse hands of the men at their sides, with the foolish look of useless husbands, to touch the handle of the baby-carriage. The children didn't know that the Right Party was going to build a new road, but they would set out along that road for cities where their parents had never dreamed of going. Or maybe they wouldn't go. Life was changing. What would happen? The Local Riding Minister had compared roads with the arteries in the human body along which life itself flows. Timoléon Tassé, who never uttered a word except after long reflection, had said:

"You take arteries: you know what they got in them's blood. But on a road you never know what's coming."

"The future!" declared the Local Riding Minister.

Worry about the future? These young fathers and mothers would leave that concern to a few old fretters and fumers. Wondering about the future seemed as futile to them as stirring up the ashes of the past. Only the present seemed real to them: taking care of their children until they could stand on the new road by themselves.

What would become of these children? What would become of their fathers and mothers when the children themselves were men and women? They would be shrunken old men and shrivelled women who would hop as they walked, like birds, bent over, trembling, subject to chills, distraught, troubled, lost, seemingly looking for another road, huddled somewhere between heaven and earth, already without a place on earth but not yet sure of having one in heaven. The young women in their enticing dresses and the young men with their heads filled with desires knew that one day they too would be in the way, and they would be silent as they watched the passage of these still untroubled innocent children.

Enthusiastic applause greeted the arrival of the national and international pickled egg champion. No one knew anyone who had even heard of such a bottomless stomach. They had awakened the champion after a few moment's sleep and hoisted him onto the back of a flatbed truck. The champion grimaced in the cool night air. Clutching the skin of his chest, he heaved a sigh that was more like a moan. They thought he was suffering from some painful ulcer, but he announced:

"I'm hungry!"

"What does the national and international champion want to eat?"

"Eggs!" the great man demanded. "I want to be the absolute egg-eater! The one and only champion! The only one in the world! The greatest of all time, before Jesus Christ and after! I want to prove to the whole entire world that a Right Party champion's a greater champion than anybody from the Opposition!"

More pickled eggs were brought. You'd have sworn the champion hadn't eaten for ages. Then one of those men who always find what they're looking for came up with a blackboard and several sticks of chalk. He attached the blackboard to the slatted side of the truck. When an egg disappeared into the champion's mouth and they were sure it had gone down never to rise again, when they had watched the lump formed by the egg slide behind the fat of the champion's neck, only then did they erase the score on the board and add the latest egg to the tally. Each time, the operation was greeted by a volley of applause. Each time the champion surpassed himself, the people grew along with him. The people of the Appalachians were no longer pitiful, for they had given birth to a national and international champion. The Right Party, guided by its Chef, had restored the national honor: it was capable of building the finest roads in the world, but it could also produce a national and international champion. Now that the people had hatched a champion pickled egg eater, was there any limit to the champions they could produce? The people applauding the egg-eating champion's fantastic feat were also celebrating champions yet to come.

"Two hundred and ninety-two pickled eggs!"

Inspired applause. Joyous dances.

"Bravo! Bravo! Let's hear it for the champ!"

"Two hundred and ninety-three pickled eggs!"

Applause. How far would the reckless champion go? How far would the people go in history? A people that produces such great champions cannot disappear. Le Chef was the champion politician, just as the pickled egg eater was the champion egg-swallower. They had children, they had a church, a school, they had the Right Party, they had Le Chef, they would have a new road, and they had a champion: life was opening up before the people who would set out along it in a fine procession.

Along came a truck towing a shed painted the Right Party's blue. On the walls big white letters proclaimed: THE RIGHT PARTY CREATES JOBS FOR THE PEOPLE. Above the door, more discreet letters read: *Verrochio*

163

Construction International. This shed would be the great builder's branch office. Murmurs ran from group to group. Verrochio: that was a big company. King of the road-builders. Some people had seen his trucks far, very far from here, at other worksites. Some had even seen his name on machines building streets in the Capital. They watched respectfully as the blue shed was towed past. In it, decisions would be made. From that blue shed, orders would go out to the workers. In that shed, the pay-cheques would be handed out. To that shed, people would go to have the unemployment stamps they'd need when the road was finished stuck in their books. From that shed, the order would come to go home if a worker criticized Le Chef or the Right Party unjustly. The new road would arise from that blue shed. People watched it as if they were looking at a box from which a serpent might pop up.

After the blue shed came strangers carrying strange tools. First, in a white shirt and work boots, came the surveyor with the theodolite that would lay out the new road. He carried it over his shoulder, with its shiny varnished tripod. To his belt was attached the long metal tape that would measure the new road. On his left, a man had slung over his shoulder a red-and-white surveyor's staff. On the surveyor's right was a man with an armful of pointed stakes to mark the line of the road. Next, at a respectful distance, came some of the village men: they bore axes, picks, shovels. They too carried their tools on their shoulders, as a soldier on parade carries his rifle. They weren't wearing white shirts like the surveyor, but red-checked shirts like the men who work in the fields and forest. Their heavy leather boots scraped the pavement, even though they were struggling to walk as unctuously as altar boys.

Hard on their heels, slowly, fighting off sleep, came a little man, a stranger no one in the region had ever seen, wearing blue overalls and carrying a wooden box attached to a leather strap on his back. Some onlookers stepped up to have a look, then immediately shrank back. They had read the word Dynamite.

The hymns were buried by the rumbling of trucks. You could sense the savage force in their steel. These trucks, whose dump bodies were transporting the earth, stones and gravel for the new road, all bore the name Verrochio.

Then came a huge bulldozer. Next, a number of iron beasts that roared so loud the singing stopped. Now only the blare of motors rose into the sky. There was a grader that stood high on giant wheels, its sharpened blade skimming the ground. There was a huge, fierce-beaked iron bird, a steam shovel followed by the strange animal that was the asphalt spreader. Never had they seen so many machines. Never in all the history of the country had a Party brought in so many machines. The days of the ancestors were over, this was the modern era of iron beasts stronger than the oxen and horses that had been relegated to the pasture. The time of the pioneers was past. They were living now in a new age. If it had been possible to create iron beasts, wouldn't the next thing be iron men and women put together with bolts and smelling of gasoline? Ah! the things they wouldn't live to see! These strange machines had taken the old road to the village. Who could imagine what would come along the new road? The crowd was no longer singing, no longer praying. It was applauding these fine machines that would build the road to the future. The powerful iron beasts growled with pleasure.

WOMAN AT WORK one sign proclaimed. A woman was holding one of those signs that indicate where road-work is being done. With blue paint, she had changed the word MAN to WOMAN. She carried her sign more proudly than if the Pope in Rome had given her special authorization (which he had never given a woman) to carry the body of Christ in the monstrance. Slowly the crowd tore their eyes away from the white-robed angels standing on running-boards, perched on truck fenders, clustered around the bulldozer, clinging to the neck of the power shovel, who were waving their hands and seemed to be singing, for you could see their mouths move.

The WOMAN AT WORK looked like a man in every respect. That was what the spectators murmured. In her sleeves, the woman's arms were as big as a man's. Her shoulders were as broad as those of a man who has spent his life grappling with something that is more powerful than a man. Pommette Rossignol, like the men, knew how to rage at the weather, she could drink beer without choking, she could tell dirty jokes; she could drive beasts and tractors, she could dig up stones and fell trees while cursing as hard as any man. Her hips, though, weren't those of a man. She had given birth to a number of children. Once, when a disrespectful individual had patted her backside, she stood up smartly and reproached him:

"I know my butt's as wide as a prairie. I haven't got a little chicken's ass like a schoolteacher. I've done my patriotic duty: I've hatched as many kids as the good God asked me to make for our country. It may spread the butt, but it's good for a woman. But you, you're a man so you can't understand. So keep your hands off what you don't understand. If you start again I'll give you a face full of fist. That face of yours looks like a hind end that's never hatched nothing but garbage."

After such ripostes, few men dared to lay a hand on Pommette Rossignol. Watching her go by, the men smiled. The women were somewhat scandalized to see this man who wasn't one, this woman who wasn't one, dragging her heavy dirt-encrusted boots. Pommette Rossignol had wormed out of the Local Riding Minister not a woman's job (writing things on white paper and making tea to serve to men with little cookies), but a real job, the kind a man does. Word had spread from house to house, from parish to parish, all through the Appalachians that the Minister had given Pommette Rossignol the privilege of working on the new road. She was famous. People who saw her in the procession recognized her without ever having seen her. There were exclamations of: "There she is!" Of: "She looks just like a man!" Or an admiring: "She looks stronger than a man!" One of the most profound remarks was made by a man; it had the level-headedness that lengthy analysis always bestows on a judgment.

"That there woman, I wouldn't be surprised if she stands up to piss!"

Amid the piety that emanated from the procession as fumes rise from an incense burner, this remark stood out like blasphemy. Giggles erupted, then laughter that echoed from group to group all down the length of the procession as Pommette Rossignol moved along. Mothers opined that the good Lord had created men and women, and that men should look like men and women like women. They realized the world was changing: the new road would lead to so many things they didn't recognize, so many things that didn't yet exist . . . Without thinking, quite unintentionally, the young women huddled against the strong shoulders of their men who, gazing into the eyes of the women huddled against them, began to think that the procession had been going on quite long enough. They were anxious to go home, with their wives.

At times, the contractor Verrochio's long Cadillac came so close to the WOMAN AT WORK that the prominent nickel-plated bumpers brushed the fabric of her trousers. Verrochio realized it and, panic-stricken, slammed on the brakes; the tires squealed, the car swerved, Verrochio's head was thrown against the windshield, then back against the seat. The same thing had happened several times in the course of the procession. He saw all the inhabitants of the Appalachians in a crush along the main street of this village, as if Christ were stopping there on the way to the wedding at Cana. For Verrochio, this road was no more important than a cow path. He, who had build sections of the national highway and streets in the Capital itself, had been condemned to act as contractor through these remote Appalachian hills. His only project was to build this road, which started at a cow-plop and ended at a horse-bun. Nino Verrochio should have accepted failure. That would have been more honorable than the humiliation of building this strip of road. Nino Verrochio wasn't very impressed with himself. In Sardinia, people killed for a lesser dishonor. Here in America, there was no such thing as honor. It wasn't part of the language. Nino Verrochio was a man from Sardinia. He was ashamed of his fall from grace. He dared not look in his rear-view mirror, for he couldn't bear to see his own eyes and think: "It's me, I'm here, and I should be somewhere else." Instead, he was part of this idiotic parade, struggling to look like a king. Maybe the procession was honoring a little saint, who hadn't even been blessed by the Pope in Italy, but its main purpose was to celebrate the inauguration of work on the new road. *He* was the one being fêted: he was the contractor, the boss, the man who would control the whole village. A henhouse. It was for him that they were praying, singing psalms. Hundreds and hundreds of villagers had come just to see him. Nino Verrochio greeted them with a discreet, reserved nod. What he wanted to do was weep. If there had been a cliff at the side of the main street instead of these devout peasants, he would turn his wheels and throw himself over the edge. Why stay alive on this earth? He had lost everything. He had no honor, because the Right Party had humiliated him. Even the Opposition had humiliated him. When the Opposition learned that Verrochio had also made a contribution to the Right Party, they accused him of being a double dealer, a bandit, a liar, a hypocrite, a spy. Verrochio shouldn't expect any building contracts when the Opposition came to power.

"If your roads and bridges are as reliable as your word, we're better off building with shit."

The Right Party had driven him to failure; the Opposition promised him failure if it replaced the Right Party. Nino Verrochio had fought the way a man must fight. He couldn't win, but he'd fought the way a proud man fights in Sardinia when he has nothing to gain. He had fought for his *onore*. That was how he had learned to live in Sardinia. Black-listed by both the Right Party and the Opposition, he would be ruined like Job, he'd have to work as a gardener again, go back to the gardens of the rich, get down on his knees and tend flowers their spoiled brats would trample. He had fought. He still had his honor.

He had fought to escape from the gardens of the rich and live on his feet, like a man. After having built a section of the national road, entire streets in the Capital, the Parliamentary parking lot where, every day, the men who wielded power parked their cars, he had been sent into exile, far from the Capital, into the forest, to this region not all that far from the asshole of the earth, to lay out a rabbit path. The local air had an acrid smell of children's piss and animal manure. He rolled up his window. Wasn't ending up here, condemned to this humiliating construction job, a greater failure than if he'd ended up with no machines, no warehouse, no buildings, ruined, stripped bare, as poor as when he arrived from Sardinia? Without this contract, the banks would have taken everything he owned. He would have kept only his shirt and his honor but he would have been able to look himself in the mirror without shame. If his *onore* was lost, why go on living? Any smile he offered in this procession was a painful grimace.

Being the contractor for this new road would mean rolling in dishonor and humiliation, like a pig in mud.

Lucia, his wife, had extorted this contract from the Minister of Roads and Bridges. The transaction had lost Lucia her *onore*. His wife, whom he loved more than his *mamma*, had sacrificed her honor to save her husband. She had come home late one night with the smell of cigars in her hair. The Minister of Roads and Bridges always had a cigar in his mouth; he lived in a cloud of smoke. Lucia had never smelled of anything but the perfumes her husband so enjoyed choosing for her, running his hands over the finely chased flasks, entranced by their poetic names, stroking the intricate stoppers, comparing samples, holding them under his nose, transported. How delightful it was then to gently kiss his Lucia's neck! Now it wasn't the perfume of rich people's flowers that dazed him. He wasn't kneeling on their lawns to tend their flowers now. Now it was he, a powerful man, master of a flock of machines and a troop of faithful employees, who bought costly perfumes for sums that could support an employee's family for a month. Her neck was softer than all his dreams.

For some days, Nino Verrochio couldn't look at Lucia. Few words were possible now. Only those everyday remarks that are exchanged even though you are silent. Lucia had come home late. She reeked of cigars. The Minister of Roads and Bridges smoked cigars. She had gone into her room. The Minister who held Verrochio under his foot like an insect, to crush him, had suddenly changed his mind. He had decreed that failure would descend on Nino Verrochio like the guillotine. He had no logical reason to abandon his threat. He had no reason to stop thinking that Nino Verrochio had betrayed the Right Party. The Minister of Roads and Bridges had threatened to throw Verrochio into the river with a rock around his neck. Why had he now, miraculously, held out a life-buoy? Why had he proposed that he build a new road in the Appalachians? It was far from the Capital. The Minister of Roads and Bridges wanted Verrochio far from the city, far from him and from Lucia. She had extorted the contract from the Minister. She had found a way to move that vindictive man: by giving herself, her body. If the Minister had agreed to save Nino Verrochio, it was because taking Lucia meant punishing Nino Verrochio even more, ruining him more profoundly. In this way, the Minister's foot ground the insect even harder. Lucia couldn't know that. She was only a woman. She didn't understand the somber games of men. She only wanted to save from ruin the man she loved. Lucia, so beautiful, Lucia, whose body felt so good when he caressed her, Lucia, his light, as splendid as the sun's rays glancing off a flower, Lucia, so much a woman that a man would die for her. It was Nino Verrochio she had chosen to love. He was certain she still loved only him, but she had flung herself into dishonor, as into the sea, to prevent him from foundering. Lucia had accepted the worst humiliation: giving herself to the man who was trying to destroy her husband. Nino Verrochio had escaped, but the light no longer shone brightly on his life.

When Lucia told him he'd obtained a building contract, her hair was permeated with stale cigar smoke, and the words that came from her mouth smelled of alcohol. How had Lucia, a woman, learned that a contract had been awarded to his firm? Such information does not usually reach women's ears. Lucia had drunk liquor. Her skirt was wrinkled and her silk blouse was rumpled. In the charitable groups she belonged to, even the musical and literary groups, she allowed herself no more than a glass of port. Lucia reeked of liquor. Had she drunk to deaden her suffering as she fell into dishonor with the Minister? Verrochio had tears in his eyes. It was life that had sullied his Lucia. Could he reproach her for not being as strong as life? Yet it was she who had saved him. Thanks to Lucia he wouldn't have to go back to cultivating the gardens of the rich. Were men born only to suffer poverty? Were those who avoided it destined to lose what they'd acquired? Was man born to lose, always to lose? Had Nino Verrochio left his native Sardinia a poor man, then got rich only to come to grief, poorer than he had been before, ruined, betrayed and abandoned? Could he dream now only of the past? Lucia had got him this meager contract: a construction job that a farmer with a team of oxen could have done. Verrochio had been the Caesar of highway construction. Lucia had been a bribe, paid to add a few weeks to the life of his business. Was he so sure his wife had betrayed him? Could he be really certain that Lucia had saved him by giving herself in exchange for her husband's salvation. Lucia had come home late, her clothing wrinkled. In the groups of literary, musical or charitable women she associated with, no one smoked cigars. Lucia never came home late, and her clothes weren't rumpled or musty like a smoke-house.

Nino Verrochio had invited his wife to take part in this ridiculous procession. She didn't want to come with him. She had reached the age, she said, where just a little extra fatigue carves another wrinkle around the eyes. Nino Verrochio had promised her that they wouldn't go back to the Capital after the procession, along the dangerous, winding mountain road; he had suggested they spend the night in the inn that smelled of fresh-baked country bread, beside the Local Riding Minister's lake. Before they slept, he would take her out on the lake in a rowboat, like two lovers from romantic times; she would wear her lace negligée and he would bring a bottle of champagne in a bucket of ice. He described the lake, as smooth as a mirror, and the moon which would give enough light so they could see, and enough darkness so they'd have to seek one another. They would come back somewhat giddy from the champagne and from the dizziness a pitch-black night bestows on your eyes. Lucia had refused to make the journey. The Minister of Roads and Bridges, who was to have taken part in the procession, hadn't come either . . . Nino Verrochio wept at the wheel of his Cadillac. Onlookers were moved to pity at the sight of this powerful contractor weeping in the procession, because of the prayers, the vigil lights and the songs.

Whispers, like those of a distant wind stirring the leaves, rustled through the crowd and moved from one spectator to the next.

"The saint!"

"What? What'd you say?"

"Here comes the saint!"

"Who?"

"Our little saint."

It was Saint Opportun's reliquary, containing what remained of the little saint who'd been boiled alive in french-fry oil. It was the bones of the village lad saved by a miracle. It was God's favorite of all the children in the Appalachians. The Almighty had taken Opportun and seated him at His left hand, upon a fold of His starry robe. On either side of the main street, men knelt on big white handkerchiefs spread on the gravel to protect their Sunday suits; the women took out little embroidered handkerchiefs, hesitated to lay them on the ground because they'd get dirty, then finally knelt and prayed. In the silence you could hear their hearts beat.

Opportun had fallen into the boiling french-fry oil. The oil had overflowed and, when it came in contact with the fire, exploded as if hell had opened its gates. The stall on wheels had burned with the unbridled violence of the flames of hell. Those who had seen the thousand fiery jaws devour the child and the stall, then saw the jaws themselves devoured, rumbling as they swallowed one another and dying in a heap of black embers and red ashes, found it hard to believe that God had willed such an accident and that His hand had pushed Opportun into the oil like a potato . . . It was very hard to comprehend. Nothing occurred on this earth, neither season nor sun nor night nor day nor rain nor snow, that was not commanded by God Almighty. More: not a single hair could grow on the head or fall from the head of a Christian, or even from a pagan, without God's having ordered it.

"Don't argue about holy matters," a woman broke in. "Men think they're too smart: they try and understand everything."

"You men shut up. Try to love the Lord and your wives a little better."

"Arguing's easier than loving."

At first the fire in the King of the French Fries stall resembled an erupting volcano, spitting fireballs on the village. Then the flames began to look like a great red tree with many branches, shaken with diabolical force by a fierce wind that tore off strips of bark which rose up to the sky like fiery birds. Then, with a whistle, the tree began to shrink, becoming small, with fewer and fewer branches, scarcely larger than a sheaf of dying red flowers, then it was a single flower and it in turn died out. "It's like the creation of the world turned upside down," declared the widow of Vital Toussaint, whose skirts had been getting shorter from one Sunday to the next ever since she'd decided to replace her late husband. When nothing was left but ashes and embers, old Charles Lépine, whom they were accustomed to see pushing his wheelbarrow through the village, filled with potatoes, turnips, a can of milk, a bottle of spring water, a child or manure, arrived on the scene.

"Sainthood is richer than gold; don't waste a drop of it; we lost the smoke so let's not lose the ashes."

He took his shovel and piously started piling the still sputtering holy ashes into his wheelbarrow. If a bone appeared, he buried it respectfully under the ashes. When everything was scooped up, Nino Verrochio's Cadillac drove past. Old Charles Lépine wedged himself and the precious relics into the procession. He gripped the shafts firmly and piously pushed. He lowered his head to avoid appearing too proud. He'd been humiliated often, had Charles Lépine. His wife barked at him like a poorly-trained dog when it thinks it sees a stranger. Never had a kind word emerged from the woman's lips. She could utter only reproaches, insults, threats; she could only keep saying how much she regretted having married that good-for-nothing, feeble-minded, clumsy, awkward, simple, impotent Charles Lépine. If any one could hear her, the shrew shrieked even louder: she was proud she could show that a woman didn't have to let herself be led around by a man, like a filly. To escape his wife's fury, Charles Lépine would rush off to his vegetable garden and pull weeds. In the winter, never answering her insults or reproaches, he would rush out and shovel snow. In the fall, he raked dead leaves. In the spring, while he waited for the storm to abate, he would walk around the trees, his eye on the gradually opening buds. Little by little, he got used to not hearing her sobs, her insults, her sorrow. Accustomed not to hear, he grew deaf. His wife had died reproaching him for still being alive. With her last sigh she cursed the woman who would surely rush to take her place in his bed. Now he was alone. Even if the Blessed Virgin herself came and asked him to marry her, he wouldn't resume life with a woman. He had forgiven his wife for the suffering she made him endure. He had not forgiven himself for once, so long ago, having married a young girl whom he loved as fire loves wood. Now old Charles Lépine was waiting to die. He feared death because he was in no hurry to continue his life in

Heaven with the angels, in the company of his wife who would start again to nag and abuse and insult and humiliate him.

Charles Lépine was carrying the ashes and bones of Saint Opportun. With eyes almost shut in prayer, he thanked God for according him the grace of carrying a saint's remains: it was the first happiness the old man had known since his youth. When the procession had stopped, he would kneel before Curé Fourré and give him the bones of the holy skeleton so they could be put on display in the church. As for the ashes, he would ask permission to put a pinch in his tobacco pouch to sanctify him from within whenever he smoked his pipe. The rest of the ashes he would suggest be preserved in the safe at the *Caisse Populaire* until the gravel was spread on the new road; at that time young Opportun's ashes could be mixed with the gravel so the road would be blessed and those who travelled on it would be protected from disaster. When cars whizzed by at those speeds young people enjoy so much, they would stir up dust from the gravel and Opportun's ashes would travel on the wind with it to fertilize and bless the forest and fields. Tears stood out on Charles Lépine's white eyelashes. At last he understood why God had made him suffer all his life: He had given him an unloving wife to purify him so he'd be prepared to receive the ashes and bones of a saint in his wheelbarrow. From the bottom of his old heart he thanked his defunct wife for making him so unhappy and giving him a sorrowful soul. She had prepared him to be worthy of receiving, as a sacred trust, Saint Opportun's ashes.

Beneath the canopy trimmed with gold fringe and braid, with Greek letters, crosses and lambs embroidered in silver thread, beneath the canopy carried by four altar boys marching as solemnly as if they were holding up the sky, Curé Fourré displayed the monstrance. At his side, the Local Riding Minister didn't know what to do with his hands. Though he had nothing to carry, he couldn't fold his hands like an altar boy or the Opposition would call him a hypocrite. He wished he were carrying some prestigious object, like the monstrance, but the disease of democracy, which had killed off the kings, had abolished all signs of power. That day, in a procession honoring works

174

being undertaken in the service of the people, the Minister was condemned by the gangrene of democracy to walk empty-handed, dressed like an undertaker, at the side of a Curé swathed in lace, an embroidered cope and a golden chasuble as if he were the Almighty in person. Yet the Local Riding Minister had the power to make the Curé obey him; he had the power to build his new road so far from the church that no one would come to Mass on Sunday. With no ornaments, with no gold or lace or monstrance, the Minister looked like a man who had lost everything. The Curé exercised power only over invisible things. Why then was he decorated so that people noticed no one else? Shouldn't the man who exercised power over visible things be visible as well? The Local Riding Minister wished he'd been alive in the days when powerful men wore golden crowns, impressive swords, bright tunics and elaborate capes, and were carried around by servants surrounded by musicians . . . That was a dream. Those times had passed. One must not regret the past, which no longer exists. Le Chef had been right on that score when he announced the opening of the election campaign.

"Remember, I'm not sending you into this election to lose. Elections exist to be won. If any of you buggers' got an urge to lose, you can resign! But here's some advice for the men that want to win. Think of the One that's never lost an election, the One that's always been in power despite the Opposition's gerrymandering. That One I'm talking about is God Almighty, the undisputed, all-time champion of power. His political strategy's easy to grasp; you can at least try and copy it. Copy the Almighty: He's everywhere and nobody sees Him. He's invisible. Do like Him and we'll hold on to power for eternity."

Thinking back on this advice, the Minister bowed his head, as if he were lost in prayer, and stepped back three paces so Curé Fourré could precede him. The monstrance gleamed with the reflections of torches. His gold-and-silver embroidered cope, strewn with spangles and precious stones, dazzled the main street like a tardy sun.

That monstrance was heavy. A wooden monstrance would be lighter, but unworthy. For the body of Christ only gold, heavy gold, was appropriate. The carved base of the monstrance was massive. The rays that surrounded the

175

lunula were numerous and long, worthy of the radiance that is proper to the flesh of Christ. Curé Fourré was out of breath. It was hard to walk and hold the monstrance in front of you at arms' length. His arms numbed by the effort, shoulders burning from the tension in his muscles, Curé Fourré thanked one of his teachers at the Grand Seminary who had given him some good advice.

"A Curé," said the old Abbé whose body was eaten away by the religion that was devouring it, "is an athlete of the Lord; he must train himself to bear witness to his faith as a world champion trains to outstrip his mark."

Curé Fourré had never forgotten these profound observations; he remembered them reverently. Before carrying the body of Christ in the heavy monstrance, he would engage in physical exercise to strengthen the muscles in his arms. For months before a procession he pumped iron. This time, he'd had to organize the procession in a hurry because the Almighty, in the great wisdom of His universal plan for the world, had caused young Opportun's miracle to coincide with the new election campaign and the announcement of the new road. Curé Fourré reacted smartly, like a good soldier. There was no question of postponing the procession on the totally legitimate grounds that his arms weren't in shape for carrying the monstrance. Curé Fourré had meditated for a moment, beseeching God to inspire his arms with the necessary strength for affirming his Christian faith.

After his prayer, he had picked up his steel weights and begun certain complicated movements to strengthen his muscles and toughen up his biceps. He whirled his arms, raised them and lowered them, then performed a number of circumductions, until he was out of breath. All this he did for the triumph of a just cause. He held out his arms like Christ on the cross, but instead of nails in his hands, he had dumbbells. Christ had endured suffering more acute than the Curé's aching muscles. He started his repetitions again: open, close, ten times, twenty, fifty. At times his chest was rent with pain, as if it had been riven by a sabre thrust, but the Curé persisted. He spread his arms wide, holding at arms' length two dumbbells that were attracted to the ground by the all-powerful laws of gravity. Eighty times, a hundred. Then it was time to flap his arms, like a bird flapping its wings, still holding the weights; he waved them faster and faster, as if trying to take flight. Ten times, thirty, sixty-seven. His shoulders creaked. His arms grew heavy and seemed about to be wrenched from his body and to fall far away, eighty-one, eight-two, eighty-three times. God was asking him to suffer so he would be worthy of carrying His body in the monstrance. Then it was time for the next phase. His eyes burned from the sweat that ran down his forehead. He attached heavy lead soles to his feet and first walked, then ran in place as fast as he could until he dropped from exhaustion. Now he had earned a rest. In the mirror his face was as red as a flask of blood. The veins on his long arms stood out in bumps. His biceps looked like the breasts of skinny chickens. Curé Fourré wasn't ready. He must repeat the exercises again — one hundred times, three hundred. God was commanding him and Curé Fourré obeyed. Because of his athletic preparation, which was equal to the great mystical exercises, Curé Fourré could carry the monstrance with dignity.

The Local Riding Minister was worried. The Minister of Roads and Bridges should have been here ages ago: before nightfall, because it wasn't easy to land in a field. When the faithful gathered in the church, the building had been shaken, the roof vibrating as if it had been dealt a blow. Yet the night was calm and the sky was peaceful. It couldn't be thunder. It couldn't be an angel from Heaven having trouble passing through the roof. The Local Riding Minister concluded that the only reasonable explanation for the shaking of the church was that a passing airplane had brushed against it. If the Minister of Roads and Bridges had brushed against the church, it would have been logical for him to land in a pasture near the church, then come and join the procession which, without him, was like Christmas without Jesus. Where *was* the Minister?

Before the ceremony, Nino Verrochio the contractor had told the Local Riding Minister that his wife couldn't attend the procession because she'd recently developed a keen interest in politics. He wouldn't say any more. Was she doing fund-raising work in a riding? Was she on a letter-writing committee? Was she going door-to-door across town, noting the names of those who seemed opposed to the Right Party's re-election? Nino Verrochio had replied that she had been given a special assignment by the Minister of Roads and Bridges. Nino Verrochio had tried to sound casual, but his face bore the sad, bewildered look of a widower. Verrochio, that smooth talker, that man who drowned you in words, who dazzled with his rings, his cufflinks, his tie-pin, his glasses, bracelets and his brightly-colored clothes, now suddenly seemed somber, lackluster, like a man who suspects he's being cuckolded. The Local Riding Minister knew the Minister of Roads and Bridges very well. He knew that if his fellow-Minister had won over as many voters as women, he'd have been more powerful than the entire Party. If the Minister of Roads and Bridges hadn't had Verrochio's wife, she'd be the only building contractor's wife he hadn't taken for himself, as a bonus. Having his shoes removed by a woman he was about to conquer was one of his great delights. Barefoot, he was fond of telling her she was the most beautiful woman he'd ever been with. He frequently compared women with voters: the less you lied to them, the less they believed you.

As for the Local Riding Minister, he used a tactic that was more effective than lying. He built roads. A lie would disappear like smoke in the wind, but a road would last dozens of years. People would travel it hundreds of times and recall: "The Right Party built us this fine road." He was a man who built the road he travelled. His ancestors had used an axe to carve out a passage for their carts and animals. Generations later, after he'd become a Minister, he built roads that ran through the fields they had worked, between the houses they had built, through the villages they had established. The ancestors were gone now, but their villages and fields remained. The Minister would disappear, but his roads would still be there when he was gone. They would be his signature upon the earth.

Building real roads, with bulldozers, stones and gravel, gave him the sensation that in another world he had also built roads, which he couldn't see, whose dust he couldn't wipe from his shoes. On the other side of life there is not merely death, but an entirely different life, and man advances along the earth, one foot on the road he can see, the other on the road he does not see. As he laid out these roads the Minister was also making his way in the other world. Was it because he was walking under the canopy, three respectful paces behind Curé Fourré, who glittered like a diamond, that he was having these philosophical ideas? He experienced such bursts of poetry and philosophy when he was piloting his plane as well. All at once, he realized that he'd been dreaming, like a schoolboy at his desk. Dreaming and philosophizing didn't win elections. You had to build. Build without dreaming, without philosophizing. Build in order to be elected. Build to remain a Minister. Build to become Premier, perhaps, when Le Chef fell. Le Chef wouldn't let himself be struck down. Le Chef would rot from within, like all mighty trees. Why become Premier? The Local Riding Minister never wondered Why? He did such-and-such a thing because he did it. He hated Why's. ("A bird that asks why it flies is going to fall.") Why? Why? That was a question for those who wonder, when death is approaching, why they have lived. After a lifetime spent wondering why they were alive, they died, without having lived, wondering why. The Local Riding Minister had lived his life with all the assurance of a charging moose. Had he just been touched by indecision? He was building this road because he wanted to win the election. He wanted to win this election because he wanted to go on enjoying his power. He wanted to rise even higher, to enjoy the giddiness that was as sweet as the giddiness he'd felt as a child when he climbed the steeple of the village church. He wanted to win this other election because he wanted to feel alive. Why? Why? The question nagged at him like a mosquito. Why? He would build many other roads. He would win many more elections. Along all these roads his people would pursue their dreams. Why?

The main street of Saint-Toussaint-des-Saints had existed since the first settler came to the forest; laying down his pack and his axe, he had decided to plant his tent in this spot, amid the bushes, the brushwood, the trees. His path had been inscribed deeper in the earth by the steps of those who came and joined him. They had felled trees and made room to build cabins. When the women arrived, they cleared space for a few animal pens. Then the path had been broadened to make room for horse-drawn carts. The main street was the path of the ancestors who had realized their dream of going into the unknown. Other men had set out with their packs and their axes, they had ventured into the forest, and far from their starting place, they had halted, studied the trees around them, the width of their trunks and the height of their boles, then gazed questioningly at the sky. In the silence, God had given an order to their blood, to their muscles, to their hearts, and they had raised their tents. Their footsteps had hollowed another path, and it in turn had been hollowed and widened by the footsteps of other men, of their women and their animals. Many years later, in Saint-Toussaint-des-Saints, Curé Fourré was carrying the body of Christ along this path that had been widened, straightened, levelled, the dust of it smothered by asphalt.

Like the ancestors, Curé Fourré had come from afar, drawn by the Unknown: not the unknown that was to be found in trees crammed together with their roots entwined, that had grown through centuries of wind and rain and snow, that had lived and died and been born of the deaths of other trees. He had been drawn by the Unknown in the bodies of human beings, which is called the soul and which, in Heaven, is called God. He had been drawn by the Unknown of what comes before life and the Unknown of what follows after death, the Unknown that existed before the creation of the world and the Unknown of what followed after creation. Instead of clearing the woods he had become a priest who made his way through the country from church to church, from village to village, always fascinated by the Unknown, always questioning his God for whom the Unknown was merely that which was known. And that was how he came to be on this old road, preparing for the opening of a new one. Curé Fourré had always been on his way to the Unknown. The road the Right Party was building was unquestionably the one that would lead him to a bishopric. One day, at the end of this new road, people would kneel at the sight of him; they would call him Your Eminence. This road of stones and gravel was also a road that God would trace in the Unknown with His fingertip, to lead him to his destiny. If, as he followed his road, the Curé Fourré should find himself not a bishop but a simple priest, he would bow his head in submission. If the Almighty wanted him as a priest in a black soutane with a humble soup-stain on the chest, instead of a bishop's dazzling frills and flounces, Curé Fourré would not be bitter. He had been born in the far-off countryside where the good Lord had come looking for him. He had snatched him away from the stable. God had been born in a stable and the young man respected that place. Curé Fourré frequently gave thanks to the Lord for lifting him off the three-footed stool where he used to sit, his cheek against the warm, swollen flank of the cow he was milking. The good Lord had chosen this servant of cows to turn him into His own honorable servant. Not many bishops in the province had been granted a miracle. The good Lord had come and plucked up Opportun in a ball of fire. Curé Fourré had read the Bible, he had studied the Old Testament in Latin; he knew that the fire which had taken Opportun was the same ball of fire in which God concealed Himself when He wanted to descend to earth: young Saint Opportun had not been burned, he had been taken away, a little earthly angel, taken to Heaven by the good Lord to sing His praises and to represent — an ambassador to Heaven from Earth — the parish of Saint-Toussaint-des-Saints. Few bishops had their own messenger at the right hand of our Father who art in Heaven. He, a humble Curé, his arms growing weary from carrying the monstrance, had his saint: Opportun. Instead of talking to God with prayers that would get lost among the prayers being offered up from all the countries in the world, as one voice is lost among the voices of a choir, henceforth he would talk to Saint Opportun, who would always want to hear the news from his own Curé Fourré and would hasten to tell the good Lord, when he sat on His lap with his little head in the white beard, the words of the pious population of Saint-Toussaint-des-Saints.

Some of Curé Fourré's flock were fleeing to the cities, in the hope of finding there the treasures of happiness and money. Those who stayed rooted like great maples would be rewarded by the sight of Jesus Christ himself, with his dusty face and rumpled robe. One night they would see a timid young man, his manners gentle because he had been educated by the Virgin, making his way to the village; he would stop at the first house and ask for water. In a foreign language they wouldn't understand, he would say: "Sitio." He would ask for cold water. They would hesitate because of his beard and his shoulder-length hair. It would be Jesus Christ. If he had already appeared on earth why shouldn't he return, and why shouldn't he return to Saint-Toussaint-des-Saints?

At the thought, Curé Fourré started. Had he committed the sin of sacrilege? Jesus Christ had come to the village, alive; Curé Fourré was carrying him in the monstrance. Busy with his thoughts, he had neglected his sacred duty. Under the weight of the heavy object, his arms drooped, despite the rigorous training to which he had subjected his muscles; the monstrance now rested on his hollow stomach. Determinedly, he lifted it and held aloft, before his eyes, the body of Christ who sowed blessings on the new road.

The paved road ended outside Cytriste Tanguay's house. After it came a ribbon of beaten earth. The road was narrow; a car could drive on it, but if it encountered another, the more fearful driver, the one who was not so brave, would have to turn toward the swamp and end up in the mud. Frequently, neither driver would yield. In the distance you would hear the sound of cars colliding, like the rumble of thunder. At haying time cars would often meet up with a wagon full of hay along this road. The driver was completely subject to the will of the farmer and his horse. The farmers never gave way. When a farmer on his load of hay saw a car, he would smile disdainfully, then tug on the reins to make his horse slow down. After that the farmer would start to hum. Astonished to hear a song from his master instead of oaths, insults and threats, the horse would shake his head to let some air in between his neck and the leather collar that chafed his worn skin till it bled. The anxious driver would lean on his horn with the conviction of a man who knows he's right to be riding in a motor car rather than on a pile of hay pulled by a deaf, blind nag. Heaving with impatience, the anxious traveller would shout the gravest insults he could invent, while the farmer heard nothing, only smiled like his horse.

Oh, life was good in the old days, thought Cytriste Tanguay, who didn't like these young people who seemed to still have their mother's breasts in their mouths and always wanted to undo what their ancestors had done. The young laughed at the road that ran past his door, saying it had as many twists and turns as a shoelace. Cytriste Tanguay was argumentative: if the elders had laid out the road that way, they had reasons the harebrained young couldn't understand: the elders wanted to keep too many cars from driving along the road.

"It's a farm road," he would explain, "not a boulevard." The elders didn't want their oats covered with dust from the road, they didn't want their grazing cows scared silly by noisy cars. Sour milk, skinny calves, miscarriages, troubled pregnancies: the elders had known how to avoid such misfortunes. The road is narrow, with curves and bumps to prevent cars with hotheads at the wheel from wreaking havoc.

"But Cytriste, when the elders built the road, cars hadn't been invented yet."

"The elders," Cytriste retorted, "were people that looked to the future. They always expected the worst, so they were always right."

As soon as Cytriste Tanguay learned that the Right Party was planning to enlarge, level and straighten the elders' road that ran through his land, he protested this injustice, this error in judgment, this desecration, this plundering of his land, and he raged at the threat posed to his animals by speeding cars whose squealing tires and honking horns would madden his cows, kill his calves and spray his oats with oily dust. Faced with such a violation of his property he left the Right Party, renounced his faith in Le Chef, and joined the ranks of the Opposition.

Outside his house, his land was bounded by a row of tall poplars, branchy, leafy, proud and solid. His new-found allies in the Opposition climbed the trees. Taking pains not to be seen, shadows swooped, brisk, eager, feline; they seemed bodiless, they seemed to glide rather than walk through the oats, bending them as they moved. Cytriste Tanguay's field seemed inhabited by devils that fled as the procession drew near. With pious care, the shadows carried buckets. They had been preparing this ambush for a long time. Every one of the eggs in their buckets had been gathered from under a hen's warm rear end, then stowed in a good warm spot to rot quickly, with a view to this great night. All the men who were in on the plot knew that the time had come. Some of the faithful had noticed shadows

183

hiding in shadow, behind the houses, jumping fences, merging with the grass. No one had seen that they were carrying buckets whose handles rattled in spite of all their precautions. Nor could anyone guess that these field-devils' buckets were full of rotten eggs.

Suddenly, from the tops of the poplars cries rang out, bird-songs never heard before in Saint-Toussaint-des-Saints: not exactly the cries of birds and not exactly human voices. The leaves of the whole row of poplars began to stir. A sudden, nauseating, slimy rain fell on the procession as it passed Cytriste Tanguay's house. It spattered their faces and clothes, it spewed slime, clouding their eyes with sticky tears. When their mouths opened to scream, they were filled with foul saliva that gagged them when they tried to spit it out. Slippery, foul-smelling snot dripped from the tips of their noses, stringy drool dripped onto their joined hands, serous fluid soaked the thin cloth of dresses as well as the heavy wool of men's suits. It smelled as bad as if every champion of every farting contest ever held in the Appalachians had come and formed one great orchestra to blow the overture that would immortalize them forever. The procession had landed in a trap. It was bombarded with rotten eggs. Prayers rose up to Heaven. It was obvious that the Devil was trying to interrupt the ceremony. Enemy forces wanted to scatter the procession like a jostled child's marbles. Someone couldn't bear that Saint-Toussaint-des-Saints was celebrating the miracles granted to young Opportun, the village's ambassador, who had so quickly travelled the long road between the parish and paradise. The procession was also giving thanks to the Right Party. Someone didn't want that. Someone didn't want thanks to be offered to the righteous God or the Right Party. Was it the Devil who was spraying the procession with malodorous rain? Was it the communists? Had they insinuated themselves into the landscape like snakes, sowing discontent, discord and contempt for the one true religion? The communists had blown up a bridge the Right Party had built. People had learned that the very eggs on the tables in the houses of Saint-Toussaint-des-Saints were communist eggs that communist infiltrators in the countryside had imported from communist countries to replace the Catholic eggs gathered from under good local hens by the pious hands of farmers who practised the true religion. That's how communists behaved. Le Chef had said so, it had been in all the papers and Curé Fourré had repeated it from the pulpit. "When the population gets used to communist eggs," he had predicted, "next we'll have to wring the necks of the fine traditional hens that have fed our children and workers for generations. Then the people will wring the necks of their Curés, their Ministers, their bishops." Was it the Devil? Communists? The Opposition? There was no end to it. They said prayers, sang even louder. The procession must not be interrupted. The enemy must not be allowed to break the chain of this procession. Each of the faithful felt he was a solid link in a chain that nothing could destroy. The air trembled with the echo of hymns.

"I say it's the Devil shittin' on us."

"Don't blaspheme," protested a voice polished by choral exercises.

"God's making us re-live the stations of the cross. When Jesus Christ was weighed down by his holy cross, the folks that scorned God spit in his face."

"Say what you want, Sister, you'll never convince me I'm Jesus Christ. I'm just an ordinary guy, though all this filth kinda makes me feel like a skunk that fell in a spittoon."

"I read the Testament and if you ask me, a good Christian ain't got the right to turn the other cheek if somebody wants to spit in his face."

Charlemagne Papillon's eyes were glued shut by the stringy shower that dripped down his face and smelled like decomposing demon.

"I betcha," said Charlemagne Papillon, "I betcha if a holy woman like Mary Magdalene was to come and wipe my face right now, there'd be a picture of it on her holy hanky. They could take it and show it in the church: the shroud of Charlemagne!"

Many people guffawed, slapping their bellies and thighs. Charlemagne Papillon's excellent joke was repeated and spread amid laughter. The hymns were gradually silenced, as a fire is extinguished when there's no more wood.

A voice protested. "In the midst of adversity, never blaspheme! We should be united in prayer."

"Miracle! Miracle! Miracle!" exclaimed Ligouri Lafleur, who was also famous for his jokes. "Miracle! I pulled up

Violette Papillon's skirt and guess what I saw on the seat of her knickers? Her old man's face!"

Not one prayer rose from the procession now, not a single song. No hands were joined. Spurts of laughter sounded like a thousand cackling hens. Now there wasn't a single Christian whose bearing was worthy of a person giving thanks to God, only bodies bent double as if suffering from colic, bodies writhing with laughter, hawking phlegm, jostling, laughing so hard they couldn't stand. No prayers, no hymns. All that was still alive in the night, in the very great procession, the greatest ever organized in the Appalachians, was Ligouri Lafleur's joke, which was repeated, heard, laughed at, repeated and laughed at again and again, because it was inexhaustibly comical.

Under his canopy, Curé Fourré stamped his feet impatiently; things weren't going according to his wishes. It wasn't yet time to send the blasphemers away. Three paces behind him, the Local Riding Minister was making a tremendous effort to maintain his dignity, for Curé Fourré had told him Ligouri Lafleur's joke, which he'd heard from an altar boy. It was obvious to Curé Fourré that he had to get through this stinking trial to which the good Lord was subjecting him, along with his flock, the better to be purified. If Jesus Christ, at one of the Stations of the Cross, had refused to carry on his procession just because people were spitting in his face, he'd never have died on the cross or been resurrected. In this respect, Curé Fourré was copying the founder of the Right Religion. He studied his flock and felt an unfailing conviction that the procession would safely reach its destination after traversing this pestilential rain, this foul cholera sent by the Devil. This trial could only be compared with one of the ten plagues of Egypt, mused Curé Fourré.

"It's rotten eggs! It's rotten eggs! It's rotten eggs!" perceived the international pickled egg champion, who had roused himself slightly.

It was a bombardment, a deluge of rotten eggs. The international pickled egg champion, almost fully awakened from his pachydermic digestion, groaned. "Them eggs are rotten." Subjected once more to his will to beat all the records, the international champion caught the eggs that were raining down around him and raced to stuff them in his mouth.

"One thousand one hundred and ninety-eight . . . (Another egg.) One thousand one hundred and ninety-nine . . . (Another egg.) Two thousand!" counted Timoléon Tassé, the referee.

What a champ! The helter-skelter procession applauded as they would have applauded the inventor of the automobile or the atomic bomb. He caught the eggs on the fly, before their shells shattered in a brownish mud, but he protested:

"They're rotten! They're rotten!"

He must not interrupt the rugged contest for the absolute record number of eggs swallowed by all the egg swallowers of all time. He was of the stuff of champions who scale the earth's highest mountains. He must go on with all the dignity of a great international champion.

Suddenly the international pickled egg champion was worried. The rotten eggs he'd downed weren't pickled in vinegar. He shuddered at the thought that his championship might not be ratified or noted in the official records. Would the rotten eggs piling up in his stomach, mixed with the official eggs cooked according to the rules and soaked in vinegar, interfere with the recognition of his championship? Only official eggs were counted. He mustn't fall victim to contrary ideas: a genuine champion must persevere. Even if his championship was no longer recognized, he must, though humiliated, behave like a genuine champion. He went on:

"Two thousand and twelve . . . two thousand and thirteen . . . "

The hail of rotten eggs could only be some perverse Opposition conspiracy. He was a great international champion; upon him rested the Right Party's honor. He would not give up, he would fight to the end, until the Opposition had run out of rotten eggs.

"Two thousand and thirty-two . . . two thousand and thirty-three . . . "

The procession was slowly advancing. As fishermen in a frail skiff upon a raging sea might probe the night, anxious to know if they will reach shore, so the faithful walking past Cytriste Tanguay's poplar trees would open an eye to see if the distant night was bright and peaceful, but they couldn't keep it open long because at once a rotten egg would shatter in their faces, and dripping albumin would form a clinging veil. Shattered shells and contaminated foam spattered clothing, seeped in everywhere and ran down the body's natural furrows. The ladies and young girls shuddered as they felt the vile fluid creep inside their clothes, muddy and cold like earthworms. Feet slithered in the disgusting drool. The faithful were skating in the stinking dew that covered the pavement; men skidded into women, married men into marriageable young girls, altar boys into nuns, and the eggs fell and fell in an endless rain. The air was unbreathable. The future brides' white gowns smelled like rotten fish. People squelched through yellowish mud that smelt worse than all the manure in the world. The faithful clung together and fell together, on their bellies, their backs, like children on the ice in winter. Their shoes slid off their feet and were planted all along their route.

Under the canopy, Curé Fourré was protected from the putrid onslaught, but at every corner the altar boys holding the posts that supported the roof had to struggle to stay on their feet. Yet they were good skaters. Walking respectfully behind Curé Fourré, the Local Riding Minister was musing. From far away, a memory came back to him, like a bad smell perceived from afar. He was a mere child at the time, still too young to go to work with his father. It was the time of year when they killed a pig. The men would help each other out. When the work was done at one farm, all the men would go to help the next one kill his pig and bleed it and eviscerate it. The child studied the pig laid out on its back. The rough table was painted with the dried blood of other animals that had died there before. With one stroke of his big knife, a man slashed the skin of the animal's swollen belly. The child had seen this several times that day, but he couldn't tear his eyes from the sight. The skin opened like curtains and heaps of red and purple intestines, braided, entangled and spotted with blood appeared like a tangle of snakes. The child was hypnotized by the sight of the animal, which was truly dead because the knife had cut the jugular and blood had spurted out. The animal was motionless, its belly cut open, but to the child it seemed that what was inside the animal's belly had not been killed. It seemed to him that all these intestines, these guts, were breathing, were moving, were going to come crawling out. He was fascinated by the life he thought he could see in the dead pig's belly. He was dazzled to see such life in the midst of death. All at once he was lifted up, snatched away and put down, like a child in a cradle, inside the still-warm carcass of the pig. As a brave little man, he couldn't cry. He couldn't scream. His heart was pounding like the heart of a cat about to pounce. He heard the men's coarse laughter. Because he must show that he was also a man, the stupefied child burst out laughing. The men found this even funnier. The Local Riding Minister had often remembered this tender scene from his childhood. He had thought he would die, so young, though he didn't know what it was to die, didn't even know what it was to live. He had seen animals die when a knife was plunged into their bodies, or a sledgehammer pounded their heads. He had not yet seen a woman or a man die. In the pig's stomach from which life had barely departed, which had not yet lost the warmth of life, he had thought he would die. He remembered it very clearly. Was death inscribed in the body and the soul in such a way that you don't have to learn it? The Minister was sure it was. The most innocent child, he thought, knows he will die, as if he has known from the outset that along the road of life, he is seeking death. In the face of it, the child is utterly powerless. All the Minister had done was run from the dead pig so he wouldn't be thrown into its open belly again. He had often told himself that his desire to leave his parents' farm was just an effort to get as far away as possible from that pig. The open belly had smelled something like the downpour of rotten eggs. Now the Minister, covered with shame, must show himself to be worthy and strong, like the Right Party. At three respectful paces from Curé Fourré, he seemed to be muttering a prayer, but he was preparing his riposte. It would contain three points. As soon as he had a chance to address the crowd, he would say: "Smell, my friends, smell: that stink in your nostrils is the smell of the Opposition!" He'd wait for the laughter to die down, then go on: "Until today they've been able to hide their shameful smell, but now as we head into an election campaign, the Opposition and their friends can't hold in the farts they have instead of ideas." That would provoke more laughter, but only from the Opposition's enemies; he must also plant some doubt in the ranks of the Opposition. He would add: "Politics is a fine thing. If the Opposition goes after the Right Party it's healthy for democracy. The Right Party wants a strong Opposition! Tonight, my friends, the Opposition didn't attack the Right Party, it attacked a procession, a religious ceremony, it attacked a little angel chosen by the Almighty from this village, it attacked good Curé Fourré who is a saint on earth; the Opposition blasphemed and profaned the body of Christ that Curé Fourré is carrying in the monstrance; that blasphemy, that unforgivable, that mortal sin will disgust all Christians who respect the true religion." No one would want to be on the Opposition side now. To bring all the voters around to the Right Party, he would conclude with: "The Opposition wasn't afraid of bringing down the wrath of God on the new road the Right Party's going to build with the good people of the Appalachian Region. Now then, let us pray. Right now! The good Lord has been provoked by the Opposition, He must be angry. Let us pray to appease Him. Let us pray for Him to tone down His punishment!" After such a speech, who could even think of voting for the Opposition? The Local Riding Minister kept turning over each of his words in his mouth.

The rotten eggs rained down, loathsome, fouling everyone regardless of status. The altar boys, angels with delicate little wings, were overcome by the gooey slime. The pioneers who had felled the forest were drenched by the drooling ooze whose acrid fumes stirred up memories of the sour smell of the dead in days gone by. When a shell smashed and an egg spattered in the warm ashes of young Saint Opportun as old Charles Lépine was carting them in his wheelbarrow, there was a faint sizzle, as if the spirit of the little saint had sighed. Old Charles Lépine, who had been imperturbable when the sloshing projectiles splattered his own face, started when, beneath the ashes which had blended with the shattered eggs and turned to mud, the little saint breathed. Old Charles Lépine had learned that to create the human race, God had taken a handful of mud and breathed on it to give it a soul: that mud had become the first man. Was God, who had already worked miracles in Saint-Toussaint-des-Saints, taking another handful of mud, this time from Charles Lépine's wheelbarrow, to re-create young Opportun as he had been, and replace him on the path of men? Rotten eggs were assailing on all sides, but old Charles Lépine didn't take his eyes off the holy ashes that were beginning to breathe.

Suddenly people realized that the rotten eggs had stopped falling. The prayers resumed softly, like fire under the ash. Hymns came back to the lips of the Children of the Virgin and the whole choir proclaimed their joy at having triumphed over the ordeal. Their clothes, like banners, were drenched in the nauseating puke, but they must continue into the night, singing the praises of the Almighty. They must give thanks to God who had seen to it that the Devil was not victorious, they must thank the Right Party for giving them the road on which the right religion had won out over the godless before it was even built. Hymns and prayers rose up as if all the villagers were declaring their joy at being alive on this earth that was sometimes a very sad place. But the procession made no progress. The faithful were bunched together. Their way was blocked.

"Don't step on us!"

The faithful at the back began to push, but those at the head of the procession couldn't move. Charles Lépine muttered. Pushing his wheelbarrow into the legs of the people ahead of him, he cleared a path for himself and disappeared, grumbling. He had decided to go home. He had taken all the rotten eggs the good Lord had willed to fall on him, but he shouldn't have to expose himself to any more danger at his great age. He had decided to go home. He was muttering. Since he wouldn't be able to scatter young Saint Opportun's ashes to sanctify the future new road, he would spread them in his vegetable garden. If the holy ashes could help the new road, they probably wouldn't hurt his cucumbers and leeks.

The procession had come to a halt because of Cytriste Tanguay. He was threatening to fire his rifle between the eyes of the first person who dared take one step forward. Never would he permit the new road to let new-fangled foolishness into his fields. He didn't want his oats smothered by the dust raised by cars that would drive past at the speed of airplanes. He didn't want his animals in the pasture driven wild by the noise of motors, which weren't natural because the good Lord hadn't invented them. He didn't want his calves poisoned by their mothers' milk mixed with the oil and smoke from automobiles. He didn't want people from the neighboring villages coming on Sundays and spreading their checkered tablecloths for picnics in his fields, and children and lovers rolling in his oats. This was his home, and he waved his rifle as a warning that no one would trespass on his lands without his permission "and no road neither."

"If you didn't get the picture from my rotten eggs, maybe my gun'll convince you!" yelled Cytriste Tanguay.

Or so a churchwarden reported to the Curé, who repeated it to the Local Riding Minister.

"Monsieur le Curé," suggested the Minister, "you take care of religion and leave the politics to me."

Fearing that chaos would get the upper hand and scatter the procession, Curé Fourré thanked the good Lord for His miracles, asked Saint Opportun to bring peace to Saint-Toussaint-des-Saints, thanked the Right Party for services rendered and hastened to give his blessing.

Young Opportun did his best to be a speedy messenger to the Almighty, for scarcely had Curé Fourré ended his prayer when the sky, which until then had been as clear as the river, turned muddy, as if a big foot had stirred it up. The sky was overcast now. Dark wads of smoke unfurled over Saint-Toussaint-des-Saints. Suddenly it shattered like a detonation of war. There was a flash of lightning. An arrow of fire shiny as a red-hot iron struck Cytriste Tanguay's poplars, illuminating the leafy branches with an incandescent light. The Opposition renegades who had bombarded the peaceful procession with rotten eggs were revealed. The bodies of the infidels fell from the trees like ripe fruit that could howl.

A violent rain lashed their faces. No one ran for shelter. Everyone allowed the good Lord's rain to wash them.

Soon bodies, clothes, the sacred ornaments all were clean again; the rain stopped. The sky was bright again. Stars reappeared. It would be a beautiful night.

The farmers were of the opinion that the fine weather would last several days, for the work on the new road.

Innocent Loiseau, the exiled collegian, hadn't taken part in the procession, for he was neither an altar boy nor a Daughter of the Virgin nor a Son of the Sacred Heart nor a pioneer nor a Knight of Columbus nor an angel, penitent, future bridegroom, pickled egg champion, contractor, cabinet minister or Curé. The procession composed of the people from his village had paraded past him as if he were a stranger, but he felt like a stranger among the other strangers who had come to the event. He hadn't stayed long. As he went home, he felt as if this was no longer his village. There had been no place for him in the procession. There was no place for him in Saint-Toussaint-des Saints. There was no place for him in this life: it was running past him like the procession where he couldn't fit in.

Innocent Loiseau had not prayed, he hadn't laughed. Life was passing, time was passing, summer was coming to an end. As an adolescent, he was nowhere in the world. He was lost in limbo. At his age he had not yet been born. Innocent was not alive. He couldn't even sleep.

Saint Opportun was happy, though, and the heavens smiled.

XVII

The rooster on the steeple
was no rooster

That night in the land of the Appalachians a heavy ema-
nation lingered like the one that remains after a fearful
combat. The battle of the eggs: under that name would it
take its place in memories. The lingering effluvium of rotten eggs would take days to disappear. Birds and fieldmice
came to feed off it. Some village women, unable to tolerate
the pestilential reek, took out mops and buckets of soapy
water and washed the green grass and the dirt of the road.
The battle of the eggs would be recounted for years to
come. Young people would remember and describe it to
their own incredulous children and to their grandchildren,
who would be sad because they lived in a peaceful time
when politics was practiced only by machines.

All night, Cytriste Tanguay had been breathing in the
sickly sweet and putrid summer breeze. The new road
would not go through his fields. He was the last sentinel.
All the windows in the village on the hillside were now
dark. The land was once again a blue ball. He saw its round
form standing out against the horizon. The night was span-
gled with light as if the sky were full of villages with lamps
at their windows. Only he was not asleep, and he would

stand alone as he defended his property. After this Opposition victory, he had considered going home like a warrior who has won his rest. Then he thought better of it. He had been a member of the Right Party long enough to know that it was sneakier than the Devil himself. Cytriste Tanguay must not sleep, for the Devil never sleeps. It was his duty to stand guard. The people from the Right Party might sneak up while he was asleep, making no more sound than a wolf; then in the morning, outside his house, he would see the new road stretching through his fields. He went on guard. Cytriste Tanguay wasn't going to be snoring on his pillow, clutching his fat wife, while the Right Party slithered about like the Devil. He watched. The silence was so deep he must be the only man in all the world who was awake. He mustn't think that way. When the sentinel thinks that he alone is not asleep, that's when the enemy looms up. He squeezed his rifle. He wouldn't hesitate to shoot anyone between the eyes who violated his boundaries. This land belonged to him. Generations ago, his ancestor had decided he would not go somewhere else to live out his life. He had felled trees, built a cabin, made children who, once they were men, had felled more trees and made more children and, once they were men, they had started their parents' lives again. Cytriste Tanguay in turn would give his land to one of his sons. Cytriste Tanguay would not sleep. He gripped his rifle so hard he was shaking. The night was too peaceful. Yet nothing was happening. The curtain of night rose slowly to reveal the day. Cytriste Tanguay heard the birds awakening. He saw the light creep slowly over the back of the hills until they seemed to rise gently in the day. Dark trees stood out from the dark. There was daylight on his land. He would continue to lie in wait for the enemy.

While Cytriste Tanguay was watching, the Local Riding Minister was asleep. The endless procession had exhausted him. He had taken a room at the Mountaintop Inn in Saint-Toussaint-des-Saints. He had asked to be awakened early to go and shake up Cytriste Tanguay. He'd push the old mule out of the way so the road-works could begin. During the night, Politics would dictate what he must tell Cytriste. The Minister trusted those sleep-filled nights when mundane matters were organized in dreams, as he often said.

The Minister snored so authoritatively the walls shook. Guests in adjoining rooms left at dawn, after an impossible night. They grumbled because they hadn't been able to enjoy a Christian sleep at an inn that claimed to be well run. "If a man's been on the road all day and goes back on the road next morning, he deserves a good night's rest!" moaned a travelling salesman who was the Maple Leaf Cookie King. Another threatened: "Next time I'm in Saint-Toussaint-des-Saints the new road'll be down and I'll wave as I drive right past this place — which ought to be called 'The Big Snore'." Trying to appease his dissatisfied customers, the innkeeper said: "Messieurs, you've never slept so close to a Minister before. The Minister *honored* you with his snoring." The unhappy customers left content — and quietly, for fear of awakening the Minister who, even as he snored, was engaged in politics. In addition, the servant girls who feared his wrath if they awakened him listened with pious respect to the modulations, the arpeggios, the appoggiaturas, the crescendi of this symphony that started in the abysmal depths of the belly and made the Minister's chest vibrate like the walls of a church when the organ is played full blast. One girl observed, "It sounds as good as a good political speech." It lasted a long time. People were waiting for it to end. It was noon when the innkeeper, uneasy at the lengthy silence, screwed up his courage and rapped on the door. The Minister started. He was soon outside, like a man who knows he helps the earth to rotate, scurrying off to persuade Cytriste Tanguay to let the new road cross his land.

Around noon as well, when the sun was very high above Saint-Toussaint-des-Saints, a farmer looked up at the church steeple. The rooster on the tip seemed to have grown. He rubbed his eyes. Had the procession, the prayers, the hymns, the flood of rotten eggs made him lose his mind? As he put it, "Believing too much is like not believing enough. Neither one does a man a mite of good." The rooster was really and truly bigger. Not only that, he had spread his wings. The farmer rubbed his eyes again. And cried for help. Bystanders gathered. Some of them realized that the big rooster was actually the airplane belonging to the Minister of Roads and Bridges, impaled on the tip of the steeple.

The Local Riding Minister, who was walking so he could shake hands with voters, met a flock of men, women and children outside the church. They were looking up to Heaven as if Saint Opportun were visible through the clouds. He raised his eyes as well. An airplane was stuck on the tip of the steeple like a great white rooster. The Minister of Roads and Bridges had spent the whole night in his plane, pinned to the tip of the steeple. Tiny men, like insects, were climbing the ladder that leaned against the narrow tip of the steeple at a dizzying height. They were, as it was explained to the Local Riding Minister, hare-brained youngsters who feared neither dizziness nor the Devil. They were risking smashed skulls in return for rescuing a Minister who'd have been better off not getting pinned up there. "If you can't steer a plane without wrecking it, what makes you think you can lead the people?" inquired a man with a mustache rusty from cigarettes. He must be in the Opposition, thought the Local Riding Minister. Was he dangerous? The mere thought of ending up so high in the air without being enclosed in the cabin of a plane made him giddy. The ground was his natural element. He must see to his new road.

"When a Minister gets to thinkin' he's the cock on the steeple it's time to vote for the Opposition," grunted Uguzon Dubois the logger.

The Local Riding Minister was shaken by what he'd heard. After such a fabulous procession there were still people who would vote against the Right Party!

When the Local Riding Minister arrived, Cytriste Tanguay was almost asleep.

"Bonjour, Monsieur Tanguay! How's every little thing?"

Cytriste Tanguay started at the voice. He thought he was under attack. He fired. The bullet whizzed past the Minister's ears and he dived into the oats. Now Cytriste was wide awake. His eyes, clear of sleep, saw how things really stood. Cytriste Tanguay thought to himself that the Right Party's bulldozer must be sneakily hiding somewhere. He fired straight ahead, into the oats, then behind and all around and into the haystacks. He fired without let-up. Roused by the combat, he heard a voice choked with fear:

"M'sieur Tanguay, I just want to to talk about politics! I'm your Minister."

"If its politics you want, Minister My Ass, I'll give you politics. Listen to this!"

Cytriste Tanguay wanted to fire at random, in the direction from which the frightened voice had come, but he'd used up all his ammunition. So then, with all his peasant strength and vigor, he seized his rifle by the barrel and started beating the oats with the butt. He struck at anything that might be hiding there.

The Local Riding Minister would probably have had his head crushed like a strawberry if, at that very moment, a loud whistle from the river, far, far away, and compressed by the surrounding hills into a more tempestuous current, hadn't struck the church. The stone steeple swayed like a tree. The rescue team clung to the ladder with all the strength in their hands. The wind tugged at their feet and the steel ladder felt as limp as rope. The steeple seemed like a ship's mast swaying on a raging sea. The young people weren't afraid. With their windblown hair in their faces, they roared with laughter. They were having the time of their lives. Once they were down on the ground, with the Minister of Roads and Bridges on their shoulders, they'd have plenty of stories to tell around a table covered with bottles of beer.

The airplane, shaken by the wind, pitched and tossed, reeled and swayed, spun, writhed, bobbed and swung from the tip of the steeple. Inside, the framework creaked. The passenger in the cabin had been waiting all night for the moment when he would come crashing into space. Then, exhausted, he had fallen asleep, lulled by the sun's first rays. Now the Minister of Roads and Bridges was sleeping like a baby. It had been a long time since he had felt so secure. The Opposition couldn't throw stones at him. The telephone wouldn't ring. No voice would plead with him to do some voter a special favor. His wife wouldn't wake him up to tear a strip off him. Happily and authoritatively, he snored away in the fine cloudless sky of his dream.

The wall of the airplane was torn. From it descended a blizzard of flat, square flakes that swirled in the sudden gust of wind. Children hurled themselves at the messages that fell from the plane. The sheets of paper took flight like frightened birds. Some of the youngsters managed to get their hands on one and they all stopped to read: VOTE FOR THE RIGHT PARTY, BUILDER OF MODERN

ROADS; VOTE AGAINST THE OPPOSITION WHO *DON'T* BUILD MODERN ROADS.

In the cabin there was a snapping sound. The Minister of Roads and Bridges woke up. "Here it comes, we're splitting in two." Then nothing happened. The Minister's heart began to race; he could feel it very high in his chest, quite close to his throat. The sensation was very much like what he had felt when the airplane took off. It was as if he was flying. Through the window he saw roofs, trees, fences, gardens, as if the whole countryside was making a fast getaway. The airplane was moving again. The wind carried it along. The Minister saw the ground come closer. The plane wouldn't be able to avoid taking a nose-dive into the fences. The oats were so close the Minister could have grasped a handful through the hole in the outer wall. All at once, the Minister of Roads and Bridges couldn't see a thing. He thought his heart had jumped into his head.

In Cytriste Tanguay's field, the oats had flattened under the force of the wind, but still he lashed out with his rifle barrel. Haystacks went rolling, possessed by the Devil. The Local Riding Minister stood and clutched his straw hat in both hands, shouting words that were carried off at once by the wind. Cytriste Tanguay couldn't hear him. The Minister was shouting at the top of his lungs. Cytriste couldn't hear because the wind was whistling in his ears, and when he saw that the Minister's face was red, as if in anger, he thought the Minister must be shouting insults at him. His landowner's rights violated, he raged and threatened and pointed his gun at the Minister. He barked the most terrible insults. The wind played with his words and erased them. The Local Riding Minister and Cytriste Tanguay couldn't hear each other.

"The new road's gonna run through here, because this is where Progress is coming!"

The farmer retorted,

"Just because the Right Party decided to go to the Devil it ain't gonna split my land in two to get there!"

The Minister was exultant.

"A road runs like a river: it's a blessing that brings good luck."

"You wanta know who'll be travelling this road of yours? I'll tell you who: dust-raisers, germ-spreaders, apple-stealers, cow-scarers, picnickers who'll drop their knickers in my oats, and good-for-nothings that'll hop over my fence without permission. And none of them's got the right to set foot on my land!"

In the gust of wind both were mute. All that either one could make out were the other's grimaces. In the battle between the Right Party and the Opposition, the Local Riding Minister and the farmer, so busy ranting and raving, saw the airplane swirl like an autumn leaf in the wind. It dived into the oats and disappeared under the curtain of golden stems like a swimmer under water. Cytriste Tanguay dropped his rifle and clapped his hands over his ears to muffle the sound of the explosion. The Local Riding Minister pulled his hat over his eyes. Forgetting their insults for the moment, they waited, straining, ready for the worst, for the detonation. Trembling, tense, powerless, they couldn't even run away. Cytriste Tanguay would die without having forgiven the Minister who wanted to tear up his land. The Local Riding Minster would die without having convinced this stubborn peasant of the virtues of modern progress. There was no explosion. The Minister of Roads and Bridges burst out of his plane, astonished to be in the oatfield, looking as if he'd just awakened from a dream. He walked up to the two men, followed by his dazed staff members.

"I thought I was dreaming, but if these oats are tickling my butt, it's no dream."

The Local Riding Minister pulled his hat off his head.

"Monsieur le Ministre, we had to have the procession without you!"

The Minister held out his hand to his colleague.

"Monsieur le Ministre, I watched the whole ceremony from high in the sky, which is fitting for a Minister of the Right Party. As our Chef says, 'You haveta look down on things.' "

"Monsieur le Ministre, you're standing in the very spot where in just a few weeks the new road's going to run."

Cytriste Tanguay picked up his rifle. The Local Riding Minister pushed the Minister of Roads and Bridges toward the farmer.

"Monsieur le Ministre, I'd like to·you to meet this gallant man, a determined patriot who defends his land as our ancestors defended their country. I'm going to ask you to be generous with him. He's going to sell the province — for an honest price — a portion of his land so the Right Party can build a road that will link Saint-Toussaint-des-Saints with progress."

"Can'tcha read," snapped Cytriste Tanguay, "it says No Trespassing."

"The Minister of Roads and Bridges will reimburse you generously: the Right Party is a generous party."

"Two Ministers don't impress me no more than just one."

"My dear man, we're going to pay for your land at the price the Right Party reserves for its friends," said the Minister of Roads and Bridges. "Besides, we'll be offering you the little rebate the Right Party gives its friends. And besides that, I wouldn't be surprised if the Minister of Agriculture asks you to raise some little calves and little bulls that'll grow up and make more just like 'em."

"It says No Trespassing."

"The law entitles us to cross your land, did you know that? If you won't accept a favor from the Right Party, maybe you'll accept the law?"

Cytriste Tanguay raised his rifle. In the silent oatfield a shot rang out in the dry summer sky with the force of thunder. More shots flew into the air, landing in a burst of smoke. Cytriste blanched. The airplane had exploded. Suddenly he was afraid.

"You didn't haveta bring the army," he said. "All I wanted was a good price for my land."

The two Ministers and the farmer talked in hushed voices; there were some guffaws, then they leaned against the fence and signed some papers. The right of way was ceded.

As the two Ministers were leaving, Cytriste called out:

"I was never really in the Opposition, y'know. Them buggers'd never'a given me as good a price as you did. I gave you a bit of trouble to get a good price out of you. Now Monsieur le Ministre, don't forget them bulls and calves!"

Shortly after that, the shed that would serve as administrative offices for the building of the new road was placed on Cytriste Tanguay's land.

201

XVIII

The insurance salesman says: "Don't lack assurance."

It wasn't the custom to knock on doors in Saint-Toussaint-des-Saints. You simply walked in, as if you were at home. Only strangers committed the discourtesy of knocking first. Montcalm O. Labranche, C.I., was from the city, but he'd spent enough time in the Appalachian Region to know the customs of the country. At every election, he had come to aid the Right Party. He had entered every house, except those where belief in the Opposition was so strong they'd set the dog on him. And so Montcalm O. Labranche, C.I., walked into the Loiseaus' house as they were seated around the long kitchen table, noses in their plates. They were digging into a dish of boiled beef and summer vegetables. Montcalm O. Labranche, C.I., greeted Azellus and his wife. After peering at each of the chairs that lined the walls, he selected the deepest one, the rocker, the one that belonged by a sacred bond to Azellus, the father. Montcalm O. Labranche, C.I., was so round he could have rolled instead of walking. He wore watches on both wrists, he had rings on all his fingers, a heavy silver chain across his fat belly and a number of gold teeth. In the summer he dressed in white, with a black tie upon which gleamed a large gilt pin. To sit down, he laboriously folded his bulk in half, revealing ankles clad in black-buttoned white spats. He sighed:

"Not getting any younger. No sir. On the road every day, you don't realize it, but time's passing by, right along with the road. Fast. Too fast, if you ask me. Suddenly you're at the end of your road. Turn up your toes and they carry you off on their back. Happens fast."

The warm aroma of meat roasted with cabbage and carrots left the kitchen, replaced by the lavender perfume of Montcalm O. Labranche, C.I.. Azellus Loiseau's thirteen children sniffed delightedly at the odor of the city. When they were grown up they would take the road, they would go to the cities.

"Only one thing in this life's a sure thing: death's out there waiting for us and we don't know what turn in the road she'll spring from."

The fat man lit a cigar. His head disappeared in a dense cloud of smoke. His belly was wadded like a heavy eiderdown. Azellus Loiseau ate, saying nothing. Montcalm O. Labranche, C.I., who was a fine talker, was trying to lead him into a trap; his insurance salesman's words were nothing but bait. Azellus ate as if he hadn't really heard what the fat, perfumed man had to say.

"When death strikes a man down at least he can have the consolation he's left his family a good life . . . "

In the stranger's presence the children refrained from squabbling or exchanging kicks under the table or elbowing each other or yanking the tablecloth to jiggle the plates; no one squalled, no one stuck out their tongue, no milk was spilled. The mother was proud of her offspring. The father thought of those who had passed away. They hadn't had much at the end of their lives: there hadn't been much of a legacy for their heirs to glean. Azellus, at the end of his road, wouldn't leave much to his family either . . . He chewed at his beef, head down, thinking the insurance salesman was right on that score.

"But if a young man, a very young man, who's just finished his first pirouettes on the road of life, is suddenly struck down by death, what does he leave his family? When the college doors re-open after summer holidays, not everyone comes back: there's some that can't continue their education. Why? Because during the summer they've died. They left the college singing like birds leaving their cage . . . "

"Our Innocent ain't going back to school. They dumped him out like a shovelful of shit. The priests don't like country kids that smell of the stable. But wasn't Jesus Christ born in a stable?"

"You know how Le Chef likes the country. He'd hate to hear that a country boy was missing out on an education. All I want to know is this: should I drop Le Chef a word about your Innocent? If Le Chef lifts his little finger, the college doors will open up for Innocent as if he was a Minister . . . Unfortunately, after the summer holidays there's some that can't go back to college . . . "

Innocent, one of the Loiseau boys, was sixteen years old. Curé Fourré and Madame Loiseau had decided to send him to college. His hands were folded on the table. He was a sensitive, pious lad who understood religious matters and the stories in the holy books better than the others. Madame Loiseau was proud that he wasn't concealing his piety.

"Dying's always sad," continued Montcalm O. Labranche, C.I., "and it's even sadder to die young. But saddest of all is to die like a thief. To take everything from your parents after they spend a fortune raising and feeding and clothing you, then just skip out and die."

He brought his cigar to his lips, but took it away without inhaling any smoke, jolted by a sudden thought that he urgently needed to share.

"In my life I've seen young men as lively as a calf in the new grass in spring — healthy, happy, laughing, cheeks like apples — fine-looking lads like your Innocent: that's his name, isn't it? I've seen fine-looking lads like Innocent, full of life, with no room in their heads for a thought of death. They figured they'd live till the end of their old age, but then just a week later they'd had their death prayers and they were buried in a satin-lined coffin. And that costs dear, Monsieur Loiseau. Death's dearer than a wedding, did you know that? Undertakers aren't reasonable men. You can't bury the dead in their birthday suits. Would you be prepared, Madame Loiseau, would you let your fine-looking Innocent be buried in the ground, with the worms and the damp? Got to take precautions. You wouldn't

be so stingy you'd try and screw handles on his body . . .
You'd want a coffin."

He pulled up several rolls of fat to gain access to his vest
pocket and drew out a card.

"Take this, Monsieur Loiseau. If you ever need it, here's
the name of the finest coffin-maker in the Capital; he doesn't
ask much and for friends of the Right Party, the price is
right."

He disappeared in a cloud of smoke. Innocent rose abruptly, knocking over a chair, and ran outside. They heard
him moaning. One by one, the Loiseau children left the
table and went outside to look, trying not to be rude to
their visitor for if they were, some random maternal clouts
would land on napes of necks.

"Innocent hasn't got a strong constitution like the others,"
Madame Loiseau apologized. "In the college, you know,
they forget how to do a man's work. He used to have
muscles like his father, but from working with a pencil his
arms are like a little girl's. Being with all those men in
robes can't be good for the health . . . Now I don't mean
to insult religion, but it isn't normal for a man to wear a
robe. It's fine to have your head full of books, but wearing
those robes, a man gets in the habit of sitting down to pee
and then he'll turn up his nose at man's work."

Innocent came back inside, hollow-cheeked, eyes wet
with tears, clutching his stomach. Azellus hadn't said a
word. Deep down he knew, with his atavistic peasant's
intuition, that the man from the city had dropped some
bait. But Azellus wouldn't be taken in. He wouldn't say a
word. Innocent went back to the table, followed by his
brothers and sisters.

The cloud of smoke dispersed around the head of Montcalm O. Labranche, C.I..

"That was a fine procession last night. I was born in the
Capital myself, spent my whole life there. And I've seen
processions, believe you me. I've seen longer ones than
that one here in Saint-Toussaint-des-Saints, Monsieur
Loiseau, but I surely haven't seen a finer one. If the good
Lord in Heaven's as pleased with that procession as the
Chef in the Capital, you're going to be deluged with fa-
vors . . . I don't know too much about the good Lord's

intentions, but I assure you — ha! ha! — sounds like insure, doesn't it? And I noticed that even though your Innocent's as pale as if his soul's departed, he's got his wits about him, because I can see in his eyes, he caught my little witticism right away . . . Ah yes. Say what you will, those colleges do our children's wits a world of good. Monsieur Loiseau, I swear to you, our Chef is fonder of Saint-Toussaint-des-Saints than all the other villages in the province, and I've been given the responsibility to tell you about some special favors . . . some *very* special favors . . . You see, Monsieur Loiseau, Le Chef's like a mother that takes good care of all her children, but fusses over the young and weakest just a little more. Monsieur Loiseau, I'm here to tell you that Le Chef knows about your son, who's going to be taken back by his college. I'm here to tell you Le Chef wants to award Innocent Loiseau a favor."

Azellus was wary. The more this man talked, the happier he was that he was wary. This man from the city smelled of perfume, like granny on her way to Mass. He'd come here to lay a trap. The peasant knew how to use trickery too. He didn't let his happiness show. Men are made in such a way that their hearts pound at the announcement of victory. The blood was throbbing in Azellus Loiseau's temples. Not a wrinkle moved on his face. Not the slightest twitch showed at the corners of his mouth. Montcalm O. Labranche, C.I., wouldn't be able to brag that he'd seen a farmer switch his tail at the sight of a handful of oats. Madame Loiseau was less honorable, her husband judged. He gazed reprovingly at her. She was as pale as when she gave birth to her children and she was sweating. It was too much for her: she picked up her saucer and fanned herself with it. As for Innocent, he was blushing. He had been honest, he'd done his school work as the good priests required. He had assiduously respected God's commandments; rarely did he give in to the pleasure associated with the impurity of the body; he loved his parents. Accordingly, he deserved God's reward. And the reward was being offered from the hands of the Right Party's Chef. Montcalm O. Labranche, C.I., had disappeared in a cloud of smoke. The children could see only his feet and his black-buttoned spats. They looked questioningly at their lucky older brother. Innocent was discovering that God was giving him a sign just as He had given a sign to Opportun. Innocent asked never to be fried alive in oil. Slowly the smoke thinned out and Montcalm O. Labranche, C.I., reappeared.

"That was a fine procession yesterday, Monsieur Loiseau. Innocent, you've been to school to develop your intelligence, tell me, have you ever seen anything as important?"

Innocent flushed a little redder. He separated his fingers. Not knowing what to do with his hands, now heavy and awkward, he picked up his knife and fork. His plate was empty. He'd never been asked such a question in college. What should he reply? Everything was important. The entire procession was important. In college he'd got used to answering questions that had only one answer: the right one. This time, there could be a thousand different replies. The Minister could be more important. Or the bulldozer. Or Curé Fourré. Or perhaps the monstrance with the body of Christ inside, or the altar boys, or the workmen — or Saint Opportun. Three thousand replies were logical, possible. He blushed and his chair seemed to melt under him. Any one of his responses might turn out to be erroneous and cause him to lose the present from Le Chef. So many correct answers that could come between him and the one expected by the fat perfumed man from the city. Innocent's father was watching him. His eyes said he wouldn't tolerate the wrong answer. There were tears at the corners of his mother's eyes, ready to fall if he made a mistake. The children whispered answers, as in school, and their murmuring made the same vexing sound as flies. Suddenly these words fell from his lips.

"If you ask me Monsieur Labranche, I believe I'd answer the same thing as you."

Montcalm O. Labranche, C.I., had been waiting for Innocent's answer, and since he had to wait for it, he'd brought his cigar to his lips. His fat cheeks were preparing to suck in the smoke when the words popped from the student's mouth. The perfumed man from the city was dumbfounded; he uncrossed his legs and gazed at Innocent, astounded.

"Without batting an eye, young Innocent, you just gave me an answer that could take you far in politics! Now I see why Le Chef picked you for a special favor. Le Chef knows a lot about politics, but he knows even more about men . . . Monsieur Loiseau, Madame, take a good look at your Innocent: you've got a great politician here, because a politician's a man with the knack for giving little answers to big questions."

The cigar was stuck in his mouth, the flabby cheeks were hollowed as they sucked in the smoke, and a grey cloud unfurled around the perfumed man. Azellus knew he'd fallen into a trap. He knew he was stuck, but he couldn't see the goddamn trap. At least he wasn't ashamed of his son. He was silent. With a corner of her apron, Madame Loiseau wiped away a tear; she had given birth to a good son: Innocent would bring honor to the Loiseau family. The boys were filled with admiration for their brother; they couldn't wait to grow up and know as much as he did so Le Chef would choose them too. The girls were as proud of Innocent as their mother.

"I'll say it again: that was one fine procession!" Montcalm O. Labranche, C.I., proclaimed again. "But what nearly brought tears to my eyes — me, with my businessman's heart — what tickled the tip of my heart was the sight of that fine blue-and-white shed that's going to be the administrative office for the new road. When I saw that shed drive up on its platform, Monsieur Loiseau, like a royal majesty, when I thought, inside that shed all the important decisions about the future of the road will be made, it brought tears to my eyes. And that didn't happen even when my own father died. This time, though, I cried with happiness, because I was so glad to see the Right Party at work for the progress of the people. Roads, Monsieur Loiseau, are the veins and arteries of a body. Are you going to contradict me, Innocent?"

The schoolboy turned even redder than before; he folded his hands on the table.

"If you ask me, Monsieur Labranche, I'd be inclined to think the same thing as you."

Montcalm O. Labranche, C.I., rose briskly, as if his body weren't encased in heavy fat. He approached the table, leaned over the plates and dishes, and offered Innocent his hand.

"Monsieur Loiseau, you should be proud to hear such judgment from the mouth of such a young man. Madame Loiseau, I congratulate you for giving birth to a son who not only sets an example for his brothers and sisters, but will be an inspiration for all the young people in the Appalachian Region. Monsieur Loiseau, in this country there's room for youth! You understand why Le Chef picked Innocent to represent him personally in the administration shed for the construction of the new road. Monsieur, Innocent will have his own telephone. Is that an honor, Monsieur Loiseau, or isn't it?"

The father knew now that he was caught in the net; he felt as if he'd been tied in a bundle. Silently, he clenched his fists under the table. Tears rolled down Madame Loiseau's cheeks. The children promised themselves they'd visit their big brother in his shed. Innocent had been honored more than he deserved.

The insurance salesman donned his white straw hat and headed for the door, pushing it as if he were about to leave without another word. Uneasy, Azellus Loiseau got up. The fat perfumed man had caught him in a trap he still couldn't see, and on top of it all he was leaving, he already had one foot on the other side of the threshold. Then Montcalm O. Labranche, C.I., turned around.

"I'm going to tell Le Chef he was right about Innocent. Your son might very well have been appointed Le Chef's personal representative in the administration shed for the new road. Unfortunately, though, Innocent's not protected. Innocent isn't covered by a good life insurance policy. Death comes too often to construction sites. You'll understand that without the protection of a good life insurance policy, your Innocent's quite a risk. If it was up to me to do the right thing for Innocent, I'd make sure he was covered by a good insurance policy."

"Exactly," exclaimed Azellus. "Must be the good Lord Himself that sent you our way; only last night, before we went to sleep, my wife and me had our heads on the pillow and we were saying it might be a good idea to take out some insurance on Innocent. But we didn't know who we could trust to ask for advice. Isn't that true, wife?"

Madame Loiseau hesitated briefly, then came to the conclusion that the good Lord wouldn't take her words for a lie and said:

"My husband and I, we didn't sleep a wink all night, we were so anxious for an insurance salesman to come. Isn't that true, husband?"

"And since the good Lord can read our dreams, he must've had a word with Le Chef . . . Insure Innocent," (the farmer thought of the trap and grew cautious), "how much would that set me back?"

"Monsieur Loiseau, I couldn't put a price on your Innocent's life. A child is a fortune, a treasure."

Azellus decided it was time to use cunning.

"If you can't put a price on Innocent's life, does that mean you'll insure him for nothing?"

The fat man put on his hat, pushed the door and set his other foot on the other side of the threshold. An army of mosquitoes flew into the house and whined around the light bulb.

"I'll tell the Chef Innocent's a talented young man, but his father doesn't understand why he has to be protected."

Azellus caught hold of him.

"Monsieur Labranche, Innocent's our family treasure. I'm prepared to go into debt till the end of my days, to mortage my animals and land, so I can buy him the best insurance policy money can buy. He'll pay us back later with his gratitude."

Montcalm O. Labranche, Certified Insurer, took off his hat and went back to the kitchen.

"Monsieur Loiseau, Le Chef's going to be a happy man. Sign here."

Azellus signed the form without reading it. He was neither a lawyer nor a notary, which was what you had to be to understand the fine print on a contract.

"I had the contract all ready because I knew you couldn't turn down a present from Le Chef. Your son Innocent is about to take his first steps on the road of life."

"Tell Le Chef we're proud of Innocent too," added Madame Loiseau.

"And thank you, Monsieur Labranche."

"If you ask me, Monsieur Labranche, I'd be inclined to think the same thing," Innocent concluded.

XIX

Photos, unlike memory, don't forget

Sautereau, the Editor-in-Chief of *The Provincial Sun*, arrived home late. He was coughing. Sweat was running down his back. To take the air from the river, he had unbuttoned his raincoat, which was not swollen by the usual breeze. The air over the city was stagnant. He would have liked to breathe fresh air, the way a thirsty person drinks cold water, but the air that entered his nostrils was tepid, sticky, fouled by all the smut in the Capital. The sun had gone down long ago, but the city still reeked of hot ashes where garbage had been burned. And there was soot and spittle on the sidewalk, broken bottles, crumpled paper and handkerchiefs, and a mixture of chemical fumes in the air; above all there was the dirt that can't be seen but in which Sautereau lived like a silent carp in the muddy water of a stagnant river. Sautereau remembered the river of his childhood; in it the carp were so sluggish from their heavy sleep they were barely alive. You pulled them from the water by running a wire snare around their bodies. Often the flesh was so rotten that the wire broke the fish's body. The carps' flesh was infested by worms that grew as long as white veins. Sautereau stopped several times and leaned against the wall. Vomiting would have been a relief. His heart was constricted, his stomach heaving, his arteries in knots. He had become like the carp in the river of his childhood. He was rotting like carp in contaminated water. As a young man, he had dived into it to save the truth. He had become a journalist so he could denounce those who betrayed the people. During his years at school he had worked at his style as a criminal sharpens his dagger, to strike those who cared more about fattening their un-satiated bellies in ever larger trousers. The silent province was steeped in rot and Sautereau remained as silent as a carp. He never opened his mouth. Through its silence, his newspaper became like the stagnant water of a polluted river. Sautereau could have become a priest and frightened sinners with descriptions of Hell; he could have become a notary and drawn up marriage contracts and wills, but he'd chosen to become a journalist. In his class at college, he was the one who had chosen to be poor and free so he could denounce the enemies of the people. Years later, he had been shattered by what young Achille Bédard told him. He was silent when, right there in the province, a mother was selling her body because the Right Party had ruined her husband. The Minister of Roads and Bridges had driven Verrochio, the shady contractor, to the brink of ruin, then rescued him because Madame Verrochio had offered her body to the Minister, in a room at the Château Frontenac, and still Sautereau was silent. He was an accessory to corruption. He had prevented a young journalist from denouncing these degrading operations. Sautereau was si-lent and forced others to remain silent in the face of all these wrongdoings. He had betrayed the young man who had decided, in college, to use words to fight for the lib-eration of his colonized, exploited, despised people. As a journalist, he had become the voice of silence. He could write an entire article without saying anything. His editorials passed over the surface of things like silence. In *The Provincial Sun* he wrote words that brought no truth, but merely flew away. God had given him a yearning for truth, He had granted him the gift of words, yet his edi-torials were as sweet as honey. Sautereau spread honey over the Right Party's filth. He didn't cry scandal. He was the silent accomplice who lived off his silence. Sautereau was ashamed of himself. If he could have vomited he would have been freed of the knot in his stomach. His shame was choking him. He had cleaned nothing in the Augean stables. He had become filth himself.

His headache was back. With each beat of his heart a hammer pounded his brain. He felt disgust at his silence, he felt hatred for himself. He was no longer a man, for a man can hold his head up to the sky and feel proud, beneath the stars, that he is a man, while an earthworm crawls with its nose in the dirt. Thus did Sautereau walk. He didn't even feel an urge to cry out his suffering to the stars. He had become one of the Right Party's henchmen, he was crawling in corruption and he had the soul of a worm. He could remain silent no longer.

Sautereau had four children and a wife, four growing children. When the Editor-in-Chief of *The Provincial Sun* asked for a raise, he was told that journalism was a form of priesthood. The authority he enjoyed in his position and the respect that position brought him were worth far more than money. Defender of the Right Party, a faithful soul, Sautereau had never obtained any pecuniary recognition like the Party's other friends. And yet the Right Party needed him. True, the party detested ideas. That was why it paid more for a shovelful of gravel than an editorial. For a long time Sautereau had borne the humiliation — he, a thinking man — of being considered less valuable than those who did not think. He had suffered and remained silent. Several times he had considered leaving *The Provincial Sun*, but where could he go? He was condemned. All the newspapers, even the Opposition's, were in the Right Party's tentacular grip. As they said in the movies, he was a marked man.

His wife Méloppée played the piano when he met her; after they were married he hadn't been able to give her the piano he'd promised. The first child had been born before their first wedding anniversary; they had to move from their cramped apartment. At the time, he was only an apprentice journalist who wrote up lost cats and death notices and summaries of the cardinal's sermons. Other children followed. He had to move to an even bigger apartment. The children kept growing. So then came outgrown shoes and clothes, and school books, skates and skis, and

213

Méloppée Sautereau still didn't have her piano. He often heard her drumming on the table, seemingly transported by her own silent music. Then she appeared to forget. Sometimes, during arguments, Méloppée would say: "It's one thing to promise and another to act." Sautereau knew she was thinking about her piano. Sautereau wished he could give his wife such a gift. He assured her she'd have her piano one day and who knows? if the Right Party stayed in power, perhaps she'd even have a grand piano in her living room . . . Méloppée had no idea of her husband's shame. Not only did he not dare raise his eyes to the stars, he no longer really dared look in the mirror at his own face, which he couldn't recognize. He wasn't that pale, drawn little man, bent over in submission. When Méloppée saw her husband so preoccupied, she would ask: "Poor man, are you tired of living? Are you thinking of giving up the fight? Remember . . . "

Méloppée used to write poems when she was studying at the convent, beautiful, great, sad poems. At a meeting of a poetry circle, she had been astonished that Sautereau, a boy, was familiar with the poets she was so fond of. Once a month, a young vicar brought the aspiring intellectuals in his parish together in the church basement to show them there was no conflict between God and culture, that, on the contrary, God was the highest, most perfect accomplishment of integral culture. These young people, squeezed into their students' uniforms and constrained in the starch of their education, recited poems by revered authors; at times they might venture to read their own verses about recent sorrows and bleak aspirations. Sautereau recited lines declaring that young people should not weep, but howl like young wolves emerging from childhood, starved for liberty, with glittering fangs to bite into those adults who made life other than what it might be and justice no longer justice. The other young poets would weep in their verses, reading them in quavery voices; Sautereau, with a politician's emphasis, denounced the guilty, the traitors, thieves, despoilers; he thundered out at his brothers who were more like Cain than Abel, who thought of the people as "an ox they were entitled to lead to the slaughter." Those who wrote poems filled with tenderness and nostalgia thought they were listening to a future Premier of the

Province. He exhorted them to stop being sad, to stop weeping, to stop thinking of themselves as wounded. They listened: they would recall his words when he was Premier and they were famous poets. Sautereau wanted to become nothing but a journalist. He wanted to help the people on their march to liberation. "A journalist," he said, "is a free man, and it takes a free man to defend freedom; a politician is not free." He would be only a journalist then. A free journalist can be as powerful as a Premier, they told him.

Méloppée's poems stopped being sad. She wrote that in the darkest walls, there are always windows, and that behind the greyest horizons, there is always a sun; and that after the coldest rain, there is always a rainbow. She liked Sautereau's self-assurance, his determination. Méloppée's father was a humble civil servant in a government office. His work consisted of tasting random samples of cream taken from farms during inspections. From him she had learned that the government was a big machine whose goal was to devour the people for the benefit of the few who controlled it. Her father had done his job conscientiously. He had tasted the cream with the diligence of a great scholar and the detachment of a saint. He had raised a big family; he had never missed a day of work; he had taken sick only on holidays. One of his favorite jokes was to say threateningly: "I'll wait till I'm dead to retire." Many other civil servants, less conscientious, less assiduous than he, had risen in the organization: they had responsibilities. Their suits were never rumpled. Their wives paraded around in new hats with feathers. The government didn't treat Méloppée's father fairly. When her poems expressed her sorrow, she was putting into rhyme her father's sorrow as well. She knew, with all the certainty of her woman's intuition, that young Sautereau was right: they must not weep, but howl like young wolves.

For Méloppée, the weeks between poetry meetings were long. Soon Sautereau would be waiting for her outside the convent where she was studying. A little later, he would walk with her to the door of the house where she lived. She stopped writing poems ("Words cannot express what I feel.") She did, however, spend many hours at the piano. She had to obtain permission from Sister Principal to come

215

back to the convent in the evening, after study time, to play. Her father had never been able to buy her a piano. It was very humiliating for him never to have earned enough money from the government to be able to buy his daughter a piano, while others who hadn't worked as hard as he now had two cars, a house, savings in the bank, and apartments to rent in the Capital . . . In the evening, Sautereau waited for Méloppée, after her piano practice, to walk her home. The streets were dangerous at night for a young girl on her own. He recited articles he'd written in preparation for becoming a great journalist. They took ingenious detours to extend their walk along the quiet streets, of which every twist and slope they knew well. They would stop, shoulder to shoulder, to look at the stars, identify some constellation. Sometimes they would walk to the river and dream they would one day cross the sea. Happy, Sautereau could not contain himself, and his lips flew onto Méloppée's cheeks while she, with all the strength in her arms, pushed him away. Soon after, she invited him to her parents' house. The apartment was tidy and modest. She introduced him to her father. "Young man, you want to become a journalist and do battle with the profiteers. In this world an honest man has a hard life."

His round little wife smiled fondly at her daughter who already had a sweetheart.

"This young man has ideals; husband, don't discourage him."

Sautereau and Méloppée saw each other frequently and married a few years later.

Sautereau distinguished himself at *The Provincial Sun*: he'd become the youngest managing editor in the Capital. The Right Party enabled him to marry. After the wedding, his father-in-law helped him don his overcoat before going out into the cold February wind, as chilly as the water under the ice on the river.

"I belong to the generation of silent men. Your generation can speak out. When you cry out the truth in your newspaper, it will mean some vengeance for me. It hasn't been fun, spending my life tasting cream. But I never learned how to do very much. Tasting cream was better than ending up in the street. So I toughed it out. The cream was like dog turds in my mouth. I didn't complain. By toughing it out, I was able to give my daughter an education. She's a good girl. Be careful with her. She's all I have to give you, son."

Soon the first child arrived. At the newspaper, Sautereau became twice as vigorous. It was said that he had the wit of a Voltaire. Some priests felt as if they'd been flayed. In letters of fire, he wrote articles in which certain cabinet ministers felt as if they'd been caught with their pants down, as they admitted to their intimates. Sautereau wielded the lash of irony. A canon wrote to *The Provincial Sun* that the most biting style is no replacement for thought. Notaries complained that such a journalist, who attacked responsible persons, sowed doubt about institutions. Sautereau had become the knight of truth. Méloppée was expecting a second child. Sautereau was recognized on the street. When strangers spoke to him, they always had a smile. The people, he thought, are in collusion with the truth. The man who tells the truth is always right. Sautereau knew how to dislodge it from the tangle of lies. They occasionally went to the movies. Sometimes, they went to admire the river. One day they would cross the sea and visit the Old Countries. Mélopée had started writing poems again, in a scribbler. While the child slept, before doing some household task, she would transcribe the verses she had first polished in her mind. Her poems were a little sad. Sautereau noticed that when she wrote love poems, they were more often about the children than about him. She would console him with a motherly kiss on his brow. Then they would bill and coo their way to bed. One day, he promised, he would buy her a piano. It would be good for the children to learn to play too, she would say.

One night he came home very late. His eyes were red. He stank of beer. Méloppée asked if he had been crying. He wanted to tell her his eyes were tired from his long hours of reading and correcting, but he answered that he'd been crying. Why? "Because I love you very much." Staggering, he dropped onto their bed. She approached him, tears in her eyes. "I want to sleep," he muttered angrily when he felt the warmth of her body. Then, more gently: "I got a raise. We celebrated it. If things work out, you'll have your piano." He was already asleep.

Several journalists, including Sautereau, who had benefitted from the generosity of the newspaper's owner, had gone out drinking beer together. There were gags, laughter, teasing, tales and jokes, all made heavy by beer. One of them decided that they didn't want to spend another minute at the tavern. The merry group left the place, choked with laughter, and went to the tavern next door, where they drank more beer, and enjoyed themselves even more noisily. Spontaneously they took a vote and unanimously decided to move on to another tavern. And they continued to celebrate, to drink, to laugh until the tears came, to repeat the old stale jokes; they drained more glasses and decided to visit all the taverns in the Capital. Sautereau wanted to know how many there were. He was told there were five for every church. To that must be added the number of canons multiplied by the difference between nuns and monks. It sounded reasonable. Those who could walk continued to the end of the pilgrimage. The last was a house whose owner rented rooms to visitors. On the top floor, the proprietor offered the services of plump country girls.

Sautereau was drunk, almost asleep, holding Mélopéé as tight as he could in his slack arms. He wept apologies in her ear, and promises that he wouldn't drink again. He swore on the heads of his children. He swore he loved her more than ever. He was awakened by guffaws and cackling laughter. In his drunken fog he recognized the faces of his friends from the newspaper. What were they doing in his bedroom?

Sautereau opened his eyes. He wasn't in bed with Méloppée, but with a fat freckled redhead. His friends' laughter was even louder now than in the tavern. He began to sob. His friends took him home.

The next day he told Méloppée, with many apologies, about making the rounds of the taverns with his friends from the newspaper, even told her a couple of the dirty jokes, but he kept to himself his odyssey to the tavern that had rooms to rent. He tried to forget the red-headed woman, but his recollection of being in bed with her slashed through his memory like a scar.

At the newspaper his friends seemed to have forgotten the humiliating episode in which their managing editor had been naked in bed, awakening from his drunkenness, with a redhead he'd never seen before. Sautereau thought it was unlikely they'd forgotten. He told himself that a man is never as drunk as he claims and that because he has the gift of memory, man can not forget. He no longer enjoyed going to the movies with Méloppée, or roaming the streets of the Capital. They might have run into his friends from the newspaper and as friends always enjoy sprinkling a little discord over conjugal happiness, someone might have made a joking reference to the redhead and Méloppée would have caught it, would have guessed everything. They awaited their second child without ever going out, without entertaining friends, as if they were alone on the earth. Sautereau no longer enjoyed seeing his father-in-law who always talked about the silence of the earlier generations, about the truth that was starting to well up, about the justice that would be re-established, and who accused cabinet ministers and civil servants alike of being "whores at the beck and call of the highest bidders."

That night in a strange bedroom with an ugly girl whose face he couldn't even recall, kept coming back to him, throbbing like a toothache. Looking at her pensive husband, Méloppée thought there must be problems at the newspaper. The second child was born. Sautereau's unpleasant memories spoiled his joy at the birth of a second son, but he smiled as if his happiness were complete. Méloppée was reassured. Seeing her husband so often sad, she had thought he didn't want the child. Now she stopped worrying. The journalist who refused to make compromises with the truth must have problems with the people who held it in contempt, she thought. Seeing him worried always made her feel proud. Her husband had problems because he was a journalist who respected the truth. He was still as pure as the young man she'd fallen in love with. She told him so. Sautereau couldn't believe his friends at the paper had forgotten the episode that had made them laugh so hard. Often they talked about that memorable night, recalling the outrageous jokes, but no one seemed to have gone to that tavern where they sold beer and rented girls. Sautereau, whose lips had rarely touched the foam on a glass of beer, had drunk as much as the others. He must have been even drunker. The liquor must have set fire to his imagination: perhaps the strange redhead lying naked beside him was just an invention of a drunken man's muddled mind. Had he got so worked up over nothing?

So much useless suffering? The redhead had appeared to him when he was drunk. That was why his friends from the newspaper didn't remember her: they'd never seen her.

The Right Party came to power. With bitter words, Sautereau had lashed out at the previous government, which was not aware, he wrote, that "the twentieth century has arrived. While airplanes are travelling faster than the speed of sound, the government is leading the people at the speed of a funeral procession." A few days after the election of the Right Party, which Sautereau celebrated with an article in verse, in the style of the odes to conquerors of Greek antiquity, one of the Right Party's men, a Monsieur Pichette, came to congratulate him and ask if he'd be interested in becoming editor-in-chief of *The Provincial Sun*. Sautereau shut the door of the office where journalists and visitors went for interviews.

"*The Provincial Sun*," said Sautereau, "already has a good editor-in-chief."

"Cut the sweet talk. Le Chef wants you running this paper; he wants you to keep your eye on the paper for him. What's your answer, yes or no? Le Chef's waiting. Where's the phone?"

"I am a free journalist, I write what I personally believe. I write the truth. And if I represent the Right Party . . . "

"Are you trying to tell me," asked Monsieur Pichette, "that when Le Chef talks, crap comes out of his mouth, not the truth? Watch out!"

The man, who was dressed in a wrinkled black suit that was too big for him, with a battered hat pulled down over his eyes, dialed a number.

"You know my boss, the editor-in-chief," Sautereau began hesitantly.

"The old guy's burnt out. We'll take care of his ashes. Plenty of civil servants spend the day scratching their nose. One more won't affect the provincial deficit. Le Chef wants new blood. Yes or no?"

"Yes."

"Sautereau says yes," Monsieur Pichette spat into the telephone. "If you'd said no, Le Chef told me to kick your ass off the paper. You couldn't've even got a job with the Opposition."

His first articles were sincerely favorable to the Right Party. A change is always a purification. He was sincere in his praises of Le Chef and the Right Party. One day, out of respect for the truth, he wrote an article expressing disagreement with a decision the Right Party had made. Monsieur Pichette, dressed in black, appeared in Sautereau's office, pushing the door as if he were going into a public toilet.

"So we can't trust our men, eh? That's what Le Chef asked me. If people threaten war you can bet your boots I'll attack first."

Monsieur Pichette took a photograph from his inside jacket pocket and tossed it onto Sautereau's desk, pounding his fist like a card-player throwing down a strong hand. At first Sautereau didn't understand. Then he recognized himself. It was a picture of him, naked and triumphant, embracing a fat girl: the redhead from his nightmares. His heart leaped and wanted to stop; he felt his flesh burn as if he'd been struck by lightning; he tried to speak, but his mouth was paralyzed. When he decided it was wiser to be silent, his mouth began to repeat:

"It's a mistake! It's a mistake! It's a mistake! It's a mistake!"

"I agree with Le Chef, Sautereau: you made a fatal mistake."

The pudgy fingers took the picture and replaced it in the inside pocket of the black jacket.

"The wife know about your little outing, Sautereau?"

"It's a mistake! It's a mistake!"

"If you throw a stone at the Right Party's windshield, just remember, I'll answer with a bomb."

The fat hand with dirty fingernails pressed his jacket, in the place where the picture had been stored.

"It's a mistake! It's a mistake!"

"Listen Sautereau: if you want your wife to know about your pastimes, just say the word . . . And that word'll be your first attack on the Right Party. Le Chef doesn't want enemies: he wants good friends. And I agree with Le Chef. Le Chef wants you for one of his good friends, Sautereau."

Méloppée saw lines wrinkling the surface of her husband's face, she saw his back becoming hunched. She assumed that he was being eaten away by his passion for the truth. Sautereau knew that the swashbuckling knight of the profiteers was dead behind him. Sautereau felt as if the blood was turning sour in his veins. He went to extremes with perfume: now he smelled like a barber shop. His nostrils were filled with a stench of decay that didn't seem to want to go away. Nothing interested him any more. Everything resembled dead ashes. As a youth, he'd been curious about everything; now, he knew too much. His mind was like the stomach of a man who has gorged himself. All day, he felt like retching. Sometimes, in a nightmare, he would vomit up his own heart. He would awaken in a sweat. He saw the fat girl with red hair. Tossing under the blankets, he wanted to run away. Méloppée held him back with reassuring caresses. He realized then that his wife was at his side and he was choked with anguish. Had he talked during the nightmare? He went back to sleep. When he awakened he realized that he no longer loved Méloppée. He no longer loved his children, who had come into his life too soon. Yesterday, he was a young man on his own and life was too much for him. Now, with a wife and four children, he could never be alone again. He could never be alone in his sorrow. If it hadn't been for them, he'd have deserted the paper. He'd have crossed the sea, seen France, the cathedrals, the ancient cities, the fortified castles, the tombs of History's great men. He had made a terrible mistake. He wanted to be a knight of the truth. Instead of setting out to do battle like a knight, he had attached himself to a woman. And as if that tie weren't strong enough, he had attached himself to children as well. If it hadn't been for them he could have escaped from the prison *The Provincial Sun* had become. Without Méloppée and the children, he could have turned down the Right Party's politics — loathsome mush that he must swallow with a smile. And his articles were supposed to give the people an appetite for another bowl! Alone he could have denounced corrupt practices, favoritism, lies, duplicity, laxity, swindling, extortion. Because of Méloppée and the children Sautereau kept quiet and, through *The Provincial Sun*, the people were exploited, duped, deluded, wheedled, ridiculed, hoodwinked, screwed, betrayed. Sautereau was silent . . . Or rather, he wasn't silent: in *The Provincial Sun* he sang like a well-fed bird pecking at the droppings of Le Chef. Sautereau sang the Right Party's praises as if Le Chef dropped golden turds.

Sautereau read his reporters' articles as painstakingly as a monk. His red pencil struck out every line, every word that ran contrary to the Right Party, every word, every line that the Opposition might have transformed into a criticism of the Right Party. Despite his precautions, his scruples like those of an old miser who examines all his coins to avoid being stuck with counterfeit, one day the black-clad Monsieur Pichette came bounding into his office, raging:

"Le Chef read your paper and he wants to know why you've got it in for him. Le Chef thought you were a friend."

And then he withdrew that cursed photograph from his pocket and tossed it onto Sautereau's desk, pounding his fist for emphasis.

"You wanted to fire the first shot," said Monsieur Pichette, "now you'll get one of our bombs in the face."

Sautereau pleaded, tried to explain his articles, he apologized, knelt, implored, swore, prayed; he wept. When Monsieur Pichette had sufficiently humiliated the editor-in-chief of *The Provincial Sun* he took back the picture showing Sautereau naked in a fat girl's arms and left, saying again,

"The Right Party don't want enemies: only friends, everywhere."

Sautereau thought that the photograph would become yellow and worn, that the fat girl would disappear, his own features grow blurred, that he would become unrecognizable; then he would be free again. Unfortunately, the picture remained sharp and bright, as if carved in stone, persistent as his black memory of that night of carousing which seemed never to end, but continued to darken his days.

Sautereau walked very slowly, to postpone the moment when he must go home. If he hadn't loved his family, he wouldn't have tolerated the humiliation or the forced labor at the newspaper, he would have fled to the other side of the sea, to Europe, where a man could be free. But because he loved his family, he tolerated the pain of his shame. He had succeeded only in becoming a dutiful slave. His children would remember only a dutiful slave, who withered like a dead tree. The Right Party was at the root of all his unhappiness. It was because of the Right Party that he'd become as indifferent to Méloppée as dry bread. A sunset over the river, with its rays turning the water to a flowering garden, mattered as little to him as the dirty sidewalks where he walked, eyes cast down to avoid the light on his face. The books that had been magic boxes for him, inhabited by kindly genies, now dropped from his hands like meaningless sand. Silence seemed more beautiful to him than music. The Right Party had killed him.

Achille Bédard, a young reporter, had brought him the information about a woman who had to sell her body in order to survive after her husband was destroyed by the Right Party, which he had served like a faithful slave. Méloppée would not sell her body: Sautereau swore that to God in Heaven.

He arrived home. He went up the stairs to his apartment. The wallpaper was coming unstuck. Méloppée no longer greeted him at the door; he looked so sad, so exhausted, she preferred to leave him to his sadness. Sautereau realized that he was humming. He would no longer be a slave. He would denounce the Right Party. Even if he lost everything, he would keep Méloppée and the children. What would Méloppée say when she discovered his secret, when she saw her husband in a fat redhead's arms? She would leave him. He would lose her. Never again would he be the slave of Monsieur Pichette. His children would remember him as a man who loved the truth.

"Wake the children," he said. "They're growing up and I don't see enough of them."

Astonished, Méloppée did as he asked. She brought them to him, sleepy, languid, complaining, rubbing their eyes. Sautereau managed to set them all on his bony knees and there he rocked them as he'd never done before, he cuddled them, kissed their foreheads warm with sleep, he rubbed his nose against their tousled heads; he murmured songs to them, songs his own mother had sung when he was a child. They fell asleep. Sautereau held the sheaf of children against his bony chest, musing that nothing in life is as good as children. Gently, Méloppée took them back to bed.

"Mélopée," he announced, "tomorrow you'll have a surprise."

"You've been very preoccupied these past weeks. Are your troubles over? You looked like someone who wasn't alive. You looked as if some animal was gnawing away at you, inside. You were suffering but you didn't say a word. But it wasn't just your silence; there was a dead light in your eyes. You didn't want me to look you in the eye. My poor father was tormented, just like you, by all sorts of worries. He had that sort of dead light in his eyes when he was seeing another woman. My mother found out about it much later. It's a terrible thing for a man with four children to be seeing another woman . . . "

"Méloppée, I'm not seeing another woman!"

"But you don't want me to look you in the eye..."

"Méloppée, I love you more than I've ever told you."

"Are your worries because of a woman?"

"Tomorrow, Méloppée, you'll find out just how much I love you. You and the children. I hope you'll love me too."

"On his death bed, when his liver had been poisoned by the germs in all the cream he'd tasted, from contaminated farms and dirty cows, my father swore to my mother that even though he went to see other women on payday, he'd never really loved anyone but her . . . If you don't love me I can understand why you'd go to another woman, but if you do love me, I don't understand why you'd cheat me, the way my father cheated my mother."

"Do you remember when I told you that a journalist is a knight of the truth? Méloppée, I haven't forgotten anything, you'll see tomorrow."

In bed, Sautereau held Méloppée in his arms and pressed her to him. She felt loved. For a long time there had been none of those caresses that inflame. Already her husband had gone from her. Méloppée thought he must be thinking of another woman. She turned over, disappointed, and let the tears flow onto her pillow. She had reached that point in her life where, after all their years together, she realized that she and her husband were no longer following the same path.

Sautereau didn't realize that Méloppée had left his arms. He didn't realize that she was crying. In his mind he was writing the article that would strike the jugular vein of the bloated pig the Right Party had become. Stained with the Right Party's blood, Sautereau would once again become the man he should never have ceased to be: "*They* have taken over the province and since *they* have been in power, sons have been selling their mother's bodies." (That was a little ambiguous. The phrasing was turgid; he'd rework the sentence.) Ever since *they* have taken over the province *they* have been slicing it up like a cake for their faithful, obedient friends. *They* have taken over the province, *they* build roads on land belonging to their faithful friends. If a friend lets them down, they don't dare kill him outright like American bandits, but they kill him all the same, by ruining him. If the wife is beautiful, if she has a bosom like bunches of ripe, heavy grapes, if she has a backside like a fine mare (she need not necessarily have a ribbon on her tail), she will please the Minister of Roads and Bridges, she will climb into his bed, he will climb onto her, and a contractor will be saved from ruin. The Church will give its blessing to the road built by a man deceived by his wife, before a crowd deceived by the Right Party . . . " That's how he would write when he regained his freedom. Sautereau would be resurrected. Sautereau would be re-born. Tomorrow.

He slept soundly, but awakened well before dawn. Unable to stay in bed on this, the day of his true birth, Sautereau got up and walked to his office. The sun wasn't up yet. The night was still steeped in the river's coolness. On that morning, merely breathing was a joy. His worn raincoat was open and hung loosely about him. In his legs, the muscles of a youth had re-awakened. He strode as if he was no longer weighed down by all his concerns. That morning, he would become a free man again.

As soon as the newspaper was open, Sautereau summoned his colleagues.

"*The Provincial Sun* is going to publish a secret report: the Right Party's scandals. The paper will print, in black and white, what a number of people have been saying to themselves. I've been thinking that 'J'accuse' would be a good headline. 'J'accuse': it will contain everything you haven't dared to say . . . "

Incredulous, the others asked questions. They couldn't believe their ears: a report on the Right Party's scandals! "Why," asked one of the senior journalists, "why must he dig up the dead? It just raises a stink."

Another said:

"It was the people that voted in the Right Party; I don't see why I should write anything against it."

Sautereau replied that the measure of a man is the amount of freedom he will assume. The freedom of a journalist was to write the truth.

"If Le Chef asked me to write something against him I'd do it, but I've got a hunch it's not Le Chef that's asking me now."

Sautereau pleaded: being a journalist was an honor. To be worthy of that honor, the journalist must bear witness to what he knew, not hide the truth from the people or disguise it.

"The editor-in-chief's had a sudden attack of honor," said one of the recalcitrant journalists.

"Nowadays honor means holding on to your job, and I need mine."

"Before I tell the truth I want to see if there's butter on my bread."

"The Right Party's corruption has spread to the news-rooms," Sautereau concluded.

"Does writing the truth mean I can tell about our little outing that night when Sautereau ended up in a double bed?"

The journalists roared with laughter. They'd never before spoken in his presence of that night of celebration and libations. Sautereau glared at his colleague with an authority he hadn't shown before.

"No blackmail will stop me from proclaiming the truth," he concluded, waving them away.

They left his office, grumbling.

"In the old days, at least we had fun."

"We miss it already; now if we have to tell the truth besides . . . "

"I'd be glad to go along with Sautereau, but Le Chef's our boss."

Sautereau completed his scathing editorial. The sentences were short. They stung like a whip. He read it aloud and the walls seemed to reverberate. He read loud enough for the journalists to hear his fury: "Truth dies if it is not expressed."

His office door was pushed open and the knob struck the wall.

"Already!" That was all Sautereau said.

Monsieur Pichette, the Right Party's man in black, came striding in with the determination of one who is about to strike. On top of the rough copy of Sautereau's explosive article, he laid down the fateful picture. The editor-in-chief couldn't stop himself from looking at it, fascinated by this man who, beyond a doubt, was himself (though it was no longer he), with a woman he didn't remember, in a bedroom that was unreal but true. The photograph was both the truth and a lie, memory and forgetfulness. It was just a piece of paper, but he was a prisoner of it as if it were an abyss where he'd fallen, mortally wounded.

"Monsieur Pichette, there's one thing stronger than blackmail: the truth."

"Sautereau, don't get so worked up, you're spitting in my face. You think your wife will like this picture of you and the redhead . . ."

"My wife knows everything," Sautereau lied, turning red. "I confessed and she's forgiven me. So, Monsieur Pichette, show me the respect you owe a man who's about to institute proceedings against you, for blackmail and psychological torture."

"Sautereau, your kids'll love to see their old man lying there beside a fat hen as if she was their mother."

Sautereau, struck dumb, restrained himself from falling to his knees and pleading for clemency. He had not given any thought to the pain of anyone but Méloppée. He hadn't thought of the pain the picture might cause his children. He could never appear before his children if their eyes had seen the photograph that dishonored him.

"Women," Monsieur Pichette went on, "forget nothing, but they do forgive, whereas children never forgive. When they're little old men, Sautereau, and you've long since turned to dust, your kids'll still be ashamed of you. Is there any finer feeling than being proud of your father? Sautereau, your kids will never know that joy. And your wife's forgiveness won't give them back their pride. Sautereau, your children will never talk about you to your grandchildren. Your daughters-in-law, Sautereau, will never let you hold your children's children in your arms. If I let this picture get out of my hands, Sautereau, you'd be better off dead. Now me, I don't wish you any harm. And neither does the Right Party. Of all the Right Party's friends, you want to be the first to spit in the face of Le Chef. Has Le Chef ever done you any harm? He says you're the best newspaperman in the province; he gave you the most important paper. Has the Right Party done any harm to the province? Remember, Sautereau, what the province was like before Le Chef arrived? Roads built by rabbits, that ran in zigzags."

Monsieur Pichette took some photographs from another pocket and spread them across the rough copy of the devastating editorial. The editor-in-chief had never seen them. Sautereau undressing the fat redhead. Sautereau waving her panties at arm's length. Sautereau drinking from her big breast. Sautereau hefting the redhead's breasts. The redhead kneeling before the naked Sautereau. His heart pounded. His forehead was split by pain. If he published his "J'accuse," Monsieur Pichette's photographs would kill him with shame; passersby who looked at his epitaph and read his name by chance would wonder:

"Is that the Sautereau, the intellectual that got his picture taken bare-assed with a fat woman?"

The passerby would continue his visit along the paths, laughing at the salacious exploits that legend would attribute to Sautereau. If he didn't publish "J'accuse," he would become the journalist who turned away to avoid looking at the truth. Méloppée wouldn't love a servile man for long. His children wouldn't long respect a father who showered praise on corruption. After his death, someone would write: "This was a journalist whose conscience consisted of keeping silent." Sautereau was condemned to shame. Destroyed, his heart racing, a migraine tormenting his head, he refused to accept his fall from grace. Life, which he had scoffed at, was given another chance in this defeated man. Suddenly he knew that he was going to live. He knew he could save himself. He knew he could escape from shame. He realized he'd got out of his chair. Never before had he stayed on his feet before Monsieur Pichette. He heard his own voice say calmly and steadily:

"Put those pictures away; they humiliate you as much as me. I won't publish 'J'accuse,' or anything else against the Right Party."

"Le Chef told me, Bark and Sautereau'll shit his pants in fear."

"Monsieur Pichette," Sautereau went on, his voice amazingly self-assured, "if you keep those pictures to yourself you'll be saving my life. I can show gratitude, but I intend to do something better."

"Watch it, I'm an honest man: I can't take big sums of money just like that."

"I want to save your life."

"Sautereau, you can save me when you aren't drowning yourself."

"Monsieur Pichette, a journalist is a man with big ears, so he hears everything. The Right Party has enemies. Monsieur Pichette, in your line of work, you have enemies too."

"I'm in no danger. Sautereau, what're you trying to tell me? Don't try blackmail. Don't try and scare me either: I've been hit once or twice in my life, and believe me, I can hit back. What're you hiding from me?"

"I won't publish the report, and if you want to find me, Monsieur Pichette, I'll be on the ten o'clock ferry for the south shore."

When the man in black had left, Sautereau picked up the draft of his editorial. He added additional evidence of scandal. His heart was beating calmly and his headache had gone. He was thinking clearly. His words were finely honed. His journalists were nonchalantly touching up their articles. Sautereau had told them he'd postpone his "J'accuse" because, as he put it, "There's some evidence I have to check, and it's best to verify our evidence three times instead of two, so that our report will be as indisputable as a sword-thrust." His colleagues, accustomed to singing the Right Party's praises, were hardly surprised by this about-face. They had seen Monsieur Pichette. They knew that the man in black carried a lot of weight with the Right Party.

That night, to get to the wharf from which the boat that plied the river between the Capital and the south shore departed, Sautereau decided to walk. The city sloped down toward the river. He need only follow the decline. The distance was greater than he remembered. He no longer had the legs of an eighteen-year-old, when he used to go down to the river, his hand on Méloppée's waist, shivering when her long hair caressed his face.

As soon as he was on board, the mooring cables were unwound and the boat left the wharf. A few minutes later and he would have missed the ten o'clock ferry. He walked between the cars, hands in his raincoat pockets. Travellers were talking about the fine weather and the recent baseball games. Would Monsieur Pichette be there? He must be waiting discreetly in some corner. Sautereau rehearsed what he would say: "Monsieur Pichette, I've found out the Right Party wants to get rid of you because you're becoming an embarrassment. Are you alone? Come with me, I know a quiet spot."

"Sautereau! Over here!"

Sautereau turned around. Monsieur Pichette, a black form leaning over a guard rail at the back, was gazing out at the water stirred up by the propeller. Sautereau approached and leaned over beside him, peering into the choppy water.

"Monsieur Pichette," he said in an undertone, "I've learned that the Right Party wants to get rid of you. Apparently you're becoming an embarrassment."

"What the hell are you talking about, Sautereau? I'm as solid in the Party as the foundations of the Parliament buildings in the Capital."

He hadn't even glanced up briefly in surprise. He was looking at the black water.

"Are you alone?" Sautereau asked.

"I've heard it said the water's a hundred feet deep. The Right Party's gonna dig a tunnel underneath, one of these days, when there's unemployment and plenty of manpower with nothing to do. You hear that? Put that in your paper, Sautereau. Alone? Am I alone? Yes, I'm alone. All alone. I got no wife. Why d'you think Le Chef trusts me? Cause I haven't got a wife. Tell me, Sautereau, why do you think the people trust Le Chef? Cause he hasn't got a wife either. That's what he says. You can put that in your paper too. Yes, I'm alone: on this boat and in my life. I haven't got a wife to scream and yell and claw my face if she sees a snapshot of my naked ass."

He had talked without straightening up, fascinated by the black water.

"Can I talk to you?" asked Sautereau.

"Get to the point."

Sautereau, leaning on the guard rail, peered at the water. It was black. In the distance, it blended with the night. The foam stirred up by the propeller was white. The Capital and all its lights seemed to be drifting, disappearing deep into the black sky.

"Talk, Sautereau!" Monsieur Pichette commanded.

All around them, the shadows were dense; there were no lights at this spot on the deck. There were no lovers billing and cooing. Monsieur Pichette knew about quiet places.

"Monsieur Pichette?"

"Sautereau, you're getting on my nerves!"

"I know a quiet place. Will you come with me, Monsieur Pichette?"

"No!" exclaimed the fat face leaning over the guard rail.

Sautereau's small hands, pushed by arms endowed with amazing strength, nudged the man in black, who swayed over the guard rail.

"Sautereau!"

The ferry boat continued on its routine course. Sautereau asked a number of passengers if they'd seen a man dressed in black. They said he was probably on the upper deck. He went up and inquired again. No one had seen the man. He stopped inquiring.

Sautereau returned to the Capital. For a long time he walked toward the upper town, but when a late bus came into sight he boarded it and slumped on a seat, tired, winded, legs wobbly. It hadn't been hard to get rid of a man. From now on, whenever he looked at the river he would see Monsieur Pichette's shadow in the water. Méloppée would not see it. Sautereau had another secret he must keep from Méloppée. Of that secret, no one had a photograph. He got off the bus and walked home. In the muggy night, some of his neighbors were performing minor tasks: sweeping outside their front doors, watering flower-beds, gossiping. He said hello to them. Sautereau was smiling. They weren't aware that he had killed a man. Neither his children nor Méloppée would ever see the indecent photographs. The river would carry far away the body of the man who had caused him so much anguish. He climbed the stairs. He was eager to see his wife and children. He arrived with all the fervor of one who has returned from a long journey. Méloppée hadn't seen him so happy for ages. She was pleased she hadn't asked him any questions: she understood that men's worries are sometimes so great, they can't talk to a woman about them.

Sautereau hesitated to touch Méloppée's body with hands that had pushed a man into the river. She offered herself. He loved her. For her it was like the old days when their only thought was loving one another. Sautereau was saved. He was free to become the man he was, as the old philosopher had put it. He loved Méloppée so ardently she thought he might be giving her another baby. They fell asleep together, reunited.

Suddenly, he woke up. A nightmare: he was falling into black water. The night was still pitch-black. He tried to get back to sleep, but he could think of nothing but the drowned man. He drew closer to Méloppée's warm body, holding her. He murmured in her ear: "I think I'll be buying that piano soon." She made no reply. She was pretending to sleep; she knew that men make promises and then forget them. Sautereau was still surprised: it is easy to kill a man. Later, he would write an article on the subject. He would conclude by saying: "Killing is so easy, it's surprising that men don't kill more often." His hands still felt the hard back of the big man leaning over the river. He still heard the muffled sound of the body dropping into the foamy water churned up by the propeller. Monsieur Pichette was going down the river, being carried out to sea with the logs and bottles and dead tree trunks. He would not come back and threaten to destroy Sautereau's life. He would drop to the bottom of the river, he would decompose, he would be erased like an old photograph from which the image vanishes. His corpse would be found, swollen like the bodies of cows that are sometimes washed up on shore. How easy it was to kill a man. A single push. It was the river that had taken the man's life. Monsieur Pichette had been attracted by the water, he had leaned over it, he had offered himself to the river, his eyes were seeking the bottom. Sautereau had barely given him a push; he had been merely the river's accomplice. Wasn't it a matter of legitimate self-defence? God had given life to Sautereau so that he could accomplish his mission on earth. Monsieur

Pichette had tried to interfere with that mission. Sautereau, now free, would be able to pursue his path. He would publish "J'accuse." He would write until his articles, like a battering ram, forced down the doors of the Right Party's fortified castle. The people would resume possession of the power the Right Party had usurped. Sautereau drew the curtain aside to look out at the street. The neighborhood was still asleep. He looked at the sky above the houses; he could wait for the light of a new day without remorse. At last, he had been born. He had spent all these years powerless, in the dark belly of a circumstance that had imprisoned him. He was free. He no longer felt Monsieur Pichette's burning gaze upon him. No one had seen him. The river had done it all. Today, *The Provincial Sun* would publish "J'accuse." Every copy of the paper would be a bomb hurled at the Right Party. Before Monsieur Pichette appeared in his life, it had been a ritual for him to press his lips against the warm forehead of Méloppée who stayed in bed, waiting for the children to wake up, while he got up to go to the paper. Monsieur Pichette had almost killed his love. Sautereau knelt beside the bed and pressed his lips to Méloppée's hair. She sighed like a woman in love.

"Life is beginning again," Sautereau whispered.

Tiptoeing, gingerly pushing the door, he went into the children's room to watch them as they slept: what was happiness if not his sleeping children, carried away by dreams they would never remember? They would always yearn for that flight into spaces detached from the earth. His children would not be ashamed of their father. It was time for the news on the radio. Every day, he listened to the news before setting out for the office. His hand trembled as he turned the dial. He set the volume very low. The reader's voice was barely audible. First came the foreign news: puzzling wars between unknown people ("Everywhere throughout the world, the expression of human wickedness depends on local customs," he had once written). He made an effort to understand, for he must explain these wars in his paper. The more he studied them, the more complex and mysterious their tangled causes seemed. In the river, the same toneless voice went on, the lifeless body of a man had been found. He had died recently. In his clothing were papers making identification possible. The corpse was clutching a black hat. In his jacket pocket compromising photographs had been found. They showed a man and woman in erotic and scandalous poses. The police would reveal nothing more. They were continuing the investigation. The man and woman in the photographs could be linked to the death of the man, dressed in black as if wearing his own mourning, the reader pointed out coldly.

Sautereau did not take his raincoat. He left, softly closing the door, he tiptoed down the stairs to avoid waking anyone up. Outside, the light was beautiful. The air smelled fresh, like water. It was a day that seemed destined to be lucky. Instead of heading for the bus that would take him to *The Provincial Sun*, he stopped for a moment to reflect on the simplest way to get to the bridge that straddled the river. His life was over. It was easy to kill a man. It should be just as easy to kill oneself. He did not remember that scandalous night, but because of it he must die. Sautereau did not remember that night, but his wife and children would never forget it. Tears would scald Méloppée's face. He would be guilty of humiliating his children. And yet, he had no more recollection of that fateful night than of a night he had never lived. The light that was painting the leaves and streaming over the pavement was too beautiful to fall on a man like Sautereau. His presence sullied it. Fortunately, the night before, at the office, he had completed his editorial, "J'accuse": that was all he would leave to the people, to Méloppée, to his children. He had no other will, no other property. He was realizing his goal; with "J'accuse," he was entering the fray; he would brandish "J'accuse" because he had become a knight faithful to the truth.

Sautereau watched the river flowing under the bridge as he leaned over the railing. He could have tolerated the pain of his own humiliation, he could have suffered being spat upon once the facts were known, but he could not bear that Méloppée or his children be touched by a single drop of spittle. His hands clutched the railing. The river was so far away, under the bridge; the arches were so high. The water would be cold. It was easier to kill a man than to take one's own life. "J'accuse" would be his vengeance.

A big black car, a Cadillac, drove by so slowly that Sautereau wrenched himself from his contemplation of the water to look at the car, which seemed about to stop beside him. The car was covered with dust, splashed with mud. It was returning from the dirt roads of the country. The windshield was spattered. He knew that face in the shadow. Wasn't it the contractor Verrochio? The car drove past. Sautereau had recognized Verrochio, a road-building contractor, a man who had become wealthy by exploiting workers. His roads melted with the spring thaw; every summer he re-did what the spring had undone. Thus he was living off the fat of the land, from the excessive prices people paid for his roads. He made generous donations to the Right Party's war chest. He handed out bribes to civil servants, MPs and cabinet ministers, and that didn't hurt business. Sautereau had once received an envelope from him marked "For services rendered." The envelope was swollen with new bills. It was Christmas and he had to buy a dress for Méloppée, toys for the children. Verrochio always paid for favors obtained. This time, he had offered his precious wife to the Minister of Roads and Bridges. That, Sautereau would expose in "J'accuse." He would leave Méloppée without ever having been able to give her a piano. Perhaps the mud on Verrochio's car was from the road his wife had enabled him to build by giving herself to the Minister. "J'accuse" was the one good thing Sautereau would have done in his life.

He sat on the parapet, eyes shut, for he was dizzy. His head ached. His head was too small to contain all his suffering. He hoped the water wouldn't be too cold. He leaned over. It is easy to take one's own life, he concluded. Now he couldn't go back.

Sautereau knew that he was dead, but he still had a few moments to think about Méloppée, about the children one by one, all four, the oldest, the youngest . . . "J'accuse," he simply wanted to whisper. A great cold hand flattened his mouth and gripped his throat.

XX

Wherein the tender-hearted discover a lump of stone at their core and the hard of heart find out they're really pussycats

Innocent Loiseau, unable to sleep, tossed and turned all night, quivering with a new strength that had just welled up in him and was working its way through his body as spring swells the buds on trees. His body was prickling with impatience. Every muscle crackled with energy. On that very night, his child's skin split, making way for his young man's body. He was in the process of becoming free. He was about to take on his first job. And so Innocent Loiseau was dressed in suit and tie while the windows were still dark. Once they began to grow pale and the street stood out from the night in the first rays of dawn, Innocent Loiseau raced to the new road construction site. From far away he caught a glimpse of the shed, all white walls and blue roof, perched on its stilts. Outside it, like animals outside the stable, stood a flock of machines all painted blue: trucks, a bulldozer, tractors, a crusher, grease-smeared crates that were padlocked, chained and reinforced with

237

crude hinges. On the wall of the shed, above the padlocked door, Innocent read: BUREAU. This was where his life would begin. Here, on the new road that had not yet been built, he would take his first real step into real life. Innocent Loiseau had been singled out by Le Chef of the Right Party. He watched the light chase away the night and wondered if the things that were happening to him were signs of destiny, inscribed in a place above the sky. On this first day of his real life, Innocent Loiseau found himself standing in an oatfield, assigned to open up a road. That same day, others would be shovelling manure or, in the cities, washing dishes in luxury hotels, selling newspapers at street corners or simply hanging around, bowed down under the weight of their useless youth. Innocent Loiseau had been enthroned as the opener of the new road. That was the mission Le Chef had entrusted to him. He mounted the steps that led to the padlocked office door. He turned around. Gazing at the oatfield undulating in the wind, he felt like the captain of a ship charged with bringing his men safely into harbor. His heart stirred: he knew so little. Now the sky was very bright and all the light of day was falling upon Innocent Loiseau who was alone on the earth. Was this one of the laws of fate? Was it the will of God? He had been designated builder of the new road. Raising his eyes to heaven, he swore he would be worthy of the task.

He sat on the office steps and gazed pensively at the oats. Then, field and sky gradually merged in his mind and he thought of the roads that God had already laid out in His spirit, roads that Innocent Loiseau was to translate into reality on earth.

Suddenly he heard motors growling. Gleaming automobiles were driving right up to his shed. A tall lean man got out of his Cadillac, pouncing like a hungry tiger. The wind blew his straw hat to the ground, but a long arm unwound vigorously and snatched it up. Innocent Loiseau got to his feet, bowing and inclining his head and torso as he'd been taught to do in college, when he was in the presence of authority. He started. A hand was squeezing his shoulder. He thought he felt claws digging into his flesh to the bone.

"I'm Verrochio," said the man in a lilting accent. "If you not know Verrochio, better run home to mamma."

If Innocent Loiseau hadn't been so well educated, he'd have pissed his pants, he was so impressed. At his side stood Verrochio, the famous contractor, millionaire, builder of roads, the man chosen by Le Chef to give the province a network of new roads.

"What's your name?"

"Innocent. Innocent Loiseau."

"Mamma mia! Innocent! Not many people could live up to a name like that! When the new road's open, you'll have to change it. Your little birdy, he'll lose some feathers!"

There was a jingling of keys. Verrochio kicked open the door.

"This," he proclaimed, "is the office of Verrochio Construction International. And inside here, Innocent or Nino Verrochio, she's the same thing, the very same. If you take orders from Innocent, it's Verrochio's orders. You're my eyes and my ears."

At the back of the shed stood a makeshift table — a sheet of plywood laid across two sawhorses. The dirty window filtered a greyish light. Against the wall, a paint-spattered filing cabinet. Verrochio clinked his key ring. He opened the filing cabinet. He checked the labels on some of the files.

"What's in here, she's none of your business. But because you're my eyes and my ears, I'm tell you: it's the list of the members of the Right Party and the forms for collecting the Party's share. The foreman, he's look after that. The foreman, he's make the road run over the Right Party's land; if the land belongs to the Opposition, we make a detour. But you, Innocent, you're my eyes and my ears, so I want you to watch out for the foreman: you write down the day, you write down the time, you make me a report. When the foreman sees you, he's crawl on his hands and knees, because Verrochio or Innocent, it's the same thing."

Innocent Loiseau's heart was quivering with delight. Never had he thought he would become so powerful so soon. His first job, and already he was a boss!

"You're my partner," said Verrochio, hugging Innocent against his bony chest.

Then he took a telephone from the filing cabinet and set it on the table, tossing the cord in the corner.

"Should I call you if there's any problems?"

"Innocent, you think I got nothing better to do than answer phone calls? You're my eyes and my ears. When I'm come, you make your report. That phone, we don't have to hook it up. Leave it on the table. The workers, they'll see you're my eyes and my ears."

Innocent couldn't resist; he went and sat on the stool behind the table and stroked the telephone. Verrochio tossed him some keys.

"I'm want you here in the office before the others in the morning, and after the others at night. If you aren't here, you aren't my eyes and my ears."

"You can trust me; I know about responsibility."

Innocent dared not ask so trivial a question as: "When do I get paid and how much?" That would insult the contractor who had given him his trust. Innocent refrained from succumbing to anything so vulgar as worrying about his salary. Instead, he asked:

"Monsieur Verrochio, what's the secret of your success?"

The contractor gazed suspiciously at the naive young man. Was it known, here in this isolated region, that he had been relieved of his duties, driven to the brink of failure, rejected by the Right Party? Had this Innocent been warned that the strip of road to be built here in a cow pasture, in the middle of nowhere, had been tossed at him like a buoy thrown at a drowning man? Had this Innocent been informed that the buoy had been tossed at him only after his wife's appeal to the Minister of Roads and Bridges? The man whose life had begun on an island parched by a blazing sun, who had begun a second life in his new country by weeding the gardens of the rich, who had risen to become a powerful contractor, didn't know what to say; he stammered, he was shaken by this innocent who blushed when he spoke to him. Innocent's question disturbed the man who had given orders to hundreds of workers, who had cut through mountains, filled in rivers, put up bridges, who had confronted Le Chef. Innocent was hoping for a magic reply, for words that would change his life. Verrochio decided not to hesitate, but to forge ahead like a bulldozer, always making an impression:

"Never accept defeat. That's my first key. The loser loses because he accepts defeat. I'm always win because I'm not know the meaning of defeat. Defeat? No such thing. That's for other people. I'm win because I don't know how to lose. Never lose: that's the first key, the key for outside. Inside, in your own house, there's another key: your wife. A man, he's worth as much as his wife. If you want to know a man, know him deep down, go and meet his wife. A man without a wife, he's dangerous. You can't get to know him, how he attacks, his weak points. No wife: that man, he's not know himself. Me, I've got a perfect wife, she's the light of my life; I live for my light. That's *amore*. I'm love her, she's love me. A wife that's loved, she's a second heart for a man. Two keys: never lose; and have a wife like my Lucia. You, do you love a woman?"

"I'm too young, Monsieur!"

"What do you love?"

"Lots of things. Books, history, nature, the good Lord, the work I'm going to do for you. And life . . . all of life . . . "

"Life without a woman, she's no life. It was a woman that brought you into the world; now you need a woman to give you life every day. A man comes into the world in the morning and he dies at night. Without a woman, there's no resurrection. Understand?"

"Monsieur, I'll wait till it's time for me to have a woman."

"If the Klondike gold diggers had waited for the gold to land on their tables, they'd've found nothing. You have to go out and look, not wait. Win!"

"You can't always win. All the great men — Julius Caesar, Napoleon, Hitler, Mussolini, all the great men have known defeat."

"Losers always give examples like that. Losers all went to the same school. Lose? I never learned that word."

Verrochio left the office, shouting at the team of surveyors arguing over their plans:

"Don't dawdle! Get to work before winter!"

The surveyors laughed. Verrochio was overflowing with Italian joy. It was June; winter was barely over; it wouldn't return all that soon.

Verrochio hopped into his Cadillac. Innocent waved as his boss drove away. In Saint-Toussaint-des-Saints the men were not so forceful. Monsieur Verrochio's power was not, like the power of animals and the village men, in his muscles; his power was elsewhere. The man had only to want things and they were done. Monsieur Verrochio had come from Italy to build roads in America. There was a mystery about Monsieur Verrochio. Was that what gave him his power? The black-robed men at the college were as mushy as porridge compared with Monsieur Verrochio. Le Chef had chosen him. To move mountains, as it says in the Bible: that's what the man was capable of. Innocent had been singled out to be his eyes, his ears. Following some mysterious logic, Innocent's path had crossed Monsieur Verrochio's. Merely being in his presence gave Innocent a power he'd never felt before.

"Innocent," the contractor reminded him from the open car door, "don't forget to write in your ledger the time the men start work and when they finish."

The door slammed. Innocent waved, ecstatically happy that he too had become a builder of roads.

The Cadillac took off with a a roar, amid a hail of pebbles and a cloud of gritty dust. Verrochio had noticed Innocent's smile. This country lad knew more than he let on. Before he was given this job in the office, he must have heard about Verrochio's betrayal, his contribution to the Opposition, he must have heard descriptions of how Verrochio had grovelled before the Minister of Roads and Bridges like a dog asking for a treat. The boy must have been told about how Verrochio's wife had saved him from ruin.

Lucia had saved him, but that salvation was more deadly than failure. To save her husband's honor, she had lost her own and destroyed her husband's too. Lucia had come home late, her hair gave off the smell of cigar smoke. She had told him he was saved. Early the next morning, he found out he'd been given a road to build in the Appalachians. Young Innocent in the office must have known all that. No doubt he knew other facts of which Verrochio himself was ignorant. Innocent was smiling. The contractor had dealt with men who were stronger than he and he'd never lost his footing. Now that his wife had given herself as a bribe, the smile of a child burned his soul like a brand. Verrochio pumped the accelerator. Tears came to his eyes. He had been a man of iron. Now he was just a man in tears.

Innocent Loiseau came up to the team of surveyors and said, swelling his voice and injecting as much guttural harshness as he could:

"When you start to work I'll write the time in my black book."

"We're thinking," came the mocking retort from a man leaning on the theodolite like a crutch. "When you're belly-button's dry, my boy, you'll know, a surveyor's job is to think!"

"I'll note the time when you start working," said Innocent firmly. "Minus thirty minutes for insulting the supervisor."

Innocent didn't stop when the laughter exploded behind him. In retaliation, he decided to dock an hour off every employee. Like Verrochio, he would win. He went back in the shed. He knew it was no coincidence that had brought him to this office. Outside this shed a new road would run, but even more, the unknown road of his destiny would pass.

Far from Saint-Toussaint-des-Saints, far from this humiliating strip of road, Verrochio wept. He had loved his wife. Even possessing Lucia, he desired her. He desired her more each time he possessed her. His wife was as important to him as his heart. She had sacrificed herself out of love. Without a doubt, her soul had been filled with disgust when she lent her body to the smoky caresses of the Minister of Roads and Bridges. What could she offer but her body? She possessed nothing because the Right Party had ruined her husband. She had paid for her husband's rehabilitation with her body. Lucia's body . . . more beautiful than the most beautiful statues in Italy, more beautiful than the girls in the magazines he bought . . . Her body wasn't in a museum in Italy or on a page of glazed paper: it was in his house, in his bed. Verrochio could caress it, he could press against its milky warmth that always mingled with some precious perfume. Verrochio wept. He turned on the windshield wipers, sure that it was raining. His abstraction made him smile through his tears. Lucia had saved him through love. She was his light and light does not lie. On occasion, at country inns or farms, he had loved the bodies of girls toughened by work in the fields; even in the Capital, at times, he had felt such ardor

243

that he sped to some house of love, but he had never loved any woman but Lucia. He felt no remorse, only a certain sadness in his soul when he couldn't fight nature. He didn't wipe the tears that slid down his cheeks. He turned off the windshield wiper.

Did she still love him? Lucia had come home from her charitable evening late. Her dress was creased. Evenings of good works don't leave you creased like that. She smelled of cigars. Charitable ladies don't smoke cigars. The Minister of Roads and Bridges was always smoking a cigar. Lucia had said hello without looking at him and told him he was saved as she fled into her bedroom. She had taken a bath. Longer than usual. In bed, Lucia had turned away sharply when he laid his hand on her thigh. Lucia had saved him, not through love but because she didn't want to be a ruined man's wife. She had sold herself to the Minister so she wouldn't be poor. Verrochio wept. He couldn't see anything. The windshield was clouded with dust that turned to a curtain of mud. It was raining now. Verrochio wept as if he had learned that Lucia had died. In future he must hate that woman, that fearful bitch who had licked the hand that promised her a pittance. He wept and he stepped on the gas. He remember that in the inn near the lake there was a girl whose bosom deserved comparison with Mont Orignal.

XXI

Onward to power!

Seated at his table, Innocent Loiseau dusted the telephone
with his handkerchief. Would he be able to return to college in the autumn, to bend over books, to sit before a
teacher who would talk about ancient things, after he had,
in real life, built a real road? Until now he had spent his
life writing on paper; now he would write in trees, in fields,
in bedrock, in hills. Rather than writing with ink, he would
write with gravel, pebbles, stones, concrete, dynamite, and
instead of holding a pen, he would use trucks, bulldozers,
steam shovels. Like a man, he was building. His surveyors
hadn't got down to work yet, but they had assembled their
instruments — stakes, pickets, chain, axes; they had unrolled plans; they were chatting. Innocent went out. He
gazed at them as Monsieur Verrochio would have done:
a gaze filled with contempt and threats. He listened, al-
lowing each word to be engraved on his memory so he
could report it to Monsieur Verrochio. The surveyors were
commenting on an item they'd read in *The Provincial Sun*.
The bodies of two men had been found in the river. One
was carrying compromising photographs of the other.

"A man that goes into politics has to win. Otherwise he's
better off jumping off a bridge."

"If he doesn't jump, he'll be pushed."

"Winning in politics often means pushing somebody off a bridge."

"Quiet! Innocent's listening."

"Innocent can't hear a thing: he knows the new road might run a long way from his father's land."

Innocent must not lose. He warned them:

"I'll tell everything."

"We could drive the bulldozer over the little bugger."

"Anyhow," said the chief surveyor, shouldering his theodolite, "those two bodies they fished out of the river weren't wearing stones around their necks. It's politics that sank them."

"All we know is, we can't know. The truth's in the Bible, not the papers."

"The truth isn't anywhere. It's in everybody's interest to conceal it."

"If we let the truth out on the roads in this province, who knows what'd happen."

"Before Le Chef, after Le Chef, with Le Chef — politics is always politics."

Innocent went back inside. He'd chop another few minutes off the surveyors' time. He must not lose. Win. He must learn to be as hard as the rock that is not defiled by the wings of a passing bird. Turn his heart to stone. A prayer rose to his lips.

"Saint Opportun, help me become a man!"

The little saint had been chosen by God, whose ever mysterious hand had guided him toward heavenly paths. Perhaps God had also selected Innocent to guide him along earthly paths? He and Opportun came from the same village. One was travelling now on heaven's unknown paths; the other was taking his first steps along earthly roads. Why should the village child now in Heaven not help out the one still on earth? From the window, Innocent looked at the sky through dust and cobwebs, and pleaded with Saint Opportun to help him never to lose. Opportun was very young to understand the meaning of his prayer, but Innocent had learned that saints possess innate knowledge. Bringing his gaze back to earth, he saw the surveyors in the oatfield, preparing to draw their first line. He noted the time.

In his Cadillac, Verrochio was weeping. He had lost Lucia. He had lost his love. He would lose his business. Ruined, he would have to go back to weeding gardens. As a humble gardener he had been poor, but he'd been so near the ground no one could think of pushing him off his pedestal. How far it was to that inn where he knew a plump girl! The strip of road to be built in these godforsaken woods was one last dream before awakening. He had won everything; he would lose everything. Such is life. You possess her, she possesses you, she leaves you. He had come from little Sardinia, poor as a stone. In magical America, the stone had been transformed into a diamond. And now those who had made him rich were ruining him. They were taking Lucia from him, a woman far too beautiful for a miserable, overly ambitious foreigner. He must forget Lucia. She was only a lovely souvenir in the memory of a wounded man. Lucia hadn't wanted to save him; Lucia had fled a ruined man the way the princess in an old Sardinian tale took flight from a leper. He had lost everything, but wasn't losing all that a man was permitted to do?

As long as he lived, Innocent Loiseau would never forget Monsieur Verrochio's advice. He had been told that the rich were miserly and tough. Yet with great generosity Monsieur Verrochio had unstintingly shared the secrets of making a fortune. Innocent would always remember the two keys: a) there is no such thing as defeat; b) have a wife who loves you. Innocent would try to forget the word "defeat." But a wife? He didn't know any women. No woman loved him. In the college, there were only boys. The black-robed priests couldn't take a woman's place. That was why he was only an angel roaming the earth, an adolescent lost among the workmen. He was nothing because he didn't have a wife who loved him. Why would any woman love him? He didn't have a fancy car to drive her to the Capital or take her dancing. He didn't know how to dance. He only knew how to skate, to kneel in chapel, and to yawn through long hours of black-robed men talking Latin. He'd never have a wife who would be the soul of the great man he would become . . . A wife: he wouldn't dare to touch her hand for fear of getting burned in the fire of her flesh.

Talk to her? He'd rather run away, because he didn't know what to say to a woman . . . Win. There's no such thing as defeat. Win. Always win, Monsieur Verrochio had said. He would learn to touch women. He would learn how to talk to them. Like a conqueror, he picked up the phone:

"Hello! Mademoiselle, I'm calling you because I want to open up my heart. I love you and if you love me, well, um . . . If you love me, you'll open up too, like me, you'll open your, um, heart, and . . . and . . . it's hard to admit you're in love and . . . and . . . if we're on the same road and . . . and . . . if we avoid collisions, we should be united in love, at the inn of happiness."

He replaced the receiver. It was hard to talk to a woman. He'd learn. Never lose . . . He was glad the phone wasn't hooked up. How ridiculous he'd have been if he'd really been talking to a woman! He must get rid of these doubts . . . And of course if a real woman had heard his romantic declaration, she'd have been won over. To win. He had been singled out to win. He went out to check that the surveyors were still at work.

The oldest was looking through a device mounted on a tripod; he was waving at a man who stood deep in the oatfield and held a blue-and-white painted stake. Another man was measuring. Still others were pounding in a row of pickets. To keep sight of them in the golden wheat, they'd been painted red.

It was along these pickets that Innocent's road would run.

XXII

Must one be snuffed out to travel at the speed of light?

After granting the Minister of Roads and Bridges permission to build the new road across his land, a shamefaced Cytriste Tanguay went back home. He was a traitor. To his friends in the Opposition, he had shown himself to be a very great general in the rotten egg attack on the Right Party, which was hiding under Saint Opportun's halo. To the cabinet ministers, he had seemed a wily peasant. Cytriste Tanguay knew he was a craven coward. He hesitated before going inside his house, working hard at being busy. His pride, his lofty pride, was gone with the wind. He was a turncoat. When his men were bombarding the Right Party's friends with rotten eggs, Cytriste Tanguay felt so tall it seemed he was towering over the poplars where his artillerymen perched with their stinking ammunition. With his rifle trained on the Local Riding Minister, he had felt so tall above the oats, the sky itself served as his cap. Now he was as reluctant to go inside the house as a schoolboy with a bad report card. He had given his wife a number of children; the children had become men and women who had in turn made children, who were growing up too fast. Yet Cytriste Tanguay was only a little man, gnawed by shame. He propped his rifle against the wall and slumped, woebegone, into the room where his old parents were waiting for death. It had forgotten to come for them.

They knew that their reign was over. They had worked long enough, seen enough days and nights, seen enough children grow up to become men, they had seen enough melting snow and flowering springs. The time had come; they were no longer hungry, no longer thirsty. They lay in their bed, waiting for the moment when Curé Fourré would come, with the altar boy and the holy water, to shut their eyes for the Final Journey.

Cytriste drew up to the bed. Would he go to his father's side or his mother's? It would be easier to confess his deed to his mother. Slowly he advanced a little further. Like a good soldier, Cytriste Tanguay had fought to the end to prevent the new road from cutting through his land, but he had laid down his rifle and capitulated for several good reasons. Now he must tell his parents. It was they who had first been opposed to the building of the road. Evariste-Cytriste Tanguay, father of Cytriste and son of Trefflé-Cytriste Tanguay, who was himself the son of Sinaï-Cytriste Tanguay, son of Désiré-Cytriste Tanguay, had decided as a man who had lived his whole life in the same house, with the same wife, and ploughed the same land, that the Right Party's government had no right to build a public road on private land without the agreement of the hereditary and traditional owner of that land. Cytriste's father had ordered him to fight the Right Party until he'd won. He had failed. Cytriste was not a man of the past. He knew that progress was like a rainstorm that multiplies harmless plants as well as harmful ones. He had defended himself against the assault, but he was more than a little proud that he had been courted by progress. His "No" had been a traditional response, because generation after generation in his family had said No to anything that might change their lives, but then he'd been quite glad to hear himself say "Yes" to the Ministers. How could he explain that to his father and mother, as they waited for death to carry them away in a black catafalque, along a road that human eyes can't see?

His mother had backed up her husband enthusiastically. For a long time they had thought as one. One felt the aches in the other's bones. The same folds wrinkled the flesh of each. The one suffered from the other's rheumatism. The words of one recounted the other's thoughts. In their souls lived the souls of five or six generations of ancestors, who didn't want a piece of land built on so much suffering to be broken up. Cytriste, a son unworthy of the treasure that had fallen into his hands, had allowed the Ministers to trespass on his sacred land. The Minsters paid dearly. Cytriste had, as they said, pulled off a good deal. ("Hard cash, hard as a Minister's heart.") How would he explain to his parents what he'd done? He was a man glad of his profit, but even more he was a guilty child. He deserved to be punished. How would he confess his misdeed? He took tiny, imperceptible steps toward his mother, sneaking up as if he were approaching a rebellious horse. He waited for the propitious moment, listening to his parents' breathing. Then all at once, as if throwing a halter over a surprised creature, he blurted out:

"I ceded the right of way."

"Can't hear you," moaned the old lady hoarsely. Her minuscule head, creased to the bone, was so light it floated on the feather pillow.

"Come closer!" the little voice commanded. "Get on your knees so I can hear your lying voice."

Cytriste knelt by the bed.

"What was it you said, boy?" asked the worn old voice.

"I said," Cytriste replied, "I sold the right of way for the new road across our property."

A skinny yellow hand at the end of an arm as thin as a broom-handle popped out of the covers, then landed with a bony sound against the face of the son whose eyes filled with tears. He was a humiliated child, overflowing with rage and vengeance he couldn't appease.

"What'd you do, son?" the far-away voice rebuked him.

"Ceded the right of way across our property for the new road."

The hand's fine bones were imprinted on Cytriste's other cheek. He realized he'd wet his pants.

"New road — we don't need no new road, do we old man?"

Under the covers, from the other pillow, came a voice as harsh as the sound nails make in boards, in the dead of winter.

"Nope, old girl, we don't need no new road."

"Don't want no new road across our property, eh old man?"

"Old girl, we don't want no new road across our property."

"So we better get up like we did in the days when we obeyed the good Lord's commandment to get up and work."

"It means we're gettin' up, old girl, like when we used to get up."

"First we better put some soup in our stomachs, old man."

"A drop of beef broth, maybe a bit of white bread, old girl, if we don't want the wind to blow us away."

Dry laughter creaked like rusty hinges.

"You're still a funny man, old man . . . "

An old bird cooed scratchily,

"Didn't have much time to make you laugh when we were on this earth, old girl, but when we're on our Final Journey, hee! hee! I'll make you laugh like you never laughed in your life!"

"But we don't need no new road to . . . "

" . . . laugh, old girl. Hee . . . hee!"

" . . . for our Last Journey, you old fool . . . hee! . . . hee!"

At the end of their lives, Amandine and Evariste-Cytriste, with their twisted, dried-out, gnarled, scraggy bodies, and their shrivelled faces, had become twins who laughed the same laugh.

The daughter-in-law, Cytriste's wife — she'd lost her own name when she joined this family — was amazed when the old folks asked for food. They hadn't eaten for days now. She'd become accustomed to their fast and recently she'd stopped insisting they have "just a bite." She'd even stopped worrying about their latest whim: the old fools were letting themselves starve to death. They didn't complain, so she left them alone in their room, where they stayed in bed like newlyweds. They didn't seem tired from sleeping too many nights together. The daughter-in-law was a little irritated when the old folks asked for soup and bread. ("At their age they get to be like kids in diapers: change their minds three times when they go peepee. Still, these two aren't at the squalling stage yet . . . But everything else, they're just like babies . . . Life's no joke.") The daughter-in-law no longer provided for the old folks' portion: if she gave them soup, there'd be less for the others' bowls. ("They're selfish, those old folks . . . Think just because they're old, they're entitled to more than the rest of us . . . But what the heck are they doing anyway, except waiting to die?")

Muttering, the daughter-in-law brought their food. She listened, irritated, to the old couple slurp their soup, lapping it, wheezing and choking; she heard them nibble the crust of bread, clucking like hens as they chewed. The daughter-in-law had forgotten how much noise the old couple made when they ate.

"Now you've got some soup in your belly, you must be feeling strong, eh young fellow? Hee! hee! hee!"

"The daughter-in-law's soup in your belly makes you strong, eh young lady? Hee! hee! hee!"

"I want more soup."

"Me too, and bread . . . Hee! hee! hee!"

"But we don't want no new road."

"No new road, hee! hee! hee!"

"Just home-made soup!"

"And bread! hee! hee! hee! hee! hee!"

The daughter-in-law was scandalized to hear them demand more food. ("They'll tear a hole in their stomachs, the old fools; they fast for weeks like Jesus in the desert, then out of the blue they decide to eat like pigs. Two feet in the grave and they still want to commit the sin of gluttony.") Accustomed to serving, she filled their bowls with beef broth and sliced more bread. If they'd decided to eat again, it must mean they'd changed their minds about their Final Journey. The daughter-in-law wished she could ask Cytriste if there was any reason why they should start feeding the two useless old creatures in their bed, but he had emerged from their room deathly pale, slamming the door so hard that one day it would break the glass, which had been hand-painted by a passing artist years ago. It would be fine with her if he smashed it to bits: they were the only ones in Saint-Toussaint-des-Saints who had such painted glass. A dark little man in a green rowboat was fishing in the blue water at the base of a high waterfall seething with white eddies, under a foam of grey clouds lit by a red sun around which black birds were wheeling. It would be fine with her if an accident destroyed that hideous scene. Then she could replace it with a nice modern door like she'd seen advertised in *The Provincial Sun*.

A few days earlier, the old folks had decided to let themselves die. They had announced, the way you announce a marriage, that they were setting off along death's highway. Why, the daughter-in-law wondered, had they decided now all of a sudden that they no longer wanted to die? They had told the whole family they were setting out together on their Final Journey because they'd lived long enough. Now, suddenly, they had demanded soup and bread. And asked for more. ("Not only won't the old folks leave an inheritance, if they start eating like they used to they'll ruin us before they go.")

Amandine and Evariste-Cytriste Tanguay had been waiting for death a long time. They had watched grandchildren and great-grandchildren grow up. They had seen the seasons return so many times, seen so many diseases pass by; they had seen so many young people grow old, they had heard everything people had to say repeated so many times, but they felt that soon the world and life would change. They didn't want to see that. They were too old to bow to new winds. They had decided they would stop waiting for death, and summon it. If they simply stopped eating, death would come. Cytriste and his wife weren't terribly worried: if the old folks wanted to die, it meant they'd come to the end of their road. They were quite right to think they'd seen enough of life.

And so Amandine and Evariste-Cytriste wanted to die. At noon one day, in front of all the children, they announced that they were setting out on the Final Journey. Then they ate their cabbage soup and a big helping of boiled beef and vegetables, asking for plenty of carrots and turnips; they finished and asked for more; and when there was nothing left, they wiped their plates with bread. When the plates were shiny clean, they announced it was their final meal. Since then, they had eaten nothing. Where had they got the idea of starving themselves like old animals tired of life? The two old folks had left the table and gone hand-in-hand to their bedroom, to wait for death to close their eyes. They'd been smiling ever since.

The old folks had announced their decision to die after Mass. Cytriste had slept through Curé Fourré's sermon. Curé Fourré just had to spread his arms in the pulpit and Cytriste fell fast asleep. His wife had listened. She remembered the sermon. He had talked about life after death. He had told about the final sigh of those about to die:

"The soul abandons the body the way a sailor abandons a sinking ship. The soul is invisible, like breathing, but your breath exists, though you can't see it. The proof that it exists is that, in winter — when the snow is hard and the icicles hanging from the roofs are sharp and glittering and the sun is bright and the wind cuts through you like a scythe and your tears freeze your eyelashes together — when you breathe you can see your breath swirl in the wind like white smoke. On those bitterly cold days, when you can see your breath, you have proof that your breath exists. Your soul, though, even on the bitterest cold days, you can't see it, but it exists. And after your body's dead, your soul exists whether it's hot or cold, it lives. Your living soul leaves your body, but if you could see it, you'd see that it looks like your body. It lives the way your body used to live, doing everything your body used to do, but invisibly. Only God will see your soul. Other souls won't see yours. You won't see theirs. Invisibly, the souls of the dead eat, walk, smoke, go to Mass, live with their families, in their houses, they plough the fields. After death, life goes on, but without the weight of your body, without the hardness of your bones. When you're dead, my most very dear brethren, your souls won't let any obstacle stop them. Your souls will pass through walls, through stone, through concrete, like water running into water. You will be weightless. Your souls will travel at the speed of light and light travels as fast as thought. Most very dear brethren, when my servant switches on a light in the living room of the presbytery, the next door neighbor (who's always spying on your Curé instead of doing penance for her sins — which would be a lot better for her eternal salvation), my neighbor sees the light in the window and thinks: Curé Fourré's servant just turned on a light. And that's the meaning of the speed of light. Your souls will travel at that speed. Your bodies will be in their coffins, sleeping peacefully. Your soul will ask itself: 'I wonder what I should do after my morning prayers today?' And maybe it will answer: 'Today, I'd like to go to Rome and see our Holy Father the Pope.' No sooner said than done: your soul will be in Rome, it will see the most Holy Father, even touch him if it wants. And that's what it means to travel at the speed of thought and light. How beautiful life will be after death, if your soul isn't driven into the scarlet flames of blackest hell from whence the souls of the damned never emerge. Most very dear brethren, you must choose: choose to have your souls locked up in the infernal gloom forever, or to travel at the speed of thought and light. Choose: a soul as free as light and thought that can go to Rome whenever it wants, or a soul locked in flames that can never escape from hell."

Since he had stopped working in the fields, Evariste-Cytriste Tanguay no longer slept through Curé Fourré's sermons. In the past, when his body was exhausted from his long day's work, the first Latin phrase was enough to send him into the realms of deepest sleep. This time, though, he had listened to Curé's Fourré's words to the end, without succumbing to snoring slumber. Amandine knew he wasn't just pretending, to please his pious old wife. He appeared to understand everything that was being said, and to attach great importance to it. After Mass, Amandine was amazed when the old man put his arm around her and drew her to him; it was an affectionate gesture from the early days of their marriage, which he'd long since forgotten.

"Amandine, life's taken us a long way, we've seen plenty of birthdays we never thought we'd see, but old girl, we ain't seen much of the world."

"We ain't seen the world. You, old man, you used to go to the Capital every year, or just about. You'd tell me about your trip, you old hypocrite, but I know you didn't tell me everything you saw. I still haven't seen the Capital."

"You weren't listening to Curé Fourré. He explained how the Holy Gospels tell us dying's just the same as living. Two good old people like us, we could be a lot happier dead than alive. We could travel. Wouldn't you like that, old girl, to do some travelling? Visit new horizons? Countries full of pagans?"

"Sure, old man! I'd'a liked to see the Holy Father's city before I died, and where our ancestors came from in the old country and the country where the Blessed Virgin showed herself . . . I've never gone past our fence-line. Sometimes I'd look out at the mountains and I'd think, far away must be a nice place. But it was only missionaries and soldiers and big shots that could go on trips. You weren't a missionary, because a missionary can't make children; and you gave me nineteen, old man, and that's not counting the ones that wouldn't come to term, hee! hee! We aren't soldiers, and a good thing too, because why bother going to the end of the world if all that's waiting is a bullet in the head? And I'm not a big shot's wife. So all that means is, we've never seen our ancestors' country or our Holy Father the Pope's city or the mountains or the blessed apparitions."

Evariste-Cytriste pressed his wife's arm a little harder against his bony, quivery old body.

"Amandine, if you wanted I could take you to see the Pope's city . . . hee ! hee!"

"Old liar, always pulling my leg. I'm not a little girl that still believes men's fibs, hee! hee!"

"You heard Curé Fourré's sermon? When we're dead we can travel faster than lightning. Amandine, if you wanted I could show you the Pope's city, like Magloire Cauchon's going to show Desneiges, and our ancestors' country (we never been there, Amandine, and it's as if we never went inside our father's house), then we could go and kneel at the mountain where the Blessed Virgin comes for her apparitions . . . "

"It'd be a nice trip all right . . . "

"Curé Fourré said you've got to be dead to take that kind of wonderful long trip . . . "

"It'd be more fun than rocking in our creaky old chairs. But we'd have to be dead, old man . . . "

"Dying's easier than living, old girl; it's like going to sleep, and then the Final Journey that comes after, it's as beautiful as a dream, but this time old girl, the dream would be real!"

"The Pope's city must be a real nice place, but what I really want to see is Florida. There's no winter, no blizzards where the village seems to be inside a cloud, it's always summer and there's trees that grow fruit; there's never any ice on the windows when you want to look outside."

"I'll take you to Florida, old girl, if that's what you want."

"Old fool, hee! hee! You trying to say you're a millionaire? You found a suitcase full of gold at the end of a rainbow?"

"When we're dead, old girl, we'll be a lot richer than a millionaire."

"Is that another one of your fibs, old man, like you used to tell me before we got married?"

"Ain't me that said it, it's Curé Fourré, and he studied the Gospels. When our old carcasses won't hold our souls any more, we'll be able to take long trips: we won't need money, we won't need roads or trains, we'll be able to travel like light."

"Old man, we're alive. You can't shake off life like a cold. Sure I'd like to die, but I've got enough life to last a century."

"Me too."

"What we can see ain't too pretty."

"We'd better die, old girl. Whadda you say?"

"Hee! Hee! Hee! Yes, old man."

"Me too, I want to die. Hee! Hee! Hee!"

"We'll take a long trip, the both of us."

"Sure, old girl. Dying don't hurt?"

"It's like going to sleep."

"And when we wake up we'll be in Florida?"

"Curé Fourré told us: our souls will travel faster than thought; you'll just think about the Pope's city and you'll be a lot farther away than Magloire Cauchon and his Desneiges."

"But Florida's where I want to go."

"Our souls'll be able to go everywhere."

"What do we have to do to die?"

"Stop eating."

"Just as well; I've had enough of the daughter-in-law's slop. If we didn't have iron stomachs we'd be poisoned."

"We'll starve ourselves to death because the good Lord hasn't come for us. Hee! hee! hee!"

"When you and me are dead, we'll sit tight on a thought, get a good hold on each other's arms, then we'll be off on the Final Journey hee! hee! hee!"

"And when we open our eyes we'll see Florida . . . "

"Yeah, I'd like to go to Florida; you're safe from winter there . . . "

Since that day they had eaten nothing. They wanted to be snuffed out by hunger like logs devoured by fire, then fly away, their souls side by side, lighter than smoke, invisible, passing through walls and flying faster than birds.

"I'll take you to the moon hee! hee! hee!"

"That's way too high, old man, I'd get dizzy . . . I'd rather be in Florida. I'd like to spend a whole winter without freezing. All my life, when winter came to the house I had frost in my joints that didn't melt till late spring. I'd rather go to Florida than see the Pope."

"Old girl, what you needed to warm you up wasn't a wood stove, you needed the sun in the house hee! hee! hee!"

"Old man, I didn't think about my own happiness very often in my life, but I'd like to go to Florida like the big shots."

"Only thing holding us back is our bodies; old girl, we'll get thin, our bodies will be like string, like wire, then they'll snap in the wind; our souls will float up like kites hee! hee! hee!"

"When do we leave, old man?"

"First we gotta die, old girl."

It took the daughter-in-law several days to understand that the two old people had decided to die. At first, she was outraged at their sin. At the same time, she saw the day approaching, after they'd gone, when she would be queen of the household. She had never ruled, she'd only been the servant. Henceforth, she would hold power. There'd be changes in the house! Wobbly old furniture to the attic! She had already picked out the lovely chrome-plated set that she wanted. She would change the colors of the walls. She would take down the huge plaster crucifix with the blood-stained body of Christ. She would open all the windows in the old people's bedroom to drive out the smell of old age that filled the room and spilled out into the house. She would get rid of their bed.

"Old fools," she protested. "They want to die . . . It must be normal . . . "

For strangers, the daughter-in-law put on a sad face.

"I don't say we aren't sad, but dying is one of God's laws and you have to obey them. Growing old is sad. Real sad."

The old people weren't eating and they weren't getting thin. The daughter-in-law calculated that at this rate, it would take them years to die. She often glanced inside to see if they hadn't "gone." She always caught them whispering secrets and snickering. That irritated her.

"Here I am worrying myself to death and those two are already enjoying the Final Journey . . . "

And now, as if they'd been resurrected, Evariste-Cytriste and his wife were in the kitchen demanding food. They cleaned their plates and asked for more. Revived, they went back to their room, snickering mischievously, and emerged wearing their work clothes. Evariste-Cytriste had slipped on trousers shiny with spruce-gum. Amandine had donned her black dress and her big grey apron.

"You're taking the tractor, eh, old man? hee! hee! hee!"

"Nope, I'll hitch up the horse like in the old days when I was young, when I was really a man. I want to wreak havoc hee! hee! hee!"

"Folks that think we're dying, they'll see we're still around hee! hee! hee!"

Taking cautious little steps, the old couple who had come so close to death their faces had already started to resemble it, tottered out to the stable, where the old horse was surprised to see them. He neighed. He had thought they were dead. For so many days, neither Amandine or Evariste-Cytriste had come to give him his portion of oats. The old horse had been replaced by a red tractor. He had been left in the pasture, idle and bored. He would have preferred to be with people, straining all his muscles like a real horse. Since the tractor arrived, he'd been forgotten. Some days, his masters even forgot to give him his oats, they were so busy playing in the belly of the red tractor. That machine had won all their affection. Idle now, he grazed. It was easier to graze, to roll on the ground, to laze about under leafy trees. He forgot the heavy burdens, the collar that hurt his neck, the sweat that scalded under the leather and the bit that tore his mouth. The horse got used to being useless. He gradually learned the pleasure of solitude, sweeter than the company of men who whip you, who hurl insults and force you to do what they can't do themselves. And then he preferred shade to light. He rarely went out. He liked the cool tranquillity of the stable.

Evariste-Cytriste or Amandine used to come and see him, give him water and oats, talk to him; they understood each other very well. Then they stopped. The horse was very lonely, but he knew that when the end draws near, everyone is alone.

Suddenly, Amandine and Evariste-Cytriste were there before him. They greeted him, prepared his oats, ran fresh water and talked about going out, about driving the horse along the new road. He heard the click of metal buckles, heard the straps of his harness rubbing together. He hadn't worn them for so long. He snorted, whinnied, pawed the ground, shook his mane. He loved his masters even more than the too peaceful solitude.

"Good to be back at work, eh horse? hee! hee! hee!"

"Those scatterbrained youngsters are freshly-hatched. Soon as they can stand up, they disown their father and mother and do exactly the opposite of what they're told."

"We don't want no new road cutting through our property."

With a movement he'd performed so many times, that he could still perform effortlessly, Evariste-Cytriste tossed the harness over the horse's back. He strapped it up.

"The horse is so happy he's laughing," said the old lady. "Hee! hee! hee!"

"What do you say, old girl, should we invite the horse on the Final Journey?"

"Ain't for me to say, old man, but I was thinking when our life's over, I'd like to go to Florida, then to the Pope's city, with our horse, like when we got married. Hee! hee! hee! Old man, do you think he'll understand he has to stop eating oats, and let himself be extinguished so his soul can leave his body and travel as fast as the good Lord's light?"

The horse dropped his head. The old couple were certain the animal was giving his assent.

"If you were to ask me, old girl, I'd say we'll be taking our Final Journey on horseback!"

"We'll ride around in the Florida sun on horseback, then go to the old countries where our ancestors came from, on the other side of the sea."

"And then the Pope's city, like Magloire Cauchon and his Desneiges . . . "

"Hee! hee! hee!"

"Then we'll go see the stable where baby Jesus came to earth, in the Jews' country."

"Horsey, you're going to have one fine trip!"

Now the horse was harnassed, the bit adjusted, the girth firmly fastened, the crupper a little loose because the horse had lost weight ("just like us hee! hee!"); Evariste-Cytriste checked all the buckles and straps, for the harness hadn't been used in a long time; they were rusty and here and there the mice had nibbled at the leather. Amandine had picked up a piece of burlap and wiped off the dust and cobwebs. Evariste-Cytriste, so small beside the horse, gave its chest a manly thump; Amandine rubbed her nose in the downy warmth of its lower jaw. Frail and feeble, they looked like two old children.

"Come on horsey, we're going to wreak some havoc; afterwards, we'll go back to fasting: no oats for you, no meat and potatoes for us. We'll become souls travelling like light. You'll come along; it's not as sad as being all alone. We'll show you some pretty little fillies."

"Old man," Amandine grumbled, "don't put ideas in your horse's head. I don't want to die to see souls screwing around when I'm dead."

"Don't be sad, we'll have a fine trip, but before we go we're going to wreak some havoc, hee!hee!hee!"

"Hee! hee! hee!"

After they'd finished wreaking havoc, the horse would go back to the stable and they, to their bedroom; he would lie down on his straw, they would lie on their bed, he must refuse to eat his oats and drink his buckets of water as they would refuse meat and potatoes. Slowly, the horse's body would be snuffed out like the flame of a candle with no wick; the old couple's bodies would be snuffed out as well; together, horse and masters, now become bodiless souls, would travel at the speed of light; Curé Fourré had promised it. Evariste-Cytriste explained it all to his horse. After they'd wreaked havoc, he would resume his explanations, because this particular horse had always had trouble understanding what was said to him. Perhaps he was a little deaf? The soul that leaves the body like the smoke from a burnt log was something he understood, but it would probably be harder for him to understand why he had to give up his oats and water, the old man thought.

Evariste-Cytriste found the old rusty mower under a tangled heap of forgotten ploughing implements: heaps of useless metal they hadn't yet dared to sell off for scrap. Cytriste, his son, could hear the clatter of iron on iron, he could hear the creaking of rust, but he didn't feel like going to see what was happening, after getting such a slap in the face. With tears in his eyes, he'd gone to hide his shame at the end of the vegetable garden, behind the runner beans. Must parents die before they stop humiliating their children? His parents had slapped him. Wasn't he a man who had his own children and grandchildren, who had launched the rotten egg war and managed to wrest an excellent price for a narrow strip of land? For Cytriste it was a terrific deal. The new road would add value to his fields, to his woods, it would bring customers for milk, butter, eggs, ducks and firewood. It was an excellent transaction. Follow progress: a man who does that can't go wrong. A man has to keep in step with the times. Cytriste Tanguay had been humiliated by two old wrecks from ancient history. The world had gone modern without their permission. He wept in his runner-beans and hoped they would die soon.

Evariste-Cytriste managed to wrench the mower from the shed. He harnessed up the old horse; the animal, who hadn't worked for a long time, was nervous and impatient. Evariste-Cytriste understood: he was tired too. A man and his horse experience many things the same way. He helped Amandine get up on the mower, then he clambered up behind her and enjoyed watching her smooth her big apron against her legs, as daintily as an elegantly dressed great lady.

"Ready to wreak some havoc, old girl?"

"Hee! hee! hee!"

Before them stretched the oatfield, as dense as a fat cat's fur. The wind came up, the oats made a bow, then righted themselves. Evariste-Cytriste remembered when this field had been standing spruce. Amandine too had seen the space scattered with scrawny spruce trees, battling one another for room to spread out branches and avoid being choked to death. Some trunks were so big you could carve a man's tomb from them. Others were as thin as a pencil. The branches were braided and woven into a dark zone a man could enter only by clearing his way with an axe. Evariste-Cytriste had felled every one of those spruce trees. Amandine had gathered the branches into piles they set alight on humid nights when the wind slept in the hollows of the valleys. They had pulled out stumps with horses, chains, crowbars, oaths, anger and sweat. The stumps clung to the earth like teeth to gums. Evariste-Cytriste had ploughed the earth. Amandine collected the stones dug up by the blade of the plough and took them to the boundary of their field to build a fence. If the stones were too big, Evariste-Cytriste would wrap a chain around them and slide them across the slippery earth, whipping his horses, hurling abuse at them. His oaths made Amandine tremble. She was afraid the good Lord would punish him for his insults by putting a curse on the child who already was forming a bump in her belly. Their land became as beautiful as a king's carpet. Such perfect oats grew nowhere else in the Appalachian Region. And their son, Cytriste, the shame of his generation, had just sold that land to the Right Party's government, so they could run a road through it . . .

The lines that would mark the boundaries of the road had already been laid down. In the oatfield trampled by the surveyors, Evariste-Cytriste and Amandine could make out the two rows of red flowers formed by the painted tips of the pickets the surveyors had stuck in their land. From their mower, the old couple could see far away, as far as the forest, the narrow red ribbon marking the edge of the new road. The horse was so happy to be outside, to be walking through the oats and pulling a mower, he seemed to be humming. And they could taste their own happiness at being together with their horse and the mower, under the good Lord's blue sky filled with birdsong. But the field of oats wouldn't exist if they hadn't created it. Like the Almighty, they gazed in astonishment upon what they had made. The row of red-painted pickets announced that part of their oats would be swallowed up by the new road. Their son Cytriste had betrayed them. These oats were gold. Their son, Cytriste, had given them to those government swine who can't tell the difference between gold and sheep shit. Even the horse knew the value of the oats, because he wasn't grazing. Their horse respected what their son had profaned. Evariste-Cytriste ordered him to get a move on. How the horse enjoyed obeying! He hadn't had an order for so long. He rushed ahead so eagerly, Amandine rattled on her seat.

"Old girl, take a good look at the fine swath we'll make . . . "

The old man cried out a hoarse command. The reins clattered on the horse's rump. The animal plunged into the oats where the wind stirred up waves as on the surface of a lake. Evariste-Cytriste brought down the blades. The neck was chopped off the first surveyor's picket and it fell into the oats, under the mower's sharp teeth. The red head of another picket fell. Again, the reins clattered, the horse speeded up, the rusty wheels screeched. Evariste-Cytriste heard his wife tittering, shaking with delight.

"Old girl, you sound as rusty as my mower."

"Old man, you're as lame as our old horse. Did you notice he's limping?"

"Hee! hee! hee!"

"Hee! hee! hee!"

The horse tottered on wobbly old legs. He hadn't walked in the fields for so long. He charged. The oats were flattened. The mower blade lopped off all the red pickets the surveyors had planted without missing a single one. As each one fell, the old couple burst into victorious laughter.

Soon they came to the rim of the forest. The line of red pickets continued through the bushes, rushes and alders; the ground was swampy. They could advance no further with the mower. Evariste-Cytriste let the horse rest a little. He quenched his thirst at a pond, lapping ecstatically, then headed for the other side, where the surveyors had put up another line of red pickets to mark the other side of the new road. Standing up on their mower, the old couple gazed out at the red line that stippled their oats. Didn't the Right Party respect anything? Above them in Heaven their ancestors were looking down at the field of oats gleaming in the sun like a piece of the sun itself. They were proud that they'd increased their inheritance. For a few pieces of silver Cytriste had betrayed them, like Judas. He, Evariste-Cytriste, would do battle with the Right Party as he'd done battle with the forest. He was still strong enough to defend himself! No one would trespass on his property! No one would invade his land!

"Old girl, we'll slice off their necks!"

"Hee! hee! hee! Old man, let me tell the horse what to do."

"That's a man's job. I'll give the order, you smack his rump."

He shouted a word. The horse reared. The old lady smacked his back with the rein. The animal shot ahead with all his ancient might, an imitation of his old spirit. He forged ahead. The wheels of the mower creaked on their old axle. Evariste-Cytriste shouted, urging on the animal, hurling threats and abuse, insulting him, then stroking him with gentle words. Amandine cracked the whip. The old couple, standing on the mower, one hand clamped to the seat, were exultant. The oats seemed to be rolling toward them like an avalanche, to cover them. They saw the red pickets fall beside the blade. The surveyors would never be able to reconstruct their line. The new road would be lost in the oatfield. Amandine lashed at the horse, who whinnied happily. Evariste-Cytriste shouted congratulations and advice. The oats were coming faster and faster toward the sharp blade which sliced off the stems. The horse seemed to have left the ground. His hooves threw sparks over the oats. Suddenly the mower took a tremendous leap into the air. Evariste-Cytriste and Amandine were thrown and went rolling in the oats. The horse could hear the cries of his old master and mistress. Thinking he must obey, he ran even faster. He possessed a vigor he didn't remember from his youth.

Evariste-Cytriste and Amandine saw the oats and the mower roll over them and a small wound opened their bodies.

"I feel my soul leaving my body," said the old man.

"Me too. It's the start of our Final Journey. Smell, old man; I just thought about Florida and I can smell it already."

"Us and our horse, we're heading off on our Final Journey. It smells like Florida. Hang on, old girl, I don't want to end up there all alone."

When Cytriste found his parents' bodies, he murmured that it was a sad fate to be mowed down like oats. He found the horse drained of its blood, tangled in a barbed-wire fence, legs shattered between the broken shafts.

He mused that on certain pale summer evenings, the souls of his father and mother would get into the cart drawn by the soul of their old horse. They would drive, invisible as the breeze, along the new road.

XXIII

The real way to govern

Le Chef didn't like to use the bell under the carpet, the one he could press with his foot. He preferred to shout:

"Thérèse!"

The oak door was double and padded with leather. His secretary couldn't hear her master, but like a well-trained dog, she knew when he had called. She brought a file on which she had meticulously inscribed in her own fine hand: SAUTEREAU.

"Ah!" murmured Le Chef.

He opened his top right drawer and took out a glass.

"Bring me a glass of water. I want to see my province clearly."

Whenever he had a difficult file to analyze, he was careful to drink only water. The secretary brought back the glass filled with water and the cool clink of ice.

SAUTEREAU. The folder contained three photographs, all bulging because they'd been soaking in water, and several hand-written pages, covered with corrections like an essay by a diligent student.

"Sautereau! Never saw him in the buff. Poor Sautereau: as out of place in a whorehouse as a nun in a synagogue. What was he doing with that female? He was more Catholic than the catechism . . . Not a man alive doesn't have his little hidden sin, a little vice he's trapped in like a dog in its collar. When you pick a man, you have to wait and take a good look at the collar around his neck. That's what power's all about. Sautereau . . . Sautereau. When I made him editor-in-chief of *The Provincial Sun*, it must've gone to his head. He must've thought: 'Le Chef's noticed my talent. Le Chef was struck by my style.' Rest easy, Sautereau: I picked you because we found these pictures in Pichette's pocket . . . Pichette, he liked little boys. The filthy pig, he liked to have little boys kiss his intimate jewels. Pichette had a collar too. When you know the vice, you control the man . . . You can't control the forces of nature, but you can control a man . . . Sautereau . . . Who'll replace him? Who will I put in Pichette's place? Thérèse!"

The secretary hadn't heard, but she came because she knew he'd called.

"You've done the necessary for the 'Sincere condolences' and the 'Tragic loss for us all.'?"

She nodded.

"That's all."

She left.

"Poor Sautereau: jump off a bridge because he was scared his wife would see his picture in the buff. Whenever a man's in trouble, there's always a woman mixed up . . . Same thing for Pichette: his wife left him when she realized he liked little boys better than women and he never got over it. Poor Sautereau! A journalist, an intellectual, a reader, chasing whores like an ignorant politician . . . And on top of all that, apparently he wanted to bring down the Right Party."

He read: J'accuse.

"J'accuse," Le Chef repeated. ("Sautereau, you poor chump, if you can't keep on your pants and tie in front of a woman, if you haven't got the brains to know if you were in the church or a whore-house last night, you're kidding yourself if you think you can take on the Right Party. Poor Sautereau: sleep in peace, Amen. But if you're dreaming, I wonder what you're dreaming about: the fat female in the picture, or your wife, or the Right Party.")

He read again: J'accuse. ("Good title. He must've had some help with that.") Le Chef noticed that a number of paragraphs began with those same words: J'accuse. ("For sure he must've had some help. That's not bad at all. I'll use it in my next speech. I accuse the Opposition. I accuse the leader of the Opposition . . . I accuse the treasurer of the Opposition's war chest . . . Thanks, Sautereau. You did me a favor in spite of yourself.") He pushed up his glasses, which had a tendency to slide down his nose whenever he was reading; otherwise they stayed in place. Le Chef hated reading and his glasses knew it.

"J'accuse.

I accuse the Right Party of forcing mothers to sell themselves to spare their children the shame of being ruined by the Right Party.

I accuse the Right Party of awarding contracts to those of its parasites who consistently give it the highest kickback.

I accuse the Right Party of never awarding a contract unless the contractor has taken a blind oath to adhere to all of the Right Party's policies.

I accuse the Right Party of fattening itself like a blood-sucker on all the road-building contracts distributed to the friends of the regime.

I accuse the Right Party of threatening any person — priest, professor, journalist, politician — whose duty it is to express opinions and judgments.

I accuse the Right Party of awarding a building contract in an out-of-the-way corner of the province to a shady contractor (whom it had earlier threatened with bank-ruptcy) because the Minister of Roads and Bridges was enjoying the intimate favors of the contractor's wife.

I accuse the Right Party of letting its friends dip into public funds. As a result, every segment of road that is built here costs ten times as much as roads built by our neighbors.

I accuse the Right Party of transforming the highway system into a vast network of theft and thieves, into a putrid, rotten cancer that eats away at every region where the tentacle of a road is to be found.

I accuse the Right Party of governing by blackmail, ab-duction, cooking the books, lying, favoritism, threats, slan-der, influence-peddling and bargaining in human flesh."

Le Chef took off his glasses and laid them on his desk.

"Sautereau . . . Sautereau . . . I see why you lived up to your name and jumped into the water . . . You were scared

of life . . . If you knew some other way to govern, Sautereau, why didn't you tell me before you jumped? How do
you expect a government to govern if it doesn't give the
people what the people want? I reward services rendered:
that's gratitude. If a government does anything different,
it ends up in opposition. The opposition isn't a party, it's
a bunch of nobodies. Sautereau . . . Sautereau . . . I wish
I had friends everywhere. You go and throw yourself off
a bridge and send yourself to kingdom come, then you
drop a little turd on the Right Party. That little squib of
yours, J'accuse, what is it but a turd in the Right Party's
face? Sautereau . . . You're an ingrate. The Right Party
put food on your plate, you and your family . . . Sautereau,
you're ungrateful and you're rude . . . (Le Chef pinched
one of the pictures between his fingertips and studied it.)
Sautereau, I'm sure you were ungrateful and rude to that
bare-assed lady. Maybe she gave you the only pleasure you
ever had in your life . . . All you could do was write an
article . . . J'accuse! I'm giving a speech tonight and I'll use
your technique against the Opposition. I accuse . . . I accuse . . . I accuse . . . I know the Opposition's vices and I'm
going to wring their neck . . . Thanks, Sautereau!"

He crumpled Sautereau's editorial and dropped it in the
big crystal ashtray on his desk; he gazed at each of the
scandalous photographs of Sautereau with the fat woman
in the brothel, then leaned them, one by one, against the
wad of paper.

"Thérèse!"

She came, thinking her life would be a lot easier if Le
Chef would ring for her because she couldn't hear him
shouting through the padded door.

"Thérèse, bring me a light."

She came back, embarrassed because she hadn't foreseen
Le Chef's wish, and handed him a box of matches.

"That's all."

She went out. Le Chef struck a match and set fire to
Sautereau's editorial, J'accuse. The fire spread to the
photographs. Le Chef watched. The article burst in the
flames, then shrivelled. In the photographs, Sautereau and
his lady-friend were writhing against one another. When
the fire was out he mashed the ashes with his pencil.

"Thérèse!"

She came in.

"Thérèse, J'accuse was a series of criticisms that friend Sautereau was levelling at the Opposition. Sautereau was striking at the very heart of the Opposition. That's why they wanted to get rid of him. The compromising photographs were fakes. Thérèse, let the police know, and let them know also that the guilty parties are to be found in the Opposition! And Thérèse, let the newspapers and the radio know that with its underhanded tactics, the Opposition killed a man of great merit. Sautereau was the flame of truth that sheds light on the road of the People. You got all that, Thérèse?"

"Yes, Monsieur."

"That's all."

She went out. Le Chef dumped the contents of his ashtray out the window and returned to his desk.

"Power may not let you accomplish great things, but it gives you the power to wipe out a few little ones. So! You don't win elections with ashes and smoke. You have to build roads . . . Thérèse! I've spotted a hot-blooded youngster at *The Provincial Sun*. I think he shows a lot of promise. We need some young blood! Bring me the file on Achille Bédard."

XXIV

Eyes rivetted on the gentle hills of Rome

When the airplane wrenched itself from the ground, Magloire Cauchon felt his heart drop into his stomach as into a bottomless well. He was sorry he'd undertaken this trip. His wife, Desneiges, had strapped herself in as tightly as she could; nothing could make her fall out of her seat. He, who had never taken a pill, had had to be vaccinated against all the epidemics that "run around in the Old Countries." Desneiges had filled out complicated forms to get a passport and official papers, then she had corresponded with a company that sold trips. They had bought a new light-weight suitcase. They'd gone to the Capital, to dress themselves in the latest fashions. After that, the suitcase turned out to be too small for everything Desneiges claimed was indispensable. When they were ready, the company that sold trips told them the trip had been cancelled for some complicated reason. Magloire Cauchon asked the notary in Saint-Toussaint-des-Saints to write some legal threats. Miraculously, a few days later, the company that sold trips told them the trip would take place after all. What a lot of worries and bother, on top of his duty as Mayor of Saint-Toussaint-des-Saints! For weeks, they'd been getting ready for this trip, though they weren't certain until they were actually on board that they'd have a place in the airplane. Once they were there, anxious because they couldn't see their suitcase, they weren't sure the airplane would be able to take off. When it had broken through the cloud ceiling and was flying above a beautiful sea of tranquil white sheep, Desneiges and Magloire Cauchon still weren't sure they'd reach their destination: if the good Lord wasn't holding the plane in His hand, it would fall like a dead leaf. There were too many passengers. It was flying too high. Soon they would be over the ocean, and it was deep. The airplane was held in place by a hair; there was nothing solid underneath it. The floor was like the mossy ground around Mud Lake, where you were careful not to step because you don't know how deep you'll sink. Desneiges had warned Magloire that people in the Old Countries were civilized and didn't shout like farmers bellowing at their cows and horses. Magloire Cauchon leaned over his wife's shoulder and murmured,

"One thing I'm sorry about: this trip made me miss the procession. Everyone'll be on show but the Mayor!"

Magloire Cauchon gazed for a long time out the window, out at the sky where he'd never imagined he'd be before he died. Yet he was alive. He was up in the sky, even higher than the clouds. The light was bright: the good Lord was nearby. Magloire Cauchon's heart was beating faster than it did on earth. He wouldn't have been surprised to see the good Lord smoking His pipe as he rocked in a cloud.

The mayoralty election would soon be held. If Magloire was honest with himself, he had to admit that his victory wasn't at all certain. And it was obvious that a photograph of him receiving a papal benediction could be a determining factor in his re-election. Who, without troubling his conscience, could vote against a mayor who had been blessed by the Holy Father, the Pope? He would be the first person from Saint-Toussaint-des-Saints to see the Pope with his own eyes. Even Curé Fourré hadn't seen him. He'd be the first — unless young Opportun, who had died like a true saint, had arrived at the speed of light and thrown himself into the Pope's lap. Magloire Cauchon would be the first living person from Saint-Toussaint-des-Saints to see the Pope. He would come home vested with a papal blessing.

In the election he'd be victorious. The Right Party would have to take account of the fact that Magloire Cauchon was King of the Appalachians. The papal blessing would put a stop to the plots being hatched against him. In the bus that took passengers from the airport to Rome, Magloire Cauchon was jubilant.

A young girl with black hair and eyes of the sort you didn't see in Saint-Toussaint-des-Saints (Magloire Cauchon peered at her as if she were some odd sort of heifer), was talking some complicated foreign language. Suddenly he recognized some words from his own language. In the guide's delicate mouth, the words were gentle, polished, round, musical. He listened, surprised, captivated; he didn't understand everything she was saying, but he watched the words as they came to the young girl's red lips. Desneiges Cauchon didn't enjoy her husband's adoration of youth. She knew that Magloire was mentally undressing the young girl. Desneiges had been warned by the women in Saint-Toussaint-des-Saints whose husbands had gone to war in the Old Countries: the women there were first cousins to the Devil. She nudged Magloire to make him pay attention.

"Look, Magloire, did you see all the old-fashioned things along the road? Houses held up by a prayer; walls as rotten as old teeth; graveyards as decayed as the dead; stumps of columns eaten away by time. Magloire, a man can't feel young in such an old country."

"Desneiges, it ain't time to slop the pigs yet."

That was what he always said when he hadn't been listening to his wife, and to keep from hearing what she was going to say. His mind was elsewhere. The young girl at the front of the bus was talking Magloire Cauchon's language. She had grasped the fact that he understood that language, and so she was smiling at him. Her voice was as sweet as a song. Magloire's eyelids were closing. He felt a burning sensation when the young girl's black eyes met his. His seat on the bus felt like fire. Desneiges could read her husband's mind.

"Magloire Cauchon, instead of thinking about perfumed sin you ought to pick up some knowledge, because when ignoramuses like you get power, they lead the people like blind men. And don't start daydreaming about that painted hussy: anything she can do I can do just as well . . ."

275

"It's an old country, all right. So old there's nothing growing in the fields, did you notice? Little dry bushes, that's all. Brooms, they call them, if you can imagine. And pine trees with branches like umbrellas."

"Quiet, Magloire, I want to listen to the guide. She may not be big on virtue, but she seems to know a lot."

With her softly lilting words, the young girl was telling them that Rome, crossroads for all the Christians on earth, had also been, in ancient times, a crossroads for tribes that travelled in caravans. The road on which the bus was travelling had been built before Jesus Christ, by people who travelled on the backs of camels, on horseback or on foot. This road had been in place for more than two thousand years, surviving rain, wars, droughts, floods, revolutions and earthquakes.

"Magloire Cauchon, I can't believe we're in Rome: it's like a dream."

"It's no dream, Desneiges, we're travelling on a road that was built before Jesus was born."

"They had better contractors then. They were Romans."

"Romans are Italians. What's Verrochio's nationality?"

"Same as the rest of your friends in the Right Party. You're all moles. Those rodents in the Right Party are making roads rot and bridges fall down. This road's older than Jesus Christ, but it's still here. That's because it hasn't been eaten away by a bunch of rodents like you and your friends."

"Desneiges, have you gone over to the Opposition?"

"Magloire Cauchon, when you ask the Holy Father to bless the new road, he'll likely do it, but he sure won't bless the profiteers that intend to nip some profit for themselves."

The pretty guide was smiling and saying things in a strange language. They were driving along a road that was older than Jesus Christ, a road that had traversed centuries, generations and empires; they were taking this road because of another one, the road in Saint-Toussaint-des-Saints which hadn't yet been built. Magloire Cauchon wanted a papal blessing for his new road. Between the two roads, between the one that was older than he could imagine and the new one, the one that hadn't yet been built, between the old world and the new, there must be a road that didn't appear on the maps but was inscribed in the minds of men, because men from the old world had come to the new, and those from the new world travelled to the old continent. Magloire Cauchon didn't understand, he was lost in a strange land, he could no longer see the tip of the steeple of the village where he was born, he was as lost as, when still a child, he'd lost his way in the forest. He felt choked. He wanted to call out, as he had in the past: Mama! He leaned over Desneiges.

"You're right, it's a dream."

"Magloire, remember that dirt road outside my father's house? When a horse and carriage passed by the house went dark from the cloud of dust it left behind. And when you passed by, Magloire, I'd watch you on your bicycle that clanked like scrap iron. One day you stopped and asked for a glass of water; then you came back for more. My poor mother thought you were the thirstiest man she ever met. Then you asked for my hand and I drove to the church in the shiny black car with my father. I was wearing my white gown. Today, Magloire, on this old road that's beyond age, like everything that's too old, I feel the way I felt when I went to the church with my father. I can't help it, Magloire, my soul's all aflutter."

"Desneiges, it's a dream."

"It's a dream, Magloire."

The young guide looked at them. She explained in their language that Rome had been built on seven hills. Her black eyes were as big as windows. Magloire couldn't stop the blush that spread over his cheeks. With her elbow, Desneiges brought him back in line.

"I knew I'd have to keep an eye on you; you can see that all roads lead to sin. Even the road to Rome."

Magloire didn't react to his wife's innuendo. He had lowered his gaze and now was admiring the young bosom that swelled her blouse.

"Hills? They're little mountains, Desneiges. Like back home: we build on hills, we lay out the roads between the hills."

"It's so beautiful, it's like a dream . . . "

Dazed by the wonders they had seen, dazzled, as if they'd been staring at the sun, by the palaces, statues, parks, the ancient ruins that the guide kept pointing out, first on one side of the bus, then the other, eyes most likely irritated by the Roman light, walking as if they were drunk, amid a flock of tourists who all looked more or less drunk, clinging together, terrified of losing each other forever among all these strangers who came from all the countries in the world and spoke terrifying languages, Magloire and Desneiges Cauchon walked into the room where they would catch a glimpse of the Pope. An old priest at the head of the herd, who seemed to know all the languages, announced that they were entering the Consistory, "one of His Holiness's private apartments," he pointed out.

"Desneiges, we're nearly at the Pope's place, get out your Kodak! We don't want to miss this! It'd be worse than missing our wedding picture."

"Magloire, the floor's made out of Italian marble!"

It was a large room lit by huge windows. No furniture: some consoles held bouquets of flowers. The walls were bare except for some that were hung with tapestries depicting scenes from the lives of the saints.

"Presentat sciabl!"

The Swiss guards in gleaming armor, bearing halberds, swung into action. The tufts on their helmets and the ribbons on their bouffant pants stirred. Old nuns dropped to the floor making no more sound than angels. The visitors shoved and insulted each other in all sorts of languages that no one understood. Desneiges, who had learned good manners from the nuns at school, smiled politely, but Magloire Cauchon had crossed the ocean to come and see the Pope; besides, he bore an important missive addressed to His Holiness from Curé Fourré. He wasn't going to let himself be pushed around by people who weren't as important as he. He pulled Desneiges along with him, skilfully warding off assaults. When everyone was inside, when all had taken their places, when they had decided to make peace and stop trying to take their neighbor's spot, there were a few more motions and a metallic click from the Swiss guards. Then came a rustling of soutanes and skirts. All at once the sun drew near to the earth; the room was flooded in light. It was the Pope!

"Your Kodak, Desneiges?"

The Pope advanced, arms wide, followed at a respectful distance by a bald old monsignor. Seemingly still saying his prayers, he spoke to the first row of visitors. What was mentioned an Italian (one Verrochio) who built "roads through the forests of the New World so that Christ can travel farther on this earth." With clerical caution, the officer submitted this letter to an adviser who asked to have it submitted to a second adviser, who decided that this pleasant letter need not rise to a higher level, while the other suggested that the Pope was particularly concerned about the propagation of the Catholic faith. His Holiness would be touched, the adviser maintained, at the notion of the Italian opening the forests of America to clear a path for the Savior of all mankind. Because of this contradiction between advisers, the officer, as was customary in such cases, called on a third adviser. After study and prayer, he suggested that His Holiness would surely be interested, on both human and religious grounds, in glancing at this letter from a humble country priest. Saint Opportun had guided the missive, which would otherwise have been stored in an immense shed for wasted words before rising as smoke into the blue Roman sky.

Here is what Curé Fourré had written:

"Very most dear Holy Father,

Forgive the humblest of your priests for tearing you momentarily from your divine dialogue.

I am first and foremost your son and the son of the Son of God, but I am also a descendant of one of those ancient families of old France who left Europe to proclaim the name of God to the savage echoes of the barbarian forests of America.

The bearer of this missive is also a descendant of those very ancient families of the Old Continent, come to pray to the Almighty on the pagan shores of the Indians' America.

The man who brings you this missive is a major hog producer who feeds the bodies of his fellow citizens; I have the mission of nourishing their souls.

The roads the good Lord has traced for men on earth are often beyond the understanding of those who follow them. And so the bearer of this missive and Your humble correspondent travel side by side, through our families in the Old Countries. The bearer of this missive thinks of his pigs, while I consider my parishioners. He wants to fatten his pigs, while I wish

he saying? Magloire, in the second row, couldn't hear, but he noticed that the Pope was heading toward some visitors being introduced by the bald monsignor. That was enough to tell him it was a mistake to settle for the second row. He knew how to control the hundreds of pigs that rushed at him as soon as he'd filled their trough. He decided to move up. A few kicks and nudges, a well-aimed shoulder placed Magloire Cauchon and Desneiges in the front row.

"Get out your Kodak, Desneiges, here he comes."

And Magloire made a dash for the old bald monsignor, announcing:

"I come from Canada, from Saint-Toussaint-des-Saints, in the Appalachian Region. I came to see His Eminential Holiness the Pope. I'm the mayor of Saint-Toussaint-des-Saints, and I raise pigs. My pork's so good I sell it to the Jews! (Stuffing his hand in his inside pocket). Our Curé, good Curé Fourré, he asked me to give this missive to the Pope's Holiness."

The bald old monsignor took the letter.

"I shall transmit it to the Holy Father who has a particularly tender love for his Catholics in the New World."

"Is your Kodak ready, Desneiges? Move it, for Chrissake!"

The Pope stood before him. Could Magloire look him in the eyes, like a man? Or should he lower his gaze to the cross on his chest? Should he kneel? Should he kiss the ring on his finger?

"You got the camera?"

No doubt he was overwrought. And tired from the long plane trip. Had he been blinded by the Holy Father's white soutane? Had he, a pig-farmer and champion cusser, who forgot to say his prayers and slept through mass every Sunday, had he been too reckless, wanting to approach the incarnation of Holiness on earth? His fine earthly self-assurance had melted like the waxen wings of that man who had flown too near the sun. His body soft as melting butter, Magloire Cauchon collapsed at His Holiness' feet.

"Magloire! Magloire! Are you dying a sudden death? Here, wait, I got the Kodak!"

The Pope knelt, the Swiss guards rushed to push back the crowd. The Pope murmured a prayer, made the sign of the cross over Magloire. With tears in her eyes, Desneiges snapped away.

"Magloire, if you die with the Pope's blessing, there's nothing can stop you on the road to Heaven."

Magloire Cauchon did not die. The Pope returned to his apartment. The tourists left the audience hall. Magloire Cauchon's eyes opened as if he'd been asleep for a long time. He got to his feet, lost, gawking, aching all over; he spotted his wife.

"Desneiges, did you get any pictures?"

His wife had tears in her eyes.

"Magloire Cauchon, I saw you lying there dead, and now I see you resurrected! My Kodak took pictures of you when you were dead. But then the Pope blessed you and brought you back to life! Magloire, you're going to win your election! The Pope brought you back to life! Wait, I want a picture of you alive!"

XXV

A letter from Ameri[ca] brings the Pope sad memories

The missive from Curé Fourré must have got lost i[n] maze of administrative procedures that had been e[stab]lished over the centuries. At the Consistory exit, the old monsignor placed on a table the various letters, par[cels] gifts and objects the visitors had given him. The secre[tary] skimmed every letter turned in by the visitors and ope[ned] every parcel. For each parcel, he filled out a form a[nd] placed it, with the contents, in another room. He inser[ted] each letter in envelopes with imprinted boxes, that he fil[led] in with a firm hand. It was a way of summarizing the let[ters.] Like thousands of other letters that arrived from all o[ver] the world on that particular day, Curé Fourré's missive [was] turned in at the registry office, where it was given a c[ode] number. Other secretaries assigned to the registry [de]partment filed Cure Fourré's missive, along with hundr[eds] of others, which were then distributed to the appropr[iate] departments. Their replies would be passed to the S[ec]retariat for Latin Letters, which would translate the Po[pe's] reply into Ciceronian Latin. The officer who read C[uré] Fourré's missive was suddenly interested: the signa[ture]

280

to sanctify my parishioners. We walk together and we often pray to God together. Monsieur Magloire Cauchon is also the mayor of our hamlet and I humbly commend him to your prayers because he's running for re-election.

The hog producer and the pastor can, then, as sons of God and of yourself, have a shared concern. Ours is a new road that's to be built upon our land. Many men from Saint-Toussaint-des-Saints will be employed there. A woman will even be working there, just like a man. Would you be so kind as to have the holy goodness to bless this undertaking with your eminent and holy hand? It seems to me, as I write, that you will not refuse your very paternal blessing on our new road to protect it against all the works of Satan.

And it seems to me that you would not refuse to bless a new road being built by Nino Verrochio, an Italian like Yourself, very most Holy Father, who came from Italy, mainly from Sardine. In his own way he has followed the way of the Lord to the New World, so far from Italy and his native Sardine, to come and build roads through the New World forests so Christ can walk farther on this earth. After all these years in a foreign land, in his soul Monsieur Verrochio is still Italian. He is an Italian patriot, not a bandit that ran away from Italy of the sort there are all too many of in America. As a loving son who expects too much, I dare to ask Your blessing on Monsieur Verrochio as well.

Through your blessing may the workers of these public works be transformed into God's workers and may the new road lead Your children to the house of the Heavenly Father.

The humblest of your priests prostrates himself and kisses Your holy feet,

Fourré, Curé of Saint-Toussaint-des-Saints."

This letter could have been stored in some obscure warehouse, but the Holy Father was holding it in his hands, filled with emotion. Such naive faith had vanished from Europe along with the builders of Medieval cathedrals.

Birds were singing in the Vatican Gardens, as they must sing in Paradise. Robins, ortolans and warblers danced joyous rounds. A *roccolatore* clapped his hands to frighten the birds and send them away where their wings would get caught in nets spread among the flowering branches. The Pope had withdrawn to his chamber. The blue ceiling represented the starry sky. The walls were hung with red and gold damask. The Pope had taken a light meal before a standing crucifix: a coddled egg, a small roast ortolan, salad, a finger of Bordeaux wine — a gift from a congregation of French nuns. He had read the humble Curé's letter while he ate. Verrochio: was this simple Sardinian, builder of roads in the New World, a sign from God? Was his story not a parable that God was telling him, through the pen of a humble country Curé, to remind him that his signal role was to be a builder of roads for the Apostles of the true religion? The Holy Father prayed to thank God for sending this message through the hands of two of the humblest men on earth, a country Curé and a pig farmer. He asked God to bless the Curé and all his parishioners, the hog producer and his animals and, most of all, his Italian compatriot, Verrochio. The name was not uncommon in Italy . . . So many names had passed through the Holy Father's memory, so many words uttered in every accent, every language. Verrochio . . . The Holy Father held before his eyes the letter from a humble Curé on the other side of the world. The words had been written by a pious hand that had not yet repudiated heavy labor. The Holy Father thought of the Apostles, whose successor he was, who, after Christ ascended into Heaven, had separated so that along all the roads, they could recount the life of the man who turned water into wine and told how he had come to earth so men could hope again. The Apostles had taken familiar roads; their successors, repeating the same message, had travelled across countries, forded rivers, crossed seas, gone through war and persecution. Verrochio . . . The Holy Father was filled with emotion, and he who was accustomed to the thousands of Catholics who came from every part of the world to kneel before him, felt his heart beat faster because of this letter the good Lord had directed to him. He would bless the good Curé, he would bless the new road, he would ask the Almighty to bless the labors of those Catholics in the hills of the New World. He would also ask God to shower His blessings on the contractor, the child of "Sardine," as the humble Curé wrote it, the Curé whose faith surpassed his knowledge of geography. That humble Italian at the other end of the world was unwittingly copying his distant ancestors, who had laid out roads throughout the known world when Rome was a mere worldly empire. He would pray for Verrochio. He would ask the Secretariat for Latin Letters to send a letter blessing Curé Fourré's flock. He would pray for them. Their faith was the faith of the Christians who followed the Apostles' first steps on a journey that would never end, for the world would never be Catholic enough. Verrochio . . . Verrochio . . . The Pope laid down his letter. The powerful here below would never have the faith of this good priest of the New World forests, nor that of the most humble crusher of stones for the road being built by Verrochio.

Many years ago, a young soldier with a pronounced accent had given him his confession. His gravest sin was that he could not return to his country: was it Sardinia? Verrochio — that could have been the young soldier's name. His face was still a child's, but his eyes had seen more inhuman horrors than most old people. The Pope was then a chaplain assigned to the Army Medical Corps, doing what he could to bring a little peace and hope to the vast violent madness that was torturing Europe. The young soldier's uniform was torn and soaked in blood. The young soldier was weeping; he lay in the grass, pulling up handfuls of earth and pounding his forehead. With gentle words, talking of his mother and of the goodness of God who loves those who have suffered, the chaplain managed to calm the young soldier, who finally slept, exhausted by his despair. His body was thin, his uniform stained with dried blood. Accustomed to sleeping amid the din of battle, he was suddenly awakened by the silence. Again the chaplain talked to him. The child-soldier wept. On roads in Greece, he had entered houses and killed terror-stricken women and children, who threw themselves against the walls in the hope of escape. He had followed men and killed them too. The soldier was not alone; he was with other children of his age. All of them had killed women and children, all had hunted down men, all had blood on their uniforms. Because they had to eat, they hunted goats and sheep and slit their throats. The blood of those beasts mingled with the blood in which their uniforms were already soaked. As they ate shreds of meat torn from animals roasted over a sputtering fire, their faces blackened with blood and glistening with the salt from dried sweat, the soldiers joked about the women and children who had pissed in terror. They all agreed that it was more fun to kill Greeks than goats. They fell asleep, as drunk as if they'd been drinking. (These children of the war had drunk only the wine of violence.) The soldier with the child's face stood up in his ragged blood-stained uniform and with vulgar words, to offend the chaplain, swore he'd never return to his country — it was Sardinia — swore he would never see his mother again because he had stabbed the bodies of so many grief-stricken mothers. He screamed, forgetting that he was giving his confession, that he could never see his mother again, because the women he had killed now filled nightmares he could never escape. He cried out, forgetting he was on his knees before a priest, that he could never again be loved by a woman, that he would be tracked down everywhere in the world by women who would remind him of those he had killed in the war. He would never be a father. But he added that he felt no regret, that he had been fighting a war and you must not regret what you do in war, because you must kill to avoid being killed, you must rape if you don't want to be raped, you must torture if you don't want to be tortured; he regretted nothing, because he had saved his own life. Confessing that he felt regret would have been lying to God, and if he were sent back to the war, he'd kill again; but he wanted to run away, to hide, to find a country free of war; and if he didn't run far away, all his memories of cries and terror would cling to him like his victims' blood on his uniform. Crying out his pain and despair had turned his words to sobs.

During his medical service the chaplain, too, had followed the Stations of the Cross that was war, in which innocent saviors — men, women and children — had been scourged, humiliated, put to death. It was two hundred and fifty kilometers of bumpy, twisted roads through steep hills and bare valleys. Behind hillocks, in bushes, on all sides deadly fusillades burst out. Overhead, airplanes roared and dropped bombs. So much needless pain. So much suffering for nothing. Why, at certain moments in history, do people thirst for so many nightmares? The chaplain prayed, heard confessions, consoled, promised Heaven — but what power did a priest have in the face of furious armies? Wasn't the young priest's impotence in the face of violence precisely the power of the man of peace who is incapable of causing pain?

The soldier with the child's face had dropped to his knees again. His sobs were silent now. And then the chaplain spoke to him.

"God forgives you. The Madonna inspires me to assure you that her Son forgives you. My son, you were a victim of violence when you killed, just like the men and women you killed. You have confessed, my son, you regret your sins. The confessor must impose a penance: your penance will be to forget; you must try and forget the sins against life you were forced to commit. As soon as you can, try and find a road that will take you far away, where there is peace. Somewhere, God has created a woman who is waiting for you, who will love you."

The young soldier got to his feet and left without another word, eyes fixed on the horizon.

"Hey, soldier, what's your name?" the chaplain had called out.

The young soldier turned his head and said his name . . . Verrochio . . . Was this the same Verrochio? Those years were so far away in the Holy Father's mind. In his memory he saw again the young soldier in his tattered, bloody clothes, he saw him turn his head, saw his childlike face, his eyes sunk deep in their sockets like one who has aged too fast, who has seen too much, he saw the mouth utter his own name, but he did not hear it. Time had erased the sound.

The Holy Father would accord the blessing as requested and he would pray for the success of his works. Verrochio . . . It was not impossible, following the great plan of the Divine Will, that the soldier was now in America. It was not unthinkable that the child stained with blood from Old World violence was the Italian now building roads in the peaceful immensity of New World forests. Verrochio . . . The letter from a humble Curé was like the flame

287

in the sanctuary lamp which declares that the tabernacle contains Christ's body: it said that the New World forest was a great tabernacle that contained the Truth of Christ.

"P.S. Very most dear Holy Father, It is with Christian pride that we tell you that the Almighty has accorded us the favor of granting us a little parish saint, who was born in our village and baptized in the water by my own hand, but the good Lord Himself baptized him in french-fry oil. Later, most Holy Father, I will send you the official request for his canonization. How many miracles does it take? The name of the little saint is Opportun: he is the son of a good Catholic."

The Holy Father smiled. Such men as this, he thought, had piled one on top of the other the stones of cathedrals that neither Satan, nor time, nor the violent madness of man had been able to shake. The Holy Father rang a bell; he asked that a reply to this simple letter be sent at once.

When Magloire Cauchon and Desneiges returned from Rome, the new road had already started eating through the countryside. It wasn't mere groundwork: they had knocked over oats, moved earth, pulled up trees, dug holes. Piles of stones were accumulating, and piles of burned roots. As soon as they were back Magloire and Desneiges took the large papal envelope, stamped and sealed with a wax seal, to Curé Fourré. They tried to appear humble as they walked down the main street, not proud, but hadn't they been to the Old Countries? Hadn't they talked to the Pope in person?

"I feel all shiny," Magloire confided to Desneiges.

"If the Pope blesses the new road, it means nothing can go wrong."

"I bet it's even good for my pigs: no more epidemics of germs!"

"Magloire Cauchon, as soon as you start thinking about money you run. You're walking too fast for me."

"Follow behind. You're a woman, that's what you're made for. Man makes the road, the woman walks on it."

With his letter from the Pope, Magloire had no doubt that he'd be re-elected mayor.

288

XXVI

Why is there cruelty when tenderness exists?

The surveyors re-worked the route for the new road. Loggers drove a tunnel through the tight-packed branches of spruce trees. Axes thudded wood, high boles rang out. Power saws repeated strident cries. Bulldozers growled with all their giant might as they pulled up stumps: they flattened the earth, filled in holes, pushed rocks away, pulled out spindly birches and razed puny firs. Loggers lopped off branches and sawed up trees. Trucks loaded with wood thundered and threw up black clouds as they extracted themselves from the mud. Loggers and laborers chided the mechanical beasts that roared and coughed up black. Brown water ran in the ruts. Mosquitoes, attacked on their own territory, defended themselves with sly belligerence. In dense clouds, they attacked as if they'd sworn an oath not to let a single man escape untouched. They bit flesh, they gouged eyes, with their lances they stole into ears, they penetrated nostrils, they bit. Exasperated men wept, men who hadn't wept when their own mothers died. Their swamps violated, eggs threatened, territory disturbed by these machines, the insects panicked. It was the end of the world. The smell of human sweat had never been so strong.

They attacked the men's flesh for a banquet of despair. The loggers knew the insects' habits. They had lit fires in buckets filled with fresh grass that would give off smoke to drive the mosquitoes away. The men worked, slogged, strained. They were hungry and thirsty. The machines rumbled, the men panted.

From his office, Innocent Loiseau saw some strangers get out of a truck. They walked in without saying hello, carrying crates. They set them down, then came back with more. Fifty crates in all.

He finally worked up the nerve to ask, "What's in there?"

"Dynamite."

"Isn't it dangerous? It could blow up."

"If you sit still, the dynamite will too. If you get excited, so will the dynamite."

The truck drivers disappeared, leaving him with that message. Innocent Loiseau had never seen dynamite before. All he knew was that it could explode. Sitting at his table silent and terrified, he did not move. If the dynamite blew up, he'd blow up with it. The crates were stacked up, threatening, fragile, powerful and sly. "There's no such thing as losing," Monsieur Verrochio had told him. He would not lose. He held his breath. Gradually, he let his breathing return to normal, and the dynamite didn't explode. He wouldn't lose. He moved one hand on the table, then the other. The dynamite did not explode. He got up. The dynamite just sat there. He took a step. Then another. Only winning existed. He took another step. The dynamite was harmless. Then very gently, but firmly and decisively nonetheless, he wrapped his arms around a crate of dynamite, lifted it, rested it against his abdomen and set it down again. It did not explode. He had won. He was no longer afraid. He had won. Since meeting Monsieur Verrochio, he'd been learning how to win. Lose was a word that didn't exist except in an old, dead language. Innocent went back to his table, heart pounding: he had overcome his fear of the dynamite. There was a reason why Monsieur Verrochio and he had met. Together, they would win many victories. And then, later, much later, as had happened in history, at the time of Brutus and Marc Antony, they would wage war against one another. Innocent would conquer his former master. Wasn't that the meaning of life? To win.

A man who wins, Monsieur Verrochio had explained, always has a woman in his life, who is his very soul: "When a woman love her man, every day she give him life; she's more than a mother." Monsieur Verrochio had such a wife. To date, Innocent had only his mother. He didn't know any other women. If a woman appeared, he wouldn't know what to say, he'd want to run away. Just thinking about a woman in a flowered dress, with the pointed bumps of her bosom, the round swell of her belly, and everything her flimsy dress would hide, made Innocent's flesh heat up as if it would melt. He mustn't let himself melt like a chunk of pork fat. He must learn to be strong if he was going to conquer women in their flimsy dresses, and not be unhinged by the secrets hidden in their bodices. He must win. His hand picked up the telephone. He must learn how to talk to women.

"Hello darling," he declaimed. "Oh darling, how you'd love me if you could see me now. I'm facing a mountain of dynamite that's more powerful than the atomic bomb. Darling? You aren't listening. I said: stronger than the atomic bomb. Right across from me. In my office. If it explodes, it will cause more damage than the atomic bomb. Yes, crates of it. About a thousand. While I'm talking to you, darling, my hand is touching dynamite. Am I afraid? Darling, do you think a little dynamite that's as explosive as the atomic bomb could scare me? You sound like my mother. Listen, darling: I swear I love you — with my hand on this dynamite as if it were the Holy Bible. You know, darling, the Gospels can't explode, but this dynamite could wreak more havoc than the atomic bomb."

Innocent Loiseau hung up. He would make frequent calls while the construction was in progress, to a woman who didn't exist, on a telephone that didn't work. He would learn how not to be silent in a woman's presence. And when his education was complete, he would turn the key in the lock of the front door of life, the second key Monsieur Verrochio had entrusted to him. Like Monsieur Verrochio himself, Innocent would have a woman who would be his very soul. Ah! since he'd been working in this office, since he'd been Monsieur Verrochio's associate, Innocent had learned more than he'd ever learned in college.

At first, some of the workers had thought they'd be able to soften up this youth. They would turn up late for work, their smiles as broad as in a wedding portrait. Innocent would note their names and the time of their arrival. He imposed fines. Some threatened to drive their boots into his "pretentious little student's butt that probably still wets its diapers."

"Insulting me is insulting Monsieur Verrochio who's giving you work, and the Right Party that's giving you a new road."

He added another, more severe fine, noting it next to the names of the recalcitrant.

"You wet-behind-the-ears little bugger, you looking for a strike?" raged one of the workers, who could have crushed the student like a wild raspberry.

Innocent, calm but pale, with cheeks ablaze, noted the name of the worker who had made the threat.

"Whether you work or not, doesn't matter to me. Because tomorrow, I'm not counting your day."

The penalized worker stepped forward, fist clenched, more livid than Innocent. Not looking at him, Innocent said drily:

"If dynamite doesn't scare me, do you think a man does?"

The worker flung breath laden with tobacco and rage in his face, then stormed away. Innocent had won. Monsieur Verrochio would have been proud of him. At college, he'd been taught to feel fondness for losers. He went back and sat at his table with the ledger where he recorded everything concerning his employees. How could you advance along the road of life if you had to keep stopping to waste sympathy on losers? Win. Win like Monsieur Verrochio. Innocent picked up the phone.

"Hello darling. You should have seen your loved one at work! This morning I was as tough with my workers as my father with his cows. You should have seen me, darling. I'm strong, I'm a winner. In the face of threats — yes, darling, threats — I was as calm as dynamite that doesn't explode. Darling, darling, won't you let me win your love?"

The black-robed priests who taught him only knew how to talk to other black-robed priests. How could Innocent find a woman who would be the key to his success and the soul of his body if he didn't know the necessary words or the essential phrases? Soon he would know how to talk to women without blushing. Every word he uttered would be uttered to win.

In the doorway, he saw a child with hair in wild curls topped by a ridiculous hat trimmed with a spray of brightly colored flowers. She was shifting queerly from foot to foot. Her little legs were perched upon high-heeled shoes so big her feet swam: a silly limping chicken. On top of the dress that was far too loose for her flat body she sported a brassiere with exaggeratedly swollen cups. From one of her skinny folded arms a handbag hung. With the other hand, she lifted the veil that hid her face. Her lips were painted so red her mouth looked like a wound. Her cheeks were made up like two red apples. Her eyes were ringed with long thick lashes that she'd drawn herself. Thrusting out her slender child's bosom, she pasted a smile on her painted lips and, showing her teeth, stuck out the tip of her tongue. Then, darting glances charged with strong light, she gave Innocent a long stare. He didn't know what to do. Her gaze burned his eyes. His legs were quavering. His heart pounded. The knot in his stomach kept tightening. If a real woman had been standing before him, he would have looked away. Innocent certainly wouldn't lower his eyes because a child was staring at him. He would win this battle of the eyes. He, chosen by Le Chef, he, assistant to Monsieur Verrochio, he who pitilessly noted in his black ledger every minute the workers wasted, wouldn't let a little girl with a smeared face, who was playing at having a movie star's bosom, upset him. He had noticed before that women's eyes are filled with stupefying light, but this was a child standing before him. (Was she twelve years old? Ten?) He held his body very erect, like a real boss. In Monsieur Verrochio's absence, he was the boss. Assuming the harsh voice of authority, he asked,

"What's your name?"

"Homélie Plante."

A cloud shifted in the sky, letting through a ray of light that crossed the dusty window and struck the little girl's crooked legs. They were marked with thin blackish streaks. Was it blood?

"Did you hurt yourself?" Innocent asked.

Her child's eyes sank even deeper into Innocent's.

"I know what a man is like," crooned the child with a smile.

She turned and went out, wiggling her hips. Her high heels hammered the floor. Her shoes, which were too big for her, had to belong to her mother.

Had Innocent Loiseau heard correctly? Had this grubby-faced child really said the serious thing he had heard? Did Homélie Plante really mean what he thought he'd heard? Was what he had thought to be blood on her legs really blood? Innocent's heart speeded up and the thumping echoed in his skull. He had never been in such a situation. He had seen Homélie Plante, he could still see her hobbling, pushing one shoe and dragging the other, through the muddy earth stirred up by machines and workmen, but he wasn't convinced that it was real. Homélie Plante approached some men who were fiercely attacking a rock with steel sledgehammers, trying to smash it. Innocent noticed that she swelled her absent torso to make the bumps on her brassiere stick out. He heard the men shout lewd remarks that sounded like spitting. It was happening in reality. He saw and heard, but he didn't believe it. When the vulgar jokes began, Homélie Plante stopped. Innocent saw that she was looking at the men the way she'd looked at him.

"I know what men are like."

She continued on her way. She hopped like a chick on her high heels, dodging the puddles. Some men who were unrolling a fence greeted her with a volley of dumb jokes. Innocent kept an eye on her. She turned to the men and thrust her brassiere out provocatively.

"I know what men are like."

Innocent heard the filthy words and coarse laughter aimed at the child. He was the eyes and ears of Monsieur Verrochio. He caught up with the child on the freshly cleared land. Innocent planted himself firmly in front of her. Wanting to order her to clear out, he realized that he was disturbed by these strange events.

"What's your name?"

She raised her head, thrust forward the tight-packed points of her brassiere and, sticking the tip of her tongue between lips hideously broadened by lipstick, she gave him her look of an angel who has had a glimpse of sin.

"I know what men are like."

Some of the workmen had gathered round. Behind him, Innocent could feel the rough leather of faces tanned by the sun, he could sense laughter about to explode.

"Can't you say nothin' else, Homélie Plante?"

In his rage, the name he'd forgotten came back to him.

"Homélie Plante, take off those grown-up shoes and get out. We're men here. This is no place for you to be playing dolls."

Her little body assumed a submissive posture. She took off her shoes and walked away. Innocent heard her repeat,

"I know what men are like . . . "

She disappeared onto Cytriste Tanguay's property. When he was absolutely sure she wouldn't be back, Innocent went into his office. He had won. And small victories were the best way to learn how to extract the big ones. Luckily, this confrontation had been with a child. With a real woman, perhaps he would have lost . . . Oh, he'd learn to talk to women! He picked up the telephone:

"Hello! Darling, you should have seen me directing operations. I'm the Napoleon, the Julius Caesar, the Attila of the new road. A strong arm, but a velvet hand."

An immense man in uniform filled the doorway. He was a policeman and there was another one behind him.

"Anybody here name of Dénommé Plante?"

Innocent Loiseau had never talked to a policeman. His numb fingers trembled as he opened his ledger. His vision was blurred.

"Yes, I have a Monsieur Dénommé Plante. In my ledger. Let me look . . . "

His fingers got entangled in the pages, which stuck together.

"Innocent goddamn . . . "

"Innocent *Loiseau*. Yes, that's me."

"Goddamn simple-minded — I don't wanta know if Dénommé Plante's hiding in your book, I wanta know where he is on the site."

No one had ever talked to Innocent so savagely. He looked up at the big uniformed man whose head almost touched the ceiling, who had a gun at his hip, in a well-rubbed leather holster. His legs were encased in leather boots and they too were well-rubbed. The handle of a dagger stuck out the top of his boot. This man was authority. The only real authority Innocent had known was that of the superior in his college. In the presence of authority wearing a gun on its hip and a dagger in its boot, Innocent thought that the authority God had bestowed on the man in a soutane was milder than what Le Chef bestowed on the uniformed policeman. He must obey this big dumb ox of a policeman like an ant that's afraid he'll be squashed by a boot. Innocent would win. He extended his arm, pointed to the forest where the men were logging, sawing, stumping and digging channels to drain the swamp.

"Dénommé Plante's out there," said Innocent casually. "Seek and ye shall find . . . "

His audacity amazed him so, he choked on his words; coughing, he cleared his throat:

" . . . as the Bible tells us."

"You're telling me if I want Dénommé Plante I should look for him — is that what you're telling me?" roared the policeman. "That's a good one! You're quite a joker! Corporal," he said to his assistant, "I didn't hear you laugh. C'mon, Corporal, let's have a good laugh! Ha! ha! ha! ha! ha!"

"Ha! ha! ha! ha! ha! Is that the kind of laugh you meant, lieutenant?"

"If you're so funny," said the policeman, serious now, "you must be from the college, eh?"

"Yes, Monsieur."

"You laugh at the power and authority that make order and morality prevail in this province? You turn up your nose at sworn officials of the police, then you put obstacles in the way of the application of criminal laws. Name. Christian name."

"Dénommé Plante isn't far away, he's just out there," Innocent hastened to point out, trying to shirk responsibility.

"Name. Christian name. Answer. Corporal, write this down. Name. Christian name. That's how you start a criminal file. Education's a fine thing: we put them in college to make them into lambs and what comes out is wolves."

"My name is Innocent Loiseau. (The two huge policemen had backed him against the wall, but he was going to win.) If I told you to seek Dénommé Plante if you wanted to find him, I said it with the greatest respect for the Holy Bible wherein lies the Truth. I said it with the greatest respect for your profession as policemen. You know how to seek and you know even better how to find."

"You hear that, Corporal? Not even a politician yet, but it lies as easy as it breathes. Just imagine, Corporal, what it's going to turn into."

"And *that*, lieutenant, is what the police'll be taking orders from."

"Yeah, but our innocent lad's still got a ways to go. Len Vinci, ever hear of him? He painted pretty pictures, portraits. Well let me paint a nice clear portrait of the situation for you. I'm puttin' my butt right here, nice and cozy, on this table; and the corporal's resting his ass quiet and peaceful on a crate — is that dynamite in there? We're going to catch our breath, take a break from life while you, you snot-nosed little brat, you're gonna go out, you're gonna walk through the mud and you're gonna bring back that bastard Dénommé Plante. If he sees a pair of handsome cops he'll get scared, he'll take to his heels, he'll jump the fence like a rabbit, and screw off into the woods. But if you go after him, Innocent, Dénommé ain't gonna be scared of a little jerk like you. He'll follow you like a trout follows a worm. And when the both of you step inside this here hut, the corporal and me, we'll pull on the hook and we'll pull in Dénommé Plante. Get the picture, little Innocent? Could Len Vinci draw it any better?"

Being humiliated, despised and mocked by the words coming from the fat foolish face with eyes like a ruminating cow — that wasn't winning. Innocent could only obey. Docile, he left the office and headed for the spot where Dénommé Plante was felling spruce trees. Innocent knew he'd find him leaning on his axe handle, stuck in the ground like a crutch, busily watching the others work. Dénommé Plante was not a vigorous man. No one had ever caught him working, but he'd always voted for the Right Party with profound sincerity. His political conviction merited a reward. Workers were accustomed to putting up with him. He did nothing. He never dirtied his hands. Never did a drop of sweat stand out in his hair, which was never dishevelled. Innocent obeyed the policeman. He felt like a beaten dog as he went out in search of Dénommé Plante, Homélie's father. His workers mustn't see that he was being obedient, nor that he was a pitiful sight. He raised his head and looked out at the horizon like a winner. He spotted Dénommé Plante. He wasn't resting on his axe handle, he was sitting on a stump.

"Monsieur Plante, you're wanted in the office."

Dénommé Plante barely took the trouble to look up. "Can't it wait till tomorrow? Like you can see, Innocent, I'm busy; I'm working . . . "

Innocent spoke as Monsieur Verrochio would have done. "Now, I said."

He turned his back without laboring the point. His order would be heard. Someone bantered:

"Little bugger sounds like he could bite."

So the workers were afraid of him. Wasn't that the meaning of winning? A joyful sense that he was respected welled up in him. Win. He turned abruptly. The workers went back to their jobs, chopping at a tree to be felled, bludgeoning a rock to be crushed, shovelling a channel to be dug, glancing at the line to be followed. These grubby workers were losers. He would win, like Monsieur Verrochio.

Innocent went back to his office. Dénommé Plante followed him: he heard the sticky earth that sucked at his boots with every step. As he led Homélie Plante's father into the shed, Innocent was merely submitting to the order of the policemen who were observing him through the dusty window.

"Dénommé," he whispered, "there's some policemen in the office."

Innocent quickened his pace. Dénommé followed the student like a beast on its way to the slaughterhouse. Behind him, Innocent heard his boots squelching in the mud.

"Make a run for it, Dénommé!"

If Homélie Plante's father fled, Innocent would be avenged for the boorish policemen's rudeness.

"Run, Dénommé!"

The man was still following him. He refused to run away, to disappear in the woods, he refused the freedom Innocent had offered.

"Dénommé, if you follow me the police will take you in."

Innocent could hear Dénommé's boots as he followed him through the mud. Innocent had offered him freedom, but Dénommé was going to give himself up to the police. It was Dénommé who would lose.

"You're a good kid, Innocent, and you'll make a good man. You're as good as homemade bread, Innocent. You're as good as Jesus Christ when he didn't condemn the two thieves, but forgave them. You wanted to save me, Innocent, but a sinner like me can't be saved, not on earth and not in heaven. Instead of choosing the road of good, I chose the road of evil. Innocent, I committed a terrible sin. I have to follow the road of evil till I'm punished."

Innocent didn't want to appear unsettled by the confession made by Homélie Plante's father. He bounded into his office and announced,

"Here he is."

The two policemen drew their guns and sprang outside.

"What's your name?" the bigger one roared.

"Dénommé Plante."

"Come with me. One false move and you're dead. We're the law. You owe one hell of a debt to society."

Along the road that hadn't yet been built, that didn't stand out yet from the mud in the fields, Innocent saw a man from his village go away between two policemen. Dénommé Plante had lost. Innocent wasn't sorry to see Dénommé Plante going away between two gun-wielding policemen. He wasn't sad to see the policemen take away a man to whom he'd offered freedom. He was getting tough. In the forest of life he would become a hardwood tree. At college, he'd been trained to be flexible, to bend with the wind. He must become like Monsieur Verrochio. Tough.

Innocent respectfully opened his ledger and, under Dénommé Plante's name, noted the precise time when he left the worksite, so Monsieur Verrochio wouldn't pay him for the time he hadn't worked. He closed the ledger like a meticulous accountant. Dénommé Plante could cause a scandal. Innocent opened the book to Dénommé Plante's page again and struck off an hour's work by way of fine. Monsieur Verrochio would approve.

He picked up the telephone.

"Hello, my love. You won't believe a word of this. It's hard for me to believe it myself, and I'm the hero of this story. I'm talking to you but I can hardly believe my own words. You know me, darling: tender, romantic, a dreamer, you've said so yourself — a poet. On your pretty lips, that may be a criticism . . . I've performed an act of unbelievable bravura. The police were here, looking for a guilty man. Do you believe me? I discovered the man and turned him over to the police myself. You have to act, darling, if you want to find out what you can do. Every man is an America to be discovered. Every action is a step in an unknown country. Darling, I dream of discovering you, body and soul. Do you ever dream of discovering me too? My love, every hour I learn a little more about winning. Will I ever be strong enough to win your heart?"

Innocent dropped the phone. He was ridiculous. If women could be won over by such nonsense, they were even more ridiculous than he. Since he'd been learning about life under Monsieur Verrochio's iron tutelage, he had a number of victories to his credit, but he hadn't yet learned anything about how to talk to women in order to win them over. No woman belonged to him as the soul belongs to the body. Monsieur Verrochio had assured him: to win, a man needs a woman. How could he learn the difficult art of talking to women if all he talked to was the cold receiver of a disconnected telephone? He'd never talked to a young girl — not one of his nasty sisters, but a real young girl, one he could love, love more than anyone else in the world, a young girl who could become one of his keys for winning in life. He didn't know any. On his disconnected telephone he exhausted himself inventing fiery phrases to impress someone who didn't even exist. He was ridiculous. No one ought to know that Monsieur Verrochio's assistant was ridiculous, that he didn't know any young girls, that he'd never talked to a real young girl, and that he told his words of love to a telephone that wasn't connected to anything.

With her chicken's body and her padded brassiere, her legs like string, her big shoes with the too high heels, her face hideously streaked with makeup, and that dried blood on her legs, Homélie Plante was not a real young girl. Had he truly talked to her? Why had the police come looking for her father? Why did Dénommé Plante denounce himself like a sinner who cannot be forgiven, when Innocent had begged him to run away to the woods to escape the police?

After Dénommé's departure, the workers were nervous; they spent more time talking than working. Innocent went out several times and hung around the groups of men, his black ledger under his arm, to make them think he'd dock them if they kept chatting. That afternoon, he glanced out his office window and saw all the workers gathered around a truck. The foreman was with them. He made a note of the time and rushed out to the meeting. These unpolished men no longer frightened him. They were all listening to the trucker, Téton Lachapelle. Innocent, approaching them, heard Téton Lachapelle talking about Dénommé Plante. Innocent decided to listen.

In the village, said the trucker, no one was talking about anything else.

Dénommé Plante had gone crazy. Till last night, he'd been an honest man who didn't drink, didn't smoke, didn't have an eye on the ladies. Last night, he'd had some kind of fit. Dénommé Plante started to abuse the new road. He had a construction job and was glad of the salary, but he criticized the new road for attracting too many men to the vicinity. Those men had the instincts of animals: they thought of nothing but coupling. He didn't like all those men going past his house. Going by, with their thoughts of coupling, the men would look at his wife. And his wife let them look, as if she didn't know that men think of nothing but coupling. Dénommé had told her to put heavy drapes at the windows. She preferred the transparent, ruffled curtains that didn't stop men who were thirsty for coupling from looking inside the house. Not only, Dénommé Plante said accusingly, had his wife not changed the curtains, the better to be seen by the men, she would go out on the veranda. When the wind blew her skirt against her legs, she exhibited herself, worse than if she were totally naked. And not only did she exhibit herself as if she were totally naked, she talked to the men who wanted to couple, and not only did she talk, she also laughed. Without a doubt they were asking her to couple and she answered with a laugh, which is a way of saying yes. Dénommé Plante had hurled these accusations, punching and kicking at the walls and furni-

301

ture. He shouted. He cried. He tore out his hair. He scratched his face. He wanted to die. He couldn't bear it that his wife, whom he loved, was giving herself to all these men coming to work on the new road, who were constantly thinking of coupling. He was sure that when he was in the fields cutting trees, his wife was back at the house, entertaining men who came to couple. He had noticed that she no longer wanted him. He hadn't learned the fancy tricks you learn in the cities; he only knew the Catholic way, not any fancy communist tricks. His way had been blessed by the Church, but that wasn't enough for the ladies since the new road had started changing the country. He understood — Dénommé cried it out — why the men smiled at the sight of him. Dénommé wanted to die. His wife had betrayed him. Clutching his head as if he wanted to tear it off his neck, Dénommé Plante cried out that not only was his wife giving herself to any passing men but his daughter, Homélie, who was only eleven years old, let them look at her too. Not only that, she would come and show herself on the veranda when the workmen were going past, thinking only of coupling. Not only did she show herself, she would stand in the wind so it would lift up her dress and the men in rut could get a good look at her panties. Then Dénommé had rushed furiously at Homélie. Thinking he was going to beat her, Dénommé's wife picked up the poker to defend her daughter. Instead of slapping her, Dénommé stopped shouting and talked almost gently, his voice filled with sobs.

"Little girl, those men are full of dirty thoughts. They want you; and they aren't entitled. Little girl, you belong to your papa."

Dénommé gently pushed Homélie into her bedroom and shut the door. His wife heard him move the bed, and realized he was pushing it against the door. Then she heard the child cry out. Dénommé's wife tried to break down the door. Dénommé began to cry out things more terrible than blasphemy. The child was wailing, screaming as if her throat had been cut. Dénommé's wife ran for help. When she returned, Dénommé had left the house and little Homélie was in her bed crying, and there was blood on her belly and thighs. Dénommé's wife looked for her husband but couldn't find him. She didn't recognize her daughter.

Homélie no longer resembled the child she used to be. "Dénommé's wife asked us to hide the awful thing that happened to him," concluded Téton Lachapelle, "but if you ask me, a terrible thing like that, nobody can hide it. Dénommé looked like an ordinary man. Who'd've thought we'd see him leaving today between two policemen, more ashamed than if he'd killed his mother."

The workers around Téton Lachapelle lowered their heads as if they were all guilty of Dénommé Plante's sin. They had lived beside him for years and no one would have guessed that Dénommé was filled with vicious madness.

"When you see a man," Téton Lachapelle began, "you can't know what misery he's carrying around in his belly. When a man gets caught by that misery, he keeps it to himself. He doesn't want to share it. When a man feels he's under attack by that misery, he wants to get rid of it himself, he wants to kill it himself. This misery was stronger than Dénommé. You know him, Dénommé never hurt a fly. Dénommé Plante did a terrible thing to his daughter, but I think it was his misery that made him do it. Nobody knows what misery can do to a man. You can't know what misery a man's got inside him," Téton Lachapelle repeated.

Innocent took a good long look at his watch so everyone could see him. Téton Lachapelle's story was extinguished like a snuffed-out flame. The workers took up their tools and moved away from the truck. They were pensive. Dénommé Plante, who had gone away between two policemen, had left among them an invisible Dénommé Plante who still disturbed them. In their throats there was the taste of shame at what he had done. They felt strange spasms in their bellies whenever they thought of what he'd done. In their heads there was giddiness, for they were trying to understand something beyond comprehension. The mystery of life was too much for their thoughts. They could not understand life, or the madness of the gentle Dénommé, a man like them, from the same part of the country, with the same winters, the same summers, the same Mass, the same school. Understanding nothing, in their impatience, their discomfort, their powerlessness, they struck the trees even harder with their axes, they attacked the ground even harder with their picks, pushed their shovels more violently into the rocky mud. What could a man do in this life, except work? When a man works, he stops thinking, and so he doesn't notice that he understands neither men nor life.

Back in his office, bending over his black ledger, Innocent struck off, one name at a time, the minutes Téton Lachapelle's account had taken from the work time of the listening men. Innocent realized that a man could commiserate with a colleague's misfortunes, but he saw no reason for the contractor to pay for sympathy time. A simple college student, exiled from his college, among men whose hands could have broken him like dry bread, he was maintaining order. Monsieur Verrochio would be proud of him. Innocent was leading the ship as if he were its captain. One day, he would be the real boss. As for Dénommé Plante, he was proud he'd handed him over to the law. He didn't feel even a pinch of remorse. The man was a brute. He knew it now, since he'd heard Téton Lachapelle's account. He knew Dénommé Plante had hurt his child, and her wound would never heal. Homélie Plante was wounded in her body, and that wound would burn all her life, like a hot coal in her belly. Dénommé had rent his daughter's soul and no scar would ever form on it. When she was a very old woman, she would still feel pain in her soul. Homélie's children, who would learn what Dénommé had done through the magic of memory that travels through the generations, on account of which nothing is forgotten, would suffer in their souls because that man had done such evil to a little girl. Because of it, Innocent was proud he had thrown a guilty man into the hands of the police.

He picked up the telephone. He wanted to spend some more time studying the proper way to talk to women. He knew he was awkward. There was just one way to learn to talk: by talking. Committing his errors, displaying his clumsiness into a telephone whose wires led nowhere, had fewer consequences than doing it in front of a real woman in the flesh (whose warmth would trouble his body and his mind, and paralyze his mouth). Into the black mouthpiece to which no voice, no breathing gave life, he struggled to talk, to win. "Hello, darling, I was thinking about you. Did you hear the terrible, bloody story of Dénommé Plante? Darling, why is there so much cruelty in life? Why do so many men choose cruelty when tenderness exists? Why do so many men choose to do evil when they could quite simply love? Love. Darling, I dream of holding your hand all my life, of guiding you through a great meadow of love, flowering with the red periwinkles of love . . . (Are periwinkles red? he wondered. Not knowing the answer, he blushed at his awkwardness. What would happen in real life if, after he'd mentioned red periwinkles, his beloved, his muse, had asked sarcastically where he'd ever seen a red periwinkle? Though he'd read so many books, he knew so little!) Darling, I've made my choice: if we're to conquer the world, if that is our destiny, we must go out hand-in-hand, armed with tenderness."

XXVII

A rebate for the baby Jesus

Outside, a voice that sounded like a barking dog was howling curses. Innocent Loiseau rushed out. A bulldozer operator, standing on his mount, was insulting all the saints in heaven. Innocent gathered that the bulldozer was stuck.

"Why can't you move?" asked Innocent.

Picotte Maillet replied, with a volley of oaths, that a bulldozer won't go through a house like a knife through butter.

Innocent didn't understand.

"Let me have a look."

The bulldozer started up and soon came to the place where it was stuck.

"Why can't you move?" he shouted, so he'd be heard over the sound of the motor.

"Because there's a shack in the way," shouted Picotte Maillet, with another stream of curses.

Monsieur Verrochio had told him, he had to win.

"Keep driving," Innocent Loiseau ordered. "Surely your machine can run over a little wooden shack."

Like a real boss, like Monsieur Verrochio's eyes and ears, Innocent jumped off the bulldozer and went up to the shack that was blocking the way. It had been built like a logger's cabin: from trunks laid one on top of another. It was brand new. Resin still dripped onto the bark. The shack had been built in the exact middle of the red pickets outlining the new road.

"Let your machine go; drive through it like a pile of feathers."

"You think I'm going to pretend there's no such thing as a law?"

"The law orders you to build the new road. Between those two lines on that land: land that's been legally requisitioned."

"I got my pride," protested Picotte Maillet, "and I'm not driving no bulldozer over the house with a poor old man and his blessed wife inside. The law's for the dying, not for bulldozers."

Was there really someone in the shack? Innocent stuck his head in the doorway. He saw two dark forms in the shadows. He heard weary breathing.

"There's somebody in that shack," Innocent declared.

"That's what I told you."

"Who do they belong to, those old folks?"

He had thought very fast, as Monsieur Verrochio would have done: if the old couple had just enough breath for one day, the bulldozer could have waited, but their lungs were solid, their breathing strong.

"The shack, it's on Guennolle Lamontagne's land; which means it's Guennolle Lamontagne's," replied Picotte Maillet. "But the old folks, a little bird told me they were borrowed . . . "

"Borrowed?" asked Innocent, amazed.

"Ain't me that said so, Innocent. I got it from a little bird. Guennolle Lamontagne sees the Right Party's cut off a chunk of his land. Guennolle, he wants a better price for it. Guennolle Lamontagne knows the law a lot better than his prayers. He knows if the government expropriates land that's got a building on it, the Right Party'll pay a better price. And if somebody's living in the shack, the price goes even higher. With two old folks, Guennolle must've figured he could make his fortune. So what he did was go and borrow a granny and grampa, seeing as how his own have been in heaven a long time, and I don't think they'd want to come down to help him pull off another stunt."

"He's leaving old people here, in the middle of the woods?"

"That ain't what I said . . . There's lots of old people. Stuck in homes like rabbits in a cage. On his wife's side, Guennolle Lamontagne's got a cousin that knows the sister of the woman that's the Local Riding Minister's secretary. The Minister's secretary, she's the cousin of the Sister Superior at the home. Which means that when Guennolle pulled up in front of Sister Superior in his hat and his Sunday suit with the wife in her flowered dress and her big purse, it made sense to the nun, when he offered to do a good deed and to take some poor old folks, who'd been breathing the old air in the home for too long, out into the fresh country air. Guennolle Lamontagne moved those ancestors into a shack in the middle of the woods. He's set his trap. And now he's waiting for the game."

"You're quite sure of all this, Monsieur Maillet?"

Picotte Maillet, perched on his bulldozer like a confident knight on his steed, couldn't quite hold back a smile. Innocent detected a hint of mockery. The young man had learned that these rugged men weren't really obedient to the less robust. Picotte Maillet was showing him the contempt deserved by a young calf who reads Latin.

"Me, I didn't say nothing, I told you I got it from a little bird."

"Poor old people! How cruel!"

"From what I heard from that there bird, Guennolle made a point of telling them, 'I'm taking you out in the woods, where it's peaceful, for a rest. And while you're resting, you'll be helping me earn a buck. After it's earned, I'll take you back to the home and give you a little cut.' Before he left the home, Guennolle Lamontagne and his Guennollette went and confessed to the Sister Superior: 'The Right Party's giving us a little present, so when we bring the old folks back, we'll give you a little rebate — for the baby Jesus."

"But those people stick to the Right Party like bloodsuckers. It's scandalous!"

"Nothing to it, Innocent. It's as simple as life . . . But you didn't hear nothing from me. And I didn't hear nothing from the birds."

"If they give the new road a name, they should call it bloodsuckers' road."

"That, Innocent my friend, is life. An infant sucks up blood in his mother's belly for nine months. The habit must stick . . . Bloodsuckers' road . . . But I'm not saying nothing: I got it from a bird."

Innocent hated the bulldozer operator's smile. Astride his huge machine, he towered over Innocent. There was a look of mockery in his yellow-toothed smile that spread to cheeks smudged with five o'clock shadow and axle grease. To avoid his contempt, Innocent must show himself to be the stronger. Win. Win. Suddenly his body shuddered as if he'd been struck by a bolt of lightning which gave him tremendous strength.

"Is that gasoline?" he asked.

Innocent had spotted a tin at the back of the bulldozer.

"Watch out!" Picotte Maillet exclaimed with ten curses, "there's gas inside!"

Innocent's white hands picked up the gasoline. He unscrewed the stopper and poured the contents over the shack, quickly, without hesitation.

"Give me a match."

Picotte Maillet held out a match, protesting:

"Don't light it, Innocent, it'll burn."

Innocent was the stronger now. Picotte Maillet, on his machine, was no longer taunting, but pleading. He begged Innocent,

"Don't set it on fire, Innocent, there's people in there. Those old folks are gonna fry!"

Innocent won. The shack stood on the site for the road that was being built by Monsieur Verrochio and he was Verrochio's eyes and ears. The people who had put the shack here wanted to exploit the Right Party and Le Chef, who had chosen Innocent. The law protected Monsieur Verrochio and the Right Party. He struck the match. A large, violent flower of fire spread and roared through the cabin. Win. Innocent felt power burning inside him. The resinous bark crackled.

"I told you Innocent, it's gonna blow up," said Picotte Maillet. "The old folks came running out like devils baptized with holy water."

The roof caved in under the flames and blazed furiously. The walls burned with a hissing sound. The new wood, cool and still wet with sap, contained too much life to let itself burn; the flames died down.

"Take that away," Innocent ordered, pointing to the blackened debris.

Picotte Maillet started his motor; Innocent looked at his watch, calculating how much time the operator had lost while he was stopped outside Guennolle Lamontagne's shack. He would subtract those minutes in his black ledger. He had won. Monsieur Verrochio would be proud of him.

Innocent won and became a man: not one of those men made effeminate by wearing skirts, like women, men who stagnated in warm colleges like jam in an overheated cupboard; not a man like his father who, from struggling to make a living where there was nothing to win, had the sorrowful eyes of one who is without hope. He would be a man like Monsieur Verrochio, a man who slashed through mountains to put in roads, a man who pushed back forests, a man who joined the countryside to the towns, a man who had built the streets leading to the Parliament in the Capital, down which drove Le Chef himself. He would learn how to win. He would win. Win like Monsieur Verrochio, like Le Chef, like Caesar, like Napoleon. Monsieur Verrochio had opened the door to real life for him. Win. Win like Innocent Loiseau. He would learn how to talk to women. Back in his office, he would pick up the telephone and apply himself to seducing the woman at the other end of the disconnected wire, who didn't yet exist. He would tell her how some wily peasants had decided to hold the Right Party up to ransom and stop the advance of progress, tell her how he'd turned out the old profiteers who thought that, because they were old, they were entitled to hold up progress, tell her how he had set fire to the shack. He would promise her that one day, on this new road, in a big car longer than Monsieur Verrochio's, he would take her away — his fiancée — dressed in a long white gown, its veil floating in the air above the car, take her to unknown cities, the countries where happiness dwells. He would talk about all that on the telephone, hesitating, searching for his words, repeating himself, he would learn how to polish his sentences smooth, he would learn to use words to win over the mind, the heart and the body of the woman who would then become his soul. Monsieur Verrochio had told him: he would win only for his wife, and he would win because his wife would give him strength.

Back at his own shack, Innocent spotted Homélie Plante. She was leaning against the wall, her high-heeled shoes clotted with mud. Her skinny legs were dirty. Makeup streaked her face and neck. An empty brassiere hung on her chest.

"I'm looking for my father," she announced.

So no one had told Homélie that the police had come and seized her father. Innocent didn't know where Dénommé Plante was now. He went inside his office without replying and shut the door.

Later, bursts of laughter from outside wrenched him from his black ledger. Children's laughter. Hoarse laughter. Vast guffaws that couldn't be contained by a child's frail chest.

An old man and an old woman, clinging together like adolescents in love, were walking past the shack, barefoot in the mud of the new road, sinking down, sliding, helping and holding on to one another. He carried his black boots, she carried her black shoes. They were choked with laughter. Her loose grey hair was flying in the wind; his bare skull gleamed in the sun. Her dress was torn and not buttoned properly; his shirt hung out of his trousers. They repeated over and over an inexhaustible joke. It was the old couple from Guennolle Lamontagne's shack, who had bolted when he lit the fire. They were experiencing forbidden joy.

Innocent watched them walk along the muddy road and disappear like a dream that would come back to him often.

XXVIII

The accountant's ledger and the devil's notebook

The spruce trees were moving back. The swamps were filled in. The streams were re-directed. Bulldozers rolled over muddy earth, rocks and stumps. The road was advancing. Trucks rumbled, their wheels stuck in mud. The foreman castigated his men who were always stopping to gripe about the mosquitoes or to tell stories that made them spit laughter.

Verrochio had come to the worksite several times. He would drive his Cadillac until the wheels got stuck and the car ran aground, its belly stuck in the mud. Then he would spring out, with his fine shoes, white socks and pale trousers. Trapped by the mud, he would grumble, threaten, hurl abuse. Nothing had been done according to his orders. The road was too narrow or too wide. The base was defective. The drainage had been neglected. The work was going too slowly. The curves were too abrupt or too long. The space hadn't been sufficiently cleared. Levels had not been respected. Frost-resistant materials hadn't been used as fill. Why had he hired these men? The cows in the next field would have given better results. Never had he seen such poor work. He had built prestigious roads before this:

Le Chef had chosen him to build the fine roads that would testify to the Right Party's genius. Why should this particular road look like nothing so much as a cow path? Were they trying to drive him to ruin? Would these workers have to be whipped? He talked, he seemed to laugh, to cry, but he was praying, pleading, whining. If his orders weren't followed, he'd close down the site and fire the workers.

"If you fire us, we'll vote for the Opposition," snickered a worker who was leaning on his shovel, listening to Verrochio's laments.

"Innocent, you gonna take off an hour, they been lazing around listening to me instead of doing their job. Innocent! You take off an hour. Understand?"

As he spoke, he was sinking slowly into the mud. The workers, faces baked by the sun and strained by the efforts of their tasks, watched him being sucked down, and they smiled a terribly tranquil smile.

The first time Verrochio threatened them like this, the men were surprised. They had feared his words the way animals fear blows. When he left, they talked about his violence and his threats. If Verrochio had landed the contract to build this new road, it was a favor from Le Chef, they deduced, because everything done in the province was a special favor granted by Le Chef. Their own jobs were favors obtained from Le Chef and his Minister. It seemed obvious that work couldn't be interrupted unless Le Chef wanted it. Before the election, Le Chef wouldn't want to interrupt any works: if work on the new road was interrupted, the workers would vote against the Right Party . . . The new road would be built, then, in spite of Verrochio's threats. So why was he ranting and raving? He represented just one vote, whereas all the workers . . . Their fear took flight like dandelion silk carried away by the wind.

After Verrochio's fits of authority they started following a ritual that took shape from visit to visit. The foreman started following a ritual that took shape from visit to visit. The foreman would explain that his men were the best workers he'd ever seen, on any job; he pointed out that his workers hadn't been spoiled by city comforts, that they still considered it quite normal to work like horses. They weren't the kind of men whose arms had been ruined by machines. Unfortunately, he would go on, it was hard to work the land here, it was tough: "It's as if the land doesn't want men to build a road across its back."

Another stage in the ritual consisted of making the contractor walk through the mud to show him the work that had been accomplished, despite tremendous difficulties. He was taken to the end of the road, where men were cutting spruce trees, the bulldozer was pushing out rocks and piling up earth for the roadbed, and the steam shovel was digging irrigation ditches.

"I wish we'd made more progress," the foreman acknowledged, "but it's no piece of cake, making a road in the land God gave to Cain."

"No excuses," Verrochio broke in, "I'm hear them all before. There's nothing can fight hard work. And that's all you need here — hard work. I'm tell you again: I'm pay you to work. No work, no wages. If I'm lose one red cent on this road, I'm shut down. Even before the elections."

The workers didn't believe him. If anyone shut down the worksite, it would be Le Chef. Their fine self-confidence spread across their ravaged faces like an insolent smile. Their eyes, scratched by dust and blazing sunlight, sparkled with obvious mockery. They knew how Verrochio had obtained the contract to build the new road.

A few days earlier, a new employee had arrived. From the sight of his hands it was obvious the young man was used to wearing gloves. The heaviest tool he could hold seemed to be a pencil. At any moment, he'd stop and write something in a green notebook. It was as if he was afraid of forgetting his ideas and had to put on paper everything that came into his head. After writing, he took up his shovel again, struggling to lift some earth, then awkwardly throwing it into the dump body of the truck. He couldn't work for long without becoming exhausted. His backbone and the muscles in his little arms were too feeble for these man's tasks. What was such a sissy doing on the new road? At its end he surely wouldn't find the future he was seeking. What route had this young weakling taken to end up here, working with men? To such questions he gave answers that didn't seem like answers. He talked more to his notebook than to men. He wasn't impolite. To all questions he replied softly, a few words, but never a real reply. Who was he? Who was this young stranger who was the same age as Innocent Loiseau? Every man questioned him. Every one tried to guess something of his secret. To all, he would give a brief reply with the sort of politeness that is learned in the calm boredom of colleges. They knew he'd come to work in the fresh air of this wild land because he had to restore his health. He'd said to someone, "restore my soul." To another, he had confided that he wanted to "start his life over." People thought that was going a bit far because, in their opinion, before you can start your life over, you have to have already lived. This youngster had fuzz on his chin. His skin was as smooth as an altar-boy's surplice. Often, he would look up to heaven, fascinated. He would breathe the air as someone might drink from a spring. Jeannot Tremblay drew attention to himself. People would look at him as at a gentle fool, bright where books were concerned, but rather dim in real life. A man can't make his way down life's highway with his nose in a green note-book. The newcomer wasn't simple-minded. When he talked the others didn't always understand. They had to ask him to repeat himself. Sometimes even twice. When they understood what he'd said, it wasn't so much true under-standing as a semblance. When he was drinking the wind of the fields with his lips like a baby's attached to the ma-ternal breast, and felt himself being observed, he would say: "After everything I've been through, I'm thirsty for clean air." Try to understand! People didn't want to insult him because he talked in such a complicated way or because his flabby arms didn't do their fair share of work. Once, Jeannot Tremblay said: "The mud on your boots and the spruce gum on your hands are as clean as spring water. I've floundered about in much dirtier substances." Watch-ing them shrug, Jeannot Tremblay added to make his words clearer: "I've come to roll in your mud to cleanse myself." If a real man had delivered himself of such a statement, one of the workers would have beat him up to show him how a man's supposed to talk, but this weak fool was sacred, like an angel.

Innocent had noticed that Jeannot Tremblay did less work than the others, that he often rested, out of breath, leaning on his shovel; he had noticed that Jeannot Trem-blay dreamed, open-mouthed, breathing in the wind, eyes filled with vertigo as he beheld the sky. He had too often seen him stop shovelling to scribble in his green notebook. Jeannot Tremblay wasted time and Innocent had decided to take a few hours off his time-sheet. Monsieur Verrochio was opposed to it: "That child, you'll have to take him like he is: it was a reporter at *The Provincial Sun* recommended him to Le Chef and Le Chef, he take pity on him, because that poor child, he's been through Hell . . . A recommendation from Le Chef, that demands respect. And a reporter's friend, you always treat him nice. So you put in your black book all the hours Jeannot Tremblay works. He's a little bandit. Now he's howling how he's go through Hell. People say he's sell his mother . . . Innocent, keep your eye on him. If a boy's sold his mother, he'll do anything."

"How can you sell your mother?" Innocent asked, thinking of the great slave markets in ancient times, unable to see what benefits a young man might derive from the sale of his own mother.

"You're a young fellow, Innocent, you haven't been through Hell . . . "

Monsieur Verrochio explained to his clerk what he'd been told when he was asked to hire Jeannot Tremblay. Saint-Toussaint-des-Saints was a long way from the Capital. With the protection of distance, Jeannot Tremblay could start his life over, restore his physical and emotional health. The young man's body and soul were more rotten than if he were being eaten away by cancer, leprosy and all the mortal sins. Far from the city, he could purify himself in the Appalachian winds.

Monsieur Verrochio entrusted Innocent to watch over Jeannot Tremblay, a bandit of his own age who had sold his mother into slavery. This Jeannot was a poisonous serpent. Innocent was walking cautiously now, like one who is aware that snakes can bite. He hesitated before entering his office; he searched the shadows with a gaze that, one day, would see the glow of the serpent's eyes. Because he was afraid, he repeated, in veiled terms, what Monsieur Verrochio had confided to him. So this tall skinny creature traded in his mother's sins. The boy deserved a beating. The workers rubbed their knuckles, itching to have a go at the youth who used his pick to scrape delicately at the earth, his pencil to scratch softly in his green notebook.

They restrained themselves. They waited. They couldn't believe that a young man who looked so harmless, so delicate and freshly scrubbed, could do anything so ignoble. On the job, he wouldn't kill a fly. Yet he had sold his own mother.

If the truth be told, they kept their distance. They were waiting for the skinny youth to make his first mistake so they could hand out the sort of punishment reserved in the Appalachians for those who have brought shame to a man's honor. They resented this Jeannot as much as if he had spat in the face of each man's mother. They despised him for his way with the pick, for his shovelfuls of earth. Wasn't this young man scattering curses along the roadway? When they saw him behaving like a bird that looks at the sky but doesn't fly, they spat on the ground. After seeing him gaze up to heaven as if he could see the Almighty in person, they went furiously back to work; they attacked the earth, the rocks, the spruce trees because they couldn't attack Jeannot Tremblay. The young sinner who was trying to purify himself with such an obvious display must be as hypocritical as he was loathsome. His repentant sinner's attitude hid something else. Finding the fires of Hell too hot, he had recoiled; he was acting the man who is suffering from burns, but when a man has tasted Hell, the memory remains deep inside him forever. When a man has known Hell, he needs plenty of Heavens to keep him from wanting to go back. Or so people said.

No one wanted to be on the same side of the road as Jeannot. People stayed as far away from him as possible. If Jeannot Tremblay greeted one of the workers, the worker would turn his head. If Jeannot Tremblay's eyes came to rest on one of them, he would receive the glance like spittle and move his hand as if to wipe it away. Jeannot Tremblay was alone. A rare weed.

Innocent Loiseau and Jeannot Tremblay were bound to talk to one another. One day at noon the venomous serpent was in the office, facing him. Innocent couldn't look away. His eyes couldn't avoid Jeannot Tremblay's eyes that, in the Hell of his life, had been burnt by visions Innocent would never know.

"Nobody will look at me," Jeannot Tremblay complained. "I haven't heard a human voice talk to me for

317

days. I know they'll soon be throwing stones. They hate me. They can't forgive me because I was unlucky. Any more than people can forgive a man who's had good luck. In fact, nothing is forgiven . . . The man who takes the wrong road isn't forgiven when he wants to take another turn. I'm going to have an accident. You represent the boss here. I want you to write down, black on white, that the accident I'm going to have will be caused by someone who doesn't forgive . . . My life has been troubled. I've crawled through terrible ordeals. I want to get back on my feet. If I can get back on my feet, if I can think clearly again, if I can find serene light for my soul, if I can convince myself that not everything in this world is rotten, not everyone afflicted with gangrene of the soul and heart, then those ordeals will have given me a knowledge of life, wisdom, and a conscience that will help me live better . . . I've been unlucky. No one wants my luck to change. They'd like to see me poured into my past, like cement. The only person who's helped me is the man who spreads corruption across the province like jam on a slice of bread. Le Chef. I saw him. He knew about my bad luck. Le Chef told me: 'I'm opening a new road in the Appalachians. The air's clean, the ground's hard. Opening a road transforms a man. When a man opens a road through forest or mountains, it makes him want to keep on going. He becomes a man with hope.' Do you hear what I'm saying? The man who gave me that message of hope is the same one who rules by despair."

Win. Innocent mustn't let himself be hypnotized by the shining eyes of this serpent disguised as a golden-tongued young man. He mustn't let himself be dazzled by phrases that writhed like poisonous reptiles. Win. How could he kill a serpent that spoke with the charm of the one that had damned Eve in the Garden of Eden? Win. Not let himself be strangled by the fine, tear-filled words in which Jeannot Tremblay wrapped himself. Win. A serpent must be struck on the head. Innocent Loiseau aimed and fired between the eyes.

"The people here know your past. They know more than you're telling us. We'd just as soon not see you and your past. Here in the Appalachians, the air's still pure and the earth is clean. They can see you coming. With a past like yours, they won't roll out the red carpet like they would for the bishop. What they want is for you not to be there. They'll help send you on your way."

"I'm condemned."

"You'd be better off leaving. The evil life you've led has given you a bad smell."

Innocent Loiseau was winning. Jeannot Tremblay turned pale. His eyes grew dull. Innocent was sorry he'd struck so hard. Jeannot Tremblay was still talking, ingratiatingly. Innocent felt sad. Immediately, he stiffened.

"I have suffered. And that word doesn't begin to express the torture that has ground my soul, day and night. I was on the verge of giving in to despair for all eternity, but I met a friend: a good friend whom I had fled because I was suffering too much. A suffering man doesn't want to share his pain. I was alone. A friend offered me his hand."

Win. Not let himself be charmed by this serpent. Innocent wasn't one of those who would extend his hand to a venomous serpent. As soon as he could, he would squash its head.

"I was about to disappear forever in the inferno my life was then, but a friend offered me his hand. I tell you that in confidence. We're around the same age, you and I. If there's one thing we can understand at our age, it's friendship. You can't imagine the horrible things that happened to me, but you can understand friendship. He was a friend I'd treated with the sort of contempt I wouldn't have wished on an enemy. I'd erased him from my life. It was as if I'd killed him in my mind. If I ever thought of him, I was sorry I'd known him. Achille Bédard, the rejected friend in question, is a journalist who's preparing to declare war on all the corruption in the world. Achille offered me his hand. He reminded me of our oath. He forced me to look out the window and see that the sun was shining, that life hadn't stopped because of one sordid hour. Achille Bédard reminded me that he and I had sworn an oath. We had placed our oath in a bottle and thrown it into the river where it would be carried out to sea. It contained our promise to help our fellow humans to a better life. We had sworn to guide our brothers along roads where they would find justice, respect and hope."

Innocent was surprised to hear so many words from the mouth of the silent employee. Listening to him wouldn't help him win. Innocent realized that this misled youth,

who was his own age, wanted to become a leader; he had
sworn an oath to that effect and cast it out to sea. To
become a leader you must win. This young man had taken
roads where one could only lose. One must despise losers
if one is to win. The slightest sympathy for losers was the
first step on the road to defeat. Innocent Loiseau was learning how to win. Only by winning do you learn to win.
Monsieur Verrochio had learned to win by winning. Those
who lose don't even exist. He must not even listen to them,
because they don't exist. He must not be moved by their
troubles, because they don't exist. Jeannot Tremblay was
facing him, so Innocent couldn't help but see him. On the
young man's face there was an invisible shadow, a mask
left by suffering. Jeannot Tremblay was no serpent. A
serpent was incapable of suffering; only men could suffer
in that way. Innocent must win. He must not let himself
be weakened by sad words. Monsieur Verrochio, who had
learned how to win, wouldn't have listened to Jeannot
Tremblay. Didn't listening to losers make you a loser too?
Innocent picked up his black ledger and said, so he could
slip away:

"It's time for my inspection tour."

Monsieur Verrochio's words had changed his life, whereas
Jeannot Tremblay's plaintive remarks, the words of his
defeat, weighed on him.

"Nobody here talks to me. Since you and I are around
the same age and you remind me of my friend Achille
Bédard, the journalist who helped me, I'd thought you
might help me too. I want to rebuild myself, because all
that bad luck destroyed me. Achille Bédard found me this
job. He knows Le Chef, because Le Chef got him onto *The
Provincial Sun*. He asked Le Chef to send me to the pure
air of the Appalachians to re-build my body through work.
Achille Bédard is one of Le Chef's men, but he's a journalist in search of the truth. Achille Bédard and I are going to study, we're going to observe real life, we're going
to train our minds, we're going to listen to the obscure
voice of the people, we're going to learn how to give words
to the silent thoughts of our people. We've sworn an
oath that we'll take power. Because you're our age, I'd
thought I could talk to you as a friend, the way I talk to
Achille Bédard . . . "

The venomous serpent had wrapped itself around him. The serpent had guessed that Innocent was a winner. Already he was talking about power.

"I thought you'd like to know the terms of that oath we sent out to sea. You know that all life comes from the sea; we learn that in Biology. The oath we swore will come back from the sea and touch the shore. When that happens, our time will have come. I'd hoped that you'd be with us. We're going to re-establish truth, justice and friendship in the Province. When I was going through Hell, Achille Bédard rekindled that dream. I came here to re-build my body through hard labor and re-build my soul by listening to what ordinary people have to say, people who live life instinctively. I need a body and a soul like theirs. I need to learn to read the unexpressed desires in my compatriots' souls . . . That's why I'm here . . . I'll develop the genuine strength of a man. This new road will lead me from despair to hope. It's here that I must assemble my first friends. It's from here that we'll set out and together we will build the road to the future . . . That's what I wanted to tell you because we're the same age and you can understand things that those men can't. I was struck by a terrible misfortune. It was a sign. At the beginning of the life of any man who's going to be important, there's always a sign. I could have stayed in Hell. But here I am building a road under the blue sky, in the Appalachian wind. The future of our Province will happen right here, in this mud. You know that at the beginning of the world, the earth was nothing but mud. Everything comes from the mud. The spirit emerges from the mud so as to order it, organize it. It's here that I'm going to carry out the oath we sealed in a bottle and cast into the river. I'd have liked to have you with us. This province needs young people. Our province needs its young people to unite and conquer the stagnant old age of power. This province needs youth. Being young means being able to win against the causes of death."

"To win?" sighed Innocent Loiseau.

"To win. Make the province win out over those who would have it die . . . "

"Win?"

"Yes. The Right Party always wins elections, but the province loses. I would like the province to win with its

321

young people, its people, its future. You're almost the same age as I am, you should understand that."

The serpent's words had Innocent absolutely hypnotized.

"Innocent, the young people shouldn't be divided. This province is being eaten away by a corrupt government. The Right Party: that's the name of a disease, not a government."

"You're very eloquent."

Innocent blushed, he was so ashamed of having uttered these words. A certain admiration had spurred him on. This Jeannot Tremblay, marked by misfortune, had sworn an oath and sent it out to sea: this young man contained a will, a strength, a destiny.

"I hope I have faith, not eloquence," replied Jeannot Tremblay. "I think a great deal. I've talked a lot with my friend the journalist. You'll meet him some day. He knows as much about corruption in the Right Party as the Curé of Saint-Toussaint-des-Saints knows about his parishioners' sins. I listen a lot. My bad luck taught me a lot: I feel as if I've lived several lives. And then there's my notebook; I often jot down what I think. When a thought is written down, it's not forgotten. I'm glad you're listening to me, Innocent. I can understand why the others don't like me. They don't like what's dirty, and my past misfortunes have given me a smell they don't like."

Innocent couldn't win out against this employee now. He would wait, keep an eye on him, he would follow in his traces and when the time was right, he'd run him into the ground.

"What do you write in your notebook?"

"Poetry. I think in poetry a lot. Poetry is thought in the process of being born; it's alive. My poetry comes from what is being lived by our brothers of the new road."

"You think they'll understand?"

"They'll understand. What I write is what they think in their desires, in their sorrow, in their submissiveness that's sometimes silent and sometimes filled with blasphemy."

The workers summed them up with mocking looks and words that whistled between the chipped teeth of their smiles.

"Some day I'll tell you . . . I'll tell you about my poor father's bad luck and my mother's humiliation . . . Let me read you something I wrote yesterday: 'Sometimes, at a turn in the road, you come upon an apple tree laden with fine fruit that gleams in the sun. You draw near. The perfume is delectable. The leaves rustle softly. You hold out your hand and pull away an apple. You place your lips on its sweet peel and press your teeth . . . Horror of horrors! it's rotten. You go to another side and select another apple. It too is rotten. All the apples on the tree are rotten. All the branches of the tree are rotten. The trunk of the apple tree is rotten. It stands up only through the strength of its decay. So then, in disgust and to prevent another traveller from being disgusted by the rot, you give the tree a little push and it collapses. There's no such apple tree, you say? But it does exist, and its name is the name of our province. All who live here are worms grown fat on its rot.' "

Innocent was astounded. He had as much to learn from Jeannot Tremblay as from Monsieur Verrochio. He must not bring down Jeannot Tremblay. Not now. Even though the rotten apple trees didn't look like the one Jeannot Tremblay had described.

"The province needs some gallant knights who are prepared to attack the tree of corruption: there's my friend, Achille Bédard, there's me, and now there's you. Others will come. By the end of this summer everyone who's working on this road will be with us."

Jeannot Tremblay was a poet. All Innocent could do was record the hours his men had worked in his black ledger. Jeannot Tremblay wasn't a poet mourning his lost youth, but one who announced the future. To win: didn't that mean allying himself with him?

"I wish I could have sworn the same oath as you and your friend and sent it out to sea in a bottle . . . "

"So you're with us?" asked Jeannot Tremblay.

"Yes."

"The road we're opening," said Jeannot Tremblay, "is already a rotten fruit. It's not being built because men need roads for commerce and freedom; no, this new road is being built to get votes. The Right Party has thrown crumbs to these poor people, and the Right Party is waiting to hear these same people sing its praises, like little birds who will then drop the turds of their votes into the Right Party's ballot box."

Innocent was sorry he lived in the Appalachians instead of the Capital. There, he'd have attended the same college as the poet and his friend. He'd have set out to conquer the province with Achille Bédard and Jeannot Tremblay. Jeannot and Achille were part of the future, while Monsieur Verrochio already was part of the past. You can't win with the past.

"Since you're with us, we must strike at once. We must bring down the first rotten fruit: Verrochio."

"Attack Monsieur Verrochio?" asked Innocent, astonished.

"You see, you're an honest citizen of Saint-Toussaint-des-Saints, and you've already been touched by corruption. Put a healthy apple up against a rotten one. What happens? The healthy apple goes bad. And that's how corruption spreads across the province."

"But I'm seeing to Monsieur Verrochio's interests here."

"Verrochio has sown rot along every road he's built. Verrochio's building this road through the Appalachians because the contract's his reward. His wife slept with the Minister of Roads and Bridges."

"Monsieur Verrochio gave me good advice. Should I believe you?"

"Innocent, do you think I'd tell you that if I didn't trust you? Do you think I'd tell you that if I didn't consider you the equal of my friend Achille Bédard? We have to start the clean-up. You, Innocent, you can talk . . . Look for young people, people our age, who want to build the future. Tell them the old power is rotten. Innocent, the men on the new road must know that Verrochio's a miserable guy who had to give his wife to the Minister of Roads and Bridges as a tax. He'd be begging at the street-corner if his wife hadn't rescued him by giving herself to the Minister. Innocent, tell your employees Verrochio's no man of iron, he's a poor worm writhing in pain, in the mud of this road that leads nowhere."

"So Monsieur Verrochio's a loser."

"With the Right Party, nobody wins; we all lose."

"Monsieur Verrochio taught me how to always win . . . "

"Innocent, what price did you pay in exchange for working on this new road?"

He hesitated, just the length of a sigh. It was too long. Jeannot Tremblay had read his silence. Innocent wanted to lie, but not telling the truth seemed contemptible.

"My father had to buy me a life-insurance policy in exchange for this job."

"You see! Your father paid a tax on corruption. Your price is the shame that you'll bear for the rest of your days, for having been in the service of corruption. Innocent, one day there won't be just the two of us, there'll be thousands, and we won't seal our oath inside a bottle, we'll make it ring out down all the roads in the province."

Innocent was dumbfounded. So Monsieur Verrochio was just pretending to be a champion, when he was nothing but a poor humiliated man: a loser. Why had Monsieur Verrochio taught him the ways of winning if he was a loser himself? Now he'd have to choose between Jeannot Tremblay and Monsieur Verrochio. What was he to do? Innocent no longer knew which man he represented, with his black ledger under his arm.

Like a great poet, Jeannot Tremblay could talk about dreams and the future and the present; logically, it seemed as if everything he said sounded like the truth and everything he foresaw for the future would come true. The sun was shining as if it would never drop behind the horizon.

When Verrochio came to the worksite his face was creased with worry. Innocent knew now that he wasn't worried about engineering, surveying, irrigation, culverts or levelling problems; he was being chewed away by sorrow at having lost his wife and by the humiliation of defeat. Verrochio had taught Innocent that you needed a wife in order to win. Innocent had made impromptu speeches into an unconnected telephone to learn how to conquer a woman. The future was elsewhere. Jeannot Tremblay had shown him he must learn how to talk to the entire province.

Innocent got in the habit of arriving at the construction site long before the others. He would leave long after the others as well. He would talk to the wind, addressing the boles of the tall spruce trees, he would harangue Mont Bonnet. The echo returned his voice filled with all the forces of nature. To crowds of spruce and starlings, he denounced corruption, prophesying that youth would come like clear water to cleanse the province, he gesticulated, his finger threatening the clouds, he shouted to make the sky tremble, he threw out words that formed circles in the branching forest as a pebble draws rounds in the river. The scrawny spruce learned before men did about the corruption from which the new road was made. He asked stones piled up by generations why they had sold their right to vote for a miserable wage. He told the stumps that, to give men the right to practice the trade that would support their families, women had to give themselves to Cabinet Ministers. To the small creatures that spend their lives hidden in damp grass, he confided the drama of Verrochio, the man who had won everything and who would lose everything. Innocent cried out the truth to the sky, to the trees, to the swamps, the echoes, the birds, to the stones . . . Sometimes during his Demosthenean exercises a cow would moo; he laughed, saying inwardly that she was agreeing with him, just like a voter. If he learned how to convince nature, he'd be able to convince a woman too. When Innocent deemed that he could tell the sun the story of a poor Italian who amassed a fortune in America, but had been saved from ruin by his wife who gave herself to a Minister, he decided that now he could tell it to the village of Saint-Toussaint-des-Saints, begging them not to repeat it. He knew what he was doing.

The next day, Verrochio drove up. He got out of his Cadillac, triumphant and regal. Instead of applying themselves to their jobs with redoubled ardor, the workers merely stared, a smile on their dry, sunburnt lips. He couldn't know that his employees were reading through his body, and that they saw his soul, humiliated, like a goldfish in a jar.

Verrochio raised his arms, waved his hands, grumbled, insulted, threatened. The men moved with the indolence of security. Le Chef needed their votes. They watched Verrochio slide in the mud like a duck on ice. The foreman appeared to be drawing up the list of problems his workers had encountered: the swamps and the bedrock, a hill whose slope the engineers had miscalculated, defective machinery. Verrochio, muttering in Italian, agreed to visit the site. The foreman led him to where the mud was deepest. A man who's been deceived by his wife deserves that. After listening to Verrochio's comments, the foreman accompanied him to his Cadillac, where he sat down, ridiculously shaking his mud-caked legs. Verrochio started the motor, but as usual, he had driven too far. The Cadillac was bogged down like a pachyderm that roars but doesn't move. The workmen watched him, smiling, not daring to laugh. They kept themselves peacefully busy. The Cadillac overheated, surrounded by black smoke.

Innocent decided to stop docking time from the workers. These people were underpaid, they did the sorts of jobs no longer done by oxen or horses. They deserved their full wages, with no punitive deductions. In his black ledger, Innocent would note only generous working hours.

The season advanced. In his soul, time passed, changing something. He was becoming a man. Along this road that was still merely a muddy rent through fields and forest, Innocent was slowly advancing toward his life as a man.

XXIX

Wherein reference is made to the famous swineherd in the *Odyssey*

That week, *The Provincial Sun* ran a picture of a bulldozer that was opening the new road in Saint-Toussaint-des-Saints. It showed stones and stumps retreating behind the steel blade. The forest was being vanquished by conquering civilization. In the past, only foresters, loggers and hunters could come this way, along with the wild animals, but the caption promised that soon, automobiles would be driving through the countryside as if it were a street in the Capital, adding: "To the Right Party, masterfully led by Le Chef, the population says, Thank you, and wishes you a long life, as good sons wish to their father."

Across the bottom of page 19, the paper ran pictures of some of the workers on the new road. In various houses and around kitchen tables, the paper was passed from hand to hand. For the next few evenings they scrutinized the grey-and-white squares in which faces grimaced, smiled, scowled, posed, tensed and simpered. Those in the pictures didn't recognize themselves; they "didn't look like that," they protested. The others teased them, laughing and pointing at goofy smiles, bushy beards, wrinkles, at eyes that squinted to avoid the camera. They re-read the caption: "The Right Party has brought to the Appalachians the modern might of machines that help men in the performance of their heavy tasks. Without exemplary, devoted workers, machines are worthless. By providing jobs on the road, the Right Party has made the right decision, just as these gallant workers will make the right decision when they vote for the Right Party. These zealous workers are building a great future for our small population." (See article by our fiery reporter Achille Bédard, page 4.)

Never before had these workers had their pictures in the paper. They had struggled all their lives like their fathers, they had worked at difficult tasks like beasts of burden, and no one had ever noticed them. This appearance in the Right Party's newspaper marked the first time they were honored. As Le Chef made all the decisions for the Right Party, they knew that this tribute came from Le Chef. And so, despite the teasing, they knew that the Right Party loved its workers: not just because it gave them work, but because it set them up as an example to the population at large. It was a great honor. People tore the page from the paper and pinned it conspicuously to the kitchen wall, right under the statue of the Blessed Virgin. In spite of all the whispering about the Right Party's dishonesty, they had to face facts: the Opposition had never paid tribute to workers. *The Provincial Sun* provided a further explanation: "The Right Party is the party of honest workers, while the Opposition is the party of those who would take hold of power. The desire to take hold of power is not constructive work, like building a new road for the populace. The Right Party recognizes the rights of the populace to go straight where it wants, without too many bumps or detours. The Opposition always wants the opposite of what the Right Party has to give. Voters: have you considered that if the Right Party is giving you a new road, it means that the Opposition will not give you a new road? If the Right Party is providing jobs for the honest workers in our land, it means that the Opposition — always seeking the opposite — would give them unemployment. Think it over. Give your votes to the Right Party and its Chef, who are giving you a new road, work, and a number of promises." The article appeared in a box above the workers' photographs.

Le Chef was particularly satisfied with the editorial by Achille Bédard, the reporter who had succeeded Sautereau, who brought to the paper a youthful outlook that Sautereau had lost. Le Chef felt that his articles crackled proudly in the air, like a flag:

THE OPPOSITION GIVES BIRTH TO A LIE
THAT REFLECTS IT AS FALSEHOODS REFLECT
THE GULLIBLE FOOLS WHO BELIEVE THEM.

Breasting with its rapier-sharp bow the waves of kindly indifference or enemy disparagement, the Right Party is opening a new road through the inhospitable territory of Saint-Toussaint-des-Saints. The local population has a warm heart, but the land is the roughest, the harshest, the most demanding, the most stubborn, most violent in God's creation: a land for strong men and women. The new road built by the Right Party with the muscle-power of the local populace symbolizes the Road to Tomorrow that is being built for us by the Right Party's M.P.s, Ministers, organizers and contractors, who are all brothers in the great family whose father is our Chef.

The Opposition does not want a new road for our population. The Opposition would like to lead our people back to that remote era when the idea of progress was not yet firmly anchored in the heart of the people. The Opposition would like our population, rather than hopping on board the prestigious, speedy train of progress, to watch progress pass them by as they stare, dazed, like cows watching a train go through the countryside.

Fortunately, the population of the entire Appalachian Region has proclaimed: We want progress! We want modern times! We want to keep up with the times! We want a new road!

The Provincial Sun is on the side of the population and joins it in declaring unanimously: "We want a new road and we're going to have it!"

What can the Opposition do? When one is powerless, one lies. Can a lie raise up the sea? The train of modern progress, of which the Right Party's ship is the locomotive ringing the bell of hope, is sailing through fair weather. With the Right Party, our people's future will be just as fair.

The Opposition lies. Unable to turn back the implacable hands of time, unable to slow down progress or modern times, unable to slow down the enthusiastic work of laborers who are creating a highway out of swamp and forest, the Opposition sullies reputations. It says that one man sells his mother, another his wife, in return for favors. When the Opposition opens its mouth dung, not human speech spews out. Birds crap and pigs do too, but the sky still exists. As for the question whether the members of the Opposition are birds or pigs, we would ask: Have you ever seen an Opposition member fly? The answer is a resounding No, NEVER! And pigs don't fly either.

Achille Bédard

P.S. Did you know that the head (so to speak) of the Opposition is called Joseph-Eumée. In Greek, he'd be called Eumaeus. And isn't that the name of a famous swineherd? You can check this mythological reference with your Curé, a man as erudite as he is holy, who is probably busy hearing the confession of the two or three people who are voting for the Opposition. The list of Opposition sympathizers is a lot shorter than the list of their lies.

The editorial in *The Provincial Sun* wasn't easy to read; people stumbled over words you generally saw only in the dictionary. Achille Bédard was an educated young man and that gave him the right to use words that aren't in anybody's vocabulary. In some people's opinion, an uneducated person who reads what an educated person has written must be prepared to follow far behind, like a farmer chasing a frisky horse. Others felt that the place for hard words was in a crossword puzzle, not an editorial. Achille Bédard was proud. His editorial, with its flamboyant fervor, brought congratulations. He received a couple of insulting letters too, but they didn't count because they were written by the Opposition. That week, a number of people cut out the editorial and slipped it into their missals, to reread during Mass, between the Credo and Holy Communion.

XXX

On the importance of having a shiggy and on the danger that it might be cut off

One person who wasn't happy was Pommette Rossignol. She had been hired by the Local Riding Minister himself, "personally." Hadn't he said that the roads of the future must be built by men and women because life is made by men and women? Pommette Rossignol was the only woman working on the new road. *The Provincial Sun* had run a photograph of the workers who were opening the road. Pommette Rossignol wasn't in it. The paper showed only men. But there weren't only men on the worksite. Pommette Rossignol didn't pin the clipping to her wall; she burned it, and spat in the fire as she did so. Did the people at the paper think she wasn't worth as much as a man? On the first day, Pommette had turned up on the job. A fat, winded man from a neighboring parish had said from his chair: "I know you girls are good at baking pies, but you don't build a road out of jam." The other idiotic men had laughed so hard they must have been worn out before they started their day's work. Men, thought Pommette Rossignol, don't like women doing the same jobs because they're scared they'll do them better. At least that's what the men on the newspaper thought. That was what she said, her words exploding and passing through walls, soaring out windows and floating over to the neighbors, who cocked an interested ear when anything was cooking in the Rossignol household. Pommette's husband, Origène, agreed. He had a weak heart; he had to shun strong emotions, avoid irritations.

"Origène, you know hard work don't scare me. The good Lord made you weak in the heart; when the good Lord made you, Origène, he didn't want you to wear yourself out; so when there was heavy jobs to do, Origène, did I look for other men to do them? No sirree, I did all the men's jobs myself. Isn't that right?"

"Pommette my love, it ain't me that's gonna contradict you."

"I work with men; I do a job a man did before me and another one'll do after; and I do it as good as any man. My arms are bigger than yours, Origène, with muscles like a man's. I even got hair on them. My backbone's as strong as a man's. I've carried seventeen children. My heart's stronger than yours, Origène, and no weaker than any man you care to name that's working on the road. So when they didn't put my picture in the paper with the other workers just because I'm a woman, I say they're being snooty. If I had a shiggy Origène, I'd've had my picture in *The Provincial Sun*. You can't work, Origène, but I'm not saying nothing against you because the good Lord made you the way He wanted. You couldn't do the job I'm doing on the new road, but nobody's snooty to you . . . Everybody respects you because you're a man and you've got a little shiggy."

"Pommette my love, my shiggy isn't all that little. It made you seventeen children."

"Women do men's jobs as easy as knitting a sock and on top of that we make babies. But the papers are snooty."

"It ain't me that's gonna contradict you."

"Your shiggy, Origène, it was the kindling — the kindling, Origène — that brought the spark, but the fire and the wood and the oven where those babies cooked for nine months was me. And I did it seventeen times! If this is the time for telling the truth, Origène, your shiggy wasn't an awful lot better than your heart."

"Pommette, my love, I got the heart and I got the shiggy the good Lord meant me to have."

"Origène, I do the same job as a man and I even do it better cause I'm scared of doing a bad job. So how come I don't get my picture in the paper when three-quarters of those men are lazy bums? How come they get all the honors? There's just one reason: because they've got a little extension and I haven't."

"But if you want one, Pommette my love, I got one . . . "

On the waxy-skinned man's grey and bloodless face, frozen by a life-force that was already atrophying, a spark of light imprinted a shameless smile. Lust had revived the dead face.

"I got a shiggy, Pommette my love, and it's yours, all yours . . . "

"Origène, your shiggy made me seventeen children. Don't you think that's a lot?"

"Your husband won't contradict you; it's a lot."

"Too much. Enough! You're gonna tie a knot in your shiggy, Origène. Seventeen children's quite enough."

"The oldest ones are starting to bring in a little cash. Me, I got my pension on account of my weak heart. And you get a good wage workin' on the new road, practically as much as a man. We're well off, Pommette my love. We could afford another one. I'd like that, having a baby to spoil . . . The others didn't have an easy time of it."

"Seventeen children's too many, Origène."

"Pommette my love, that shiggy of mine, it's like a little animal. Skipping, wriggling, climbing, squirming, nervous, jumpy, ambitious, curious, generous, joyous, jealous, capricious, dependable, rude, stormy, sighing, flamboyant, galloping, agitated, dancing and full of imagination . . . "

"Origène, that's enough! Don't blaspheme!"

"We're gettin' a fine new road. If we want people to travel on that road, we haveta make babies. The two of us won't last forever, you know. My heart's half dead already. And every one of the children you carried around in your belly took a little piece of you when they came out. You ain't brand new either, Pommette my love . . . One of these days we'll be passing on . . . We'll be taking a road the Great Contractor built long, long ago . . . And when we're gone, what use will the new road be if there's no little feet pitter-pattering along it? That's what you oughtta be thinking about, Pommette: the future: let's make a baby!"

"Origène Rossignol! Just because you've got a shiggy you think you're one of the Three Magi with his magic wand. You think you got the right to scatter your seed whenever you want. You think the harvest's all fun and games for me. I already gave you seventeen children, Origène, seventeen. They'll make more children, just like we did. That'll be plenty of people to travel the new road."

"You know my heart's no stronger than a sigh. I'm half-dead, I got less than half a heart. I'll be dead and gone before the new road's even finished. When I'm dead and lying in the graveyard with not many people dropping by for a visit, I'd like to know there's a child I planted specially to celebrate the new road. Pommette my love, I figure I could even smile from my grave when I think about that child."

"Origène, I'm gonna cut off your shiggy."

The anger that rose to the stout woman's throat was transformed into a husky chuckle mingled with echoes of the amorous calls of wild beasts. A wan light glimmered on the pasty face of the man with the damaged heart. Grimacing, he uttered a feeble, almost a silent gasp.

Shiggy! The word had come to Saint-Toussaint-des-Saints after the visit of a preacher priest, a sort of missionary in a white soutane who stood in the pulpit waving his arms, pounding his chest and punching the marble with his fist. To his flock, Curé Fourré had become something like a notary. Curé Fourré knew as much as the notary did about tithes, taxes, boundaries, deferred contributions to charitable works, mortgages and loans, but once a week, on Sunday, he put away his account books and read the Holy Gospel. The preacher priest, however, made the stone walls tremble and the ceiling shake when he announced the imminent coming of Satan, announced that his kingdom was expanding, that Satan was threatening soon to conquer the village. The preacher priest, travelling from church to church, had even crossed the ocean, gone to lands so distant that winter couldn't touch them. He had done battle with Satan on all the highways in the world. He had been hunted, imprisoned, tortured and starved by pagan infidels. He had been exposed to the naughty temptations of women who had little virtue, and less religion than the snake in the Garden of Eden. All along the roads he travelled, he had proclaimed God's supremacy. When he came to the village his skin was baked by strong winds and blazing sun, he was fat and pot-bellied and he knew the villagers' sins as if they'd already confessed them. Those sins, he said, shouting and pounding his fist on the pulpit, were the first stones the Devil had put down to erect his own Church of Evil, which would be a lot bigger than the true Church of Good. It was the preacher-priest in his white soutane who had first mentioned the shiggy.

He pointed a threatening finger, the finger of God, at the assembled flock. He gave them a searing look that burned the eyes of the faithful. "Don't be hypocrites, brothers and sisters: you commit sins of the flesh more often than you bring children into the world. Brothers and sisters, every time you commit a sin of the flesh you give birth to a tiny little everlasting devil who'll prepare the way for Satan. Every time you don't bring a child into the world, you're killing one of the good Lord's children, another of God's children who'll never travel along the roads of the universe and sing the greater glory of God." After that, he explained that a very learned German named Sigmund Freud — he pronounced the foreign name Shigmund — had studied the difference between men and women. The great scholar had discovered that women felt deprived because they didn't have (and here he took a deep breath) "a little extension like the man's." The preacher assured them that if that was how things were, it was the good Lord, in His wisdom, who had made them thus. The difference, the extension, must be used for the greater glory of God — that is, to bring about the birth of children who would sing His praises. That night, in a bed warmed by the passion of two bodies seeking to join into one, in deference to the great scholar, the word shiggy was born, and spread through the village as fast as a rumor.

"Cut off my shiggy!" repeated Origène, laughing as if he had lungs of steel and a heart of stone.

"Don't laugh," Pommette threatened. "Origène, your heart's as full of holes as an old saucepan that's cooked too much food; don't you think I'm worn out too? But I've spent my whole life as a mother and now I gotta be the man. I gotta work harder than a man to make other people forget I'm a woman. And while I'm doing a man's work all day long, you want to plant another child. If you can't hold back, Origène, you're gonna go and get your shiggy cut off. Because I don't want no more babies."

"Pommette my love, my golden apple, do you mean you've had enough of my shiggy?"

He was still laughing between his words.

"Origène, my work on the new road's too hard."

"Pommette my love, I can feel my life drifting away. The only part of me that's still alive, like when I was alive, is my shiggy."

"Origène, I'm gonna cut it off!"

"Pommette, all I want is to make a baby with you before my heart dries up like a leaf that's about to fall. Before a man passes on he should sow a little life. Touch me, Pommette my love, my body's like ashes, here, touch . . . "

"Origène! Let go of my hands!"

She sprang back and gave him a look that told him Pommette, his love, was ready to bash him — frail though he was. Pommette's fists were clenched, her arms a mass of taut muscles ready to fling rock-hard fists at him, her husband, her sick husband, with his scarred heart from which the life was draining away. At the end of his life, as it was about to be extinguished, all Origène wanted was to give his Pommette a little tenderness.

"Pommette, my love," Origène purred, trying to touch her heart and soften it.

"Origène, I'm gonna cut off your shiggy."

"Pommette, my beautiful sweet love-apple . . . "

"Origène, you'll have to use plenty of sugar and honey too if you want to clear out the taste of that new road's mud from my throat."

Her fists opened, her muscles relaxed. Had she finally been moved? Origène didn't dare approach her. Perhaps her muscles would strain, her fists clench again. A gentle voice, a voice he'd seldom heard, a young girl's voice flowed from the body that no longer looked like a woman's.

"Origène, it's hard, working on the new road."

Pommette had demanded a man's job and that was what the Minister gave her. Like the men, she wielded an axe.

Berated by jeers and ironic remarks, she had felled spruce trees, she had split roots, clenching in her woman's hands the handle of the axe that burned her blister-covered palms. Every blow of the axe resounded in her head as if she had been struck along with the tree. Like the men, she had crushed rocks. Lifting the sledgehammer above her head which was buried under wind-tangled hair, she gathered all her strength, the strength of a woman who must not be weaker than a man, and brought down the sledgehammer, puffing and heaving; when the lead bounced off the rock, she felt as if her arms were being wrenched from their sockets. Like the men, she had transported crushed rocks and piled them up in anticipation of culverts to be built. In a group of mocking, blaspheming, vulgar men, her job had been to fill the trucks with earth. Following a rhythm established by the crew leader, each person was to throw his shovelful of water-heavy dirt into the dump body; if the rhythm was broken, all the shovels would stop and reproaches would fly out; the insults were more ferocious for the woman than for the men, because she was alone among these men, who worked faster in the hope of seeing her faint from exhaustion. She never fell. She had been assigned to filling in an embankment and she toiled with a sledge-hammer, ramming in cedar stakes whose sharp points were worn down by the stones. "Pommette, you can't ram that in; that's a man's job!" A greasy smile would spread across the men's faces as their lewd eyes explored her body. Another said: "Even your Origène can't ram in a little stake." More laughter made her feel as if they were spitting on her. Pommette held her tongue, sweated and kept pounding. Her muscles had never strained so hard. Her heart hadn't beat so fast when she gave birth to her children. She pounded desperately to make them forget she was a woman. She pounded with the anger that came from knowing these men despised her and desired her body. The most comical of them all asked: "If your Origène's too weak to drive in a stake, Pommette, who was it made your babies?" Tears sprang to her eyes and she almost wept like a little girl who can't take any more of her brothers' teasing, who is so bitter she can't believe that life is beautiful and wants to die because she's so unhappy, she thinks there is no greater suffering in the world. Because she had lived, because she had given birth, because she had often painfully scraped her hands, Pommette Rossignol held back her tears and declared: "My Origène was so good at doing what you do to make babies, your wives would rather do it with him than with your droopy little shiggys." She held back her tears and saved her husband's honor from these men who despised her. Just as it felt as if her soul was going to burst into tears, Pommette had to burst out laughing louder than the men, she had to force her voice to make her laughter rise up higher in the sky and spread out farther above the forest; and she must pound her stake harder and more often than the other workers.

"Origène, it's hard work. A woman can't make a baby and build a road at the same time."

"Pommette my love, don't just think about yourself. You have to think about the children we could have — about the children waiting out there in unknown lands for a man and a woman to prepare the way so they can come down and live a good life on earth . . . "

"I won't stop at your shiggy, I'll cut your tongue off too."

"Pommette my love, it's because my heart's half dead that you're wearing yourself out and getting exhausted. You're working like a man because your own man can't work like a man any more. Pommette my love, I'd like to make another little Rossignol just to prove I'm still alive. If you gave me that child, you could brag to the village that you'd done everything for me. When a woman does everything for her man, people respect her . . . When my heart's all frizzled like a dandelion, you'll be a widow, Pommette my love, a widow people respect. You'll be able to hold your head up and have your pick of all the men who've been looking for such a woman for so long . . . "

"Origène, I read in *The Provincial Sun* about a doctor in the Capital that went to the States and learned how to cut off shiggys."

Origène howled with amazing vocal strength for someone in his weakened condition. He squeezed his legs together, protecting his honor with delicate pale hands while his eyes pleaded for mercy.

"That doctor in the Capital," Pommette went on, struggling to sound reassuring, "he doesn't cut the way they cut steers on the farms. He learned how to cut in the States. They said in *The Provincial Sun*, he just cuts off what he has to. The man doesn't lose his honor."

"Oowww!" howled Origène.

"If you only knew how hard the work is. Laying that road through bedrock, Origène, ain't like slicing bread."

The bedrock had been cleared of the earth that covered it. It was a thin layer; that was why the fields were so stingy. It was schist, rock that was foliated but solid: it was impossible to strike off a flake even with a hammer. The stone was scattered with flecks of mica that glittered in the sun. The jackhammer with its long steel bit dug deep holes in the bedrock that would later be stuffed with dynamite. It was almost as if they were fighting a war, the foreman had said. Digging into stone is violent work. To pierce it you must be stronger than the stone. The jackhammer is more restive than a wild horse. It takes pigheadedness to pierce rock. The machine is powerful, it wants to break away. With both hands on the handles, men must hold it back, force it to stay in one place and stamp out a hole the size of a buttonhole. Dust from the stone fills your eyes. You choke if the wind changes direction and blows the chalky cloud in your nose. Then you jump along with the machine. The jackhammer's bit sinks into the bedrock but whenever the bit is jolted, your body receives a jolt too. Pommette Rossignol held the machine in a virile grip. Shaken up like this, your body becomes too small for the water it contains; the water wants to come out with the greatest urgency. For men, it's easy: they see which way the wind is blowing, then release the floodgates. For a woman . . . Holding back the water that seethed inside her like Niagara was no easy matter. It was an ordeal, a genuine ordeal, almost as bad as the fires of hell. And then she had to contend with the men's looks. Pommette Rossignol realized that she'd been given the jackhammer, the hopping machine, because it would make her bosom jiggle. The men couldn't take their eyes off her dancing breasts. Seventeen children. All fed on natural mother's milk. That makes a bosom. Her generous bosom, which had satisfied the appetites of seventeen babies, was shaken by the jackhammer; it leapt, fell, fluttered, wriggled, undulated, rolled, dan-

340

gled, swung, rippled, palpitated inside her shirt, and the men observed it all. Innocent Loiseau looked on no less ecstatically than the other men. Finally, Pommette Rossignol could no longer tolerate the men's devouring eyes, peering like thirsty infants. Her body no longer felt the pounding of the steel bit, but the sting of all their gazes as they tried to pierce her shirt. She could no longer bear the torment of their stares. She shut the air intake valve. The machine spat a great sigh. She laid the jackhammer on the bedrock. With a gesture like Curé Fourré's embracing his assembled flock when Mass was over, Pommette Rossignol unfastened her shirt buttons and spread her arms. Her great white bosom surged out, blinding as the sun. The men blinked and looked away. Pommette threw her shirt down on the bedrock, picked up the jackhammer, opened the air intake valve, and once again the machine started hopping, chewing at the bedrock, and her breasts moved like great white birds. The men dared not admire them too long. Dazzled, embarrassed, pitiful, blushing, unable to joke or even to laugh, they picked up their tools. Innocent went back to his shack. Jeannot Tremblay scrawled a reflection in his green notebook. When they were far away, Pommette put her shirt on, muttering:

"What happened to the men around here? One look at a tit and they turn into babies."

Origène was insistent.

"I've got a weak heart, I'm a dying man just asking for something with his last breath: I just want to plant another baby . . . My last descendant . . . "

"The new road's no place for a mother carrying a child. It's hard work, Origène."

Moving like a man who was no longer altogether in the land of the living but who hadn't yet arrived at death's dark kingdom, he advanced toward her, with caressing hands. Pommette recoiled from all this gentleness.

"Origène, listen!"

And she explained again why she didn't want a child. She explained that a doctor in the Capital knew how to perform a little operation he'd learned in the States, just a little cut that didn't show, but prevented babies. She assured him everything would be like before. It wasn't the

341

whole shiggy that was cut off, just a tiny little vein. She insisted. "Your shiggy'll still be there after the operation, like it's always been."

"Pommette my love, just let me make another couple of babies: the ones the good Lord wants us to make. Afterwards, if I haven't passed on, we'll go see your doctor in the Capital and I'll get my shiggy cut off."

"Origène!" Pommette screamed, "seventeen children from one woman is enough!"

"Pommette my love, you're saying no but deep down you're thinking yes."

And feebly but feverishly, he began to unbutton his pants.

"Origène!"

Innocent Loiseau had stayed behind in his office. After a day filled with mechanical droning and the coming and going of men and machines, he enjoyed these moments of calm and silence. He made notes in his black ledger, checked his addition, prepared his reports for Verrochio. Then he had got in the habit of standing on the bottom step of the stairs to his office and addressing a speech to the wind, the machine, the trucks, the bags of cement and barrels of oil. He denounced corruption and announced the future. He was learning to speak in order to take power. Sometimes Jeannot Tremblay stayed with him. Innocent did not talk then, but listened. Jeannot was a great modern poet.

That night, their conversation was almost religious because of the great respect they expressed for the unpolished men who were being exploited on this worksite. It was interrupted by shouts and vulgar words that the echo shamelessly repeated. Past the shack and disappearing onto the mud of the new road came a very pale skinny man pursued by a fat woman brandishing a butcher knife. The man wept and pleaded, his voice like a frightened woman's. The fat woman was swearing, her voice harsh, like a man's:

"Origène! I'll cut off your shiggy myself!"

XXXI

A wound inflicted on the earth

In one of the poems Jeannot Tremblay read to Innocent, he compared the new road with a wound inflicted on the flank of the earth while men were battling it in order to tame it. Such a notion would never have occurred to Innocent Loiseau. It was more than a thought: it was a poet's vision. True, it's not normal for the earth to be criss-crossed with roads. And it was quite true that men had to destroy flowers, trees, birds' nests, animals' dens, streams and swamps in order to establish their domain. It was true that man had declared war on nature. Innocent had studied history at the college and he had seen that man had been induced no longer to live according to nature (for he would still be an ape in the jungle), but to develop and evolve in opposition to nature. Man had undertaken to cultivate, to build and to make roads. That was the history of humanity which Jeannot Tremblay had summed up in a few words as beautiful as diamonds. Innocent Loiseau knew that his own thoughts were never so rich. His mind could encompass only small details of everyday life, whereas Jeannot Tremblay could distinguish the beginning and end of the world in the smallest pebble. Innocent was condemned to

343

note in his ledger when the employees started work and when they put their tools away and stopped the machines. Jeannot Tremblay, though, declared that the new road was a wound dealt out to the earth; he stated that the more the earth suffers, the more men live, and that the less the earth resembles itself, the more men would resemble the destiny they were creating for themselves. Jeannot Tremblay, who stood facing Innocent, was almost his age; his trousers were muddy from the earth for the new road that was drying on them, and he was a poet. Innocent Loiseau was not a member of the family of great minds, but he was glad to have the privilege of meeting Jeannot Tremblay. If his thoughts were so profound, wasn't it because he had learned how to look at life when he was living in Hell, as he put it? Every one of the great minds in the *Manual of Literature* had also known hell. Innocent deduced that despair was the doleful womb that gave birth to great minds who would see life differently from men who hadn't suffered. Innocent Loiseau had not yet experienced hell. He was glad to have the privilege of being invited by Jeannot Tremblay (and by his friend Achille Bédard, the journalist) to share their oath. "Soon the wound will be scarred over," said Jeannot Tremblay, reading from his green notebook, "and the scar will be a road toward the summits of tomorrow. Tell me: will civilization be something other than a scarred wound?" Jeannot Tremblay left then and Innocent Loiseau sat at his table for a long time, hypnotized by the poetry Jeannot had left behind.

The next day, Innocent observed his laborers bent over their tasks. His thoughts were still steeped in Jeannot Tremblay's poetry. These men were working without knowing they were engaged in a war against nature; they didn't suspect that the more they disfigured nature, the more they resembled their own destiny. He would have sneered at their ignorance if Jeannot Tremblay hadn't taught him that the first stage in the march toward power is to instil a conscience in those who don't have one. The role of Jeannot Tremblay and of Innocent Loiseau then, was to teach the men who were digging in the earth and the other laborers that they were building a road and, with it, a civilization. Without that conviction, their presence here was preposterous. That was what Jeannot Tremblay had said.

Some of the workers were milling about, dragging their feet in the mud, slowly pushing their machines and stopping to chat as if they didn't want the new road to advance, as if they wanted the construction to last a lifetime. Others kept digging, excavating, felling, sweating, forging ahead as if they'd decided to finish the construction that very day. Some, naturally, insulted others.

"Le Chef's a soft touch: he gives jobs to guys with one arm that can't hold a shovel, and legless cripples that can't put one foot in front of the other."

"If the new road's the road to the future, at this rate it'll be finished too late."

"Plenty of guys work because they don't know what else to do with their hands."

"There's some that work because they're big enough hypocrites not to show their laziness."

XXXII

Everything flies away;
only dreams remain

Charlemagne Saint-Ours wasted no time arguing. He knew
what he had to do before the foreman did. He never took
the time to gaze up at a bird flying across the sky. He only
stopped to flick off with the back of his hand the drops
of sweat that clung to his mustache, as narrow as a
knife-blade. Charlemagne was in a hurry. He was impatient
with the other men's flabby arms. In his opinion, the trees
weren't felled fast enough, the bulldozers ("as lazy as the
men") weren't powerful enough to deal with stumps or
rocks, the trucks got stuck in the mud for the fun of it.
This road seemed to be attached to him like the line of
cars behind a steam engine. He was only a day-laborer,
but he knew roads. (Turning up with his papers, he would
say "Monsieur, I've worked on the roads all my life. Ask
anybody that's worked on the roads, anywhere, if he knows
Charlemagne Saint-Ours. Maybe he's forgot the name of
the Minister of Roads and Bridges, but he'll remember
Charlemagne Saint-Ours.") He would struggle with his
hands, arms, back, with all his heart, while others dawdled.
No one wanted this road to make progress. No one wanted
to see the end of it. Did they think this was a party? Some-

times you have so much fun at a party you wish it would last forever. Those were the thoughts that went through the mind of Charlemagne Saint-Ours. He toiled away, trying not to think: thinking doesn't build roads.

Charlemagne Saint-Ours remembered all the roads he'd ever worked on. He talked about them as if they were people he'd known very well. His roads were alive. Each had its own story. He remembered their curves, their hills. He had never met another man who had opened so many roads. He had opened roads in every region of the province. He'd opened roads on the other side of the world, as he put it. He valued this experience as much as if it were a halo. People respected him. They didn't laugh at him, didn't insult him — but they didn't copy him either. Why was he in such a rush to finish this road?

Charlemagne Saint-Ours had got his start on the streets of the Capital. He had, as he said, mended all the holes in the streets so the MPs wouldn't break their necks ("when they tied one on"). He had opened roads through fields, around the city, so country-dwellers could come to the Capital. Further away, he had opened roads through forests so that city-dwellers in the Capital could go out to pick fruit, to hunt and fish. Then war broke out. Far away, they needed roads that would lead to airports. Charlemagne Saint-Ours opened some of those. There were times when he didn't even know where he was, he'd gone so far, farther than he ever thought he'd go. He wielded his axe, he pointed his pick, he dug up stones. Sometimes the places were so quiet, the echo repeated the "Oof!" of his panting breath. He donned a soldier's khaki uniform, but his only weapons were his axe, his pick and his shovel. He didn't hear much about the war. He lived as if no war was being fought. He opened roads. Then a truck with a khaki canvas cover arrived unexpectedly one day and took him even farther away, to open another road. And one night he was deposited on a boat. There were hundreds of other men like him who hadn't been told where they were going. For more than a week they were at sea where they were tossed about, sick, thinking that man was made for the roads on land, not those on the sea. Then things became calm. They were told that they were disembarking on the soil of England. Charlemagne Saint-Ours was shoved into a truck that followed roads as tangled as a skein of wool, then he was driven into a country like a dream. Charlemagne Saint-Ours learned that he was in Scotland and that he was a member of the Third Company of Foresters. Charlemagne Saint-Ours was assigned to build roads to victory, or so he was led to believe. He saw no difference between the roads that were opened for war and those being opened for peace. He wondered where these roads were going. They seemed to lead nowhere. Charlemagne Saint-Ours was just a soldier. He wasn't entitled to know. Fortunately, the roads were making progress. ("Even if a road leads nowhere, better a road that goes nowhere than one that doesn't go at all.") That was how he consoled himself. With the road still unfinished, a truck picked him up and drove him to an airplane. After it wrenched itself from the ground and started climbing up above the clouds and Charlemagne saw the land disappear in the distance, he felt as if his heart didn't want to be up there with him. His heart had tenacious roots. Were they returning to the province? No one had told them. A soldier doesn't ask where he is going. It lasted for hours. Flying was an ordeal for Charlemagne. The aircraft might fall. And because there was a war, it might be shot at like a wild duck. Sometimes there were waves in the sky, like the ones at sea. Sometimes the airplane would drop like a stone, then bounce back. Sometimes the motors growled and the plane seemed stuck, like a truck caught in the mud. He preferred the roads on land to those in the sky. They touched down, then took off again after the gas tank was filled. The men weren't allowed to get out. They touched down several times and always took off again. This went on for days. Then a truck came and drove them to a boat which, several days later, let them off in a forest. It wasn't a forest. It was the jungle. ("The jungle's full of weeds higher than the spruce trees back home. They haven't even got any roads.") You couldn't see the sky, you couldn't see the land. The jungle. The enemy might be waiting in ambush. Charlemagne Saint-Ours opened the road for those who would follow. He had no axe but "some kind of big butcher knife, a sabre, a machete. In that country they called it a parang." The name of the country was Burma. ("Aside from me, I never met a soul that ever went there. The Burmese jungle. As hot as if you were buried alive in boiling mud.") When he breathed, his nose and mouth took in not just air but mosquitoes. ("When you looked at a man all you saw was a black ball of mosquitoes sucking his blood. Even in the eyes. When the blood started pouring down his face another kind of even hungrier mosquitoes moved in.") It was always night. The light couldn't penetrate the jungle's tangled roof. He hadn't seen the sky for weeks. He had opened a road. He had walked but had not seen the ground covered with leaves, branches and roots tangled among woven vines. Slashing broadly, he advanced. Often he stepped into banks of fog as dense as a white squall of snow. He had to win every step in the jungle. He had to bite each step out of the limp wall of vines and branches and leaves. He made progress, but he was caught in the jungle like a fly in a spider web. At any moment there would be a stinking, muddy flash as a snake darted at him. He would slash it like a vine. His legs were on fire. Leeches ("as long as garter snakes") ate through the rotten leather of his boots and the cloth of his pants; they would clamp their mouths to suck his blood, then dig their sharp little teeth into his flesh. It was impossible to get rid of them: there were too many and they stuck. His legs swelled. He slashed, slashed. No enemy appeared, so he had to keep his anger and hatred to himself. The rain fell endlessly: warm piss, an acrid stench. His hands burned as if he were holding hot coals. The rain tenderized his flesh. It softened calluses. His hands bled from gripping the handle of his parang. They were covered with as many blisters as the cells in a wasps' nest. His clothes were torn by brambles sharp as a cat's claws. His arms were lacerated. Mosquitoes quenched their thirst on the blood. Little worms came and nested there. He must advance. The enemy had to be somewhere. Charlemagne Saint-Ours, guided by someone with a compass, slashed and slashed at the wet green wall where hard and soft were all confused, a wall that seemed to be walking in front of them, along with them, a wall that kept closing around them like a foul-smelling sea. Waves rolled over him, impossible to repel, though he tried relentlessly. Rattan, bamboo, rhododendron, vines, leaves as sharp as blades, mushrooms, hills of slimy moss: a never-ending bush. The absent enemy was an obsessive presence. In the end, he had almost forgotten he was Charlemagne Saint-Ours. His skin had been stained with a mixture of coffee, iodine and lampblack; a filthy rag had been wrapped around his head, another around his waist. Some days he was ordered to march with his chest thrust out and head high; other days, he was ordered to bend down, to make his body smaller. Depending on the day and the territory, amid the jungle's quiet disorder, Charlemagne Saint-Ours learned that he was Chinese, Malay or Hindu, a sikh, a gurkha, a sakai, Thai, Tibetan or Kachin. He was forbidden to speak his own language, even to swear. Because of the enemy he must express himself in grunts, as if he were speaking a tribal language. Charlemagne Saint-Ours was a fine sight, decked out like a wild man of the jungle! He had lost weight. His bones protruded from his yellow skin. Suddenly the blade of the parang rang out: it had struck a steep cliff hidden by a curtain of leaves. He must clamber like a monkey, cling to vines bristling with thorns; his weakened arms must lift his body, hoisting heavy sacks along with him. At times the jungle opened up and he would be carried along on the tumultuous current of a river hidden by the vegetation. At other times, a fissure covered with brush and moss would open like a mouth. The jungle devoured some of his companions. But still they advanced in a dense cloud of mosquitoes, of fierce gnats starving for flesh and thirsty for blood.

When Charlemagne Saint-Ours recounted his adventures, the young people laughed because they'd never heard such a liar; their incredulity didn't bother him.

"You youngsters can't understand, you've been brought up in luxury. Before your mothers gave you milk they killed all the germs . . . My generation lived through a war."

The young people roared with laughter.

"You said yourself, you never even saw the enemy's nose."

"An invisible enemy's worse than one you can see. I fought a war by opening roads. I fought against the jungle. And in the jungle of Burma I had my great dream."

"A great dream!" they jeered.

"It'll come true one day, you'll see . . . "

He'd been saying that ever since he came back from the war, on all the roads he'd worked on:

"I had a great dream, back when I was making a road through the jungle, during the war . . . Monsieur, I went to the other side of the world to fight a war. And some day you'll see my dream come true."

Charlemagne Saint-Ours was always in a hurry. He always worked harder and longer than the others. He wanted to reach the end of the road before the others. At mealtime, when the workmen were leaning against the hood of a truck or sitting on the blade of a bulldozer, Charlemagne Saint-Ours would declare:

"I spent my whole life opening roads, and you can whine all you like, but let me tell you, opening this road's like slicing a sugar pie."

The others were incredulous. Charlemagne Saint-Ours had fought a war and hadn't even seen the enemy. They enjoyed listening to him. There had never been such a great liar in the region.

"In this life," Charlemagne Saint-Ours would tell them, "everything flies away. Nothing lasts but dreams. If writing lasts, that's because it's a dream. My adventures in the jungle of Burma have faded like bonfires and the wind's blown the ashes away, but some day I'll show you the dream I dreamed in the jungle."

Sometimes Charlemagne Saint-Ours made the kind of speech a sensible man doesn't make. Or so people thought, but didn't say: he was such a good worker. He never criticized anyone for not doing his share. He minded his own business. He was determined, and nothing could distract him from the road. "He thinks he's still in the jungle," they would say. If Charlemagne Saint-Ours was a little odd, it was because he'd been a soldier. They knew that soldiers took special pills to make them stronger. The pills upset their minds a little. Some women didn't recognize their husbands when they came back from the war, those pills had changed them so much. The soldiers had been exposed to poison gases released by the enemy and those gases had scrambled their brains. Charlemagne Saint-Ours had never met the enemy, but perhaps he'd breathed their poison gas. For a man to wear himself out working, for a man to take so much pleasure from work wasn't normal, or so they thought. For a man to talk about his dream like

351

a lover talking of his beloved wasn't normal, but no one spoke ill of him. He knew far more about roads than anyone else, even Verrochio. He never spoke ill of anyone. He only talked when it was his turn. He had done what no one else had done. No one else had gone to Scotland as he had. The others didn't even know that a country like Burma existed; Charlemagne had laid out roads through the jungle there. It wasn't normal, but they couldn't help respecting the man.

"That dream of yours, Charlemagne, it wouldn't by any chance be some tall tale, would it? Is it true?"

"I could put that dream on paper for you, black on white."

"Was it as hot in your jungle as it is today, Charlemagne? We're melting like pigs in a frying pan."

As had happened so often in his life, Charlemagne saw incredulous eyes turn his way: eyes that couldn't imagine that someone else had seen what they had not.

"I know you don't believe me. In the jungle you never know where you are, you can't find your way . . . You don't know where you are, where you've come from . . . "

Skeptical smiles spread across mouths that were fiercely chewing pork and bread, lips smeared with mustard. They weren't lost. The road was under their boots, the church steeple was pointing at the sky, the sun was in the south, the village was that way, their house was the third on the left after the post office, or across from the general store, or the yellow one on the other side of the knoll. Charlemagne Saint-Ours hadn't known where he was since he came back from the war! But you couldn't tell him that. They respected a man who had risked his life for his country and hadn't come home dead. He was aware of the incredulity in the other men's eyes.

"Life is like a jungle."

The workers shoved soft drinks into their mouths .

"Life's like a jungle. If a man's lost in the jungle he looks at his compass; a man who's lost in the jungle of life looks at his dreams. A dream is the compass of a man who's lost. I have my dream. I look at it and I know where I am. The dream tells me where to go. A few more strokes with my pick and shovel and I'll be there. And my dream will be as real as earth and wood and stones. A few strokes of the pick . . . It's easy here. I remember another time, another place . . . "

His words took Charlemagne Saint-Ours back to the jungle. The enemy was hidden there, but he didn't move, didn't show his face, he was as silent as death. With his next step, after he'd lifted a leaf the size of an umbrella, Charlemagne might be struck down. The days had the rotten smell of death. Shadows decomposed amid the hot odor of rot. The nights were cold. Wet clothes turned as cold as ice. Would they light a fire? The enemy lay in wait. The bush soldiers shivered as they tried to sleep in the black night. Sometimes they were so exhausted they were able to sleep without being bothered by the hideous insects that devoured them as if they were corpses. Sometimes they decided the enemy couldn't spot their fire and the order was passed to light a match. The dampness turned the sulphur pasty. If, miraculously, the match did light, the bamboo was too wet to kindle. During the day, they shuddered in the nauseating heat. At night, they shuddered from the cold. Sometimes it crossed his mind to stop advancing, to stop eating, to die as if falling asleep, numbed by the insects and leeches, but he remembered that he had a road to build. Then he got up and resumed the struggle against the soft green wall that didn't stop them from making progress but kept them from going through. The idea of building a road was what kept him alive, was what kept them from dying. In the night made darker by the silent presence of death, this road through the jungle closed around his companions and himself like green water. Turning on his bed of leaves to take the weight off his sores, flailing his arms in a pathetic struggle against the omnipotent insects, he listened to the night. The jungle had slept through the day in a vaporous torpor. The night awakened everything that had been asleep. The leeches became even thirstier. Now they wanted not just blood but flesh and bones as well. Grasshoppers burst like sparks sputtering from a dry-wood fire; you could hear their feet alight on leaves with a clicking sound; they cried out that they were alive, male and female called to one another. Cicadas chirred. Toads the size of rabbits shrieked and hopped under the ferns as if all the stones in the jungle had started to jump. Families of monkeys that had slept

353

through the day woke up, squabbling. The father intervened with his dictatorial Waw! Waw! The wild pig grunted and moaned like a tired ghost. Great birds hopped from branch to branch. Hornbills bent over awkwardly, falling from leaf to leaf with strident cries. These nights were harder than the days. Sleeping was harder than walking and opening the road. ("It was no sugar pie like here.") Charlemagne Saint-Ours repeated again what he'd said so many times, but no one believed him because they thought that if his stories were true, Charlemagne wouldn't be there, alive, to tell them.

"What kept us there was that we were a group of soldiers, but together we were just one man, with one thought: to build a road to get out of the jungle . . . the dream . . . "

And he repeated once again the story told so many times. Even if it had sprung entirely from a lonely man's imagination it would have become true, for truth exists not merely through facts, but through the insistence with which they are recounted. He repeated the story of a handful of men from every country in the world, who communicated by imitating the sounds of birds. Because of the hidden enemy they had to be not men but jungle beasts; they would probably have become true beasts if they hadn't had the job of building a road through the gigantic foliage. Charlemagne Saint-Ours had often thought of it: they had become almost beasts, no longer speaking a human language, no longer living in human houses, no longer walking on human roads. When they looked at one of their number they saw not a man but a wretched suffering body, torn, bloody, swollen with bites, bruised and bony. Lost, adrift in the jungle, they dug out a passage. The idea of the road kept them from being beasts. Without that stubborn idea, they would have obeyed the law of the jungle: they would have killed to put an end to their own suffering. But as Charlemagne Saint-Ours said, men who cling to a road are men who cling to a dream. He said that all roads lead to a dream; and as long as man holds on to his dream, he does not become a beast, he does not die. ("If I hadn't had my dream I'd've never got out of the jungle. I couldn't be telling you that it'll soon come true.") And once again, he told his story. From living in the slimy humidity, from having their skin covered with blood mixed with sweat, from being soaked in the sticky sap that dripped from vines, ferns and leaves, and because of the insects that hatched their eggs in that mingled filth, their bodies were covered with fuzz that was probably greyish (it was hard to see colors exactly in the jungle). Their skin was covered with hairs as when, far back in time, men were not yet men. This hair wasn't like their beards or the hair on their chests; each strand was a tiny poisoned dart. A single one could make a man weep. But Charlemagne Saint-Ours never stopped slashing with his parang. He lashed out with the desperate relentlessness of a man who is trying to kill a wild animal that doesn't want to stop living. ("Our bodies got moldy in the jungle like bread when it's too damp, but bread doesn't suffer, it doesn't scream when it's asleep . . . We were lost in our pain like we were lost in the jungle . . . Bread doesn't suffer, but it doesn't dream either.")

The workers on the new road chewed and said nothing. They had never known such misery, and they were quite happy not to. They weren't rich, but the good Lord had never tortured them like this. There were times when they'd have liked to leave Saint-Toussaint-des-Saints, travel to the cities on the other side of the hills, leave the Appalachians, but they had stayed behind with the trees that didn't move and the church that would stand for centuries. Their lives were peaceful and sometimes they got bored. Certain Sundays had seemed endless. Certain seasons had dragged on and on. They'd had time to watch themselves grow old. They were glad they'd stayed. Never had they suffered disasters as great as those who had gone away; never had they known the happiness of those who had been lucky elsewhere. They weren't obliged to go away just because a road was going past their houses. They shouldn't be unhappy because they'd stayed behind. That Charlemagne Saint-Ours who claimed he'd suffered so much was just a liar . . . And what's better than a good laugh to chase away worry, doubt, perhaps even envy.

"Hey Charlemagne, that fuzz you talked about, you say it grew *everywhere*? And when I say everywhere I mean — everywhere?"

Guffawing, the workers who had been swept along by Charlemagne's story found themselves on familiar ground once more, in their own country, they found themselves back in their own lives. It was like taking up the refrain of a song you know too well.

"When we see Charlemagne's dream come true we'll know if he's lying or not."

"A couple more chops with his pick and you'll see . . . "

And then he started to tell about the hideous deaths he'd seen. He had seen his companions die: they had burst, their bodies had been torn apart. They had died of internal strangling (or so the survivors said). Charlemagne described it all in detail: he had seen a heart bounce against the trunk of a locust-tree and roll on the ground. Once a snake had lashed out, level with the ferns at his feet. Moving just as fast, he swung out with his *parang*. When the sections stopped wriggling he realized that he'd cut through a length of intestine that had spilled out of one of his companions who had burst. Sometimes they heard only a rubbery sound like a balloon; the man who had exploded into bloody chunks, had landed on the men in a greasy, bloody, stinking human rain. Once, in the midst of huge mushrooms with caps bigger than pumpkins, Charlemagne spotted a leather boot like the ones all soldiers wear. One of the other men, he thought, must be taking a nap . . . How could he be sleeping when the road hadn't been cleared? He pulled on the boot to awaken the man. The boot stayed in his hand. There was still a foot inside it. A length of leg jutting out of it was being shared by leeches, ants and flies. There was a label on the heavy sock. He read the name of one of his buddies who had burst a few hours earlier. The explosion had projected the foot far away. Charlemagne Saint-Ours didn't omit any details. Rather, he emphasized what others would have left out. The workers chewed their lunch which smelled of butter and mustard, their eyes stupefied. They had forgotten they weren't supposed to believe this man; Charlemagne Saint-Ours had travelled so many roads, seen so many things, he wasn't an ordinary man. And he continued to explain why his companions blew up. It was because of the leeches. They were covered with bites which had swollen up. Their bodies were a mass of blisters. The still-thirsty leeches bit at the swellings. The men swelled up even more. And then they bit again, sinking their tiny teeth into the flesh. The men swelled more and more. They couldn't breathe. Their noses had no nostrils. Their lips and cheeks were so puffed up, the mouths couldn't open. Their intimate orifices were completely blocked. Charlemagne multiplied the descriptions, added details, specified colors, found the words to suggest the odor, demonstrated the size of things, mimicked movements. They understood very well why the poor soldiers had broken like eggs. When Charlemagne was finished, the workers felt the good Lord must love them because He hadn't condemned them to explode.

"When you build roads in the world, you learn about life, because life follows roads. And roads follow the dreams of men."

"Dream!" exclaimed one of the laborers who rarely opened his mouth. "I once knew a man who had a dream. Well, actually I didn't know him, I knew his father. Well, actually I didn't know his father either, but I worked for his father's brother. His father had some stores in the Capital. But him, the man, he knew as much about work as an Eskimo knows about palm trees. His mother's father had some sawmills in the province. I didn't know him. Because I was working for his father's brother, his cousin's father who didn't work either. Anyhow, that man's mother inherited some money and then she died. Her son inherited a fortune . . . And that's the man that had a dream."

In his convoluted way he told the man's story. The dream of this man who had inherited so much money was to travel. All he wanted was to travel. Once his mother was buried, he went to the notary to collect his inheritance, then he had someone drive him to the airport. The man got on the first plane. At the next airport he boarded the first plane that was leaving. And he continued his travels, from airport to airport, from one continent to the next, from one country to another, never wanting to get out on the ground, disembarking at an airport only to board another plane, travelling everywhere and nowhere, crossing countries and oceans, travelling around the world in every direction without leaving his seat in the plane, travelling without travelling, seeing nothing, sitting perfectly still because he stayed in his seat and saw nothing, but always in motion because the airplane was always taking him somewhere else. He truly went nowhere and he remained alone with himself. Then one day he realized he'd run out of money, that he'd squandered his inheritance, and he came home. He wasn't unhappy because he'd realized his dream. He had travelled everywhere and gone nowhere. He had travelled all the roads in the sky without going anywhere. Of his travels, nothing remained: soap bubbles that had burst. But there was always his dream . . .

"Actually," said the laborer, "I didn't know the man, but I heard about him."

"We're all little soap bubbles that burst," Charlemagne Saint-Ours declared sententiously.

"Women are stronger than that!" Pommette Rossignol assured them.

"Man or woman, they're nothing more than their dream. I learned that in the jungle. A dream's more important than a man's blood. A dream can't be attacked by leeches or mosquitoes."

"You go on and on about that dream of yours, Charlemagne Saint-Ours, but you don't have much to show for it!"

"The new road's gonna be there this afternoon."

Their bodies filled after their meal, the workers returned to their various tasks. The bulldozers started up again. A number of strapping spruce trees had been felled when suddenly Charlemagne Saint-Ours made a gesture like God wanting to make the world stop turning.

"Stop! Stop!"

His voice was covered by the bulldozer that purred with well-lubricated mechanical happiness every time some obstacle appeared in opposition to its brute strength. Only the other men who were working with picks noticed his agitation.

"Here's my dream! Here's my dream! Right here!"

There it was, the piece of land where Charlemagne Saint-Ours would realize the curious dream he had conceived so many years before, in a country so far away it seemed no longer to exist. He had built so many roads to reach this piece of land where his dream would become reality! He had laid out this trail in the jungle of Burma and now, suddenly, on the other side of a nightmare, he had awakened. He realized that they had crossed through the jungle. When they saw soldiers on the plain, his companions and he — haggard, tattered, hallucinating, broken like ship-wreck victims (cast away by the sea of greenery) — opened fire with the ferocity of those who do not want to die; they fired with the feverish anxiety that came from knowing the enemy was present everywhere in the jungle but never visible; they fired to erase that enemy from their fear. Here on this plain there was no enemy, there were friends who did not answer the attack; they appeared when the ghostly survivors' ammunition was exhausted. Then Charlemagne Saint-Ours threatened the enemy with his *parang*. Even after he was convinced that the enemy was not the enemy but friends on the same side in the war as he, he still refused to put down his *parang*. He was taken to a bed with blankets folded according to army regulations. He turned them back to look for reptiles, leeches and spiders between the sheets, extracting them one by one to flush out mouths avid for blood. Though he found nothing, he would not relinquish his *parang*, which he laid under the pillow he punched with his fists to overpower all forms of life. And then, in the air and on the sea and along roads where trucks jolted through devastated countries, he had come home where he'd never done anything but build new roads. ("I was a man that couldn't stop. I never felt as if I'd arrived. I had to keep moving on. I needed to build my own road. Then I had a revelation that showed me I was building roads to arrive at my dream.") Charlemagne Saint-Ours had climbed up on the trunk of a spruce tree the bulldozer had overturned, and he was dancing.

"My dream's right here!"

Word had reached Saint-Toussaint-des-Saints that one of the workmen on the new road had bought a plot of land. The first interpretation was that Le Chef was re-warding a faithful servant by ceding him a small plot of land on which he could build a house and hunt and fish while waiting for death. People were very surprised to learn, in the course of those conversations that streak through the village, taking sustenance at every house, that the buyer had actually paid. He'd paid the full amount in just one installment, taking the carefully ironed bills from his pockets. Through his work on the new roads, Charle-magne Saint-Ours had amassed the necessary money for his dream. ("Dreams are a kind of alcohol that doesn't cost a thing, but there always comes a time when you have to pay, when the dream is over.")

"My dream's right here!"

The work went on, but Charlemagne Saint-Ours had stopped. He left his pickaxe planted in one of those anthills that formed a hump on the surface of the ground. He wasn't an employee now, he was a landowner.

"I'm calling it The Plains of Saint Opportun, in honor of the little saint who guided my footsteps toward the realization of my old dream."

In the Capital there was a very famous park called the Plains of Abraham; it had been the site of an important battle in the country's history and Charlemagne Saint-Ours wanted to honor his land with this glorifying reminder.

"The road goes right up to my land. Now my land can become what the good Lord wanted it to be. In a way it was the good Lord's hand that pushed me toward the Plains of Opportun . . . Excuse me, I have to write to the Heads of State involved."

It was obvious that he was leaving the job. Why should he write to Heads of State? Charlemagne Saint-Ours's fellow workers didn't ask too many questions. The foreman was near by. They had to get back to work. It wasn't the first time an ordinary man, a man from the Appalachian Region, a modest, unimportant man, ignorant and poor, had written to one of the world's great people: the Pope, the Queen of England, the President of France or Russia. Every time it happened, some disturbance in the man's brain was disclosed. ("Say what you like about all roads leading to Rome, us and the Pope don't belong to the same family. You gotta be crazy to write to the Pope. Writing to Le Chef's about as far as a healthy man can go. After that . . . ") Not only had Charlemagne Saint-Ours — a man who shovelled dirt — decided to write to Heads of State, he'd left his job and seemed not to remember that he'd worked every day of his life . . . He had seen too many roads, he'd lost his way . . . Or so people said.

On the fence that ran along his property he put up a sign with the following painted in red: "Plains of Saint Opportun; Charlemagne Saint-Ours, Proprietor. DANGER. No Trespassing."

The workers on the new road saw him every day on their way to work. He sat on his fence and waited. His beard grew. His skin turned brown from the sun, but also because he stopped washing. Charlemagne Saint-Ours really had written to the leaders of various countries; the postmaster confirmed it. He had addressed letters to distant countries and the stamps had cost a week's wages. Charlemagne Saint-Ours had no secrets from his former companions who sometimes stopped by to see him. He explained that after travelling along so many roads, he knew about life. That, no one could deny. He told them that the war wasn't over, that it would come back just as snow storms come back, and ice and droughts and death. ("Look inside your houses: husbands and wives bickering, children squabbling, lovers arguing; when the whole world gets involved, family quarrels turn into wars.") He was right. You couldn't contradict him. He'd spent years laying out the roads along which the war had travelled.

"Why fight wars in cities to destroy cathedrals and houses, to crush children, pregnant women and old people under the rubble? Why destroy what generations in the olden days have built? Why fight wars that destroy whole countries, when you can pick the winner on a lot smaller piece of land where there'd be lots less destruction? Why fight terrible wars that need thousands of cannons and millions of bombs? On a smaller battlefield there'd be fewer weapons, fewer bombs. On a small battlefield there'd be fewer soldiers, and fewer deaths. Why fight a war in countries like the jungle, where you have to be a snake to live, where men explode before they can fight? You should be able to fight a war on a clean little piece of land like the Plains of Opportun, where the mosquitoes are bearable and the two sides could get to it by travelling along a fine new road, with no mud or bumps. That's what I wrote to the Heads of State. I've realized my dream and it'll be a favor to all humanity. I'll spare suffering and destruction and lives. In the future, any wars will take place on the Plains of Saint Opportun."

To see Charlemagne Saint-Ours so early in the morning, bearded and damp with dew, to hear him talk that way, wasn't it part of a dream that had broken away from sleep? The workers listened to him amazed, mouths agape, arms dangling, eyes dazzled. The man wasn't wrong. Just because something had been done in a certain way for a long time didn't necessarily mean that was the best way. Charlemagne Saint-Ours was suggesting a new way to fight wars. He wasn't wrong, but they were rather upset by his words. Charlemagne Saint-Ours was logical, but his words that were so clear, so easy to understand, concealed something incomprehensible, a touch of madness that kept the men from fully agreeing with him. Some mystery veiled by those words aroused a certain discomfort and they didn't like it.

They recalled that during the war, soldiers had been enveloped in poison gas. It was rumored that a little madness always remained in the brains of soldiers who had fought a great war.

One morning Charlemagne Saint-Ours got off his fence and approached them, saying:

"I've got answers from the Heads of State. They're confidential, but I can tell you that the next world war's going to be fought right here, on the Plains of Saint Opportun."

"Charlemagne," said one of the workers, "I hope you'll be able to control the noise from the explosions, because my mother-in-law's real nervous."

"All right!" said the foreman, "Let's get busy. If the war's gonna be over here, we'll need a road to get the hell to the other side."

On the following mornings, the men on their way to work saw Charlemagne Saint-Ours sitting on his fence. He was waiting for the warriors. The workers said hello as they passed. Then they stopped saying hello. In the end, they were jeering:

"Hey Charlemagne, how's the world war? Started yet?"

"I want three tickets for your war."

Charlemagne Saint-Ours had tears in his eyes. Why were people so cruel to those who had realized their dream? Why did they always mock those who were working for the good of humanity?

In the end, he stopped hearing the workers drive past in their trucks. The aged and dirty man perched on his fence like a strange bird no longer saw them. He was waiting for the warriors.

XXXIII

Hear the story of a woman who ate chocolate

Innocent Loiseau had to admit he was scared. He was in no immediate danger. His shack was not about to blow up like a ship struck by a torpedo. Shattered stone would not rain down on his roof. The explosions occurred far away from the office, but when the whistle sounded three times to announce an imminent detonation, all his muscles tensed and he felt paralyzed. His eyelids closed. The only thing he was capable of doing was let his head drop between his hands, which covered his ears. With muffled explosions, the dynamite tore apart the tight-packed bedrock. He hated the shock that shook his cabin and made the windows shudder. Every time, there was the same tension, the same irrepressible start, the same uncontrollable surprise. He had to bow to the evidence: he was scared. When the warning whistle sounded his heart thudded, his hands shook, his eyes flickered. Was he so timid? He would never be able to win. He had first to conquer his own fear. Why was he tense and trembling when there wasn't the slightest danger? The fear that now encrusted his muscles and his soul was overcoming him. Innocent had to overcome his fear so he could overcome himself. In one of their conversations, Jeannot Tremblay had told him that a man wasn't made just by his parents, but by an entire people, by that people's history. Innocent was discovering that his fear was far greater than himself. This instinctive fear wasn't part of him. Was it part of a people? The fear that gripped him was more than simple fear of an explosion, it was a fear of living, of dying, an indefinable fear, an unjustifiable fear, a fear born of ignorance, a' fear that was born of suffering too. Innocent Loiseau told himself he must conquer his own deep-rooted fear. He trained himself not to be startled by the detonations. He taught his hands not to tremble on his desk. He kept his knees from wobbling when the dynamite exploded. He struggled to master his pounding heart. Outside his office, he persuaded himself to come gradually closer to the chunks of bedrock that the dynamite would crush so the road would be level and without the inclines there were on the old roads built by the Opposition. Seven days later he had triumphed over his fear. Now he was as indifferent to the explosions as his workmen. He had overcome the fear inside him that came from elsewhere, that extended back beyond his time and perhaps even his century. At college, he'd never learned that a man must first dominate his fear. On the contrary: he'd been taught that the ancient Greek thinkers considered fear the beginning of wisdom.

"If a man is to win," said Innocent, "he must not be afraid."

"If a people is to live," Jeannot Tremblay replied, "it must not be afraid."

There will always be people to exploit fear.

"A frightened people is a dominated people."

"Men become free at the moment when they shed their fear."

Innocent was glad he was no longer afraid. All his life he would remember this summer on the new road. He would never be the same again. The road had shown him another self. He had learned that a free man was one who was not afraid, that a free man was one who knew how to win. Sometimes he was sad because there was no woman to help him win. One day, a woman would come into his life. Innocent just had to prepare for her. During the day, he often picked up the telephone (which still hadn't been connected) and talked to a woman who existed for him somewhere, but couldn't hear him. Methodically, he learned to talk to her in order to captivate her. His finest victory that week came when he picked up the dynamite into which the shot firer had inserted the detonator, pulled out the wooden peg that blocked the hole which Pommette Rossignol's jackhammer had drilled in the rock, and placed the stick of dynamite in the hole, being very careful to keep the detonator's two thin strands from catching on the rough spots on the wall. Dragged down by its own weight, the dynamite dropped to the bottom of the hole. Grandpa Dynamite, the sapper, a silent, scowling old man who hadn't uttered a word since he said yes to his wife on his wedding day, handed him another stick. Innocent dropped the dynamite into the hole, letting the detonator wires slip through his hands. In this way, Grandpa Dynamite had him fill the hole. Waving him back, Grandpa Dynamite knelt and packed down the dynamite with a stick of wood. Innocent watched him, then drew nearer. Like Grandpa Dynamite, he knelt beside the hole filled with explosives, placed his hands on the stick of wood and told the shot firer he wanted to have a go. The dynamite-laden bedrock could explode and tear him to shreds like the bedrock. He pushed the stick of wood onto the dynamite with all his might, to pack it even tighter into the bedrock so it would explode with even more force. He pushed on the stick without trembling, repeatedly. He was frightened. It could blow up. He'd be dead before he heard the roar. His heart was beating too fast, but he mastered his fear. Grandpa Dynamite lit the wick. They stepped back, taking shelter behind a spruce trunk. The explosion heaved up a violent sheaf of crumbled bedrock that fell in a heavy rain, clattering against leaves and trunks. Innocent didn't start. He kept his eyes open and observed how the eternal bedrock had crumbled like bread. After this feat of valor, Innocent went to the phone and gave a lyrical account of the events. If the woman of his dreams had actually existed at the other end of the line, and if the wire had been connected, she'd have been forced to admire him. Innocent didn't like this thought which had just occurred to him. He didn't want to be admired, he wanted to win. He started mentally choosing the words for the speech he would deliver to the horizon, to the spruce woods before him and to the distant steeple. "Working to tear apart its chains makes a people strong." He was proud of his aphorism. Remembering Jeannot Tremblay, who always jotted down his thoughts, he wrote it on the wooden table. What a summer! Never in his life had he learned so much! When the work on the new road first started, Innocent Loiseau was still a babe-in-arms newly released from the college with its black-robed priests. When the road was open Innocent would be a man, ready to take his place in real life. He had been able to keep his hand from trembling when he held a stick of dynamite and now he would be able to face danger with serenity.

The shattered rock had been loaded into trucks that clattered and moaned as they wrenched themselves from the deep ruts. Then the dump body tipped the debris into hollows filled with brown swamp-water. Starting now, the trucks were truly the kings of the new road. The dump bodies unloaded mountains of crushed bedrock. Bulldozers spread it out. The excavators used long heavy rakes to level the gravel. It was a fine thing to see the mud being turned into road. This rubble was the base of it: when it was piled up and hardened, it would receive the gravel.

One morning, the truckers reported to the office, their dump bodies empty. Téton Lachapelle was dead. The news burst like a blast of dynamite. Some, struggling to keep a tear from running onto their cheeks, others, sucking on cigarettes so they could hide in the smoke, decided they wouldn't move a stone until the day after Téton Lachapelle's burial.

"How do you expect us to work when one of our friends, a man like us, our age, is lying there cold and dead? Only yesterday he was driving his truck flat out, to pass us and pile up more trips. He was ambitious, Téton Lachapelle, but he always had a joke. He was ambitious and he always wanted to win the race, but we loved him."

"Téton Lachapelle was the best man on the construction site, even counting Pommette Rossignol!"

"If a man dies in an accident, if he's run over in his truck, you can say it's the good Lord's will; but Téton Lachapelle himself decided to snuff out the life the good Lord gave him . . . "

"One day you're laughing with a man, the next day he's dead. He'd decided to kill himself but he was laughing all the same."

"If a man that's decided to end to his life hears a joke he probably thinks: might as well laugh now, tomorrow I won't be able to."

"Remember? Téton Lachapelle often said, 'You can't know the misery a guy's carrying around in his belly . . .' Remember that?"

"I heard him say it often."

" 'You don't know the misery a guy . . .' Sure . . . I remember."

"He'll never say it again."

"He'll never say, 'You can't know the misery a guy's carrying around in his belly . . .' "

"And we'll never know what his misery was . . . "

"When's the burial?" asked Innocent Loiseau.

"In three days."

"Three days!" the foreman roared. "You mean you're stopping work for three days to celebrate with the dead man? I got a timetable to respect, deadlines to meet, a contract to carry out. This road's gotta be finished before the election. Le Chef needs a new road. And snivelling over a dead man won't get it built. Let your wives do the crying, that's what they're good at. Téton Lachapelle won't know the difference. And if he does, he'll be happier to see tears running down pretty faces as sweet as cake-icing than down your gloomy mugs. Téton Lachapelle was proud of his work on the new road and he'll be proud to see you guys at work. Téton Lachapelle understood that working's a privilege. He'll never work again because now he's stretched out on his back forever. I'm telling you to get back to work like nothing happened, even if poor Téton Lachapelle took his own life with no reason and no explanation. Friends, we're going to plug away even harder because Téton Lachapelle's keeping an eye on us from his silk-lined coffin!"

The foreman was a man of iron. He wasn't impressed when a bulldozer lumbered toward him or a charge of dynamite blew up under his nose. He was a man who never stepped back. He was a man who talked in the same way to trucks, bulldozers, excavators and men. He had tremendous authority over his men. When the workers heard him they did what they always did: they obeyed. They turned to go back to work, but they were checked by a lament, a sort of muffled sob. It was the foreman: he was hugging his belly as if he'd been wounded. His face, worn by pain, was rent by a great sob. To hide his sorrow, the foreman turned his back on the men and, spying a big stone, bent down and tried to lift it. The stone was too heavy and he stood there, powerless, exhausted. His broad back shook. He sobbed:

"Téton Lachapelle was our brother: we can't work when our brother's spending his final days on earth . . . "

Innocent Loiseau went inside, opened his black ledger and in big block letters wrote: DAYS NOT WORKED: MOURNING FOR TETON LACHAPELLE. The employees did not go home. They leaned on the hoods of their trucks, sat on the bulldozer blade, stood in the mud, hands in their pockets, numb with sorrow. Their voices were muted as if they were trying not to be heard by Téton Lachapelle's soul. They talked about him. Bit by bit, they reconstituted his final days. Each remembered a few sad words, each had noticed some concern in his eyes. Each man was struggling to make sense of Téton's death. Each one searched the preceding days for a sign foreshadowing his ultimate despair. Yesterday, Téton Lachapelle was alive and laughing. A few hours later, Téton became his own judge and sentenced himself to death. They told stories. Remembering, their memories stirred other memories to life. They talked as if the breath of their words could revive the breath of life in Téton Lachapelle's body. Words stirred up memories. Téton Lachapelle's life was like a fire of words whose flames could burn up time. Each man was hypnotized, for along with Téton Lachapelle's life, his own life was being consumed. They had spent the same time together; they had had the same childhood, the same youth; they had set out together upon their life as men. Suddenly, Téton's life had ended. It was a little as if their lives were ending too. Why had he killed himself? He had left a letter in his truck: mysterious words no one could understand. Some of them thought that instead of such an ambiguous explanation, it would have been better if Téton had left without a word. He had written with a hand that didn't even tremble. How could a man about to administer his own death write without trembling? ("When I'm hunting, once I take aim at my deer I shake from head to foot and it's not even me that's gonna die, it's the deer." — "When they phoned me to say my old mother who was almost ninety-nine had died, I shook so hard my pants fell off; and it wasn't me that was dying, it was my old mother.") Aside from signing his name on contracts for buying trucks and on his marriage certificate, Téton Lachapelle hadn't written a word since elementary school. Yet he'd written without trembling, without hesitating and without making a single mistake. His farewell message had no doubt been ready for a long time. When he came to unload gravel or rubble, telling stories that had them rolling on the ground, he probably had the message in his head. In school, Téton could never remember a single rule of grammar; he was the champion — international, the teacher specified — at making mistakes in a single composition. Now he had written a message without a single error. His teacher would have been proud of him: he had died without insulting the school or his mother tongue. "I'm going because I'm incapable of loving." That was the message he had left. "I'm going." That they understood, it was easy. "Because I'm incapable of loving": that meant nothing. It wasn't the way Téton Lachapelle usually talked. Pommette Rossignol, who read a lot of magazines full of pictures of women with all kinds of cosmetics on their face, all sorts of paint around their eyes and all manner of harnesses to hold their bosoms up or bellies in, told them she'd often read similar phrases. Téton's wife was a great reader who subscribed to many magazines. Perhaps Téton had copied his farewell message. In school, they remembered, Téton always managed to copy the description of autumn, a river or a snowstorm from a book. ("He had a gift for finding descriptions in books, he had a nose for it.") It was odd: copying out your farewell message, like homework. The reason he gave to justify his death was even odder. "Incapable of loving." Nobody kills himself for that. They would never understand even if his death was explained like two and two are four.("Curé Fourré does a good job on the mystery of the Most Holy Trinity, but we can't understand because it's incomprehensible.") In the end, everyone agreed that Téton Lachapelle had been working very hard lately, and that in his fatigue, over the long nights when he was driving his truck to the Capital, sometimes after a day on the road as well, he'd probably been brushed by madness. ("There's winds of madness that come up at night; you can't feel them but if they touch you it makes your mind reel.") "I'm going because I'm incapable of loving." These words meant nothing. ("Téton Lachapelle went off the beam.") "Incapable of loving": hadn't Téton married the most beautiful girl in the Appalachians? All the men in the region had desired the beautiful Blandine. For her they had gone far away to forest worksites or to big city factories, farther than the Capital; they had worked endless days, interminable weeks, everlasting months, to amass a small fortune to lay at the feet of the beautiful Blandine; they'd gone into debt to buy sparkling, speedy, chrome-decked cars and implored Blandine to get in; they had ruined themselves to offer Blandine, at dances, bottles of wine made for the mouths of princesses. Often they had fought to establish their right to approach Blandine, the right to ask her to dance. Finally, Téton Lachapelle was declared the winner. Blandine was seen only in Téton Lachapelle's truck, the big red truck with a motor that bellowed like a rutting bull. Téton waxed and polished it every Saturday so he could parade around Saint-Toussaint-des-Saints and the neighboring villages with his Blandine. The running board had been made for a man in work boots, not a young girl with legs of porcelain and a skirt like a swirl of crinoline. The boys always tried to be present at a ritual more beautiful than anything in the movies: they watched Téton Lachapelle grasp Blandine's slender waist and lift her up so that her dazzling bosom grazed his torso, then he held her by the strength in his arms while her dainty feet sought the steps. The boys marvelled at the sight of such delicate legs moving, the wind swelling her skirt to show, in a flash, her lacy underpants like a magic flower in a forbidden garden. Blandine's laughter thrilled their hearts a little more. The radiant lovers set off in the red truck. The others, who had never possessed Blandine, became as sad as if they had lost her. They couldn't see the other girls, because they didn't look like Blandine. None had such blue eyes or such an adorable chin or lips that never pursed in a sorrowful pout. None had breasts so round, inviting a man to rest his head after a hard day. None had such a slender waist, that seemed made to be held in a man's broad hand.

Today, Téton Lachapelle was dead. He had taken his life because he was "incapable of loving" that woman.

"Blandine had changed a lot . . . "

"You looked down on us because hatching babies made us ugly," Pommette Rossignol protested, "and now you look down on women because they don't make babies any more. What do you men want anyway? No matter what women do, you look down on us."

Pommette Rossignol had her claws sharpened to defend herself against these men who thought that they possessed the only truth.

"What you want, Pommette Rossignol, is to geld your husband and then all the other men."

"What women want is equality. Everywhere. That's why they dream about cutting off our shiggys."

"I hear you," said Pommette, "and it makes me sad to think that you men with your empty heads and your limp little shiggys are preparing the province's future."

"What makes me sad is, Téton Lachapelle isn't here with us."

Peace returned to the group. Slowly their expressions mellowed. The melancholy thoughts of each turned slightly to himself. So many things they couldn't understand. Life held so many secrets, so many mysteries.

"Death's like love. You never know when it'll come for you."

In other circumstances everyone would have guffawed and kept laughing for a long time. The joke would have been repeated around the table at suppertime, and again they would have laughed.

Today, Téton Lachapelle had taken his life. Yesterday he was hauling gravel, working faster than the others. To-day, he had fled to the land of death because he was "in-capable of loving." Never had he said that he couldn't love his Blandine. Never had he announced that he wanted to kill himself. Never had he given anyone to understand that he wouldn't come back to the new road. "When you see a man you can't know all the misery in his belly." These

371

words were the only sign of his distress. Who would have suspected that Téton Lachapelle was talking about himself? He had to die before they knew.

"The one that goes always wants to teach something to the ones that stay behind."

They recalled that Téton hadn't always been the round-faced man who knew the latest story, who tossed comical invective at his fellow workers and sang the same old love songs in a voice that drowned the sound of his truck. Before he married the beautiful Blandine, Téton was made of stone: he never smiled. Téton always wanted to be the toughest. He was the truck-driver who carried the heaviest load, the one who drove the fastest. Even if he spent three days on the road without sleeping, it wouldn't cross his mind to be tired. The man was made of stone. Winning over Blandine had been harder than plucking a wild strawberry. Other suitors put sugar in his gas tank. Impassive as stone, unperturbed, he took it apart, drained the ducts and, as patiently as stone, waited to find out who was responsible. In the dance hall, Téton spotted the joker, who collapsed under an avalanche of blows. Next came those who had slashed his tires one Sunday and those who had taken Blandine in a car and driven into the night, and those who had prevented him from driving his truck along the road to Blandine's father's house. Téton stood motionless. The joker's friends came to save his honor. Téton took their blows without flinching. He landed a few himself. Now a number of them struck out. Téton didn't fall. He resisted. He stayed on his feet. He didn't cry out when he received a painful blow: the silence of stone. Finally, unable to bring Téton down, they gave up and left the dance floor. After a hard fight it's common for a man to cry; there were no tears in Téton's eyes. Those who had seen him remembered very well. There was only blood. The endurance of stone. At that moment, Blandine was in the room. It was for her that he had fought. He made his way through the dancers, who stepped back to let through this tough, bleeding, sturdy man who gave off an animal smell as he moved and a sort of electricity you could feel as he passed by. He walked up to Blandine and his big hand, with bleeding knuckles, grasped Blandine's well cared-for, perfumed little hand with the strength of a trap snapping shut. Pulling her behind him, he crossed the dance hall, went outside and led her to his truck, where he hoisted her up onto the seat. The motor started. No one was tempted to put sugar in his gas tank now.

"Did you notice," asked Blandine, "the orchestra kept playing while you were fighting? Every time one of you landed a blow, Homère hit his drum. It was nice, but the orchestra's too small. What you needed was a big band, like they've got in the Capital. Did you hear . . . ?"

"I didn't hear nothing. Only the beating of your heart."

He had laughed. Blandine had never seen him laugh. She thought Téton was made of stone. She told others about it. It was she who told about the first time Téton laughed. That night, they clattered through the night in the truck. They travelled all the roads through the Appalachians. A man can do many things for a woman: he can even be reborn so that he no longer resembles what he was when he came out of his mother. Blandine melted the stone. Since he'd fallen in love with Blandine, Téton was no longer as hard as stone. Blandine's body was a fire that could melt the hardest man. Wild men, drinkers, rowdies came and licked her hand like big ingratiating cats. Blandine gave Téton his second birth; he became a man the others had never known: he smiled. The people who lived around him were no longer enemies to be defeated. Instead of standing among them like cold stone, he offered warm gestures and words. Was Blandine giving him a better understanding of life? Surely she was the one who was awakening tenderness in the stone; her fiery young girl's warmth was transmitted to the stone. Blandine asked for nothing, she wasn't ambitious, she wasn't looking for the richest husband, she didn't suffer because she didn't live in the Capital where men could buy their wives whatever they desired. She wasn't a hypocrite, she had nothing to hide, she lived only in the present moment, like a flame that glows with what it burns. Téton was a new man and that new man had decided to take his own life.

Other men would have bought a luxurious limousine and ushered Blandine into it. Téton, after taking her by the hand in a way that told her he'd never let her go out with another man, bought only trucks, always red but with ever bigger wheels that raised it higher and higher, with running boards ever more inaccessible, with ever more immense dump bodies, with ever more sophisticated nickel ornaments, ever more elaborate and gleaming radiator grills, ever more streamlined fenders: his trucks were great fine savage beasts of steel. On the hard leather seat, Téton Lachapelle and Blandine travelled all night long down out-of-the-way roads. There was no end to their discoveries. Blandine talked: every bump, every cloud, every spruce tree that stood out against the sky, every lighted window, every animal cry, every creature frightened by the head-lights, every pair of glowing eyes along the road and every star made a sheaf of words spring from Blandine's lips. For Téton, it was as beautiful to listen to as a sheaf of flowers is beautiful to look at. At times, she was still. Then Téton would say two or three words. Without knowing it, he was learning how to speak. Often Blandine's reflections were unexpected. He would smile, and without knowing it, his face was learning how to stop being stone. On this earth a man must meet a woman: Téton had just met his and he knew he'd never seek another. He also knew that he would never have a truck beautiful enough to be worthy of transporting his treasure along the Appalachian roads. He had won her; now he must live so as never to lose her.

He wanted to give Blandine everything. He worked as hard as ten men. ("I'll go out in my truck and bring you every jewel in the world.")

Téton didn't seem triumphant after winning Blandine. Rather, he looked like the one in charge. Blandine was a forbidden fruit. When they saw her gaze at Téton, the other young men were no longer entitled to dream about her. Yet she had become even more beautiful. Her bosom was filled with sighs that raised it in a way that made you giddy. Her lips bore a smile that made her look as if she was distributing kisses when she talked. Above all, her eyes glowed with the light of a person who is in love with life.

The workers dreamed about Blandine and Téton on their leather seat, driving along the bumpy roads, heads lolling, wrapped in the night that huddled against the windshield, enclosed as an egg. She looked at the powerful hands clutching the wheel, their strong wrists, while he tried to see beyond the beams of his headlights, happy that Blandine was there beside him. All the men his age had wanted her, but only he had her on the seat beside him. He was happy to be in love with this young girl who was so beautiful that the boys didn't look at anybody else when she was in the dance hall. She danced like music. She was so patient she had even managed to make her lover dance, though his feet knew only how to push the pedals of his truck along winding, bumpy roads. When he held her in his arms, close to his body that burned with the heat of Blandine's body, he dared not look at her. She was as beautiful as a dream.

"Why'd they call him Téton? That's not a very nice name."

"It was a nickname."

"But why Téton? There's lots of nicknames you can give a man without calling him a tit."

"I never heard his real name. In school it was always Téton. He used to get into fights on account of it."

"It was in school Téton learned to be as hard as stone. When a child fights because the whole school calls him a name, it makes for a hard child, a lonely child."

No one could remember the name the priest had given him at his baptism.

"Poor Téton, spent his whole life here in Saint-Toussaint-des-Saints, part of our big family, and he died with nobody knowing his real name."

"No, I'd say, Poor us. If we can't find out the name of a man that lives with us we don't know much about life."

The church bell sounded the mournful notes of the death knell. It was as if God's tears were falling on the village. The houses clinging to the hillside around the church seemed to be in mourning. Each note that fell from the steeple reverberated in the sky where it made circles like a pebble tossed in the water. No motor rumbled, no cow lowed, no horse whinnied. The birds were silent. There was only the sad lament of the knell that was no longer coming from the steeple, but from the deep bosom of the earth. Rising up and saddening the sky, the echo's voice choked and became a sob. Yesterday, it was Téton's laugh that they heard.

Téton Lachapelle and Blandine: theirs was the most beautiful wedding ever seen. Blandine's gown was as lovely as the queen's that they'd seen in the paper. Her train was so long she had to ask all the grade one girls to carry it.

The little girls were all dolled up with their hair in curls. In their brightly colored dresses and crinolines they looked like wildflowers. Téton had paid a little extra so the choir would prepare some special songs. He had also made an offering to the organist. The church in Saint-Toussaint-des-Saints didn't seem large enough. They needed a cathedral like the one in the Capital, a cathedral like in Rome, so much power and joy filled the music that celebrated the day when Téton Lachapelle and Blandine Laframboise were married. Téton also made a donation to the nuns' good works in Africa; in return, the sisters had woven garlands of flowers and draped them on the statues in the Stations of the Cross, and tied a bouquet to every pew. The church smelled of the sky and looked like a garden. The church was filled with the celestial light of angels: you could hear the fluttering of their wings. Téton Lachapelle had paid a double tithe to Curé Fourré, asking him to light all the candles, all the votive lights, all the tall candles on the lateral altars, all the electric lights in the niches, all the fluorescent halos above the saints, all the chandeliers on the ceiling and all the festoons of stars that framed the pictures. Téton Lachapelle was beaming like a beautiful day when spring is driving winter away forever. On this, his wedding day, he wasn't a man decked out in his wedding suit, he was a sun dressed up as a man. Blandine bathed in the light. She truly looked like a flower with all its petals open to drink in the light. She sparkled like the dew when light plays in it. What fine children they would make! No bachelors came to this wedding: probably they didn't want to see so much beauty escaping them. A number of young girls were at the ceremony and they were paying heed to Blandine, learning how to be beautiful.

"Too much beauty's no good for a woman; it's almost a disease; too much beauty in a woman just means a pack of trouble."

That day the bells rang more joyously than when they had announced the end of the war. Téton had slipped a bill to the altar boys who pulled the ropes. The bells proclaimed to the Appalachian hills that never had a young girl been as beautiful as Blandine on this her wedding day and that alas! never would she be so beautiful again. Who could forget this wedding? For the occasion, Téton had

376

bought a new truck, more powerful, taller, more nickel-plated, more streamlined than any other. He had decorated it with ribbons and flowers. They got in the truck that was as ornate as a papal chair, with silvery tailpipes as long as organ pipes that gleamed in the sun; they uttered cries of joy, then disappeared in a cloud of dust. The others watched the cloud for a long time as it travelled down the road. They had heard it said that Téton Lachapelle was taking his Blandine to a hotel in the Capital that admitted only Le Chef and his Right Party ministers. You don't often see happiness in a lifetime, but on the day Blandine and Téton Lachapelle were married, people knew they'd seen happiness with their own eyes. It even showed in the photographs. Today the knell was tolling. The photographs were ridiculous. They showed a happiness that was false, for Téton had taken his life because he was "incapable of loving." The cameras had been unable to capture Téton's anguish. Despair that drives a man to death doesn't show up just like that, like a fly. A man doesn't decide to kill himself, just like that. A man who kills himself does it because, in his mind, it's as natural to take your life as it is for others to sit back and wait for death. People said so after the knell had finished tolling. In their wedding pictures Téton wasn't smiling as much as Blandine. Only today did people know that he wasn't as happy as he pretended. If the idea of death had already taken root in his soul, it must have been painful for him to feel happy.

After their wedding ceremony and their honeymoon in the Capital, Téton Lachapelle and Blandine Laframboise moved into a cozy place they had rented over an apartment where two old deaf people lived. The curtains were always drawn, the blinds lowered. It was hard to know what was going on inside, but people imagined. They weren't too pleased to see the windows completely obstructed. The newlyweds were shut inside a box no one could open. In Saint-Toussaint-des-Saints, people liked to be able to glance in windows and see other people at the table or getting ready for bed, see them moving around in their houses and arguing, know whether they were heating up leftovers, see the woman doing her ironing, checking the hem of her dress before she went out, see children doing their homework. If they looked inside other people's houses they shouldn't close up their own. If everyone had closed up his house like Blandine and Téton, there would have been nothing to see. Blandine and Téton were in hiding. They were newlyweds with their own little secrets. How was their apartment furnished? How was it decorated? What color were the walls painted? Or were they papered? No one knew, and so much secrecy irritated the village. If someone in the village wrapped himself in too much secrecy, he became an outsider. Outsiders would never be loved like brothers and sisters. Blandine and Téton Lachapelle had become outsiders. He was never seen except at the wheel of his truck, through the sun glinting off the windshield. People could hear his truck rumbling late at night when he came home from a long trip, and early in the morning — frequently still in the middle of the night — as he was leaving on another. Occasionally the truck would be gone for days at a time: Téton had gone to America, or over into Canada. During his absence the apartment windows remained impenetrable. Blandine didn't go out. They didn't see her parading around like other happy young women. Was Téton so afraid of losing his treasure that he shut her away when he was gone? She didn't go out when he came back either. People realized that with such a beautiful wife Téton would want to spend as much time as possible in bed. But it wasn't good for a woman to be shut away. When women are shut away they fade, just as the fur of caged animals becomes dull. The more a woman is shown to others, the more she is looked at, the more beautiful she becomes. Was Téton so jealous that he couldn't tolerate other men's eyes looking at his Blandine? Was she so happy she was numb, like someone drunk on alcohol? All that remained to the curious was their imagination. Everyone was curious . . . And anyone with any imagination had his eyes riveted on the newlyweds' blinded windows.

It was easier to understand Téton. This rented apartment, in a house the old couple had "cut in two" to bring in some money, wasn't worthy of the most beautiful girl in the Appalachians. He wanted to lodge her in a castle he'd have built of stucco, with arcades like the ones on those Mexican haciendas he'd admired in Blandine's magazines. He would have the house built on the hill near the church, where there was an oatfield he would buy and transform into a flower garden where the children could play. But happiness has its price and dreams cost dearly. Téton drove himself hard. He needed lots of money. He knew that money is the magic substance that turns dreams into reality. Téton worked days, he worked nights, he worked weekdays and Sundays, he worked on Saints' days and government holidays. He transported sand or pigs, wood or sheep, potatoes or natural manure for the lawns in the Capital. At the same time, he carried love letters, business letters and parcels on the front seat beside him. Neither the days nor the nights, neither the weeks nor the months were long enough for what he had to do. Téton Lachapelle's powerful truck travelled endlessly toward the Capital, toward America or into Canada, in search of a fortune. People said he'd become very rich if his truck didn't kill him one night, at some unexpected bend in the road. Many women wished they had a husband like Téton, who worked to get rich and set up his wife as she deserved. They thought they understood. They knew that Blandine had always been a proud woman. When a young girl is so beautiful that the boys all dream about her every night, murmuring her name, she is entitled not to be modest. Blandine knew she was the most beautiful girl in town. She must have decided not to show herself until Téton had built the luxurious castle he sometimes described to the other workers.

They were wrong. It took time for them to find out. They had known Téton was like a motor, unable to do anything but spin, but work. He started telling stories brought back from his travels. Téton, who in the past had hardly taken time to catch his breath, now let his motor idle as he told a story. At first the other men were so surprised they couldn't laugh. Only Téton would guffaw. Sometimes he would stop a truck coming in the opposite direction; he would roll down his window, tell his story and take off again, laughing to himself, leaving the other man baffled. Téton, formerly as solitary as a bear, seemed to be seeking company, the warmth of friendship, laughter and talk. After their initial surprise, the men decided his stories were funny. They gradually got over their surprise and let themselves laugh. Téton was comical, he enjoyed

379

laughing as much as work, and being married to Blandine had softened his hide. Blandine was making a new man of him. Or so they thought.

They were wrong, but didn't know it right away. The women learned the truth. They used to make quilts from multi-colored scraps of fabric, rescued from worn-out clothes and sewn together with taste. The women also patched together fragments of sentences Téton had dropped, scraps of confidences shared by some individuals who had actually gone inside Blandine's door, to repair an appliance or ask for a charitable donation. Our two lovers also had families . . . and what a son or a daughter hides in the depths of himself or herself, the family will recount. The women patched together all these scraps of confessions, admissions, gossip and rumors, they joined them with the thread of feminine intuition which teaches so many things, and with the thread of experience. Gradually the coverlet of the life of Blandine and Téton was stitched together. When Téton died, everyone realized the women weren't as wrong as the men had maintained.

" 'Incapable of loving': if Téton really wrote that to explain why he was killing himself, in a way Téton died of sadness."

"Blandine didn't get fat from nothing," said Gornouille Larivière, a truckdriver like Téton, but a bachelor. "Blandine fattened up on Téton's sadness."

"Blandine didn't get fat from a wasp sting."

After the knell had draped Saint-Toussaint-des-Saints in a heavy cloud of sorrow, the workers on the new road looked at the dark windows of the life of Blandine Laframboise and Téton Lachapelle, and it seemed that they could see better than ever. Death sometimes opens the heavy curtain that conceals life. They recalled how things had happened. Together, each man added to the women's accounts his own anecdote, his observation, his recollection, his word or his silence, and together they reconstituted the story of Blandine and Téton.

If it's true that a rolling stone gathers no moss, a truck that rolls along the road day and night, transporting all the things men need to have transported in the perpetual motion that is life, a truck that rolls along like the frenzied beating of a heart in love doesn't bring in a fortune. That was what Téton realized, he who had promised the princess of the Appalachians a castle worthy of her beauty. All those hours at the wheel exhausted him. He came home worn out, his muscles stiff and sore. After all the bumps and ruts and turns and washboard roads, followed by other roads as flat as sleep, he felt like a rock that has gone through a crusher. As he pushed the door of his apartment he felt, not desire to see Blandine and hold her in his arms, but regret that in a few hours he must leave her and get back in his truck. Wealth was running ahead of him like a wild horse. Blandine was in bed. She was waiting for him. She was eating chocolate and crying because her husband was never with her, because he was always out in the world somewhere, travelling the roads. The pillow was wet.

"I've been crying because I love you too much."

Blandine hadn't combed her hair, hadn't put on her clothes. She had waited for her husband in bed. Famished when he got up after loving his Blandine, face wet with his wife's tears, Téton Lachapelle went to the kitchen. Hunger seared his stomach. No sooner would he fall asleep, holding Blandine's blazing body close to him, than it would be time to leave again. He loved her, but he spent his days and nights away from her, in his truck weighed down by their maximum loads so he'd be paid more, following roads that took him far from Blandine. Why didn't he just stay with her, since he loved her so? It would have been easy not to leave her, but those who truly love must part. He would have shown insufficient love for Blandine if he spent his days and nights with her, joined in love. He showed much greater love by leaving her to go and earn the fortune that would buy the hacienda his dreams had already built.

"Why don't you stay in my arms?"

"I'm hungry, Blandine. I haven't had time for a bite since morning."

He opened the refrigerator. The shelves were bare.

"I've got some chocolate. Come here."

Blandine's voice was so enticing, Téton had already stopped being unhappy at finding nothing to eat. He went back to bed. Blandine arranged the chocolates on her bosom. Bending over, Téton picked them up in his teeth one at a time. Blandine's hands took his head and pressed it hard against her breasts. Her husband's lips kissed the soft flesh. Téton fell asleep. How had the men learned such an intimate secret? One day he had recommended this magical method to a co-worker who was too worked up to get to sleep, after being on the road too long.

"It puts the nerves to sleep," Téton had pointed out.

"You make that up yourself?"

"No, I read about it in one of Blandine's magazines," he lied.

Téton confessed everything while seeming to say nothing, to be as secretive as a strong-box. After they learned this, the workers made lewd remarks about bringing home chocolates they bought in towns along the roads they travelled.

Blandine had reigned over the dance halls; the orchestras played her favorite tunes when she entered like a ray of light. People watched her dance as admiringly as they would watch a bird in flight. As her body moved, the slender shimmering of her gown hinted at fascinating mysteries. Some of the boys stopped dancing and stared. Now only her husband would look at her. The white sheets on the bed were grey. Blandine didn't even think of changing them. Tufts of dust rolled across the floor; she didn't sweep them up. Her wedding bouquet had dried in its jar and she just left the petals on the table. She no longer got dressed. Her clothes were piled in a corner of the bedroom. She stayed in bed and wept because Téton left her to travel the roads in his truck. She ate nothing but the chocolates he brought her.

"Tomorrow," Téton suggested, "I'll take you with me."

"No, the place of a woman who loves her husband is at home. I love you."

"But Blandine, if you come with me the day will be more beautiful."

"No. It's a woman's lot to miss her husband and I want to spend my day missing you."

Téton was delighted that Blandine loved him so much, but he didn't comprehend the full meaning of her words. He went to his mother-in-law for an explanation.

"My handsome Téton," said the older woman, wrapping a maternal arm around his shoulders and hugging him to her big bosom, "you're a good boy and I know you want

382

to be good to Blandine. You say you want to understand her. Téton, don't try and be so crafty, don't try and figure everything out. A woman's made in a way men can't understand. She loves you. Be happy with that. She loves you in her own way. Take my Blandine's love, without asking for explanations. When a woman loves a man it's a gift. So many men aren't loved . . . Let yourself be loved, and love Blandine."

One Sunday, Téton Lachapelle wasn't working on the road. After he had cleaned his truck, changed the oil, made some minor repairs and got his vehicle ready for the road the next day, Téton wanted to go to church with Blandine, arm-in-arm, like a real lady and gentleman, well-dressed, shoulder-to-shoulder, and walk together to one of the front pews. Blandine nervously refused. She couldn't go out because her clothes were too tight. She could no longer wear any of the clothes she had bought when she got married. Téton thought she might like to go to the movies and see a fine love story.

"I don't want to see any love stories. Our love story is the best one of all. I don't want to look at anybody else's."

"They're showing a funny movie on the other side of Sixty Acre Mountain. With the truck . . . "

"Do you still love me? You're gone all week and come Sunday you make up all sorts of excuses not to stay here in our little nest with me."

They spent Sunday in bed, loving each other and eating chocolate. Blandine's breasts had become weighty clusters. Her little belly was rounded now and overflowed onto her thighs. Her feet were grey. Her toenails were long and rimmed with black. Blandine's hands were no longer as white as whipped cream. Her body was no longer scented like a field of flowers. Before her marriage she used to dab perfume on herself. Now a fuzz of dust had accumulated on the flasks of scent Téton had given her. Blandine's flesh had the stench of cream gone sour. Her limp hair drooped onto the pillow. It hadn't been combed for ages. The pillows were smeared with melted chocolate.

"You ought to change the sheets," he heard himself say drily.

Wanting to correct himself, he said with tenderness enclosing his anger,

"We've been married for several weeks now. You should change the sheets, my love . . . "

"I love you too much. It's like being drunk on love. My love, will you wash the sheets?"

How did you go about washing sheets? He remembered seeing his mother boil hers in bleach. He applied himself to doing that, filling the apartment with fumes that brought tears to his eyes. Washing sheets was no job for a man. A man who drove a truck all day should be able to look forward to a little rest before he sets off again.

At work the next day, Téton teased one of the other truckers, who replied,

"Now you're washing the sheets, do you wash Blandine's little panties too?"

Téton Lachapelle's truck took off like a racing car in a cloud of pebbles and dust. The other man regretted his attack.

"I was just kidding, but I guess I really hurt his feelings."

The knell had tolled. Fields, trees, stones, the Appalachian hills were sad because Téton Lachapelle had chosen the land of death over this beautiful land, a land so harsh her children have hoarse voices. People suspected that poor Téton had washed plenty of things besides sheets. They also knew that if Téton played the fool, it was to draw a laughing mask over the sad man he had become. He tried to make others laugh to forget that he was crying. ("When you see a man you can't know what misery he's got in his belly.")

Blandine didn't go out; the people in the village had been happy for Téton. According to an old saying, when a man marries fire, he shouldn't be afraid of getting burned. Blandine was fire wearing dresses that were too bright, with crinolines; those dresses were fire that made men's blood seethe. Téton Lachapelle had married that fire in the presence of Curé Fourré. People expected him to suffer some burns, they expected to see poor Téton consumed and become a little heap of ashes in the hollow of Blandine's blazing hand. A man must always pay a price for his wife, both men and women agreed on that score. Rather than pay, Téton seemed to have been paid and gotten rich. He was laughing now. He who earlier had thought only of holding the wheel of his truck, making it go ever faster, ever farther, carrying ever heavier loads, in ever more powerful trucks, now would stop to tell a story, joke with a fellow-worker, ask a riddle, then leave, laughing, hurrying to make up for lost time. People had been expecting Blandine to give her husband the slip as soon as some handsome young man in a new suit approached her, but she became a real stay-at-home. As the heart does not leave the body to wander and make mischief, so did Blandine stay at home, waiting for her husband the bread-winner to return. Then she would fill his repose with caresses so that when he set off again he would be a new man, restored by love. That was what the villagers thought as they peered at the windows always veiled by curtains, at the door that was never opened.

Blandine, they reasoned, was a star plucked from heaven. A treasure. When a man possesses a treasure, he is bound to feel some anxiety, some concern about being robbed. Téton feared being robbed of his Blandine. She was a diamond. Men always want to possess a diamond, and those who cannot buy one try at least to hold one in their hands, heft it, watch it sparkle; that was what Aurore Lapierre, the jeweler's wife, had said. Blandine had known lots of boys. She knew her own worth; Téton wasn't the only man who had sparks in his eyes when he gazed at her. ("A woman's a woman," people said; "she knows what she's worth but not what she wants.") Téton kept her cut off from the world. He didn't want another man to come along and steal his star the way you pluck an apple. He shut his diamond away. He imprisoned his love. He drowned her in chocolate. People knew that Téton bought boxes of chocolates in the Capital. Blandine would have been quite happy to go out, those people thought, and show herself, before age had extinguished her beauty, to go out and display herself in a short dress that would show off her gleaming body when she danced, she would have liked to light up sparks in the eyes of other men besides her husband. She would have liked her husband to see desire in strangers' eyes, she would have liked other married couples to be jealous of them, but she was shut away by Téton like a diamond in a strong-box, like a star in an impenetrable cloud. People thought that for a long time, especially when they saw Téton who looked happy, like a man who is his wife's master. So many men walked beside their wives like dogs trained to pee where they're told; the village was gratified to see Téton act like a man who ruled his wife. Téton Lachapelle was the master and if he had put his Blandine in a cage, that was his right. The proof was that he was always happy. That, too, was what the people in Saint-Toussaint-des-Saints thought.

Now that the notes of the knell had fallen like heavy tears, the villagers suspected they might have made a mistake. The man who had taken his life was the one who had wanted to escape; the man who had wanted to escape was the one who had been shut up inside. Téton had wanted to run so far away from his diamond, from his star, that he had taken his life. He had decided to flee into death because there he could never be locked away again. Had Téton Lachapelle been so unhappy with his Blandine?

He had mentioned to Timoléon Tassé that Blandine had lost any desire to go out. ("It was like she'd shut away her youth, double-locked the door and thrown away the key.") Timoléon Tassé told him not to complain: everybody knew women who went out more than their husbands would have liked. ("Every man's got his own sorrow," he had said.) People remembered remarks they hadn't understood at the time.

"Funny how a man's death helps you remember."

"But who understands death . . . "

Blandine was gifted for love, and if she loved her man so much, she must have known what she was doing. Some of the other women dreamed of loving their husbands so absolutely. A few confessed to Curé Fourré that they didn't love their husbands enough. Shouldn't Téton Lachapelle be happy to have so much love for himself? When they saw Téton's gleaming truck drive by, some women couldn't stop themselves from dreaming, guiltily, that if they had husbands like Téton, they would have shut their doors and windows too. They would have liked to be loved absolutely, infinitely, like Blandine, their lives consisting only of love. Some more passionate women wouldn't even let such a handsome man go out . . . How good it must be to know you were loved like Blandine. And then their thoughts came back to their own houses. They were not loved like Blandine and they didn't love like her. Their love had the taste of dry and rancid bread.

Téton Lachapelle went home, his eyes burned by the light of the countryside he had travelled through, the bones in his back ground from jolting along the bumpy road, head heavy with the thoughts that teemed in his solitude, arms stiff from restraining the wheel of his powerful vehicle. He rushed to Blandine's bedroom. The sheets had been tossed to the floor, open magazines lay scattered all around; everywhere there were bits of candy wrappers, and the sheet was stained with chocolate.

"Blandine, are you sure chocolate's good for your health?"

"When you aren't here, chocolate's the only thing that's good."

From the middle of the bed, with no clothes on, she held out her arms. Her whole body seemed to rise up like bread dough, seemed to swell; her waist, her thighs, her neck were ringed by rolls of fat. Her delicate features were mired in fat. The Blandine he had desired and won now was lost. The light in her eyes seemed sticky. Clothes were scattered on the floor all over the room; had she tried to dress herself? She had certainly spent the day in bed. Her hair was plastered to her head. It hadn't been washed for a long time. Runnels of melted chocolate stained her hands. Sweat had left trails on the grey flesh of her drooping breasts and ballooning stomach. Something was rotting in the room. He'd see to that another time. Blandine was calling him.

"Oh no," she protested, "I stayed just as you left me this morning; I want to stay just the way you love me."

Téton Lachapelle knew that where love is concerned, men can be a little foolish. He knew more about the motor in his truck than his wife's emotions. He decided to pick up some tips from his godmother, who had been the reason for the death of her three husbands.

He asked, "Do women usually get fat after they're married?"

"Godson, if it isn't a baby that's making Blandine swell up, it must be love. In either case you've behaved like a man, and your godmother's proud of you."

"Aside from that, is it true that after women are married they have the habit of . . . umm . . . of neglecting the dust around the house?"

"Now listen here, godson. Curé Fourré gave you a young girl so you could make a woman out of her — in the biblical

387

sense, that is. Now, it takes time to make a woman. Let time take its course. What do you want in your bed anyway, a woman or a vacuum cleaner?"

His godmother had advised him to let time take its course. Blandine would discover not only that she was as beautiful, lively and bright as before, but more beautiful and better, for she would have become a woman. Every time he came home he found more dust. A rotten smell greeted him when he opened the door. The mattress drooped lower and lower under Blandine's weight as she got fatter and fatter from devouring chocolate. Téton started washing her; she would make cooing sounds as he scrubbed the masses of limp soft flesh.

"Oh, how I love it when you love me!"

On the fat joyous face where the flesh jiggled like clotted milk, on the fat chocolate-smeared lips, Téton Lachapelle occasionally saw a glimmer of Blandine's former prettiness. He soaked the sheets, picked up the candy wrappers and scattered clothes, tidied the magazines, washed and caressed and perfumed Blandine's huge body, then opened the windows to let in the cool night air.

"Oh, I love you so much I feel as if I've died and gone to heaven where we don't need our bodies any more and only love is alive forever."

Bent and exhausted, Téton collapsed into bed, then embraced his fat wife. His arms were too short to wrap around her ever-swelling body; he fell asleep, unable to take pleasure in so much love.

One day he asked a fellow worker, Méthode Mouton, if when he was alone with his wife, she ever recited phrases she'd picked up in magazines. He was surprised when the other man replied,

"When a man's loved he doesn't need to be told, he knows it."

"When my Blandine wants to tell me she loves me, she says words she learns in magazines."

"Weird words. If you don't understand them it's like she isn't saying them to you."

"Blandine loves me too much," he murmured, then got back in his truck and called out,

"If I could, I'd sell you the surplus."

When Méthode Mouton told this story, no one had to point out that, once again, Téton Lachapelle had hidden his sorrow in a hearty laugh. That morning the workers no longer heard his laughter, only the sorrow in the off-hand words of a man who would never return again.

By absorbing himself in his work, Téton Lachapelle was finally able to start building the palace he had dreamed of for Blandine. When the villagers saw Téton and Blandine's house going up they became concerned. How would a humble truckdriver pay for such a castle? It was the biggest house in Saint-Toussaint-des-Saints. Neither Curé Fourré nor the doctor nor Pigeon the notary lived in such a palace. ("Curé Fourré, the doctor and the notary haven't got a Blandine," Téton retorted.) People came from far away to admire it. Never had they seen such huge windows: the house had hardly any walls. They would be safe and sound in this house, but with the impression they were living outside. The roof, which was very high and very steep, was pierced by skylights. Through them, Blandine could follow the cloud of dust her husband's truck stirred up as it travelled over the backs of the hills. When the house was ready, Téton had flowers planted. Never had anyone seen so many flowers in a garden. Everyone thought Téton knew about nothing but axle grease and the parts of his truck, but he had selected the flowers as a princess selects her jewels. One night his truck pulled up, laden with crates. His furniture. The crates bore the name of the most fashionable store in the Capital. It was in that very store that Le Chef bought his furniture, the salesman had assured him, asking him to keep it confidential. Sumptuous drapes hung at the windows. This house had its secret too. Blandine had never asked God for so much happiness. Téton had reported her remark the next day, as they were loading his truck with stones, making sounds like thunderclaps.

Now that she was living in her castle, the villagers thought they might see Blandine again. A woman cannot keep her happiness to herself. A woman likes to show off her happiness. Téton promised former friends that soon they would go out together as they'd done in their youth, go out dancing. The night when they might revive their youth was postponed several times. Apologizing, Téton claimed he had to be on the road. He promised they'd do it another time. As the next date approached, Téton would withdraw, always with a solid pretext: work that he couldn't give up. When you earn your living transporting earth and stones, people thought, it can't be easy to live in a palace. Often, Téton would drive along in his truck, unaware that night had given way to day, unaware that dawn was chasing out the night. He drove like a man who had no need to stop. On the seat beside him, there was always a box of chocolates.

"It's good for love!" he would joke.

"When a woman eats chocolate she isn't thinking about cheating on her husband."

"Blandine will never cheat on me!"

"If you trust a woman that much you must love her."

"All roads come to an end," he had said.

"Yup, that's exactly what he said," Uguzon Dubois remembered. "They were practically his last words. Right afterwards, he started up his truck and drove it full speed into a maple tree at the side of the road. The tree was blown to smithereens, but its roots stayed in the ground."

Blandine didn't answer the people who brought the tragic news. They called; they waited for her to answer. As there was only silence, they dared to enter the luxurious house. They lost their way in all the rooms, then found a bedroom where a fat woman lay naked in greyish sheets, unsurprised, indifferent to their presence. Her greasy hair was plastered to her face. Apologizing for bursting in, the villagers asked for Blandine ... The fat, smelly woman shrugged and picked up a chocolate.

"Instead of going home and re-living that story while we wait for Téton Lachapelle's funeral," said Méthode Mouton, "I'd just as soon stay here on the new road, and work to bury the sadness of life."

It must have been sensible advice, because all the workers who had thought they were too unhappy to work while Téton Lachapelle was waiting to be buried went back to their tools or their machines.

"We can work just as well while we're in mourning."

XXXIV

Men do not hear the prophet's voice

Those cries: it was Jeannot Tremblay. Like Our Lord in the Gospels, he was calling to the workers from a rock. Still numb from the shock of losing Téton Lachapelle, they retraced their steps. They were probably going to learn something about the man who had arranged his own death, with a smile. Perhaps they would be given a better understanding of his tragedy. Or were they going to hear some new anecdotes? They gathered around Jeannot Tremblay, who proclaimed:

"At this hour of profound sorrow, only poetry remains intact. Though powerless, it possesses the gift of consolation."

"Intoxication?" asked an interested voice.

Jeannot Tremblay clutched the pages of his green notebook, which were being stirred by the wind. Innocent Loiseau was amazed. His friend who was so timid, so discreet, was addressing all the workers:

"My sorrowing friends, listen to the voice of poetry."

Weeks before, Jeannot Tremblay never said a word. He didn't let anyone look him in the eye. He was afraid they might read his hateful secrets. Now, miraculously, Jeannot Tremblay had come back to life. He had picked up his

391

youth where he abandoned it. Jeannot Tremblay was once again on the road to the future. Achille Bédard, his friend on *The Provincial Sun*, had pointed him toward the new road. He had arrived there in a weakened state, his muscles lazy and humiliated, a lump of remorse in his throat, his soul quavering dizzily in the face of the abyss he had only just escaped. He had learned how to work, and in the process learned how these uncultivated men lived. He had been working on the construction not of the new road, but of his own life. Innocent was proud to see him standing on a rock, notebook in hand. Jeannot Tremblay watched the workers gathering, bowed down by sorrow at the loss of one of their companions, who had taken his life because he could no longer love a woman. In his green notebook Jeannot Tremblay had jotted down: "It was life he could no longer love."

Most of the workers were there. Taking a deep breath, Jeannot Tremblay spoke in a firm voice that everyone could hear before the wind scattered his words. He read. Innocent Loiseau noticed that the hands that clenched the green notebook were trembling. He must talk to the workers so he could learn how to talk to them. Jeannot Tremblay had explained to Innocent that when a leader talks to his people, there is more than ideas, more than words, more than a voice, there is also something that cannot be seen, that cannot be heard: and that was the true language with which Le Chef touched his people. It must be something that could be learned and he'd learn it, Innocent decided. Jeannot Tremblay declaimed:

Men O men of my generation, weathered by rough seasons

Men with hands toughened by violent tasks that still give tender bread to your children

O men who have heard the voice of the knell in the steeple that was the voice of death,

Now hear this poetry, the voice of life.

You who have heard the knell, the voice of yesterday,

Now hear this poetry, tomorrow's voice.

Men of my father's generation, men who have made children

As my father has done and who will make children

As you have done

Men of my father's generation, already you belong
to the past
You have inherited bitter bread
And I would share that bread, I would share it with
your children
Let us share the pain so each man's pain will be
reduced
Men of my father's generation you have inherited
a land
But that land is bitter bread
Men of my father's generation
Of that land, you should be kings
But you stand here like the men of my father's
generation
Men with picks, men with shovels, men carrying
buckets of water, carrying axes
You are slaves who should be kings!
You are stones, you are the earth
With which usurpers build the roads to their own
wealth
Men O men of my father's generation, you have
been taught the roads of heaven
But earthly roads have been forbidden you
Stop being stones, stop being earth, stop being slaves!
Be kings!
Between history and the future
Men of my father's generation and sons of my own
generation,
Let us build the roads to liberty
That will lead to wealth
That we will share like brothers
Sons of my generation, men of my father's generation
And sons of the generation of our sons
Like brothers
We shall share history, bitter bread and festive days
And mornings, and days of toil and hopes,
Like brothers
We shall share the history of the past and the history
of the future
We shall share liberty
Men of the generations of fathers of sons and of
grandsons

We shall not leave a single crumb to the usurpers
Abandoned and alone along roads that will lead
only to loss
Men of our fathers' generation your sons will give
you liberty
Your sons will become your fathers
Men of my father's generation, you have been taught
the roads that lead to heaven
Your sons will guide you along the roads where we
shall walk, heads high and free, upon the earth.

Innocent Loiseau, his black ledger under his arm, would
never be able to talk like that, neither to women nor to
men. To have such fine ideas Jeannot Tremblay must have
suffered greatly. Is it not through suffering that thoughts
mature? Innocent regretted that he'd never suffered. He
had been unhappy at the priests' college. Many times in
the big dormitory he had wept into his pillow. Was that
suffering? All the days resembled one another as if he were
Sisyphus, condemned always to start the same day over
again. It was more boredom than suffering. Great men
had been carved by pain. Suffering might have destroyed
Jeannot Tremblay's soul, but instead it had made him live,
it had matured him. Now Jeannot Tremblay could go forth
into life and distribute his ideas like fine fruits. His poetry
was like a fruit: it provided nourishment. When Innocent
had found a woman perhaps then he would learn how to
suffer. He knew that in life a man often suffers because
of a woman he loves; perhaps he would suffer when he
fell in love. Then his thoughts would mature; he too would
be able to utter words that would move the hearts of men.
He was proud to have a friend like Jeannot Tremblay who
had sworn an oath to become his people's guide. He was
proud to have been invited by Jeannot Tremblay to join
him and his friend, the journalist at *The Provincial Sun*,
who was preparing the way. Jeannot read. His voice was
powerful. His voice, too had matured in pain. To be worthy of his friends who had a great destiny, he would learn
everything he had to know so that he too could win. Win.
Win. Verrochio was right. That was the most important
word in the dictionary. Win. He would learn.

The workers didn't linger. This strange shy boy who stood on a rock like a prophet, like Moses, was delivering an incomprehensible speech. Slowly they went back to their machines and their tools. Jeannot Tremblay went on reading. At the end, only Innocent Loiseau was still listening. Win. He would dock Jeannot Tremblay the number of minutes it had taken him to read his poem. Jeannot climbed down from his rock, unhappy because he couldn't keep the workmen until the end of his poem. He confided his disappointment to Innocent.

"No words are more eloquent than a man's death," Innocent replied, to excuse the workers.

"Life is more eloquent than death," Jeannot assured him, bending down to take up his shovel. "Let's get this road built, fast!"

XXXV

Will an adolescent decipher the enigma of love?

The horn blew insistently.

"Innocent, somebody wants you!"

It must be Verrochio. And yet it didn't sound like his horn. This one sounded reedy. He hurried. He tried to run as fast as the mud stuck to his boots would let him. The horn sounded impatient. It wasn't Verrochio's. If Verrochio were kept waiting for a moment he got furious and the horn, in its own way, hurled oaths.

It was just a little yellow car: a model he'd never seen. It was the yellow of a daisy's heart, of the underside of a warbler. Innocent approached the car.

"Is it you, Innocent?" asked a woman's voice.

The light on the windshield and windows kept the woman hidden in shadow.

"I'd like to talk to you.

The door opened and a long leg unfolded, slender and brown, a little foot hugged by a delicate sandal sought a place that wasn't too dirty to set itself on the ground, and during this movement the yellow dress opened, was pulled up high on the leg, and in a head-spinning motion revealed the other leg, which was now elegantly unfolding. The other foot alighted on the ground. The bare thighs gleamed. Innocent waited for the woman to pull the yellow skirt over her knees, but it probably didn't occur to her. The youth didn't know where to focus his embarrassed eyes. She stretched her travel-weary legs. He thought the woman hadn't noticed his flushed cheeks. She held her pose. To control his giddiness, he picked up a good-sized pebble and, very responsibly, threw it over the shoulder of the road. He came back to the car, promising himself he would win.

"So it's you, Innocent," said the lady, who didn't speak with the rough Appalachian accent.

As she got out of the car she leaned over and, in the low-cut neck of the yellow dress, Innocent saw the gleam of breasts. At this moment of great privilege, Innocent shuddered, his heart pounding inordinately hard. He decided that winning meant not looking away but admiring this gift that the unknown woman had brought him here, in broad daylight. He had never seen live breasts before. The women in Saint-Toussaint-des-Saints hid theirs behind the thick cloth of dresses fastened at the neck. They had learned in the nuns' schools how to flatten the diabolical bumps that induced fevers in men. Innocent had spent a lot of time observing and comparing breasts in the photographs of paintings and sculptures in his illustrated dictionary. He had see many paper breasts, but never any made of flesh. He felt a sort of hot breath in his eyes. He concentrated all his efforts on looking. This vision would last longer than he'd hoped. The woman let herself be admired.

"I was telling myself, that Innocent must be a good-looking boy . . . "

She walked toward his shed. The women in Saint-Toussaint-des-Saints didn't walk that way. Her hips swayed as if they were trying to tear the yellow dress. Her arms were wound with bracelets that gleamed and clinked. She didn't walk, she danced. If the girls in Saint-Toussaint-des-Saints had twisted their spines this way, they'd have been followed by all the males, young or old, wanting to see, and Curé Fourré would have excommunicated them. Behind her, Innocent Loiseau had forgotten how to walk. His boots didn't want to alight where he aimed them. He had seen how men walk when they've drunk too much beer; he was walking in the same languid way. The woman had intoxicated him.

"I've wanted a confidential chat with you for a long time, Innocent."

"With *me*? Confidential?"

Innocent didn't know how to talk to a woman. At the black-robed priests' college he had won a certificate of merit for eloquence. In this woman's presence he forgot his vocabulary. What he wanted to do was to touch. Touch. He couldn't. Or talk. Verrochio had told him about the importance of a woman: she was a lamp in the night, like the soul in a man's body. He knew no women except his mother. There were featherbrained girls studying at a convent not far from his college; their squealing got on his nerves. His head was empty and speech had deserted his mouth.

"Innocent, I'd rather talk with you in private than on the telephone . . . . "

"Uh . . . the telephone . . . ummm . . . "

Did this unknown women know that he used his telephone to practice seducing women? The word *telephone*, on which he was positive she had placed a certain emphasis, took his breath away. She pushed open the door to his office and walked in. He followed her. What was he to do? He was the boss, he would go and sit behind his desk.

"Verrochio saved on the interior decoration: not even a sexy calendar . . . "

"I took it down, Madame."

These words were a stroke of genius. He was proud. He wasn't so awkward after all; he knew how to talk to a woman.

"Innocent, you're a little liar: you wouldn't have taken down a picture of a young girl in a short, low-cut dress."

"Umm . . . "

She looked around. Innocent had to circle her to get to his chair. Walking close to her was like passing a blazing fire. The women in the village didn't have that effect. He sat behind his table, opening his black ledger to put on a bold front, and felt the woman's warmth again, on his arms and belly. She pushed the door shut.

"I wouldn't want anybody to know our little secrets, Innocent . . . And neither would you . . . "

Where was she taking him? He wasn't naive. No woman would get the better of him. He wouldn't let himself be led down a path where he didn't want to go. He stiffened his back like someone who is resolutely waiting.

"Innocent, aren't you going to ask me to sit down?"

"Umm . . . unfortunately there aren't any chairs."

"Oh Innocent! We'll just have to make the best of things." And jauntily, she sat on the crates piled up along the wall.

"That's dynamite, Madame! Dynamite!"

"I know, Innocent, I know. Dynamite is less explosive than some young men . . . "

A slow smile opened her beautiful painted lips, revealing pearly teeth. She gazed at him with that endless smile of hers that disturbed him more and more. Why was she looking at him like that? What was she hinting at? What was the use of everything he'd learned at the black-robed priests' college if he still acted so foolish in a woman's presence? She crossed her legs and in doing so raised her skirt. He saw the movement of mysteries in the shadow that played upon her thighs. She didn't pull her skirt over her knees as the village women would have done. They stayed bare and an odd light glinted off them even though it was dark in the shed. He thought it was the damp heat that was making it hard to breathe.

"Have you ever loved anyone, Innocent?"

"Umm, yes: my mother, my father, my brothers and sisters . . . "

She laughed a laugh he'd never heard before. Her mocking laugh told him it was possible to love someone besides his father, his mother, his brothers and sisters . . .

"Is that black book very important to you, Innocent?"

He was clutching the ledger in both hands, clinging to it as if it were an object floating amid a shipwreck. He set the ledger down slowly, so she wouldn't notice; imperceptibly, he slid his hands across the table. Now his hands embarrassed him; they were superfluous.

"Have you ever loved anyone, Innocent?"

In a peal of laughter and a swirl of curls she threw her head back and Innocent saw her breasts bounce against the fabric of her yellow dress. Then she brought her head forward again and looked him in the eyes. He was unable to look into this woman's eyes with their long, slowly flickering lashes. Innocent lowered his gaze. The neckline of her dress was gaping. Innocent could see there only troubling shadows.

"Oh, you'll know when you're in love . . . Innocent, are you afraid of a woman in love?"

He wasn't afraid but would she think him impolite if he went and sat beside her? He didn't know this woman. Win. The precept echoed in his mind as persistently as the electric buzzer that roused the college dormitory. Win. He could win nothing from this strange woman. She was there, with her body. He gazed at her, dazzled. What secret force was paralyzing him? Was it the stranger's beauty? Was it the robed priests who had taught him that desire for a woman comes from the Devil?

"If you aren't afraid, Innocent, if I'm not so ugly I scare you, come and sit beside me. I have some confidential things to tell you. Come, sit down!"

He got to his feet. Either his legs were melting like butter or the floor of the shed was quicksand. He made his way with difficulty to the crates where the strange woman sat enthroned.

"Innocent, are you afraid of dynamite?"

This woman wanted to win. He prepared his answer like a hunter who aims so his arrow will strike the heart.

"Madame, I have held dynamite in my hands. I used a pointed wooden rod to pierce a hole in a stick of dynamite so I could insert the detonator. No, Madame, I'm not afraid of dynamite."

"But you're afraid of a woman, Innocent. You're sitting so far away."

This woman must not win. Moving confidently, he pressed closer to her. She must know now that he wasn't afraid of a woman. Should he touch her shoulder with his own? Win. Win. Win. If he hesitated he was lost. There was no such thing as losing. Innocent pressed his shoulder and arm against the bare shoulder and burning arm of the strange woman in the yellow dress.

"So, Innocent, you aren't afraid of holding a stick of dynamite in your hands."

"Madame, I didn't even tremble."

"And if you were holding a woman . . . "

The stranger turned her head toward him. Between the lashes that rimmed her lids in a perfect ellipse, her green eyes stared into his. He felt that she could read his soul and he wished he could hide it by slamming a cover as if it were a book. Win.

"Umm . . . Madame, if I were holding a woman in my hands I wouldn't tremble."

Win. Never stay in one place. Advance. Always move forward. One more step. One more stride. One more desire. Win. Like a conqueror. The strange woman's brown knees showed under her dress, which had crept up her thighs. He decided to put his hand on the knee. Win . . . His heartbeats echoed in his ears. He was bewildered. His troubled soul wriggled in his body like a fish in a net. The stranger was aware of his discomfort because her lips mocked him with a subtle smile. He couldn't bear the woman's gaze any longer. To keep from trembling he struggled to tense the muscles in his arms and hands, but he had lost control of his body. Win. Win. Always go further. With a conqueror's might, Innocent's hand gripped the strange woman's knee. His fingers clutched incandescent flesh.

"My hand isn't shaking," Innocent declared.

"Innocent, you aren't holding a woman, you're holding a knee."

She placed a light kiss in his hair, above the temple, gently.

This woman was the devil. It was so hot in his shed. The flames of hell must be blazing invisibly in the shadows. He must not be afraid, mustn't let himself be scared to death by fairy tales. Win.

"Innocent," she began again, "I'm going to tell you some very intimate secrets."

He had let his hand glide very slowly onto her thigh; he would never have imagined a woman's thigh to be so muscular and soft. Win. One move at a time. Slowly his hand nudged the skirt.

"Innocent, do you feel something through your whole body, as if your soul was dancing a wild dance?"

"Umm . . . no, Madame, I don't feel anything."

Win. Be stronger. Don't let the enemy know your feelings.

"Innocent, I know you're burning like the fire in a chimney. When someone's truly in love, Innocent, it's like being under a spell. Innocent, love is magic."

She had leaned over to whisper. Her warm breath caressed his ear. Her bulging torso, offered to him, opened over a haze of lace.

Innocent's hand leapt to the button. His trembling hands, his numb fingers began to unfasten her bodice. The woman kept him from tearing the cloth:

"Innocent! Innocent!" she reproached him, chuckling and trying to hold back his avid hands. "Innocent, what are you doing?"

Feverish fingers stabbed at the buttons; the strange woman grabbed his wrists but in his excitement Innocent didn't know if she wanted to stop him or if her hands on his wrists were caressing him. Her bodice opened and her breasts appeared, held back by delicate lace.

"Innocent!" the strange woman moaned.

His finger touched the lace, grazed the flesh through the lace.

"Innocent! Innocent, why . . . ?"

Invested with sudden strength, with unexpected daring, with a brand-new brutality that he enjoyed, he pushed the woman onto the crates of dynamite, he hoisted his body onto hers, gripping her legs in his. She did not resist. She merely said:

"Innocent, I understand. You're young, you're curious about life, but it's impossible to learn everything in one day. You're too impatient."

Stretched out on the crates of dynamite, her dress hiked up on her thighs and open on her breasts, the strange woman smiled wanly. Innocent's eyes filled with tears.

"Innocent," she said, not fastening her dress, not moving, "I'll have to tell my man everything. Repair the damage you've caused, Innocent. Do up the buttons."

Why was this woman still there? He wished she had disappeared along with his shattered dream. Obediently, he brought his fingers close to the tiny objects made of shell that were her buttons. The strange woman took his hand in her soft hands.

"You'll remember me for the rest of your life. You'll never forget me. Every time you love a woman, you'll think of me. Innocent, I don't want to be an unpleasant memory for you."

This time there was no mockery in her smile, but a light that was wonderful to see. She brought Innocent's head toward her and pressed it against her bosom. Innocent discovered there the perfume of his dreams. The woman spoke softly, the way you speak in the confessional:

"Men with unpleasant memories become hard like rocks. Innocent, I'll never say a word to the man I love, who loves me. He has a great many unpleasant memories. Men with unpleasant memories have trouble loving. Innocent, I want to pass through your life like an angel . . . I want the beating of my wings to linger on long after, every time you're happy. I want to be a pleasant memory. Innocent, I love a man who loves me. I love being in love. I love being loved. You're a child, Innocent, I can feel your heart beat. Love is natural. It's not loving that's a sin. Do you love to be loved, Innocent?"

"Umm . . . yes," he murmured, lips kissing the delicious breast through the lace.

"I don't want to be an unpleasant memory, Innocent. You will think of me often. When I'm an ugly old hag, you'll still see me young, as I am today. In your memory I'll never become old or ugly. You will preserve my youth. I'll be young and beautiful as I am today, as long as you're alive."

He had never heard anyone talk this way before. The strange woman was talking as if she had the gift of knowing the future. He had never heard a voice so gentle. Never had anyone murmured such sweet words in his ear.

"Oh, Madame, give me a pleasant memory! Let me see you naked!"

Had she seen him glancing nervously toward the door of the shed?

"Don't worry, Innocent," she said, "I drew the bolt."

So she did know the future. She knew in advance what was going to happen. She stood and took off her high heels. The secrets of life were being revealed to Innocent in the hush of fabric slipping down the skin of this woman whose name he didn't know. The light that came through the window to touch her body created effects like dancing flames.

"Innocent! What are you making me do?"

Innocent thought he was dreaming again. He looked, he tasted, and it was as delectable as a fruit stolen from the Garden of Eden.

"What about you Innocent, aren't you going to take off your clothes?"

Still in his dream, he hopped out of his boots and clothes like a frog, with gestures that made the lady smile. He threw himself at her, he kissed her body; he felt neither flesh nor bones but something immaterial, like air beneath him as if he were flying. Perhaps the young man and the strange woman, clinging together as if each had saved the other from peril, did fly. When they opened their eyes they were lying on the crates of dynamite. Innocent was crying. He had become a man. She took his head in her hands again; with the tip of her tongue she wiped the tears, then placed a kiss on his forehead.

They dressed in silence. Innocent no longer felt any desire to look at her. He heard machines. He was no longer in a dream. He was sad.

"Innocent, I hope you won't say anything to the man I love, who loves me . . . "

She was dressed now. She tidied her hair with a casual toss of her hands.

"Innocent, I came to have a private conversation with you."

"Ummm . . . . yes, Madame."

"Innocent, I know you're the boss here. I know you make a note in your black ledger of everything your employees do well, everything they do badly, everything they don't do and everything they should have done. I know you write down the time of everything that happens. Innocent have you ever loved? I'm not saying want to love or dream of love. I'm saying Love. I love a man who loves me. Adolphe Cerisier."

"You love Monsieur Cerisier?" asked Innocent in amazement.

"And he loves me."

Adolphe Cerisier was the only employee on the site whom everyone called Monsieur. Verrochio was no longer given this sign of respect. Monsieur Cerisier wore white gloves when he drove his grader. He was, it was said, the king of

404

the graders. He had graded roads in far-off lands. He could lay out miles and miles of road without a bump. He wore overalls as white as a notary's shirt. Though he worked in the mud and dust his shoes gleamed as brightly as a bridegroom's. In the morning he didn't start up his machine until he'd dusted it. The other operators let the dust and mud accumulate on their machines. The thicker the crust of dirt the prouder they were. It was their war wound. Swabbing it as delicately as some fragile object, Adolphe Cerisier would meticulously wipe away every trace of his labor. Adolphe Cerisier operated his machine gently. To him, building a road with gravel and stone was no rougher work than a painter dabbing watercolors on white paper. He was an artist of the grader. He was famous right across the province. He spoke only to other artists. Hardly anyone spoke to him. The foreman once made a few suggestions but Adolphe Cerisier reminded the man with one phrase that only he knew the secrets of a fine smooth road. The excavators, loggers, and truckers left their shirts open or rolled up their sleeves to show off their strength. Adolphe Cerisier stood a head taller. He would look out straight ahead of him, over their heads, farther into the distance. His nose was baked by the sun. It was as if he smelled rather than saw. His wavy hair wasn't tousled like the other workers', turned by mud and sweat into poorly-made birds'-nests. He had silver hair as neat as that of movie stars in magazines. Was he muscular? His shoulders were as broad as two men standing side-by-side but with his white overalls you couldn't tell. These were as white and spotless as a hospital. People respected this man, who was a member of another race: the race of artists. He talked differently. He came from the Capital. He would arrive at work precisely on time; he left again precisely on time. Innocent had never been able to dock him a single minute.

"You love Monsieur Cerisier?" repeated Innocent, flabbergasted.

"And he loves me," said the lady in the yellow dress. "It's on account of him that I want to talk to you, Innocent. He loves me but he's a man and he loves all women. I understand, because I'm a woman and I love all men. You don't know how handsome Adolphe is! Only a woman's eyes can truly see him. All the women love Adolphe. And

405

I understand because I'm a woman and all the men love me. Innocent, I love being loved. It feels good. There are so many people who aren't loved, so many who are hated. I understand why Adolphe loves to be loved. It's not worth being born if a person isn't loved and doesn't love. The only thing that's good in life is love. If two people meet who love to love and be loved, it's a fine thing, it's beautiful. When you see that, it makes you not want to go to Heaven. Despite all my respect for the good Lord, Heaven can't be any more beautiful than a place where a man and woman are in love. Innocent, I'll pray to the good Lord to guide you to a road where you'll find love. Adolphe told me about you. He knows your name. He thinks you're too polite. He's afraid you'll never learn bad manners. He says that if you want to be somebody, you have to forget your good manners. Adolphe's met a lot of people in his life . . . He knows a lot and knows his way around. He's handsome. And he loves me . . . But he's always off on some far-away road; it's his life. He's unhappy unless he has a road to build. When a man's far away he won't be alone for long. Innocent, it isn't good for a man to be alone. And it isn't good for a woman to be alone either. Solitude is death. To stay alive, a woman needs a man and a man needs a woman. Along all the roads Adolphe travels, there's always a house that opens where he can love and be loved. I understand that: there are plenty of houses where I've loved and been loved too. That's what I wanted to tell you in confidence. I know you'll understand me. After his week of work Adolphe comes back to the Capital and we love each other until Sunday night. Oh Innocent! you'll learn how to love a woman . . . He loves me so much. I'm happy and then it's Sunday night. He has to leave me and come back here, to the worksite. I watch him go away, carrying his suitcases like an immigrant and I tell myself that I'll never be so happy again.

"Adolphe Cerisier leaves me on Sunday night so he can get back up on his machine here, on Monday morning. Adolphe is never late. If he was, I think he'd confess it to the priest. So he leaves me on Sunday night. I'm always sad and he is too, because he likes to be with me. He laughs with me. He's a man who laughs, Adolphe, but I know you've never seen him smile. When he's on his machine he's always preoccupied: all he thinks about is making the road as smooth as possible. You know, Innocent, Adolphe's past the mid-way point of his life; his hands are strong but they shake a little. When he's driving his grader he needs a firm grip. They have to know just what they're doing at the controls of the blade. Adolphe doesn't want the trembling in his hands to show up on the road, so he's very careful. Adolphe is a little sad because he's already reached the top of the hill and now he's going down into old age. His eyes aren't as good as they once were. Looking at life too much hardens the eyes. Eyes that do a lot of looking get hard, just like hands that work a lot. When he leaves me on Sunday night he's sad. A man is sad when he leaves the woman he loves. The woman he loves is sad as well. Adolphe Cerisier gets back on the road. He drives across the plain, he comes to the hills and suddenly the road seems long. His car doesn't seem to be making any progress. He thinks of the bed that's waiting for him at the inn. A bed with white, starched sheets, but no woman. Adolphe built the roads through these hills, he knows all the houses. He knows the one where he won't be allowed to sleep alone. So he stops. Adolphe loves to love. I understand, because I too love to love. There are people who don't love to love. Innocent, I hope that you'll . . . "

Innocent went back to his desk. He had listened to the strange woman but he hadn't really understood. His head was agitated, like leaves blown in the wind. He looked at her, dazzled. The strange woman's hands were gesticulating, folding and unfolding, clutching one another, opening and then closing again.

"Instead of leaving me on Sunday night to go and sleep in a strange house, Adolphe could stay with me till Monday morning. Adolphe would be late starting up his grader, but if you wanted, Innocent, you could forget to note it in your ledger. It would be as if he hadn't started late . . . If you wanted, Innocent, you could spare me a lot of sorrow. I cry all night long from Sunday to Monday, thinking about Adolphe who isn't in my bed . . . I cry so much I'm going to turn into a wrinkled old woman . . . Innocent, if you didn't put anything in your black book, Adolphe would stay with me on Sunday night. I wouldn't cry, I'd be happy and he'd be happy. On Monday morning he'd get up before the sun rises over the Capital; I'd wake him myself. His coming to work late wouldn't count: during the week he'd be so happy he'd make up the lost time. All he'd need would be for you not to put anything in your black book. Adolphe's a proud man. He knows you're proud too. Adolphe has watched you; he told me you'll go far in life. A man as proud as Adolphe Cerisier would never come and ask you not to note his lateness in your black book. Innocent, I, the woman he loves, who loves him, I'm asking you not to make a note when Adolphe Cerisier comes to work late on Monday morning. Will you give me that happiness?"

The strange woman had lent herself to Innocent to obtain this favor. She had paid in advance for what she wanted to buy from him. A few moments earlier, he'd been happy; his chest was too narrow to contain the beating of his heart. Now his eyes were filled with dry sorrow. His heart was frozen in resentment. Win. Verrochio was right. He must win. Always win. If a man doesn't win, he loses. The word had magic power: it made Innocent as tough as steel, as tough as a man who wins.

"I want to see you naked again," he said coldly.

She didn't notice the hardness in Innocent's voice, for she replied very tenderly:

"Innocent, you'll think of me often and I don't want to be an unpleasant memory. I'll think of you also and I want you to be a pleasant memory as well."

She came up to him and kissed him warmly on both cheeks.

"Innocent, you won't put anything in your black book, will you?"

The woman went away and left Innocent smarting and distraught. There was a taste of ashes in his mouth. He'd be obliged to turn a blind eye now when Adolphe Cerisier came to work late. The woman was leaving, certain that Cerisier could spend Sunday nights with her. What was she leaving Innocent? Solitude. Nostalgia for a too-brief ecstasy, the memory of the warmth of a woman who had touched him with no more reality than a fragile breeze. Win. The strange woman was leaving him a loser. Had he really possessed her? Yes, he had embraced her beautiful golden body. Yes, his sweat had mingled with hers. Yes, their mouths had been joined. With a sob that echoed his birth-cry, he had lost his seed in that woman's body. She was leaving him a loser. His ecstasy was already a memory.

Is memory more real than a dream?

He must win.

"Madame, in the maple grove nearby there's a cabin and a road where you can hide your car. I could love you again . . . "

She had stepped across the threshold. She came back. Innocent thought she was going to unbutton her dress. She leaned over to kiss his forehead, then turned so briskly that her skirt swirled around her legs.

"Remember, Innocent, a satisfied man is more unhappy than a man with a desire."

The door of her car slammed, then the engine started up. The yellow car drove away cautiously. The strange woman didn't turn around to look at him.

At his table, he opened the black ledger. He couldn't dock Adolphe Cerisier even one minute. He shut the book. He hadn't dreamed. What he had just experienced was quite real. His sorrow proved it. How puzzling was the love of men and women! He turned to the black book again. He flipped through it. He stopped again at Adolphe Cerisier's page. It didn't bear a single unfavorable mention. It would stay as white as the overalls he worked in. Innocent had the power to prevent that woman from being unhappy on Sunday night, he even had the power to make her happy. Such power was greater than noting lateness in a ledger.

Innocent Loiseau was no longer an adolescent ignorant of life. He had known a woman, as the black-robed priests at the college put it. All along his road, they had taught him, man would encounter woman; afterwards, he'd never be the same again. The strange woman had done the soft warm things of one who loves, but she did not love him because it was Adolphe Cerisier she loved. She couldn't love a student as much as Adolphe Cerisier, who had a gorgeous car gleaming with chrome, who had graded all the roads in the province. He wished that she didn't love Adolphe Cerisier. He was jealous. Innocent wouldn't have been sad if she had loved only him, but she loved to love, she had said so, and she loved not only Adolphe Cerisier

409

and him, but all men. Love was filled with puzzles. He should have been happy, but he was weeping. He felt lost in his own body. His man's body was drifting around his soul like a too loose garment borrowed from somebody taller. To whom could he confide his sorrow? He was alone. His hand moved toward the telephone receiver. Now he didn't need to learn how to talk to a woman to win her over. He was ashamed of his ridiculous monologues into a disconnected telephone, talking to a woman who didn't exist. It was a childish game. From now on Innocent Loiseau was sentenced to real life. And so he went out, his black book under his arm, to inspect his men and his machines.

XXXVI

Wherein reference is made to the inability of great men to be happy

A few days later, Innocent Loiseau was surprised to receive a letter from Jeannot Tremblay, who had disappeared without a word. The envelope was as thick as a novel.

Dear Friend,

The other day, after the workers on the new road turned their backs on me as I was exhorting them to liberty, I went away. I didn't want to remain with people who refuse to hear the music of the word liberty. My heart was filled with grief. Are only those who are already free able to tolerate the word Liberty? Those workers are used like beasts of burden. A handful of oats could make them forget that they're men. For them, a little money is freedom. Those beasts of burden, who are our brothers, do not feel the harness on their backs or the bit between their teeth. They obey reins that force them to turn left or right. Their masters do not care if the beasts have enough to eat or if the bit hurts their mouths or if their burdens are too heavy. For them, a road is a pencil stroke on a piece of paper.

411

That was why I stood on a rock like the Apostle and preached liberty and dignity; I urged them to hope, I asked them to seek other reasons for living besides mere submission. I used human language to address beasts of burden who were ruminating their oats. And I went away sad. Those beasts of burden, who are my brothers, should aspire to more than a handful of oats. My words could not make them understand. Innocent, I couldn't make my own brothers understand me!

I shared in my brothers' toil, I used the same tools, I shoveled the same earth, like them I had crushed stones, diverted streams, dried up swamps, I had learned their crude language, their hearty oaths. At the inn I danced with their daughters or wives — and yet they turned their backs on me. All peoples on earth once spoke the language of poetry, their first language. It was their final language too, for poetry has been rescued from oblivion and will prove to be more durable than all their buildings of stone. The men of my province do not hear poetry. They're only interested in oats. They haven't yet reached the stage of the first human language. That was what I was thinking about as I walked along, carrying my valise. My sorrow was much heavier than my baggage. I, who wanted to kindle on the horizon a fine dream for the men of my country, I who wanted to lay down a road they could follow to reach that dream, I who swore an oath to do so, who sent that oath out to the sea which is the source of all life and to which all roads on earth lead, I had been unable to speak to the men of my country. Somewhere I had forgotten the language of my family. I was sad, for when I lost that language I lost my family too.

The trials I've endured have made me an outsider. An outsider wanders until he finds a place where someone will willingly listen to his outsider's language. No one wanted to listen to me. I had to go away. I shall have pleasant memories of our conversations, Innocent. You, like me, are an outsider among those men. They don't speak to you, they don't listen to you. In any case, what could you tell them? That was why you and I were able to talk to one another. The two of us spoke in the language of outsiders. And we understood one another. But we don't know how to talk to the men who build roads. We don't know how to talk to men whose backbones are as strong as horses. My own troubles have broken me like a toy that a big foot has stamped on. I can talk to no one but myself, I can listen to no one but myself. And you, Innocent, cannot talk to them because you have not lived; you know only the stinking breath of your soutaned teachers who believe that God speaks through their mouths, as if there were such a thing as Truth. The only Truth comes from *dreams*! My friend Achille Bédard and I swore that we would realize our dream. We deposited our oath in the sea, which is eternity on earth. That is our truth. I won't forget you, Innocent. I had to go away. If you share our ideal, swear your oath and cast it into the Famine River, which will take it to the St. Lawrence which in turn will take it out to sea. And then we shall be together again. Our people are lost in the very forests they have cleared for passage. We should climb a mountain and study the horizons so we can point out the best direction. We aren't mere passersby, we are guides.

And so I was walking along the shoulder of the road. I didn't know where I was going, but I knew that I had to go. From the fields on either side of me came the chirring of cicadas, like fragments of light. Perched in swamps or spruce trees, birds twittered, warbled, chirped. Families of partridges were twittering. In the pastures, horses snorted, cows mooed, horses whinnied. In chicken-coops, hens were cackling. From one farm to the next, dogs were barking, while I silently listened to the voice of the world. I, who had never been able to talk to my human brothers, told myself I must learn how to speak with the simplicity, the beauty, the music of nature. We don't know what it means, but it is beautiful and it helps us to live. And that's our mission, Innocent: to help, to show our people how to live. The concert was so fascinating I was barely walking; I'd almost stopped so I could listen. Creation was talking to God who had

413

made it and God was listening. If we want to be guides, we must listen to what creation says to God. If our words resemble what creation says to God its creator, we will be listened to, Innocent. The more I listened, the more I discerned different voices, calls, laughter, demands, fears, threats. I thought, a poem should contain all that.

I started. A yellow car had pulled up beside me, almost touching me, and I felt touched by the animal warmth that was stored under the hood.

"Would you rather walk or travel at the speed of the time you're living in?" asked a woman's voice inside.

Her window was rolled down. I bent over.

"I was listening to the birds."

"Was it beautiful?"

"It was more than beautiful: we don't understand, yet at the same time, we do."

"Men and women think they're very important, but as far as the good Lord's concerned, we're probably only crying and cooing and weeping amid the voices of all the animals and tiny creatures that rise up from earth into Heaven."

"No woman's ever talked to me like that, Mademoiselle."

It was true. She wasn't vulgar like some women, who treat their toenails as if they were the hanging gardens of Babylon.

"One must speak in a special way to a young man who stops by the roadside to listen to the birds."

Even in the Capital, even around Parliament and the Château, you don't often see women so beautiful. She was more like the kind of woman you see in magazines. In her yellow dress, she seemed to be wearing a sunbeam. She got out of her car and came toward me. I was suffocating. The mere presence of a woman like that has the power to melt steel. She stood next to me and listened with me to the fields. I could hear nothing but the beating of my heart. It was pounding so, I was sure she could hear it too. She was so close to me my shoulder felt the warmth of her bare arm. I wanted to speak — but what would I say? My only language was the pounding of my heart. But I mustn't

414

just stand there like a lump, stunned by the living beauty of this apparition. I had to say something. In my troubled mind I managed to gather up a few words which I then strung together as best I could, until it sounded more or less like a sentence!

"All those birds, those insects, those small animals have been sharing the earth with us for centuries. We do not know them. They're strangers. We don't know their language, yet they possess knowledge, experience, culture. They have their own sorrows and hopes. And that must be what they talk about, but we don't understand them. What is that cicada telling me? Is it announcing a birth or a death? Is it declaiming a poem about the summer sun? And the horse that's whinnying in the distance, is he talking about love to his mare or rebelling against the labor imposed on him by man, that puny two-legged animal with superior airs? Is the barking dog on the other side of the hill telling us a wolf's at large in the woods or explaining to all the echoes some cosmic law we haven't yet deciphered? And the butterfly — it must be talking, but we don't even hear it. And the frogs in their pond — they know plenty of things about mankind. And . . . "

"Sssh! Stop making useless sounds, young man, and listen."

She was right. I was talking too much. The woman's presence disturbed me. I was tossing off words and clinging to them to keep from losing my balance, but words are smoke. She was right. Her blazing arm was pressed against my shoulder. She listened; I was silent; my heart beat even faster. Suddenly she turned to me:

"You talk like a book. I don't understand what the animals say and I don't understand you either. But it sounded nice. When you talk to a young girl you must pay her lovely compliments."

"I don't want my words to confuse matters, I want them to shed light. The Word is light."

"You aren't going to recite the whole Bible!"

She turned her back sharply and her yellow dress shimmered blindingly. Innocent, why did God make women so beautiful? There isn't a doe, a ewe, a cat, a flower or a bird as beautiful as a woman.

"Where are you going, young man?" she asked. "Home to mother?"

"I'm not going home to my mother."

I spoke more curtly than I'd intended. Innocent, you know about the troubles I've had. You know I haven't yet recovered from them. The simple word mother makes my whole body tense.

"Why not come along with me?"

I stowed my suitcase in the back of the car and got in beside her. Have you ever sat by a woman who smells like all the flowers in the world, who is wearing a flimsy skirt that creeps up on her suntanned thighs? Her delicate little feet danced on the pedals. She drove straight ahead, often gazing directly into my eyes. Innocent, my poor friend, I think of you in your dark shed where you can see nothing, where not even life can enter. You're not even connected to life (like your telephone, Innocent). I was traveling along the roads of real life. You're a prisoner of your youth, while I was spinning along beside a woman as beautiful as you could wish, along the road that leads to the sea. And here's how it happened.

We drove through fields of oats, through undulating hills, groves of scraggy spruce and rocky pastures. The road was rolling underneath the car. I felt as if we were motionless in the yellow car, while the whole earth was spinning hypnotically. The lady didn't speak. I looked at her. Her lips were slightly parted in a smile and her teeth were gleaming. Her hands held the wheel gently, delicately, with the fingertips. Men drive cars as if they were leading cattle; she maneuvered hers with the precise motions required by fancy work. Bracelets jingled at her wrists. I looked at her arms: they were finely modeled, smooth. I thought, chance could not have produced so beautiful a form, such beauty in an instrument (for an arm is only a tool). I felt certain that a perfect God, a brilliant sculptor, had formed this woman's arms. I told myself that such perfect instruments could also close around the body of a man. These thoughts raged through my

416

mind, but I kept them to myself. There are silences that must be respected and others that must be filled with words. Later, I shall record these observations in my green notebook.

Her dress was cut very low: in it you could see the roundness where her breasts began. The position of her arms — stretched out to the wheel — opened the bodice even wider. I could see her breasts, revealed in a froth of lace. Innocent, you'll learn that there are two things a man cannot look at without being blinded: the sun, and a woman's breasts. I know what it is about them that blinds us, Innocent: it's their power to burn the wings of Icarus. Ever since man was born he has possessed an innate knowledge of his own end, he has been inwardly burned by a yearning for his own death. If that desire for death weren't fastened to him like an implacable law, he would not die. If he possessed an urge for life as powerful as his urge for death, he would have everlasting life. Burned every day by his yearning for death, man is fascinated by everything that can procure his death, everything that can burn his great invisible wings and hurl him into abysses where he will be crushed in sorrow. Innocent, woman gives man wings by giving him life, but she has the power to burn those wings as well. Man is attracted by woman as the earth is attracted by the sun that gave him life, where one day it will come to grief. Such were the thoughts I was inwardly formulating.

A great American writer named Herman Melville — do you know his work, Innocent? — said that man will always be fascinated by the sea because man was born of the sea. The sea covers the perpetually secret roads that life has taken in order to come into being. Along what roads has this miracle been accomplished? The sea, like an egg, contained this wonder. I am facing the sea now as I write to you, Innocent. It has been millions of centuries since man left the sea, but his memory recalls it still, as it recalls his mother's womb.

Similarly, man is fascinated by woman. At the same time as she gives him the splendid gift of life, she condemns him to die. As death is the corollary of life,

417

so woman gives her children both life and death simultaneously. When man looks at woman, he remembers that she has given him life, and he dreams of plunging into life to its very depths, to its source; and his heart beats faster so he will forget death. That's what I was thinking of as I admired that woman, who drove her car as beautifully as if she were at the controls of the entire earth. Why should someone think of death when he is travelling in a luxurious car with a woman as beautiful as a desire? Men who have an exceptional destiny in store for them (like you and me and Achille Bédard) possess, as well as their dream of happiness, the inability to be happy. I thought about the men I'd worked with on the new road where you still are, I thought of the roads my father had laid out, I thought of all the roads that are unknown to me, of all the roads that are inviting me, and I told myself: in the end, every road leads to death. Isn't it true, Innocent, that at the end of his road a man finds only death? People like us, Innocent, should live as if they were on their way not to death but to eternal life. You, I and Achille Bédard are not among those who lie down and wait for death to close their eyes. All those ideas were exploding in my brain as I gazed at the fine fruits inside the young lady's yellow dress. I've summarized them so you can appreciate my light-headedness. The young lady said,

"You're a good boy. You're trying to look inside my dress but not to tear it off me."

I tell you very frankly, Innocent, even though I was marveling at her delicate neck and splendid bosom, I was thinking mostly of the toiling men I'd met on the new road. No one steals the souls of horses, but those men had been robbed of their souls. The men I saw on the new road were neither hopeful nor hopeless, they neither desired nor dreamed, they didn't want to take flight, they didn't seem to love and they didn't try to understand. Someone had stolen their souls, leaving behind only two-legged horses who rented out their muscles for a little food and beer. Innocent, it's up to us and our friend the journalist Achille Bédard, to restore those men's souls. A mighty soul is essential, Innocent. Restoring the soul to the people of our province is a way of sharing our own souls, just as Jesus Christ shared His bread with the multitude. That's what I was thinking. Innocent, I swear I had nothing else in mind, even though I was dazzled by the electric beauty of the woman who was leading me down a peaceful road.

"You can unbutton my dress if you want."

And so I drew the first button through the buttonhole. I was no more adept, I assure you, than if I'd been handling a blazing coal. I unfastened all the buttons and her beautiful sun-baked body appeared amid the folds of her yellow dress, like a siren emerging from the waves.

Was she driving her car a little faster? Was it my heartbeat that had speeded up? Her gaze was fixed on the road ahead. With calm indifference, she let my hand glide along her beautiful bronze skin.

"You'll remember me for a long time, young man. What's your name?"

"Jeannot."

"Jeannot, your thoughts will return often to the woman you met by the side of a road. Jeannot, I don't want to be an unpleasant memory for you. I would like to be your very finest memory. Jeannot, I love to love and I love to be loved. Do you love to love and be loved? Life and love are the same thing. Without love there is no life."

(Innocent Loiseau could read no further, his eyes were so full of tears. He had possessed a treasure and now it was being taken from him. That woman had wanted to be a pleasant memory for him and now she wanted to be a pleasant memory for someone else. Innocent had been betrayed. He trembled. He bit his tongue. That strange woman would be the most wretched memory of his life. She had made him a man: an unhappy man. Was it worth the trouble to become a man in a woman's arms if a man must suffer, be deceived, betrayed, deprived, humiliated? Innocent didn't want to read any more of his friend's letter. Was he still his friend? The strange woman in a yellow dress was a spider who wrapped men in a web of tenderness, then poisoned them with sorrow. "I want to be a pleasant memory for you." She had made that vow to Innocent, she'd made it to Jeannot. Innocent would remember only that he had been deluded. Why did she want so much to love when loving causes pain? He knew now why men appear so sad: no doubt they were the victims of love's shattered illusions. Innocent wanted only to weep and he loved the huge sob that was choking him. What did he have to love except his sorrow? It was his sole companion. With it, he was a little less lonely on the new road. He would often feel that delicate pain which reminds a man that he has lived. He must conquer his sorrow. He forced his hands to stop trembling, his eyes to stop weeping, and he continued to read Jeannot Tremblay's letter.)

"A little later, we had to slow down at the outskirts of a village. I buttoned up the dress to conceal her body from the eyes of the population. Shrugging, she opened it again and the car drove past the brightly colored little houses on either side of the single quiet street. So then my hand sought her heart. Innocent, you poor withered field flower, you cannot imagine the head-spinning delight of holding in your hand a woman's heart that beats and beats, faster, faster, faster. Innocent, don't look for the heart of life anywhere but in a woman."

(Once again tears filled Innocent's eyes. Never would he forget the woman in the yellow dress; every time he thought of the strange woman, she would wound him again. Suffer. Be silent. Conquer sorrow.)

So then I said:

"Mademoiselle, the sun has loved your body very much."

Poetry is useful, Innocent. I tried to touch the hearts of the men of my province with poetry. They turned away from me as if I were speaking a foreign dialect. From now on my poetry will speak to women.

"If I were the sun, I would love your body too," I went on.

"Why should the privilege of loving my body be restricted to the sun?"

Yes, Innocent, you read correctly, those were her very words. What she said was more beautiful than a whole anthology of poetry! I didn't dare ask her if she read poetry; I was cautious. You'll learn, Innocent, women's answers to our questions are often deceptive.

"Young man, when I look at the world I see two sorts of people. There are those who love and those who hate. I still don't know if it's possible to choose between hating and loving. Young man, I love to love. I know that I could hate, but loving makes me happier. I love to love and I love to be loved. What about you, young man?"

"I? Well, I think that love is life . . . Loving is giving. Life is a gift and living is giving."

Do you believe me, Innocent, we talked that way, Innocent, for long minutes. She'd picked me up by chance on a road in the middle of nowhere — a young man whom life had wounded. Miraculously, Innocent, I was no longer sad, I was almost happy. A woman was carrying me away, toward the unknown; an adorable goddess, she was taking me away in her yellow carriage, as the prophet in the Bible was carried off in a fiery chariot. The goddess of love drove faster and faster, we passed through villages like flashes of fire and love.

And I, Innocent, I was thinking: men build roads on earth, take on careers, they submit to routines, participate in movements, but deep down, Innocent, perhaps men only submit to the law that governs their trajectory like planets in orbit. We think that we choose, but we only obey. I was sitting next to that unknown young lady, in her yellow racing car. You'll say that chance had brought us together. Perhaps, Innocent, chance is a law whose implacable and omnipotent nature our minds cannot grasp.

"Young man," she said, "I love a man who loves me. I enjoy it when my body is loved. A woman's body possesses everything a man's body is looking for. Ah! I know men and I know life. If a man says, I love a woman, he means that he loves a woman's body. Man can love only the body. Is it possible to love a soul? The soul is a dream. A woman's body is the soul made flesh, the dream come true. Young man, I can see that you love my body. Aren't you happy, young man?

421

My body can give you happiness. I'd so much rather give happiness than sorrow. Down all the roads that you will follow in life, you'll meet merchants of sorrow who'll do their best to sell you their sorrow. I don't like sorrow; I love to love and to be loved. If the good Lord didn't agree with me, do you think He'd be up there in His Heaven, smiling down on us? The beautiful light that illuminates the earth is the good Lord smiling down from Heaven on two little terrestrial animals that He created so long ago, He no longer remembers. If the good Lord didn't enjoy seeing you desire the body of a woman whose name you don't even know, if He didn't enjoy seeing me desiring to love and be loved, do you think that He, who is all-powerful, would let us drive along this road? If He didn't like creatures who want to love, He'd crush my car in His hand like a flower, or open up the mountain ahead of us so the road would toss us into the ravines of Hell. But you can see, He's smiling at us. If you loved my body even more, young man, I know that His light upon the earth would be even more beautiful."

That woman was talking about love the way a bird twitters. She talked about the deepest truths as if she were saying: here's a stone, a dandelion. Innocent, we must be like her, we must live! That young lady loves life while others treat it like a disease. They think the only remedy is death and they take powerful doses of it every day. For that young lady, life is a beating heart. She took genuine pleasure in simply listening to it beat. She loves everything that can make it beat faster. Innocent, we can never live as simply as that young lady. You and I will never be able to believe that if the light on the fields and hills is beautiful, it's because God is happy to see us love. Innocent, you and I and Achille Bédard carry a heavy little stone in our hearts that will always prevent us from feeling as light as a bird in the sky. That heavy stone makes us look sad. It's the stone that we want to bring to the construction of the great road men are building out of their mis-understandings, their vices, their despair and disap-pointments, and in spite of everything, with blind hope. Innocent, you and I and Achille Bédard, like the great geniuses of the world, want to make our contribution to the progress of mankind who, having emerged from the sea that receives all the secrets of our past, is now aiming at heaven where the answers to all questions are hidden. We cannot be hearts, happy at the mere sound of their own beating. We want to learn, to guide, to give. That's what I was thinking of too, amid the blissful confusion that was dazzling me. The yellow car struck sparks of sun that landed in the fields.

"I love a man who loves me. You mustn't think you can take his place, young man," she told me with a certain tenderness. "He's a man who spreads gravel the way a great painter spreads his pigments. His name is Adolphe Cerisier. He's a man as fine to look at as a well-lived life. He's a man who loves to love. A man who loves to be loved. A man who loves women's bodies. Young man, does your hand feel how my heart stirs when I say his name? Pay close attention! Adolphe Cerisier! Do you feel my heart? I believe that men are a gift from the good Lord to women. Unfortunately, Adolphe is always far away, always working on some remote road he's opening through a forest or a rocky hillside or a swamp. Adolphe Cerisier works on the new road not far from where I found you. When he comes home he wants me to be beautiful. He wants my body to be beautiful because he loves to love and he wants to dream about me during the coming week. Young man, look carefully: do you think my body would be more beautiful if I had a darker tan?"

Innocent, you'll understand that I was open-mouthed. Looking at her body was like looking at lightning. I must weigh my words like a diplomat. I couldn't tell her that she could be more beautiful. First of all, she *couldn't* be more beautiful. She was the most beautiful creature I'd ever seen in flesh or photograph. I babbled,

"You're so beautiful Mademoiselle. The summer light couldn't make you any more beautiful. It's you who beautify·the summer."

"Liar!" she said, with a smile that made her teeth cast glimmers on her lovely lips. "But such lies are the

423

truth for women who love. We're always prepared to believe them. If you can already lie so well, you will learn to love."

I couldn't stay in the car. I wanted to run through the fields with her. I could have flown above the forest. I felt my body crack like an eggshell. I felt vast wings sprout on my back. My chest couldn't contain my breath. I was a prisoner in her car. Finally, I threw my head, the way a man might throw himself from a moving train, into her wavy hair. My lips sought her neck and drank at length from her sweet flesh. That fountain filled me with peace. I took my seat again. She told me quietly,

"Adolphe Cerisier loves me and the more beautiful I am the more he'll love me. I'm all pale; I'm as pale as an old nun. Young man, don't you think I need some sun? Not only sun, I need the sea. It's not good for a woman to be alone. Young man, will you come with me to the sun and the sea? Will you come, young man?"

(Innocent's tears spilled onto his cheeks. The strange woman was betraying him with Jeannot Tremblay, his best friend. He was humiliated. His soul was filled with the bitter taste of hate. Jeannot Tremblay, with his wheedling words was a liar, a fine talker. Now the tears that spilled from his eyes were no longer tears of sorrow but of rage. He hated his friend, his lying false friend. He despised the unknown woman. He blushed with shame at having touched her. Suddenly his whole body shuddered as he thought she must have given him some disease. And he wept even harder, overwhelmed by sudden panic.)

Now here I am at the sea, "the sea that is perpetually renewed," as the poet said. Here I am with a woman who is like the sea, always foreign and intimate, always the same and always new: the woman who is perpetually renewed, I might say.

(Jeannot Tremblay had gone to the sea, the sea that disappeared behind the horizon, while it was Innocent's fate to be a prisoner in his dark shed, with a window encrusted in grime and cobwebs, it was his fate to be alone between a telephone that wasn't even connected and a ledger where he made notes of useless letters and numbers.

The new road had led Innocent nowhere, whereas Jeannot Tremblay had gone to the sea, as in a marvelous dream, with a woman who was taking him on a journey to the land of love. Why was Innocent a prisoner in his shed? What law decreed that Jeannot would take the road that led to the sea while he, Innocent, must stay shut up in the dark, dank shed built of wood that was rotting away like some forgotten thing? Was it fate that confined him to the remote shadows while Jeannot proceeded to conquer the sun, sea and woman? A prisoner of his family, of his father's authority and his mother's good advice, prisoner of the black-robed priests' college, prisoner of this shed at the side of a road that led to nothing — was that his fate, his nature: to be shut away, in chains?)

Innocent, my dear friend, I won't describe my days and I won't describe my nights. In a close friendship it's permissible not to share certain secrets. There are things a man does in his life that demand to be kept secret. I'll tell you only that I'm happy. After so much misery am I not entitled to some joy? I'm not sad at the thought that my happiness soon will end, when the time comes for Gracieuse to go home to her Adolphe Cerisier. I assure you she'll be more beautiful than she's ever been. The sea loves her, the sun loves her body, and I think I make her happy too.

As for me, I reflect a great deal. It's good to look out to sea and think. With the constant motion of the waves creating their endless life, with the unfathomable water endlessly creating waves that endlessly die, I cannot have superficial thoughts. I can't forget the oath I swore with my friend the journalist Achille Bédard, but perhaps it's our own modest fate, Innocent, to peacefully follow a secondary road, while you stay where you are, at the end of your new road in the middle of nowhere. I think, I reflect, I love.

Your friend, Jeannot Tremblay

(Innocent folded the letter and inserted it at the page he'd started for Jeannot Tremblay in his black ledger. He had stopped crying. With that woman, he had lost his soul. Gracieuse. He hadn't even known her name.)

XXXVII

Can life be changed?

At *The Provincial Sun*, Achille Bédard, the editor-in-chief, didn't have much to write besides a brief daily editorial. The Right Party was buying more and more space: advertisements singing the praises of the government and Le Chef arrived pre-packaged and ready to print. The young journalist scarcely had to touch his typewriter: *The Provincial Sun* wrote itself! He filed his papers. Le Chef had told him one day that before he tried to put the world in order, he should start with his own desk and bookshelves. Le Chef had added:

"You've seen pictures of the great leaders, men like Hitler and Caesar, Napoleon and Mussolini and Stalin: do those men have messy offices?"

"They inflict their mess on the world!" Achille Bédard replied.

"Achille Bédard, I've caught you with your pants down, thinking!" Le Chef reproached him. "Write as you're told, don't think! I don't pay you to think."

The young editor-in-chief was suffering, but he held his peace. The other journalists let the Right Party stroke them, their pens switching like the tail of a purring cat. The proud young journalist raged, but he remembered what he'd learned from poor Sautereau, who had gone off his head. Achille Bédard, kept on a leash, obeyed. Perhaps that was better than thinking, than having a head like a steam engine, than having headaches and being all alone, with ideas no one wanted. A good employee, he complied with Le Chef's demands. Not thinking would make him like everyone else: his ideas would be those of everyone else and he'd be able to understand the people. He would be noticed for his obedience. Perhaps he'd become a Minister. It was a question not of thinking, but of time. The future was before him. He need only make progress from day to day. Achille Bédard worked hard to keep his ideas to himself. His editorials were a vigorous expression of his boss's ideas. They were nudging him into the future. Despite his youth, Achille Bédard was already editor-in-chief of *The Provincial Sun*. The future was before him. Somewhere, Le Chef was watching him obey, observing him write. Achille Bédard's face was no longer emaciated like that of someone who thinks too much; his eyes weren't red from the worries that too many ideas always cause. The future was before him. He need only approach those who had already reached it. He need only follow their path and their thoughts; by doing so, he would arrive at the same place. Rimbaud had said that life must be made over. Yet that poet was incapable of changing his own trousers when they were dirty. Change life: now *that* was pretentious. *Either* life has been created by an infinitely perfect God who made the world the best way He knew. When you know all the life that is contained in a single dewdrop, you realize you can't begin to imagine everything the universe contains. So that wanting to change what God has made, wanting to change what you don't know, what you can't even imagine, is very pretentious indeed. Poets give voice to man's pretensions. And those are very grand illusions. *Or* life creates itself. And then a law has prevailed, a necessity, a force more powerful than any possible coincidence: who are those people, little unimportant strokes of fate, who think they can change life? All that was left for men was to follow life as if it were a road passing through countries of which they knew only the outlying areas. Change life . . . All that one could do was live.

At the black-robed priests' college, Achille Bédard could not discipline his intelligence. The smallest scrap of information loosed an avalanche of ideas that left no room in his head for the knowledge he was supposed to store away for exams. His teachers considered him undisciplined, over-sensitive, flighty. One had written in red on one of his exams: "This is the product of a flighty mind governed by no rules, no duties, discipline, goals or faith. This student will follow his own path in the same manner. Lacking a goal, he will be like an intellectual beachcomber. Lacks the desire to follow the road the good Lord has laid out for him, and indicated through the teachings of his masters." He sometimes imagined the inside of his head like a min-uscule celestial vault where millions of ideas spun around one another like small fiery planets. What went through his mind was far more fascinating than the lessons taught by old priests with rotten teeth and soup-stained soutanes. They recited lessons they'd repeated so many times they no longer had to think about what they were saying; they droned as if they were trying to put their students to sleep. Their words spat saliva. Their snores reeked of tobacco. He had become editor-in-chief of *The Provincial Sun*. His teachers had been wrong.

XXXVIII

Innocent receives the gift of winning women over with words

Tires crunched along along the gravel. Innocent rushed to the door: he had recognized Verrochio's Cadillac. Since the strange woman had passed through, Innocent had been waiting. The noisy mechanical routine of the construction site was of no interest to him now. He was waiting for something, for someone to turn up. Ten times a day he looked up at the open door, hoping to see in the lighted square the woman whose flimsy yellow dress drifted in the breeze. He no longer left his office. He no longer went out to catch the workers lying down on the job. He stayed in his office for fear of being out if she returned. Before his open ledger, in which he no longer wrote anything, he waited. He didn't like to acknowledge that he was waiting for the woman, because he knew she wouldn't come back. A dream never does: it passes. What would happen to him now?

Innocent sensed that there was another life, as if the life he saw with his eyes was merely the shadow of a life that was more real. He had become a man, but nothing had changed. He was waiting at the place where a new road began. Life seemed to have stopped, yet it was just starting.

One of the bulldozer operators, Trophyme Laroche, had worked on highways in the land of California. He often described the roads there — their loops tangled like spaghetti. He described how people would lose their way on those highways and never get off them: out of gas, they would continue on foot and never find their way home. They had got lost amid all the loops and junctions that twisted and crisscrossed, the turns that were split into even more loops, the spiraling exits and entrances, the tangled upper and lower levels. With his own eyes, Trophyme Laroche had seen abandoned cars and desperate people who had lost all hope of ever finding their way. Innocent remembered the stories Trophyme Laroche would stretch out and embellish. Didn't they reflect what he was living through? Hadn't he lost his way, solitary and desperate? The strange woman wouldn't return. No one would come to him. It was he who must walk his man's life along the new road. No one would walk in his place. He was a man, but he hadn't shed the childish habit of waiting for someone to take his hand. Wasn't becoming a man like becoming an orphan? To be one's own parents? Ideas swirled in his head. Innocent waited.

Since Jeannot Tremblay's letter, he had been sad. He had been deceived by the woman, deceived by his friend. Did becoming a man mean accepting sorrow? It was through his troubled thoughts that he heard the purring of his boss's Cadillac.

Innocent wasn't quick enough to go and greet Verrochio, who was already bounding into the shed.

"Innocent, is everything clean? Good, the dynamite's neat and tidy."

Verrochio glanced around quickly.

"Innocent, you're my best clerk. I'm gonna give you my most precious thing while I'm inspect the road. I've invested a fortune here, and now I want to see if I make a profit. My Lucia, she's no got feet for walking in mud, and she's no got the skin for mosquitoes. (Verrochio turned toward the crates of dynamite and bent over for a better look.) You gotta be *very* careful with dynamite."

430

He peered into Innocent's eyes, smiling oddly. Innocent had never seen a smile on his tense features before. Now, suddenly, Verrochio was smiling. Making a great show of smiling. He wanted his smile to be noticed. His smile contained a mystery.

"It's dangerous work, building roads. Takes big machines, big motors, power, dynamite. It's dangerous. Building a road, it's dangerous. Cut through stones and bedrock, open the forest, take the top off a mountain, all that takes power: and power, she's dangerous. Power, she's always hurt somebody . . . It's like love, Innocent: love, she's always hurt somebody . . . You're a good clerk, Innocent, and I'm trust you with my prize possession — my Lucia!"

Verrochio left the shed the way he'd come in, hopping over the little staircase. "Trust you with my prize possession." What did he mean? Verrochio returned, springing on his long elastic legs.

"Innocent, here's Lucia, my wife. I'm give her to you, Innocent — but watch out! Lucia's a beautiful woman, beautiful like you never see before and you never see again. I'm leave her alone with you. You understand, Innocent? Watch out . . . Be careful . . . I want you to have nice manners with Lucia . . . I was your age once, Innocent, and I was like a young stallion. Innocent, I don't want you to get dirty ideas. Innocent, when Lucia's standing in front of you I'm want you just to think about beauty. I want you to look after her like she was the Pope. When women are Lucia's age they know that tomorrow, in the mirror, they'll see the old nightmare that used to be just in their heads, printed on their face. They're scared to get old, Innocent. Old is ugly. And ugly, it's the only thing a woman's scared of. So when a woman's the age of my Lucia, she likes young boys like you; she's think she can borrow some youth. Innocent, I want you to respect my Lucia. Innocent, Innocent — don't stand there like a little saint: I was your age once, I know boys your age, they're like stallions. Innocent, can I trust you? Lotsa people they cheat me, but not you, Innocent, because you're my eyes and my ears on the new road."

"Monsieur Verrochio, I'll look after your lady as if she was my own mother."

"Innocent, don't talk like that: boys they're always make their mother suffer. It starts when they're born and it's never end . . . Do you think I make my mamma happy when I go to the war and not write because I'm ashamed of what they made me do, and of all the blood I saw along the way? Ever since I leave Sardinia to come and build roads in America, my poor mamma, she spend her whole life crying. If the soil of Sardinia's dry, it's because of all the salty tears of mammas whose sons have left the island. I caused my mamma so much pain, Innocent, I never want to see her again. Innocent, don't hurt my Lucia. My Lucia's like the light. She's made for happiness. But alas! at the end of all the roads I'm build, I don't find the happiness I wanted for my Lucia. Do you understand me, Innocent? I'm no crazy. See how I build this new road, as fine as a nun's handwriting. A crazy can't do that, Innocent. My old friends, they turn away, they say I'm crazy. They say my Lucia, the light of my life, made me crazy. My Lucia, she's stay with me through my ordeal. I was ruined and my Lucia, she's stay with me. I'm pull myself up and my Lucia, she stay with me. If I have to go away, my Lucia she's no want me to go by myself . . . So I want you to respect my Lucia, Innocent. Don't try and seduce her. Every young man that's got any guts, he wants to seduce the boss's wife. I know, I put horns on the heads of plenty of bosses. But nobody can touch my Lucia, Innocent, not a clerk and not a Minister. Understand, Innocent? Respect my Lucia."

Innocent nodded. Verrochio was nervous: the man controlled many men and many machines, yet he was always afraid that someone would dash cold water on the fireworks of his fortune. Innocent had never seen him so worked-up. These past weeks he had been dejected, broken; his drooping head made him look ashamed: the pernicious shadow of spiteful gossip must have weighed heavily on Verrochio's shoulders. That morning, Verrochio had the determined look of someone who will win, the look of a conqueror. On his way out he turned to Innocent:

"Innocent, I know you're take good care of the dynamite. Dynamite, she helps put the road through when the hill's too hard. It's power that mows down what stands in your way. You have to take good care of it. Dynamite's like women: you have to respect it."

Verrochio liked to philosophize, but that morning his words seemed to come from a mind loosened by alcohol. Was it possible? Verrochio's life hadn't been easy. It sometimes happens that overburdened men try to relax with alcohol. Innocent had never smelled alcohol. There was another man in Verrochio's body, an alien brother. Something had happened, or was about to happen.

Verrochio returned with a black-haired lady, wearing a long gown as if she were going to a ball. Her fur stole came unfastened and Innocent caught a glimpse of gleaming bare white shoulders. She was tall. The silk clung to her thighs. A rope of pearls glowed when the stole fell open. Now she kept it closed, and the fingers of the hand that held the fur sparkled with rings.

"Innocent, I'm trust you with my prize possession: show her around and take good care of her."

Verrochio bounded outside, leaving Innocent alone with Madame. What can a humble employee say to a lady — a lady who looks like a queen, a queen all dressed up for a ball? She dared not move in the dark dusty shed, filled with a damp and musty smell, with the oily odor of stored tools and the greasy perfume of dynamite. Madame Verrochio seemed frightened. She looked at the window, all grimy with dust and cobwebs and imprisoned insects, then uneasily turned around. She remained standing. Innocent couldn't offer her his chair; she would have dirtied her dress. He had abandoned his struggle with the gritty dust. Now he merely blew on the table before he set down his ledger, and he himself sat in the dust. Nor could he suggest that she sit on the crates of dynamite. Another strange woman had sat there and ever since he had been a most unhappy young man. He had conquered happiness, but all that remained now was sorrow. The oily crates of dynamite would spoil her silk gown. "Neither cast ye your pearls before swine": When he was at the black-robed priests' college, Innocent had often meditated on that phrase from the Bible. Madame Verrochio was a pearl. Why had her husband left her in this dirty shed? Innocent could not ask Madame. He could say nothing to her. He dared not smile, because he knew his smile would be ridiculous. He pretended to be very busy with his black ledger.

"So you're Innocent . . . My husband's very fond of you . . . I couldn't give him a son, so when he sees a resourceful young fellow like you he thinks of himself at your age, and he thinks about the son he doesn't have. He thinks very highly of you. I believe he's considering giving you more responsibilities."

Innocent rose to his feet, excited by his boss's affection and pleased because Madame Verrochio had broken the silence. Filled with joy, he opened his mouth, but the words wouldn't come. What was he to say to this lady who had shared such sweet confidences with him? To break the silence, he unbuttoned his shirt and stripped it off; generously, he spread it over the crates of dynamite.

"If you'd like to sit on my shirt, Madame, you won't ruin your lovely dress."

"Innocent, you're a very charming young man. Your mamma must love you very much."

With grace and dignity, she sat down. The women of Saint-Toussaint-des-Saints didn't possess such elegance. For Madame Verrochio, it seemed less important to sit than to accomplish — with her legs, with the slightly raised folds of her silken skirt, with her shoulders and breast and hair — beautiful movements, tracing graceful lines in space. Not only did she sit, she created beauty as she moved. The bodies of the women of Saint-Toussaint-des-Saints didn't possess such delicate litheness. Madame Verrochio was a lady from the Capital. One day, Innocent would take the road that led to the Capital. He would meet great ladies. One day he would know what it was that a woman wanted to hear. All at once, Innocent realized what he must say to this lady.

"Madame, I know your husband loves you more than anything in the world. He told me he owes all his victories to you."

Madame Verrochio smiled modestly. Glad that he'd spoken and almost triumphant at having won a smile from the great lady, he wanted to be more gallant still and pay her another compliment.

"Everyone who works here knows it's because of you that the new road is being built."

Innocent hadn't completed his remark when his lips were frozen. What a hideous thing he'd said, thinking he was

434

being subtle! He felt himself blush. He couldn't erase what he'd said. His face was aflame. Madame Verrochio had lowered her eyes. She was no longer smiling. Innocent must try to make amends. What could he say?

"Everyone here in Saint-Toussaint-des-Saints is very fond of you, because without you, Monsieur Verrochio wouldn't have built the new road."

Why didn't he just keep quiet? Now he'd committed another, more horrible gaffe. He must pull himself together. Words and ideas were jockeying for position on his lips.

"We know that if it weren't for you, Madame, the Right Party wouldn't have built the new road."

He shouldn't have said that either. Madame Verrochio had lowered her head.

"Without you, Madame, a number of people, including me, wouldn't have jobs. We thank you. We know you saved your husband from ruin."

What had he said? Did he have a fever? Was he delirious? Why couldn't he shut up? He had said aloud everything that should have remained buried in silence. How awkward he had been! Why did he become as crazy as a caged squirrel as soon as a woman approached? He had thrown in this lady's face the rumor that had spread as far as the remote forests outside Saint-Toussaint-des-Saints, that she had obtained a favor for her husband by giving herself to the Minister of Roads and Bridges. Yet Innocent intended to be gallant to his boss's wife. Why didn't he just throw himself in the lake with a stone around his neck? How could he be so awkward and still live? Innocent didn't disappear. He could only stand there, paralyzed, ridiculous, powerless, shameful, adolescent. He could neither speak nor be silent. The lady raised her head and said softly, not looking him in the eyes:

"In our life together my husband has given me some marvelous days, and I've given him some as well . . . Today, I think he wants to give me another marvelous day. He wanted me to visit the new road. This road is important to him. My husband came close to the depths of despair. He lost almost everything. Men like my husband cannot lose altogether. They've helped so many people there's always someone to extend a hand to them. There will always be someone to help my husband. He won't be alone. After coming so close to ruin, my husband is starting a-fresh. This road is like the first road he built, when he was young. My husband is starting his life over here, and I want to help him. My husband has become like a young man just getting started. My husband is going to become the most important contractor in the province. If I've helped him, I'm proud. He's proud too: for the first time in our life together, he's invited me to visit his worksite. He insisted I get dressed up as if I were going to a ball. Sometimes I think my husband loves me too much. He thinks I'm a queen, though I'm only a woman."

Innocent thought of a compliment, one that would erase his earlier blunder.

"Madame, you're a heroine for us. You sacrificed yourself in the cause of the man you love. Monsieur Verrochio is right to see you as a queen. Madame, you are a queen, here in my humble shed . . . sitting on a throne of dynamite."

"Is it dangerous?" she asked with exquisite delicacy.

This woman was not nearly as thin as the strange woman Innocent had undressed. (That other woman had run away to the sea with Jeannot Tremblay, the poet who had abandoned his oath in order to sleep with a girl at the seaside.) Madame Verrochio wasn't tanned: her skin was like milk. Her bosom wasn't pointed like the strange woman's, it was round. Her belly didn't look as if an iron had flattened it, it was round. Her thighs were round too. Beneath the silk, her legs too appeared to be round. Innocent felt an urge to touch the woman's body, to brush the white flesh of her regal bosom. Perhaps he would succeed in possessing Madame Verrochio as he had possessed the unknown woman.

"Innocent, come sit beside me. I want to talk to you."

Had Madame Verrochio guessed his desires? He was convinced that women could read men's desires. He drew near to her, proud and ashamed, but he felt like a man. He knew that sense of feeling his flesh warm with that fire that can stir a woman.

"Innocent, my husband has suffered a great sorrow. I think he still feels stricken. Come close to me, Innocent, and tell me what you know."

She took his hands in her own. Innocent felt himself melting — body, words, ideas. Why had this woman —

another strange woman — come here to the new road? He felt an urge to tear her dress so that her beautiful white body would burst from its shell. He told her how Monsieur Verrochio had given him good advice for the future. Monsieur Verrochio had told him how to win in life. If a man didn't win, he had said, life wasn't worth living. A man who didn't win was not a man. Monsieur Verrochio had taught him that in order to win, a man must have a woman, and that he must win for her and through her. Monsieur Verrochio would have been nothing without the woman whom he called the light of his life.

"Innocent, do you think he still loves me, after all his misfortunes?"

Why was she asking him these hard questions? He wasn't Verrochio's confessor. Or his friend. Innocent's only desire was to see this woman naked. He replied, without thinking:

"With a woman like you, a man can only love her more and more!"

Madame Verrochio brought her beautiful silk-draped bosom closer to him and kissed his brow. Her lips stirred up a flock of wild ideas, like agitated birds. How could he have invented such a reply? In ordinary life such a remark would never have come to his lips. He felt a certain pride. Hadn't he already won a kiss from this woman? Was it because he knew how to talk to women? Had he mastered that difficult art?

"Are you sure he still loves me, Innocent? Sometimes I think he must hate me now. He's a different man. He's experienced great misfortunes. Some misfortunes make a man; others can unmake him."

"Madame," Innocent insisted, "I'll never forget how Monsieur Verrochio loves you. It's the greatest lesson in life that I've learned."

"I wish I'd known my husband when we were your age, Innocent. How good it would have been to travel that road together. Life is a one-way road; it's impossible to turn back to the place where you set out. That road always leads to the unknown. My husband is upset. Is he afraid of the future? I think he's afraid our road is leading him back to our past. My husband has had a hard life. I wish he and I could have lived through those difficult times together at your age. Innocent, you're at the beginning of the road.

437

You have all sorts of qualities you don't even know about yet. You have a great beauty you don't even suspect. Every woman must want to be your mother. You'll be tempted to gather many flowers as you make your way along your road. Try to gather only the ones that are so beautiful they'll last forever. Pleasant memories never die."

Would Innocent speak the words that had sprung to his mind? He thrilled with quivering pride: he knew how to talk to women. He unclenched his lips and the words slowly poured out.

"Madame, you are a flower I won't forget."

Gently, he laid his head on the hair that fell in waves on Madame Verrochio's shoulder. She bestowed a perfumed caress on his face.

"I am a poisoned flower. I have been touched by death."

Innocent was shaken by these unexpected words. With perfumed hands, Madame Verrochio lifted his head and looked at him mildly.

"You'll see, Innocent, it's hard to know if the trace that's left is a trace of life or death. My husband must have been like you when he was your age. I couldn't love him then: our roads were so far apart."

Win. Win. Conquer this woman. A great fire had burst in him, a desire to burn.

"Madame, let me kiss you as if I were your husband when he was my age."

The queen gave an astonished laugh. A bright light illuminated her eyes and she offered her lips like an unforgettable flower. Innocent brought forward thin adolescent's lips, above which was dotted a skimpy mustache. What was the source of those magic words that charmed women? His lips grazed the lady's. Then they drew apart, astonished, the mature woman and the youth face to face, strangers. Madame Verrochio adjusted her hair, drew her gown around her legs. She regretted the kiss. She wanted to forget it, he was certain. He wanted the kiss to endure in his memory. His heart was pounding. He wanted his heart to pound just as hard whenever he remembered her lips. She was running away. She was escaping him. Win. Win. He had already seduced an unknown woman. He had received the gift of speaking to women. He must speak again. Win.

438

"Madame, when your husband was my age he must have wanted to cover your breasts with kisses."

"Innocent!" she exclaimed reprovingly.

"Madame, let me love your breasts the way Monsieur Verrochio would have loved them."

"Innocent!"

"You wouldn't have refused Monsieur Verrochio when he was my age."

"Innocent, I'm not your age." (She was smiling now.)

"Madame, you're passing through my life for the first time; you will leave and perhaps you won't come back. Don't you want to leave me with an undying memory?"

"Innocent! Do I hear what I think I'm hearing? How can such words come from the mouth of such a timid boy?"

"I'm tell you, Madame, I'm loving you and I want to kiss your heart."

Innocent didn't recognize himself. Without reflecting, he was imitating Verrochio's lilting accent; he had spoken as Madame Verrochio would have heard him if she'd known him as a youth (but Verrochio was a poverty-stricken young immigrant then, and she was a rich young girl.) Surprised at his unexpected boldness, he grasped the shoulder of his boss's wife and declared:

"Madame, I'm love you!"

"Innocent, you're a little liar. You should never say those magic words to a lady — an old lady."

"But I'm a young man, and a young man, he has to love . . . "

Innocent was scandalized at his new-found power to talk to women. Madame Verrochio smiled at her young conqueror's boldness. He had pressed his brow against hers. She felt his breath, that of an impatient young bull. He drank the air scented by her woman's warmth. Her lips bore the smile of a woman stirred by a madness she didn't hold back. As a poor, ambitious, enterprising youngster, her husband must have been like Innocent, with his clothes that were too big for him and a greedy appetite to travel as far as possible along the roads of the world. Madame Verrochio peered into Innocent's brown eyes, starred with deep flashes, she peered at his broad forehead under unkempt hair, at his narrow nose, at his mouth that seemed ready to bite into the whole earth like an apple; she looked at his hands that were not yet scarred by any wound, but were impatient to grasp. She had seen this young man before, she knew him: he was the young Verrochio, the man she loved. She saw him as she'd seen him in her dreams. He was the youth she had often regretted not knowing. This young Verrochio, steeped in the air of his native land, was at her side, telling her in his musical language:

"I'm love you. Is the first time I'm love a woman."

Madame Verrochio wasn't altogether prepared to be possessed by her dream.

"Innocent, if you keep lying like that you'll drive the women wild."

She was smiling, but he saw a shadow of sorrow darken her eyes. She was thinking of the man she loved. No doubt he had lied as much as young Innocent.

"I'm swear, I'm loving you."

"What a fine talker you are, Innocent. My husband must have talked like you. But where did you learn to turn a mature woman's heart upside down?"

He felt a hint of fear that he wouldn't be able to find the words to win over this woman.

Should he answer in his own voice? Should he imitate Verrochio? Win. Win.

"You don't love me, Innocent."

"I'm want to kiss your breasts."

When he was a young man, her husband had not kissed her bosom. He was so poor then, so famished, he desired nothing but bread. She had cradled his head on her breast, made heavy by the preoccupations of a man who was building roads, but she had never felt there the lips of an adolescent feverishly discovering life.

"I'm want my lips on your breasts."

With infinite gentleness, Madame Verrochio's long perfect fingers unfastened her bodice.

"There's so little love on this earth," she said, uncovering her bosom.

XXXIX

A crime that makes a lot of noise

Verrochio was walking in the gravel that had been carefully spread by Adolphe Cerisier's grader. The pebbles clinked under his feet, making music he liked to hear. He listened to it as he had listened to his first road sing under his feet. Now this new road was his last. From road to road, from highway to highway, he had come at last to this new road. He would build no more roads. The Right Party had driven him to ruin. Lucia had got him this strip of road in a godforsaken corner of the Appalachians, but Verrochio couldn't build roads any more in a place where his wife had had to humiliate herself to save him. Lucia had given herself out of love, but she had caused him to lose his *onore*. Lucia was no longer his light, but a shadow who created a weight around him. Verrochio was a man of Sardinia, a man of light. He was unhappy that Lucia had become a shadow. He didn't want any shadows in his life. Lucia still loved him, but all her love couldn't dissipate the shadow. The people around the Minister of Roads and Bridges joked about a beauty spot Verrochio's wife apparently had right over her heart. He had met with the officials of the Right Party to find out how to submit a bid;

441

they suggested he name his wife president because "Madame can conduct negotiations with an expert's iron hand in a velvet glove." Verrochio didn't dare show his face in the restaurants frequented by the people involved in highway construction: government officials, contractors, surveyors, political organizers, those people who sold machinery or gravel, shysters, those who bought and sold lumber, land dealers, insurance salesmen specializing in coverage of heavy machinery, influence peddlers, dabblers in just about everything, speculators in secret operations, tax-collectors, policy-mongers, collectors of unpaid dues to the Right Party's war chest, buyers of used machinery, evaluators of anything that could be evaluated, buyers and sellers of scrap metal, suppliers of beer, heating oil and gasoline, shareholders in limited liability companies, first- or second-mortgage brokers, out-of-work foremen: all these people had dust in their hair and on their shoes, they all talked and laughed loudly (a habit left over from jobs where they had to make themselves heard over the roar of machinery), they had black fingernails, they drank a lot of beer (because they'd got in the habit of being permanently thirsty from construction dust), they talked unctuously about Le Chef and the Right Party, for the roads fed them in the same way that God's little sparrows pecked their food from horse manure; these paunchy men with pointed noses looked like huge overfed birds. It was among these people that Verrochio had lived, among them that he'd lost everything. He had lived with them even longer than with his father and mother, longer than with his wife. They had been his friends. Now they laughed as they described the stages in his downfall: crude laughter that made their fat bellies shake with glee.

He had lost everything. He was so poor now that the clinking of pebbles was music to him. The workers were amazed: they had always seen Verrochio sitting imposingly at the wheel of his Cadillac, rolling the window down just far enough to talk to the foreman. Now, like an apparition, the boss — the contractor — stood facing them. He spoke to one of the laborers.

"We not see much of each other, my good man," he said. "I'm Verrochio, your boss."

The other man was rooted to the spot.

"You got children, my good man?"

"Yeah! Eleven alive and kicking, three that's passed on and one or two on the way, not to mention the ones the good Lord's keeping for later. We built a good road here: it ain't just for the mosquitoes . . . "

"Keep plugging away at your wife, my good man. Children is riches, is happiness. A man without children is a sad man."

"How many kids've you got, Monsieur Verrochio?"

The contractor patted his cheek, a childish caress, and kept walking, without replying. The laborer scratched his neck. A truck was coming. Verrochio waved to the driver to stop.

"I'm Verrochio," he said to the driver, who held out his big hand. Verrochio clasped it like a boss who wants to demonstrate his power.

"We hardly know each other," he said, "hardly at all . . . "

Taking a handkerchief from his pocket, he wiped the mud from the door so the letters that formed his name would be visible. He took off his hat and gazed for a moment at the door where his name was displayed. He put back his hat and snapped at the truckdriver to stop wasting time. He continued his walk. He gazed admiringly at the fine gravel. Behind him, he left roads. His chest swelled with pride. He held his head higher. The sky seemed to be copying the blue of his machinery, but a storm was gathering: black clouds were tumbling onto mountains untamed by his roads. A man's life wasn't long enough. He had built roads the way a man traces his beloved's name in the bark of trees. He liked to build roads. And he loved his roads as a breeder loves his animals. His roads were alive; they moved, they ate, they grew, they got sick, they reproduced, they kicked, they forged ahead. He loved this new road. He knelt and gently stroked it. (Some of the employees who noticed these goings-on were sure Verrochio had spotted some technical flaw that they'd be hearing about.) He scratched the gravel the way you scratch a cat's back, then took some pebbles and put them in his pocket, cautious as Hansel and Gretel. Throughout his life, all the roads he'd built were pebbles he had scattered, the way Hansel and Gretel scattered crumbs. Was he so afraid of losing his way? Was he so afraid that he'd never go back to Sardinia? He had never returned to his island. He'd always been too busy strewing pebbles. All these roads, built with more fervor than he'd ever accorded his beloved wife, were leading him here — that is, nowhere — where he had knelt down to caress the gravel. Were these roads that unfurled one by one quite useless then? He rattled the pebbles in his hand. If he followed these roads backwards, they would take him to Sardinia, to his childhood, his roots. He would never return to Sardinia. A ruined man loses everything but his pride. He would not return to his island as poor as when he left. As a young man, he had left Sardinia amid the sorrows of war; now as a grown man he did not want to go back there amid the sorrows of failure. How could he tell them in Sardinia that he'd built the finest roads in America — he, a ruined man who owned nothing but a few pebbles? How could he tell his brothers, who owned nothing but some sheep, that he had driven flocks of bulldozers, trucks, tractors and powerful machines into the forests and plains of America? He had lost everything and now possessed only the power of speech. Who, on his island, would believe the fine words of a man who came home as bereft as when he'd returned from the war? How could he tell his brothers, who were poor, that he had made a fortune and then lost it? Verrochio could hear their laughter, hear their big hands slap the table in rhythm with their laughter. He had even lost Lucia. Could he tell his Mamma that he had lost his fortune and his wife? Of what use had been the life his mamma gave him?

A bulldozer was parked on the shoulder. Some of the workmen nearby saw a man come up to the machine as if it were some rare beast. They recognized Verrochio. Mocking banter was followed by stifled laughter. Now that Verrochio didn't have a wife he was interested in bulldozers! ("Look at that — the guy made a fortune building roads and he's taking his first look at a bulldozer!") Verrochio slowly drew near the iron beast. The men watched his strange behavior. He walked slowly around the bulldozer. They noticed his hand touching the steel. Verrochio was stroking the bulldozer. He was talking to the machine, but his employees couldn't hear: "You been a good creature, you do good work; you don't know, but you not work for

444

me no more. You help make Verrochio rich, but you can't save him from ruin." The employees snickered. If, they mused, their wives were to amuse themselves illegitimately with men, they'd never try to take their minds off their troubles by stroking bulldozers; each of them would take it out on his wife until she didn't have a tear left to shed. That was the behavior which separated real men from a decrepit wreck like Verrochio. The contractor tipped his hat and lingered at the bulldozer like someone saying farewell in a graveyard, then put his hat back on and continued walking.

He inspected the spruce trees on either side of the road as attentively as if he were conducting a census. He peered at the sky as if looking for a sign. As black torrents of clouds rolled by, he smiled. He watched his shoes alight on the new road, he listened to the music of his footsteps on the gravel. Verrochio was probably drunk, the employees thought. If they'd lost their wives they wouldn't go and soak up drink like a miserable barrel, they'd beat the man who had taken their wives until he'd lost all his appetites. This Verrochio who claimed to be a builder was dragging himself along like a fallen leaf. Now the man was so pitiful that they held back their laughter. Wasn't it always sad when a man suffered because of a woman? They could mock a man, but not his sadness.

Verrochio approached the men. They stopped watching him and went back to work. They would have preferred poor Verrochio to go by without noticing them. He didn't look like a beaten man now: he was walking erect, head high, and he looked like a contractor who had the power to drive through mountains, to divide the forests and create jobs for poor people. As he made his way toward them he was the king of the roads. They bowed respectfully. Verrochio wouldn't go back to Sardinia. His Mamma was old now, like the old women in black who came together to weep at burials, their skin as dry as the earth of Sardinia. What would he say to his Mamma? She had given him Sardinia and he had left it. His Mamma had given him life and he wanted to snuff it out. He had never gone back; he'd always been hunting his fortune. When you hunt, you don't leave the game until you've caught it. Verrochio had

445

chosen the hunt over quiet visits to an aging woman on a poor island. He would not go back to tell her: "I caught my fortune but she got away!"

His orbit ended here. He completed his final round. On all the roads he'd built people travelled, as free as birds. His roads opened the way to their desires. All the roads he'd built had brought him here, to this place on earth where he could hear the beating of his heart. He stopped walking so the sound of pebbles pressing one against the other wouldn't cover his heartbeats. The noise of motors, of machines, of tools and money had always covered the sound of life coursing through his heart. He dropped his head, bringing his ear as close to his chest as possible. He listened. The breeze carried the distant rumble of a grader. He identified Adolphe Cerisier. At certain times, when love set him ablaze or when his hand signed a contract, his heart would beat especially hard, but he'd never stopped to listen to it. He thought he'd never listened to the music that supplied life to his body. The life in his body's inner routes obeyed his heart, but what heart did the life on these man-made roads obey? Where was the heart of the world? He raised his head and questioned the sky. Unmoving, listening carefully, he tried to discern the heartbeats of the world. Cicadas were chirring, dogs were barking, machines were roaring, the chirping of birds burst from the tall grass, and Verrochio could not hear the heart of the world. Pebbles clinked beneath his feet. He thought that the gravel was making music on all the roads he had built.

"Verrochio's using liquor to forget about his wife," said some workers gathered around a culvert they were finishing.

The men had never seen him venture so far onto the worksite. They'd never seen him walk. When he was near them they doffed their hats but held back their laughter. Wasn't it comical to see a man looking for the wife he's lost? *They* knew how to hold onto their wives. If *their* mare had jumped a fence, they'd know how to bring her under control . . . Instead of howling or getting drunk, a good thrashing: it was good for the mare and good for her master . . . How could this man expect to command men if he couldn't make a woman obey him? *They* couldn't obey a man in tears. Laughing behind their caps was one way of disobeying.

446

"Don't be afraid," Verrochio told them, "I'm do what you do, I'm do your jobs, I'm do it with my own hands. Don't worry!"

Why should Verrochio think they were afraid? The workmen would never be afraid of a man who cried because his wife had gone grazing in a Minister's field.

"We aren't afraid but we wanna know if our new road's built right."

"She's the best built road I ever saw. And I'm say thank you. I'm tell Innocent, my clerk, to add a little extra to your wages."

He gazed at them for a long time, then went away.

He walked slowly. He stopped before all his employees and promised them a bonus in their next pay. Now and then he would stroke a bearded laborer's cheek. At once a rumor began to circulate that Verrochio was offering a bonus to the men who let him pat them. ("Now that his wife sleeps with Ministers, maybe Verrochio goes for men.") He would stop when he saw a worker, introducing himself as if he were a stranger. Some times he realized that he was. He would assure the man that his sweat would be rewarded. He would take his hand and clasp it for a long time. These men resembled the man he had been. He had been covered in mud like them, bent toward the earth, on his hands and knees in the gardens of the rich. He had managed to get to his feet. He had built roads for other men. Now he was ruined. He didn't want to go back to the gardens of the rich on his hands and knees. Lucia wasn't his any more. Night had fallen over the earth. Verrochio gazed at the machines. If his company's name was covered by mud, he cleaned it off. Then he greeted the operator:

"Building roads — what a blessing! We could've been building prisons!"

What was the meaning of this bizarre inspection? the workers asked. Verrochio smelled not of liquor but of perfumed mouthwash. Was his mind deranged? People muttered that immigrants from far-off countries lose their minds a little because of the new language they had to learn, which got mixed up in their minds with the one they'd learned at their mothers' knees; their memories of the old countries got mixed up with the new country; the past was confused with the present; they ended their lives not knowing where they were, recognizing neither the old country nor the new one. Was that happening to Verrochio? Yet he wasn't an old man. He had worked like a slave. He was rich because he could take advantage of the favors of Le Chef and the Right Party. What good was being rich if it made you as miserable as a beaten dog? Better to be poor and able to split your sides laughing.

He looked at his road like one who is moved by a letter from a distant loved one. He should have been happy. An airplane crossed the sky. He watched it fly past. He would not return to Sardinia. As a wealthy man, he hadn't dared go back lest his fortune wilt there like a neglected plant. He had been afraid to see his poor house in Sardinia. Now he was too poor. The airplane passed and the sky closed behind it.

He had thought he'd enjoy introducing himself to his employees. They took no pleasure from seeing him or from his promised bonus. He had thought he'd enjoy breathing the country air. He discovered he was indifferent to the air, as the air was indifferent to him. He had thought he'd enjoy walking on his road. He found he was apathetic. He felt eternally indifferent to the light of day. His promenade was over. Everything around him had lost its value. Verrochio walked quickly now, as if responding to some urgent call. His wide trousers were draped about his narrow legs as he strode. He looked furious. He no longer seemed drunk. The laborers were expecting a storm. Black clouds had gathered on the hilltops.

Outside Innocent's shed, Verrochio looked up to the sky. He had worked the land. He had spent more time looking at the land than at the sky. When he closed his eyes for sleep he saw pebbles, not clouds, roll past his eyes. He thought he'd stop for a moment to gaze at the sky which contained all that was unknown from past and future. It interested him no more than the gravel under his shoes. It was probably going to rain. There would never be enough rain, he thought, to wash all the filth from the earth. He was tired of the dust and mud that clung to his body and his soul. All his life he had spent in the earth, like a corpse. It would never rain enough to drown those who had plotted his ruin. Neither the earth nor the sky was his friend. Everywhere there was indifference. This was the morning of indifference. He was surrounded by indifference to his ruin. Now he must make haste. He bounded into Innocent's shed.

"Is Madame Verrochio still here, Innocent?" he asked without humor.

"Yes, Monsieur."

He approached Innocent and bestowed on him the gaze of a leader, a contractor, a man who knows how to win. Innocent felt his boss's gaze sink into his like the flaming stake Ulysses had driven into Cyclops' eye. Now that he knew how to talk to women, he must get in the habit of not looking away when a man spoke to him.

"Innocent, I'm hope you were polite and respectful and you no forget you're responsible for my treasure.

"Oh, I assure you," said Madame Verrochio, all soft, tender smiles, "Innocent acted like a real man."

Monsieur Verrochio kept his gaze fixed on Innocent's eyes. He laid a fatherly hand on his shoulder.

"If a man respects another man's wife, I'm honor that man."

Innocent knew he should have kept silent, but the words came out and he couldn't hold them back.

"I hope one day I'll be able to love a woman like Madame Verrochio."

"Did you hear that child, my dear?" asked Madame Verrochio.

He didn't give her the blazing look that Innocent had sensed in his eyes.

"Innocent," said Verrochio, "everything that happen, she's happen because of women . . . Now I'm need dynamite. Without dynamite, nobody can get through."

Madame Verrochio loved her husband. If she hadn't loved him she wouldn't have looked at him so tenderly. Innocent was a loser. Every time a woman appeared in his life, he lost. Each time he thought he was winning, but he lost. If Madame Verrochio loved her husband, why had she held Innocent in her arms? What was love anyway? The strange beauty in a yellow dress loved only her Adolphe Cerisier, yet she had lent herself to both Innocent and Jeannot Tremblay. Madame Verrochio loved her husband. If Verrochio hadn't come back so soon Innocent would have possessed her as he had possessed the beautiful

449

stranger. What was love anyway? Was it the flames that flared up when a man and woman were together? Was it a mixture of confessions and secrets? Was it a sort of thirst? A dance? An urge to give and to conquer? A cure for solitude? Love was like a book written in mysterious characters. He would learn to read. He would learn how not to lose. Win. Win. He had learned how to say the magic words that would unfasten women's dresses. He had also learned that once women had been conquered they preferred another man to him. Was it his fate, then, to pick up the crumbs of love that fell from the tables of the rich, as it said in the Bible? Was love a game?

"When things are blocked, dynamite unblocks them!"

Verrochio picked up a crate.

"Monsieur Verrochio, I've learned a lot of new things from you," said Innocent.

"I'm hope," the contractor said dryly, "you're not learn nothing new from my wife."

Love was truly mysterious. This man and woman were looking tenderly at one another and suddenly the man had expressed a doubt, as if he were administering a slap. The enigma of love.

Verrochio stood up with his case of dynamite, looked questioning at Innocent, then at his wife, who lowered her eyes. Verrochio talked very harshly.

"If you find a woman like mine, I'm hope you don't find ruin at the end of your road."

He went out, carrying a crate of dynamite.

"Do you want another crate, Monsieur Verrochio? I'll help you."

"No, Innocent, stay with my wife. She's like youth . . . "

Verrochio went out, and now there was only silence. Madame kept her eyes lowered and Innocent wished she wasn't there. The silence was as heavy as remorse. Innocent had known a happiness as sweet as milk. Now the silence was trying to erase what had happened, trying to turn a moment's happiness into oblivion. Why did women make Innocent so unhappy after they'd made him happy? He would learn how to win happiness too. Love was a sad enigma.

"I'm need lots of dynamite, many many crates," Verrochio announced.

"Let me help you," Innocent repeated.

"At your age, if I was a young man, with a woman like Madame Verrochio, I'm no leave her. Innocent, don't help me, you'll be sorry. Some jobs, a man's gotta do by himself."

"Let me help you anyway."

"Innocent, you a good boy to want to give a man a hand, but a polite young man, he should take care of a woman that's alone . . ."

He took out another crate of dynamite, then came back for another, sighing heavily at the effort required to lift it. Then he asked:

"Innocent, you're give me the detonators and the wire? She won't blow up by herself, I need what it takes."

Cautiously, Innocent held out a carefully packed box of detonators and a spool of wire.

"Can't I help you?" he asked again, trying to ingratiate himself.

Innocent had never seen Verrochio do a job with his own hands and he was worried when he saw him carrying crates of dynamite and preparing a detonation.

"Madame," he asked, "do you know what your husband wants to blow up?"

She smiled in a way that made Innocent want to press his lips once more against the fine red fruit of her own.

"My husband has always made a big fuss over little things. A pebble to him is like a mountain. To blow up that pebble, he uses the force you'd need for a mountain. My husband has always used too much force."

She opened her arms so invitingly that Innocent flung himself at her, embracing her firm, sculpted body. She held him then like a child. Innocent wrenched himself away from her happy warmth.

"Innocent! Innocent! You got the exploder? Where you put the exploder?"

"Innocent," said Madame Verrochio, "don't despise me. You're the only person who wants to love me."

"Innocent! Get the exploder ready. We need a big explosion. It's the only way to unblock everything. Wife! Wife! We're at the end. Time to go somewhere else . . . No! No! Not Sardinia!"

"Innocent," said Madame Verrochio, "you've given some youth to an old woman who is no longer loved because she has loved too much. Innocent, you're like my husband I didn't know when he was your age. You're like him, Innocent, I know you are. At your age my husband must have been gentle like you. Innocent, don't lose that. You don't build roads with gentleness: you need dynamite too. But don't lose your gentleness, Innocent. You'll never lose it altogether because I'll remember. You know, Innocent, memory doesn't die. Because of you, Innocent, I shall remember the tenderness of the husband I didn't know when he was a boy like you."

"Innocent! Let go of my wife, *Seductore!*"

Verrochio burst into the shed like a knight come to rescue a beautiful captive.

"Innocent," said Verrochio, "I like you because you try to win — but Nino Verrochio, he's win always!"

Gallantly, Verrochio offered his arm to Madame. Innocent watched them go out. Their dignified solemnity was hardly appropriate to his dusty shed draped in cobwebs.

"This is a great day!" Verrochio proclaimed. "This new road, she's the end of all the roads I build. We're come to the end of something and the beginning of something else."

Innocent observed them. She was mincing along the gravel. Verrochio's steps were longer, more impatient. He opened the door for her. She disappeared inside the Cadillac. Innocent saw Verrochio coming back.

"Innocent, when everything's blocked you need a big explosion. Have you got the exploder?"

Verrochio wound the wire around the first contact screw, then wound the second wire around the second contact screw. He made certain the lever that produced the electric current was firmly engaged and couldn't slip down.

"Innocent, listen to me. We need a good explosion. Listen carefully. I'm go away in my Cadillac, with my wife. When I shut my door, you shut your office door. I start up the motor. Listen carefully. When I blow the horn three times — three times, remember! — you push the lever to send the electricity into the wire that's plugged into the dynamite that's going to unblock everything. Understand?"

"Yes, Monsieur."

"Remember, Innocent. You must WIN. Lose, that doesn't exist. You remember, Innocent? Win!"

452

Verrochio, walking like someone on his way to conquer the world, went back to his car. He got inside. He shut the door. He turned around to be sure Innocent was shutting the door to his shed. Innocent obeyed. He heard the motor starting up: an orchestra! Some day Innocent too would have a luxurious car. Its motor would make symphonic music instead of the noise like a backfiring tractor that Appalachian cars made. The motor was turning, but it seemed to Innocent that the car wasn't moving. He dared not open the door to look. The horn blared twice, three times. Obediently, Innocent pushed the lever. A roar like thunder shook the shed, then all was silent. Innocent opened his eyes. The crates of dynamite were still piled up in their place. The door was open. His shed hadn't been blown up. He could move. He got to his feet. He was not in pain. He went out. His shed was still in place. Men came running. He took a few steps. Not far away, outside his shed, drops of blood spattered the gravel. Much farther were scattered bits of metal.

"Verrochio told me," Innocent kept saying, "he told me he wanted a lot of dynamite to unblock something. What was it he wanted to unblock?"

"It's his life that was blocked, Innocent, his life."

"All his life," said another, "that man used dynamite to open roads. It seemed like the most natural thing to open a road to a better world."

Innocent recounted a hundred times what had happened. He was the last one who had talked to them. It was to Innocent that he had said his last word.

"Win," Innocent repeated. "Win. That was his religion."

"Innocent, it's you that killed them."

XL

Wherein a new character appears who is both powerful and weak

Philémon Boileau, whose hair was neatly combed and parted, never had dirty hands. His car gleamed. There was never any dirt under his fingernails. His well-pressed trousers were never rumpled except at the seat, because he spent the whole day sitting down. He never got out of his car. He remained at his post. He wouldn't even let himself be tempted by the strawberries sparkling in the grass.

In the past, he had worked very hard. He'd killed himself on the job, he would say, yet he wasn't dead. He was alive but he lacked the strength to work. He was as short and skinny as a wisp of straw. But his wife Aubépine still clung to her husband's arm, convinced he was omnipotent. Hadn't he given her twelve children, or thirteen? Philémon loved children. He loved his wife, he had never abused her, never beaten her. He always said her soup was the best he'd ever eaten. He never complained if the meat was burnt. If there was a decision to be made, Philémon never contradicted her, but said: "Do what you think is best, because if you can give me children, you know things I don't know."

On Sunday, he took his wife to church and walked with her to their pew. Then Philémon Boileau went home and put his twelve children, or thirteen, in the car; all knew their place, all knew how to bend or where to place a leg or arm, how to fold a knee or elbow. He would push them through the door; first the biggest, then the smaller ones, who waited their turn to be packed in like sardines. Back at the church, he would pull them from his gleaming car one at a time and go back inside with all his progeny in tow. His wife couldn't help smiling at her gently disciplined family.

Philémon Boileau had been a strong man. Even though he'd always been the smallest and sickliest of the workers, the one with the narrowest shoulders, the flattest chest, the smallest hands, the skinniest arms, he was amazingly strong. In fact, people wondered how such a small man should be so strong. Nothing was too heavy for him. In those days — now alas! bygone — he started work before the others, struggled harder, left later, and it was said that back at home, he lavished warm attention on his wife, because Aubépine was always smiling and jolly, while other wives were nagging and irritable. Philémon Boileau must have a secret.

Suddenly, like a well that dried up, Philémon's strength vanished. He could no longer lift his ax. Once as nimble as a squirrel, now he took frightened little steps like someone after an operation who is afraid the incision will open and his guts land on his feet. He hadn't had an operation. Whatever made the little man so strong had been extinguished. The doctor told him he couldn't work any more.

"Will my Philémon still be able to look after me and plant a few more children before he dies?" asked a worried Aubépine.

"Medical science can only tell me that your husband will never again be able to fell a tree or lift a shovelful of earth."

"Philémon can't work any more but if I understand you right he can still love me . . . "

"Medical science makes no pronouncements about love."

Since Philémon Boileau's enforced convalescence, Aubépine had had four children, or five. Philémon loved his wife, but he wasn't working. The children were always eating and the more they grew, the hungrier they were. Aubépine declared:

"It's time we prayed to baby Jesus to take care of us like he takes care of his little birds. We mustn't worry. We'll just pray. The Bible says not to worry about tomorrow. The good Lord's going to give our family a miracle."

"My chubby love, I'm sure you're right."

"The whole family's going to get washed and put on our Sunday clothes and go see Curé Fourré. We'll ask him to pray to the good Lord with us and ask for a miracle. He's on pretty good terms with the good Lord. If Curé Fourré's on our side, the good Lord can't say no; He wouldn't let a good Catholic starve to death when the father's worked his heart out doing his Catholic duty, while He was just feeding birds that don't even go to Mass."

"My chubby love, with your brains and your muscles it's you that ought to be head of the family. I'm a human wreck; only thing I'm good for is to be framed and put up on the wall with my defunct parents."

A tear dropped down Philémon Boileau's cheek. Aubépine wiped it with the tip of her plump ardent finger and said with a smile as lovely as a summer day:

"You're still alive and kicking, Philémon; do you know you've planted another little one in my belly? And he's kicking and squirming like nobody's business. So you can still do some things that I can't . . . "

Philémon threw himself at her like a child seeking shelter, and Aubépine wrapped her arms around the little man.

Curé Fourré was moved by the afflicted family. He recommended to the Local Riding Minister this admirable father, this exemplary family, this couple who had increased the population of the province. Philémon Boileau learned that they needed him on the new road.

"I can't work," he wept. "I can't stand up without getting dizzy. I've got biceps the size of a cherry. I haven't got the strength to hold a pencil. Even if I could write. I can read a little but by the end of a sentence I'm exhausted. Bury me: I'm no good for work or for life. And I could never give my beautiful Aubépine another baby."

"Don't die right away, Philémon Boileau; wait for the election. You can still vote. Take the time to vote for me,"

456

said the Local Riding Minister. "Thank the good Lord with your prayers and thank me with your vote . . . And your wife's . . . You must have children old enough to vote?"

"I can't work," whimpered Philémon Boileau. "My chubby love, my Aubépine, threw out all my work clothes. All she kept was my Sunday suit to bury me in."

"Dress yourself like a boss; nobody's giving you any orders on the new road."

He received his first pay in the mail before he'd even shown up at work. The Local Riding Minister was as good as the good Lord, Aubépine decided. A man from the Right Party explained that to show his gratitude, Philémon must turn over ten per cent of his salary to keep the Right Party's charitable fund afloat. Aubépine and Philémon talked it over and decided to contribute twenty per cent instead. Their gratitude was not excessive. Hadn't they been blessed by a miracle? The following week the special adviser's pay had been increased. Their gratitude grew apace, and they agreed to turn over a quarter of Philémon's salary to the Right Party's charitable works.

Philémon wore his best clothes to his job on the new road. His car had been waxed and polished until it gleamed. The foreman had been given instructions by Verrochio, who had been given instructions by the Local Riding Minister. He greeted Philémon Boileau respectfully.

"Monsieur, as special adviser, would you be good enough to park your car in the shade, beside the clerk's shed? You'll be near the phone in case you find yourself in a state of mortal weakness. Stay in your car, think about your good advice, and I'll come for you if I need you. Don't talk to the clerk. You're a special adviser. A special adviser doesn't talk to anybody who isn't a special adviser. So — silence."

"Are you a special adviser?" asked Philémon.

"No, I'm the foreman."

"Okay, I won't talk to you either."

"Silence! Silence! Silence is the base of a political party, just as a bed of stones is the base of a good road."

The responsibility of a special adviser seemed very heavy to a feeble man exhausted by hard labor. He didn't want to complain: he had orders not to speak to anyone who wasn't a special adviser. He sat in his car and waited for a day, a week, two weeks; then he stopped waiting. He arrived before the other workers, he parked his car in the shade and he stayed in it. He didn't speak to anyone who wasn't a special adviser.

To Innocent Loiseau, the foreman had said:

"Philémon Boileau's the Local Riding Minister's man. What he does doesn't concern you. You don't have to talk to him. You don't even have to see him."

The workers didn't understand what purpose was served by a special adviser. How did he keep busy, sitting in his car? Probably he kept an eye on the new road for Le Chef. They had no desire to expose themselves to his gaze, so they avoided his car. Philémon Boileau was all alone. He watched the hands of his watch make their way around the dial, he watched the sun make its way over the fields and forest. Never had he heard so much peace and quiet. He who had always worked like an ox was discovering that it was possible to live without working. He who had wrecked himself at work discovered that rest was less tiring than work. When he had worked he was poor. Since he'd been resting he was less poor. The Local Riding Minister must be pleased with him, since he'd given him yet another raise. In gratitude, Philémon turned over thirty per cent of his salary to the Right Party's charitable fund. It was more pleasant to be a special adviser than to do odd jobs. In his car, with the windows rolled up to protect him from the occasional gusts of wind that brought the morning coolness or the forest damp, Philémon was happy. He kept the windows shut too because he didn't want his happiness — fragile as smoke — to disappear in the wind. He enclosed his happiness in his car the way rich people seal their jewels in hermetic vaults.

They could see him from the outside, consulting papers, unfolding maps, turning every which way; they could see him tracing distances with the tip of a pencil, making notes in a book, arranging files. They didn't know if Philémon Boileau had special knowledge, but he seemed very competent at the job of special adviser. Probably he'd taken correspondence courses. The Right Party let the people know that education was the road that led to wealth. The Party had put up billboards along the roadside to encourage the people to follow the path of education. Since the Right Party had been in power, everything could be learned by correspondence: religion, accounting, horticulture, electronics, Chinese, everything. A young girl from Saint-Toussaint-des-Saints even made a baby by correspondence. After that particular correspondence scandal, Curé Fourré had unblessed the post office, then reblessed it. So it was quite possible that Philémon Boileau had learned how to be a special adviser by correspondence. His hands, toughened by hard labor, had learned paper work. You could see him in his car: he looked as comfortable amid his papers as Pigeon the Notary. Philémon Boileau worked with a pencil, Philémon Boileau, Special Adviser on the Building of the New Road: who'd have believed it?

XLI

Advice to an editor-in-chief who sees circulation dropping

Citizens who wanted to find out what the Right Party was doing to find concrete solutions to the Province's problems ("The Opposition is spit; the Right Party is cement and pavement.") read *The Provincial Sun*. Unfortunately, the Ministers' faces that appeared every day, their speeches that were printed every day, their promises listed every day were all too familiar. Politics seemed less interesting than in "the good old days." People didn't read the newspaper, they skimmed it, they turned the pages. They used *The Provincial Sun* to start their fires. The citizens put off renewing their subscriptions. Despite urgent appeals from *The Provincial Sun*, which declared that freedom of the press was a bulwark against atheistic communistic dictatorship and that every citizen concerned about the future of his children and his race ought to subscribe, circulation was dropping. Le Chef was concerned about the loss of the readers' loyalty. If they tired of the Right Party's paper, they'd read the Opposition paper and abandon the Right Party.

"Even if they don't read *The Provincial Sun*, they can use it to wipe themselves," said Le Chef. But even for that intimate task they preferred the Opposition paper.

His verdict fell during a meeting of his Ministers:

"I think *The Provincial Sun*'s getting dull. The Right Party's as bright as the May sunshine falling on the Province, but its paper's as grey as October rain."

At *The Provincial Sun* they announced a visit by a sales specialist who would restore the paper's magic touch. Building roads wasn't enough to win an election: the people must be told as well that the Right Party put roads where the Opposition let brushwood grow. And who would report the news? *The Provincial Sun!*

The sales specialist arrived. He was an ex-army corporal who had taken part in the Normandy landing. He had seen his fellow soldiers go through the meat-grinder. He had felt their blood on his clothes. He had, as he put it, "sold death on the idea of life." When peace was restored, he came home to his province. He had taken over a door-and-window-maker, a small family business, and transformed it into a big factory. He followed advice from shady lawyers and lost control of the company. He had to run away. He travelled across America, always selling something: brassieres, perfume, shoes, hats, agricultural products, insecticide, pills, houses, animals, rugs, lumber, land, cakes, travel. He was not a rich man. More interested in selling than in making a profit, he was a man who knew the people; he'd sold something to every citizen in the province or his cousin. "Only thing is," concluded the supervisor of the Right Party's organizers, "the man's my father. It'd be tricky to give my own father a job."

Le Chef interrupted:

"The Right Party is one big family with one father: me. When the Opposition disappears, there'll be just one big happy family, without all the friction the Opposition creates. And as far as your father's concerned, if I say there's no conflict of interest, there isn't any."

When ex-Corporal Oscar Marteau arrived at *The Provincial Sun*, he had a red nose, a languid walk for a former soldier, and he reeked of whisky. The leading contributors were waiting for him around their conference table. They had stacks of reports and piles of newspapers to establish comparisons. Around the conference room blackboards awaited the ideas that would emerge from the discussion.

Ex-Corporal Oscar Marteau, sales specialist, took a seat in a waiting chair. He pushed away the carafe of water and asked to see *The Provincial Sun*. He had never read it. He didn't read newspapers. He gathered his information in bars and taverns. When the news came out in *The Provincial Sun* it was already old, he said. He hadn't opened a paper for years. He quickly leafed through *The Provincial Sun*, grimacing as he'd done at the sight of the carafe of water.

"Needs women," he announced.

"What do you mean?" asked an anxious Achille Bédard, the editor-in-chief.

"Women. You know what a woman is. Run pictures of women."

The next day, *The Provincial Sun* announced a new feature: the female saint of the day. Beneath a portrait of the Italian Saint Maria Goretti, Achille Bédard published a brief prayer. Ex-Corporal Oscar Marteau came to see if they'd followed his advice. He looked at the saint's picture in horror. That wasn't exactly what he'd had in mind. A good salesman knew how to take advantage of circumstances and he deemed, with the clarity sometimes bestowed by alcohol, that there was something to be said for the idea of publishing a saint's picture, along with a prayer. He declared:

"That's exactly the sort of thing to do. And now you've satisfied the people that like saints, you've got to think about the people that like tits. A paper's got no future without tits. Don't you ever listen to the people? They don't say read the paper, they say look at it. So give 'em tits to look at. Otherwise your paper's on the road to ruin. Tits: that's what keeps us all alive."

Hoboes in rumpled clothes and run-down shoes, smelling of alcohol (they spilled as much on themselves as they drank) would come to the offices of *The Provincial Sun* claiming they had important news to sell. In a way, ex-Corporal Marteau was like them, but he was a sales specialist too; delegated by Le Chef himself, he commanded respect. He had fought in the war. Young reporters who'd never had the blood of their fellows on their clothes felt that irresistible respect which comes to those who spend their lives in a chair when they encounter those who have trod untraveled roads.

In the lower left-hand corner of page 12, under a torrent of blond hair, appeared the head of a young girl, her eyes enough to melt a man, her open lips offered as if to kiss the moon; her low-cut blouse revealed a landscape of magic mountains where a man would want to lose himself and become a child again, so he could drink. The caption read: "A morning smile from Nancy, of Denver, Colorado." That morning, on thousands of breakfast tables, the paper stayed open for a long time at that page. Word spread quickly that *The Provincial Sun* had become interesting. Along their routes, trucks distributed thicker piles of *The Provincial Sun* than usual, just as ex-Corporal Marteau had predicted. The farmers didn't often get a chance to see such lovely female landscapes. More copies of the paper were sold. The next day, following the sales specialist's orders, *The Provincial Sun* didn't publish any pictures of women without clothes.

"When somebody's thirsty you just give him a sip of water, then let him get thirsty again. And after that you give him another sip," explained the smelly character who commanded everyone's respect. His cynicism was more effective than the profound thoughts of the editor-in-chief, which hadn't been able to attract readers' attention.

Two days later, in the lower left-hand corner of page 3 and the lower right-hand corner of page 7, appeared two pictures of women; one seemed to be wearing nothing but the ribbon that encircled her protruding breasts; the other appeared to be covered in fur, like a rabbit, but the rabbit-skin was open at her bosom and seemed to bring the lovely flayed creature boundless joy, because she was smiling as if she was in heaven. That issue of the paper was more precious than gold. The illiterate were miraculously able to read. That morning even Opposition sympathizers read *The Provincial Sun*. The women were amazed at their husbands' interest in politics. When they came up to see what articles the men were so engrossed in, they turned the page, brows furrowed with concern.

"Wife, things are going downhill all over the world."

Eyes blurred by dreams they couldn't confess, they resumed their reading. "Meet Molly, from Columbus, Ohio:

she is smiling, dear reader, as she thinks of the same thing as you." And for the thirtieth time they would turn to the other page: "From Tallahassee, Florida, Joy warmly invites anyone with a rabbitskin . . . "

"You're certainly taking your time over the paper today," a woman complained to her husband.

"Sometimes politics is hard to figure out . . . "

Ex-Corporal Marteau had a victory celebration before he came back to deliver a rather muddled speech about sales and why people buy.

"There's just one way to go about it: fill your paper with American tits. Less ideas, more tits!"

He predicted that a few readers ("women as flat as ironing boards"), some nuns and the odd priest of indefinite sex would complain to the newspaper, but their complaints must fall on deaf ears. Ex-Corporal Marteau had allowed for no risqué pictures to be published for a certain period. During that time, the paper would run letters of complaint, from dissatisfied, scandalized and frustrated women. Readers would ask themselves: "What are those holy nellie hypocrites so steamed up about? There's no immoral pictures in the paper." When the complainers saw the next set of pictures they'd leap indignantly and make a fuss, but they wouldn't write because they would have already written.

"Get the picture?" asked ex-Corporal Marteau. "One: A few days' drought. Two: Publication of letters from angry readers — they're entitled to be heard. In a democracy, priests and women have the right to piss and moan. Three: After the drought, the deluge: American tits will roll over the people like derailed trains full of grapefruit. If your circulation doesn't triple, I tell you it's not worth having political ideas. If I don't triple your circulation, it'll be the first war I've lost. And I'm not about to lose a war in my province — I already won a world war!"

Ex-Corporal Marteau's automatic memory made him click his heels and puff out his chest as if it were draped in medals, then he staggered to the nearest tavern.

"Give the people tits and they'll swallow the Right Party's ideas like mother's milk!"

A peaceable avalanche of breasts was loosed on the province. On every page in the newspaper and several times on a page, top to bottom, left to right, were pictures of young women displaying their bosoms. Circulation tripled. The head-spinning bosoms seemed alive and breathing. Ex-Corporal Marteau came back twice a week: he walked around the newsroom, then went down to the printshop, proud as a king and drunk as a sad old man.

"Load your paper with tits! You don't need articles!"

His drunkard's words landed in Achille Bédard's face like spittle.

"Stuff it with tits!"

When the journalists heard this statement of principles, young wolves and old alike went to the window for a breath of air. The polluted air, the sun-warmed pavement, the sooty factory emissions seemed pure compared with the breath of the old World War Two leftover, the former brassiere salesman who now sold breasts. Circulation had tripled. Everywhere, readers opened their newspaper as carefully as if they were unwrapping a precious gift. *The Provincial Sun* was interesting again. The Brothers of Catholic Schools bought extra subscriptions "so the good brothers can be better informed about life in the world," as their superior explained. The Institute for Old Priests and Retired Canons ordered additional copies; their director wrote: "Our holy elderly priests once were gloomy; now they're in seventh heaven as they peruse your finely crafted articles, so graciously presented, with such harmonious, elegant lines."

The most stinging humiliation came from Le Chef who congratulated all the journalists in a letter. "You've brought *The Provincial Sun* back to life," he wrote. "Not only have you insured your own jobs, but your smiling declaration of the truth has put you squarely back on the road to the hearts of the populace, and the Right Party on the road to re-election."

When Achille Bédard read this letter, his stomach contracted. The food he had eaten rose to his mouth. He rushed outside to vomit. He choked with spasms, vomiting up his shame. He was disgusted to be where he was. He had sworn an oath, which he'd sealed in a bottle and cast into the St. Lawrence, that he would devote his life to the liberation of his people. The bottle had drifted toward the wall where he was vomiting his self-disgust.

"Can't go wrong with tits, boys!" declared ex-Corporal Marteau who emerged from the newspaper building without falling downstairs, thanks to the astonishing sense of balance often possessed by drunks. By the wall he saw young Achille Bédard, moaning and convulsed by spasms.

"It's a terrible thing," reasoned ex-Corporal Marteau, "to think that a newspaper — the weapon of truth and liberty — is in the hands of people that can't hold their liquor. They're loaded when they write their articles, and it shows. Liquor's not for youngsters my boy . . . Anyway, fill 'er with tits!"

Ex-Corporal Marteau made his way to the tavern. His career as a salesman wasn't over. He was no longer worried about his future. He remembered the brass bands of his past. Their jaunty music accompanied his steps: he had just won another war. His chest was broad enough for some more medals.

XLII

The world is a map

Since his appointment as special adviser on the new road, Philémon Boileau had been bringing his copy of *The Provincial Sun* to work. When he got tired of looking through his windshield at the leaves moving, at birds flapping their wings as they hopped from branch to branch, at Verrochio's blue trucks and machines going back and forth in their clouds of dust, and at the men dragging their tools, he would unfold his newspaper and look at the dense, narrow columns of print. He had been warned that any effort could have disastrous consequences for his weak heart. Some of the words were hard to read: when he got to the last letter he couldn't remember the first ones. The letters were much too small. Reading hurt his eyes. However, a photograph in the lower left-hand corner of a page didn't strain his eyes but felt as gentle as a breeze — not only to his eyes but all through his body and even in his blood. He lingered over the picture. Gradually his heart felt young and strong again. He had the impression that the mop of wavy hair in the photograph was moving, as if it were alive: the lips smiled a little more broadly over sparkling teeth; the eyes shone and looked into his; it seemed to him that the young girl's abundant, opulent bosom was breathing, rising with every breath. He placed his hand on the bosom and it felt warm, like flesh. Philémon Boileau came home humming and that night, after supper, he spent a long time re-reading *The Provincial Sun*.

"You're taking a lot of time with your paper today, Philémon," said his wife Aubépine.

"Don't forget, wife, I'm a special adviser. I have to know what's going on."

He gazed at length at the blond hair swaying in the breeze, at the winking eyes, the lips that smiled a disturbing message, the breasts that were offered like delicious fruits. He didn't have to read the caption, he knew it by heart: "Maureen, 18 summers and two fine grapefruits, sends you warmest greetings from the girls in El Paso, Texas, where she's known as the blonde bombshell." Where was El Paso, Texas? Far away. Girls like that certainly didn't live in the Appalachians. In his region he'd never seen such fiery animals. The next day he cut out Maureen's picture and put it in his glove compartment. El Paso? They couldn't make girls like her around here. At the garage where he stopped for gas, he bought a map of the United States and put it in the glove compartment with Maureen's picture. Back at his job on the new road next day, he looked up El Paso on the map. It wasn't easy: there were so many names and he was looking for just one. Hundreds of names were printed one on top of the other. By the end of that afternoon, he'd finally spotted El Paso, Texas. Philémon Boileau stuck Maureen's picture on his rear-view mirror. That afternoon, he studied the map to find the shortest way between Saint-Toussaint-des-Saints and El Paso. The roads of America were all intertwined like the hay in a hay-rick. The job took many hours. Twenty times he headed in the wrong direction. Fifty times he ended up on roads that didn't lead to his destination. A hundred times he forgot the name El Paso. When he was positive he'd found the road that led to Maureen, he took out the sharpened pencil he carried in his jacket pocket ever since he was named special adviser, marked the road from Saint-Toussaint-des-Saints to El Paso and, at the bottom of the map, at the foot of the United States, below El Paso, which he circled with a trembling hand, he wrote Maureen's name. That way, a thin pencil line joined Philémon Boileau and Maureen. Several times he followed the curves on the map and made the journey to El Paso. He went there so often he was sure that, one day, he'd be able to travel there for real. Maureen wouldn't be a stranger to him.

The Provincial Sun published pictures of young girls in frilly, furry, transparent négligées as seductive as a good sin. The most beautiful girls in the United States took part in the newspaper's contest to find the most beautiful bosom in the world. Philémon Boileau watched them vie with one another with dainty impudence, shameless but smiling like children afraid of the dark. All these children of God had been formed in the same way, but each had her own charming differences. Philémon Boileau compared the photographs and noted that the good Lord hadn't created any two in the same manner: each bosom had its special subtle differences — its own curve, point, or swelling.

At first, Philémon Boileau wondered just what he was supposed to do as a special adviser. He was worried that the days would go by like a melting candle. Sitting in his car for days on end — he who had broken his heart by working — he felt as ill at ease in the profession of special adviser as he was in his new shoes, in his tight suit made for the runty body of a city man. Since the revitalization of *The Provincial Sun*, since lovely young women had been sparkling like little suns in the black sky of tight-packed type, Philémon Boileau was less nervous when he went to work. In the beginning, he would set out trembling and fearful, after a night of troubled sleep because of all his worries. A special adviser, he lived in fear that someone would ask his advice. What could he say? He knew nothing. And if he lost his job as special adviser, how could he feed his large hungry family? He didn't even have the strength to love his Aubépine. She worried as she saw his face become more gaunt from day to day. In bed, he twitched and squirmed like a frog under pursuit. Aubépine watched her husband fade away. She wondered if Philémon would see the end of the new road. She even had a moment's pride: if her husband should pass away while the new road was being built, his position as special adviser would make it no ordinary death. She had thought that all the people working on the road, all the operators of the big blue machines, the businessmen from the Capital would file past his grave, she calculated that the Local Riding Minister

469

would have to come to the funeral of a special adviser. She assumed that during an election campaign, the Minister of Roads and Bridges, who was responsible for building the new road, would be present as well. Imagining the church on the day of his funeral gave her a burst of pride. Her husband was an important man and she wouldn't be an ordinary widow. She felt such fervent love for her dear departed that her heart throbbed . . . He wasn't dead yet. Alive, her little husband seemed pitiful and less dazzling than in his own funeral procession.

Philémon Boileau stopped wasting away. His health came back. He slept better, more peacefully. One night Aubépine awakened in a wonderful dream of love: her husband had found the strength to love her. Next morning he left the house singing, a rolled-up copy of *The Provincial Sun* in his jacket pocket. As the children waited for their breakfast, Aubépine dropped a kiss on his cheek.

"I think we made one last night."

"Aubépine, don't forget you're married to a special adviser!"

"I'll tell Curé Fourré the good Lord worked another miracle."

She hugged him; he was embarrassed in front of the children. Politely, he pulled himself away.

"Gotta be going," he apologized. "I need a quiet minute to read my paper; a special adviser has to be up on the news."

"What's happening in the world? You look so happy, there must be good things going on."

"Aubépine, how'd you like it if after the kids grow up, you and me get in the car and drive down to the States? There's lots of beauty in that country."

"Philémon, there's more life in you every day!"

She moved closer and gave him another kiss. Her lips grazed his shaven cheek, scented with "Heavenly Flower" toilet water. The children were amazed at all this affection, not hidden away behind the closed bedroom door but out in the open. They snickered and didn't know where to look.

"I'd rather stay home with you, Aubépine, but the new road needs its special adviser."

The other workers saw Philémon Boileau in the shadow of his car, between shafts of sunlight that glinted off windows and windshield, peering at maps that he turned over and over. They saw him shifting papers, writing on them, filing them. It was clean work he did, the special adviser, work that didn't get his hands dirty, or his shirt collar. It wasn't a job for a real man, because a real man needs fresh air and wind, he needs heavy things to move, powerful things to tame, hard things to break. The special adviser stayed in his car, turning sour like milk in the sun. He held so many papers, he must be more important than they'd thought. His maps must be geological maps or surveyors' maps or some other complicated science. The way he was concentrating showed that not a single mistake was allowed. Philémon Boileau was working with a pencil, like a notary. He must have taken correspondence courses . . . He was the best special adviser they had ever seen . . . He was a powerful man, this special adviser, and they were afraid of him.

Philémon Boileau didn't know how important he was. His car parked by the roadside, shaded by whispering leaves, he was busy with his "little suns," as he called the women whose pictures he cut out of *The Provincial Sun*. He hadn't been so happy for ages. His heart didn't beat hesitantly now, like a toy with a worn-out spring, it beat as it had when he was twenty, nineteen, eighteen, whenever he saw a young girl. His heart was no longer filled with doubt, his heart no longer feared, his heart was living quite normally. Philémon Boileau gazed at his "little suns" until he was absolutely dazzled. Philémon Boileau could feel the flesh through the printer's ink; he could feel the little heartbeats of the pretty American girls. He was so happy he forgot he'd once been a condemned man.

He had put together a complete collection of all the enticing pictures that had been published under ex-Corporal Marteau's orders. He could name them: Betty, Sue, Janet, Margy, Dorothy, Agatha. He knew the color of their eyes. He knew the places where his "little suns" lived: Salt Lake City, Utah; Nashville, Tennessee; Oklahoma City, Oklahoma; Santa Fe, New Mexico; Indianapolis, Indiana; and Hollywood, California.

471

Thanks to ex-Corporal Marteau's clever tactics, circulation of *The Provincial Sun* had tripled. The ingenious old man, who had experience in life, had warned them at the newspaper:

"What goes up's got to come down."

He was not mistaken. People had no doubt got used to the lovely pictures the way you get used to happiness; two weeks later, readers weren't buying *The Provincial Sun* quite so avidly.

"And now," ordered ex-Corporal Marteau, "we bring out the statistics. People are impressed by statistics."

Above the smiling "little suns" appeared enigmatic numbers. Readers were quick to realize that they represented, in American inches, the dimensions of the young girls' chests, waists and thighs. It became a game in the province to compare photographs and numbers. There were bets and arguments. Men compared the pictures with their wives or girlfriends. They appraised the numbers (blown up or too low). Each had his own theories, his own experience. Some were incredulous, others believed everything. People argued, flew into a rage. Circulation soared.

Soon Philémon Boileau's maps were smudged and smeared. All the roads were blackened by the roaming pencil. Too many cities had been circled, marked with a name. In the end, the maps were unreadable. Travelling in his dreams in search of his "little suns," Philémon Boileau had become familiar with the roads of America. He knew their numbers, he was acquainted with all their curves, with the mountains they climbed, the bodies of water they passed, the states they ran through. He knew the names of all the states, where they were located on the map, what other states formed their boundaries. When he read "Angela of the angelic smile is the ambassador from Baton Rouge, Louisiana — an ambassador who knows how to make a man feel right at home," Philémon knew the exact distance that separated him from her "starry eyes," from her "bosom as deep as the sea, that comes at you like two rocks where sailors have foundered, drawn by the Siren's song," as the caption put it.

Philémon Boileau had noticed at the doctor's that each patient had a card on which his name was inscribed, along with a list of his complaints, his cures, his visits to the doctor. It seemed like a good idea to use the same method for his "little suns." He glued the pictures to a sheet of paper, inscribed the young girl's name, her city, her measurements, the color of her hair and eyes, he calculated the number of miles that separated him from her, and — just as in his grade school days — assigned her a mark from 0 to 100. He had assembled several hundred files.

At work during the day, as his car rested under the foliage, he arranged his cards in alphabetical order, he learned the information on them by heart, he calculated statistics and percentages. He played teacher and pupil, asking himself questions: "What city does Laura live in?" If his answer was correct, he gave himself a point. Above all, though, he peered at the photographs, his eyes blank from dreaming. The workers who saw him in this state of contemplation assumed that being a special adviser required a lot of thinking, and that it was better for a man to work than think.

Philémon Boileau's reputation grew. If he had so many papers to deal with it meant he had power. If he spent so much time with his papers, it meant he had serious problems to deal with. If he had such serious problems, it meant being a special adviser was a very important position. Philémon Boileau knew nothing about how important he'd become. He filed his cards, updated them, checked the order, filled in statistics, checked distances, compared eyes and hair, counted teeth, analyzed curves, sought out special details and slipped into total ecstasy, no longer dwelling on earth but in that marvelous space where desire mingles with dream like two beaming lights. Hand-in-hand with one of the beautiful Americans sprung to life from her photograph, he walked down the road his pencil had traced on his map, walked through the land of happiness at the speed of light. His heart was racing as it had the first time he held Aubépine's hand.

Suddenly his car crashed. The windshield shattered into brittle flakes. The car was raised up by a powerful wind, then dropped on its wheels and bounced like a rubber ball. The explosion had flung all four doors open. Philémon Boileau had been projected onto the back seat. Stunned and sore, he pulled himself up. His ears were buzzing. He looked out the shattered windshield, the open doors: all was calm. A gentle little breeze barely touched the leaves, which scarcely dared to move. He emerged from the car. The breeze smelled of gunpowder. All the glass had disappeared, but the car wasn't even scratched. He walked all around it. His files had vanished. His "little suns" had flown away. The shock had wrenched them from the car and now the breeze was carrying them away.

Nancy! Agatha! Doreen! Joan! Debby! Dorothy! He sped after them but the wind was travelling faster than he. The "little suns" were rolling along, nudged by a sinister force. Philémon Boileau ran faster, hands outstretched. The "little suns" were escaping. He had nearly caught up with Maureen when he felt his heart wrenched apart. It wouldn't beat any more. Philémon Boileau was holding a card on which he tried to read Maureen's name, but his eyes didn't want to see. As they closed, they let themselves be filled with the smile of the "little sun." Philémon Boileau didn't ask if it was the smile of life or death.

Much later, when the wreckage of Verrochio's car was picked up, one of the laborers who had gone for a pee happened upon the body of the special adviser stretched out on a pile of young girls' photographs.

"There was as many of them pictures as daisies in the field," he explained as he recounted his discovery.

Another man added:

"I wonder if that new road's taking us to life or to death."

"There's death on every road," said the water diviner Odilon Santerre, who always wore a black necktie.

XLIII

Wherein the false beauty of the world will be revealed

"My dearest love, I've just killed a man and a woman. Now what do I do?"

Innocent Loiseau howled into his telephone: "I love you! I love you!"

He had collapsed in the dried mud that covered the floor. His tears blinded him, turning to mud the road dust stuck to his face. Innocent sobbed, called for help, swore eternal love. There was no one at the other end, there was no woman whom he loved and none who loved him. His telephone wasn't connected.

Innocent had killed Monsieur and Madame Verrochio. The explosion was so violent they probably hadn't even been aware of it.

The workers had come running to the site of the accident. Some gazed at the hole ripped open by the detonation. Others sifted through the debris, bringing out one of the Cadillac's doors or the crumpled trunk or a tire, the muffler, buckled like a cigarette butt, a torn seat with its stuffing coming out, the remains of the battery, the radiator, spark-plugs, a bone fragment found on a spruce bough.

With heads bowed, they walked through the fields on either side of the new road, circling the trees, bending down to spread bushes, kneeling to comb the grass with their fingers. Each piece of wreckage was greeted like a trophy and the mortuary silence was replaced by applause and cries of victory.

Innocent emerged from his shed, carrying his black ledger. He had forgotten to note the time when the men had stopped working. With tears in his eyes and the smile of one who was trying to be polite and kind, he told them:

"I blew up Monsieur Verrochio and his wife."

"A good thing you did!" said the day-laborer Janvier Mouffette.

Innocent turned to the man, gazed at him with the tear-filled eyes of a child, pointed an accusing finger and reproached him in a surprisingly powerful voice.

"What you just said is worse than what I did."

"Don't worry, Innocent, you did what you had to: Verrochio was the king of the new road. You wanted to take his place. You see it in the papers every day — the pretender gets rid of the king . . . "

"Don't cry, Innocent . . . Most of us hated Verrochio."

"A man that chases after power is short on love," declared Pommette Rossignol.

Not listening, Innocent Loiseau walked among the village women come to see if the explosion had hit their husbands and repeated:

"I'm the one that set off the explosion. I blew up Monsieur and Madame Verrochio."

He was choked with sobs. Sorrow gripped his heart and soul. As a young man, Verrochio had left his little island in Italy. He had followed roads that brought him to harbors and ships. He had disembarked in America. He had followed the road to the Capital and from there he followed other roads. His way of following a road was to build it. For years he followed roads that he had built himself. Where had those roads taken him? To an explosion that shattered his car and his body like glass. His long trek on this earth had no meaning. Sobbing, Innocent thought that the earth's long orbital journey through the universe had no meaning either, because one day it would explode like Verrochio's Cadillac.

"I killed them."

Head weighed down by sad thoughts, his heart bursting with emotion, Innocent laughed nervously and announced through his tears:

"I killed the Verrochios!"

He laughed and laughed, his shoulders shaking, he choked with laughter. His eyes filled with tears. On this country road he had undressed women and he had killed!

A police car. Lights flashing. Siren shrieking. The workers ran toward the policemen who scrambled out of the car as if they could have prevented the tragedy.

"Monsieur Verrochio is dead! Madame Verrochio is dead!" the workers exclaimed.

Innocent was Verrochio's eyes and ears. A dead man has deaf ears and blind eyes. Now Innocent must see nothing, hear nothing. He moved away from the onlookers and went back into his shed.

"Innocent blew them up," explained Janvier Mouffette. "He said so."

Another police car pulled up amid a storm of dust, urgent wails and lights that slashed the air.

"There's two dead. Innocent killed them," insisted Trophyme Laroche.

"Where's the bodies?" asked one of the newly arrived policemen, who had to be the chief, because he was looking at the others as if they were shit.

"We're holding the guilty party, Lieutenant," said one of the policemen, congratulating himself on his speedy action.

"We can't find the bodies," said another.

"If there's no bodies there's no guilty party," the lieutenant said drily.

"Innocent's back in his shed," Uguzon Dubois pointed out.

"He's a good boy," said Pommette Rossignol. "I tell you, that child's no criminal."

"I'll talk to him," declared the police chief.

He made his way toward Innocent's shed. The workers followed. Seeing the onlookers congregating behind him, he gave his men an order.

"Get rid of that mob, I don't need an escort. Don't let anybody leave. No pissing in the fields — somebody could try for a getaway. There's no crime, there's no guilty party, there's no body, but while we're waiting everybody's under suspicion."

Another police car pulled up, travelling so fast it couldn't stop on the gravel that shot out under its wheels, and nearly ploughed into a dozen workers.

The police chief knocked on Innocent's door. A voice sobbed:

"Come in."

In the shadows, his face illuminated by the light from the window, the policeman saw a sobbing youth, cradling a dynamite detonator in his arms. The policeman approached him. Slowly, with calculated movements, he took a pad and pencil from his pocket and said simply:

"I'm here to listen to whatever you want to tell me."

"I was sitting there, on the crates of dynamite," Innocent confessed eagerly. "I took pleasure with Madame Verrochio."

"Sexual?" asked the policeman.

Innocent nodded.

(The policeman wrote: "Had sex with victim.")

"And her husband came back."

"You're very young, Innocent. Was it the first time you'd done what only a man has the right to do?"

"No, I took pleasure with a beautiful young woman who wasn't as fat as Madame Verrochio. She went to the States with my former friend, the poet Jeannot Tremblay, who's a friend of Achille Bédard, the editor of *The Provincial Sun*, who's a friend of I e Chef."

The policeman kept taking notes. His pencil couldn't move fast enough to write down all the words. His suspect's intentions were good, but he was taking him very far. The officer decided to bring him back to his main concern.

"You had your fun with Madame Verrochio and her husband came back . . ."

"Yes, then he went out again with the dynamite. And he came back for more dynamite. And then he came to get his wife and he said: 'It takes dynamite to blow up what has to blow up.' And he said: 'When you hear my horn, push the lever on the detonator.'"

(The policeman couldn't write down all the words that poured out of the suspect. He caught only a few — "fun . . .

478

woman . . . husband . . . dynamite . . . horn . . . " They would be reference points and his memory would fill in the blanks.)

"Well, did you hear the horn or not?"

"Yes."

"And what did you do?"

Innocent Loiseau knew what the policeman had asked, but he needed to think. He wished he could make time stand still. He hadn't lived as much as a man who has come to the end of his years, he had taken only a few steps on the road of life and the world didn't seem to him like a very nice place. He had only walked on a peaceful country road, under a spotless sky that God had not yet deserted. What he had seen wasn't beautiful. Death always killed life. Innocent had done nothing to save life. He'd done nothing to make it more beautiful. Was life worth the trouble? Innocent asked the policeman to repeat his question.

"What did you do — after you heard Verrochio's . . . the victim's horn?"

Innocent took a stick of dynamite from a crate, inserted a detonator and held it out to the policeman. He attached the two detonator wires to the exploding device. He tightened the two brass screws. The world was not beautiful. Innocent hadn't been able to do anything to make it more beautiful. He had killed a man and a woman. Jeannot Tremblay had not been able to beautify the world. The writers of all the fine books in the college library had not been able to beautify the world, nor had Madame Verrochio or the stranger in the yellow dress. Behind the false beauty of the world, death prevailed.

"What did you say?" Innocent repeated, as if he hadn't heard.

The policeman realized that the child was very disturbed. Approaching him, he laid a fatherly hand on his shoulder.

"When Verrochio blew his horn, what did you do?"

"What did I do? I remember very clearly. I brought down the lever like this . . . "

The shed went flying like a hat tossed in the air and shattered into fragments that fell like black snow. The explosion threw the bystanders to the ground as if the new road had been yanked from under their feet. Some were deaf for days.

As for Innocent, his body was never found. They looked in vain for the police chief. They didn't find Verrochio or his wife. Great black birds wheeled overhead, shrieking impatiently. They swooped down in the tall grass, squawking and squabbling. Birds kept soaring into the sky with a piece of food dangling from their beaks.

Fortunately, Philémon Boileau's body was found before the birds arrived.

Innocent's empty coffin was followed to the church of Saint-Toussaint-des-Saints by the Minister of Roads and Bridges, who kept rubbing his eyes with his white handkerchief, by the Local Riding Minister who lit two dozen votive lights, by the life insurance salesman who had given Innocent a protection his father wouldn't complain about when he cashed the cheque, and by almost as many people as had followed the coffin of young Saint Opportun. ("Opportun was no more a saint than my Innocent," his mother thought.)

Curé Fourré delivered the eulogy. He explained that Innocent had joined Opportun and that the two village children, whom the good Lord had decided to call back to Him, made two more saints in Paradise. Unbelievers, apostates and atheists slandered God: they accused Him of having unnecessarily taken the two children's lives. Curé Fourré pleaded with his flock to say instead that God had turned two children of Saint-Toussaint-des-Saints into angels, cherubs, two little saints who would help the inhabitants of Saint-Toussaint-des-Saints to follow the proper road, the only road that would lead them to Paradise.

The Local Riding Minister began to dream and prayed God to give Curé Fourré a long life so he could deliver the Minister's eulogy.

XLIV

The best letters always come too late

If Innocent had gone home for supper as usual, he'd have found beside his plate this letter sent from the seaside by Jeannot Tremblay.

Dear Innocent, my friend,
You told me once I was the greatest poet you know. I don't want to write poetry any more. I just want to live. Poetry = life. The lady who brought me to the sea is a much greater poet than I am, even greater than Victor Hugo (and he had quite a life, the dirty old man), or Rimbaud or Homer. Being at the seaside with the lady in yellow is being with the sea itself, though she hasn't written one damn line and doesn't even know what a verse is. Poets spend their time polishing their verses and hunting for words till they forget about life, and just live in their dictionaries. Innocent, you know about poets' premonitions. I have to tell you about my dream. I had a dream about you. I'm sure you'll want to know what you were doing in it. Poets can sense the future, so be careful! Be careful of the dynamite in your shed!

Innocent (how you deserve your name!) I dreamed you were lying on your crates of dynamite, doing things to a woman that weren't very Catholic. I can laugh at it now, because I know it would never happen: you're too foolish. You'd rather work than live. The hottest thing you've ever touched is that black ledger where I suspect you noted that I was the worst laborer on the site. Let me tell you, I regret every minute I spent building that fucking road. If my contribution to the road was no more than two shovelfuls of dirt, it was too much! All those wasted weeks gave me a lot less satisfaction than seeing my lady in yellow lazily move her big toe in the sun, here at the seaside . . . You see, I haven't yet shed my poet's bad habit of writing instead of living. Words, words, words, as Shakespeare said. And he wrote so much, I don't imagine he had much of a life. When you write, you follow the roads of the world as your imagination invents it. The road of life is the road of the body . . . I've forgotten to tell you my dream, I mean what comes next . . .

I saw you next to the dynamite with an older, fatter lady than the lady in yellow, a lady in black. (You're too innocent, you have to live! It's urgent! Live, Innocent. Life's out there waiting for you with wide-open arms. The road's before you, Innocent: take it, run away from your shed, from your family, from Saint-Toussaint-des-Saints, from yourself!) And in my dream the lady in black had unbuttoned her black dress. Your lips were seeking the source of Life.

As I write that, Innocent, I realize it really was a dream. I can't see you doing favors to a woman in real life. You're too foolish. All you think about is work. Does the sun work? Does the water in a river work? The stars? Trees? Time? The sea, does the sea work? Only slaves work. You want to win, Innocent, you think of nothing but winning. Man cannot win because he must die. One who is sentenced to death cannot win. Does the sea care about winning? Does time care about winning? A flower? Summer? How can you think about winning when you forget to live?

How can you think about winning when your movements, your thoughts, the way your body develops and wears down, follow a road that nothing can move? That road was followed by our ancestors who didn't know they were following it and it will be followed by all our descendants, if the explosive, flaming toys we've invented don't kill them off.

Innocent, I'm bothered by that dream. A poet's dreams are eyes that pierce the world. Poets see better than bystanders anxious to win. A man who wants to win is nothing but an anxious bystander. I swear now that I never want to win again. I don't want to win, I want to lose. I don't want to guide my people, I want to lose my way. I don't want to lay out the roads of the future, I want to go astray. I hope that bottle containing my solemn oath and Achille Bédard's will be picked up by a wave that's indifferent to everything, even its own movement, and smashed against a rock. Such indifference gives it its strength and its eternity.

It's a very bad habit, being a poet. I envy people who aren't obsessed with words. I envy people who use words like tacks, to fasten a thought to the wall, like a poster in a travel bureau. Words are the particles of my body that come together, separate, regroup and divide again. So — I was saying, I dreamed about you and it worries me. A poet's dreams always come true for the simple reason that they aren't dreams, but a clear look at the reality of the world.

The next part of my dream frightens me, Innocent, I'm shaking as I write it. Listen to me, and get out of that shed where you dream about victory. Life isn't there: that place is filled with death. Get out of there, Innocent, as fast as you can!

Innocent, in my dream there were tears in your eyes. Were you crying because of those women? Loving isn't a disease, Innocent. Not loving is. In my dream I told you, "Innocent, if you must cry, cry from happiness!" Then I saw you open the crates of dynamite and I saw you insert detonators in the sticks of dynamite and I saw you attach the wires to the exploding device and I saw you looking not quite so sad. And then I saw you press the lever. I couldn't help you.

Since I had that nightmare where I saw your body scattered like a handful of seeds a farmer tosses in the earth, I've been worried. I'm telling you, Innocent, get out of there, run away from death and go out and hunt for life. Life is beautiful, Innocent. Stop thinking about winning. Living is winning. Stop dreaming about finding your way. There's no way to find. Stop thinking about wanting to win: you must lose, and lose yourself. You must drown in life as a drop of water drowns in the sea: that's how the drop of water becomes as huge and powerful as the sea.

Innocent, dear friend, you are the only human being I encountered on the site of the new road in Saint-Toussaint-des-Saints, and ever since that dream I've been afraid for you. Run while your legs can still carry you, run for your life. Look, while your eyes can still see. While your hands can still touch, touch. While your mouth hasn't yet become cold and still, sing. While your heart is beating, make it dance from loving life, and listen to it as I listen to the sea, which is an immense heart. Innocent, all the roads on earth come from the sea and all roads lead to the sea. You've never seen the sea. I'm not leaving this place. Innocent, why don't you run away from that idiotic, deadly new road? Come and gaze at the sea. You still haven't flung your body into it, Innocent, you haven't flung your body into life. Innocent, stop being so afraid of loving life.

Your friend,
Jeannot Tremblay

P.S. I'm not going back to the Capital; the lady in yellow left me in tears. I thought she was sad about leaving me, but she told me she was crying with love for a man in the Capital who would unfasten her dress and see her body as brown as chocolate. I'm staying here at the seaside. From her, I've learned to love. Men exhaust themselves building roads, they kill themselves because some want to go here, others there.

They do away with each other because some want a curve toward the right, others a curve to the left. Life is a sea and men are drops of water that form and strike against other drops and disappear into one another. The man who claims he can tell the waves in the sea what road to follow is mad. The man who claims to be guiding men is no less mad, but he's been elected and so we follow him . . . Innocent, you think I'm cynical, but when I look at the sea I see life . . . That's not a new image, I know . . . Life's an old story too, but I'm discovering it, I who am just starting to live, and that's enough to write a new story of which I know nothing but the inevitable ending . . .

Innocent, come and join me, instead of following the road like an ox inside his fences, making his way to the slaughterhouse . . . Live, Innocent! Doesn't that mean losing your way in life!

J.T.

XLV

How a character has the impression that he's already lived his life

Le Chef telephoned Achille Bédard, the editor-in-chief of *The Provincial Sun*, to congratulate him. The newspaper now entered every house in the province, delivering the Right Party's message. Le Chef added:

"When it comes to men, Achille, I've got a nose for them, I can smell them. The good Lord gave me a long nose and I can smell 'em through and through, down to the smell of their shit. Achille, when I put you on the paper my nose told me you'd be the best man. You've resurrected *The Provincial Sun* and I say you're the Right Party's golden tongue. Through you, the populace will learn the real truth. Achille, if I listened to my heart I'd give you a raise, but I know you enjoy working for the truth. You and me, Achille, our reign's not over. The populace needs us. You, the golden tongue, you'll help them understand why the Right Party's the only road to the future and why I'm the best guide. Achille, it's with men like you that I build the Right Party."

Involuntarily, Achille wiped his face. Every word Le Chef uttered was like spittle. The politician had congratulated him and Achille had never felt such shame. Le Chef had called him a "golden tongue." He was horrified by every word he'd written for the Right Party. His fingers hesitated on his typewriter as if they'd been dipped in filth. "Golden tongue?" Rather, Achille had been gagged. He was disgusted with himself. *The Provincial Sun* was a pigsty. He had come to this paper a budding journalist, eager to learn his trade. Achille wanted to use words to re-kindle the embers beneath the ashes and make a great memory-fire that would light his people's road to the future, a fire that would warm hands stiffened, mouths chilled by silence, hearts that doubted or despaired. Everything had been taken from the people but their language. That language had held them together and Achille wanted to make it finer, richer, more luminous, he wanted his language to crackle like dry wood as it burns. With a memory of the past and a dream of the future, his beloved people would be able to cast off its yoke and walk along the roads of liberty. When Achille had joined *The Provincial Sun*, he intended to take over the newspaper and use it in the interest of the people. Instead he served a few dishonest clowns.

Achille had failed. He hadn't taken control of the newspaper, it had taken control of him. Instead of being the one who proclaims the truth, he had become the Right Party's "golden tongue." Instead of painting the future of his beloved people, he had written hundreds of captions under photographs of girls: "Vivacious Jane offers her perky bosom, like a heady bouquet of exotic blooms." Achille Bédard had signed an oath and placed it in a bottle that was cast out to sea, that he would change the lives of his people into a precious stone that glowed like liberty. Here he was prostituting his language to describe mammals sold by the piece, by butchers who specialized in carving human flesh. Vomiting would not relieve his shame. He wanted to write editorials that would strike like lightning; instead he wrote shameful trash. And Le Chef had congratulated him for it. If the newspaper's circulation had increased, it wasn't because of his editorials or even the stupid, smutty captions he concocted, but purely because of the pornographic pictures it was running on the advice of the sales adviser, ex-Corporal Marteau. The shameful captions could have been written by one of the pimply-faced youths sent by the Right Party, the way he himself, Achille Bédard, had been imposed on the unfortunate Sautereau. He wanted to avoid the humiliation of asking someone else to do the job. He hadn't wanted some young journalist to learn, because of him, that writing could be degrading both to oneself and to one's readers. He had secretly condemned himself to the bondage of writing the words for this filthy task.

A secretary put a letter on his desk. He picked it up eagerly. He wanted something to think about besides his disappointment. It was a letter from his friend Jeannot Tremblay. A surprise. Some weeks ago, Jeannot had sent him a message announcing that he wanted to start his life again, to pull himself out of the dark hole his life had become. Achille Bédard had helped him find physical labor in the far-off countryside where the air wasn't filled with the putrid fumes of human misery. Achille had suggested that to rebuild his body, he take up "the tasks of the poor but honest people who trudge along the roads of life like beasts of burden, neither too unhappy nor too happy." After that Jeannot grew silent but, Achille Bédard thought, "apple trees in winter's grasp are silent as they prepare for their rebirth." He knew that a letter would come one day. He tore open the envelope. The telephone rang.

"Achille!"

It was Le Chef again.

"Achille, have you ever thought, you got a lot of responsibilities on your shoulders for such a young man? You know, for such a young fellow, you aren't half bad? Reviving a dying newspaper and breathing youth into it, that's quite an accomplishment! Congratulations to youth! I was right to team up with youth. But with a sly devil like you, Achille, I'd best keep my eyes open.

"Achille, there's been some accidents on the road the Right Party's giving the population of Saint-Toussaint-des-Saints, in the Appalachians. Go have a look there. Apparently it smells fishy . . . Maybe the Opposition's already there. Vultures! Don't forget to put holy pictures in *The Provincial Sun*: find some martyrs gushing blood. The Right Party defends the right religion. Go have a look at that new road. They'll tell you everybody that took the road came down with the disease of sudden death. Must be the good Lord's will. Could the good Lord be in the Opposition?"

Le Chef hung up and Achille took the letter from its envelope and unfolded it. Le Chef wanted him to go to the new road where the accidents had occurred. Probably Le Chef needed *The Provincial Sun* as a screen to hide things too shameful to mention. Achille Bédard must obey.

"My dear friend Achille,
"This is the last time you'll let me call you friend. I've learned a little and changed a lot. In our conversations — do you remember? — we used to do our best to look at life more keenly. Awareness was what we sought after most, but there's one thing even more desirable: the total absence of awareness. Achille my friend, I don't want to follow you any longer along that rough road where there's no more happiness than in a monk's cell. I spent some time with a lady who was love: love like a fire that feeds on itself. I was unable to catch that woman in the act of not loving: she loves her man and all men, she loves ants, the cockroaches in cupboards, the rain, the sun, the sand, the wind, the day, the night. She loves. And she bestows happiness. She gives herself and she always has more to give. She was like the sea that never stops giving. Achille, are you capable of love? Do you love something? Do you love someone? Do you love yourself? You love our people, you'll say. And because you love them you want to change them, to guide them. That woman who loves so much doesn't want to change anything. She merely loves. Her love leads to revolutions. Because she loves, I am no longer the same. Achille, you do not love, and because you do not love you cannot make a revolution. You want to guide our beloved people, but when one loves one does not guide: one gives. Wanting to guide people is not love. You want to guide them because you're afraid of being alone. The man who loves is not alone. I know you're alone, Achille. I remember how alone we were during our long walks through the windy streets of the Capital. How could we claim to guide our people if we are alone? There is a great distance between us and the people. We do not love them. I want to love, Achille! LOVE. I want to love like the lady I told you about; she cannot

489

feel despair, she cannot be alone, she loves! She went away, with her body that's as beautiful as an unfurling wave. I stayed behind here at the sea. The sea is all of life: you do not guide the sea or try to change it. Like life, it changes by itself. I don't understand it, I love it, I am learning. I don't ever again want to make the effort to understand. I want only to love. Achille, I want to forget the bottle that one night, in our green adolescence, you and I cast out to sea. I hope our bottle shattered against a rock, that the sea-water has mixed with the ink of our oath and erased it.

"Achille, look at the sea. It can teach us a great lesson. The sea has no direction, it does not follow a path: the sea contains billions of roads that are formed and unformed, that crisscross and weave together and come apart. The sea is made of roads that erase one another. It is made of roads that get lost in other tangled roads. I no longer want to follow a road. I don't want to lay out roads for others. Life is like the sea; it is nothing but movement. It has no direction. To lull their concerns, men have invented theories that give a meaning to the movement of the seas, of the air and the planets. The only meaning is a movement that is transformed into other movements. I don't want to find my way, I want to lose it. The sea with its demented rolling does not follow a straight road.

"When you read these words, Achille, smile, because I'm no longer unhappy. Whatever you think, I . . . "

Achille stopped reading this gibberish. Jeannot Tremblay's words escaped him like quicksilver which cannot be grasped. He didn't crumple the letter. He was surprised to see, instead, his hand laying Jeannot's letter in the basket of correspondence to be answered. He should have thrown it in the wastebasket. Jeannot Tremblay was betraying him. Jeannot was spitting on their profession of faith. Jeannot was spitting on their adolescent dream. Achille would walk alone. He would receive more sprinkles in his face than the spittle Le Chef had blessed him with. He'd toughen up. He'd become a man of iron. He was so tired. He saw the sheet of paper in his typewriter and it filled him with loathing. He was tired. He wouldn't let his friend Jeannot get lost like this. He would write to him. He would show him the rainbow in the sky toward which they must walk. He would re-kindle the colors of their dream. Jeannot Tremblay's soul had suffered so much. He was letting himself slide into ruin because their dream had been dashed. Achille would bring back the rainbow. He was very tired. Would he have the strength to fight off the seduction of the languid sea and restore the rough road's fascination? Achille was tired. He hadn't crumpled Jeannot's letter because, perhaps, it was easier to put it with other correspondence to be answered than to accept the brutal fact that he was now alone with his dream. His head felt as full of dust as a vacuum cleaner bag. He wished he could run away to the sea and drown his thoughts. He stiffened his body. The poison in his friend's letter was having its effect. He must rise and stand erect and confident. His fate was to light a path for the people, to invent the phrases that would give them the desire to live. Achille was tired. On the sheet of paper in his typewriter he read: "Dashing Dianna's broad smile and restless breast give the honest worker a place to dream and rest his tired head." He re-read the caption and didn't throw it in the waste-basket. He even thought it was rather well put.

"Monsieur Bédard, don't forget you're going to Saint-Toussaint-des-Saints. The taxi's waiting," said the secretary.

Achille Bédard had never been so tired. After a few hours on twisting, winding roads, he must visit the site, meet people, find witnesses, hear their garbled accounts, make them start over, listen ten times to the same descriptions, ask the necessary questions, discover the truth under crazed accounts, under muddled evidence. Once he had learned the truth, he must communicate it to the readers of *The Provincial Sun* and make it acceptable to Le Chef. In the taxi, he told himself he was not tired but disgusted. He was more dishonest than Jeannot Tremblay. His former friend was guilty of betrayal while he still maintained his belief in the oath they had cast out to sea. He was lying to himself, he could not accept the truth. He would write to Jeannot. Great men had always known a number of deaths before they were born and became their true selves. Was Achille experiencing death so as to be reborn? He was exhausted. The light of day felt like sand in his eyes. Nothing surprised him: neither the sun nor flocks of clouds nor the play of wind and light in the fields. His body was made of sand and his soul was elsewhere.

Once he was there, Achille Bédard examined what debris had been found. He displayed tremendous interest: bodies and souls had been pulverized and invisible particles must be clinging to them. He listened to accounts by workers who had seen nothing, but had heard the explosions; he listened to hypotheses, deductions, suppositions. He had them tell what had happened during the summer. He had them describe Innocent Loiseau, he asked questions about his behavior, his work; he had them tell about Verrochio's visits, he asked questions ("Did he seem sad or discouraged? Was he nervous? Preoccupied? Was he aggressive with his employees? Was he often drunk? Were there women in the Cadillac with him? Did the workers know that Verrochio was on the verge of bankruptcy? Had Innocent ever been seen with a woman? Could that woman have any link with Verrochio? If Verrochio had committed suicide why had Innocent blown up his shed? Did the workers have any reason to believe that Innocent might have been the murderer? Did they think Innocent might have killed himself because he had committed a crime? Did they know what his motive might have been? Why had Innocent killed himself along with a policeman? Why should he have wanted to get rid of the policeman? Could the policeman have wanted Innocent out of the way because he knew too much? What was it that Innocent knew? Had there been any compromising transactions? What was the meaning of the mysterious notes found in the policeman's notebook? What was the meaning of the words "pleasure . . . woman . . . husband . . . dynamite . . . car horn?") Achille Bédard listened to embarrassed responses, to droning, stammering, confused stories, to nebulous evidence, contradictory versions, weighty insinuations, to self-promoting lies, to tearful oaths, to attacks on earlier testimony, passionate arguments, contradictory versions, to depositions under oath. He questioned, verified, argued, discussed. A wave of details unfurled on him as if each question had burst a dam.

Why had Jeannot Tremblay's letter been as desperate as a suicide's? His friend was putting an end to hope. Did

Achille Bédard himself still believe in the oath he had sealed up in a bottle drifting on the sea? His newspaper looked like that street in Amsterdam where girls display themselves in windows. He who wanted to be the guide had become a brothel-keeper.

Achille Bédard had to write his article about the accidents on the new road. He must forget his sorrow, forget his fatigue, forget his lost friend. In the car his head swayed in rhythm with the bumps in the roadway. Sleep would not have wiped out his disgust. His article must be more forceful than anything the Opposition would write. Achille Bédard must foresee what the Opposition would write and defuse the bombs it would place under Le Chef's conquering feet. It was easier to write a ten-word caption under two pneumatic breasts. That thought made him even more disgusted with himself, because he would rather write feeble pornography than the truth. His conscience refused to admit that like Jeannot Tremblay, he was trying to forget the oath in the bottle. He must not close his eyes or surrender to his fatigue. He kept his head from nodding as the car jolted along. He had to think. When he got back to the office he would write his article, then go off to forget everything in the sleep of utter exhaustion.

He listed the facts: 1) The death of Verrochio, a road-building contractor ousted from the group of Right Party's favorites with exclusive rights to contracts; Verrochio had been restored to favor following the dubious intervention of his wife, a pretty woman whom the Minister of Roads and Bridges found attractive. 2) The death of Verrochio's wife, one of the most beautiful women in the Capital, known for her dignity; a lay saint who was always part of anything beautiful that happened in the Capital: a concert, a very formal Mass, a charitable work. Rumor had it that, to save her husband, this woman had committed a greater sin than she could probably ever imagine: giving herself to another man. It had never been proven. Did this too perfect woman have her secrets? Was it possible to live such an honest life? Verrochio had been seen in hotels with women whose beauty or reputations were less exalted than his wife's. Perhaps this couple's love story contained secrets, lies, suffering, a tragedy. The Right Party's presence and influence had been deciding factors in both their lives. 3) The death of the young clerk, Innocent Loiseau. He had taken his life after the Verrochios' car blew up. Why? Coincidence must be ruled out. A link was being established between the explosion of the car and the explosion of the clerk's shed. What was there between Verrochio and the clerk? (When a man of action has given his all in battle, he gets tired; the warrior sometimes seeks out easier prey.) Some employees had seen Madame Verrochio go into the clerk's shed. Innocent might have felt remorse and, to erase it, killed the person at its source. To disguise the motive for his crime he'd killed an innocent person at the same time. (Who? Verrochio? His wife?) Surprised by his crime, feeling lost and overwhelmed by guilt, Innocent had chosen to die. He had been relieved of his duties by the Right Party's organization. Verrochio was in disfavor after he'd benefited from the Right Party's generosity. Verrochio had built roads on which scandal was mixed with the rubble. In disgrace, had he talked too much? If he disappeared, disappeared at the same time as a probable enemy, an enemy who knew too much, was it because Innocent had been the instrument chosen to silence the Italian, who would have found it hard not to say too much? The workers had also seen a woman in a yellow dress enter the shed; this time, they had noticed the door was shut. Others had seen and heard the clerk talking to women on the telephone. When the work was getting underway, a little girl dressed as a woman had come to his shed. Homélie Plante was no angel. Other employees had noticed that Innocent had a special friendship with a rather spineless individual, a young stranger who worked by himself, as if he didn't know how to talk to ordinary people. Once, like a madman, the young city fellow had climbed up on a rock and delivered a fanatical, incomprehensible speech. That was Jeannot Tremblay, Achille recognized him. What was the link between Innocent's suicide by dynamite and the psychological death of Jeannot, who was letting himself sink into his image of the sea? 4) The death of a policeman. Why had Innocent led to his death the policeman come to question him? Probably the policeman had found the key to the mystery, the link between Innocent and the deaths of Verrochio and his wife. Innocent wanted to destroy that link and the policeman had found him out. Or else the policeman had accused the young man; Innocent knew he was as innocent as his name, but all the evidence was against him; realizing he was a prisoner of circumstances, he had opted for the only defence that was left: suicide. And he'd taken with him the man who was the immediate cause of his suicide, the policeman. 5) The death of Philémon Boileau, a special adviser to the Right Party, who spent his days in his car, studying papers, to whom no one had ever talked and who had never talked to anyone. He had died for no apparent reason, face down, surrounded by photographs cut out of *The Provincial Sun*, cards bearing weird information about the beauty of girls, their measurements, distances in miles, some vague addresses; the wind hadn't blown away all his papers and the weight of his body had pinned down a few. 6) The accident of an unfortunate truck-driver who had taken his life because his wife ate too much chocolate. When they married, she was the prettiest woman in this godforsaken part of the country. Her husband couldn't forgive her for becoming fat and round and soft, with buttocks like pumpkins and breasts that could feed an army. 7) The death of an old man and his old wife. The accident had occurred on the route of the new road. The old couple didn't want the road to cross their land. Almost on their death bed, they had got up to fight. They had climbed onto an ancient mower to cut down the stakes the surveyors had planted on their land. The old couple had been mowed down along with the stakes and the hay. 8) Many other deaths had been recounted in the local language, with syllables swallowed as though the people had nothing else to eat: some old folks had simply dried up like trees; a child had drowned in boiling oil on the night of a religious and political procession to celebrate the inauguration of work on the new road.

Throughout his trip all the talk was about death, never life. It seemed that along this road, only death existed. Achille Bédard did not understand. So much death along this new road. Why? There must be a link. This new road led to death the way other roads lead to the sea. Achille Bédard would write an article.

The car drove up inclines, then descended; Achille Bédard's heart leaped to his throat, then dropped to the pit of his stomach. How could he shed his acrid self-disgust?

Instead of standing upright like a man who is following his star, he was crawling: he was seeking his star not in the azure sky, but in the mud of politics. He rolled down his window so he could breathe. During the most difficult moments in his past, Jeannot must have felt this same self-disgust. Achille couldn't comprehend all these deaths. The Opposition would denounce the Right Party, accuse it of sowing consternation, desolation and destruction even in the most peaceful corners of the countryside. This political buffoonery was so ridiculous! There wasn't the slightest desire to understand, the slightest urge to find a meaning in these disasters. Life, death — were such matters important to the Opposition or the Right Party? The car drove over the bridge across the river, he saw the walls of the Capital, he climbed up the three steps to *The Provincial Sun*. The smell of tobacco pricked at his nostrils. He was impatient to sit down at his typewriter and hear the keys click in a fury of inspiration.

His colleagues were astonished to see him pound his typewriter with the frenzy of someone beating the drums in a savage celebration. The headline lashed the white page:

IS THE RIGHT PARTY SOWING DEATH?

"The Right Party wants to win the election. The Right Party wants to harvest votes. The Right Party pays cash. Road-building is common currency in certain neglected areas.

"The Right Party has undertaken to build a new road in Saint-Toussaint-des-Saints. No one asks if the road leads anywhere. The poor, admiring, grateful population are tossed truckloads of sand and gravel, as they themselves toss grain at their hens and turkeys.

"Along that new road, death has struck, as these good people say. Death has struck several times, in a disturbing way, with worrisome insistence.

"Even Le Chef is concerned. But don't interpret that as magnanimity: rather, it's a case of a party leader who sees the estimated number of supporters — and their votes — dropping. Le Chef sent me to the site of the massacre. I was his delegated embalmer. Fearing Opposition criticism, Le Chef sent me to bend over the corpses, not to listen to what their cold silence had to say, but to be a make-up artist, to slather pretty colors on their incomprehensible deaths.

"I saw death, I asked questions, I listened and looked, but I do not understand.

"I do not understand these deaths, but I would understand yours, Chef, if I learned tomorrow that you'd been felled by a heart attack as you read these words. Understand what I'm saying, Chef: I want you to be so angry that your heart explodes; that your fundament, to use Rabelais' fine word, bursts, that you're emptied of all your shit, that your head falls in your shit and no one can tell one from the other. Honorable Chef, if you were to die that way, I'd understand it. What I don't understand is the deaths of those poor innocent people. But just because I don't understand it doesn't mean I'll be quiet.

"God gave me the gift of speech. I have perverted that gift, Chef, I've used it to repeat your words. I've used my own words to clothe your ideas — the belches you think are ideas. I have profaned my gift. I wouldn't be surprised if God took it away because I've used it improperly. But even if I were deprived of that gift, I would find the words to rejoice at your death.

"Today, though, I must talk about deaths that I don't understand. In the face of death one must speak. Chef, the people elected you to help them create life. Instead, you bring forth death. What is death? I don't know, I can only see it as the ruin of life. Chef, death appears along the new road because you ruin life. You ruined Verrochio's life, first through success, then through failure. You ruined Madame Verrochio's life because the virus of corruption runs through your government like venereal disease. A young clerk, Innocent Loiseau, was a victim of corruption in spite of himself, because your government teaches people not life but corruption. You cynically maintain that flowers spring from corruption. The only flower that springs from your government's corruption is death, with thorns dripping blood. You're a poisoner, Chef. Death is your mistress and your child.

"I consider you guilty of moral and political corruption which beget death. I declare you guilty of the deaths of these poor innocent victims. You will receive your punishment in all fairness tomorrow, when you read this article in *The Provincial Sun*, for which you have less respect than a pair of socks."

Achille Bédard didn't re-read what he'd written. He had listened to his heart and his heart didn't make mistakes. He took his article down to the composing room. He didn't hang around. He read the front page headlines, skimmed a few articles he'd cut to make room for his editorial, then went back to his apartment. The wind smelled of the sea. Breathing it was a joy. He was no longer nauseated. He was no longer tired. The sky above his head resembled a vast river; he remembered evenings when he and Jeannot Tremblay would take long walks in the night, with the captivating sense that they were the first men to walk on the earth, filled with the intense mystery of the future. They talked about their people who had followed difficult roads through history, a small group of men and women with strong arms and hunger in their bellies. Rather than deceive their people, as others had done, rather than plunder their pitiful resources, Achille and Jeannot Tremblay wanted to give them their lives. That was the oath they had sealed in a bottle that was floating somewhere on the sea. Jeannot had already betrayed it. Jeannot would always be on the run, because he would always want to be as far as possible from his painful past, from an adolescence the Right Party had ruined. Before the ever-receding sea, he had found what he was seeking: to flee, to disappear, to fade away. Achille, though, had not forgotten his oath. He had betrayed it without forgetting. His oath was an obsession: it was as clear and precise as a neon sign in the night. For too long he had been like a sheep, submissive to the Right Party's wolves. In his articles he had bleated. Now he had written his editorial. Tomorrow the wolves would go back to their dens. He walked with his head high, like one who believes in the future. Today, at his typewriter, Achille Bédard had become a man again. His eyes saw far away, and very high above him he seemed to see the glimmer of a bottle, floating in the night.

He fell asleep quickly; happiness carried him into a sleep devoid of memory. When the doorbell rang he was far from the things of this earth. It rang several times. When he finally heard it he pulled the warm sheets over his head, swearing that it hadn't rung. It persisted. He decided not to answer. The bell was shattering his eardrums. Sleep was stronger. Now someone was banging on the door. Forcing it open. Tearing it from its hinges. He sat up in bed. Fierce pounding shook the wall. The door gave way. The light slapped his face. Three big men in black suits and hats hurled themselves at him. One pulled an envelope from his pocket, took out some photographs, peered at them, snickering, handed them to his acolytes who peered at them with the same drooling snicker; then he took them back, peered at them again, snickered, and flung them at Achille. The photographs exploded in his face. He saw himself naked, with a naked woman. He had seen only one naked woman in his life. Only once. His friend Jeannot Tremblay had been celebrating that night. Jeannot Tremblay had phoned him at *The Provincial Sun*. They hadn't seen each other for ages. They had laughed on the telephone, and finally they met. Girls were fluttering all around. They had drunk and Achille ended up with a naked girl in a green-walled room. She had thrown herself on the bed and with vulgar words, ordered him to hurry. ("Take your pants off if you got anything inside.") Humiliated and ashamed, his heart contracting, he had taken off his clothes, thrown himself on the bed. ("I hate men you have to teach everything," the tart had said.) She had got up while he was still sighing, pushing him away. Then she went out, slamming the door. He had wept for a long time in the night, in the old streets of the Capital. Achille had often regretted this adventure. He had never told Jeannot Tremblay about it. Rarely did a day go by when he didn't think about the girl with the repulsive sweat.

"Before he delivers lectures in morality," grunted a rough voice, "a wise man makes sure he's got his pants on."

Achille Bédard recognized his skinny body in the picture, his face on which life had not yet carved the lines of all his cares, the girl . . . To avoid facing up to the truth, he tried to tell himself that he was still asleep, that he wasn't awake, that the three men in black were only the shadows of a nightmare, that his door hadn't been bashed in, that the pictures were only unreal images of his memory. Achille Bédard had been working too hard. Was Sautereau's sad end coming to haunt his sleep? The cold wall against his

499

back reminded him that he wasn't asleep in his bed. The breath of the three men reeked of tobacco and beer. This nightmare was occurring in his waking life.

"Did you decide to pull a Sautereau and spit in the face of the Right Party that feeds you?" roared one of the men.

"You remember how Sautereau's fine career ended? He jumped off the bridge and into the river, him and his fancy ideas . . . "

"Sautereau was another one that made a sneaky attack on the Right Party . . . "

One of the men in black picked up the pictures and analyzed it:

"Skinny . . . a plucked chicken . . . couldn't satisfy a woman and he wants to change the world . . . Anybody got a magnifying glass to look for the gentleman's sexual parts?"

Another man came up to Achille and pressed his portly body against him. The great mass, mushy but powerful, pushed Achille against the wall:

"We don't want to sully your reputation, Achille. We don't want to publish these filthy pictures. There's too many sexy pictures as it is: they give people the wrong ideas. All we want is a nice little honest article, like the honest workers that lost their lives doing an honest day's work. They built a road so the honest citizens could go where they wanted honestly. Going where you want is freedom, isn't it? When the Right Party builds roads, they're giving freedom to the people. You can't disagree with that, Achille. So if you agree, it should be easy to put it in the paper, in black and white."

"As far as we're concerned," said the third man in black, "we wouldn't want to soil your reputation. We wouldn't want to publicize pictures that would make three or four generations laugh. We're men. We understand a man needs a woman sometimes. Those victims of the new road at Saint-Toussaint-des-Saints are heroes. *The Provincial Sun* can't insult them. We'll tear up the compromising pictures and you'll pay tribute to the honest workers who died doing their duty on a road the Right Party's giving to the good people of the Appalachians."

The pudgy fingers carefully shredded the pictures. Nothing had been destroyed, thought Achille. Somewhere there were copies of these pictures on file. They would spatter his life again at the next opportune moment. The big man in black flattened him against the wall.

"I'll correct my article," suggested Achille Bédard.

That wasn't the answer the man in black wanted: he pushed Achille against the wall again.

"I'll write another article," he conceded.

The big man pushed harder. The wall cracked. He stepped back. The other man tossed the shredded pictures like confetti. And they went out.

That's what happened to Sautereau, Achille Bédard concluded. Sautereau's story was beginning again. They were forcing him to assume Sautereau's role. The three men in black had forced him onto the shadowy road that Sautereau had taken. Achille Bédard looked at his watch and got dressed.

Everything was simple now. He wondered if he should take his raincoat. The night must be cold. He draped the coat over his shoulders, went out, shut the door, dropped the key in his pocket. He would not write a tribute to the Right Party. He would not use his typewriter to transform corruption into flowers for the Right Party to offer the people. He would not correct a single word in his editorial, "Is the Right Party Sowing Death?" He saw the bottom of his life like clear water. He would never write another word. The night was unusually clear. He would never have another thought. He headed for the bus. Sautereau had trembled as he wrote his articles. Achille Bédard didn't want to live under a threat.

Sautereau had borne his pen like a heavy cross, people had flagellated him, spit in his face. Why? Why had Sautereau accepted so much suffering? Achille Bédard refused to be condemned to forced lies. Why had Sautereau submitted his intelligence to lies for so long? He had a wife. He had children. Did it mean that love could lead a man to commit the aberration of serving what he despised? The hatred he must have felt for the Right Party, whose praises he sang, must have spread to his family life. Love shrinks back when hatred spreads out. Achille was alone, he had no wife to love or hate. The bus stopped in front of his house. He boarded it. Had Sautereau taken the bus to the bridge? He remembered that Sautereau had also boarded the bus. He remembered as if it were a personal memory. His memory contained Sautereau's recollections.

A few heads were immersed in *The Provincial Sun* of the previous day. He wouldn't write another article for the paper. Had Sautereau seen readers immersed in his paper? He recalled that he had. The bus turned several corners, drove up some hills and into the middle-class neighborhood. Achille Bédard knew those houses. He would not see them again. The bus moved into the new section. The houses sparkled like new toys. He would not see them again. These houses had been built with the help of the Right Party. The sweat of the poor had been the water in the cement for their foundations. He would never again see Jeannot Tremblay, his poor friend who had betrayed him. Jeannot had lost his way, looking at the sea, and now Achille was riding a bus toward the river that went to the sea. Their friendship was lost, but the two young men were united by the profound mystery of the water between them. Everything was simple; everything was clear. He no longer needed to think. Feelings were useless. He knew where he was heading. He was Achille Bédard, not Sautereau. No one was making any mistakes. Achille Bédard wouldn't tolerate the lash or the kicks in his side with the sad mute soul of a beast of burden, submissive to the Right Party's humiliation. Everything was simple. Achille Bédard could no longer live, think, write like a free man; he would no longer live. The night was very clear. He was not a submissive man. Everything was simple: he would dive into the river, and perhaps his soul would find his oath amid the distant waves where his future was being prepared. The Right Party's men in black could publish their vile pictures on the front page of *The Provincial Sun*. Since he would have disappeared into the water heading out to sea, the pictures would compromise only those who used them against him. He had made a mess of his life. His death would be a success: a terrible denunciation of the Right Party. Everything was simple. Everything was clear. The thoughts that whirled through his mind were quite useless.

Achille got off the bus. He was in no mood to look at the Capital all speckled with yellowish light. He didn't need that image. He went along the sidewalk that led to the bridge. Everything was futile except his steps that led him to his destination. He would have no need of the muffled pounding of his heels on the cement. Soon his shoes would be useless. He refused to think of his family. He wanted to refuse the childhood memories that were coming back to him. The past was superfluous. Only the present moment was necessary. Would the water be cold? It was while he was walking toward the bridge that the water felt coldest. It was useless to fear that the water would be cold. He didn't want to be afraid. He didn't want to think. Everything was simple. In the light of the new day, he was already no longer alive.

He passed a car parked next to the sidewalk, a shiny sports car: it seemed to be yellow. The car was perched on a jack. The person who was changing a tire stood up. It was a woman and she was wearing a yellow dress. She reared as if she meant to display the form of her body under the dress.

"Monsieur, would you be so kind as to help me?"

He did not stop.

"Monsieur, help me! I've come from far away. I went to the sea. I'm tanned from the sun and the sea. I'm a little bit cold because . . . Help me; I'll make it up to you. Monsieur, are you man enough to do a woman a favor?"

Everything was simple, he was walking toward the river, everything was clear, he was heading for the bridge.

"Men like you don't deserve to live in a world where they're lucky enough to have women!"

He did not reply. He made his way along the bridge, he walked to the middle, with no thought, no memory. He stopped. He leaned over. The water looked cold. He straddled the parapet and without crying out, without thinking, without remembering, without shutting his eyes, he jumped into the water that flowed underneath. His heart was wrenched from his chest. He had felt the same hideous sensation in nightmares. The water had a cutting edge like a guillotine. He was dead, but he felt the current carry his body away. With a movement he could not suppress, his hand clutched a bottle, and the five fingers were fused to it. He thought his hand was gripping the bottle that contained the oath signed with his blood and the blood of his friend Jeannot Tremblay. He felt a smile spread across his face, already rigid in death. They would find the oath in his hand; it would be published. It would be a great article that would fall like lightning on the Right Party that had killed him, that had killed Sautereau and the others.

His body was carried very far. Much later, they found Achille Bédard's corpse washed up on an island, amid the grass where hunters had come to shoot ducks. His hand, its skin in shreds, was clutching a bottle filled with mud.

XLVI

What is a good friend? And what is a good friend's good friend?

Le Chef's private secretary, Thérèse, had the gift of passing through his padded office door like a pure spirit. Le Chef started when he saw her standing before him.

"You'll give me a heart attack one of these days! I'll turn blue as if I had a face covered with varicose veins. Spare my heart, Thérèse, don't come in without warning. My heart's pounding as if I'd lost an election."

"Chef, I brought your foreign language dictionary because the American Governor wants to talk to you on the telephone."

"Did you make him wait?"

"No, Chef. The American Governor buys your lumber, your iron, your electric power, your cows and your asbestos: when you have a customer like that, you don't make him wait."

"Thérèse, make the American Governor wait! He has less respect for me, the Right Party's Chef, than he has for his morning turd. Make him wait! A turd you wait for is a turd you respect!"

"Chef, the Governor can't wait, he's already on the phone."

"Tell him to wait."

"Here's your foreign language dictionary."

She set it before him as mildly and respectfully as a nun.

"Chef, you mustn't humiliate somebody who buys your lumber, your asbestos, your cows, your iron, your electric power . . . "

"I've got no choice; if I don't sell to him he'll take it for nothing. The American Governor thinks my Province is his own back yard. He's never looked at a map. He thinks I'm part of his territory. Make him wait!"

The private secretary picked up the receiver.

"Mr. Governor, this is our Chef."

"*Maudit*, Thérèse, I said make him wait! Who runs this province, Le Chef or you?"

"Talk foreign, Chef, the American Governor doesn't understand your mother tongue."

"I know that, Thérèse!"

"Come on, Chef, talk foreign. Mr. Governor, our Chef was very, very much busy but our Chef is running very very fast to answer your phone call."

"Allô Mister Governor. The Chef of the Province and of the Right Party is speaking to you."

"Mon cher ami, don't you like me any more? I buy your lumber, your electric power, your cows, your asbestos, and when you have a chance to help out one of my dear friends, who buys electric power, lumber, asbestos and cows from me, you treat him like an enemy. If I wasn't the politest of all the American Governors, I'd fly into a rage. In politics, do we mistreat the friends of our friends? Mon cher ami, écoutez: I have a very good friend who owns a sparkling lake full of rainbow trout. My very good friend has a modest cottage on the shore of his lake. It's his private retreat where he goes for rest and love, if you get my meaning. He travels by hydroplane. It's a little corner of heaven on earth. There isn't even a road to the lake or the cottage. Did my very good friend ask you to build him a road? No! Did he tell me, 'Governor, since you buy lumber and cows and electric power and asbestos from the Province, could you ask Le Chef to build a road so I can get to my lake?' No, my good friend never asked me that. And Chef, have I ever said: since I buy your lumber, your asbestos, your cows and your electric power I want you to

506

build me a road so my good friend can drive up to the door of his peaceful little cottage on the shore of his sparkling lake? No! I never asked you for that. I'm angry, Chef. Très très angry. Chef, you've built a road in a village by the name of Saint-Toussaint-des-Saints. My good friend's crystal-clear lake is at Saint-Toussaint-des-Saints. The very same place. Chef, you're building a road at Saint-Toussaint-des-Saints that runs two miles from the lake that belongs to my good friend who buys electric power, cows, lumber and asbestos from me. Chef, did you ever think of putting a little bend in your road to bring it closer to my good friend's lake? No! Chef, you put your road far away from my friend, as far as if he was an enemy. The new road thumbs its nose at my friend's lake — my friend who buys your lumber, your asbestos, your cows and your electric power from me. Chef, is that how you do politics? Chef, does politics mean neglecting your best friends? A friend, Chef, is someone who buys something from you. The only friend you can trust is one that buys something from you and pays for it. Chef, do I pay you a good price for your electric power, your cows, your asbestos and your lumber? Does my good friend pay me a good price for your electric power, your lumber, your asbestos and your cows? And you, you go and build a road miles from his crystal-clear lake, without putting in a little bend so I can drop in on my good friend who's your good friend too! I'm an angry man, Chef — the man who buys your electric power, your asbestos, your cows and your lumber. When you insult one of my good friends, you're insulting me. I'm very very angry!"

"Thérèse," ordered Le Chef, his hand over the receiver, "go look in the dictionary and see how you say unbuild in foreign."

Her trembling hand leafed through the dictionary. Gasping, she searched:

"Hurry up!"

"Unbuild isn't in the foreign language dictionary."

"*Maudits* Americans! They're so tough they never have to unbuild anything."

"Mister Governor," Le Chef began, "listen to me. Verrochio, the contractor, built the new road at Saint-Toussaint-des-Saints. When I found out he'd built the new road

507

without a bend to go to our very good mutual friend's lake (who's going to go on buying my electric power, my cows, my asbestos and my lumber), when I found out that Verrochio the contractor had insulted our good friend I kicked him out like a man's never been kicked out before. He landed in a thousand pieces, Governor! He won't be building any more roads."

"Chef," muttered his private secretary, "it wasn't you that blew up Verrochio. I don't like it when you lie like that. Though it's true, politics is no place for the truth."

"Governor, I'm angry too! The new road will go to our mutual friend's lake! Something was built wrong and we'll unbuild it! Yes sir!"

XLVII

A race to happiness: Plenty of love and plenty of scrap metal

The new road led nowhere, but it was finished. It was waiting for houses that would bring forth other houses; stables would be added to the houses; and vegetable gardens, fields, oats, wheat, buckwheat, rye, alfalfa would push back the forest. Then the new road would be an old road. The new road was beautiful. The high sun turned pebbles into diamonds. The entire population of the Appalachian region was assembled. In the spring, the place was nothing but a cowpath, swamps, ruts and mud, punctuated by stones. Thanks to a miracle by the Right Party and Verrochio's machines, there unfurled before astonished eyes the most beautiful new road in the province. Le Chef was a great leader! The Right Party was a great party! With their fine road the inhabitants of the Appalachians were as proud as a great people. The Right Party would win the election. Le Chef would be re-elected to give the populace what was wanted. The population chatted, prophesied, swore, then they gazed at the new road in silence.

A blue ribbon — the color of the Right Party and of the late Verrochio's machines — barred the entrance. Beside the ribbon stood Curé Fourré, the aspergillum dripping holy water onto his hand and, on his right, the Local Riding Minister. The Minister of Roads and Bridges was late again. Curé Fourré was impatient to give his blessing, despite the absence of the Minister of Roads and Bridges.

"I have to give the sacraments now. The good Lord can't spend the whole day plugged into a poor priest like me."

Behind them, jostling their way onto the new road, were cars that had been waxed until they shone like shoes, freshly painted trucks, horses with ribbons in their tails like first communicants' braids, tractors, bicycles, children rolling worn-out tires, baby carriages filled with squalling infants, men, women, old folks come to see the new road before they died, boys trying to snuggle up to girls, then more cars, more trucks, and dogs and cats, all ready for the big race.

Curé Fourré's upraised arm came down, three times it came down, shaking the aspergillum, and the holy water spurted out and landed on the gravel: now that the new road had been blessed, it was complete.

"That was God's turn, now it's yours, Monsieur le Ministre," said the chivalrous Curé Fourré.

"God's had His turn, now it's the Devil's . . . You didn't say so, but that's what you think, Monsieur le Curé. I know you. You think like the Opposition."

The Local Riding Minister brought his lips to the microphone and began:

"Friends, dear . . . "(The loudspeakers squawked and turned the politician's words into electric crackling.) He began again: "Dear friends of the Right Party.

"Our holy father, good Curé Fourré, has just given his blessing to the new road that the Right Party has given to the good people of Saint-Toussaint-des-Saints and to everyone in my Appalachian riding. He thought he was blessing the construction, but he blessed its demolition . . . Let me explain, dear friends: not only has the Right Party built you a new road, now it's going to take it apart! My most very dear friends, has the Opposition built you a new road? No. Has the Opposition demolished a new road? No! Dear friends, the Right Party considers that the work of men's hands is a blessing. Construction of the new road is now complete. Instead of laying off the employees, the

Right Party hereby announces another shower of jobs! Thanks to the Right Party and its Chef, workers will be able to work on the deconstruction of the new road."

His voice, swept along by his oratorical flight, boomed in the loudspeakers, but frenzied applause covered it in endlessly unfurling waves. Curé Fourré dropped his aspergillum into the altar boy's holy water basin and withdrew to the church: comprehension of the things of this earth was beyond his mystical spirit.

The applause ceased. Now it was time for the Minister to cut the ribbon with the scissors of honor. He opened the way.

All the motors, filled with power and fury, roared at once. They were the hearts of the iron beasts gathered here in a motley and frenzied troop. The earth trembled, for the iron beasts were stamping, furiously, impatiently. The troop emitted long metallic laments, spat clouds of burnt oil, as they called to some creature on the other side of the horizon. Amid a cloud of dust and a smell of burnt rubber, cars ran at one another, trucks crashed, motorcyclists shot into the air, horses kicked at cars, some moved backwards thinking they were advancing, others drove into the fields unaware that they had left the road. Each was prepared to die to be the first one at the end of the new road. If they died they wouldn't really have died because people would talk for a long time afterwards about who had been the bravest and fastest. The thick dust was mixed with oily clouds. No one knew where he was, no one could see ahead or behind. They clutched their wheels, kicked their accelerators to make their beasts go faster, strike harder, charge with enough force to move mountains. The machines shrieked mechanical cries. Life would never be the same again. Now the drivers were nothing but passion, transported by a demented current to the end of a road that stopped abruptly in the middle of reeds and swamps. The mechanical cavalcade mixed with the animal cavalcade, the fury of wheels and hooves raised up a huge ball of dust that rolled along the new road. The crowd watched, they jostled, stamped their feet and issued orders as if someone might obey them. The ball of dust roared like thunder; at any moment now, lightning would slash the dust like a saber. What a wonderful day! The old people had tears in their eyes; leaning on canes, legs gnarled by rheumatism, hands tormented by arthritis, they were sorry they had arrived in life too soon, before there was pleasure. Today's young folks could have the pleasure of killing each other in cars more powerful than a hundred horses, whereas they had gone through life slowly, docilely, following the slow pace of their wives always burdened by the weight of the child to come, and by the heavy tread of horses accustomed to the routine of labor. They hated the impotence of their age. Youth was entitled to all forms of happiness. Sad, useless, filled with dreams that had shriveled inside them, they stamped their feet in irritation at the entrance to the new road, while the young people drove along in a race to happiness. If the young could have so much fun wasn't it because of the old people who had laid out the first roads? Hadn't the old people made the young ones? Gradually the old folks grew less sad, gradually the rheumatism and arthritis in their bones subsided. They were not merely old age: their youth had just bounded forward in powerful cars and on motorcycles; their youth was belting along toward the end of the new road. Their youth would win the race! And they stamped their feet as they'd once done when they held the woman of their dreams in their arms.

The participants in the race couldn't see the road because of the dust, but they could feel it under them like a wild horse trying to unseat its rider. If they couldn't feel it they'd be lost.

The new road had provided an exit for Tarte's Hill. That name was never uttered without spitting afterwards, to clean out the mouth. Tarte's Hill wasn't part of Saint-Toussaint-des-Saints, but of the neighboring municipality. Tarte's Hill was a path hollowed out by cattle on their way to pasture. Tarte's Hill was muddy, stony, full of ruts. Tarte's Hill would never become a new road because the Tartes were in the Opposition. On numerous occasions people had tried to explain the Right Party's benefits, but the Tartes didn't understand. ("You can't help people that don't want to be helped.") In the past, Tarte's Hill had just been open to the neighboring municipality. Now the new road opened its other end to Saint-Toussaint-des-Saints. The Tartes were famous for their old, worn, battered, rusty cars. Even grimier than their cars were their horses. You couldn't tell what color they were, so thickly were they encrusted with mud and manure. The Tarte girls were as beautiful as princesses, it was said, but no one had ever come near them because of their foxy smell. The Tarte girls dressed like men. The Tartes didn't have their own personal clothes: everybody wore everybody else's. No one had seen the shape of the young Tarte girls' bodies: their clothes were baggy, stained with mud and shiny with spruce gum. And yet, the sight of their gleaming eyes in their dirty faces made men dream. Their griminess must conceal wonders. No one had ever seen.

The Tartes had a reputation for firing at night at any shadow that didn't shout its name as it moved. Many times, aspiring boys had crawled through the grass to one of the Tarte's houses, to surprise a Tarte girl as she was taking off her clothes. None of this foolhardy lot had ever had the courage to press his nose against the windowpane. Their fear of a rifle blast in the face exceeded their courage. They would erase their disappointment by declaring:

"If the Tarte girls were all that beautiful they wouldn't be in hiding."

The Tartes lived in a dozen houses built up the side of the Hill. Never had they been touched by a drop of paint. They were made of wood from trees they'd felled themselves and sawed into beams and planks. They forged their own nails. They bought nothing. The women baked their own bread. The men raised animals for meat. The women never bought a dress. The men wore suits sewn by the women. Nothing from outside ever came into the Tartes' houses. The girls stayed with men of the tribe. They didn't need strangers to make babies.

The elders in the Appalachians remembered when people used to throw stones at the Tartes. The Tartes were renegades, they had denied the true religion. The Tartes were children of Judas. The Tarte ancestor had been a traitor. His name was Judas and his children were the children of Judas. Whenever a Tarte passed by, some malediction always struck: a cow would break her leg; a crying child would choke to death in its crib; the hay in a barn would suddenly go up in flames as if the devil had set fire to it. Gradually, contempt replaced the stones. People would turn away to keep from seeing them. After a Tarte passed by the women would take out mops and soapy water and clean the sidewalk.

According to village accounts, the first Tarte, Judas, was a wealthy man, a judge in the Capital. He held the scales of justice in an iron hand. He knew good and evil and professed that they were two waters that did not mix. He did not confuse the guilty with the victim. When he handed down sentences, he talked as God might have talked when one of His creatures disobeyed the law. The judge spoke with so much justice, the guilty thanked him when they received their sentences.

One day, Judge Tarte received a legal notice concerning unpaid taxes. His Lordship had not paid the taxes due. Was it fair that the rich pay taxes? They brought wealth to the land, while the poor brought only their poverty. Therefore the rich should not be punished. Upon reflection, it had struck His Lordship Judge Tarte as simple justice that he not pay taxes. The government thought otherwise.

Judge Tarte had not paid a cent of taxes for many years. The sum now due was considerable. Interest had accumulated, the interest had been compounded, multiplied. A percentage had been added as penalty. If Judge Tarte had paid his debt he'd have been naked in the street, without even his wig to put you-know-where, to keep him decent! That was what people said.

Would the Judge pay what he owed? He recognized his legal obligation to do so, but he declared that the obligation had been imposed by a government that was attempting to muzzle justice. The Government notified him that he must pay the amount due in three days' time.

After endless arguing, Judge Tarte concluded that the best way to avoid paying his taxes was to have his debt wiped out. He had to ask a powerful man to intercede. The Bishop of the Capital and Judge Tarte had started out at the same school together. Life had summoned them onto different paths, but those paths had frequently crossed. It often happens that Justice and Love are invited to the same banquet. The Judge and the Bishop often harked back to the fine days of adolescence when their young brows had not yet been marked by great concerns. The

514

Judge had several times helped the Bishop to direct the spiritual affairs of the Church through the labyrinth of man's material laws. Judge Tarte decided that the bishop could help him. Men in lofty spiritual spheres sometimes have an astonishing sense of material matters and a downright metaphysical skill at dealing with them. Judge Tarte knelt before his bishop and asked him to intervene with the Government. The bishop issued a fraternal reprimand: paying one's taxes was a way to share one's bread with those who have none.

Judge Tarte objected that priests pay no taxes. The bishop replied with an ascetic smile that priests were the servants of God and had to settle accounts only with Him.

"My son," said the bishop, "I ask you to pay your taxes as would any man who loves his starving neighbor enough to give him food and drink."

With these words, the bishop left his old classmate. The gap between adolescence and maturity was dizzying.

Judge Tarte still refused to pay his taxes. The scandal burst. The judge was relieved of his duties. He had to pay. He sold his house. In spite of safes, keys, clever combinations, and secret hiding places, the tax investigators found everything they were looking for, even the rolls of bills in mattresses and other crumpled bills in ladies' shoes.

Judge Tarte became simply Tarte. He was the most isolated man in town. No one said hello, not even people who pitied him. Every day he resembled Judge Tarte a little less. Tarte was a stranger lost in the Capital. He was adrift in a peaceful madness.

The man who no longer talked could still listen, thought a missionary of a new religion who, for months, had been travelling through the Capital, knocking on all the doors, offering his message of hope. Tarte did not send the missionary away.

The missionary of the new religion told how Christ had not ascended into Heaven as was generally believed. With the gift of flight that he had received at death, Christ had fled to America. America was then an unknown country, but Christ, who knew everything because he was God, knew that it was full of people, some of them highly civilized, others very primitive. Christ lived with the nomads and he also lived in highly developed cities. He met people who

515

ate freshly-slaughtered animal flesh and others with a so-phisticated knowledge of wines. Christ evangelized the il-literate and held discussions with philosophers who could read the messages of the stars.

Ever since, the teachings of Christ in America had spread like a magnificent untamed vine. Over the centuries, Christ's splendid vine had not died. It had propagated, following the roads that link cities, forest paths, inland rivers and rapids and rivers that run to the sea.

"The vine of the Lord," the missionary assured him, "has spread to you, so that you can cultivate it."

Tarte listened. The pain that had made him a silent old man disappeared at the remarks of the missionary, who was breathing words of warmth on him. Tarte came back to life like a tree caressed by a sun-filled wind at winter's end. The missionary said:

"Like those who have heard the words of Christ in Amer-ica, you should leave and follow the road the Master will show you. Take women when you leave: Christ tells you to take as many women as possible so you can fertilize them and produce children who will disseminate the word of Christ throughout America."

In Saint-Toussaint-des-Saints, they said it had happened that way. Many recalled the strangers' arrival. They were dirty and poor, with many children, with women who cried, many women, with horse-driven carriages filled with crates and sacks, with dented old cars filled with children and sacks and women. They had bought land and started build-ing shacks along a road the cows took on their way to pasture. When it was learned that the leader of these gyp-sies was called Tarte, the muddy road was given the name Tarte's Hill. When it was learned that they were members of a new Church that had come to convert the Appalachian Region, and when they realized that every man had several wives, a wall was erected between the shacks on Tarte's Hill and the neighboring villages, as thick as it was invisible. The evangelism of Christ's disciples in America had no effect. People were deaf and blind to the missionaries' pres-ence: Christ's vine had fallen on barren soil. If no one set fire to their shacks to drive out these immoral atheists, these sinners, these spreaders of false religion, it was not out of Christian charity. The most honest villagers acknowledged that they were afraid of the diabolical brotherhood. After throwing stones, they decided to show their contempt peacefully. People simply acted as if the Tartes weren't there. When they sold them flour or other essential goods, they pretended that they weren't Tartes. When they bought animals or game from them, because their prices were the lowest in the area, they pretended that they weren't Tartes. When the Tartes told how Christ had come to evangelize America, people simply acted as if they weren't talking. When one of the Tartes turned up with his five wives and his arms full of children, people turned to avoid seeing them and waited until they were far away, then called for death and disease to strike the apostates who were leading such a dissolute life and scattering upon the earth children who were damned at birth.

While a magnificent ceremony to celebrate not only the inauguration of the new road but, at the same time, its "deconstruction," as the Local Riding Minister had announced, was taking place at Saint-Toussaint-des-Saints, another ceremony was being held at the entrance to the new road at Tarte's Hill. No Minister was present, nor was there a priest in a ceremonial surplice and gilded chasuble with a gleaming aspergillum. There were only Tartes. Those who had joined the community had lost their own names. If they lived on Tarte's Hill, they were called Tarte. In the end, they forgot their real names. Gradually they started to look like a family, even bearing a family resemblance. They were Tartes, all gathered together at the place where Tarte's Hill joined the new road. The many children whimpered, teased, chased one another, hid their faces in the loose dark garments of the women, all of whom seemed to be the mothers of all the children. With their lined faces, stooped backs and rough hands, the men seemed old. Tarte, the leader of the clan, spoke:

"The first apostles of Jesus were persecuted, tortured and stoned on the roads of evangelization. Our community at Tarte's Hill has received threats and insults; people despise us, but we haven't suffered much. I don't know if the good Lord has protected our community or if He just forgot us when He was doling out His sorrows. Let us give thanks for what He has given us and for what He has not given us. The Province is large, America is vast. When I

517

turn my eyes to our humble houses, when I see our children playing, our flocks grazing, our women working — blessed women of the Church of Christ, Evangelist of the Americas — when I think of my life of prayer, when I think of my brothers who till the fields and fell trees, I realize that, overwhelmed by blessings and numb with simple joy, we have neglected our duty to teach our distant brothers that Christ has come to America to spread His good word. He travelled the roads of His time, He took paths through impenetrable forests, He rowed on tumultuous rivers, jumping rapids, He slept in birchbark tents, He preached the divine word to tribes that were fiercer than beasts. The happiness we have been given by the truth we possess has made us lazy. In our humble houses, that are warm in the winter and filled with the good smell of children, we have forgotten we are Christ's missionaries in America. Brothers, Christ the Evangelist has worked a miracle for us; he has given us a new road at the end of our humble hill. It is a clear sign that he wants our community to take to the road again. Go on, brothers, get in your cars! I bless you. Be the first to drive on the new road and mark it with the traces of Truth!"

In cars and horse-drawn carriages overflowing with baggage and squirming children, the Tartes burned with divine fervor.

Their dented, rusty, muddy caravan set off slowly. The apostles of Christ, Evangelist of the Americas, felt that Christ himself was guiding them. The caravan crept slowly along the new road. A huge cloud was rolling toward them. Was it the sign of a storm? A sign from Heaven? What was it? The missionaries believed that a flash of evangelizing truth illumined their way, but they were already dead.

From far away, at the entrance to the new road, the villagers gathered at the starting line saw fire surge up from the ground. Was it the Devil's flames? A roar of fire reverberated over the Appalachians. Then everything was silent. The people could see tongues of fire lick the sky, then fall to earth as black smoke. Then there was no more fire. Only a huge black cloud. The wind came up. There was an infernal smell of decay. The smell was worse than any carrion.

The silence overwhelmed the crowd. Black birds plunged into the sky above the bridge where Tarte's Hill joined the new road. They climbed back very quickly, as if they didn't like what they saw.

Once again, death had dealt a hideous blow to the new road. No conqueror would return. No one had got to the end of the road. The racers had come to the end, not of the new road, but of their lives. In the game of life and death, death was victorious. It triumphed amid a silence more poignant than cries, a silence mightier than the wildest bravos. Everyone, men and women alike, was waiting. They would not accept the verdict.

"Since they aren't coming back, we'd better go to them," suggested the Local Riding Minister.

Curé Fourré's eyes were riveted to his prayer book as he muttered invocations. How many dead must he absolve this time? Did God take pleasure in stubbing out, with a flick of His fingers, the lives of His children taking a little pleasure on the road of life? Was God so evil? Curé Fourré didn't want to believe so. No one would come back from the race. Could a God who killed like this be perfect? Shaken by his daring thoughts, the priest crossed himself. The black birds had alighted.

The people clustered tightly behind Curé Fourré and the Local Riding Minister, like a frightened flock: all those who had built the new road with their own hands, those who had watched the work, those who had sold their land to the new road, those whom the new road had dislodged, those who had not had the privilege of working on the road, those who had felled spruce trees, those who had rolled stones, crushed rocks, those who had driven the machines, children who had played among the machines and the workers, those whose brothers or cousins had taken part in the mad race, women and young girls, women whose husbands had built the new road, young girls whose sweethearts had worked on the new road, mothers carrying babies who had been born during the construction, young girls who had dreamed of walking with their sweethearts under the starry sky above the new road, bystanders from the other side of the Appalachians, people who were going to vote for the Opposition, women who had watched their

519

husbands at the table, so exhausted after a day's labor on the new road, young girls without sweethearts, in brightly colored dresses that stuck to their bodies, Pommette Rossignol who had worked as hard as a man (she'd spent the morning letting out her dress, and it wasn't easy because her fingers were more accustomed to a pick-handle than a needle) and everyone whose life had been touched by the new road were slowly marching. Their steps barely disturbed a pebble. A dreadful calamity had struck. They walked with the calm prudence of someone who knows he is venturing in a wild animal's territory. They walked silently, without singing. Some wept. They came to the smashed cars, the cars of the racers from Saint-Toussaint-des-Saints that had smashed into the Tartes, those of the Tartes folded into those of the racers from Saint-Toussaint-des-Saints, dead cars, their drivers wedged into the battered metal. Fate was inevitable. Life was powerless against death. Smoke blackened the sky. Death was all-powerful. They bowed their heads. Was there anything beautiful to see beneath the sky?

The smoking, crumpled ruins of cars, their metal crushed, overturned, all tangled and piled up together, had climbed on top of one another like hideous insects trying to devour themselves. There was a stench of burned flesh. The crude lumps of rusted metal resembled the sights they'd seen on television, in countries where war was raging. The procession approached cautiously. Not everything seemed dead in the disaster. The battered metal, swollen with contained rage, might still explode. They drew near cautiously, as if death were not death. Suddenly a car tumbled over the others with a sound of moaning metal. A small explosion whistled in a burst of smoke. People advanced, arms shielding their eyes, holding their breath, waiting for the explosion. Nothing happened. They advanced further, stunned to see cars crumpled like paper on the floor of an unruly classroom.

What a race it had been. They would remember. Many times the story would be told of the lightning roar of motors, the hail of pebbles, the ball of dust in which the cars were travelling at top speed, then the metallic clap of thunder, the explosion. Generations yet to be born would ask to be told of the great, historic race on a new road that led nowhere but to death.

The procession stayed at a respectful distance.

"A race like that," said Pacifique Loignon, "you don't see in the cities."

"That race was better than the international championship of the international leagues," declared Pierre Papillon.

"Our boys come from a race of champions," said Trefflé Buisson. "Did you see them take off like jets? Official champions wouldn't be fired up to take off that way."

"All the tears our women have shed won't wipe out the fact that our children could go faster than anybody . . . Christ!" said Uguzon Dubois.

"In our century," philosophized Oriflamme Santerre, "humanity is always trying to go faster than fast. We tear around as if we couldn't wait for the end of the world. We shouldn't do that; there's nothing that can't wait. Better to be late for death. Don't explain that to the youngsters: they want to suck before they're born, make love with women before they've sucked their mother's breasts and die before they've lived. Go fast . . . faster . . . nothing in this whole world travels fast. Not even the speed of light! If it takes thousands of years to reach the earth, that's because it's in no hurry. How many centuries did it take to turn a monkey into man? And it's not even done yet! Only man is in a hurry."

"That doesn't mean a thing!" protested Violette Papillon, in tears. (In the heap of cars mangled as if they'd been crunched by monstrous mandibles, she had just recognized the fox tail that her man, Anténor Bourgeon, had tied to the hood ornament on his car.) "You talk and talk," she went on, "but my Anténor Bourgeon looked me in the eyes, he held me in his arms and said, 'Watch me, Violette Papillon, watch me go. I'm gonna win that race! I'm gonna bring you the prize . . . ' My Anténor Bourgeon went to his death and now he's offering it to me; that's a man that knows how to love a woman!"

"I've heard people brag," declared Pulchérie Lépine, "but I never heard a person brag like you, Violette Papillon. My Fortunat was in the race too. My Fortunat wanted to get to the end of the new road before anybody else. My Fortunat went even faster than your Anténor, Violette Papillon. My Fortunat left without even looking at me. When a man loves a woman he doesn't look back when he leaves, he looks where he's going. My Fortunat set out to win the championship. Because he loved me. Me too, Violette Papillon, I had a man's love. And if he knew he was dying, I'm sure he said: 'I'm dying for my Pulchérie and my death's a finer victory than being the first one at the end of the new road.' Me too, I was loved. My Fortunat died for love too. There's love in that mashed-up scrap metal! Fortunat's love isn't dead!"

The women were comparing their love and their pain, embellishing their lovers to forget that they were dead. The men they loved grew as those grow who have passed beneath the yoke of death. Their cries scattered in the sorrow that they held in check. These women's bodies had suffered more than once, giving birth to children; now the pain of losing them was even greater. They had borne events dictated by an ineluctable law that they must accept because it was the law of God. This time, they crossed their fingers to keep from raising clenched fists to heaven.

The men examined the cars that had been tortured, burned, reduced to shreds. The accident had done a thorough job. The cars couldn't have been more twisted. So many young men dead; there hadn't been such a sight since the war. Everyone had lost sons or nephews or cousins. Someone of their blood had been reduced to pulp in the cars. They learned that a man must look at death without anger, without fear, without regret, without sorrow. Against death, man could not be victorious. A man must not feel powerless in the face of death, but filled with power because he is alive. People struggled as hard to hold back their tears as when they were pulling up stumps or crushing rocks or subduing a recalcitrant horse. Tears had the force of waterfalls; they overflowed eyes. Humiliated, they wiped their eyes on the sleeve of their jackets, then shook them in disgust.

The children were misbehaving all around. They cried out as they climbed the mountain of debris. It was as much fun as playing in a wagonful of hay. They pointed excitedly at their discoveries: blood flowing down the door of a car, a face flattened against a windshield patterned with cracks like a spiderweb, a hand at the end of an arm clamped inside crumpled metal. The children had seen birth and death; it was part of life, like ploughing and eating. They had seen lambs and pigs being bled, they knew that an ox has more blood than a man, they had seen animals being gutted, they had seen foxes nosing around in viscera, they had seen organs wrenched from a belly and thrown on the floor where they moved as if they still contained life. The children were indifferent. They were filled with youth. As long as they possessed youth, nothing could be taken from them. Their parents had reached the age of grief and sorrow; the children were still at the age when life is as beautiful as our dreams. And so they were having fun. In their own way and according to their own casual spirit, they too were running a race; they were trying to find the largest possible number of human parts.

Guédine Lacroix wasn't crying. He called himself a thanatologist, as it said on the imitation marble plaque screwed to the wall of his house. Everyone knew he was only an undertaker. People in the Appalachians had a rather surly attitude to death. If you were going to spend eternity on your back, you needed a pretty good reason. Therefore customers were rare. Guédine Lacroix dreamed when he read in *The Provincial Sun* about the number of deaths that occurred on roads elsewhere. His colleagues, who were no better than he was at bleeding a corpse or making up a dead face to give it an appearance of *joie de vivre* were getting rich, while he had to struggle to make ends meet. Sometimes he would go for months without "hooking a single burial." The thanatologist's "farewell salon" stayed empty, the paper flowers gathered dust, the specialized material was unused; it was waste space, unprofitable real estate. Guédine Lacroix did his best to sell a few coffins in advance by offering enticing bargains to reward foresight. He suggested tombstones of marble or plastic "that won't crack when it freezes." He offered "all-inclusive services," including total funerary care guaranteed for at least four days, dress suits, coffins, all the flowers a body could want, transportation to the cemetery included, along with sad music to accompany the lowering into the grave. The inhabitants of the Appalachians never bought anything until they needed it. Each one strived to live longer than his grandparents, all of whom had died "in their hundreds." If Guédine Lacroix looked sad, it wasn't just because of the occasion. He'd come to the wrong place to ply his trade. Like a starving dog, he roamed the Appalachian roads in search of his next client. He knew everyone who had reached the age of an imminent end. He inquired about their health or illness. He never expressed the hope that they'd get better. He never passed on good news. He never repeated a joke. He accorded life all its sorrow so people would want to leave it. Guédine Lacroix despaired at the sight of people so attached to life.

"Basically," he said, "life doesn't deserve so much attachment."

Guédine Lacroix felt someone's eyes look through him. He looked up and saw fat Gornouille Pesant, bearded and dirty as ever. A smile spread across his grease-smeared, frog-like face. Guédine Lacroix knew that Gornouille Pesant had caught him thinking. The smile on his teeth, yellow from the tobacco in the cheap fat cigar he chewed, was transformed into a laugh that creased his eyelids and drowned his eyes in the bloated flesh of Gornouille Pesant's cheeks. Guédine Lacroix couldn't hide his happiness from Gornouille Pesant: for a thanatologist, the mountain of damaged cars was full of gold. He dropped his head like a naughty child. Gornouille Pesant too was far from unhappy. All these wrecked cars meant business would be looking up. Guédine Lacroix, in turn, smiled a broad smile that crossed his face, his cheeks puffed up, though they were so lean the bones jutted out, and he burst out in a laugh that he hid behind a small, white, over-washed hand. Gornouille Pesant felt his secret thoughts being disclosed and dropped his head, blushing. The two businessmen drew closer together. Their shoulders touched. They would work together. Gornouille Pesant had the equipment needed to saw and cut and open the metal, to pull the shattered, twisted vehicles apart. He, Guédine Lacroix, thanatologist, had the necessary tact to look after the squashed bodies. Without talking, without a single word, they agreed to collaborate. To seal the contract, they added their voices to the prayer Curé Fourré had launched.

Gornouille Pesant would sell the scrap metal at a hefty price, while Guédine Lacroix would respectfully bury the dead. It was a pure loss; the bodies would decompose, uselessly, in the earth. The thanatologist knew that not everything in the cadavers should be thrown out. Certain elements could be recovered. If old metal had some value, Guédine Lacroix told himself, why shouldn't an old chunk of bone? Why shouldn't the skin on a body? ("There's lots more chemicals that are still good in a body than in an old motor.")

Gornouille Pesant had started modestly on the Appalachian roads, travelling from door to door, from house to house. He asked people if they had old metal to throw out; he would take care of collecting it "as a favor," he explained; "I'll clean up, clear away and make room for all the new things you'll be getting." He climbed into attics, rummaged in sheds, crawled into cellars, combed the rockpiles in fields where people junked old tools and ploughing implements. Now Gornouille Pesant bought scrap metal all over the province and even farther afield. He even bought entire bridges. He sometimes went to parties in the Capital, where only the rich were admitted. On those days, Gornouille Pesant washed and perfumed himself and wore a lace shirt. Guédine was honored to have the great man beside him.

"I hear they're closing down the new road," murmured Gornouille Pesant. "Something about free trade with the United States."

"That stuff's too complicated," said Guédine Lacroix. "For ordinary people, a road's just a road, but to the government a road means politics."

"Guédine, you 'n' me, we can't really complain . . . (Gornouille Pesant jerked his nose toward the wrecked cars.) That road's bringin' us a pile of business . . . You'll have paint and bodywork to do on the corpses, and I'm sure I'll find a few good pieces in that scrap."

"Gornouille, you 'n' me, we're men of the road."

"We spend more time on the road than on our wives."

"Death may be my business, but I haven't got a stone for a heart. I get a little sad thinking about all those young people that lost their lives on a road that, when all's said and done, was pretty short."

"They wanted a race, Guédine, and they got it. They died having fun. They can't have any regrets. Better to die having fun, Guédine, than live in boredom . . . You 'n' me, we weren't made to die in a race. Our life is meant to go slowly, taking time to see what's in front and out back of us and along the sides of the road."

"You 'n' me, we've seen a lot of death . . . "

" . . . and lots of iron eaten by the years."

"When I think of my life I realize I've spent it going from one death to the next."

"When I think about mine I realize I've gone from one piece of rusty metal to another piece of rusty metal . . . "

"Life's like iron: it rusts, it breaks, it comes undone."

"It's not always fun, picking up broken bodies."

"And it's not always fun picking up rusty iron."

"You 'n' me, we can go on, but them, they've reached the end; it's over."

They had talked like this during the prayer, while seeming to be reciting the words. Guédine Lacroix, the thanatologist, and Gornouille Pesant, the scrap dealer, had tears in their eyes.

"If little Saint Opportun really found the road to heaven, he'd send us a miracle, he'd resurrect all these dead so the race could start over and we'd know who got to the end of the road first," said Guédine.

Laughter shook their shoulders, made Gornouille Pesant's belly sway, hollowed Guédine Lacroix's skinny face and mingled the tears of their sorrow with those of the tremendous joy of men who, in the face of adversity, were capable of standing on their own two feet, of putting their hands in their pockets and getting on with their business.

On the other side of the mountain of scrap iron and dead bodies, the Tartes were gathering their thoughts. These women who worshipped Christ, Evangelist of the Americas, were weeping. These men who had renounced the religion of their forebears and who would vote for the Opposition tightened their lips and clenched their fists. Their souls were palpitating with anguish. The Tartes bowed their heads in misery. The passing wind carried the pious words away. Was the hand of God punishing His community just as, according to the Bible, it had loosed the fire of Heaven upon the cities of the damned? Had it traced a sign in the sky for the apostles of Christ, Evangelist of the Americas? Crippled with arthritis, Tarte, the patriarch, rose amidst his people, swaying; death was already seeping into the bones of his body and into his muscles. In his brain, however, he felt as if he'd been given back the intelligence of a child for whom everything is simple. Tarte loathed his uncomfortable old body, but he was glad he'd been released from the spirit of a young man who doubted everything and wanted to understand everything. At the end of his road, to his great joy he was a child again. He spoke to his disciples in a poor old voice wet with sobs.

"The hand of God is giving us a sign. God doesn't want us to take this road. Let us go back to our houses. Let us wait until His Wisdom is vouchsafed us through another sign. Let us love our women, let us make children to replace those we have lost. Let us make more children than we lost. Then life will be stronger than death and the Good Word more eloquent than silence! Let us go back to our houses. While our children sing psalms of gratitude to our Creator, all the men of our community will devote themselves to the noble task of fertilizing the women whom the good Lord has given them in His great generosity, as He gave us the land to make it fruitful. May the tears we shed at the loss of our sons, brothers and cousins be transformed into joy at the thought that we are responsible for spreading Christ's message in America, a message of joy on this earth that is threatened with the sorrow of Hell."

Tarte could have continued even longer. Christ, Evangelist of the Americas, was breathing the appropriate words into his mouth. America had not been built with words alone. He turned toward his community's hamlet and walked. His people followed.

As for Curé Fourré, he told his flock whose tears had drowned his prayers, useless in the face of so much distress:

"My most very dear brethren, God is reminding us that all roads lead nowhere but to death. We are all crying because we don't want to admit that fundamental truth which Christ has taught us."

The sobs were more powerful than his words. His voice was the voice of a man who still had hope, while the silent pain all around him was tipping souls into despair. His wretched words were but the feeble breath of a man already subjugated by death. For those who were weeping, he could do nothing. Curé Fourré gestured to the Local Riding Minister to take over.

The politician puffed himself up.

"Through my humble mouth, through the poor words of a man who's afflicted today by the death of so many young champions who would have done honor to our race, the Right Party offers you its most sincere condolences, while we wait for Le Chef himself to communicate his own personal grief. The Right Party would also draw your attention to the silence of the Opposition, whose heart is hard and who does not understand the sorrow of others. The Right Party understands its people and not only does it give you its condolences, it offers consolation too. As of tomorrow, we're going to demolish this sad new road. As of tomorrow, we're going to erase this road where you have had so many sorrows. As of tomorrow, we're going to plant trees in the place of the trees that have been cut down. We're going to dig swamps in the place of the swamps that have been filled in. All the land will return to its owners. All expropriations will be canceled. Those whose houses have been moved will see our trucks put their houses back where they were. We shall plant grass and oats. The new road will disappear and you will even forget it. But the Right Party doesn't just know how to demolish, it also knows how to rebuild. In the name of the Right Party, which is at your side in hard times, I announce that we're about to start building a new new road that will run closer to our beautiful lake. I am announcing that all those who provided enthusiastic work for the construction of the old new road will be re-hired. As for all the old people who worked themselves to the bone during their lifetimes, the Right Party believes it's only fair to reward them now, too late, far too late; the old people will be put on the payroll. Finally, the Right Party will hire and put on its payroll all those valiant champions who gave their lives today to demonstrate that they belong to a race that is alive and strong."

A powerful murmur crackled, rose, spread across the fields and up to the sky. The Minister listened to the applause, delighted, then turned his eyes toward Curé Fourré: politics had triumphed. The Curé, modest and useless, bowed his head and stared at the pebbles around his feet. The applause persisted, grew weaker, declared itself anew, gradually calmed down, then it stretched out, withered, became a breath and was silent. A religious song welled up, convinced, conquering, to thank Heaven. All the notes of the hymn rang out, more vibrant than the salvo of applause. Curé Fourré looked away from the pebbles around his scuffed shoes. The Minister feigned not to notice the triumphant look that lit up the priest's face.

"With you and me as guides, the people will be happy."

"I point them on their way to heaven," said the Curé modestly.

"I build roads for them on earth," said the Minister.

"Do our roads lead anywhere?"

Slowly the procession turned back to the village. Gornouille Pesant would smash open the cars. Guédine Lacroix would extirpate the champions. Fine services would be celebrated in the churches in the Appalachians. There would be sermons, political speeches. The bulldozers would come back, the cranes, the planters of spruce trees, then more bulldozers and more cranes, with trucks and other machines. They would fell spruce trees, they would dig trenches, they would crush rocks, they would drive the machines. They would build another new road!

Someone heard a child crying in the tall grass by the side of the already old new road. The child belonged to no one. Abandoned. He howled even louder at having been found than when he lay in the grass beside a green frog.

"I baptize him Opportun-Innocent," Curé Fourré decreed.

Where did he come from? Where was he going?

Everything was about to begin.

he saying? Magloire, in the second row, couldn't hear, but he noticed that the Pope was heading toward some visitors being introduced by the bald monsignor. That was enough to tell him it was a mistake to settle for the second row. He knew how to control the hundreds of pigs that rushed at him as soon as he'd filled their trough. He decided to move up. A few kicks and nudges, a well-aimed shoulder placed Magloire Cauchon and Desneiges in the front row.

"Get out your Kodak, Desneiges, here he comes."

And Magloire made a dash for the old bald monsignor, announcing:

"I come from Canada, from Saint-Toussaint-des-Saints, in the Appalachian Region. I came to see His Eminential Holiness the Pope. I'm the mayor of Saint-Toussaint-des-Saints, and I raise pigs. My pork's so good I sell it to the Jews! (Stuffing his hand in his inside pocket). Our Curé, good Curé Fourré, he asked me to give this missive to the Pope's Holiness."

The bald old monsignor took the letter.

"I shall transmit it to the Holy Father who has a particularly tender love for his Catholics in the New World."

"Is your Kodak ready, Desneiges? Move it, for Chrissake!"

The Pope stood before him. Could Magloire look him in the eyes, like a man? Or should he lower his gaze to the cross on his chest? Should he kneel? Should he kiss the ring on his finger?

"You got the camera?"

No doubt he was overwrought. And tired from the long plane trip. Had he been blinded by the Holy Father's white soutane? Had he, a pig-farmer and champion cusser, who forgot to say his prayers and slept through mass every Sunday, had he been too reckless, wanting to approach the incarnation of Holiness on earth? His fine earthly self-assurance had melted like the waxen wings of that man who had flown too near the sun. His body soft as melting butter, Magloire Cauchon collapsed at His Holiness' feet.

"Magloire! Magloire! Are you dying a sudden death? Here, wait, I got the Kodak!"

The Pope knelt, the Swiss guards rushed to push back the crowd. The Pope murmured a prayer, made the sign of the cross over Magloire. With tears in her eyes, Desneiges snapped away.

"Magloire, if you die with the Pope's blessing, there's nothing can stop you on the road to Heaven."

Magloire Cauchon did not die. The Pope returned to his apartment. The tourists left the audience hall. Magloire Cauchon's eyes opened as if he'd been asleep for a long time. He got to his feet, lost, gawking, aching all over; he spotted his wife.

"Desneiges, did you get any pictures?"

His wife had tears in her eyes.

"Magloire Cauchon, I saw you lying there dead, and now I see you resurrected! My Kodak took pictures of you when you were dead. But then the Pope blessed you and brought you back to life! Magloire, you're going to win your election! The Pope brought you back to life! Wait, I want a picture of you alive!"

XXV

A letter from America brings the Pope sad memories

The missive from Curé Fourré must have got lost in the maze of administrative procedures that had been established over the centuries. At the Consistory exit, the bald old monsignor placed on a table the various letters, parcels, gifts and objects the visitors had given him. The secretary skimmed every letter turned in by the visitors and opened every parcel. For each parcel, he filled out a form and placed it, with the contents, in another room. He inserted each letter in envelopes with imprinted boxes, that he filled in with a firm hand. It was a way of summarizing the letter. Like thousands of other letters that arrived from all over the world on that particular day, Curé Fourré's missive was turned in at the registry office, where it was given a code number. Other secretaries assigned to the registry department filed Cure Fourré's missive, along with hundreds of others, which were then distributed to the appropriate departments. Their replies would be passed to the Secretariat for Latin Letters, which would translate the Pope's reply into Ciceronian Latin. The officer who read Curé Fourré's missive was suddenly interested: the signatory mentioned an Italian (one Verrochio) who built "roads through the forests of the New World so that Christ can travel farther on this earth." With clerical caution, the officer submitted this letter to an adviser who asked to have it submitted to a second adviser, who decided that this pleasant letter need not rise to a higher level, while the other suggested that the Pope was particularly concerned about the propagation of the Catholic faith. His Holiness would be touched, the adviser maintained, at the notion of the Italian opening the forests of America to clear a path for the Savior of all mankind. Because of this contradiction between advisers, the officer, as was customary in such cases, called on a third adviser. After study and prayer, he suggested that His Holiness would surely be interested, on both human and religious grounds, in glancing at this letter from a humble country priest. Saint Opportun had guided the missive, which would otherwise have been stored in an immense shed for wasted words before rising as smoke into the blue Roman sky.

Here is what Curé Fourré had written:

"Very most dear Holy Father,

Forgive the humblest of your priests for tearing you momentarily from your divine dialogue.

I am first and foremost your son and the son of the Son of God, but I am also a descendant of one of those ancient families of old France who left Europe to proclaim the name of God to the savage echoes of the barbarian forests of America.

The bearer of this missive is also a descendant of those very ancient families of the Old Continent, come to pray to the Almighty on the pagan shores of the Indians' America.

The man who brings you this missive is a major hog producer who feeds the bodies of his fellow citizens; I have the mission of nourishing their souls.

The roads the good Lord has traced for men on earth are often beyond the understanding of those who follow them. And so the bearer of this missive and Your humble correspondent travel side by side, through our families in the Old Countries. The bearer of this missive thinks of his pigs, while I consider my parishioners. He wants to fatten his pigs, while I wish

282